Jonathan's
JOURNEY

Jonathan's
JOURNEY

ARTHUR HAMILTON

Library of Congress Control Number:		2014916019
ISBN:	Hardcover	978-1-4990-6894-8
	Softcover	978-1-4990-6895-5
	eBook	978-1-4990-6893-1

In reading *Jonathan's Journey*, you may recognize names of people, places, events, etc…I purposely tried to work-in true places and events of history. Nontheless, this novel is completely and absolutely fiction.

This book was printed in the United States of America.

Rev. date: 09/05/2014

To order additional copies of this book, contact:
Xlibris LLC
1-888-795-4274
www.Xlibris.com
Orders@Xlibris.com
552049

CONTENTS

In Gratitude

For their support, and much-needed help, I would like to thank the following, and hope I didn't forget someone:

Lynda Mozel
Mike Jefferies
Judy West
Anita Dawkins
VGMB – Grace Moose

ACKNOWLEDGEMENTS

I have a lot of people to thank for their encouragement along with the following: Virginia Grace Moore, for her editing and suggestions early before getting sick; Judy East and Mike Jefferies editors of the local newspaper in my little town; Anita Dawkins for coming up with the title for this manuscript and a possible sequel and last but not least, Lynda Mozel, for all her computer work in my behalf.

PROLOGUE

Diary of Margaret Rose (McAllister) Hamilton

October 24, 1835

Married at last, and to a man I truly love. It was worth all the naughty behavior. I have the man I wanted, Jonathan Henry Hamilton, and I need no longer worry about the matches Mother kept making for me. And what a wedding it was, some say the largest ever in North Carolina. Friends and family are here after traveling many miles and days. Brother Allston came all the way from Chic Wood in South Carolina, and Uncle Silas is here from Baltimore, Maryland. I now have a wonderful extended family. My new father and mother by marriage, Alex and Martha Hamilton, are so nice to me. And new brother Drew is more rowdy than Jonny. But I am too tired and sore to decide how happy I am. I hope I can talk my Jonny out of moving us out of Bethania. I will update this later.

CHAPTER 1

There it was again.

Click-a-clack. Click-a-clack.

What the blazes is that? Jonathan thought, still in a dreamy stupor.

Click-a-clack. Click-a-clack.

"Damn that blasted noise!" Jon tried to open his eyes. One was stuck, and the other saw nothing. It was very black. His mouth snapped open in a yawn, and the resulting exhale of air smelled like a water closet. The brain was finally starting to function, and Jon suddenly felt sopped.

"Buggers, I'm wringing wet!" The bed under him was soaked. Alert now, he smiled broadly. "I wonder if it's from the covers or the cockelling?" He reached back and patted the hump under the heavy quilt. Jonathan Henry Hamilton had just married Margaret Rose McAllister, daughter of Master Samuel McAllister the Second, of the Bethania Plantation in North Carolina.

"I wonder what time it is. It must be blamed early. I cannot see doodly."

The *click-a-clack* sounded again from outside, and Jon was now determined to find out what the blazes had awakened him. Toes touched carpet, and long bones stretched upward. Suddenly, Jon's head was wrapped in rough cloth. He thought he heard a crack mixed with the *click-a-clacks*. He knew he had tangled with the velvet canopy of Maggie's huge bed. Freeing himself, Jon peered into the dark room.

"There must be a cussed window here someplace." He staggered to his left, arms pointed straight ahead. He found a wall and palmed his way forward. His hand caught the drape just as his toe caught the chair.

"AHHHH! Hell's fire, that smarts!" A groan sprang from under the canopy. Jonathan spread the heavy drapes open and peered through the lacy curtain. Beams of light created strange dancing shadows, and a sinking North Carolina moon still cast a light on the activity below.

"Lordy, we must be fifty paces above the ground!" Jon now focused his eyes on the commotion in front of the mansion. A broader grin stretched his cheeks.

"Maggie. Wake up, Maggie dear. Our carriage is waiting." Not a stir emitted from under the quilt. House bounder Mose D. had already hitched two horses to the large wagon. Jonathan recognized Sloggy and Smutty, his team number fifteen.

Click-a-clack. Click-a-clack.

Mose was leading a second team of horses to the front of Sloggy and Smutty.

"Good job, Mose. That wagon is loaded too heavy for Slog and Smut alone. I'll bet Maggie has everything but the chamber pot in there." Jonathan had forgotten the tiredness, sore loins, and stubbed toe. Excitement boiled in his veins.

"At last it's here! October 24, 1835, Migrate Day." Jonathan glanced back at Maggie's huge featherbed. The light from the window seemed to magnify its size. The four shiny cherrywood posts stretched the red velvet canopy. The only thing out of place was that hump under the quilt.

"I'll fix that," he said. Jonathan leapt onto the quilt and heard that crack again. "Wake up, Maggie. Arkansas is waiting." Strange noises and moans emitted from the quilt. Jon started patting and rubbing the hump. Finally, some red hair emerged from the quilt, along with some unintelligible mumbles.

"It speaks." Jon increased his rubbing.

A slow cracking voice muttered, "What time is it?"

"Time to get those kajoobies out of this crib and ready for Arkansas," said Jon, who jumped up and sprang to the other large window.

"But it's still dark."

"Of course, it's dark, my silly little pullet. We are leaving at dawn. Remember?"

The red hair disappeared back under the quilt, accompanied by more moans. The flickering lights of torches below announced the two huge dark torsos approaching the carriage portico. Mose was leading another giant, a big gray horse named Corker. Master Samuel had grudgingly given up Corker to the newlyweds last night at the wedding reception. "Nineteen hands at the shoulders and can outpull any team on Bethania," the master had said.

"I sure hope he's well broke," said Jon to himself, "and docile."

He noticed the hump still lying still under the quilt. Taking a deep breath, he put forth a high shrieking whistle. The quilt jumped; and the red hair, pale limbs, and long white shirt appeared. Jon was surprised to see clothing but still enjoyed the sight of his beautiful wife.

"When did you cover the apple cart, Maggie?"

"When you finally wore down and fell asleep."

"The last time I noticed, you were a buffer."

"Like you are?"

Jon suddenly realized his nakedness. He turned around. "Sort of like this," he said.

"Do you like my chemise?"

"Looks like a shirt to me. I can still see the little nipper."

"I put it on when I was writing in my diary. I was cold."

"*Cold*? You must be a trifle batchy, Sissy. It's hotter than the fires of hell in here."

"Stop calling me Sissy! I told you only Daddy calls me that. You know I don't like that name."

Jon laughed aloud. He knew how to rig Maggie's attic. "Your daddy is now my daddy too, so I'll stop calling you Sissy when we are on our way to Arkansas, and dandy Daddy can no longer call you Sissy either. So get dressed, Sissy."

Jon glanced back outside as the shoe hit his back. Bounder Mose D. was now tying Pasha to the back of the wagon, beside Corker, who dwarfed Pasha. Pasha was the pure white Arabian stallion Master Samuel had purchased and had gelded for Maggie's twenty-first birthday.

What a magnificent creature, Jon thought. The custom-made silver studs on Pasha's halter sparkled as they caught the torches' lights. Jon was thinking about feeding all these animals over the long journey to Arkansas, and he was glad that Mose was coming along. Jon barely heard the testy words from Margaret Rose that "he wasn't your daddy," and "Sissy wasn't going to Arkansas. Maggie might," etc.

"Well, what should I call your daddy? Master Samuel? Father-in-law? Pop-off McAllister?"

"I think he would like Papa Sam," quipped Maggie.

"Okay, but if he takes back the horses, you're walking to Arkansas!"

"He won't. You know I can talk him out of anything."

"Talk? It's *con* him. Anyway, the rig to Arkansas is loaded and ready for the Hamiltons."

"Oh, why don't we just stay here in my room for a few days of rest and roger? We're in no hurry."

"Oh no you don't, my pretty plum! This trip was part of your vows. No back-bantering now!"

Maggie grinned and gestured to Jon. "Perhaps I might persuade you in another way."

Two long strides and Jonathan was on top of Margaret Rose. "Persuade away, my pretty piece, and see where it leads you."

Thirty minutes later, Margaret worried. "I hope Nunky Mose gets all my holdings in the wagon."

Jonathan answered with a kiss and swat to Margaret's derriere, "I told him to only pack the raggery we need for the trip."

Diary of Margaret Rose (McAllister) Hamilton

October 24, 1835

I must finish my notes from last night. The wedding was an affair to remember. Jonny called it a babbling bear garden. But am I happy? I fear today will be my last on my beloved Bethania. Oh, how can I survive without dear Daddy, and my mother and brothers? Dear me, I miss them already! Thank goodness I'll have Nunky Mose and Nanty Ella along and was able to talk Daddy into letting me bring Buel along too, even though I know Jonny was opposed to it. Poor Jonny has a load to handle and worry about. But I have faith in my new husband. I love him madly, and I'm proud to have his child swelling in my belly. Oh, what a day this has been . . .

Jonathan's plan was to head due west, along the Yadkin River; find the Boone Gap through the Blue Ridge Mountains to Fort Patrick Henry; then take the Wilderness Road to Kentucky. They would then follow the Cumberland River to Nashville. He had heard rumors that the old Daniel Boone trail was now a corduroy road, dangerous to horses. *Maybe it's better now*, thought Jon. They would soon see. By the time his son was born, they would be on their new plantation in southern Arkansas. But what if it was a fluff?

Jon smiled, as he patiently waited for Maggie to appear from inside the Mansion of Bethania. He thought he wouldn't mind having a daughter either. Mose and he would be able to farm his plantation.

"Wow, I'll have 320 acres of farm. That's over four times what brother Drew will inherit," Jon said to himself.

Jonathan's thoughts turned back to the crowd that was assembled under the portico and the heavy load in his wagon. It was now midmorning, and Jon had said his goodbyes to the crowd several times and held steadfastly against the demands, "please," and sobs of the master's family.

"If you stay, I'll give you all the farm you need, bordering the Yadkin," pleaded the master, Samuel McAllister.

"Thank you, Master Papa Sam, but I am excited about this chance. Arkansas is a new adventure, and I must try it. Maybe someday we'll come back and take you up on your generous offer."

"But you are both too young," sobbed Susan Ashley McAllister, mistress of Bethania and Jon's new mother-in-law.

"I am twenty years old, and Maggie is twenty-one. How old must we be?" was Jon's answer.

"Would it not be better if you and Mose went first, started your farm, then come back or send for Sissy and Ella?"

"No, ma'am, Mama Sue. Maggie must be with me to get the full 320 acres."

Susan was now sobbing uncontrollably. Jonathan had to chuckle. Even bent over sobbing, Susan McAllister was a head taller than Master Sam. Jon was sure glad Maggie resembled her mother instead of her father.

Jon was anxious to get started. He sucked in a deep breath, and his shrill whistle pierced the gossip of the crowd. "Maggie, get crackin'!" he shouted. Red hair appeared from the hand-carved double doors.

"Just a minute," came the return.

"Dammit, you said the same two hours ago. Snap to it, or you will end up a new grass widow!"

Jon thought that Mama Sue should be happy if that happened.

Around the corner of the mansion appeared Jon's older brother, Andrew, leading the big red horse named Dandy. Jon felt relief from his mother-in-law's sobs, and beckoned Andrew to his wagon.

"About to cut out, brother Drew?"

"Yeah, brother, I should have trotted long ago, but I had to rejigger the head."

"Got tangle footed, huh?"

"Tangle footed and obfuscated."

Both brothers laughed. "How was the poke party, brother Jon?"

"You should know, Drew. I saw you playing slap and tickle with that Johnstone grinch."

"Ha! Yeah, brother Jon, too bad she had her whole bee along."

After a few chuckles, Andrew asked, "How are you going to feed your herd?"

"Well, I have some grains in the boot, but I fear not near enough."

"You need another wagon, maybe a buckboard."

"The master has already given me a pile. Dare I con him for more, brother Drew?"

"Bamboozle him out of his skivvies if you're able. It's your last chance."

"Righto. I'll try."

Jonathan now suddenly felt pangs of fear that he may never see his family again. "Will you tell our sister goodbye for me?"

"Bet your trimmings I will. Did you talk with Mother and Dad?"

"Mother didn't cotton to the sprout in the kilter."

"Do tell. The little boot showed through Maggie's fig out."

"I know, and Mother saw it. I thanked them for the Hawken and told them I'd see them again soon."

"Gum gripper!"

"Bite bear, brother. I will see you all again."

"Time will tell, gummer. Take good care."

"I will. So long, brother Drew."

Andrew jumped up on Dandy's back, turned his back to Jon, and rode away through the iron gates and on to Salem.

"Damn. I thought I could keep my lids dry."

Margaret Rose was now flitting through the crowd, hugging, kissing, sobbing, and bidding farewell to each. Jonathan had to chuckle at the names and shapes of house bounder and fellow traveler Ella's offspring. Nine were lined up in a row. Master Samuel McAllister had a special name for all his slaves, which he called "bounders." There was the oldest, Lenny Lightbark McAllister, who was the son of Master McAllister "for certain," Maggie had said.

He's a lot older than I am, thought Jon, who didn't know the next two, a very black pear-shaped Nan and a dark brown Tom, who was much shorter than his siblings. Jon had seen him working in one of the tobacco barns. Jon recognized the tall light-complected Andy Androsterone, who maintained the houses on Bounder Row and was secretly charged with the job of getting as many Nans pregnant as possible "to increase the master's holdings." The next was the tall buxom Esther Blowby McAllister, a creamy tan beauty. Then Buelah Botcherbuns, who was Maggie's maid and close friend. Next to Buelah stood one of Jonathan's favorite bounders, Danny Doubleclutch, a teener with light skin, who helped get the teams ready in the mornings and back in their diggings at night. Jon hadn't realized that Danny was one of Ella's sons.

"That wet nose is a fireball. I wish I was taking him along to Arkansas." Jon studied the next two, a dark girl, about fourteen or fifteen, and a very black boy, probably about twelve. Jon wondered where the others were. Maggie had told him that Ella bore thirteen children. The nine present were a strange sight, tall and short, young and old, and ranging in color from honey to coal. They all knew that this would be the last time they would ever see their mother, yet strangely all stood silent, waiting their turns to kiss and hug and convey their grief and goodbyes. Quite the opposite effects were being displayed by the whites, even though they all felt certain they would meet again in a few years, when good roadways were carved through the Blues. Maggie started down this lineup with her hugs, which she seemed to prolong with the oldest, Lenny. She almost skipped Esther in favor of her own maid, Buelah. They openly cried in each other's arms. Maggie turned toward Jonathan, seemingly ignoring her father.

"Can't we take Buelah along?"

"Where would we put her and how would we feed her?"

"Daddy will help. Please?"

"Ask your father. We need a buckboard too."

"Like hell! I've given you a bundle already! I might as well move to Arkansas with my doings!" bellowed Samuel.

Margaret Rose scrambled back to hug and plead with her much shorter father again. "Please, Daddy! You know we need all those things to survive."

"I don't want you to go, Sissy. Stay, and you two can have all you need."

"But I promised Jonny. It's part of our vows. You wouldn't want me to lie, would you? Please, Daddy?"

Master Sam looked around at the assembled crowd, pausing to look long and hard at his sobbing wife, Susan. Maggie was hugging and kissing him very intensely. "Please, Daddy," she said again.

What's this? Jonathan thought. Jonathan thought he had detected a tear running down the mockered face of Master Sam. "I did see it, right into his dundrearies," he said to himself.

"Alright! Dammit to hell, take what you need." Samuel turned away from his daughter's clasp and wiped away his tears with the bottom of his vest. Maggie and Buelah started hugging and crying together, and were joined by the happy mother of Buelah.

"Ella, it's time to name the little nipper before you all depart. Bring him here."

"Yassa, Massa Sam."

Jonathan watched as Ella appeared from the crowd, pulling the little burrhead, which Jon had judged to be about twelve.

"Holy hell, another passenger?" Jon muttered. "Let's see. That makes Mose D., Ella, Buelah, Maggie and I, and now this little legbiter. Maybe Papa Sam is right. He should go to Arkansas, and I'll stay here and run Bethania."

"I hereby christen thee Chipper Cheechako McAllister, the happy rookie," said Master Sam of the burrhead.

Scattered applause ripped through the crowd, but Jon noticed the rigid silence from the row of Ella's offspring. *Master Sam had now christened all thirteen of Ella's sprouts, even sired some of them*, a smiling Jonathan thought.

"The more the merrier! Blast, I've got two fine teams of horses pulling a new heavy wagon full of Maggie's dowry, tools, cotton, corn and tobacco seeds, plants, some food, money, a conniving wife, a giant bounder with his wife, daughter, and sprout, an extra banger of a horse, and Maggie's prancer Pasha. And now another buggy! Hell, I'm bloated! Mose, will you go to the carriage house and pick out a buckboard? Put your grub in it, along with feed and grain."

"Yassa, Massa Jon," said the big bruiser as he headed for Barn Row.

Master Jon? Jon thought. He must remember to tell Mose that he was a free man and would share the new farm with Jon. As soon as they got off Bethania, all of his group will be free, including himself, Jon thought.

Ella was quietly saying goodbye to her boodle, and Jonathan wondered if she and Mose would want to keep their names that Master Sam had tagged them with. He grinned at the thought of their names: "Mose Dasilvalentis McAllister," meaning big, strong, yet meek. Jon's grin became even wider, from ear to ear, when he thought of Ella's name: "Ella Elevated McAllister," named for the position of her legs every time Master Sam saw her. He was laughing now as Master Sam approached.

"Now, son, you can head south to Salisbury and Charlotte, and catch the road west to White's Fort in Tennessee. I think they now call it Knoxville. There's a good road from there to Nashville, and I hear a corduroy road to the Mississippi. But I think the better way would be north to Abingdon, and catch the Great Valley Road to White's Fort and then the Nashville Road."

"Thank you, Papa Sam, but Maggie and I decided to trot up the Yadkin through Boone's Gap. That way, we can see the Cumberland Gap, and follow the river to Nashville."

"But Boone's Gap is a corduroy. Those horses are too valuable to lose!" Sam bellowed through his baraclave. "And besides, the river is difficult to cross west of here!"

Jon was relieved to see Mose driving a buckboard with another team of horses. "I promise I'll be damned careful."

"Just the same, I'm not losing another team."

"How will I pull the buckboard?" Jonathan asked.

"You bamboozled me out of Corker. Use him! He can pull this big wagon alone." The pitted face of the master was popping.

"Righto. Thank you, Papa Sam. Danny, will you take Corker back, and you and Mose rig a single yoke on that buckboard so Corker can pull it?"

"Yassa," came the answer from bounder Danny Doubleclutch, who jumped up on Corker and led Mose and his carriage back to the barn. Jon flopped his tall lean frame on the manicured lawn in front of the mansion. He was getting dandered.

"This adventure is becoming a blunderbutt." He wondered if they would ever get cleared out.

Mistress Susan was again crying openly, head down in her facecloth, her red beaver tail sticking straight out behind her. Maggie enveloped her in an embrace. "It will be fine, Mother. I'll be back to visit in no time at all."

Not very convincing, blown through tears, thought Jon.

"Buelah, start the ball rolling. Climb into the wagon and find a comfy seat behind the bench."

"Yassa." Buelah Botcherbuns didn't need any help. She kissed her boyfriend, Buff, and jumped up into the wagon.

"Maggie, it's time to get those dazzle sticks into the wagon."

Margaret Rose was still comforting her mother. "Just a minute."

"No! You've gobble-gummed long enough. Get cracking!"

Maggie gathered her family into a wailing huddle. Her three younger brothers, Sammy, Virgil, and Miles, joined in.

"Okay, Jonny. I'll be there in a minute."

"Damn. I think I'm going barmy," Jon reflected. "If I don't split soon, I'll go cockamamie. Ella, you, the boot, and Chipper will ride with Mose in the buckboard."

"Yassa, Massa Jon." One last review of her lot, and Ella grasped the hand of little Chipper and strode toward Barn Row. Jon saw nary a tear.

"That's the last time she will call me master." One more time, he mentally checked his list of booty. "Hell's fires, I finally think I'm ready!"

From the huddle, Maggie called out, "Jonny, Daddy wants to know if you can use a cow."

"I've got a batch of animals already. What in the hell would I do with a cow?"

"Milk for y'all and meat if you need it!" bellowed Master Samuel McAllister. "Mose drinks a lot of milk, and the Chipper can use it as well," he added.

"Hell's bells, bring it on! The more the merrier!"

"Lenny, run to the carriage house, and have Mose tie on a cow," ordered Sam.

"Yassa," Lenny hurriedly headed for Barn Row.

"Doesn't this just cap the climax?" Jon asked no one in particular. He noticed the outstretched hand of master overseer, Lental McRae, and grabbed it in a hearty shake.

"Looks like ye be a-gettin' that farm after all, Jon Hamilton."

"If I ever get on the road, Jock."

"Not to worry, son. Ye'll be a movin' along soon."

"I hoped to be moving this morning."

"Denny, you worry. Ye'll be a-still making the Yadkin by nightfall. It be a lunchin' time the now."

"Well, I ain't hungry. If we don't cut out soon, I'll be a gone coon." Jon turned in Margaret Rose's direction. "Get in the wagon, Maggie!" he shouted.

That brought a chuckle from Lental. "Ye kinned this wen ye marry her."

"Yeah, right. If she dallies on the trail, I might leave her in the Blues." More chuckles from the pair and a final handshake.

"Take good care of yourself, son. I'll be a listenin' for a word from ye. I should be a goin' along to keep the eye on ye."

"Might as well, Jock. I'm getting a pile. But we won't have any bounders in Arkansas."

"Then I be a-stayin'. I need the job. Good luck, Jon Hamilton."

"So long, Jock, and thanks." Lental headed back to the barns.

"Okay, I'm ready," said the tear-stained face of Maggie.

"And just in time." Jon felt relief as he saw the buckboard coming, pulled by Corker, and Mose was driving. It was leaning to one side, even though the little wagon was stacked. Ella and Chipper sat crammed on the bench beside Mose.

"It's about midday now," figured Jon, as he helped his pregnant wife climb onto the wagon's bench. Buelah squealed and hugged Maggie, as Jon surveyed his boodle. Danny and Lenny jumped off the buckboard and lined back up with their siblings, who were waving to Ella. The cow behind looked to be young and well-shaped to Jon. "Tie her on beside Pasha, behind the wagon."

"Yassa, Master Jon," came the deep voice of Mose, who stepped from the buggy to handle the command.

"Mose, from now on, it's Jon."

"Yassa, Mas . . . Yassa, Jon," Mose said with a big smile.

"You follow me so you can watch the wagon and animals."

"Yassa, Okay, Jon." More smiles.

"Okay, let's get cracking, and blow Bethania." Jon ran to the lead wagon and paused. He reached into the wagon's boot and brought out his birthday present from his family, a brand-new St. Louis Hawken. He grabbed the flask, poured the powder and ball down the barrel, and rammed it home. Then he placed the cap under the hammer and fired into the air. "Arkansas, here we come!" he shouted. Jon then leaped up onto the bench. "Let's scoot before something else happens."

Tears were running over Maggie's freckles. "Will I ever see them again?"

"I promise, my pretty plum." Jon yelled at Danny, "Hey, Danny, what are the names of the lead team?"

"Team numba five, Jake an' Red," came the reply.

Jon now noticed they were a handsome pair of Chestnuts. "Roll, Jake. Up, Red! Go, Slog. Go, Smut!"

The heavy wagon started down Carriage Way. Screams, waves, hollers, and cheers ripped the air. Maggie blew kisses from wet cheeks and lips. Buelah was even crying, as the strange band slowly made its way through the tall, fancy-patterned iron gate of Bethania.

"I'm hot," Maggie said for the fourth or fifth time.

"So am I," was Jon's retort, "and your feet hurt."

"How did you know that?"

"Because you've been tongue waggin' all afternoon."

"Have you been listening?"

"I told you not to dress so plummy."

"I know, but I had to dress fine for Daddy's last viewing."

"He couldn't see you through the tears."

"You didn't see Daddy cry. You're just gum-beating."

"His baraclave was dripping on his eelskins!"

"Liar." Maggie slapped at Jon's arm, "You big bunco bunny!"

Jonathan was laughing. "Where did you learn that blabber?"

"From you." She laughed. "Let's stop, Jonny. I've got to loosen my strappings."

"We've stopped twice already. We need to catch the Yadkin before dark."

"But this bodice is burning me up!"

Poor Maggie, thought Jon. *She's got to be comfortless in all that garb.* "Okay, my pretty plum. But I want you to get out of all that frock. Whoa, Red! Whoa, Jake!"

"Well, maybe not all, Jonny. That would be embarrassing."

Both wagons came to a stop. Jonathan jumped down, then helped Maggie and Buelah touch ground. Mose started fetching a bucket of water for the animals.

"Let's grain them a little too, Mose."

"Yasser, Massa, er, Jon."

"No more master! That goes for ya all!" Jon shouted. "We're all starting a new life, free."

The three women were walking away, through cut tobacco stalks. "And, Maggie, we're not going to be embarrassed by each other. Before this trip is over, we'll all be wearing Eve's togs."

The women were now about two hundred feet away, and their giggles and chatter were easily heard. Little Chipper was helping Mose with the watering. No one knew for sure if Mose was Chipper's father, as Ella was only given permission to marry Mose a couple of years earlier.

"Buelah and I want you to be the first in Eve's togs, Jonny!" shouted Maggie through the chitchat. "Is it Okay if Buelah and Ella help me too?"

"Mmmm. I'll have to think about that." Jon could see that Maggie was out of her flowered dress, and was being helped with the straps of her undergarment. "Throw that damn thing away!" he yelled. More giggles.

"Haven't you got other things to do besides gawk?"

"That's going to be my life-long job." Jon wasn't sure if he was heard through the flap jaw. He checked the sun, getting close to the hills ahead. They must have treaded for four hours or more by now. *The river's got to be close*, he thought. It was difficult to judge how many miles they had traveled over the rolling humps of the Piedmont.

Mose was balancing two buckets at once, feeding the lead team, while Chipper was watering Pasha. It was a good thing Mose thought of those buckets.

The women were headed back now, and Maggie had her flowered dress on again. Jon wondered what bundling she had under it. He grinned. He was going to find out. "Did you leave that cotton drag behind?"

"None of your business!" Maggie retorted.

"Oh, but you are my business now, and don't forget it, my pretty." Jon wrapped his huggers around her, hands probing.

"Enough of that now, big boy. Help me back up."

"With pleasure." He grabbed left hands, and grabbed rump with the right. Maggie squealed, planted her foot in the wagon, and kicked. Jon jumped back. She had some undergarments on under the flowers.

"Where's that whip, Buelah?" Maggie jokingly asked.

"Oh my. It's under the seat."

"Throw it, Maggie. No place for blacksnakes in this family," Jon said.

"I'm keeping it to keep you in line," she replied.

Jon observed that Mose and Chipper had now finished with the animals, and were putting buckets away. "Okay, gang, let's pad the hooves. Next stop is the Yadkin."

The wagons slowly moved west, chasing the glaring sun. It seemed a long while later that this odd band peered over a steep bank, observing a long, narrow valley, heavy with trees. "The river should be in those woods," said Jonathan.

"It had better be," teased Maggie, "or your demise will be duly recorded in my diary."

"Over daar," pointed Mose. Eyes followed the direction of the long, strong black arm, to an opening in the forest. They could see the river, and Jon thought he could see the Boone Road on the other side, at least two miles away.

"How much rope did we bring, Mose?" asked Jonathan.

"We has plenty to get down," was the reply.

"Good. This hill looks blamed steep."

"Sho 'nuff is. We needs da horses pullin' back."

"We can use Smut and Slog as cock horses to let the wagons down slowly. But I'm worried about the animals."

"I be walkin' 'em down," said Mose.

"Yeah. Let's put down the hammer. It's getting late."

"We starts with Corker. He breaks trail."

"Righto. Let's tie down the fixens in the buckboard. Mose, will you get the braids pinned to Smut and Slog?"

"Was yu means, Jon?"

"Oh, sorry. Will you attach the rope to the buckboard and to the team?"

"Sho 'nuff."

"How far down do you reckon, Mose?"

"'Bout long as Barn Row."

"Damn. That's probably three hundred feet. Better put an extra grip on these tie-downs."

The buckboard was finally ready. The big Corker stood ready at the brink. Mose had the rope tied to the back axle and stretched to team fifteen in the distance, to the rear.

"You've got the bone breaker, Mose. What would you like me to do?"

"Yus stan' here and keeps dem ropes straight."

"Okay, but who will handle the ribbons?"

"Ella handles hosses fo yers."

"Righto, but I want you to harness up to the buckboard."

"Yassar, I do. Ease dem slows forward, Shogar."

"I's do, Daddy," was Ella's reply, as she hurried back to handle Smut and Slog. The stage was set.

"Good luck, Mose. When you're ready," said an anxious Jonathan. Mose gave a signal forward, as did Jon to Ella, many yards behind.

Corker shied as Mose talked him forward. The two giants started over the edge. "Easy, big Corker. Comes, big fella." The soothing voice of Mose helped, as Corker started downhill, front legs rigid and inching forward, one tiny step at a time, as the hind legs acted as drag, pushing back on the forked tongue of the buckboard.

Maggie was hugging Buelah and Chipper, as they peered over the edge. Jon was digging in heels, as if he were anchoring the tow. He felt relief that Mose was doing the frightful work. Mose had a hand on the bridle, taking Corker a step at a time, as slacking rope allowed.

Inch by inch, then foot by foot, the small heavily loaded wagon rolled, skidded, and slid down the hill. Jonathan judged that they were over one hundred feet down, when he noticed an even steeper grade just ahead of Corker and Mose.

"Hold it!" Jon hollered down, and raised his arms at Ella, who stopped the team. "How goes it, Mose? Looks scary!" he shouted.

"We be fine," came the answer.

"Is that a big drop-off ahead?"

"Yassa. Is only ah small drop. We be ready."

"Okay, easy does it." Jon gave the "come on" wave to Ella. He thought he could still hear Mose's steady voice talking to Corker as the two disappeared. Jon heard the C-R-A-C-K and felt the tension slacken in the rope, as the buckboard slipped out of sight.

"Whoa!" he shouted, and waved frantically at Ella. He could hear the sounds of tumbling plunder and a whinnying Corker. "Mose, are you busted?" No answer. "Hold them steady, Ella!" Jon shouted, as he jumped over the edge and propelled himself down the rope. The gaze over the drop-off was frightening. Mose was trying to free himself from the overturned buckboard. He was talking to Corker, who was tangled in the harness and trying to stand. "Hang on, Mose. I'll be right there." Jon could see the rear axle was torn from the buggy on one side, but the rope was holding it fast. "How bad are you hurt?" he asked as he lifted the corner of the wagon and unhooked Mose, then helped him up.

"I's not sure, Jon. I's hasta helps Corka." The two men struggled to get the huge horse free from the harness.

The big horse fought to right himself, all three slipping and sliding in the loose soil. Finally, Corker was able to get his front legs straightened and sat on his haunches. He was even huge in that position. Jon was amazed that Mose seemed unhurt, as he stood soothing Corker.

"Easy, Corka. Oo dem any bones broken?" Mose rubbed and patted the big horse's sides and flanks. The horse jerked when Mose touched his right rear leg.

"Whoas, big Corka," as he felt the heavy thigh. "I's walks him on down ta dem bottom," he said to Jon.

"Are you hurt, Mose?" Jon could see Mose's cotton drilled shirt and pants were torn.

"I's fine, juss needs to get dem down."

"Okay. Just a minute." Jon scrambled to the buckboard and unhooked the rope. The buggy slid down the hill.

"Maggie!" he shouted, "Have Ella bring the team forward."

"Okay, Jonny. Is Nunky Mose hurt?" came her reply and question.

"He says no. He's a bruiser, but we're not sure about Corker. Ease the toggles slowly." The rope started sliding down, through Jon's large grippers.

"Tie yourself to the rope, Mose."

"Yassa." Mose looped the rope around his waist and grabbed the straps of the horse's bridle. "Alrights, big Corka. Easy now, big fella."

The sharp incline was only fifty or sixty feet, and then continued at about a forty-five-degree angle to a leveling some one hundred feet below, where the slope was slight through the trees to the Yadkin.

Thank God for small favors, Jon thought as he lowered himself. The belongings were scattered below. Jon raised his head and voice to Maggie. "Bring 'em to the edge."

"Alright, Jonny. Please be careful."

At last they reached the leveling. Jon waved at Maggie, who stopped Ella and team fifteen.

"How bad is it?" Maggie yelled down to Jonathan.

"We'll answer that when we've taken stock."

Mose was walking Corker ahead then back, giant with giant. Corker had a slight limp, favoring the back leg. "How is he, Mose?"

"No broke bones. I's has some horse grease in dem buckboard."

"We'll find it." Jon started taking inventory. The water was gone, but could be replenished easily at the river. The grain made a path down the hill from the crash site.

"How many barrels of grain did we have, Mose?"

"Threes," came the answer.

Jon noted that one was crushed, and the other two were damaged. One was still about half full, with a pile on the ground. "We can salvage this grain. Do we have a shovel?"

"Yassa. One bes in dem big wagon."

"How about this buckboard?" A quick check showed that besides the axle being torn loose, the bench was gone, and the right fork of the tongue was broken. *That's what muddled Corker's leg*, thought Jon.

"We's can fixes da wagon. Tools be in big wagon."

"Okay. I'll spring back up and bring back Buelah and the sprout, and some tools. Maybe we can get this plunder picked and the axle fixed before dark."

"Yassa."

Jonathan started the first of what would be several trips up the rope, hand over hand. Maggie met him at the top with hugs and tears. Ella still held the team steady, about thirty-five or forty feet from the edge. "Take the team back, Ella."

"Yassa, Master Jon."

"It's just Jon, Ella."

"Yassa, Jon."

"Okay, Maggie darlin', I need to harness Buelah and Chipper to the end of the rope. See if you can dig out a shovel and the tools from the wagon's boot."

"Alright, Jonny. It sounds like you are continuing on."

"You bet your bubbaloos we are continuing! Arkansas is waiting for us. Let's get crackin'!"

"Buts I's skeerd. I's can't goes down," cried Buelah.

"We're going down together. Your blankets are down there, and I have a job for you before dark."

"Buts I's skeerd," she sobbed.

"It will be fine, Buelah. I'll be with you soon." Maggie was trying to settle Buelah down.

"Chipper's not scared. Are you, Chip?" asked Jonathan.

"Nossa," said the little trooper.

"Good boy." Jon pulled up the end of the rope and made a loop for himself. He was glad Mose had thought to throw strappings into the wagon, and he lashed Buelah to the rope, then Chipper just ahead of her. Maggie had found the shovel, and Jon slung it down the hill. He found one of Maggie's bonnets and wrapped some tools and wire in it, and tied it to his waist. He thought he'd best take all the tools. He grabbed the wire and wired down the lid of the wooden toolbox and strapped it to the rope ahead of Chipper, then strapped the bonnet back to his waist. Jon hugged and kissed Maggie, and pulled the loop up to his waist.

"Ready, Ella?" he called, and she waved. "Okay, let's get a wiggle." Jon motioned Ella, and backed off the edge. He grabbed the screaming Buelah's waist and helped her over. Chipper jumped down, both black hands holding tightly onto the rope. Twice in the first few steps, Buelah's feet slipped out from under her, but Jon was there to catch her.

"We're all doing fine," he said, but only got sobs from Maggie's body servant. They passed the crash scene, and Jon started flipping scattered articles on down the hill. Ella had Smutty and Sloggy in a perfect rhythm, and the trip down seemed too easy to Jon.

"Whoas!" hollered Chipper, about fifty feet from the bottom. Jon repeated the order loudly to Maggie up above, as the tools from the box in front slid past them.

The box had broken from the rope and slipped out of its wires. Jon grabbed the box as it tumbled by him.

"Pick up the tools," he directed. Chipper got several pieces and handed them back to Buelah.

Mose was just below them and said, "Lets dem tools slide on down, Jon, and I's grabs 'em."

"Righto." Jon pushed the box on down, and Mose caught it. "Do you see any more, Chip?"

"Nossa."

Jonathan noted that most of the articles from the overturned buckboard had now been pushed and gathered at the bottom by Mose. As they reached the bottom, Mose was rubbing horse liniment on Corker's hind leg. Jon helped free Buelah and Chip, and found the shovel and buckets that Mose had stacked.

"Take this shovel and scoop up this grain into the buckets," Jon said to Buelah.

"I's does it," said Chipper.

"Okay. Be careful not to get dirt in with it."

"Yassa," said the munchkin, who short-handled the shovel like a pro.

"Good boy. Buelah, will you sort out and stack all our booty so we can load it tomorrow?"

"Yassa, I's dos."

"Good. Is Corker better, Mose?"

"Yassar, I's thinks so. I's greases him good."

"Okay. Then let's see if we can fix the buckboard."

"Is everything alright?" came Maggie's voice from above.

"Yes. Relax the team. You and Ella start unloading the wagon."

"Why do that?"

"It's too heavy to horse down the hill."

"Okay, Jonny, will do," answered Maggie.

Mose had already straightened the axle, and Jon could see the U-bolts were in place but were ripped from the floorboards. "How do we fix that, Mose?"

"I's gets dem axe and cuts dem tree. You's splits 'em."

"Sounds like a smasher." Jon found a splitter and hammer, and the two tall men headed for the woods. Mose found a few trees to his liking, and only a few strokes from the powerful man's axe fell an eight- or nine-inch tree. He then bucked it at about four feet. Before long, Jon had them split down the middle. They carried the logs back to the buckboard. Jon was amazed at the prowess and skills of the gentle giant, Mose.

"You're a wizard, Mose. Where did you learn this?"

"I's be carriage house bounda foe yars."

"I'm lucky and tatted to have you and Ella along."

It was almost dark when these two wagoners had splints holding the axle fast to the buckboard, and the tongue fixed with another splint.

"Just like new, Mose. Thank you."

"It's be workin' orights, buts be down in back."

Jon took that to mean that the buckboard would slant down in the back, as Mose had to split the axle blocks so the U-bolts would poke through the splints.

"That's peachy, Mose. Just so it travels."

"Its travas, oright. I's sleeps with Ella under it."

"That's right! You need Ella down here, and I need Maggie up there. Looks like we sleep apart tonight."

"Yassar. Ans Buelahs an' Chips sleeps heer too."

Ah-ha! This will be our honeymoon all over again, thought a grinning Jonathan.

"Hey, Maggie, you and Ella wrap the rope to the wagon."

"Okay, Jonny. Are you coming up?"

"Bet your bloomers I'm coming up, and Ella's coming down. You and me, my fine fluff." No answer to that.

Soon he heard, "It's ready, Jonny." Jon gave a yank on the rope, and started up, hand over hand. He was getting good at climbing and repelling. *Hell, I'm half monkey*, he thought, as he reached the top.

"Ready, Ella?"

"Yassa, I's be ready." Ella scrambled over the edge.

"Wait. You all need food. It's in the wagon."

"I'm starved," said Maggie.

"Yassa. We's need food. How we's gets it down?"

"Not sure, Ella. What's in these buckets?"

"Thisens collards, thisens hominy, chics peas, an' corn pone."

"Which ones do you need for tonight?"

"Collards, hominy, corn pone."

"Drat. Those buckets will spill on the way down."

"Can we bring them all back up here?" asked Margaret.

"Nice try, my pretty plum. But all their night wrap would have to come back up also."

"We's gets by wit corn pone, Massa Jon."

"Ella, it's Jon, not Master Jon." Ella smiled and curtsied. "Okay. We'll wrap up some corn bread and tie to my waist. I think we had better rewrap the rope to the team."

"Oh, nosaar. I's make it down oright," said Ella.

"Are you sure?"

"Yassa. I's ready, Mass, ah Jon."

"Righto. Let's go then. I'll be back in a jiff, Mag darlin'."

"But it's too dark, Jonny."

"That won't keep me away, my little minx. Come, Ella."

Jon stepped down over the ledge and, with one hand, helped Ella. "Just lean against me, keep a solid grip on the rope, and take small steps backward."

"I's will, Jon," came Ella's shaky voice ahead of him.

The ageless black woman and young white male eased their way down the hill. Jon figured they were about a quarter way down when Ella's feet slipped and she started to fall. Jon wrapped his long arm around her and blocked her fall with his body. "Are you alright?" he asked.

"I's fine. Hows far ta go?"

"A long piece yet. I'll steady you. Take off your shoes."

"Yassa. I's do. Whars I's puts dem?"

"Here in this bag with the cornbread."

"Yassa."

Down the pair went, Ella slipping and clutching rope, Jon keeping her in front of his frame and trying to let the rope slip through his right hand, which he now realized was getting sore. It was too dark to see, but Jon knew when he entered and passed the sharp incline. He suddenly had an idea to wrap his leg around the rope, and it helped the pressure on his hand, but was creeping up his leg to his crotch. *Thank God we're almost there*, he thought. Jon could see that Mose had gathered wood and started a fire below.

"Almost there, Ella."

"Yassa, Jonny." Smiles and relaxed tensions spread to all on the rope and below the rope. Mose climbed up to help the last few feet, and embraced his wife.

"He's surrounded her! She's disappeared!" Jon exclaimed under his breath. "Now, is everyone all set?"

"We makes do fine," said Mose.

"Jonny, what's happening?" came the call from above.

"I'm on my way back up, Maggie. Get the pad ready."

"Be careful. Are you sure you can make it in the dark?"

"With you at the top, I can run up the rope!"

"I said be careful, you big lummox!"

"Get ready. Here I come. I'll see you all in the morning."

All the ex-bounders said goodbye, and Jon started up hill. He was struggling with the sore hand, but kept climbing. Maggie kept asking how he was doing. "Are you there, Jonny," and "Where are you, Jonny?"

"On the path to passion!" he answered. He was feeling frisky. "Aaah help, I'm falling!" he yelled.

"Jonny, Jonny, are you alright?" from above.

"Dos yuz needs help, Jon?" from Mose below.

"Nah, I'm fine."

"Jonny, don't scare me like that!"

"BOO!" Jon's head appeared at the edge. He still couldn't see Maggie, nor she him. She started forward. "Stay there, Maggie. Just talk to me."

"I'm right here," she said. He started in that direction.

"Speak, Maggie dear."

She had snuck around the wagon. "I'm here, Jonny."

Jon veered a little to the left. Margaret crept back to the rear of the wagon. "Over here, Jonny."

"Okay, you can stop playing games."

"Why? You were playing games coming up the hill."

"I apologize. I'll never do it again."

"Liar. Just stay there. I have a lantern."

"Well, light my fire, baby!"

"I don't know where the lights are. Why don't you go back down and bring a light from the bonfire?" she teased.

"Lordy, you are baffy in the brain box!" Both laughed, as Maggie lit the lantern. Jon pulled her to him and planted a long wet kiss on her. "Ready to play, bouncebutt?"

"No. Cool down. I'm hungry as a bear."

"Oh yeah! I almost flipped my lid! What's for supper?"

"Mama packed some food in the wagon."

"Great! Food and futz. Let's eat!"

"Can we have a bonfire too? I'm cold."

"You're cold? Again? Don't fret. This womb wizard will warm you. The only fire sticks up here are ready to romp."

"Settle down, Jonny. There's room for us in the wagon."

"You first. I'll help."

"Sure, like you did earlier?"

"It got you up in a hurry."

Maggie and Ella had unloaded much of the pile, and had stacked what remained to one side, leaving room for the honeymooners to squeeze together, just as Jon liked.

"Mama fixed some apple butter for the corn bread."

"We're not very blamed organized. They have the fire. We have the pots and pans. They have the cook! We have the hunger. Oh well, let's eat. I'm hungry and horny."

"So what's new, big man?"

"This may be our only time alone for the next five hundred miles."

"You're not very subtle, Jonny."

"No need to beat the bush!"

The canoodling was fast and furious. Maggie quickly handled Jon's blue veiner.

"Good thing our clan can't see the buggy bounce."

"They're probably fast asleep, like you should be, Jonny."

"Not a bad idea." Jon rolled onto his back and closed his eyes, pulling Maggie on top of him.

"Jonny, will the horses be alright?"

Jonathan rose up in a hurry. "Damn. We better tie them down."

"I'll help you. I hope Pasha is alright."

"He is. Let's see. We have a couple bales of hay."

"Right here, Jonny."

"Okay. You grab the lamp and come with me."

"Just a minute. I've got to put some clothes on."

"Oh no you don't, my little tart. Grab some shoes and jump down here.'

"Alright, Jonny."

Pasha was still close, and luckily the two teams were still harnessed together and hadn't strayed far. But the cow was nowhere to be found.

Mose heard the commotion from below. "Is ya all ahrite, Jonny?" Mose's voice pierced the dark.

"We can't find the cow, Mose."

"We finds him in des mooning."

"I'm an airheaded modocky."

"It's be orites, Jon. He's not go far. Good night."

"Good night down there." To Maggie, Jon added, "Let's give them some hay."

One team of horses was lashed to the left side of the wagon, the other team on the right. Pasha took the same place he had been all day, at the rear.

"We'll give them each a nice little bundle," said Jon.

"Alright, Jonny. But we'll have to break both bales."

"Yeah. Let's make a mat with the remainder, to sleep on."

"That sounds wonderful."

"And let's leave a small pile for the cow, just in case."

Jon noticed the quilt. Maggie hadn't forgotten it. They spread the remainder of the second bale of hay on the floorboards then put a blanket over it. Next the quilt, which Jon lay on and Maggie climbed under, and another blanket over both. Several minutes passed before Jon realized that Maggie had become silent. He felt her shaking, and opened his eyes. Maggie was writing in her journal, tears running from her eyes. *She is a wizard, finding room to write*, he thought. "What's the matter, Maggie?"

"You know I miss them."

"I know, darlin'. Maybe some sleep will help."

"If we could have only gotten away from Bethania!" she sobbed.

"We'll be across the river tomorrow."

"But will we ever see them again?"

"Bet your buns we will, no blowing off." More silence. "Look at it this way, Maggie. We're spending the night on our own property."

"What do you mean?"

"This is the land your daddy was going to give us if we stayed put on the plantation."

"Say, Jonny, I do believe you're right!"

"What's say we celebrate our holdings, Maggie darling. I stole a bottle of your daddy's corn juice."

Frowns turned quickly into smiles as Jon dug into his bag under the wagon's bench.

"If Daddy knew this, he would run you out of the country."

"Ha, he already has!"

Diary of Margaret Rose (McAllister) Hamilton

October 24, 1835

Our first day on the road to Arkansas, and we had a disaster with the buckboard, which overturned trying to descend a steep hill. More of this in tomorrow's entry. Enough to say we're still on Bethania. For the first time in my life, I wish it were smaller! I fear the pain will remain until we have put Bethania behind. Will I ever forget this day? The voices of friends and family still ringing in my ears, the parting hugs and kisses, still warm on my lips, and the tears not even dry from my cheeks. The word farewell still stings in my heart. Leave it then to my Jonny to warm our innards, and our souls, with Daddy's corn liquor.

The wagon shook violently. It woke Jonathan and Margaret with a start. Maggie hugged Jon in fright. "What's happening, Jonny?" More shaking.

"What the blazes is that?" Jon was quickly putting on his nether garments. "Oh, my aching bones."

"I'm scared, Jonny." The wagon seemed to come up off its wheels on the off side.

"I've heard of earthquakes, but I've never seen one," said Jon. "You better put on some togs." He slipped into his trousers and jumped out of the wagon. The horses were nervously prancing and pulling on their reins. Jon noticed that the cow's pile of hay was still on the ground, untouched. The rope contracting and then tightening was the cause of the shaking. Jon stepped toward the edge of "Hamilton Hill," just as Ella and Mose's faces appeared. *No wonder the cussed wagon was shaking*, Jon thought. They were lucky the wagon didn't tip over down the hill.

"G'morn', Jonny," said Ella.

"This is a pleasant surprise." To Maggie, he said, "It's Ella and Mose, Maggie."

"I'll be out in a minute."

"Maggie thinks there are only sixty seconds in a day." Jon smiled. Both Mose and Ella laughed, and Jon was happy that they understood and appreciated his humor.

"Dem cow no show?" asked Mose.

"No. I was just about to go looking," Jon lied.

"Orites. Ferst I's has dem bucksboard tied ta rope."

"What's your plan?"

"We's pulls dem up an' has breekfiss."

"Sounds good. We use the buckboard to transport our booty. I'm starved."

"You're always hungry," came the voice from the redhead in the wagon. The red-haired beauty stepped out wearing a colorful cossack.

"Ferst we's ties dem rope ta dem teams," said Mose.

"Okay. They're still harnessed together. I'll bring Slog and Smut around."

The rope was tied to team fifteen, and Jon watched as Ella backed them, and the buckboard started up the hill. Jon waved at Ella's son and daughter at the bottom.

"Keep your eyes on the buggy."

"Yassa," came the echoes below.

Jon noticed that the steepest area was now flattened some, as the buckboard hadn't disappeared as it climbed steadily. Mose busied himself separating team five from their harness, as the buggy emerged at the top. It looked funny to Jon. It sloped down to the rear; Mose had a bench, and had built up the boards in back with a part of the tree he cut yesterday. *Does that darkie ever sleep?* he wondered.

Mose gathered wood from the buggy's bed and started his bonfire. Ella and Maggie produced a Dutch oven and some fixings.

"What's for breakfast?" asked Jon.

"None of your business. Wait and see," said Maggie.

"We's goes now an' find dem cow."

"Right, Mose." The two men climbed aboard Jake and Red bareback and started their hunt. "I'll see you back here in a piece, Mose."

"Yassar. I's goes back an' circles about."

"Righto. See you in a beat."

Jonathan headed north through the rotted sot weed. He became aware that the ground was gradually descending. The brush became thick, so he stopped. From his perch atop Jake, the slope seemed to continue.

"Lordy, I hope this doesn't drop this easy all the way to the river. Maggie will bury me in her journal! It must drop off," Jon said to himself.

Jon turned to the right, and started a circle. *That danged cow couldn't have vanished*, he thought. *There was no food around here for her.* Jon thought only jackasses were that stupid.

"Damnation, I may as well muddle on back. I'm blamed hungry."

Jon was the first back to the wagons.

"No luck, Jonny?" asked Maggie.

"Not unless Mose has found the bugger."

"I was hoping for some milk with our breakfast."

"Well, you're in for a treat. We have some of Momma's eggs, hot meat, potatoes, and flapjacks."

"We's goes whole hogs," said Ella.

"Good. I can eat pork."

"Hold on, Jonny, till Mose gets back."

"Yeah. Forget about that bloody cud muncher!" Jon hollered into space. "Let's eat!"

"There's he be." Ella pointed in the direction that Jon had first headed. "I's sees no cows."

"Well, I'm sorry, Maggie. It's my fault we lost her."

"It's our fault, Jonny," Maggie said with a grin.

Mose pulled up to the wagon. "Whoas, big fella," he said to Red, and he swung down.

"Hell's fire, he can almost step off that horse," observed Jonathan. "Maybe we can buy another cow ahead."

"You're just jaw-jocking, Jonny. There is only wilderness ahead," answered Maggie.

"There are communities in them thar hills, my pretty plum."

"Like what?"

"Like Sycamore Shoals, and Fort Patrick Henry."

Silence gripped the two couples, as their hunger became very apparent. So silent, in fact, that Maggie heard Chipper and Buelah at the bottom of the hill.

"We need to save some for Chipper and Buelah."

"We's puts food in pots," said Ella.

"Good idea. The lid on this Dutch oven should keep it from spilling. Are you finished, Jonny?"

"For now." He turned to Mose. "What's the plan, Mose?"

"We's puts dem food an' grub ins dem buckboard an' backs dem down, puts Pasha in forks. I's walks dem down."

"Alright. Let's get the food buckets and these pots in the buckboard. What are these poles for?" asked Jon.

"Dems helps dem horses an' wagon down."

"I like it. You're a crust, Mose. Let's do a trial without Pasha this first run."

"Yassa. Bas I's be walkin dem down."

"Can we put any more in?" It looked like about a third of the pile on the ground had been transferred.

"Dat be's 'nuffs, Jon."

"Okay. We're ready for the trial run. Lash to the rope, Mose."

"I's do, Jon."

Mose and Jon pushed the buggy over the edge, as Ella eased team fifteen forward. It seemed to work well. In one spot, the buckboard strayed to one side in the rear. Jon had Ella back the team until it had straightened, and the buckboard again descended in a true line, reaching the bottom unscarred. At the bottom, Mose, Buelah, and the Chipper quickly unloaded the wagon.

"You's has breakfass now," said Mose, then walked the wagon back up the hill.

"That worked great, Mose. What's next?"

"Same plan, Jon, but we's walks Pasha down now."

Mose had thought to bring Corker's harness, and put it on a shying, prancing Pasha. Both Maggie and Mose managed to settle him enough to get the gear on. It was much too big for the beautiful animal, but Mose used strappings to cinch it up, as Jon fed Pasha the hay left for the cow.

"We's puts him backwers in forks," said Mose.

Both Maggie and Mose talked steady to the frightened lifter. It took a lot of work and determination to get Pasha strapped between the forks of the buckboard's tongue, facing the buggy.

"Maybe the wagon will block his view of the hill, Mose."

"Yassa. I's hopes so. We's both walks him down."

"Good! Let's try it."

The women had loaded the smaller wagon with most of the rest of the ground items, and all was ready. As the buggy's rear dropped over the edge, Pasha again balked.

"Whoas der, Pasha. Whoa, big Pasha." Mose's voice helped the struggle to get the white beauty started down the hill. Mose and Jon had a hand on the bridle as Ella and team fifteen walked them down. By the time they were a third of the way, Pasha had settled down, and the trip went surprisingly well. At the bottom, Jon grabbed Mose's hand.

"Mose, you're a hummer!" Jon was amazed at the size of Mose's hand. *Damn,* he thought, *I have a big hand, and he swarms it!*

"Yassa, but nex we's brings dem big wagon down."

"I guess you planned to bring the cow down this way."

"Yassa. Dem cow den Pasha."

"Yeah, well, I don't think that big wagon will be easy."

"Nossa, but we's manage." Mose D. untied the buckboard. "You's put grubs in dem wagon," he ordered Chipper and Buelah.

"Yassa," came their answer.

"Mose, you rehauled the buggy well. It did its job."

"Yassa," he said, as he signaled Maggie above to haul back.

At the top again, the men started pulling the big wagon around to get it backed to the hill.

"Is my horse alright, Jonny?" asked Margaret.

"He made it down swell, darlin'. Will you put the rest of that booty back in the wagon?"

"We just took it out," Maggie teased.

"Not just! That was yesterday!"

"Maybe I should go down with the wagon, Jonny."

"Will we need Maggie up here, Mose?" asked Jon.

"Yassa. We's both walks dem wagon down an' needs Missy Maggie to spot."

"There's your answer, my pretty plum."

With the rope secured to the wagon's tongue, Jon and Mose signaled Ella forward and pushed the wagon to the brink and beyond. As the back wheels rolled over, the wagon shook out of control for a second, but then settled itself. Team fifteen inched forward, and the front wheels followed the front for a few feet, then Ella halted the tow. Mose and Jon grabbed straps and started tying the wheels to the side rails, so the wagon would only slide, not roll.

"We's uses dem poles an' breaks dem wheels."

"In case the wheel straps break?"

"Yassa."

The two men strapped themselves to the front of the wagon.

"I think we're ready, Mose."

"Yassa, we's ready," replied Mose.

Jonathan gave Ella the forward signal, and the wagon started slowly sliding down the hill. Jon was glad Maggie stayed above, as every few feet the wagon wanted to turn. Maggie would signal stop, and Ella would back the team up a step or two to straighten the wagon, then slowly edge on down. Even with the light load, the big wagon put a strain on the rope. Jon hoped and prayed the rope wouldn't snap. Past the crash site slipped the wagon and its guides.

CRACK! Both men and Maggie waved "halt" at Ella.

"What in tarnation was that?" asked Jon.

"It's bes an' spokes broke an' dem back wheel."

Jon pushed his pole behind the front wheel, copying Mose's lead, then worked his way around to Mose's side. A spoke of the back wheel was missing, and Mose was turning it to restrap the wheel to the sideboard.

"Reckon that will hold her?"

"Yassa. We's close to bottom. We's orites."

"One spoke doesn't hurt the wheel, does it?"

"Nossa. It bes fine, Jon."

"Okay. I'll get back to my side."

"We's keeps dem tongs straight," said Mose.

The men grabbed the wagon's tongue and signaled Maggie. Again, the wagon strained on the rope and slid down the hill. Pushing and pulling by the two big men kept the wagon headed straight, and soon they were close to the bottom. Suddenly, the rope started popping at the tongue.

"Gets away!" shouted Mose to Chipper and Buelah.

"Hold it!" shouted Jon up to Maggie.

The rope snapped, and the two men couldn't hold the wagon. It picked up speed the last twenty feet to the bottom, turned to the side, and slowly rolled onto its near side. Mose and Jon scrambled to the bottom. Chipper and Buelah had heeded Mose's warning and had cleared the area.

"Jonny, is anyone hurt?" came the redhead's call.

"Everyone's fine," was Jon's retort. "Any damage, Mose?"

"I's thinks it be's alrite, Jon."

"How are we going to right it?"

"We's uses dem Corker."

Jonathan slipped the harness onto Corker, while Mose gathered stakes, which he drove into the ground around the near-side wheels. Then he found a short rope in the buckboard and tied one end to the near sideboard and looped the other end around Corker's huge chest.

"Orite, big Corker, pulls, big Corker." The powerful gray draft lunged forward toward the hill. The stakes kept the wagon stationary as it came upright.

"That was peachy, Mose." The two men could find no other damage to the wagon, but the contents inside were scattered about.

"You's picks up dem fixins, an' loads dem rest."

"Yassa," came the responses of Chipper and Buelah.

"We's brings down dem Nans and horses," said Mose.

Mose gathered the poles and sledge and tied them to the rope, which Ella had finished lowering to the bottom.

"Righto," said the amazed Jonathan. "Back 'em up, Maggie."

Up came the rope, pulling the men once again.

"Lordy, I'll be tickled when we blow this hill," said Jon, as they walked upward. By now, the soil on the hillside had been loosened up, and Jon asked if that would cause problems getting the horses down.

"Nossa, Jon. Dem drays digs right in."

"Good."

At the top, Jon grabbed the reins of team five and walked them to the edge of the hill.

"We's takes dem one at a time," said Mose.

"Okay, I'll walk Jake down, and you bring Red."

"I want to go with you, Jonny," said Margaret.

"I guess we don't need you up here anymore."

Mose skillfully looped the rope behind Jake's front legs and around the chest. Jon strapped Maggie to the rope behind the horse and grabbed the bridle.

"Hang on tight to the rope, Maggie. Let's roll, Ella."

Mose guided the rope forward as the newlyweds tread downward.

"Are you doing Okay, Maggie?"

"Just fine, Jonny darling."

"Damn. This is too easy. Something else has to happen."

"No, it doesn't. We've had enough happen already, Jonny."

"Right you are. Jake acts like he descends hills every day."

"My arms are getting tired, Jonny."

"Rest them at the bottom, my little kitten. Be careful here, Maggie. This little drop-off is where the buckboard overturned."

"Alright, Jonny. Can we get by it alright?"

"Like a fox in a hen house. Hang on, darling, we're almost there."

Buelah was waiting for them at the base, and gave Maggie a boodle of hugs and squeals. Jon broke in, and gave Maggie a squeeze and a smooch.

"Okay, Mag, maybe you two can sort out and pack the wagons. I'm headed back up for Smutty." He freed Jake and signaled Mose.

"Bye, darling. Be careful."

Hand over hand climbed Jonathan, now used to this hill. At the top, Mose took the rope and bundled Red.

"I's be right back," he said to Jon, grabbing the bridle and jumping down.

Jonathan thought he had heard pounding coming from above earlier, and now noticed that Mose had driven the poles deep into the ground near the edge. *That bruiser had earned his freedom many times over already, and they hadn't even cleared Bethania*, thought Jon.

The big chattel and the chestnut reached bottom, and instantly, Mose started back up. Jon waved Ella back fast to taut up the rope ahead on him. Jon hurried back to Ella and separated Slog and Smut, as Mose stepped up onto the level ground. He carried the harness and led Smutty forward. Finally, he could see the light at the end of the tunnel. "Two to go," he mumbled.

Mose and Ella met at the rope's center and hugged each other. She was tiny next to him, and Jon could see why Mose was called the "Gentle Giant." Mose put his special tie-down on Sloggy, and Ella led him back to the rope's end. Then Mose tied the front end to Smutty, and Jon was ready to take his turn at the helm.

"I's takes Smuts down wit Ella," said Mose.

"Are you sure?"

"Yassa, Jon. I's wans handles Corker. You's drags wit Sloggy."

"Righto. I'm still not sure how to get Sloggy down."

"We's do, you's see."

Jon and Ella traded places, and the ex-bounders were ready to descend. He watched as the black bodies and dray disappeared over the edge, and he walked Sloggy forward. The Slog was having some difficulty holding steady.

"Easy, Slog. That's a lot of weight you're dragging."

The descent seemed to be very smooth. Only once did the tension on the rope vary. Jon stopped Sloggy.

"Whoa, Slog, whoa. Stay, Slog." Jon took a chance, and ran to the edge.

"Anything wrong, Mose?"

"Nossa. We's fine," came the response. "Brings dem Slog ons."

"Okay," said Jon, running back to Sloggy.

"Come on, Slog. Slow and easy."

At last the darkies reached the leveling. Even though Jon wasn't quite to the edge, the rope slackened, and he halted Sloggy. At the edge, Jon saw Ella hugging her children, and Mose switching rope from Smutty to Corker. *Here comes the big test*, he thought.

"Loops dem ropes behind stakes," called Mose.

The two stakes had been driven three to four feet into the ground, about twelve feet apart, by the giant.

"Okay, Mose. Now what?"

"I's uses Corks drags. You's walks Slogs down."

"Righto." Jon thought he could hear Mose talking to Corker, as he coaxed Sloggy forward over the edge. The stakes were holding, and the man and beast edged downward. Jon could see that Corker and Mose had started up the hill at a steady pace. Jon wondered what would happen when they both reached halfway. He reached the crash site when he heard the CRACK from above. The rope slackened, and Jon and dray slid slightly. Mose quickly backed Corker a few feet until the rope again tightened.

"Whew! The second stake is still holding."

"Wens dem oda stake breaks, stops, and holds still."

"You mean you planned for the stakes to break? Are you blunderheaded?"

"Yassa. Corka drags you's to dem bottom."

"Let's burn the hill then."

Jon and Sloggy were three quarters down when the second stake snapped. The slack came down the hill. Both Jon and Mose were struggling to hold their horses. When he finally had Sloggy stopped and dug in, Jon noticed that Mose was pulling up on a rope from below. It was another large stake and the sledgehammer. Mose started the pounding with powerful strokes, and drove the stake deep into the hillside. With the smaller rope, he secured a double loop around the stake. Mose then turned Corker around and walked him downward. Corker pawed the ground with his front legs, almost in a prance, while his hind legs and brechen strap dragged down the hill. Mose talked the Corker to the bottom, while acting as a human drag. When the long rope was again taut, Mose hollered up to Jon.

"Orites, Jon, brings dem down."

Amazing, thought Jon, as he walked Slog to the bottom. Corker was again walking up the hill, as drag. At last, at last! He was doing a jig, when Maggie joined him. Soon all were dancing around. Jon ran to the big wagon, grabbed the corn juice, and passed it around.

"Sorry, not you, Chipper."

When the bottle came back to him, he raised it toward the hill. "I gaggle this grog to Hamilton Hill, and hope to damnation that we never see another like it."

As Mose busied himself harnessing the horses to the wagons, Jon reflected on the casualties caused by Hamilton Hill. "Let's see. Water and some food and grain lost, two bales of hay used up, three broken barrels and many items in disarray, one cow lost, one horse slightly injured, one buckboard partially wrecked, with makeshift repair, one spoke broken on the wheel of the big wagon, about a day of valuable time lost, and three quarters of a bottle of hooch downed! Damn, Arkansas better have rich soil!"

All was finally ready, and Jon figured he still had a half day or more to forge the Yadkin River. Jonathan's strange clan started north, down the now gentle slope, the lead treading brush.

"That opening in the trees should be just ahead."

"That's good, Jonny. That brush is battering the horses."

"Yeah, and it's getting thicker. Come on, Jake. Go, Red." The lead was shying and dodging the brush as it rubbed across their flanks.

"Whoa, Red. Whoa, Jake." Jonathan stopped the lead and jumped down from the wagon, placing a block in front of the wheel. As he looked to see a better trace, Mose approached with a machete and proceeded to strike the brush with long, sweeping blows, sending the brush flying.

"Walks dem teams behin' me," he instructed Jon.

"Okay, Mose. Hang on to the ribbins, Maggie." Jon glanced back and saw Ella gripping Corker's bridle and the Chipper holding the reins of the buckboard. The group proceeded behind the strokes of the powerful Mose Dasilvalentis, and soon came to the clearing and what seemed to be tracks of a very old road, running through the opening to the left, and up the hill to the right.

"Hell's fire! Don't tell me we were paralleling a road. I'll blow my brain box if we did!"

"And the pages of my diary would burn up. Turn left, Jonny. We don't want to know," said Margaret Rose.

They all heard it. "Mooo. Mooo," came the clear, distinct sound of the missing cow from up the hill.

"Gloree be's, dems bassie's moos!" exclaimed Mose.

"Hell with the cussed thing."

"Now, Jonny, you know we must go find it," said Maggie.

"Looks like we're going to find out where this road goes," Jon said to Mose.

"Yassa. We's frees dem lead horses."

"Mooo. Mooo," came the frantic cries. Mose unharnessed team five and jumped astride Red. Jon followed suit aboard Jake, and they headed up the hill. The tracks switched back and forth through the brush at a steady rise.

"What a dufus I was. Not to stir around, before that bummer of a hill."

Mose jumped down from Red, and again started mowing down the brush with the machete. The mooing came from the brush a short distance above, as the pair reached a sharp hillside of only thirty or so feet.

"You's goes back, an' gets dem shorts rope, Jon."

"Righto." Jon turned Jake around and disappeared down the cleared trail, while Mose continued hacking at the brush, now turning away from the cow's moos.

When Jon again appeared at the base of the fall, Red was alone, and Mose was nowhere in sight. "Where are you, Mose?"

"I's up here wit dem cow," shouted Mose from above.

"How did you get up there?"

"Dems trail leads up here. Stays there. I's brings her down."

In a short time, Jon heard then saw Mose descending the gentle incline, with the stray cow in tow.

"You cussed grass guzzler, you run off again, and I'll tie knots in your udders."

"Moo" was the reply. The five "animals" made their way back down the incline and met some cheers.

"She's probably awful hungry, Jonny."

"An' she need milkens," added Ella.

"To blazes with her. She can wait until we reach the river."

"Don't be so thick-headed, Jonny. We all can use some milk."

All agree, and Maggie and Buelah searched for some cups. Mose grabbed a bucket and started to milk.

"We's gets corn pones fo' dinna," said Ella.

"I's does it, Papa," said Chipper. Mose instructed the eager little pickaninny with the milking.

He called Mose "Papa," thought Jonathan. "That will be your job each morning, Chipper."

"Yassa," came the boy's answer.

After a meal of the bread and milk, Jon decided he would attempt to name the cow in the fashion of his father-in-law. "I christen thee Abby Varmintus Absquatulates Hamilton."

"And what is that supposed to mean?" asked Maggie.

"The disappearing varmint."

"That's pretty good, Master Jonny, but I'll just call her Abby."

With Abby tied once again behind the big wagon, the gang turned west through the opening in the trees, toward the Yadkin River. The "road" had been over the stumps left from the falling of the trees. Mose again led the procession with the machete, and Jon tried to lead team five around and astraddle the stumps. It was slow going. Twice a heavy wagon wheel became stuck in a rotted stump, and Mose had to loosen Corker from the buckboard and pull it out.

Finally, the band reached the river, as the "road" swung north beside the waterway. The Yadkin seemed wide and swift. The two men surveyed the situation. The river, road, and rocky hill all seemed to collide a mile ahead.

"Do we take a chance, Mose?"

"We's follows road."

"Right, you've got the bean."

The trail between water and sticks was level, and free of thick brush. The river still flowed strong, as the valley narrowed. Jon could see tall grass along the Boone Road, across the Yadkin.

They needed to get the animals into that grass, Jon thought. Suddenly, the river and road met at the base of the stone mountain. Jon was fascinated at the sight of a partially collapsed log building against the mountain.

"This is it!" he hollered, and jumped down off the wagon.

"This is what?" Maggie shouted after him.

Jon didn't answer. He was already fumbling through the rubble, as his clan watched.

"Jonny, what is it?"

"I believe this is the spot that my father mined gold. Look, the rock wall has been cut into, and this looks like an old sluice!"

"You mean the one my daddy bought?"

"Righto. That's the one."

"Daddy said it was a bust."

"Yes, but my daddy made enough to connect to the farm."

"I wonder if there's still some gold here."

"If there was, your daddy would still be mining it."

Jon pushed some rubble aside and came up with a round rusty metal object.

"What is that, Jonny?"

"A danged keepsake. Might have been a sluice pan."

Mose was studying the river as Jon approached.

"What's your thoughts, Mose? Go over?"

"Dem olds road crosses here, Jon."

"Yeah, and I can see where it comes out over there."

"We's takes dem chances here."

"Okay, the water runs flat here. What's your plan?"

"I's not sure, Jon. Corka goods swimmin'."

"Sure seems swift for this time of year."

"Yassa. Muss be rains an' dem mountains."

"We need to find out how deep she is."

"Yassa. I's takes Corka crost wit ropes."

"Are you sure, Mose? Looks blamed scary."

Mose grabbed the long rope from the buckboard and made his special halter around Corker.

"You's be's careful, Daddy," said Ella.

"Yes, I'm worried, Nunky Mo," added Maggie.

"I's be's orites." Mose swung up on Corker, and the big horse stepped into the water. "You's feeds rope, Jon."

"Righto, Mose. I'll wrap it around this tree, just in case." Jon made a quick loop around the tree, and Mose urged Corker forward. The swift current did not deter the big dray, as he strode into the water slapping at his flanks. "If our luck holds, we can drive the wagons across," said Jon to anyone listening. "That must be a road bed."

No answer forthcoming, as the ladies and boy held their breath. Mose was now two-thirds of the way across the wide channel.

Suddenly, the bed gave way under Corker. Jon saw Mose grab the rope, as he and the horse were swept downstream. Jonathan ran around the tree, making a second loop. That seemed to hold the rope from slipping. Margaret screamed and held Ella in her embrace.

"Stay back, so I can see!" Jon shouted at Maggie.

"Okay, Jonny." The three women and boy retreated to the wagon. Jon could see Corker and Mose treading water at the end of the rope.

"Can you unhook the lead team, so I can haul them back?" he asked the women.

"Yassa. We's do," answered Ella.

Over the sounds of the river, Jon could hear Mose. "Looz dem rope! Looz dem rope!" Mose hollered.

"I think he wants me to let out the slack," mumbled Jon. "Is he serious? They can be swept away!"

"Looz dem rope!" came the call again.

"Okay, here goes." Jon eased the hold, and loops began to move, lengthening the tow. Jon looked out over the water and saw Mose and Corker start swimming to the opposite shore. He reversed his trip around the tree, making only one loop, and the rope easily slipped through his hands. The current had swept them down the river several yards, but the huge man and horse found ground again and walked up the incline on the west side of the Yadkin. Mose waved, as he walked the big horse back to line up with the old roadway. He then freed the rope from the horse and tied it to the closest tree.

"Ties dem rope da dem tree," Mose shouted.

Ella had team five unhitched; and Jon tied the rope to Jake and Red, backing them to make the rope taut across the Yadkin, tree to tree. When he finished tying the rope to the tree, Jon noticed that Mose was already halfway across the river, swimming back.

He must have another of his great plans, Jon thought, as he grabbed the huge black man's hand. The dripping wet giant headed straight to the buckboard and grabbed the axe.

"What's your plan, Mose?"

"We's bills raffs." In little time, Mose had a large tree dropped, and was cutting it into roughly six foot lengths. Then a second tree, and a third. "You's splits dem, Jon. Gets teams harness, missy."

"Righto." Jon wondered how Mose learned this trick. The huge man placed several small logs from the top of the trees parallel, then, with the help of team five, laid two very long, large logs on top of the rollers, facing the river, about five to six feet apart. Mose and Jon then began laying the split logs across the big timbers, making a deck. Jon took the splitter and hammer, and trimmed the round bottoms of his logs, so they would lay flat on the timbers.

"You's gets dem straps, missy," Mose instructed Ella.

"I's do, Daddy," as she hurried to the buckboard.

Mose and Jon then tied the deck down, using the straps to fasten every second or third log to the big timbers.

"Will that be strong enough to hold the wagon, Mose?"

"Nossir. We's makes stronga." Mose then produced two long poles, and laid them across the ends of the deck, again facing the river. These poles were lashed every few feet to the big timbers under the deck, making a sturdy raft.

"Do we take the big wagon across first?"

"Yassar, Jon. We's takes big wagon." Mose grabbed the shorter rope and tied it to the bow of the vessel.

Jon wondered what Mose was going to do with that, as he stood in amazement as Mose grabbed the machete and whacked off the long rope at the tree, creating a second shorter rope, which he tied to the aft of the raft. Mose then pushed it down the rollers and into the water, to one side. *What now?* was all Jon could think, or ask, as Mose led the teams, pulling the big wagon forward to the water's edge. Mose then unhooked the two teams from the wagon and led them out into the water then lined the raft back in front of and under the wagon's front wheels. He then took the small rope, tied one end to the tongue of the wagon, and short-ended the other two teams, five and fifteen, in the water.

"Ella, you's rides Jake an' pulls wagon on raff."

"Yassa, Daddy."

Mose picked up Ella and lifted her onto the back of Jake, waist deep in the river. Jon picked up blocking.

"We's holes raff straight, Jon. Orites, missy, pull dem wagon."

Ella urged the teams forward, deeper into the water. The big wagon stalled at the raft. Mose and Jon pulled on the front wheels, and it jumped forward onto the deck. The wheel started to turn, but Mose grabbed the tongue and held it straight, as Ella's teams pulled the wagon forward. The raft sank down into the water under the weight. The men blocked the wheels as Ella slackened the rope.

"We's takes sum loads off dem wagon," said Mose.

Jon tried to hold the raft and wagon steady, as Mose walked out into deep water and backed the horses up against the raft.

"Holes dem teams back, missy," he told Ella.

"I's do, Daddy."

The two men emptied a part of the booty from the wagon, and the raft lifted back on top of the water.

"I guess we're about ready," said Jon.

"Nossa, nots ready yets, Jon. We's lashes down dem wagon."

Mose walked back to the trees and brought back two more small poles. They fit through the spokes of the wheels, and the man lashed them to the ends of the decking.

"Now we's ready," said Mose, as he retied the end of the small rope to the bow of the raft. The other end was looped around his waist.

"Are you going to pull the raft yourself?"

"Nossa. I's swims across an' helps Corka pulls raff."

"Okay, Mose. When do we send the animals across?"

"We's cans swim dem teams five now, and Pasha an' Abby cow an' dem raff."

The horses were freed from their harnesses, and Mose jumped aboard Jake.

"What should I do, Mose?"

"You's rides raff an' keeps straight. Ella keeps raff straight. We's backs Slog wit drags rope."

"He wants you to anchor the back rope aboard Sloggy."

"I's knows, Jon. I's do," said Ella, who jumped up on Slog and took up the rope attached to the rear of the raft.

Jon squeezed onto the raft, and grabbed the rope stretched across the river. Mose started across the Yadkin, riding Jake and pulling the reins of Red. Across the river they went, while Jon and Ella waited and Buelah, Chipper, and Margaret watched.

Again, the horses and Mose ended up swimming the final leg of the crossing. He then swung the rope he carried around the tree and then around Corker. Mose signaled to Jon on the east side of the Yadkin, who wrapped an arm around the long, taut rope. Ella held the trailing rope aboard Sloggy. Corker started to pull. The raft, carrying Jon and the big wagon, floated into swift water. Soon the deep part was just ahead. Jon held fast to the big rope. He looked back at Ella and Slog, who were upstream in the area of the old abandoned mine and now entering the water, drag line taut, holding the raft true on course. The plan and skill of Mose once again proved valuable to Jon, as the raft snuggled up to the west bank. Corker held the raft fast. The men could hear the women and boy cheering on the other side. Mose harnessed team five and hitched them to the wagon, while Jon freed the straps to the poles, holding the wagon in place.

"Get, Jake. Up, Red." The team lunged forward, and the wagon's front wheels bounced off the raft onto land. The teams struggled to get the heavy wagon rolling up the gentle incline.

"Blocks dem wheels, Jon. Whoa, Red. Whoa."

"Righto." Jon stopped the load from rolling back. Mose led Corker to the front of team five and short-roped him, changing from the raft to the tongue of the wagon.

"Ups, Corka. Get, Red." Corker dug in his heels, and the wagon easily climbed to level ground.

"You're a wizard, Mose. Corker didn't even need team five."

Mose unhooked the three horses from the wagon and again secured the business end of the small rope to the raft.

"What's next, Mose?"

"You's goes back an' bring Abby cow an' Pasha, and Buelah, missy, an' Missus Maggie back."

"Good. We'll finally get Maggie off Bethania."

They gave the signal for Ella to haul back on the rear line, and the raft carrying Jon slipped across the water, Corker on drag. Jon looped his arm around the big line and floated across the Yadkin with ease.

"Okay, Maggie, Mose says you and Pasha, Buelah, and the cow go next. I think we can take Chipper too."

"Alright, Jonny. Is it safe?"

"Like pounding salt. Nothing to it." Jon threw some of the booty aboard.

"I's skeerd, Jonny," said Buelah.

"You can hang on to me and Chipper. He's a crust."

The cow, Abby, stepped aboard the raft with ease, but Pasha was a different story. He was prancing, shying, and even lifting on his hind legs. Maggie and Jon held fast to his halter.

"Come on, Pasha. It's alright, sweetie," coaxed Maggie.

They were finally all aboard, Jon's arm wrapped around the big line, Buelah holding onto Jon's belt, Chipper holding Abby, and Maggie holding and talking to Pasha.

"Let's get rambunctious," said Jon, as he signaled Mose across the river. The raft lunged forward, almost spilling the group, but smoothed out and floated across the stream. Jon chuckled as he watched Buelah.

"You're almost white, Buelah."

"I's nevah goes near dem watah again!" she sobbed.

"Then I'll have to bathe you in lye." That brought looks from both Buelah and Maggie.

"You're not funny," stated a stern Margaret Hamilton.

Jon was grinning when the raft stopped in almost the exact same place as the last trip. Buelah scrambled off, and Chipper led Abby. Mose helped Maggie get the frightened Pasha onto solid ground.

"Free at last, huh, Maggie?"

"What do you mean, Jonny?"

"You are free from the confines of Bethania."

"Yes. I hadn't thought of that."

Jon pulled Maggie to him and kissed her. "Congratulations." They hugged.

Mose had unloaded the booty. "I's goes back with you's, and we's brings back alls ress," he said.

"Righto. You work the drag with Corker, Maggie. One more trip and we're all free of Bethania."

Signals given, the raft skimmed across the ripples. Back on the plantation side, Mose and Jon brought the buckboard to the raft. It was loaded, but the black brute pulled, and Jon pushed from behind.

"Hell's bells. We didn't need the horses," muttered Jon.

With the small wagon in place and blocked, Mose again went searching for a couple of small poles, and lashed down the wheels. Jon loaded the remainder of the booty onto the raft and climbed aboard.

"Can we make it all this trip, Mose?"

"Yassa. I's ties Smut to dem rear an' raff. Ella, you's sits an' dem buckboard. I's backs rear with Slog."

Mose climbed aboard Sloggy and untied the main line from the tree and lashed it to Sloggy.

Jon took one more look around. "Goodbye, Bethania. Thanks."

The raft eased into the water for the last time. All went well, as long as Mose and Slog held fast in one spot with their two ropes. Mose jumped down to the ground. "Whoas, big Sloggy. Whoa, big fella."

Mose hoped that Sloggy would stay put with the big line taut as he ran upstream with the drag. Mose was about to the end of the drag line, and walked the end of the rope into the water.

Jon looked back from the raft and saw that Mose was in the water struggling. He hung onto the big rope, anchored steadfastly by the dray, Sloggy. Mose was now chest high in water, as the raft reached the drop-off.

"Hols on dem big rope, Jon!" he yelled, as he let loose the drag line. Jon wrapped both arms around the long rope. It was slacking, giving way. Jon looked back to see Sloggy slowly giving ground. Mose was trying to hurry out of the water, talking to Slog. "Whoas der, Sloggy. Whoas."

The horse was trying to haul back, but the current was dragging him toward the water. Jon hung on with all his might.

"Maggie, back Corker fast!" he yelled.

Jon saw that Chipper had heard him and was running to Corker and Maggie. Jon looked at Ella, who was sitting very silently on the makeshift buckboard bench. Mose had now made it out of the water and grabbed the big rope, stopping the current's pull and Sloggy's slipping.

"Saved by that starker again," said Jonathan, in relief.

Corker pulled the raft quickly to the shore. Jon jumped off and helped Ella down. He could see that Mose was hollering something, but he was having trouble hearing.

"Corka . . . big ropes!" Jon knew what to do. He anchored the tow rope to a tree. Then he untied the big rope from the tree, left the loop around the tree, then harnessed the rope to Corker. He waved to Mose across the Yadkin, who was astride Sloggy, and started the pull of the main line by Corker. The big ex-bounder and beast waded into the river.

Soon it was time for one last swim. Mose hung on to the rope as Corker pulled the horse and hunk to shore. All was across, and it was time for another celebration. The last of the corn juice was downed by a wet Mose and a relieved Jonathan, who could see that his new bride was quietly gazing across the water at Bethania.

Jon threw the empty bottle into the river.

"That's Bethania corn. We'll soon be drinking Arkansas rice." Jon hugged Maggie and walked her back to the big wagon.

"Come, my pretty plum. We've work to do."

"Alright, Jonny. Do we have to travel up that road today? I'm tired, and I'm sure Nunky Mo is tired."

"Tired and wet . . ."

Jon could tell that midafternoon was past them, and after the experiences of this day, a good rest was in order.

"Okay, gang. Should we rest or travel?"

"Rest. We's ress. Ress dem hoses," came the responses.

"Righto. Mose, do you have any dry banyans and trousers?"

"Yassa, Jon."

"I's stishes Daddy's shirts wen we's ress," said Ella.

"Alright. While you get out of those wet clothes, we'll get the teams hooked up to the wagons and get everything set."

"I thought we were resting, Jonny."

"Yes, but I saw some great grass for the animals back down the river about a mile."

"Orites, we's goes down riva," said Mose in a commanding voice, as he shed his wet skins. "You's brake down dem raff an' saves straps," he commanded Buelah and Chipper.

As the clan made the short distance down Boone Road, Jon's mind was busy wondering if Mose was taking a leading role in this adventure. *It would be gormless to buck that giant*, he thought, *and he would hate to play tanglebutt with him.* Hell, he couldn't. Mose was his right arm. Jon found a likely spot with tall grass beside the road. He jumped down from the lead wagon.

"Does this look alright to you, Mose?"

"Yassa, if you's like."

"Good. Let's set up and hobble the animals." Jon felt a big relief with Mose's answer.

"Yassa, we's do."

The men formed a "V" close to the road and unhooked the animals from the wagons.

"I's handles dem hoses, Jon."

"Okay, Mose, I'll get our water replenished and find wood for a fire. This place is horse heaven."

"Yassa. Chips, you's milks Abby cow for supper."

"Yassar," came the boy's response.

"We girls will get things ready for a big supper."

It was big, alright. "Boston" was on the menu, of Bullock's Heart, Boston baked beans, Boston brown corn bread, and fresh milk from Abby, thanks to Chipper.

The sun had long since hidden behind the mountains, and darkness approached. Jonathan surveyed his "clan," all gathered around the bonfire.

"This has been one wild Sunday. You all were hammers, and I'm very proud of you." Cheers rang all around.

"Nunky Mo, you have a beautiful voice. Will you sing for us?" asked Maggie. "Maybe a church song."

"We's all sings," said an excited Buelah.

Mose started a song that Jon had heard several times on Bethania. Mose had a smooth deep voice:

> *"O broders, dons gets weary*
> *O broders, dons gets weary*
> *O broders, dons gets weary*
> *We's lans on Canaan's shore"*

All the rest joined in the singing:

> *"We's lans on Canaan's shore*
> *We's lans on Canaan's shore*
> *Wen we's lans on Canaan's shore*
> *We's meets forever more"*

Jonathan and Margaret applauded and cheered.

"Let's have a happy song, a free song," said Jon.

"Okays. We's do," answered Ella.

The group started chanting over and over a catchy tune.

"Thars a bedder days a-comin'
Will you's gos along wit me?
Thars a bedder days a-comin'
Go sound dem jubilee"

The blacks started the "Juba." In unison, they slapped their knees then clapped their hands. Next, they struck the right shoulder with one hand, the left shoulder with the other, all the while keeping time stomping their feet and singing. Jon and Maggie joined in with them, having trouble keeping up at first. They no sooner had the motions down, when Chipper jumped up and started dancing to the beat, around the fire. Buelah followed suit. Soon the entire clan was dancing in the circle, singing the tune. The singing and dancing lasted well into the night. When the group finally settled back down, they began to realize it was late.

"Is time we's hits the sacs, Daddy," said Ella.

"Orites, Mama. I's tired."

"You should be tired, Mose. You worked your butt sticks off."

"Do you have enough blankets, Ella?" asked Margaret.

"Yassa, missy, we's do."

Mose grabbed the machete and wacked away at the tall grass. The rest chipped in, making a "mattress" around the fire. Jon laid the quilt over it. Maggie slipped out of her shoes and climbed under the quilt.

"We have blankets, Mag. Let's sleep on top of the quilt."

"But I'll be cold, Jonny."

"Damned if you will. I'll take care of that, my buckboard bunny."

"Jonny, behave. We're with company."

"We are not company, my pretty plum. We are family."

Maggie retrieved several blankets from the big wagon and started spreading them over the quilt.

"Two are enough for me, Maggie."

"Not for me. I'll be cold."

"I promise you will not be cold. Fold that sweat-soaker over you and put one more blanket on top."

"Alright, Jonny. That will give me four blankets to two."

The newlyweds slipped under the warmers. Jon's grabbers found cossack and blouse, as he snuggled to Maggie.

"Stop it, Jonny. You're embarrassing me," she whispered.

Jon gazed to the other side of the ashes. Chipper was already asleep, and Buelah lay quietly next to the boy. He noticed Ella only partially under the blankets, large black breasts exposed. Mose climbed under the blankets in a state of nature.

"No one is watching us. How can you be embarrassed?"

"Shush, Jonny. Go to sleep!"

"Like hell! Come on, darling, shed those togs."

"No, Jonny. I'll be cold. Please go to sleep."

"I'll give you my drawers to wear afterward."

Maggie started giggling. Her sounds were soon drowned by the grunts and moans by the buckboard. Jon rose to see Ella's blankets bouncing over a huge hump.

"Look, my little fluff," Jon whispered, "Mose and Ella are pounding ground. Why can't we?"

"Please, Jonny. I need time to get used to this."

Jon settled back and lay quietly. The grunts were finally replaced by snores, and what sounded like sobs.

"Are you crying, Buelah?" Margaret called out.

"I's misses my Buff," came the reply.

"I know, honey. I miss my whole family. It will be alright."

Buelah was soon quiet. The only sounds were the sputtering of the dying fire.

"Are you alright, Jonny?"

"I'm sad."

"Why?"

"He's one up on me."

Maggie giggled again.

Diary of Margaret Rose (McAllister) Hamilton

October 25, 1835

Today, the most difficult of my life, was also a very trying day for all, but especially my poor Jonny. First, he feared the loss of Nunky Mo, on what he later dubbed "Hamilton Hill." He did suffer the loss of supplies and a damaged wagon. He also faced the loss of our cow, Abby, only to find her again on an old road, climbing and descending that very same knoll that would have saved us all the pain of Hamilton Hill. Again, Jonny feared the loss of Nunky Mo, crossing the Yadkin River, swift and swollen from rain. But I fear that I have caused his ultimate distress, by my refusal of intimacy in front of our group. Yet, alas, we are separated from Bethania, and strangely I am much more relieved about this adventure. My husband has promised my reuniting soon with my family . . .

CHAPTER II

Margaret Rose McAllister

January, 1835

"Mose! Bring the mistress to my study immediately!"

"Yassar, Master Sam." House bounder Mose Dasilvalentis McAllister knew his master meant business. The giant slave touched one of each of the four steps, as he rushed up the grand stairway to Mistress Susan's room. As footfall touched carpet, the staircase shook, and as massive hand rapped solid cherry door, the wall seemed to shake.

"Missus Susan! Missus Susan!"

"What is it, Mose?" came the voice from behind the door.

"Massa Sam say he wans you's."

"Yes, Mose, I'll be right down."

"He's say now, Missus Susan."

"Yes, Mose, I'm coming." The big door opened, and out stepped the tall, slender frame of Susan Ashley McAllister, mistress of the plantation Bethania. The striking dark red hair, squeezed into a ball on top of her head, seemed to bounce, as Susan hurried to the top of the staircase. Her graceful strides clashed with the shuffling of the huge slave.

"Where is the master?"

"He be's an' dem study."

"Thank you, Mose. That will be all."

"Yassar, Missus Susan."

As Susan strode past the great hall of Bethania, she wondered what her husband was fretting about this time. "I'm certainly in no mood for another fight," she muttered. As she knocked and entered the master's study, Susan could see the pits had disappeared from the mockered face of Samuel McAllister II, visible only at the cheekbones, above the bristling baraclave, which disappeared behind his desk.

"What is it, Samuel?"

"It's your daughter again!"

"Oh my, what has she done this time?"

"She managed to get herself expelled again!" Sam flung the message he had just received at Susan. Without being asked or told, Susan sat in the open chair and braced herself.

January 14, 1835

> *Samuel McAllister*
> *Bethania Plantation*
> *Salem, North Carolina*

> *Dear Mister McAllister,*

>> *It grieves me dearly to inform you of the suspension of your daughter, Miss Margaret McAllister.*
>> *When the board took similar action last year, I was able to reverse the ruling. But the breaking of this school's rules has continued, and this time I must concur with the board's decision. The integrity of this school may be at stake.*
>> *You have been very generous in the past, and I have been instructed to forward our most sincere gratitude for your contributions. We look forward to another noble and unselfish donation this year.*
>> *Miss McAllister will be allowed to continue her residence here until the end of this month. Please accept my sincere apology for the resolution of the board.*

>> *Yours Truly,*
>> *A. D. Dumfries*
>> *Master of Deans*
>> *Salem Women's College*

Susan sat quietly for a moment, then folded the letter and placed it back on the master's desk. Samuel could see tears welling in her eyes.

"Well, say something."

"You never told me about the last time."

"The last time!" Sam shouted. "The hell with the last time! What about this time?"

"Please don't scream at me, Samuel." Luckily, Susan had thought to bring a handkerchief. "You were the one who insisted on sending her there."

"You bet I did. Your tutor Wilder was costing a pile."

"Sam, he's the same tutor you had teaching Allston."

"I should have sent Ally to Charlotte."

"I would like you to send Sissy there, Sam. That's where young James Johnstone is attending."

"Are you still trying to mate Sissy with him?"

"The Johnstones have wealth, Sam. That should be to your liking." Susan had managed to settle Sam down some, and the pits returned.

"That would be a good way to rid ourselves of her."

"Sam! That's no way to talk about our daughter. She has always been your pride and joy."

"Yes, I know. It does seem a relief to have her away for a while, though. Maybe I will send her to state."

"Fine, Sam. Now what about the other boys?"

"They're getting their schooling. What about them?"

"You know the teaching they're getting at your bounder's school is a very poor grade, Sam. They need tutoring."

Sam jumped off his chair, the pits disappearing again. "I'll be damned if they need tutoring!" he shouted. "Just look at me. I never had much schooling."

"But you inherited Bethania, Sam. You and Silas both inherited your wealth." The tears were returning.

"Damn your sassiness. I have worked hard for my wealth. How dare you imply otherwise? Get out of my study! I'll handle Sissy's problems myself."

Susan rushed out of Sam's study, her face buried in her handkerchief.

"And my name is Samuel, not Sam!" he cried out after her.

Susan rushed into the waiting arms of her personal body servant, Elsie Existentialist McAllister, named for Sam's belief that she was always in a fog.

"I's hear dem shouting, Missus Susan." Elsie held Susan close as they walked to and up the grand staircase, the sobbing uncontrolled. "It be orite, Missus Susan. I's bring you's some milk and friss cookies."

"Thank you, Elsie." Susan entered her room.

"You's welcome, missus." As Elsie walked down the hallway to the rear entrance of the mansion, she passed the master's study. He was still cursing as he spotted her.

"Where are you going, Elsie?" he yelled.

"I's bring Missus Susan milk, Masser Sam."

"Make it sour milk. That's what she deserves."

"You's a bad man, Masser Sam."

"Bite your tongue, floozy, or I'll send you to the field."

"Yassar." Elsie tried to hurry out the back door.

"And send Mose here right away."

"Yassar."

In a very short order, Mose appeared in the study doorway. "You's send for me, Master Sam?"

"Yes. Go to the carriage house and hitch up the Landau. You and Danny are taking me to Salem."

"Yassar." As Mose D. shuffled out of the mansion, he was met by Elsie, who tried to rush past the open door of the study.

"Elsie!" shouted Samuel.

"Yassar, Masser Sam."

"Tell the mistress that I'm headed for Salem. Not sure when I'll return."

"Yassar." Elsie hurried up the hall, past the great dining hall, and up the stairs.

"Masser Sam say he head for Salem," she informed Susan.

"Thank you, Elsie. Better remind him to wear his Albert overcoat. It's cold outside." The tears were over.

"I's no tells him. He mad at me."

"Yes, at me also. I'm sure he will remember."

"Or maybe he freeze."

"Shush, Elsie. These walls have ears." Susan smiled.

"Yassa, missus." Elsie smiled back.

The sleek carriage cut through what appeared to Samuel to be an isolated bank of fog. The bitter cold was causing the breath of team eight, young Danny Doubleclutch, and big Mose Dasilvalentis to form a fogbank.

"Are you and Danny alright, Mose?" Sam asked through the speaker tube.

"Yassa, Master Sam."

"Then get to toweling. It's going to be dark before we get there."

"Yassar!" Mose knew that meant sleeping in the traveler's slave house. "Wit' dem nassy niggers," he mumbled.

"What?" asked the freezing Danny.

"When we's gets an' Salem, you's stay neer me."

"Yassa, I's do."

"Gettup, Tiny. Gets, Waldo." The big sorrels increased their gait. The two black bounders sat on the hard cold Dickey, the air biting their hands and faces.

While in Salem, I must remember to place an ad for another overseer this spring, thought Samuel, as he sank down in his luxurious cab seat of white morocco skin. He wrapped himself in a blanket and laid his head back into the cushioned headrest. He pulled out the letter he had so recently received and read.

"A. D. Dumfries. I wonder what the AD stands for. Hmmm . . . Another dumb Dumfries! He's going to be dumbfounded when he sees me answer this letter in person."

The Landau sped across Bethania's cornfields, and finally onto the carriageway.

"Whoa, Tiny. Whoa, Waldo." The coach came to a stop.

"Why are we stopping, Mose?" The sudden lack of motion had brought Sam out of his nap.

"It be's too dark, Master Sam. I's light dem lamps."

"Alright. Be quick about it. I'm getting sleepy."

"Yassa." Another short snooze, and Sam was awakened by the clacking of hooves on the cobbled street of Salem.

"Mose," Sam spoke into the tube.

"Yassa, Master Sam."

"I've changed my mind. I was going to spend the night in the Traveler's Tavern, but take me to the hotel instead. I can sleep better there."

"Yassa, Master Sam." Mose was relieved at this change in plans, as the hotel had slave quarters in its basement, much cleaner and safer than the tavern.

"Whoas, Tiny. Whoa, big Waldo." The custom carriage slowed to a halt in front of the Salem Hotel. Nothing or nobody was stirring. Sam took the handles of his overnighter, and stepped out of the Landau.

"Stay here with the horses."

"Yassa, Master Sam."

Samuel walked into the well-lit, yet quiet lobby. He grabbed the bell at the counter, and shook it hard. No answer. He shook it again.

From a back room came the response, "I'm coming. Hold your horses."

"I have two servants holding my horses, and I want a room."

From the rear door came a little old man in a state of half dress, thin gray hair in his face. He stumbled behind the counter and began searching for his spectacles. The stubble on his wrinkled old face made Sam chuckle. The old man found and hung his specs over his ears. He looked at the heavy hair on the face of the visitor and also started to chuckle.

"My name is Samuel McAllister, and I demand a suitable room for myself and a bed for my servants."

"Alright, Sam, I have a—"

"It's Samuel McAllister, not Sam."

"Yes, sir, Mister McAllister. As I was saying, I have my best room available, facing the street. Just up those stairs and turn right. Room number twenty-two." He handed Sam a key, and started from behind the counter.

"Just a damn minute. I need a bed for two servants."

"All they need to do is walk to the rear of the building, walk down the stairs into the basement, and find a spot. That will be fifty cents more."

"And where are your servants?"

"It's past eleven o'clock, Mister McAllister. They are home in bed."

"Get them up, *now*! I expect them to feed and stable my horses, lock up my coach, escort my servants to a bed, and bring me something to eat."

"Yes, sir, Mister McAllister. I'll get to it right now."

"See that you do. I'm hungry and very tired."

"Yes, sir. Let's see, sir. That will be two dollars for the rooms."

Sam reached into his pocket and pulled out a gold Eagle. "That should take care of it."

"Yes, sir, it certainly will."

"Then get cracking." Sam took the key and headed for the stairs.

"Yes, sir. Right away."

"Oh, yes, my servants are likely very cold. See to it they get plenty of blankets and food." Sam relished his power over the hotel clerk.

"Yes, sir." The old clerk was getting flustered.

"And I'll need an early wake-up, with hot water, soap, and towels."

As he reached the top of the stairs, Sam heard banging on a door and, "Get up quick, Bobby. Run and get Joe and Nell up." Sam smiled as he found room number twenty-two.

The dancing wasn't helping Danny and Mose keep warm. They wondered what was happening in the hotel lobby. Even team eight seemed cold.

"Gos look an' dem window."

"Yassa, I's do," said Danny, who quietly peeked in the hotel door glass. He shrugged his shoulders at Mose. "I see notin'."

"Massa Sam has retired," said Mose.

"Whats we do now?"

"We's gets in dem coach." The two bounders scrambled into the Landau. At last they found warmth. The coach had two blankets. Mose grabbed them and stepped out.

"Wheres you's go wit them?" asked Danny.

"I's puts dem on hoses." The blankets fit loosely over harnessed drays, but Mose felt they helped.

Mose climbed back into the cab, and soon settled in the luxurious seat, much too small, but comfortable. His slumbering had just started when the hotel seemed to come alive with activity. A young man in his teens charged out the lobby door and ran down the street. Next an old man appeared, putting on an overcoat, and approached the Landau. He peered into the cab.

"Someone will be here shortly to shelter the horses and this Milord. I'll take you to your quarters."

"We's stays with dem hoses now," said Mose.

"Alright. Do you need a place to sleep?"

"Yassa, after we handles hoses."

"Alright, bring them this way."

Mose and Danny climbed back out of the carriage, relieving the load on its springs, and led the team behind the elderly man, around the building and into a barn in the alley. Mose and Danny busied themselves, unhitching the team.

"You can use these stalls, and the Milord will be fine right there. I'll lock the barn door."

"This be's a Landau, sir."

The old man lit a lantern, and now gazed in awe at the size of the slave. The lantern started shaking and almost dropped from his hand.

"Y-yes, it be a Landau, if you say so. I-I'll be right back and escort you to your quarters."

"Orite, we's waits here," said Mose.

The man ran out and disappeared into the rear of the hotel. Mose and Danny found hay for the horses. Before long, the same young man, who ran down the main street earlier, came out of the hotel.

"Y'all come along with me," he said in a heavy drawl.

Mose reckoned that he was a teener. *A poor white boy*, he thought.

"Maybe we's shou stay wit hoses," said Danny.

"I'll take care a that. Y'all come along and git some vittles and sleep," said the boy. "I'll lock this here barn."

"Orite. We's turns in, Danny," said Mose.

The lantern led the bounders into the hotel, and down the steps to the basement. There was a room on one side, no door, with several blacks sleeping in beds.

"Them thar is hotel workers," said the white boy.

In several places were small piles of straw, and Mose wondered which one they would sleep on. In a far corner were two small empty cots.

"Y'all sleep here. I'll bring some vittles."

Danny quickly stretched out on one bed.

"We's be on sleep soon," said Mose.

"I'll be a gettin' food now."

"Orite. I's thanks you's, sir."

The young white man rushed back up the stairs, leaving the bounders in the dark. When he returned several minutes later, the two men were sound asleep.

The pits had vanished, and the beard was ruffled. Sam had worked up another anger, as he stormed into the school lobby, past the receptionist.

"May I help you, sir? Sir, you can't go in there."

There were doors on either side of the hall. The first room was empty. A large woman sat behind a desk in the room across the hall.

"Hello, sir, are you lost?" she asked, as her door slammed shut.

As Samuel approached the next door, the receptionist took hold of his arm.

"Sir. Please, sir. May I help you?"

"I'm here to see Dumfries," scowled Sam.

"Well, please come back to the lobby and I'll get him."

Just then, Sam noticed the sign on the last door: Master of Deans.

"Never mind. I've found him."

The door with the sign swung open roughly. In stepped a comical-looking, pear-shaped man with a long heavy baraclave, followed by the receptionist. Mister Dumfries sat behind his desk, talking with a little lady, whose gray hair was styled in an Anne Boleyn mob.

"What the . . . What is your business here, sir?"

Sam produced the letter from under his overcoat and slung it at the headmaster. The little lady stood to leave, a frown then a glare on her face.

"Please don't leave, Missus Crady. This involves you." The little lady reclaimed her chair.

"You are here to question the actions of the board, I presume?"

"You can be damn sure of that!" shouted Samuel.

"Well, sir, may I introduce you to Missus Crady. She is the mother of your daughter's roommate."

"So it was your daughter who got my daughter expelled!"

The little lady came out of her chair. "Why, you hairy dufus, it's the other way around! Your daughter is about to get mine expelled!"

"Please take a chair, sir, so we can discuss this like adults," said the schoolmaster.

"There is nothing to discuss. I demand that you reinstate my daughter! I built this college, and I'll see to it that you and this board of yours get run out of the state!"

"I'm sorry, Mister McAllister. I cannot do that. Your daughter has been injurious to this school, and she has to leave."

"Injurious be damned, you dumfuss, what could my daughter do here that she is injurious?"

Mister Dumfries picked up a small bell and rang it vigorously. In a matter of seconds, the receptionist poked her head in the room.

"Yes, sir?"

"Send immediately for Miss Crady and Miss McAllister."

"Yes, sir." The door closed as quickly as it had opened.

"I believe everyone should be present before we go into detail of your daughter's shenanigans. Please sit down, Mister McAllister."

"Shenanigans? You are the shenanigan, Dumfuss."

"My name is Dumfries, Mister McAllister."

"Dumfries, Dumfuss, they still have dumb in them. I want to know what my Maggie did that was so terrible."

"She had a black man in their room," said Missus Crady, "and now she has my daughter in trouble."

Sam's jaw dropped down. "She what?"

"Yes, sir, Mister McAllister, one of our grounds men was caught with your daughter, partially undressed. He was shackled and sent to Charleston to be auctioned."

"My daughter wouldn't do that. He must have forced himself on her. Don't you discipline your flunkies? What's his name? I'll buy him and whip the truth out of him." The normally mockered face was clear and bright red, and the beard was wet where the chin should have been.

"I can't give you his name, Mister McAllister, but I assure you that he will be punished enough. He was well on the way to becoming a free slave, and now he will be bound for the rest of his life."

"That's not enough. I should put him in the rice fields. A case of malaria will cure him or kill him."

"Why kill him? It was your daughter who instigated this mess." Missus Crady was shaking a finger at him.

"Don't you shake your finger at me. It was probably Miss Shady Crady who instigated it."

"Miss Crady wasn't in the room at the time of the incident, Mister McAllister. We don't feel she was involved at all, but we need your daughter to verify that."

"And this time, I hope she tells the truth," said Missus Crady, staring at the long beard.

"Why you little ringtail. My Maggie doesn't lie."

"Please, Mister McAllister, no name calling. Your daughter tried to claim that Miss Kathryn brought the black man into their room and had a sexual encounter with him," said Master Dumfries.

"And it's *my* daughter who wouldn't do that."

"Well!" Samuel jumped back up out of his chair. "If your daughter wouldn't, and my daughter didn't, then it never happened. Where is the featherheaded liar who said they did? Bring him in here, Dumfuss."

"Please sit, Mister McAllister. There is no question that the incident happened. Your daughter has admitted involvement, and two people witnessed it."

"They're all liars!" The little exposed part of Sam's face was now a glowing red. "Maggie is a dignified young lady. I'm sure there has been a mistake, and I demand her reinstatement!"

"I'm sorry, Mister McAllister, but with Miss Margaret's previous record, the board will not consider her reinstatement."

"That was also a lie!" shouted Samuel.

"Mister McAllister, you seem to forget that your daughter also admitted to smoking and drinking on campus, both strictly against the rules."

"Why is she still here? If my Kathy did that, she would have been expelled long ago." Missus Crady was now on her feet alongside Samuel McAllister.

"Because my money built this college," answered Sam.

"Both of you please sit down. I'm sure the board had its reasons for allowing Miss McAllister to remain after the previous incidents. But this time, their decision is final."

"Incidents? What else has this spoiled girl gotten away with?" The face of Missus Crady was also now red.

"Nothing else. Mind your own cussed business!" shouted Sam.

"I believe this matter is Missus Crady's business, Mister McAllister." To the angry little woman, he said, "Miss Margaret ran away from this campus once, Missus Crady, and was found two days later in the Salem Tavern in the company of a rowdy."

"And she wasn't expelled then?" quizzed the gray-haired lady.

"Yes, she was, and later reinstated," answered Mister Dumfries.

"And I want her reinstated this time!" blasted Samuel.

"We have given your daughter plenty of circumstances to adjust with, Mister McAllister, and she has chosen to put this school's record in jeopardy. Now she must go."

"You must go, Dumfuss. I'll get the governor—"

Just then, the knock came at the door, and the receptionist entered, followed by Margaret McAllister and a much shorter blondish girl, named Katheryn Crady. Both went immediately to their parent, Maggie making a show of hugging and kissing her father.

"Hi. Daddy. Thank you for coming."

"Maggie, I want to know what happened here."

"Kathy . . ." Maggie thought better of using the same lie with everyone in the room.

"Yes? Kathy did what?" insisted Samuel.

"Ah, Kathy and I were away from our room, and this man snuck in and scared me so badly that I started to faint, and the man caught my fall just as the mistress came in the door."

"See there," Samuel barked at the master of deans, "it wasn't my daughter's fault."

"Miss Katheryn," said Mister Dumfries, "I want you to tell us what happened, and remember your stay here is on the line."

Tears welled in her eyes as Katheryn looked at Maggie, then her mother, and finally to Mister Dumfries. "I saw Maggie mixing with a black man in the gardens and then sneak him into our room, so I stayed away."

"You're a liar!" shouted Margaret. "Daddy, it didn't happen like that at all."

"Yes, it did, Miss Margaret. Her story blends exactly with other witnesses. Thank you, Miss Crady. You may return to your room," said Mister Dumfries.

To the glares of Maggie and her father, Katheryn and her mother, arm in arm, started to exit the room. Tears were streaming down Katheryn's cheeks, as she approached Maggie and said, "I'm so sorry, Maggie. Please forgive me."

"Why you little gum-wagging grassback. I'll get even with you!"

"No, you won't." Mister Dumfries rang his bell. "You are to leave this campus within this hour."

"Yes, sir?" The receptionist must have met the Crady ladies at the door.

"Have Miss Crady identify, and have Miss McAllister's belongings brought to the lobby."

"Yes, sir." The door again closed.

"I don't believe we have anything more to say to each other, Mister McAllister. Thank you for coming."

"I've got one hell of a lot yet to say, Dumfuss, and I'll be saying it in Raleigh."

"I'm sorry you feel that way, sir, but this is a private school, and Raleigh has no control over our board."

"Well, I have some control over your wages, and they're going to get damned slim."

"Come on, Daddy darling, let's barrel out of here."

"Okay, Sissy. You haven't heard the last from me, Dumfuss."

As Margaret led her father by the arm, out the door, Sam said, "I sure gave him the Jesse."

"I'm sure you did, Daddy."

As the McAllisters walked down the hall, Sam realized that he hadn't taken off his overcoat, and it was heavy with sweat. He started to remove the coat.

"Leave it on, Daddy. It's not very warm outside."

They walked past the receptionist, who stood and said, "Goodbye, Miss Margaret, and good luck."

"Bye, Mary. Good luck to you."

As soon as they stepped outside, Sam felt the chill. Mose and Danny were shifting feet back and forth, trying to stay warm. Maggie ran ahead of her father to the hug the huge bounder, red hair bouncing.

"Hello, Nunky Mo." Her arms strained to encircle the neck of the shy giant.

"Hello, missy."

"And, Danny, how are you?"

"I's be fine, Miss Maggie."

"Let's get inside the Landau, Sissy," said Sam. To Mose, he said, "As soon as they bring Maggie's dry goods, take us home."

"Yassar, Master Sam," replied Mose.

A long silence prevailed as Sam settled into the Morocco skin and spread a blanket over his baraclave.

"Why?" he finally asked.

"Daddy, it was the way I said. Kathy was to blame."

"Don't lie to your father! That little Crady fluff is as innocent as I wish you were. Just looking at her, she was as white as these cushions."

"Then you're calling me a liar."

"I just want to know why, Sissy." The pits were back.

"Oh, Daddy, that place is *so* boring."

"I'm paying for the best instructors available."

"But they didn't know near as much as Jimmy, Daddy."

"Do you mean your tutor, Mister Wilder?"

"Yes. He has more head matter than all these deans."

"I wanted you to learn the social graces."

"Mother has more grace in her feet than these muddlenobs, Daddy. I already have more grace than them."

"Well, don't you think it's about time you were showing it?"

"Yes, Daddy, I will."

The conversation was interrupted by the sounds of Margaret's raggery being loaded onto the carriage.

"Mose?" Sam spoke into the tube.

"Yassar, Masta Sam?"

"I almost forgot. I need to stop at the Salem newspaper office."

"Yassar." The Landau headed for Main Street.

"Are you going to pop off about the college, Daddy?"

"No. I need to advertise for an overseer."

"Do you have enough bounders, tools, and horses for another gang?"

"Why, yes I do, Sissy." Sam was both surprised and pleased at his daughter's sudden interest in the business. "Tobacco is gaining all over Europe, and England is now buying cotton as fast as we can produce it."

"I thought they were supposed to be our enemy."

"They were, but that's all been forgotten."

"Try telling that to Uncle Silas."

"What do you mean, Sissy?"

"I don't think he'll ever forgive or forget them for what they did in Baltimore and Washington."

"I guess you're right about that."

The clacking of team eight's hooves on the cobbled street stopped the conversation momentarily. The rhythm was irregular and slowing. Samuel didn't know that Mose was searching for the newspaper office. The street was busy with white folk, but Mose could find no blacks. He spotted a white woman standing alone at a street corner and pulled up team eight.

"Pardon me, ma'am, I's looks fo dem newspaper."

Anger gripped the face of the lady. "How dare you? I don't speak to niggers."

Samuel slid open the window of the Landau. "Then speak to me. My servant was asking where the newspaper office is located."

"Turn right at the next corner. It's on the right."

"Thank you, ma'am. I already know where it's located."

"Well, you are very rude." The lady turned sharply and marched down the boardwalk, her umbrella striking the walk, and bustle-bouncing under her coatee.

"And you, ma'am, are very snooty!" he hollered back at her. "Turn right at the next corner, Mose."

"Yassar, Master Sam."

Sam sat back in his cushions and shared a good laugh with his daughter.

"Pull up here, Mose."

"Yassar."

"I'll be back in a split, Sissy."

"Okay, Daddy."

Sam turned the knob on the door with the sign *Salem Chronicle*, and stopped at the counter.

"Yes, sir. How can I help you?"

"I should like to place an ad in your paper for the entire month of February."

"Yes, sir. If you'll write it on this pad, I'll see to it."

Sam took the pad and pen, and wrote:

> *Hiring overseer. Steady employment March through October. Good pay and board, with ample time off. Apply at Bethania Plantation.*

"Thank you, sir. That will be one levy per week."

Sam dug into the pockets of his pantaloons. "I have five flips and one levy."

"That will be fine, sir. It will be spread each week of February. Thank you."

"Pleasure doing business in your establishment." Sam walked out the door and into the Landau, with a grin under the beard.

"Is something funny, Daddy?"

"I just took that flunderhead for a levy."

The clacking was now in fine rhythm, as Mose headed team eight west out of town. Margaret was soon faced with tongue and teeth, as Sam started yawning.

"Why are you so tired, Daddy?"

"I didn't sleep very well at that blame hotel."

"You mean you were here last night?"

"Yes, and I was *so* fired up over your expulsion that I tossed and turned most of the night."

"You could have slept in your own bed and came here in plenty of time this morning."

"I know, Maggie, but I wanted to get away from your mother and Elsie."

"Elsie can rattle your brain box, can't she?"

"I told her I was going to put her in the fields."

"You can't do that, Daddy. She is Mother's special servant."

"Better she than me."

"It would be nice if you did pay more attention to Mother."

"I've given her everything she ever needed. What more?"

"She needs some caring and respect, Daddy."

Their voices were quickly rising in pitch. "I don't get any caring or respect from any of my family."

"Yes you do, Daddy. You're just too bullheaded to accept it."

"Bullheaded, huh? If I was half as bullheaded as you think I am, you wouldn't be going to college."

"Good. I'd rather stay home!" screamed Maggie.

"Well, you're not going to!" Sam shouted back. The pits had disappeared again.

"What? Are you going to expel me from my own home?"

"Maybe I will if you don't start using some of those graces you say you have."

"You would never notice them if I did!" she screamed.

"Try it and we'll see, Sissy."

"You want me to apple-polish your backside?"

"No. Just act like a lady. That would help."

"You don't act like a man to Mother."

"That's none of your affair!" Sam was beet red and shaking.

"We better quiet down, Daddy, before you pop a cork."

At last there was an ear-splitting quiet, and Mose and Danny breathed a sigh of relief outside the Landau. Margaret noticed the pits slowly returning. "Looks like everything is back to normal," she said.

No answer. More silence.

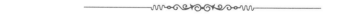

"I'm considering sending you to state, in Charlotte."

"I don't want to go there either."

"That's where your mother wants to send you."

"Mother? Why would she want to send me there?"

"She has visions of mating you with that Johnstone boy."

"Bull. She knows how much I dislike that lamebrain."

"That family is wealthy, Sissy. Your mother wants that for you."

"Mother wants me to be miserably wealthy?"

"I'm sure she feels that money makes you happy."

"It hasn't made her happy."

"What the hell is that supposed to mean?"

"Oh, come on, Daddy. You know Mother hasn't been happy in years."

"And I suppose that's my fault?" The pits were vanishing.

"Yes. It's both our faults, Daddy."

"She's had everything she's ever wanted."

"Let's not start that again."

"Then stop blaming me for your mother's unhappiness."

"Are you truly happy with all your booty, Daddy?"

"Of course I am."

"Think about it, Daddy, and don't lie to yourself. You have wealth, title, property, and slaves, but are you really happy without love?"

"My family loves me, I'm sure."

"I love you, Daddy, but you really don't give anyone else a chance to love you." Silence again sat in, as the sleek Landau skimmed over fields of corn and tobacco stalks, appearing like stakes in the ground. Maggie was again home on her beloved Bethania.

The luxurious carriage descended into the lush valley, full of neatly arranged buildings, across the McAllister creek and onto the circular drive up to the mansion. Even in midwinter, the setting was spectacular.

"Anyway, Daddy, I don't want to hurt Mother's feelings, but please help me convince her that I have no interest in either North Carolina State College, or James Johnstone."

"What does interest you, Maggie?"

"A good man and a family."

"And James Johnstone can't give you that?"

"I said a good man, Daddy. I'm afraid James Johnstone will turn out just like you."

"See what I mean? You're blaming me again."

Maggie giggled. "I'm sorry, Daddy. I love you, in spite of your brazenness."

"Brazenness be damned. Anyway, you're too young to be raising a family."

"My Lord. I'm almost twenty-one years old. Now I know what your problem is, Daddy."

"And what is my problem?"

"You want me to be Daddy's little old maid."

May 1, 1835

"For me? Oh, Daddy! He is lovely, so princely. What kind is he?"

"Full-blooded Arabian gelding, Maggie." Samuel McAllister the Second, wealthy owner and master of the Bethania Plantation, thought himself very uppish and fancy, in dress and manner. In fact, he was quite the opposite, with his patched eel skin trousers, and his favorite vest of pig skin and slave cloth. Stern with his family, servants, and slaves, which he called bounders, Samuel had trouble controlling his only white daughter, Margaret Rose. "Happy birthday, my sweet."

"Thank you, Daddy. I love him! He's *so* beautiful, and white as snow." Maggie was hugging, rubbing, and patting the pure white silky coat of the majestic animal, held fast at the reins by house bounder Mose.

"Isn't he beautiful, Mother?"

"Yes, he is, Sissy. Be careful. He may not be completely broken in," came the response from Susan Ashley McAllister, mistress of Bethania. Tall, slender, and always well dressed, Susan was in sharp contrast with her husband. She was trim, neat, and statuesque; he was a head shorter, pear-shaped, and unkempt. She with long, clean red hair, stacked neatly high on the back of her head in an "a la giraffe," he with long brownish hair, in no particular style, covering his neck, collar, and ears, and a beard starting at the line where ears should be, to meet and cover the tip of a large, pointed proboscis, covering half of his heavily mockered face, then running all the way down to his waistline.

"What is his name, Daddy?"

"His name is Pasha, and he is the great-grandson of Salum the Magnificent of Alexandria," boasted Sam.

"In Virginia?" Maggie was trying to climb on the shying animal.

"Well, yes," said Sam with a hidden smile. "Alexandria, Virginia, by way of Alexandria in Egypt." Samuel spoke and strutted as if addressing a convention of plantation owners. "Salum and a brood of mares were captured and shipped to Virginia by William Eaton after the Tripolitan War." Samuel was speaking to no one in particular, and no one in particular was listening.

"Help me up, Nunky Mo."

Holding tightly to the reins, Mose shifted his big round eyes toward Master Sam and Mistress Susan.

"Better not now, Sissy. He has no saddle, and looks skittish," cautioned Susan.

"Go ahead, Maggie. Help her up, Mose," answered Sam.

"Yassa."

Samuel enjoyed, and made a habit of, belittling Susan at every chance. He never let her forget the indebtedness her Ashley family incurred to Sam's father, and his foreclosing abruptly on the Ashleys, for no good reason, when he became the master, gaining the small Ashley plantation, "Chic Wood," in South Carolina, and the arranged marriage, in eighteen-eight, to a very young Susan to boot, all to undebt the Ashley family. Despite this, Susan remained a loyal wife, a brick, even spirited until recent years when she became certain that two slaves had been fathered by Sam. Since then, she had worn a solemn Friday face.

Mose's hand acted as a stirrup, as he grabbed Maggie's foot with one hand and lifted her onto Pasha's back, all the while holding the reins steady. The weight on his back caused Pasha to prance and try to lift, but the powerful grip of the bounder held him back.

"Sam, she's going to fall off," cried a terrified Susan.

"Nonsense. Hold fast the reins, Mose."

"Yassar."

"Give me the reins, Nunky Mo. I want to ride him around the barns."

The big eyes again rolled over to the master. Susan was shaking her head no.

"Please, Sam. I'm afraid Sissy can't handle him."

"Nonsense," he said. "She's a better rider than either of us."

It was just then that Pasha jumped and tried again to rear up. Susan covered her face in fright.

"Whoa der, whoa, Big Pasha," said Mose.

The soothing voice of the gentle, giant bounder immediately had an effect on the pure white horse, who stood very still and erect.

"Maybe you should walk him around, Mose, so he can get used to Sissy's weight."

"Yassa, Master Sam. Come, Pasha." The horse started prancing.

"No, Daddy. I want to ride him. He's my birthday present."

"I know, Sissy, but I shall need to purchase a burick saddle in Charlotte. That will help you balance."

"You're not dressed to be riding, Sissy. It's shameful the way your legs are exposed in that dress," Susan added.

"Nonsense. There is nothing shameful about my daughter."

Susan hated the word "nonsense." She felt it very degrading. Sam used it often to silence her in public. She wasn't going to let him do that to her this time, she thought. "You want her to start showing the social graces? Well, get her down off that horse! Besides, it's time for her to come in. She has a pile of presents in the hall, and some sweet cheesecake for supper."

Susan wasn't sure if Sam even heard her. She was now afraid that if he had, he would find a way to get back at her for sassing him.

"Better get off him now, Maggie. It's time for your birthday party. Put Pasha away, Mose."

"Yassa, Master Sam."

"I want to ride him, Daddy. Look, he's already getting used to my weight. I'll be there in a few minutes."

"Each morning you will see to it that one of my trotters is saddled, and someone accompanies Maggie and Pasha."

"Yassa, Master Sam," Mose quickly agreed.

"I don't need any company. Watch this, Daddy. Give me the reins, Nunky Mo."

"I said not now, Margaret Rose. It's time for supper."

To the amazement of all assembled, even Sam, and to the relief of Susan, Samuel McAllister had put his foot down to his daughter. He strode like a peacock into the big house, followed by a much-easier-breathing Mistress Susan. Her personal house servant, Elsie Existentialist, was waiting for her at the door.

"You place be's ready for supper, Missus Susan."

"Thank you, Elsie." They fell in, arm in arm, behind the master, as he shuffled to the great dining hall. The hand-carved double doors were open, and house bounder Ella Elevated McAllister was waiting for the procession. She curtsied to the master and led him into the dining hall and his proper place at the head of the long, wide table of Tennessee red cedar, with white Appalachian pine chairs and trim. The table was said to be large enough to seat three dozen people, and was placed in the center of the huge room, which seemed to be divided in the middle by partial walls on each side. This created the "his and hers" half of the great hall. The two halves were similar and dissimilar, similar in the forms of large crystal chandeliers, which hung from the ceiling in the center of each half, and seemed to verify the claims of the table's length and capacity. There were matching candelabras, which were removed before each supper, so as to afford the visual contact between the master and mistress at either end. Dissimilar were the wall decorations. Large tapestries, and wall-mounted trophy heads of animals, from Sam's hunting forays, lined "his" three walls, while statues and portraits of a few McAllisters and many Ashleys covered the red velvet walls of the "hers" half.

Susan's end of the long table had several wrapped birthday gifts, commemorating Margaret Rose's twenty-first birthday, so the McAllister family gathered around the master's end of the table. Brothers Sammy, Virgil, and Miles, aged sixteen, fifteen, and ten, respectively, had already taken seats on the master's left side, and Elsie now assisted Mistress Susan to a chair immediately to Samuel's right side. There was also a place setting of white china with royal blue rings to Susan's right, soon filled by a pouting red-haired and red-cheeked Maggie.

"Is you's ready fo supper now, Mistress Susan?" asked Ella.

Susan turned to her daughter. "Would you like to open your presents now or after supper, Sissy?"

"Open the little one first!" said an excited Miles.

"Miles Mattergasser McAllister!"

"Yessir!" The ten-year-old boy jumped up and stood at attention.

"Did anyone speak to you?"

"No, sir, Father."

"Then sit, and keep quiet."

"Yes, sir, Father."

Samuel noticed the glares from Susan and Maggie.

"And what is bothering my two ladies?"

"You know how much I dislike that name," said Susan.

JADA

Here is a copy of
Pat Novel I hope
you will read it
and hopefully in my
"I DO" — Thanks
Pat

"I do, and I like it."

Mattergasser was the first in a long series of what Samuel felt were humorous, characteristic handles.

"You promised me that you would change it."

"So I lied! Just look at how it fits. My son is a cracker brain. He knows when he is allowed to speak."

"My son is not a cracker brain! He is a very intelligent boy, and you are harming him by not allowing him to speak!"

"Nonsense!" shouted Sam.

"You think you are an army general, Daddy! You treat my brothers worse than the bounders!" yelled Maggie.

"That's nonsense." The pits were disappearing.

"Please stop." Tears were running down Susan's cheeks. "Must we fight on Sissy's birthday?"

"Sit here, Mother, so I can be between you two." Margaret helped Susan move one chair over.

"I'm teaching my sons some much-needed discipline." The three boys sat very still, afraid to speak.

"They don't need more discipline, Daddy. They need affection."

"We have five children, Sam. With tutoring, they can be outstanding citizens." Susan had settled back down.

"Don't start that again. Let's eat. You two make me hungry."

"Not until I've opened my gifts."

"Alright. Get to it, Sissy, before I decide to leave."

"Calm down, Daddy. I want all my family here for my birthday. I wish Allston was here."

"He couldn't be here, Sissy, but he sent a note," said Susan.

"Oh, good. I'll read it when I open his gift. Is everyone all settled, so I can start?"

"Yes, we are, honey. Go ahead and start." Susan tried to show a smile.

"I would like to start by thanking you, Daddy, for Pasha. But even more important than that, I would like to see the love and respect for each other to return. That would make this my best birthday ever."

"And in honor of your birthday, Sissy, I have decided to change Miles's middle name," said a brash Samuel.

"Oh, Daddy, that would be wonderful. Wouldn't it, Mother?"

Susan didn't answer. She had a stunned stare at Sam.

"How about Miles Matterhead McAllister?" asked Sam.

"That's just as bad," said Mistress Susan.

"Nonsense. It shows that intelligence you say he has."

"It is an improvement, Mother."

"I still dislike it. Why can't he have a common name like John or Robert?" asked Susan.

"Daddy wants both given names to start with the letter *M*."

"Well, how about Matthew or Milton?"

"Yes! Miles Matthew is a wonderful name, Mother. Do you like it, Miles?" asked Maggie.

"Yes."

"How about it, Daddy?"

"It doesn't have any crust. I shall decide on a name."

"Please, Daddy. We like it, and Miles likes it. It would be another lovely birthday gift. Please, Daddy?"

"Well, alright. Just for you."

Applause and hurrays broke out all around. Even Ella and Elsie applauded.

"Thank you, Daddy dear. Now, in honor of my little brother, Miles Matthew McAllister, I will open the little present that you brought me first."

Margaret quickly opened the little wrapped box, revealing a brooch, with a large blue stone circled with small diamonds.

"Oh, Miles, this is beautiful!" Maggie ran around the long table to hug and kiss an embarrassed boy. "Where did you get a gem like this?"

"From my mom," said the bashful boy.

"It belonged to your grandmother Ashley, and I gave it to Miles, who wanted to give it to you," said Susan.

"I love it. Thank you, Miles."

"You're welcome."

One by one, Margaret unwrapped the stack of birthday gifts. Virgil gave his sister a satin turban with a muslin band and gold looped fastener, while Sammy gave Maggie a Bonaparte hat. The three boys also gave their sister a very large wooden crate setting on the floor.

"What is it?" asked Maggie.

"Open it and find out," said Sammy.

"We'll help you," volunteered Virgil.

The boys had hidden a crow bar under the table, and proceeded to rip open the wooden box.

"Oh my, it's a trunk!" gasped Maggie.

"A gold-lined Saratoga Travel trunk, made in Fayetteville," boasted Master Sam. "I, ah, the boys bought it in Salem."

"But, Daddy, I'm not going anywhere."

"Someday you will. You're not going to be 'Daddy's little old maid.'" Both Maggie and her father grinned at that.

"Well, thank you, Sammy, Virgil, and Miles. I have the best brothers in the world."

"You're welcome," came the simultaneous response.

"We have the best sister in the world," answered Miles, who noticed the cold stare from his father. He had again spoken out of turn, but was relieved when his father remained silent. The brief silence was broken when Maggie's personal servant and friend, Buelah Botcherbuns, entered the room.

"I's brought you's sumtin', missy."

"Oh, how nice, Buelah. Thank you so much!"

"You's welcome, missy. Opens it."

The package turned out to be a cotton blouse shirt. "And it's handmade, too. Thank you."

"You's welcome, missy. Mommy Ella helpt me make it."

"Thank you, Ella, and thank you, Buelah."

"You's welcome," as she exited the room.

There were still three packages left, and Margaret picked up the largest of the group. Inside, she found three dresses and a Bolero jacket, all homespun, by her mother. One was a straight neoclassical dress made of gossamer satin; one was a Trafalgar evening dress, also of satin; and a redingote coatdress.

"Oh, Mother, these are so nice. I love them. Thank you. I can surely tell what you are doing when you remain in your room for hours at a time."

"I hope they all fit you, Sissy."

"If they don't, I know where to get them sized. Thank you so much."

"You can try them on later. There shouldn't be any major adjustments."

"I will. Now I wonder what this heavy package is." Maggie read the little note. "To my darling daughter, from a proud father. Happy birthday."

"Thank you, Daddy. What is it? It's very heavy for its size." She shook it, and it rattled.

"You'll have to open it to find out."

The package turned out to be a shiny white porcelain horse, like Pasha, with a key inserted in the belly, attached to a beautiful gold necklace. Curiosity got the better of her, and she turned the key. The belly opened, and a pile of double Eagles spilled over the floor. The boys ran around the table and helped their sister pick up the pile and fill the belly back up.

"Oh, Daddy. I don't know how to thank you enough."

Samuel was satisfied his gifts to his daughter had outshined all the others combined. The belly locked again; Maggie pulled the necklace over her head.

"When you spend it, spend it wisely." Sam now seemed to fancy himself a cross between a philosopher and an investment counselor.

"I will. Thank you, Daddy. I love you."

Maggie rushed to the head of the table and embraced her seated father. Red curly hair mixed with brown baraclave. The remainder of the family witnessed the show of affection in silence, wondering if they were worthy of a similar hug.

"You're welcome, Sissy. Now let's eat. I'm as hungry as a bear after hibernation," said Samuel.

"We can't eat yet!" an excited Sammy Junior blurted out.

"There is still one present left!" shouted Miles.

"Miles Mattergasser McAllister."

The boy leapt out of his chair to attention. He knew that he was in trouble, speaking out of turn again.

"Yes, sir, Father."

"Oh, Daddy, cool the bean. Miles meant no harm."

"His name is Miles Matthew, Sam," added Susan.

"Yes, yes, I forgot. You may sit quietly, son."

"Thank you, Father."

"You're correct, Miles. I do have one more present." Margaret picked up the neatly wrapped red package with a big white bow, under which she noticed a note.

> *My dearest Maggie:*
>
> *I wanted so much to be in Bethania for your twenty-first birthday. Unfortunately, it is rice planting season, and I couldn't get away. I hope your twenty-first is as great as mine was, and I look forward to seeing all of your gifts soon. Please record them all, so I won't miss any of them when I visit this summer. I love you, and miss my family.*
>
> *Your Loving Brother,*
> *Ally*

Margaret's older brother, Allston, had shipped the red package upriver from father Samuel's other plantation, Chic Wood, in South Carolina, which Sam had taken along with the young Susan Ashley, as a settlement of debt from the Ashley family to Samuel. Sam had immediately rendered Susan pregnant and deliberately named the boy Allston "Ashley" McAllister, so the steal of these prizes would always be remembered. Maggie lifted the heavy package and shook it, hoping to guess its contents, but to no avail.

"It's so pretty. I must take care not to tear it."

"Hurry up and open it, Sissy. My supper is getting cold."

Maggie slowly and carefully opened her last package amidst many anxious eyes. A large black book, with golden hinges and a buckle, appeared from the red wrap.

"Oh, look. It's a diary. It's beautiful."

"Did you notice the words to record all your gifts in Allston's message, Sissy?" asked Susan.

"Yes, he was giving me a clue." Maggie smiled.

"Okay, Maggie. Sit down now so we can eat."

"Just a minute, Daddy."

Margaret gave her mother a long hug. "Thank you, Mother." She then walked around the table to hug each of her three brothers.

"This has been so wonderful. Thank you all." Margaret hugged her father again and found a hairless spot to kiss. "And thank you for Pasha. This is my best day ever. I cannot imagine a better twenty-first birthday."

"Now we have a special birthday supper for you, Sissy. Chicken fixin's, oysters, and macaroni," said Susan.

"And a gumbo soup with rice from Chic Wood," added Sam.

"It sounds delightful, and I'm really hungry."

"Then sit, and let's indulge," said the master.

Just a hand clap from the master, and the huge hall came to life. Ella could be heard giving directions, along with the clomping of bounders' shoes hurrying in and out of the rear of the mansion. In came three Nans, aprons covering their clean cotton-drilled dresses. They carried the first course, an apple dumpling, the dough a rich golden brown color. As quickly as they appeared, the kitchen bounders left. Very soon, they reappeared with the second course, the Nans carrying soup and saucer dishes, all in rich bone-colored china with a royal blue border that marked the craftsmanship of Williamsburg. They were followed by a buck in another apron, carrying a large tureen of gumbo soup. The two women were afraid to ask what all was in the soup, but they recognized several vegetables and the rice, and an okra flavor. Ella followed with Maggie's favorite cracklin' bread, wrapped in a towel for warmth. Fried chicken in fixin's were next, along with coleslaw. The fourth course was Carolina coast oysters, fricasseed in a rich gravy over McAllister rice. Margaret wasn't sure what the "main" course was, but she was getting very full. By the time the fifth course was served, the Italian macaroni shaped in the form of small pies, only Master Samuel was able to eat it. They all watched as Sam gobbled down his portion. One signal from Maggie, and Ella brought a towel so the birthday girl could wipe gravy and soup from her father's heavy beard. When he finished his macaroni, Maggie offered Sam her portion. This was the first Sam noticed that only he had eaten the fifth course.

"Eat your meal, boys. We waste no food in Bethania."

"But we are very full, Father, sir," said Sammy Junior.

"And we would like to save room for the surprise," added an excited Miles.

Once again, Miles had spoken out of turn, and the angry look from his father confirmed his fate in advance.

"Go to your room."

"Yes, Father." Tears were forming in the boy's eyes.

"Yes, what?"

"Yes, Father, sir." Miles started to leave.

"Oh please, Daddy, let him stay," pleaded Maggie.

"He really didn't do anything wrong, Sam," added Susan.

"Nonsense. I wouldn't send him away if he hadn't done something wrong."

"What wrong did he do, Daddy?"

"He knows not to speak unless spoken to!"

"But he was spoken to," said Susan.

"Nonsense."

"Yes, Daddy, you spoke to him when you ordered them to eat their macaroni."

The pits turned a reddish color, and Sam quickly started in on Maggie's macaroni.

"May I call Miles back, Daddy? Please?"

Samuel only nodded his head as he continued filling face.

"Please bring Miles back, Nunky Mo."

"Yes, missy." Mose was quick to return, the boy's arm lost in the grasp of the large hand.

Maggie grabbed her mother's handkerchief, already getting some early use, and wiped away the tears on Miles's face.

"Welcome back to my party, Miles. Please take your seat quietly, so not to disturb your father."

Mistress Susan beckoned to Ella. "Please have these plates removed, and the last course brought in."

"Yes, Mistress Susan." Ella gave the signal, and the kitchen bounders again appeared and gathered the plates of macaroni, along with Sam's empty plates.

Sam now noticed the plates of untouched food leaving the room, and when he spoke, Margaret wondered if her father really was a disciplinarian, or just still hungry.

"Hold it. I said we do not waste food here."

"We can put it in the cellar and have it tomorrow, Sam."

"Oh, Daddy, don't be a stick in the mud. It wouldn't be wasted if Nunky Mo and Nanty Ella ate it. Now would it?"

"No, I guess not, Sissy. I guess they can celebrate your birthday a little too."

"Did you hear that, Nanty Ella? You can divide that macaroni with your family."

"Yes, missy. We's thanks you's."

"Now you may bring the final entry, Ella."

"Yes, Mistress Susan." Ella disappeared, and minutes later, there appeared her loveliest daughter, Esther Blowby McAllister, carrying a large cheesecake. The eyes of Margaret and Miles were fastened on the colorful cake. The eyes of the remainder of the family were fixed on the tall, creamy-tan-skinned house bounder. Master Sam dressed his house servants well, all in matching black with white trim. He had ordered low-cut dresses, especially for Esther, to show her ample bosom. Samuel Junior and Virgil were enjoying the view as much as their father. The three kitchen bounders followed Esther with plates and a knife, but no one noticed them. Margaret and her mother became solemn and red-faced, and had anyone noticed, Susan's face was very angry. Esther placed the cheesecake on the huge table and curtsied, giving the McAllisters an even more vivid view, then took the knife in an attempt to cut the cake.

"That will be all, Esther. We'll cut the cake ourselves," came the command from Susan.

"Yes, Mistress Susan." Another deep, defying curtsy, and all eyes watched the exaggerated swaying exit.

"I should have named her Esther Sidewinder, instead of Blowby," said the grinning Samuel to a loud silence.

"I thought I had ordered her out of the house and into the field." Susan's voice shattered the silence.

"I ordered her back." More silence.

"Ella."

"Yes, Mistress Susan?"

"From now on, Esther is not to serve my meals."

"Yes, Mistress Susan. I's so sorry, Ma'am."

Margaret grabbed the kitchen knife and started cutting the cheesecake, hoping to calm the atmosphere.

"Ella, from now on, if Esther is serving, no one is to serve the mistress."

"Yessar, Master Sam." All eyes noticed the tears stream down the cheeks of the mistress as she stood to leave. Maggie grabbed and hugged her mother.

"Please don't leave yet, Mother. Please have a piece of cake with me."

"Alright, Sissy." Susan sat back down, making use of her handkerchief. Margaret handed a piece of cake to each of her family. She might as well be cutting cake for a wake, she thought. Everyone ate in silence.

"This has been a wonderful birthday. Thank you all again. The prizes and the food were better than I ever could imagine." Maggie's words broke the quiet spell.

"May we be excused, Father, sir?" asked Sammy Junior.

"Have you all cleared your plates?"

"Yes, sir, Father," came the answers in unison.

"Then you are excused, my sons."

"Thank you, Father, sir." The three boys each hugged their mother and sister, wishing their sister a happy birthday.

When the boys reached the door, they suddenly stopped.

"Father, sir?" The voice of the previously silent Virgil Solomon McAllister penetrated and changed the atmosphere. The third son of Samuel and Susan McAllister was the prankster of the family, and had been silent all too long.

"Yes, what is it?"

"I just wanted to remind you of my birthday, on the thirteenth of next month."

"What? You dunderhead, are you getting saucy with me?"

"Oh no, Father, sir," said the fifteen-year-old boy, "but you forgot my birthday last year."

The reminder was embarrassing to Master Sam, and comical to the others, who were trying to keep straight-faced.

"Nonsense! Have I not fed you, and clothed you, and housed you for the last fifteen years?"

"Yes, Father, sir."

"Then what more could you want?"

"A horse like Pasha, to start with, Father, sir."

The straight faces would no longer be kept; and all, save Susan, broke out in laughter.

"What in Sam hell are you all laughing about?" The pits vanished in a hurry from Samuel's face, which turned so bright red, that the bed of whiskers seemed almost white. The laughter increased.

"Keep it up, and I will will Bethania to the ivory." The laughing stopped abruptly.

"Now, Daddy dear, please don't get angry. We were just having some fun on my birthday." Maggie stood and gave her father another hug and kiss, and the pits came back.

"My sons obviously have a lot to learn."

"Virgil was just bantering with you, Daddy."

"And as for you, my virgin Virgil, work hard and no dallying, and someday you may be the recipient of my charitable inclinations." Sam's chest was swelling.

"Yes, Father, sir. Good night, Father, sir." This sentence was difficult for Virgil, and the laughter of the three boys could be heard in the hallway. The hair under Samuel's nozzle bristled.

"Someday those boys will learn the virtue of patience and controlling greed."

"Yes, Daddy. And you are the best of teachers," said a grinning Margaret.

"The boys are not greedy, Sam. They would just like to be treated equally," said Susan tersely.

"Nonsense. They have everything they need. I need some more Chic Wood rice. Ella!"

"Yassar, Master Sam?"

"Send Esther in with more rice, and that gravy."

"Yassar, Master Sam." Ella disappeared from the room. Margaret quickly scooted her chair next to her mother, and wrapped an arm around her before Susan could leave. The mistress had a cold stare at her husband, but the tears gave away her true emotions.

"How could you, Daddy? You are the dunderhead. Why hurt Mother like that?"

"Because I'm still hungry. How dare you call me names, after what I have just done for you."

"If it would bring the love and affection back to my family, I would gladly give it all back."

"Nonsense, Sissy. You are just like me. Like father, like daughter."

"There is no one like you in the world, Daddy. You could have asked for someone else to bring more rice."

"I like to look at Esther."

"Perhaps I should take off my clothes and run around Bethania 'a la natural.' Would you like that, Daddy?"

"You do, and I'll take back all your booty. There is a lot of difference between Esther and you, Sissy."

"We're both your daughters."

With that statement, Susan jumped up to leave, her handkerchief now soaked. Maggie again stopped and hugged her mother.

"I'm sorry I said that, Mother. Please stay a while longer. Maybe we can get something settled, once and for all." Susan's crying was now uncontrolled.

"We don't know that!" barked Samuel, "There are a lot of light-skinned bounders running around here. They can't all be mine." The crying increased.

"Knowing you, Daddy, they just might all be yours."

"Nonsense. I'm a practical businessman, and . . ." The statuesque body of Esther appeared in the doorway, and a smile displayed even white teeth, which went unnoticed. A tureen of three-quart capacity, in the now-familiar white-and-blue pattern, was balanced on Esther's head, and she displayed a great talent of keeping it steady, given the swaying below it. This too was unnoticed. Far too many steps eventually led to the head of the table, where Esther dipped into a deep curtsy, giving the master a breathtaking view.

"Mo rice for Massa Sam." The smile broadened. Both hands reached upward, grabbing the tureen and placing it just under the right breast of the lovely house bounder, still bent at the knees. Samuel now noticed the large spoon in the rice, and a shaky hand dipped a spoonful of rice, and emptied it on his cake plate.

"Thank you, Esther. You have a pretty smile."

Margaret was sure she detected a grin under the hair mass.

"Thank you's, Massa Sam." Esther rose back up, and a broad smile graced her face.

"You oyster gravy, Massa Sam," said Ella, ladling a couple of spoonfuls over the rice. Esther noticed Mistress Susan across the big table, her face buried in her hands, and her handkerchief and body were shaking.

"Is mistress orite?" she asked.

"Mother is fine, Esther. You may leave now."

"Yes, missy. Thank you's." One more curtsy, and the keisters wiggled away.

The only noise the next several minutes was the quick stabbing of rice into the hair-encircled cavity of Samuel. Margaret used her royal blue cloth napkin with lace trim, to wipe rice and gravy from her father's hair bed.

"Speaking of rice, I shall be headed back to Chic Wood and Georgetown tomorrow, and I'll bring back a bundle of rice."

Margaret and Susan looked at each other. No one, other than the master, was speaking of rice.

"Will I be getting a burick saddle, Daddy?"

"I suppose so, yes. I must go to Charleston anyway, to purchase another reaper and gin."

"Oh, thank you, Daddy."

"Is there anything I can get for you, Susan?"

The mistress dried her eyes, swallowed her anger and pride, and said in an unsteady voice, "I should like some rolls of cotton cloth, velvet brocade, and silk. And I can always use more calico."

"Starting on Virgil's birthday presents, Mother?"

"Yes, I already have." A slight smile appeared on the swollen face of Susan.

"Granted!" said Master Sam.

"Thank you again, Daddy."

"You're welcome, Sissy. Now, is there anything else?"

"Only that you have not told us about the tall, handsome man you hired as overseer, Daddy."

"What about him?"

"Is he available?"

"No, he is not! And you are much too observant for your own good, Sissy."

"Oh, Daddy, don't get all waxy. Where is he from, and how long has he been here?"

"His name is Jonathan Hamilton, and he is the son of a one-horse clay eater near Salem."

"You mean I missed him while I was in college?"

"Probably not. Leave him alone."

"What gang is he overseeing?" Maggie was paying little attention to her father.

"None of your business, Sissy. Don't you go playing futz with any of my overseers. I expect you to stay as pure white as your horse, Pasha."

"What, and let my father play futz alone?"

"What I play is nobody's business!" shouted Sam. The pits disappeared in a hurry, and Maggie noticed a shaking baraclave.

"On the contrary, Father, your playing around with the bounders is what has caused all our family's problems." Maggie's freckles disappeared the way of Sam's pits, replaced by a face to match the red hair.

"Nonsense!" Sam rose from his captain's chair and pounded the table. "How I run this plantation is not the issue." It was Maggie's turn to jump and pound the table.

"Nonsense to you, Father!" she screamed. "How you run this plantation has caused issue, Lenny and Esther, just to name two."

"Stop it, you two!" Mistress Susan jumped up, and ran out of the great hall, sobbing uncontrollably.

"Oh, dear, I have upset Mother again."

"Worry not, Maggie. I seem to upset her every day."

"Well, Daddy dear, there is a reason why you upset her every day."

"Nonsense. I see no reason for the mistress to be upset. When it comes to my bounders, I have only attempted to increase my holdings. I have a clear conscience!" A moment of silence was smashed by a roar of laughter from Samuel. Eventually, Margaret could no longer hold back her anger, and she joined her father in laughter.

"And I suppose you have been pure and untouched?"

"My purity has not created an issue, Daddy."

"Thank God for that!" More ringing laughter, which finally ended in a few minutes of silence.

"Is he married?"

"Who?"

"Your new overseer, Hamilton? Did you say Jon?"

"Margaret! I said leave him alone. I don't want him spoiled by you."

"Are you forgetting that I am now twenty-one and the daughter of the ultimate bouncebutt of North Carolina?" This time, the huge table and captain's chair shook violently from the master's laughter, joined by Maggie.

"Would you rather I bedded Lenny and Will?" The laughter ended as quickly as it began, and the pits vanished, replaced by a red mat.

"Lenny! My Lenny?"

"The one and only, Daddy."

"I forbid you to mess with Lenny. Why, he's practically your brother. I'll ship him to the Indies!"

"Relax, Daddy. It was just a suggestion. Maybe I'll take after Willy."

"And just who in hell is Willy?"

"Wilbert Aims, your overseer."

"Damn it, Sissy! He is married."

"A lot of difference that makes to you! Besides, he is sweet on me."

"I'll have that bugger blacksnaked and shipped out of the country."

"No need, Daddy. I can handle him."

"That's what I'm afraid of!" It was Maggie's turn to laugh at her father's uneasy stare.

"Then it has to be Mister Hamilton, Daddy."

"It doesn't have to be anyone. Just because you are twenty-one, you can stay pure until I find someone suitable for you."

"Oh, and just how pure were you at twenty-one? Dang, how cussed pure were you at eleven?"

Father and daughter seemed to be taking turns at laughter. This one, by Samuel, didn't last long.

"Stop swearing, Sissy, and leave my purity alone."

"I will if you leave my purity alone. Agreed?"

"I don't make deals with my offspring. I want you to behave. I'm not ready to be a grandfather."

"Why not? Just another munchkin to add to your holdings. That would make me a part owner of Bethania. Besides, Allston will soon be getting married at Chic Wood, and you don't expect him to keep his prong on ice. He might already have a chic or two in Georgetown. Like father, like son."

"Nonsense. Ally would tell me if he was playing roundheels. Would you?"

"No. Some things are better off unsaid." A grin covered Maggie's face. She knew she had Samuel worried.

"Well, I'll find out, and you and he will have hell to pay."

"It's a big plantation, Daddy, and my indiscretions are not broadcast all over the Piedmont."

"Nor are mine."

"Ha! You were the most famous father at college."

"Oh, and I suppose my daughter had something to do with that?"

The grin got even broader, and was shared by Samuel. "You, above all else, know how hard it is to keep a secret, Daddy."

"I hope you and I have no secrets, Sissy."

"Okay, Daddy. I'll let you know when it happens."

"When what happens?"

"When I have Jonny Hamilton corralled, of course." With this sentence, Maggie jumped up and started out of the room. "Have a good trip to Chic Wood, Daddy, and thank you *so* much for my wonderful birthday."

"Hold it! Where are you going, Sissy?"

"To cheer up Mother. You hurt her pretty badly."

"Me? You were the one spreading names and accusations, Maggie."

"Do you think that Mother is some kind of rumhead, who doesn't know what is happening?"

"No, she is a wizard. I just wish she would understand that I need to broaden my holdings."

"How many broads do you need, Father?" This brought only a few chuckles, and Maggie started out the door once more.

"Maggie?"

"Yes, Father?"

"You really haven't been playing roundheels with Lenny, have you?"

Another big grin covered Maggie's face. "Like father, like daughter." She blew her father a kiss and disappeared. Sam realized that he had accomplished nothing in his bid to keep his daughter straight and had laid an egg in efforts to keep her away from his overseer. He didn't know whether to curse or smile in his frustration. Sitting alone in the great hall, Sam decided what he really wanted. It would take some of his special skills.

"Mose."

"Yessar, Massa Sam."

"I have decided to return to Chic Wood tomorrow on my boat, and I want you and Lenny to go with me."

"Yessar. By boat, Massa Sam?"

"Yes, by boat. Do you still have the brand on your leg?"

"Yessar, I's do."

"And the pass I wrote for you a couple years ago?"

"Yessar, I's do."

"Alright, Mose, I want you to harness a buckboard, load it with ten days' supply of grub, ride on down to my boat tonight, and prepare it for the trip."

"Yessar, tonight, Massa Sam?"

"Yes, Mose. It's only a couple hours on the Salisbury road, and you can sleep on the boat.

"Yessar. But, Massa Sam . . ."

"Yes? What is it?"

"Dem Pattyrollers, deys catch me in dem dark, and deys whips me, Massa Sam."

"Nonsense, Mose. That's why you have a pass."

"Yessa. Massa Sam? Do I's row all dem way?"

"You and Lenny. And if you like, we can take another, maybe Danny, who is driving me down in the morning."

"An' Ella too, Massa Sam?"

"No, Mose. She has no pass or brand."

"Yassa." Mose had disappointment painted on his face.

"You'll only be away from her for ten days."

"Yassa."

"Do you want Danny on the trip with you?"

"Yassa, Massa Sam."

"Alright. On your way. I'll see you and Lenny tomorrow."

"Yassa."

"We may take in an auction in Charleston."

"Yassa." That brought back some very unpleasant memories for Mose, who was auctioned himself, fresh off the boat from his native Africa, many years before. Mose shuffled out of the hall and out of the mansion. Samuel was halfway to his goal.

"ELLA."

~~~~~∿w•๏◦Q◟◦◟◦◦Q◦◦◦w~~~~~

Diary of Margaret Rose McAllister

Friday, May 1, 1835

My first entry in my new diary, thanks to brother Allston. Oh, such a lovely twenty-first birthday. Jewelry, clothes, and a Saratoga trunk from my dear brothers; dresses of silk from Mother, and the most wonderful gift of all, Pasha, a beautiful, pure white Arabian horse from Alexandria, from Father. I shall treasure him forever. Only one gift would have beaten all, had I been granted it, that Daddy must show more respect and kindness toward Mother. That the love they once displayed for each other be rekindled. Even as I write, I know that Mother is in her room, sewing or reading, and Daddy is in his chamber room with Nanty Ella. And what shall I do to ease the pain they must have, and the pain I feel for both? I shall engross myself with Pasha, and the new overseer, Jonny Hamilton. He does not know of it, but he should beware!

~~~~~∿w•๏◦Q◟◦◟◦◦Q◦◦◦w~~~~~

May 30

The polished black hooves struck out again and again, in perfect rhythm. Pasha spun on his hind legs in a clockwise circle. The silvery mane and tail glistened in the morning sun. Suddenly, never breaking that rhythm, he twirled back counterclockwise. Maggie rode gracefully in her new burick saddle.

"See how easily he learns new tricks, Nunky Mo?"

"Yas, missy. But he dance so pretty. Why's you's wans ta lifts him?"

"I will answer that one day." Margaret grinned.

"Yas, missy." House bounder Mose Dasilvalentis started to swing his huge frame onto the big chestnut.

"I think I shall ride Pasha alone today, Nunky Mo. I have Pasha mastered."

"Yas, Missy Maggie, you's sho does. I's was goin' ta take you's ta gangs four again. They be ready fo' you's."

"Thank you, Nunky Mo, but I shall go south again this afternoon."

"But, missy, you's done gone south every day."

Another big grin split the freckles. "I like the scenery." Maggie lightly tapped the pure white Pasha's sides, and he danced to the south.

"Yas, missy," shouted Mose to the white rump.

The dark green stalks of the tobacco plants were now over a foot tall, and stretched as far as Maggie's eyes could see. "Straight as a Cherokee arrow," her father always bragged. She could see a gang ahead, busy thinning the stems, and Maggie was certain it was gang nine. She became positive when she saw Overseer Wilbert Aims running toward her, waving his arms and calling her.

"Get up, Pasha." The black hooves stretched and pounded the ground between rows, very swiftly passing gang nine and its overseer in a blur, turning southeast.

"The beef whit," Maggie muttered as she flew past. "Ever since I dallied with him that day, he thinks I am his canary." Gang nine shrank in the distance. "I'd rather have Lenny!" The grin was back. "My half brother!" She was chuckling now. "Hell, I'm trading both of them for Jonny!"

The gait of the erect white animal now slowed back to a prance as the crop changed from tobacco to corn. Before she even saw gang twelve, Maggie knew that after nearly an hour, she was close to her target, Jon Hamilton.

"Okay, Pasha. Let's see that special prance."

Gang twelve appeared ahead, as Pasha danced between rows, sometimes straddling a row, facing the gang of field bounders and prancing sideways. Even on the rich dirt, the steady thump, ta-thump of the hooves made beautiful music. Maggie noticed twenty pair of wide eyes staring at her. *But where was that special set of peepers?* she wondered. Suddenly, she saw the tall overseer, standing close to the nude Nan. He flashed shiny white teeth as Pasha pranced by.

That smile better be for me, thought Maggie. Now Pasha hopped, one at a time, over several rows of the cornstalks, gracefully landing between the narrow rows. When he had hopped enough rows to be past the gang, Pasha then returned to prancing sideways in the direction whence he came, this time facing twenty keisters and a like number of eyes.

"Keep them thinning, Levi," Maggie thought she heard.

"Yassa, Masssa Jon."

Headed back past gang twelve, Maggie was much closer to her prey and the nude bounder, whose very black kazoo stood straight in the air and appeared to Maggie to be as wide as two rows.

Maggie didn't think she had anything to worry about, since she looked much better than that, even in her clothes. The overseer had his back to the a-la-natural nanny, and he was smiling at Maggie, who waved to him. He waved back and said, "Hello."

"Hello yourself." She smiled. She now tugged at the reins and shouted, "Up, Pasha!" The sleek white horse reared up on his hind legs and pawed the air in the direction of the overseer then again pranced on past the gang.

"Bye!" she yelled, and waved goodbye.

"Bye yourself!" came the return.

Maggie now turned the horse straight, prancing back in the direction of gang nine.

"Yahoo!" Maggie shouted, as she distanced the horse and herself from gang twelve. "Success!"

Diary of Margaret Rose McAllister

May 30, 1835

. . . And today I finally received a wave and a hello from JH. Now I know he is interested, the poor, handsome man. Tomorrow I put my plan into action. As I said before, beware, Mr. Hamilton . . .

May 31

It was early, very early for Margaret, seven thirty. Activity abounded in the large bedroom of Margaret Rose McAllister. The personal house bounder, and friend, of Maggie, Buelah Botcherbuns McAllister, scurried about the third floor room, fetching and returning a wide assortment of clothing for her "Missy Sissy."

"I's swears, missy, you's will melt in all dem wraps." Buelah had been Maggie's constant companion since their childhoods. "My Salt and Pepper," Master Samuel had quipped many times. She's "like a sister," Maggie had quipped many times. Maggie now tried on a pair of shocking and fancy-laced silk undies.

"I will be fine and fair, Buelah. I hope even irresistible."

"I's afraid you's will."

"I shall wear the red cotton dress, Buel."

"Oh, my Sissy. It be *so* short, omose to dem knees!" gasped Buelah.

"I know. It will be even shorter in the saddle."

"Tee hee! Missy, you's is shameless!"

"Yes, I know." Maggie's chuckle matched the tee hees. Margaret Rose raised the short low-cut dress over her head and let it slide down her slender but ample body. It barely covered her pretty knees. *And yes, it was shameless*, she thought, having put on no other undergarments. She grinned happily. "Good and tight. Maybe Jonny will think me shameless." More chuckles.

"You's is lovely, Sissy. You's dress even mashes you's red hair."

"Not really, Buelah, but I want it to clash."

"Missy, is you's wearin' dat dress to's church?"

"No, Buel. I shall wear it to school."

"But dis be's Sunday. Der be no school today."

Easy to see why Daddy named her Botcherbuns, thought Maggie. "I'm going to teach an overseer."

"Buts dem overseers be in church toos."

"One is in the field. I made sure of that."

"What's you's teaches him, Sissy?"

"About birds and bees."

This made Buelah pause. "We's has many cardinals."

"Oh my! That's the wrong kind of birds, Buelah."

"Oh. I's sorry, missy. I's not learns 'bouts birds ans bees yet." Maggie saw the hurt in Buelah's eyes, and walked over and hugged her.

"It's alright, Buel. You will. Would you like to wear this dress sometime for Buff?"

"Oh yes, Sissy! Thens I's be shameless too!"

"That you will, and Buff will love it!"

Bare legs covered burick saddle. Just as Maggie had thought, she was having trouble keeping the hem at the halfway point between knee and derriere, with the steady jolt of Pasha's prancing.

Maggie hoped the darn thing wouldn't creep too far. She wasn't ready to give him that much of a view. Maggie tugged again at the hem, and wished she had decided to drive a buckboard. "Calm yourself, Maggie," she mumbled out loud. "It may *not* be too early to give him a thrill. He'll love it." Endless rows of tobacco stalks and the warm May sunshine made the cotton dress cling as well as creep.

Perhaps that is good, thought Maggie. She just didn't want to lose her curls. To herself, she said, "Stop fretting, Maggie. Damn it. My plan is going to work like a clock." The constant reassuring was taking effect, and Margaret was feeling brave as gang twelve appeared ahead.

"Okay, Pasha, prance and get ready to do your new trick!" The handsome white horse seemed to understand and started his showy prance. Maggie noticed the overseer straighten up, smile, and wave at her. "It's time to lift, Pasha."

On cue, Pasha reared up on his hind legs. "Stop it, Pasha! Whoa Pasha!" Maggie screamed. The hooves came down, and the rear legs rose up and kicked out. Pasha repeated this maneuver again, this time kicking higher. Maggie could see Jon Hamilton running toward her, as Pasha again reared up.

"Stop it! Whoa! Please, Pasha. Whoa!"

Suddenly, he was there, grabbing the silver-studded bridle with both hands. Pasha swung around, almost lifting the tall overseer off the ground.

"Whoa, boy. Whoa there," said the man, but the horse continued swinging and lifting. Jon grabbed an ear with his left hand and pulled on it.

"I said whoa!" he shouted at the white animal.

"Whoa, Pasha!" ordered the "distressed" rider.

The horse stopped and became rigid, almost throwing the overseer to the ground. A quick smile graced the red lips. "Thank you, Mister Hamilton."

"Are you alright, ma'am?" he huffed.

"Of course, I am. Are you?"

"Yes, why do you ask?"

"Well, have you not noticed me riding past every day for a week?"

"Certainly, I have. Do I look blind and airheaded to you?"

"Then why haven't you tried to stop me?" Maggie flashed a wide smile, as she watched his eyes trace a line up her bare leg.

"You might bite!" The first nonquestion changed the smile to uneasy laughter.

"Are you afraid of me?"

"No, I'm afraid of the horse." More laughter.

"Well then, why not help me down, and I promise I won't bite." Maggie swung her right leg over the saddle, and grinned broadly when she saw his eyes bug out. It took him a few seconds to gain back his composure.

"Will my job be on the line if I do?"

"Of course not. Are you batchy?"

"Bashful. I like my job."

"I suppose you do, with your Nans running around naked." They both glanced at the nude bounder then back to each other and smiled.

"Her name is Lucee, and she has been whipped but still refuses to dress out here in the field."

"I'm not worried, as long as she doesn't get you so excited that you can't do your job."

"Thank you for your concern. I manage my job alright, without getting too excited. Lucee sags at the top and spreads at the bottom. Not very exciting."

"Well then, help me down, and maybe I can excite you a little."

"You already have." The tall, lean overseer stepped up to a pair of shapely legs, now slightly parted, so he could reach up to Maggie's waist. He tried to avoid looking down, as he lifted her off the saddle and lowered her to the ground. Her arms immediately encircled his neck, and her tall warm body molded against him. The forty black eyes were again watching, as he started to feel very uncomfortable. It suddenly occurred to Jon that his hands still held her waist. His long arms pushed her back, and a red face proclaimed, "Please, ma'am, I want to keep my job!"

"I'll even see to it you get a promotion." Maggie grinned at the overseer's awkwardness. "And my name is Maggie, Jon Hamilton, not ma'am." Her arms wrapped around the overseer again.

"I know who you are, Miss Margaret. I'm not as feathermobbed as you think."

"Good. Then you know how unhappy my father would be if his daughter were rejected."

"Uh-oh. I'm being bamboozled into a schleppy position. Excuse me, Maggie, I need to get back to work."

Maggie had a firm hold around the tall man's waist, and only laughed as he struggled to free himself.

"Poor baby, you love being backed into a corner."

"Maybe, but not in an open field!"

"Well then, perhaps we can make other arrangements." Maggie giggled at the clumsy efforts of the trapped man, who seemed to gain strength after her last sentence. He partially freed himself from her grasp. They both noticed gang twelve had completely stopped working.

"Levi! Do you want to keep your job?"

"Yassa, Massa Jon."

"Then you and the gang better get a wiggle on."

"Yassa, Massa Jon."

Margaret started laughing out loud at the results of the order from her man.

"What's funny?" he asked.

"They're all fannies and elbows."

"Yes, well, if you'll excuse me, Miss Margaret, I'll get my fanny back to work."

"Stop worrying about your job, and start worrying about me." Once again, she reached for him. He stepped to one side and grabbed her arms.

"Like I said, I like my job." As Jon eased his grip on Maggie's arms, she broke free and again embraced the tall young man, who was still and quiet.

"Did you hear what I said a few minutes ago?" No answer. "Would you have supper with me and my family this evening?"

"Thank you, but the wider the distance from your father, the better I like it."

"Don't worry about Daddy. I can handle him."

"Besides, I'll be working here until dusk," he said.

"No need of that. You can pack it in right now."

"I'm sure your daddy would like that!"

"Daddy doesn't even know you're out here."

"What?" He pulled away again. "What do you mean?"

"Come back here. Don't be so bashful."

"Ma'am, if I'm bashful, you're brazen."

"The name is Maggie, Jonny." She laughed.

"Well, Maggie, what did you mean when you said your daddy doesn't know we're out here?"

"Don't get mad, Jonny, but I ordered Lental McRae to send your gang out this morning." The tall overseer pulled away from Maggie.

"Let go, ma'am. Of all the blubberheaded . . ."

"Please don't get mad, Jonny."

"You're a real rooker! Levi!"

"Yassa, Massa Jon?"

"Load the gang. We're going in."

"Yassa, Massa Jon."

"And make sure Lucee puts her clothes on."

"Yassa, Massa Jon."

The gang's boss took Maggie's arm and walked her back to her horse. He started to help her aboard.

"Give me one more hug, Jonny."

"You are a bold one, Miss Margaret."

Maggie giggled, as the object of her boldness wrapped his long arms around her waist.

"Mmmm, yes, and you love it."

"Guess I kinda do at that," he answered, as she squeezed and rubbed tighter against him. He squeezed back. Maggie chuckled, as she felt the results she was getting from her rubbing.

"Will I see you about six o'clock, for supper?"

"I don't think so. I'm not ready for that yet."

Maggie liked that answer. It wasn't an outright no, and she now knew that she had him in her grasp. She let go of him, and easily swung up onto the burick saddle.

"Then I'll see you here tomorrow."

"I reckon you will, Maggie."

Maggie opened up with a big smile. Her dress was hiked around her waist, and the big overseer was getting a good view as she blew him a kiss and turned Pasha's head to the north.

"Maggie?"

"Yes, Jonny?"

"It wasn't a week. This was the sixth day."

"Yippee!" she exclaimed, as she rode away.

Jonathan watched as the streak of red on white vanished.

Diary of Margaret Rose McAllister

Sunday, May 31, 1835

Captured! And there is no escape for poor Jonny. I'll have him boogying in the barn soon . . .

Friday, June 5

The hot North Carolina summer was at hand. June came steaming in like a lion. Corn and tobacco stalks were shooting fast into the air. The master was hoping that he would get rain periodically. "This could be our best crops ever," Samuel had said several times to his overseers. Margaret McAllister was not concerned about the crops. She was headed east on her beloved horse Pasha to see the only overseer she cared about. The corn was left to itself to grow and produce. Overseer Jon Hamilton had not graduated to the big moneymaker, tobacco, which made much more plunder for the master, but needed constant attention. Margaret needed constant attention also, and today she was out to get it. The past five days had produced an ever-increasing closeness and connection, almost to the point of "futz in field," and Maggie's hankering for the big man had reached the boiling point.

"Today's the day," she said, either to Pasha or herself, as gang twelve came into view between rows of sot weed. Jon Hamilton spotted Maggie even before she saw him, and he was coming to meet her. As they met, he reached up and lifted her off the saddle and into his arms. Passion mounted, as mouths mashed, hands explored, and tongues wrestled. Two bodies were pressed together, and Maggie was enjoying the pressure against her riding togs. Suddenly, the overseer separated himself from her.

"This is barmy. I must get back to work."

"Still afraid of Daddy?"

"Afraid of myself, and your daddy."

"Daddy knows I'm after you."

"You're after anyone with trousers."

"Not anymore, Jonny. Just the ones you're wearing."

"That's good. I'll save them for you."

"Jonny, take me for a ride in the wagon."

"You are daffy. I've got a gang to watch."

"Please, Jonny. Just for a few minutes. Levi can handle the gang. I brought us some dinner."

"What would your father say if they run away?"

"They wouldn't dare. I'll tell Daddy that I ran them off. Besides, they know they would be flogged and put in stocks."

"I don't think that would bother Toby."

"Please, Jonny." Maggie ground into the overseer. "I have something to tell you." She kissed him with force, her tongue playing with his. It worked.

"Levi, come here!" he yelled.

"Yassa, Massa Jon." The bounder bounded over.

"Levi, Miss Margaret and I are going for a ride and have lunch. Can you keep a watch for me?"

"Yassa, Massa Jon."

"Stick close to Toby. If he runs off, you will be punished with him."

"Yassa, Massa Jon."

"If I'm not back soon, let them have their lunch."

"Yassa, Massa Jon." Levi ran back to gang twelve, and Maggie gripped Jonathan around the waist. She took Pasha's bridle and began walking to the wagon. She tied the white animal to the rear and walked back into the long arms of the overseer.

"Where would you like to go, the corn or cotton?" Jon asked, as he helped Maggie up onto the bench.

"Very funny. There's a little creek a mile or so north of here. Maybe we can find shade there."

"And seclusion? Get up, Slog."

"That too, darling, unless you want twenty eyes watching us. They have already been tongue-wagging."

"No wonder I've been getting strange looks from the other overseers."

"They're probably jealous."

"I would be," said Jon, as Maggie squeezed up against him. The team and wagon expertly straddled a straight row of tobacco plants, stretching far into the distance. After what seemed a hundred smooches and feels, they reached the end of the row and a patch of trees. The overseer pulled team twelve under some branches and stopped.

"Where's the creek?"

"I don't know, Jonny. I heard there was one here. At least we have shade." The kisses started again and soon turned into foreplay. Maggie took Jon's hand, and they stretched out in the wagon's bed. The foreplay continued, hot and heavy, for several minutes. Finally, the overseer let go of Maggie and sat up.

"Wow. I need to catch my breath."

"I'm too much for you, huh?" she teased.

"Much too much. I need to eat something to gain my strength back."

This brought a chuckle from Maggie, as she jumped out of the wagon and grabbed the bag attached to the burick saddle.

"I brought some corn dodgers and meat, and some ketchup I stole from the kitchen."

"Sounds wonderful. Let's lay that blanket under the trees." They started on the dodgers.

"Do you always have a blanket with you?"

"Yes, in case one of my gang gets sick."

"Are you sure it isn't for you and Lucee?"

"Ha! Don't get snooty. It would probably take three blankets for her." Their laughter eased the tension between them, and they ate their dodgers between kisses and hugs.

"What was it that you wanted to tell me?"

"Only that I want you right now."

"Whoa!" exclaimed Jon. "You are brazen! If your father got word of that from those tongue wagers, I would be the one in stocks."

"I told you not to worry about Daddy. He is pudding in my hands."

"Hell, he'd make pudding out of my butt!"

Maggie pushed the overseer down on the blanket, and climbed on top of him.

"You know you want me, and I want you, so what are you waiting for?"

"Rain! Let me up, Maggie. I need to eat and get back to work."

Maggie was making it very difficult for the lanky man to get up. She was kissing him passionately, and tongue-jabbing him. Her hand reached down to the bulge in his trousers. He grabbed the hand and pulled it, and his head away.

"Maggie, you really are a scrubber."

"And you love it, you big starker."

"Maybe so, but I also love my job, and I'm afraid the two don't mix."

"We could do it right here, Jonny, and no one would find out."

"I'm afraid they would, Mag. You know how the rumors spread around here, like grease on axles."

"That's twice you've used the word 'afraid.' I believe you really are. What are you afraid of, me?"

"Yes, you, and your daddy, and of losing my job, and of making a little boot in the kilter."

"You can't make me with child, Jonny, unless I want it."

"And you're crazy enough to want it."

"Oh, Jonny. Please do me now. I need it."

"Sorry, darling. I'm just not ready for that yet. I've got to get back to the gang."

"You're as ready as you'll ever be," Maggie said, as she again reached for the spot on his trousers. Jon grabbed her hand, pulled her up to him, and kissed her. He then grabbed the blanket and leftovers, and walked her back to the wagon.

"Jonny, I'll be in barn five tonight, at seven and thirty. Please be there."

"I don't know, Maggie. I have to think on it."

"I'll do the thinking for you, Jonny. Just be there. You won't regret it. alright?"

"I won't make any promises. I'll see."

"That's fair. Please try, Jonny. I want you so badly."

"I want you too, baby. I'll try."

With that, the two headed back down the tobacco row. No chatter, just touches, squeezes, and smiles. When they approached gang twelve, they noticed them still working hard, weeding and trimming.

"Have you had lunch yet, Levi?" Jon shouted.

"No sa, Massa Jon."

"Why not, Levi?"

"Dem lunch be's in dem wagon, Massa Jon."

Maggie and the embarrassed overseer glanced at the food under the bench, and started laughing.

"I'm sorry, Levi. Come and get it now, and you can have some extra time for rest."

"Yassa, Massa Jon."

He helped Maggie down from the wagon and onto Pasha.

"Remember, barn five, at seven and thirty," she said, quite loudly, to Jon.

"Shhh, Maggie. I said we'll see," he answered.

She pointed Pasha west. Smiling, she stuck out the five fingers of her hand at the tall man. He waved goodbye to her, and she again showed five.

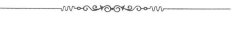

Diary of Margaret Rose McAllister

Friday, June 5, 1835

I thought I had him ripe and ready. I waited for him in barn five, but my Jonny didn't show. THIS TIME. I shall try again tomorrow, and the next day, and the next. I shall not be denied . . .

"One animal was missing in barn five last night." Margaret Rose had ridden Pasha again into the eastern tobacco fields, and again she was wearing the short red dress she used as a "persuader." It was working well.

"This animal couldn't get away. I think Jock McRae was up all night," was the overseer's reply.

"He probably knows about us," said Maggie.

"Yeah, and he is trying to save my derriere."

"Maybe I should talk to him. I can have him sent back to the field, or even fired."

"No, Maggie, don't do that. Jock is a good man, and a friend."

"Then maybe you should talk to him."

"Okay. I'll talk to him this evening."

"Good. I'll be in barn five again tonight."

"Oh, Maggie, I don't know. I'm still scared."

"You want me as much as I want you, don't you?"

"You know I do, but the timing isn't right yet."

"Nonsense. There's no time like the present, Jonny, and you need it as much as I do."

"You can tell?" They were grinding into each other.

"Mmmm, sure can, big boy. Barn five has a wonderful bed of straw," she teased.

"Now just how do you know that?"

"I was there last night, remember? And I'll be there again tonight, waiting for you."

"What if I don't make it again? I may have—" Maggie stopped his negative thoughts and words by kissing and tongue-dipping.

"Then I'll have to teach Pasha a new trick."

"And what would that be?"

"Chasing an overseer into barns."

"Hmm . . . Don't want that. There are too many overseers on Bethania."

"Then try to meet me in barn five tonight."

"I will try, Maggie, but no promises."

Diary of Margaret Rose McAllister

Saturday, June 6, 1835

He escaped my grasp one more time. The third time will be the charm. I'll see him tomorrow in church . . .

June 7

The generosity of Samuel McAllister the First had made Bethania a popular and busy place on Sundays. He had developed a park directly behind the original plantation house, with the overseer's house and slaves' quarters to the south, and his row of barns to the north. Then, in 1789, a fire started in the kitchen, to the rear of the house, and had it not been for the slaves forming a water line from McAllister Creek, the great house would have been a total loss. To show his gratitude, the first master built his new kitchen twenty-five yards behind the main house, and behind that, the first North Carolina church west of Salem. White people traveled many miles from all directions each Sunday morning for ten o'clock services. The slaves then had their own services on Sunday afternoons. The Sunday of June 7, 1835, was no different in the old church, except for one red-haired beauty, searching the crowd for a tall overseer. The neck-craning made her parents uneasy.

"What are you looking for, Sissy?"

"Nothing, Mother. Just seeing who is missing."

The service had begun when the door opened, and the lanky young man tip-toed in and took a seat in the rear. Maggie almost missed him, but she knew he was there. Somehow she would make contact.

The proceedings had now lasted over an hour, and sensing its near-end, Margaret excused herself and walked down the aisle. As she reached the door, she glanced at the young handsome man and motioned with her head to meet outside. His little shake of the head told her that he understood, but everyone was watching. The service ended, and the crowd started to leave. Maggie spotted her man near the front of the crowd, and flashed the five fingers. She saw him again shake his head yes, and noticed his smile. She was again excited.

"Are you here, Maggie?" She heard him enter the barn, and was shaking with anticipation.

"Over here, Jonny." She smiled as he heard him stumbling in the dark. "This way," she whispered. As she sensed his closeness, she thought she could even smell him. She stepped forward and smothered him with hugs and kisses. His response was more intense than she had known. He helped lower her onto the straw, never separating the locked jaws. The sounds of heavy breathing, moans, rustling straw, and many animals permeated the air.

"Why are you so late?"

"Sorry, baby. This is the quickest I could get away."

"Mmmm . . . you're forgiven."

Diary of Margaret Rose McAllister

Sunday, June 7, 1835

Victory! Now I know why I wanted Jonny so much. He is insatiable, a real goer. My derriere has straw burns! I believe I am his first. I know I will be his last . . . He even thanked me.

Love is grand! The remainder of June was a boogering blur. The young lovers couldn't get enough of each other. Barn five had at least two wild animals. They were determined to meet every night possible, and they even resorted to amusing activities to escape from prying eyes. Several times Jon Hamilton dressed up in his best clothes and saddled a horse, pretending he was going home to a "sick mother," then rode around the mansion to Barn Row. Maggie complained of suffering from the "hot June sun," and announced that her trick training and riding with Pasha would be in the evenings. Even so, they knew that most bounders were fully aware of what was happening, and were waiting for the explosion when the master found out. The lovers were pushing their luck, but couldn't help themselves. Yes, love *is* grand!

"Where were you last night, Jonny?"

"I just couldn't get away, my pretty plum."

"I know. It's getting harder and harder to get away."

"We need some new signals. The other overseers think my mother is near death. She either has to go coon or get well soon."

"I will wear something red when I ride out to see you, if I can get away."

"Mmmm. I love that red dress."

"You love what's in it."

"That too. But you don't ride out to my gang every day. So how will I know those other days?"

"Do you need it every day?"

"You bet! You've spoiled me, my pretty plum."

"Well, I'm supposed to be training Pasha each evening that I'm free, so if you don't see him in the first stall, I'll be here waiting."

"Dandy idea. I hope I never see that horse again."

"But it's easier for me to get away, Jonny. What about a signal from you when you're available?"

"Damn. That's a tough one. Hmm . . . It's a bummer to think when I'm here with you."

"That's because you've got one thing on your mind. Where is your room in the overseer house?"

"It's the last room on the left."

"Well then, maybe you can put something outside your window. I should be able to see it from the house."

"Righto. I have a shiny pocket chain watch that I got last year for my birthday," he said.

"I'd be worried that a bounder may steal it."

"Nah, I can anchor the other end of the chain, and most of the bounders will be in their shanties in the evening."

"Okay, darling. I'll look for it."

"And I'll look for that red dress."

They had time to recoup for another session of loving.

"When is your birthday, Jonny?"

"It's coming soon. July eighteen. Why?"

"Oh, just wondering. I'll have to give you something special for your birthday."

"You've been giving me something special every night."

"I'm glad you think so, lover."

Diary of Margaret Rose McAllister

July 2, 1835

Have I created a monster? There is no letup in this man, and I love it, and him. I know how it will hurt Daddy and Mother, but I must, AND WILL, marry him.

Is there ever too much of a good thing? The lovers in barn five didn't think so. July was flying by, the signals were working well, and any consequences of this torrid affair were out of their minds, for *they* were out of their minds in love. Margaret and Jonathan were about to discover how much is too much

July 18

Gang twelve was now in view, but Maggie wasn't thinking about any prancing by Pasha, any little wagon trips, or any new signals. She was plain *scared*. The overseer was running to greet her, seemingly equally excited. They met with the usual fervor.

———

"Jonny, do you love me?"

"Does a bear crap in the woods?"

"Please, Jonny, I have to know."

"Of course, I love you. Why do you ask?"

"Because I love you desperately . . ."

"Well, that's a smasher."

"And I need to see you tonight."

"And that's a banger."

"I have something I need to tell you, Jonny."

"Great. I have something to tell you too."

"Then I'll see you tonight, for sure?"

"For sure, my pretty plum."

With that, Maggie broke from their embrace and jumped back into the burick saddle. The overseer watched her fade into the distance, and then returned to his gang.

The lovemaking was fast and furious, and some rest was needed. Maggie cuddled close to Jon.

"What is it you have to tell me, Maggie?"

"I was just going to ask you the same question."

"I asked first, my pretty plum."

There was a long lull, as Maggie searched for words.

"You really do love me, don't you, Jonny?"

"Yes. I already told you that."

"I know, but I've got to be sure."

"You can put that in your trunk, sugar. I don't know what I'd ever do without you now."

Another lull, as Maggie was squeezing Jon firmly.

"What is it, Maggie?"

"I'm late with my female curse." Yet another lull. "Did you hear me, Jonny?"

"Yes, but I don't know what you mean."

"Really?"

"Really. What does that mean, baby?"

"Yes, baby! I might have a baby in my belly."

"Wow!" he exclaimed.

"You really didn't know what the curse means?"

"Well, you're the old geezer of this twosome."

"Is 'wow' all you can say, Jonny?"

"What would you like me to say?"

"That you're happy you're going to be a father."

"I'm trying to imagine what your parents will say."

"Unhappy. They will be unhappy. What about you?"

"Uneasy and unsure."

"Unsure of what to say, or do?"

"Well, it might be a false alarm, but I don't think so."

"Yeah, you once told me that I couldn't make you with baby."

"I might have lied, Jonny."

"How soon will you know for sure?" he asked.

"Maybe by this time next month. If it's true, what will you do?"

"Maggie, I won't let you down. I do love you."

"Thank you, Jonny. I love you too."

"Now we must decide how we're going to tell all this to our parents."

"I'll figure out a way to tell Daddy," Maggie said.

"No, baby. I should be the one. I'll ask both."

"Ask them what?"

"For permission to marry you, of course."

Maggie hugged Jon extra close. She raised her head and kissed him. Her cheeks were wet.

"Why are you crying?"

"I'm happy."

"That makes good sense!"

That drew a chuckle from Margaret. She was ready to show her appreciation, but he wasn't ready any longer.

"I think I should be with you when you ask Daddy."

"Why?" he asked.

"Because I know him, and how to handle him."

"Okay. What part of the day is he happiest?"

"When he's eating. I'll bring you to supper."

"I don't think I'll be able to eat much, Maggie."

"Well, we don't have to worry about it until I'm sure."

"Thank heaven for that. Wow!"

"Wow what, Jonny?"

"Wow, you sure know how to throw a birthday party."

"Oh, Jonny, I'm sorry. I forgot it's your birthday."

"You forgot? Well, please don't ever forget again!"

Maggie tried to make love, but Jon wasn't responding.

"What's the matter, Jonny?"

"I'm worried. Hell, I'm *scared*."

"I was too, until tonight. Now I'm sure you will make a good husband and father. And I'll make you a good wife, I promise."

"Wow, a father of my own little sprout."

Maggie couldn't see it, but she was sure he was smiling. She could feel him responding.

"Let's put a cap on our vow to each other, Jonny."

She didn't need to ask again.

"Happy birthday, Jonny."

"Mmm, my best one ever."

At last they were able to relax in each other's arms. And relax they did. Endless minutes were spent exploring each other's bodies. Margaret noticed Jon's hand kept going back to her stomach.

"You can't feel it yet, Jonny."

"When will that happen?"

"Probably in two or three months."

"I guess I'll have to spend that time feeling here."

"Mmm, yes, don't ever forget that spot," she moaned in the darkness. "Jonny?"

"Yes, my pretty plum?"

"What did you have to tell me?"

The overseer reached around in the dark, until he found his trousers. He handed Maggie a piece of paper.

"What is this?" she asked.

"It's a newspaper ad."

"Well, how am I supposed to read it in the dark?"

"Sorry. Can we light a lantern?"

"We better not, Jonny. What does it say?"

"Let's take a chance and light the lantern."

"Alright, but it better be important."

"Trust me, it is." The tall overseer stood, and tried stumbling about the barn, looking for one of several lanterns. Maggie was amused at the sounds.

"Damn. I wish I were an owl," he said.

"Come back, Jonny. There's a lantern over here." She had the lantern lit by the time he returned. As he settled back next to her, she studied his lanky body.

"This is the first time I've seen you, Jonny."

"You mean out of my togs?"

"Of course, you big lummox, and I love what I see."

"Get to the ad, my pretty plum."

"Do you like what you see, Jonny?"

"I'll have a life-long itch for what I see."

Maggie smiled and handed Jon the lantern, and then read the ad.

Arkansas Needs YOU!

The next state in America, Arkansas, invites you to come plant your roots and seed into rich river bottomlands, ripe for the taking. One-hundred-sixty-acre parcels, along the Arkansas and White rivers, are open to any white man or woman willing to take up the plow and become an Arkansawyer. Register in our new state capitol, Little Rock.

Maggie read the ad twice, and looked at Jon curiously.

"What does this mean, Jonny?"

"Will you come with me to Arkansas?"

"Are you batty?"

"I've never been more serious. I want to marry you and take you into the Arkansas wilderness."

"But, Jonny, I love Bethania."

"More than me?"

"You know how much I love you, Jonny. But Bethania is my home, where I was born and raised."

"And bred!"

"Don't joke, Jonny. This is serious. If we stay, we could partly own Bethania someday."

"If we move to Arkansas, we will be full owners of land, instantly."

"But that would be so primitive," she mused.

"Primitive, yes, but also exciting, adventurous, and clean, with only each other to rely on."

"You mean we wouldn't have any servants?"

"That's what I mean when I say clean, Maggie."

"But I would miss Buelah, Nanty Ella, and Nunky Mose. Couldn't we bring them along?"

"Not as servants. I don't want slaves on our land."

"How would we get the work done, Jonny?"

"With these, our own two hands."

A long silence ensued, as Maggie thought about this development. The thoughts scared her.

"Would you still marry me if I said no to Arkansas?"

"Yes. But I would be unhappy living in that big house."

"And I would be unhappy away from Bethania, and Mother and Daddy. And you would be farther away from your family."

"Well, we have some time to think on it, Maggie."

"I love you, Jonny, and I want to please you."

"And you do please me, my pretty plum."

"I promise I'll think hard about it."

"Good. That's all I can ask."

"I guess we better get back to our houses."

"Righto! Thank you for agreeing to be my bride."

"You're welcome, my husband-to-be."

"We better douse the lantern before we're seen, baby."

"Yes, I'll put Pasha away. See you tomorrow?"

"I'll keep a watch out! Good night, darling."

"Good night, Jonny, and happy birthday."

Diary of Margaret Rose McAllister

July 18, 1835

Missus Jonathan Hamilton. Doesn't that sound wonderful? . . . It was so easy and thrilling. Jonny actually wants to marry me, and I want to marry him, whether or not I'm with child. I got my man on his birthday. . . . I hope he forgets about Arkansas.

The whole world was becoming suspicious. The lovers were constantly dodging prying eyes. Maggie's man was spending much more time in the field, with the tobacco plants needing suckering and worming. Once, when she had snuck out of the mansion, Maggie put the halter on Pasha and led him toward the back of barn five, only to be startled by barn bounder, Danny Doubleclutch.

"What are you doing here this late, Danny?"

"I's sorry, missy. I's not finish wit bedding dem horses."

"Well, go turn in, Danny. I'll finish the job."

"Yassa, Missy Margaret."

"And don't startle me again like that."

"Yassa, Missy Margaret."

Another incident happened in early August. Margaret's father and mother had yet another argument over the tutoring of the boys, and Maggie spent much longer than she expected comforting her mother. When she made her way to barn five, she noticed that Pasha was not in the first stall. What had happened? Had Jonny been there already and not found her waiting? Was he pulling her own signal on her in jest?

"Jonny? Jonny are you here?" No answer, and she was positive that he was angry with her. Then she remembered that she had forgotten to put Pasha away following their lovemaking the previous night, and one of the bounders, probably Danny, had put Pasha in another stall. When she saw Jonny the next night, it was the first thing he asked.

"Were you here last night, Maggie darling?"

"I was here late."

"Well, I'm sorry, darling. I had the watch laid out, and it turned out I couldn't get away."

Relief, thought Maggie. "It's alright, Jonny."

"Are you sure yet?"

"Not yet, Jonny. Another couple of weeks."

Summer was racing by, and it would soon be time to harvest. Maggie knew when that happened, she would see very little of her man. Nothing was happening with her natural cycle, either. She was now becoming certain of her condition; and it was time to condition herself, and Jonny, for the storm ahead. The conditioning started exactly one month after his birthday, following a session of "point and poke."

August 18

"Jonny?"

"Yeah, baby?"

"I'm sure." There was a pause, then an embrace.

"Really? I'm going to be a father?"

"Yes, I'm positive now."

"Oh, baby, that's a smash! Don't that beat all?"

"Are you happy, Jonny?"

"I am happy, I'll be a pappy! Can I feel it?"

"Not quite yet."

"Then how can you be sure?"

"Well, I again missed my curse, and this morning I got sick."

"Strange signs for a baby!"

"Now we must decide how to tell Mother and Daddy."

"Don't forget my parents too. I'll tell them this weekend," he said.

"Oh, you're going to be away this weekend?"

"Yes. I told you that a month ago."

"Oh, sorry, Jonny. I forgot."

"My sister has a birthday on the twenty-fourth."

"What's her name?

"Mary. Mary Jane. My sister will be twenty-two years old."

"She's older than me."

"Yup, and this may be the last time I see her."

"Why is that, Jonny?"

"She is about to marry a man from Savannah. Hmm . . . maybe I'll beat her."

"When do you plan to marry?"

"Oh, whenever I find a pretty redhead to knock up!"

"Very funny. We should set a date, Jonny."

"Will tomorrow be too late?"

"Be serious, Jonny. I don't want a big belly showing in my wedding dress."

"Well, then, will tomorrow be too late?"

"Daddy would probably be even more angry if I take you away during harvest season."

"True. Let's see. The harvest should be in by this time in October. Will that be too late?"

"I'll be showing then."

"Maybe we should marry in the cornfield during harvest and exchange cobs instead of bands."

"Jonny, be serious. I think we should wait until the harvest is in the barns."

"Okay. So we're talking about the last of October."

"Can we make it the third weekend in October?"

"That will be cutting it close, Maggie."

"I wish we had a calendar."

"You want to marry on a Saturday, right?"

"I think it would be better on a Friday."

"Okay. Let's set it the Friday in October after the twentieth," said Jon.

"Alright, lover. Let's seal that with a kiss."

"A kiss? Hell, let's seal it with a poke!"

Maggie's giggles turned to moans as they sealed the deal Jon's way.

Afterward, Maggie asked, "We don't have any bands, do we, Jonny?"

"No, but I'll get some."

"How?"

"Well, I know my brother and sister will have birthday gifts waiting for me. I'll just exchange them for bands in Salem."

"I'll miss you this weekend, Jonny."

"Want to come along?"

"I'd love to, Jonny, but I better not. At least not until our wedding plans are announced."

"And when is that fateful day?"

"It's going to have to be soon. Mother will want to start making plans right away."

"Let's get it over with as soon as possible. The sooner, the better, darling," he said.

"Alright. You're leaving Friday?"

"I was going to, right after I get the gang in."

"Then let's do it Thursday evening at supper."

"That's the day after tomorrow."

"The night after tomorrow, Jonny. I'll arrange it."

"Will I be going home Friday in a coffin?"

"I hope not, Jonny. Just try to keep your calm, and after you ask for my hand, let me do the yelling and arguing. He's used to that." Jon didn't answer. "Let's see . . . I'll sit you next to Mother, so you can charm her. She'll love you, Jonny."

"Well, what are you afraid of? Your daddy likes me too, doesn't he?"

"Yes, he does, until our affair and plans of marriage are announced. He'll be furious when he finds out we're going to have a baby."

"Just tell him he'll never see his grand-munchkin."

"What do you mean, Jonny?"

"You'll be having it in Arkansas, I hope."

"Oh, yes, Arkansas. I had hoped you had forgotten."

"It's our big chance to start anew, darling." Maggie fell silent, so Jon held her close. "Please, Maggie."

"Oh, Jonny. I'll be a good wife. I'll follow you anywhere."

"Wahoo! We'll leave the first Saturday after harvest."

"You mean the day after the wedding?"

"Righto, my pretty plum."

"Alright, but I need to have Buelah or Nanty Ella along."

"We'll work on that after he gets the good news."

"It will be one more piece of bad news to him."

"You're really going to have to sweet talk your daddy, Maggie. We'll need lots of supplies for the trip."

"Let's make the announcement first, Jonny." The stage was now set.

Diary of Margaret Rose McAllister

August 18, 1835

. . . Our wedding date is set for October 23. It may be in Bethania or on the trail, depending on my father. We will find out soon. I love my family, but I also love my Jonny . . . enough to leave Bethania?

The table was set at "hers" half of the great hall, with the boys on one side, Jonny and Maggie on the other, the mistress at the end.

"Jonny, Mother asked you a question."

Margaret noticed that her betrothed was gazing around the huge dining room. She bumped him back to consciousness.

"Huh? I'm sorry, ma'am, what did you say?"

"I asked if you liked collard greens, Mister Hamilton."

"Yes, ma'am, I do. I haven't had them very often."

"Why not? They're cheap to grow!" The coarse voice of Master Samuel McAllister rumbled from the far end of the long table.

"Well, sir, I guess it's because we only had room for a small garden."

"Nonsense."

"Papa, please come down here and sit, so we can talk to each other without shouting."

"I like it here, Sissy," Samuel replied. He turned his attention to Jonathan. "How big is your farm?"

"A little shy of eighty acres, most of it cultivated."

"And you don't have any bounders?"

"No, sir. Just Dad, my brother, and I, until this year. I'll find out tomorrow how they're doing without my help."

"You're going home? For how long?"

"Just for the weekend, sir. My sister's birthday is coming soon," said the very uncomfortable overseer.

"So you have one brother and one sister, Mister Hamilton?" Maggie's mother was keeping the small talk alive, and Maggie was wondering how long it would last before her man got to the point. She hoped he would at least wait until her brothers had departed and supper was over. *No sense wasting food*, she thought.

"Yes, ma'am, and my sister is about to get married, and that will leave only my brother to help my father with the crops."

"Where is your farm, boy, and what kind of crops does your father grow?"

"Mostly cotton, sir. It's about five miles south of Salem."

"How much cotton?"

"About fifty bundles, more or less, sir."

"And no tobacco?"

"Yes, sir, about ten acres, but it's mostly mundungus."

"What is that?" asked Maggie, as she placed her hand on Jonny's lap under the table. She knew he was very uncomfortable, having to answer all these questions from her father, and she thought the hand rub would help comfort Jonny. She smiled when he pushed her hand aside.

"Discolored sot," answered the master.

"How are your father and brother going to handle that farm without you, Mister Hamilton?"

"I'm not sure, Missus McAllister. I'm going to help them on weekends, but they will have to learn to do the job themselves. I won't be around any longer, after this year."

"They need bounder slaves, just like the rest of us."

"My father doesn't believe in having slaves, sir. He will probably have to hire some help."

"You're not going to be there anymore?" quizzed the mistress of Bethania.

"No, ma'am. My brother will be getting the farm, so I'm looking for some land of my own."

Margaret breathed a sigh of relief. She was sure that her man was going to mention Arkansas, and they had agreed that she would bring that up last.

"All the more reason for bounders. Those damned Yeoman farmers ought to stay north of the Mason Dixon anyway!" bellowed Samuel.

Maggie could feel the tension through the overseer's leg, which Jonny again freed from her hand. She thought she had better intercede.

"Jonny's sister is marrying a man from Savannah."

"How nice. It seems all young ladies feel a need to get married and raise a family," said the mistress, to Maggie's surprise. *This would be a good time to upset the cart*, Maggie thought, but she kept quiet.

"Nonsense. Most of the time, it's just an excuse to get away from home," growled Master Sam. "It would be much cheaper if they just had their sprouts at home, and be done with it."

Maggie was amazed at how the conversation was progressing, and she couldn't hold back any longer. "Does that include me, Daddy?"

Samuel busied himself with the collard greens.

"No, it doesn't include you, Sissy," said Susan.

"Why not, Mother? A few more bastard McAllisters would be to Daddy's liking, I'm sure."

"Stop it, Margaret! We have company."

"Sorry, Mother." The room fell into silence. Maggie could see the hard stare coming through her father's hair. The main course of pork and hominy, hot corn pone with chitlings, and cabbage was served. Maggie noticed that her fiancé had an appetite to match her father's. *So far, so good*, she thought, as the house bounders scurried about, picking up the dishes and serving the dessert. She noticed Jon was studying the dish. "Apple pan-dowdy, just for you."

"Thank you all. This is a wonderful dinner," said the lanky young man, pushing a hand off his lap.

"We call it supper here, Mister Hamilton."

"Oh, I'm sorry, ma'am. I'll have to remember that."

"How did your father acquire that farm, boy?"

"He had a gold mine on the Yadkin River, and you bought his claim, sir. He used the knob from the mine to tie down the farm. He just barely makes enough off the crops to cover his payments."

Maggie and Jon both noticed Sam's face turning red, and the pits started to disappear.

"Is anything wrong, sir?" asked Jonathan.

"Daddy gets growly when he thinks he has lost a rap to anyone, Jonny," answered Maggie.

"He didn't," said Jon. "My father worked hard to make the mine bring salt."

"So that was your father who bamboozled me?"

"No, sir. My father never bamboozled anyone."

The men's voices had raised a couple of notches, and Maggie thought she had better cut in.

"Daddy thinks he lost a pile in that mine deal."

"You couldn't have, sir. My father did well there, and he was sure he was close to a load," said Jon.

"Well, that load never appeared!" shouted the master. "Your father sold me a griefer!"

"I'm sure my father would buy that mine back for the little you paid for it, sir," came the overseer's reply.

"Here it comes," Maggie mumbled. "I'd better speak up."

"You must not have dropped much, Daddy. You still have your first Levy." This brought laughs from the boys, who had remained very quiet through the meal.

"Ridicule today, sob tomorrow!" Sam hollered. He enjoyed holding inheritance over his family's heads. "Get to your rooms, boys. You're excused."

"Yes, sir," came in unison, then in turn, the boys kissed their mother and sister, and shook hands with Jon.

"Glad to have met you, Mister Hamilton," said Sammy Junior.

"Great to connect with you, cracker," from Virgil.

"Good night, sir," was Miles's comment.

"Good night, Father, sir," again in unison.

"Now, if we can all keep calm, Jonny has something he wishes to ask of you, Daddy." Maggie felt it was time to get the fight started, now that the boys had left.

"The way he sassed me? The answer is no."

"How do you know what he's going to ask, Daddy?"

"I'm not giving him anything. Neither he, or his dad will ever take anything of mine again!" Sam shouted.

Maggie placed her hand on Jon's leg again, trying to settle and soothe her lover's anger.

"Maybe we ought to put it off, Jonny."

"Like hell!" shouted Jon. "I've probably lost my job anyway, so there's no time like the present!"

Jonathan grabbed Maggie's hand and pushed back at her. He stood up to address the plantation master, who was intensely watching the young couple from under heavy eyebrows. "I would like your permission to marry your daughter, Mister McAllister."

"You what?" Sam came up out of his chair.

"I love your daughter, and I plan to marry her."

"Why you young flunky! You'll marry her over my dead body! The answer is still no! Get out of my house!"

"I love him, Daddy, and we have set the date."

"Please, Samuel, this is no way to treat a guest." No one seemed to hear Susan.

"I said get out of my house, before I have Mose throw you out on your ear!"

"Yes, sir, I'm going, but that don't change nothing."

"I'm making the changes!" Sam shouted after Jon. "And you'll be hearing from me tomorrow!"

"I can hardly wait," came the answer from the door.

Maggie got up from her chair and followed Jon out the door.

"Where in hell do you think you're going?!" shouted Sam.

"To see him out, and kiss him good night."

"He can find his own way!" snapped Samuel.

"I'm not as ill-mannered as you, Daddy."

Maggie hurried out of the hall and caught up with the overseer at the back door. As she held him close, she was aware of his shaking from anger. "It's alright, Jonny. He'll not stop us."

"My father never conned anyone. Damn him for saying he did."

"I know, Jonny. Daddy just said it in anger." Maggie tugged at his neck and kissed him passionately. She knew when he had settled back down, as the shaking had ended.

"We hadn't even reached the good stuff yet," said Jon.

"Well, wish me luck, because I'm going to spill the beans."

"I should be in there with you."

"It's alright, Jonny. I can handle it. I may end up sharing your bed in the overseer house, though."

"You're in enough trouble already, baby."

"I'll go tell him, then meet you in barn five."

"Not tonight, Maggie. Don't you know when you're well off?"

"I'm well off when I'm with you."

"By the way . . ."

"Yes, Jonny?"

"You look beautiful tonight."

"Thank you, Jonny. Do you like my dress?"

"You bet. Flowers in all the right places." The lovers hugged and kissed for several minutes.

"I had better get in there and get it over with."

"Good luck, baby. Should I wait here for you?"

"No, Jonny. You'll hear the results soon enough."

"Okay, my pretty plum. Please tell them thank you for the dinner."

"Supper, darling. I will. Good night."

"Good night, baby. Maybe I'll see you in my bed."

"If you do, that means we pack and leave."

One more kiss and hug, and Jonny headed for the overseer house. Maggie watched him disappear into the dark, then took a deep breath and walked back inside.

"Let's get this over with," she mumbled.

The first thing Maggie noticed as soon as she stepped into the great hall was that her father had moved to the "hers" end of the huge table, to the left of her mother.

"Come in and sit, Margaret Rose," Sam said sternly.

"Yes, Father." She strode briskly to the table. "Jonny says to tell you thanks for the supper."

"Are you out of your mind?"

"Yes, Daddy, I believe I am. I'm going to marry him on October twenty-third," Maggie said matter-of-factly.

"Like hell you are!" Samuel came up out of his chair, baraclave bristling. Maggie noticed the tears already rolling down her mother's cheeks. She jumped out of her chair, across the table from her father.

"I am, and you're not going to stop me. Either here, or somewhere else, the choice is up to you."

"Damn your insolence! I forbid it!" Sam screamed.

"Forbid it to hell and back, Daddy. I am twenty-one and will do as I please."

"I'll run him out of the state before I let that happen!" Father and daughter stood eye to eye across the wide table, portraits shaking from the outcries and table pounding. Neither noticed the mistress was openly weeping.

"He is already going out of state, and I'm going with him!" In the heat of the shouting, this last sentence seemed to go unheard.

Suddenly, Susan spoke. "Please stop shouting at each other." Her voice was drowned out by the table pounding and rage.

"You're going nowhere, Sissy! I forbid that too!"

"I love him, Daddy, and I'll follow him anywhere he goes, whether you like it or not!"

"He's nothing but a clay eater and a flunky! He's not suitable for you!" The yelling continued.

"I'll be the judge of that for myself!"

"I swear, I will disinherit you, Maggie!"

"That's the last time you'll ever threaten that one on me, dear Samuel!" This brought Susan out of her chair, which overturned. The chairs and table were getting a workout.

"Stop it!" Susan screamed through her tears. "I insist we talk this out like human beings!"

"Sorry, Mother, but I'm not giving in."

"He is not in your class, Sissy," said Susan.

"I don't care, Mother. He is the man I love."

"You don't know the meaning of the word!" shouted Sam.

"And I suppose you do? Do you love Mother? Do you love all the Nans you dally around with, Daddy?"

Samuel's pits had been long gone, and his face was now sun-burned red. Susan lowered her head, crying loudly.

"This is not about me! It is about your love life, which is about to end!"

"Like hell it is! It's only just begun!"

"You are my daughter, and you'll do as I say. I forbid you to see that conjurer again!"

"You seem to forget I'm twenty-one and on my own, Boss!"

"Twenty-one or eighty-one, as long as you are in my house, you will do as I say!" There was no letup in the volume of Sam's voice.

"Okay, Daddy. I'll leave tonight!" No letup in the volume of Margaret's voice.

"I said you're going nowhere, and you are not seeing that Hamilton boy again! He is not in your class!"

"Would you rather I twaddle with Lenny?"

This brought a quick silence and glare from Samuel. "You know the answer to that is no. That would be even worse."

"He is a McAllister. Isn't that in your class?"

The Mistress Susan again rose out of her chair. "Margaret Rose! Stop that kind of talk!" The mistress slammed the dessert dish on the table. "Both of you sit down and act civil!"

Both combatants sat down in shock and stared at Susan. Maggie had never heard her mother speak out before. Silence gripped the great hall for an instant eternity.

"There are many young toffs with the wherewithal to satisfy us both, Maggie." Sam was trying to remain calm.

"It is not my responsibility to satisfy your wherewithal, Daddy, though Lord knows I have tried, and the only man satisfactory to me is Jon Hamilton." The master and his daughter stared at each other from across the table.

"You must marry into your own class, Sissy. We want you to be happy." Susan calmly addressed her daughter.

"Are you happy, Mother?" The hurt showed back in Susan's eyes. Maggie had her answer.

"If you need to get married, we could arrange for you and young Master Johnstone to . . ."

"Mother!" Maggie broke in on Susan. "You know I have no use for that podunker James Johnstone. How dare you even bring him up? You are a good example of an arranged marriage."

Tears again were popping from the eyes of the mistress.

"That will be enough of that, Maggie," said Sam.

"Well, I do have a need to get married to Jon Hamilton. He is the father of the baby I'm going to have."

"And what is that supposed to mean?"

"I fell off the roof, Daddy!"

"Oh no, Sissy! Say that isn't so!" Susan was having trouble holding back the tears again.

"It is so, Mother. I have one in the basket."

"And what is that supposed to mean?"

"It means I'm going to have Jon Hamilton's baby."

"Like hell you are! I will not have it!" Samuel came out of his chair with such force that it tipped over.

"You're too late, Daddy. I am having it, not you!" Maggie's chair stayed upright this time. Mose D. straightened Sam's chair.

"Dear God, Sissy. How could you?" Susan's handkerchief was sopping wet.

"How dare you!" roared Sam. "You are a disgrace to the name McAllister!" The pits were gone.

"Why? For doing the same thing you've been doing for years?"

"Damn you and your sassiness! You can tell that clay eater that he's fired!"

"We're going to have to accept him as our son-in-law, Sam, to keep Sissy's honor," said a teary Susan.

"Nonsense. We can send her down to Chic Wood to have her nipper"

"Alright, Daddy. Jon and I will get married in Chic Wood."

"When are you going to listen? You are not going to marry that one-horse Casanova!" Sam was again pounding on the table.

"When are you going to listen, Daddy? I am marrying him and having his child!"

"I see what that bickerhead means, when he said he was looking for land. He wants some of mine."

"He doesn't want any of your land, Daddy. I wish he did."

"And what is that supposed to mean?"

"It means that as soon as we're married, Jon and I are headed for Arkansas."

"Arkansas! Why in the devil's name would he want to go to Arkansas? That's nothing but wilderness!"

"For the first time tonight, I agree with you. But Jon saw a newspaper ad that Arkansas is giving away river bottomland and becoming a state."

"Dear me. We will not even see our new grandbaby." Susan was now using the apron over her dress to ward off tears.

"Jonny has promised me that as soon as the roads improve, I can come home to visit," said Maggie.

Samuel had that sinking feeling. He sat down easily, and held his head in his hands. "How could one person so ruin my life?"

"Nothing is ruined, Daddy. Jon will make you a good son, and me a wonderful, caring husband."

For once, Samuel sat in silence, head in hands. Susan's quiet weeping became ear-shattering.

"Don't cry, Mother. It will be alright."

Susan paused and took a deep breath. "I saw what you were doing to that young man under the table, Sissy."

"What?" Samuel again exited his chair.

"Cool down, Daddy. I was only touching his leg."

"In front of your brothers and the mistress?"

Once again, Maggie felt the need to return to her father's shouts with some of her own. She jumped back up out of her chair, and this time, it tipped over. "I suppose you have never played with anyone's legs, black or white, Daddy?"

"Not in front of my family, Sissy."

"Stop it!" Susan was again out of her chair. "We must find a solution to Sissy's problems, calmly."

"I have the solution!" shouted Maggie.

"And what might that be?"

"That you two sit down and accept the inevitable. That Jonathan Hamilton and Margaret Rose McAllister will be husband and wife. You gain a son and a grandchild, and I become an honest woman."

Samuel and Susan McAllister sat down in silence. Susan wept quietly, and Maggie witnessed something she hadn't seen in years. Her father reached over, grabbed, and held her mother's hand. Tears even popped from beneath heavy brows. This had been a strange supper!

"What day did you set for the wedding, Sissy?"

"October twenty-third, Mother. It's a Friday."

"That's too late, Sissy. You'll be showing by then."

"I know, Mother, but Jonny wanted to be fair with Daddy and wait until the crops were all in."

"Can you talk him out of the move to Arkansas, Sissy? I'll give him some land."

"I tried, Daddy, but he is determined." Margaret watched in disbelief as her father's tears soaked through his baraclave. "It will be alright, Daddy. We'll need a lot of help from you to begin with, but I know that Jonny and I will be very happy together. You'll see."

"I guess I better get started with the dresses," said a much calmer Susan. "I have some cotton cloth and silk, but you will need to travel soon to Charleston, Sam."

"Yes, Mother. Make a list, and I'll leave tomorrow." Margaret again was stunned at his reply.

"Oh, one thing more," said Margaret Rose.

"Sissy, please don't hurt your father anymore."

"What is it now, Sissy?" said the weary master.

"Our invitations may get snubbed. I want Buelah to be my bridesmaid, and Nunky Mo and Nanty Ella in my wedding."

"If any of them snub us, I'll bury them."

Diary of Margaret Rose McAllister

August 20, 1835

Dear Me. In the course of reaching my goal, I have injured my father and mother, I pray not permanently. I know that Jonny will make them proud. I can hardly wait until morning to tell Jonny of my success . . . I know now the depth of my parents' love for me, and mine for them. That love will endure forever.

Mistress Susan and daughter Margaret both knew something was very wrong. Master Samuel McAllister was not eating! Bullock and beans was one of the master's favorite dishes, and he was still picking at the first helping. The women gave each other signals.

"If you boys are finished, you are excused."

"Thank you, Mother." The three had become experts at speaking in unison. They each rose and bade good night to all present, with kisses and a handshake. Virgil bowed and kissed his sister's hand.

"Daddy, what is eating you?" quizzed Maggie.

"Why do you think something is eating me?"

"Because you're not eating!"

There was a silence of several minutes, and the ladies determined that the problem with the master was serious. His pits were vanishing. "I received a letter today."

"Come on, Daddy. You get letters every day."

"This one was from your overseer's father."

"He's your overseer, Daddy, my future husband."

"What did the letter say, Sam?" asked Susan.

"He demanded a dowry, damn him!"

"That's the custom, Daddy."

"To hell with custom! Nobody makes demands on me. I will not allow it!" The pits were gone.

"Now don't get snarly, Daddy. He was just doing his duty. He couldn't have asked for much. I think we have almost everything we need."

"What did he ask for, Sam?" questioned Susan.

"He demanded a wagon, horses, and a bundle of other things for the move to Arkansas!"

"Sounds like things they will need, Sam," said Susan.

"I had hoped Arkansas had been forgotten."

"Hardly. Jonny talks about it every day."

"And just where do you see him every day, Sissy?"

"In the field, barns, overseer house. Everywhere."

"No wonder his work has gotten so sloppy."

"Daddy! Jonny is working very hard for you. He is putting in more hours than any other overseer."

"His reports are sloppy, and often late."

"I'll tell him to cut back on the hours, so he can write a better report."

"Like hell you will, Sissy! You just leave him alone so he can do his job."

"Like hell I will, Daddy! He is my fiancé, and the father of this hump, and I'm not seeing enough of him now." Each sentence got louder by a crescendo.

"Perhaps you would like to bundle with him."

"We would both like that, Daddy. It couldn't do any more harm, but he won't move into this house."

"I have asked him several times to supper, but he politely refuses," added Mistress Susan.

"What's wrong with him? Does he think he's too good for us?" A simple question from simple Sam.

"Of course not, Daddy. Jonny thinks you hate him, and he doesn't want to do anything to upset you."

"He really seems to be a kind and courteous young man, Sam."

"Thank you, Mother. He really likes you too. You don't hate him, do you, Daddy? He thinks the world of you."

"No, Sissy. I don't hate him. I can't hate my future son-in-law. I just hate the idea of the lad taking my daughter to Arkansas."

"We'll be visiting often. Who knows, maybe when he gets there, in the wilds, he'll want to come back."

"I already know him well enough to know that isn't going to happen," quipped Sam.

"Then maybe you can come visit us in a couple of years. We both would like that."

"Well, that sounds like a good idea, Sissy. I think I would like that too."

"Good. Then you'll give us the wagon and horses we need for the trip?"

"Whoa! I didn't say that."

"Please, Daddy. We may not survive without them."

"It wouldn't hurt us any, Sam, to give them what they need." It was good to have Susan on Maggie's side.

"Well, I'm not going to change either of your minds, and I can't let you go empty-handed, so I guess I haven't much choice."

With that, Maggie jumped up and hugged and kissed her father. Tears ran from Susan's eyes.

"Thank you, Daddy. I love you. Both Jonny and I love you."

"Nonsense! You both love my pile!"

"That too, Daddy. Jonny will learn to be just another chip off the block."

"Hmm . . . A very expensive chip."

"You love it, Daddy. You can't take it with you."

"Nonsense! They're building banks all over hell now." All three McAllisters had a good laugh over that. Even Susan forgot the tears and laughed loudly.

"I guess I had better get back to the dresses."

"How's it coming, Mother?"

"Wonderful. Elsie and Ella are both working wonders. Your dress and Buelah's will be ready for a fitting soon. I thought I would make black slacks and gray coats for Jonathan and his brother, if that suits you, Sissy."

"That sounds great, Mother. That will match Buelah's and my dresses."

"And what would you have me wear, Mother?" Maggie was beaming over the way her father was treating her mother lately. Not the best, but no recent arguments or fights.

"You pick a color, Sam, and I'll make outfits for you and I, and the Hamiltons to match."

"How about red, to show your joy?" quipped Maggie.

"How about black, to show our sorrow?" quipped Sam.

"We'll wear blue, to show neutrality," quipped Susan.

"And what are the bounders wearing?" asked Sam.

"All of the other attendants will be dressed in white," answered Maggie.

"Even the whites?"

"Yes, Daddy. I want them all dressed alike."

"That should create quite a stir."

"This whole wedding will create a stir, Daddy."

"How about the male attendants wearing white trousers and black coats?" asked Susan.

"And the women in all white?"

"Yes, Sissy. That should make a better contrast."

"Wonderful, Mother. Will you have time to do all of this?"

"Yes. I better get busy."

"Alright. I'm going out to the overseer house."

"Sissy?"

"Yes, Father?"

"Tell him I don't hate him, and would like to talk with him more often. I would even like him to move into this house if he has a mind to."

"Thank you, Daddy. I'll tell him."

Sam was left alone to eat his bullock and beans.

Diary of Margaret Rose McAllister

September 10, 1835

. . . Jonny and his brother will be dressed alike, as will Buelah and I, "to scare off evil spirits and confuse kidnappers." Ha! Some of these customs are funny . . . Daddy has promised everything we need for the big move to Arkansas . . .

The wedding did cause quite a stir. The small church at Bethania had the banns read three times by its regular pastor, Benjamin Homster. The *Salem Chronicle* carried the news of the approaching wedding all across the Piedmont. Curious Carolinians came from miles away to verify the many rumors. They were all true. At the front of the grand staircase stood a lone bagpiper. The crowd filled the huge foyer and portico, the carriage porch. People had to squeeze back to make a pathway from the stairs through the foyer and portico, and onto the lawn, where an arched trellis awaited the wedding party. They gasped as the first two coming down the stairs were a black boy and girl, carrying a basket of rose petals and the wedding bands on a white cushion.

Next came the attendants. The crowd gasped again, as the huge black frame of house bounder Mose Dasilvalentis, wearing black coat and tie with white trousers, came down the stairs with bounder Ella Elevated on his arm, wearing a floor-length white muslin gown, and carrying evergreens.

As the piper played, each of the attendants, in couples, walked down the stairs and through the huge, hand-carved doors. Next in line came Margaret's oldest brother, Allston, with Miss Jennifer Johnstone, from Salisbury. Then Samuel McAllister Junior, accompanied by the pastor's wife, Missus Rebecca Homster. Last of this group was the comically prancing Virgil McAllister and the breathtaking house bounder Esther Blowby. The people thought it strange when next came the groom's father, Alexander Andrew Hamilton, accompanied by the Mistress Susan Ashley McAllister, he in an appropriate blue suit, and she in a sky-blue silk gown with full skirt, and carrying garlands and pine boughs. Now the groom, Jonathan Henry Hamilton, appeared at the top of the stairs in a gray coat and black tie, trousers, and shoes, and carrying a sash of the Hamilton tartan, and accompanied by his mother, Martha Moreley, in a seashell aqua gown of ankle length, with an empire waist. She was carrying a green wreath full of red holly berries.

Excitement now built, as the crowd awaited the appearance of the bride. At the head of the grand staircase now appeared the best man, Jonathan's older brother Andrew Hamilton, wearing the familiar gray and black, and the maid of honor, and very black, Buelah Botcherbuns. Her short, curly black hair and shiny black skin seemed to illuminate the elegant gown, white to the waist, with tight bodice and a necklace, and a neckline of lace, and off-shoulder flowing sleeves. The skirt was long blocks of dark and light gray, separated by blocks of white linen, floor length, and loose at the waist. Buelah carried a bunch of mistletoe and pine.

All eyes now viewed the bride, in the same grays and whites as Buelah's dress, her back-length fiery red hair covered by a long veil of lace. She carried the family Bible. At Margaret's side stood her father, the master of Bethania, much shorter than his daughter, with a waist-length graying baraclave covering a good portion of his light blue suit. A few chuckles spread through the crowd, which quickly turned to gasps, as the bride approached the bottom of the stairs. Her loose waistline failed to cover up the swelling. The crowd closed behind the father and daughter, swaying to a brisk wedding march from the piper.

Through the huge double doors and over the trampled rose petals covering the portico, they marched, and finally the wedding party stood at the pine and red rose-covered trellis and altar. The last few steps seemed to show a slight limp by the bride. The spectators wondered if Maggie was wearing a bustle, as the slight outcropping of the rear of the gown was highlighted by blue ribbons. This would be explained later as something old, something new, something borrowed, and something blue.

The wedding itself went without a hitch. The bands were exchanged and vows repeated. When asked to speak now or forever hold their peace, the crowd remained silent. A broad grin covered Jonathan's face when Margaret vowed to love, honor, and obey. The grin continued as he lifted the veil, revealing the bride's lovely face. The kiss was long and passionate, causing some uneasy chuckles from the viewers. As Pastor Homster pronounced them husband and wife, Jonathan placed the tartan sash over his bride's left shoulder and, using a long hairpin, secured the sash to the gown at the waist. The crowd now squeezed the path back to the foyer, and Chic Wood rice was thrown at the newlyweds, replacing the rose petals.

Inside the doors, the wedding party formed a reception line. The crowd scrambled into the line, so they could ensure themselves a place in the grand dining hall, set up to seat one hundred and sixty people, a little over half of the huge crowd. The grand dining table had been pushed to one side, to accommodate fifteen additional tables. Pine boughs and roses decorated the head table. At the center, where the room divided, stood the tall multilayered cake and a three-foot-tall candle, seated in a polished silver holder, both surrounded by a floral bouquet, and a large object covered by a white silk cloth and, strangely, a clump of the herb dill.

One side of the table was occupied by the wedding party, backs to the wall. A dozen other people claimed seats at the grand table, making a total of twenty-eight, with an open area facing the crowd. That open area became the focus of the first event of the reception after a snack of homemade sweets and the never-before sampling of ice cream was served. Jonathan's brother took control, and became the master of ceremonies.

"Ladies and gentlemen, our first event will be the jumping of the broom." With that, the bride and groom circled the huge table. With the assistance of Nunky Mo and Nanty Ella, they each jumped forward and back, over a broom handle. "Brother Jon and sister Maggie are now truly married!" shouted Jon's brother, Andrew. "I have a couple of announcements, friends. Perhaps you noticed that the bride was wearing something old, something new, something borrowed, and something blue. Inside her shoe, Maggie is walking on two old coins, a sixpence and a levy."

Maggie stood and removed her shoe. She showed the coins to the crowd and received cheers. Andrew continued, "The new is the brooch Maggie is wearing. It was a birthday gift from her youngest brother, Miles, and this is the first time she's worn it." Again, the people applauded. "You will notice the brooch also has a blue stone." More applause. "The borrowed item is the McAllister family Bible, and the blue is the tail ribbons, as well as the brooch."

After another short applause, a lady at the end of the head table stood and asked a question. "What was the ribbon wrapped around?"

Maggie again stood and whispered something to her new husband. Amid gasps and screeches, Jonathan reached up under the bride's gown and unhooked a small pouch. He emptied its contents on the table. There was a piece of bread, a piece of cloth, a piece of wood, and another coin.

Andrew explained the meaning of these items. "The bread, cloth, wood, and coin are meant to ensure that the newlyweds will have enough food, clothes, shelter, and money in their future together. I would now like to draw your attention to the silk bundle on the table next to the wedding cake. Inside that silk cloth is a sieve, and on the table in front of you, along with a memento for each of you, is a small envelope. Anyone wishing to donate to the newlyweds are asked to place it in the envelope, and place the envelope into the sieve, at any time. Thank you."

The room erupted into chatter. Several people rose and shoved their envelopes under the cloth and into the sieve. Andrew rapped a cup to bring the crowd back to silence.

"Folks, it is time to light the unity candle, symbolic of two people uniting as one," said Andrew. Mister and Missus Hamilton each lit a candle from their seats to the right of the groom. Samuel and Susan McAllister did the same from the left of the bride. They walked around the ends of the long table to the tall "unity candle" in front of the newlyweds, and together both sets of parents set it aflame.

"All single ladies are now invited to gather in the foyer, where the new Missus Hamilton will toss her bouquet from the top of the stairs."

A large group of ladies headed for the grand staircase to join many others, who were unable to find seats in the dining hall. With the assistance of her new husband, Maggie climbed to the top, turned her back to the people below, and threw her bouquet over her shoulder. There was much applause and screams, but neither saw just who caught it.

"It is time for the wedding supper!" shouted Andrew from a few steps up the grand staircase. "All of you who haven't been able to join us in the grand hall, don't worry. You will all be fed, here in the foyer." House servants, many of whom had to be recruited from other plantations, scurried about, serving the masses. It was a very elaborate meal of ham, turkey, salads, biscuits and jellies, and more ice cream made with ice, and unfamiliar to most of the crowd. It was a hit.

"Before we cut the cake, I have a couple more tasks. You all should have wine on your tables. I would like to propose a toast to the newlyweds." All present stood and raised their glasses to the head table. "Tonight starts a new adventure for Jon and

Margaret. May their journeys in life be ever happy, and may the Good Lord protect them all their days, in the new state of Arkansas."

"Here, here!" shouted the males in the audience, as all drank to the newly married couple.

"Now for my contribution to this ceremony. On the long head table is a clump of dill. Eating the dill is supposed to create lust. Let's all encourage Jon and Margaret to eat it now."

It was obvious that the lust was not really needed, but the crowd cheered and clapped as the newlyweds chewed and swallowed a good portion of the herb.

"The wedding cake is much too large to sit on Maggie's head, so the bride and groom will now cut it, right where it sits."

Jon and Maggie needed help from their parents. The servants scurried about, serving. A lot of the standing-room-only audience in the foyer did not eat. The cake was not big enough to accommodate the multitude.

"We're almost finished with the reception, folks. You will be happy to know that our wonderful hosts, the McAllisters, found a Celtic band to play dance music for you out in the foyer and Partico. They are gathering now at the altar." The crowd started filing out.

"One more thing before we leave!" shouted Andrew. "I am now requesting brother Jon to remove his tie." Jonathan stood, took off his tie, and handed it to Andrew, who proceeded to cut the tie in little pieces. "These pieces of the groom's tie are for sale at an Eagle each, to help the newlyweds."

Some grumbling about wealthy people beating the drum for donations could be heard, mingled with the chatter, as the throng emptied the great hall. Ceileigh music filled the air, as the newlyweds initiated the dancing. The tall lanky groom displayed three left feet, and the bride guided him along the small space at the bottom of the grand staircase. Again, some gasps were heard, as the white best man and black maid of honor joined in the first dance. The parents were next, and soon the dance areas in the foyer and portico were packed. The McAllisters' corn liquor and wine flowed freely. Everyone seemed to enjoy themselves.

The shivaree had started, and soon the bride and groom were looking to disappear. The dill was working, at least for the groom. The bride was aware of this, and teasingly threw kisses at her husband as she continued dancing with all the men, who had formed a line for that purpose. The party raged on.

It was well after midnight when the last of many tricks was performed. The female attendants grabbed the bride and hustled her up the grand staircase to her room, while the male attendants held the groom at bay. The crowd continued their dancing, but all eyes were focused on the balcony. Finally, the women reappeared, pulling Maggie into view, wearing a white nightgown. Whistles and cheers erupted. The new bride looked stunning and appealing. The long red hair covered both shoulders and flowed over her breasts. The male attendants raced up the stairs in single file, joined by many other men. A few had to stay behind and hold back the groom.

The ladies led the bride back into her room, then stood guard at the door, allowing one man at a time into her room for a couple minutes, much to the worry and concern of the contained groom. As each man reappeared at the balcony, they made gestures of satisfaction to the groom below.

Finally, all who wished had their turn. To preserve his energy, the tall groom was carried up the stairs to Maggie's room. The crowd cheered as he was pushed into her chamber. The audience was shushed to silence, as many ears became attached to the heavy door. Whispers abounded, as tales of tearing clothes and creaking of bed springs were passed down the stairs and through the crowd. Suddenly, by arranged time, several men fired their rifles in unison outside, and the crowd roared its approval. The shivaree had just begun.

Diary of Margaret Rose (McAllister) Hamilton

October 23, 1835

. . . An affair to remember . . . a babbling bear garden . . . but am I happy? I fear today will be my last on my beloved Bethania . . . I'm proud to have his child swelling in my belly . . .

CHAPTER III

Jonathan Henry Hamilton

April 1835

Hot and cold, that's North Carolina. The sun was warm, but the breeze was bone-gripping. Jonathan sat in front of his brother Andrew, and now realized he had been outsmarted. The wind seemed to blow westward from the blues, and now as the Hamilton brothers turned north toward Bethania, Jon was certain it came from the North Pole, straight into his face.

Poor Dandy, he thought. Dandy was getting the brunt of the blow. Hell, the horse's back even felt cold through his kentucks. He should have left Dandy's blanket on.

"Are you gum-gabbling at me, Jonny Boy?"

"No . . . Y-yes. Let's switch kazoos. Too much weight on Dandy's shoulders."

"Smart choice, but no chance, brother. I'm comfy right here, with you blocking the wind."

"I'm getting wrathy. I may have to give you Jesse yet, to get that backseat."

"Little chance, Jonny Boy. Just remember this was your idea, not mine. We can turn around now, and the cold would be at my back."

"Sure, then I can be a slave to you the rest of my life."

"We don't hold slaves, remember? I'm willing to share."

"Then we both would starve."

"You're muddleheaded, brother Jon. Our family hasn't starved yet."

"It's not being muddleheaded to want your own land, Drew, and I'm sure not getting any of yours."

"Okay, you're oxheaded then, if you think you're going to earn any land as an overseer."

"Treat me nice, my astatine brother. I may own this Bethania plantation someday."

"Dig my bones up when that happens, and we'll party, Jonny Boy."

"Get stuffed, Andrew. I'm going to be a success."

"Ha! Speaking of stuffed, let's stop and have a bite to eat."

"Sounds good. I'm hungry and cold. What do we have left?"

"Some pork and corn dodgers. I need to stretch and walk a little. I'm about to freeze my flummox off, Jonny Boy."

"I suppose you learned about your flummox at state?"

"Mine, and a few others."

They both laughed at that. Jon found a small patch of pines along the road, and the horse and Hamiltons huddled out of the cold wind. The dodgers were hard, but filling. Dandy even ate one, along with a couple of apples.

"It's not too late, Jon. We can still make it back home before dark."

"No way, brother Drew. I'm going whole hog."

"See what I mean? You are oxheaded."

"Maybe I can get the mistress to cotton up to me, and get some land from her."

"Fat chance, brother Jon. Why don't you go whole hog, and kill the McAllister family?"

"Sure. Just my luck they'd have the other half of the family scattered all over the south."

"Maybe they have an ugly daughter, Jonny Boy, one who can't get anyone else."

"If they had a fluff, the master would probably have her locked up in a chastity belt!"

"So what? You marry her for the rhino, brother Jon. You'll have slaves for the rest."

"Ha! Would you like a burr-headed nephew?"

"Wear a boogie bun, you flounderhead."

"Pound salt, modocky! Don't you worry. I'll get some land somehow."

"Hokay, I won't worry. Just remember, you'll always have diggings on the farm."

"Thanks. Let's get going. My future is waiting."

"Roger. I'm still taking the backseat."

"Like hell you are!"

The brothers scrambled onto Dandy's back. Jonathan, the bigger of the two, rode the rump.

The low-rolling hills of the Piedmont seemed to stretch forever. Jon sensed they were now on the Bethania Plantation, as the frozen-looking ground had rows of evenly hacked brown cornstalks, sticking up six to eight inches out of the dirt. Andrew steered Dandy between the frozen stalks.

"Looks like things are sloppy here at Bethania."

"I noticed. Father always made us pull them up and torch them."

"You're going to have to straighten them out, Jonny Boy."

"Hope not. This sod is hard."

"So is my keister. Let's trade places."

"Bite horse, brother Drew. We're about there now."

"Damn, we should be. We've been riding all morning."

"How far do you think we've trooped, Drew?"

"Feels like fifty miles, but probably twenty."

"Maybe Master McAllister will put you up for the night if I get the job."

"How can he refuse a harlot's favorite like you, Jonny Boy?"

"Get cheeky, and I'll have him send you home."

"Dandy and I would like to make it back to the farm tonight anyway."

"Not tonight, brother Drew. I need that smooth babble-gabble of yours to land the job."

"We'll see what happens, Jonny Boy."

Now that Jonathan was riding in back, the wind seemed to die down, and the afternoon's rays warmed the stiffened joints of the Hamilton boys. The landscape had also changed. The dead cornstalks were gone, and Jon wondered if the cleared, fertile fields were for tobacco or cotton, or something else.

"We'll soon be rubbing vestibules to the fire, brother Drew."

"You may not be so air-nobbed after all. I can smell sot weed. This must be the tobacco fields we're treading."

"Righto. That means the barns are close."

The stout legs of the big red horse, Dandy, broke over a knob, and before them spread a beautiful, flat green valley. Jon and Andrew squinted through the afternoon sun at the rows of buildings laced with trees. They sat in the valley's center, and fields of cattle grazed in pastures on either side.

"Behold, Andrew, before us lies Bethania."

"I'm impressed. Just this valley outsizes our farm."

"Your farm. This one will be mine."

"You're as wacky as your sister. Let's get down there."

"Righto. Forward, Dandy. Dinner is on the table." Dandy handled the weight of Jon and his older, but smaller brother, well. He seemed to sense that he too would soon be fed and rested, and quickened his pace down the gentle, sloping hill.

As the terrain quickly leveled again, a smooth road crossed a bridge ahead and seemed to divide a grove of trees in the distance. The bridge crossed a swift-flowing brook, and the brothers jumped off Dandy. All three filled their bladders, and Andrew pointed at the line of trees.

"Feed your pupils on that, Jonny Boy."

Through the grove, the Hamilton boys had their first glimpses of the huge white mansion.

"Even that outsizes your farm, brother Drew."

"Are you ready to deal with slaves and slave holders, brother Jon?"

"I think so. I'll try to treat them as humans, as Father said."

"Then there is no time like the present to get started on your conquest."

"Righto. Forward, Dandy. My new life awaits me."

As the house grew larger, it resembled the great manor houses in Scotland that Jon's grandfather had spoken of. It looked as though it were three stories tall, with a set of four huge, round pillars in front, reaching to the top, outlining a large portico. The portico was divided by a balcony two-thirds of the way up, outlining the second story.

"Think you can find your way around that shed, Jonny Boy?"

"Not sure. That porch would hide the farmhouse."

Through the stand of trees, the road forked, creating a loop and climbing slightly to the big portico, about four hundred feet straight ahead.

"Your first big decision, overseer. Left or right?"

"Right it is, brother Drew, and right is the course I intend to steer."

"Well, good luck. It's a long walk back to the farm."

Dandy halted within the confines of the giant pillars, as if he were pulling a golden-gilded carriage. The portico floor of polished stone made an unusual clacking sound under the hooves of the dray, Dandy. The brothers leaped off Dandy's back, and Jon strode up a step to the hand-carved wooden double doors. He pulled the golden rope, and heard ringing inside. He nearly lost his balance when the huge doors were opened by the biggest black man he had ever laid eyes on. *Wow, what a weald*, Jon thought. He must be twenty hands and twenty stone.

"Ah, I'm here to see Mister McAllister about the overseer job."

"Goes to rear. Massa Sam will see's you's there."

"Righto. I have my brother and plower with me."

"Yassa. They's goes to rear. Massa Sam will see's you's all there."

The big slave covered both doors, and Jon decided to eat ego, and headed around the mansion.

The rows of manicured barns and outbuildings came into view. The back side of the huge house looked as impressive as the front. Four evenly spaced doors lined its length. A second house, bigger than the Hamilton farmhouse, stood directly behind, with a covered walkway to the mansion, some sixty or seventy feet. Both male and female slaves ran in and out of it.

"Maybe it's their quarters," Jon figured. "Hell's bells, they have it better than we do!"

"Which door do we rattle, Jonny Boy?"

"Not sure, brother. Let's wait in the walkway."

From the first door they had passed, the giant black slave reappeared, squeezing head and shoulders out. His huge hands and face showed wrinkles, and his hair was peppered. Jon judged him to be midaged.

"Massa Sam will see's you's now. We's feed an' beds horse."

"Righto. Let's dazzle, brother Drew."

The door opened to a long hall, but the brothers couldn't tell how long, as the huge frame ahead blocked the view. A big hand rapped on the first door to the right.

"Who is it?" came the loud response inside.

"Two young'uns to see you's Massa Sam."

"What do they want, Mose?"

"They wans overseer jobs, Massa Sam."

"Good. Bring them in."

"Yassa, Massa Sam."

The giant black man pushed the door open and stepped aside. The first view was of animal heads hanging on the walls. Then, as the Hamilton brothers entered, the master came into view behind a desk to the rear of the room.

What a wacko, thought Jonathan, as he scanned all of the hair behind the desk. Andrew started chuckling, and Jon tried to elbow him quiet.

"What the hell are you laughing at, boy?"

Jon felt his job flying away. His own brother was trying to sabotage it, right off the bat.

"Sorry, sir. I was just looking at that funny animal there on the wall," Andrew answered.

"That is a beaver, son. Haven't you ever seen one before?"

"No, sir, I haven't."

Jon's panic drained away, and he was thankful for his brother's quick wit. He was also having a lot of trouble keeping a straight face at the sight of the master. Only his head and shoulders were visible above the desk, and only a little face was showing behind gobs of hair.

"I've never seen one either, sir," he said.

"Well, small wonder, I guess. They've been about hunted to extinction in the Blues."

"I've come here for the overseer job you advertised for in the newspaper. I have the ad here in my pocket."

"I don't need to see it. I wrote it!"

"Yessir."

"And what about you, son? You looking for a job too?"

"No, sir," said Andrew. "I'm just accompanying my brother."

"Oh, too bad. I need a couple of good men."

"My brother can do the work of two men, sir."

"Lock jaw, dummy," Jon said under his breath.

"Why are you so late? It's the first of March already. The ad has run for a month," said the master.

"Sorry, sir. Our father just went to Salem last week and brought home a newspaper."

"That's alright. Are you sure you don't want to work too, son?" the master asked Andrew.

"No, thank you. I've plenty of work at home."

"Have a seat, boys. Have you ever been an overseer before?"

"No, sir," said Jon.

"Well, have you ever handled bounders before?"

"No, sir. I don't know what that is."

"Servants, boy! Do you know what slaves are?"

"Yes, sir, I do."

"Well good. You're not completely dufus. Have you any farming experience?"

"Yes, sir. We live and work on my father's farm."

"Now we're getting somewhere. Cotton and sot weed, I presume?"

"Yes, sir, and some corn."

"Good. I pay twelve dollars a month, plus meals and room, and most Saturday afternoons and Sundays off. Is that satisfactory?"

"Yes, sir. More than satisfactory, sir."

"And I don't expect you to do the work of two men. I do expect you to get a full day's work out of your gang, and your reports in on time. Is that understood?"

"Yes, sir."

"Do you have any questions?"

"Well, um, yes, sir."

"Speak up, boy. What is your question?"

"The report, sir. I can't spell like my brother."

"Neither can I. Don't worry. Lentil will show you how to write the report."

"Thank you, sir. Can my brother stay the night?"

"Yes, I suppose he can. It's too late to go back to Salem today. He can stay with you in the overseer house. Any other questions?"

"No, sir, and thank you, sir."

"Save your thanks, boy. We'll see if you can handle this job. It's not as easy as it looks."

"My brother will be your best overseer, Mister McAllister."

"I hope you're right, son. One more thing, before I call Mose to take you to the overseer house."

"Yes, sir?"

"You will notice that there are far more Nans than Toms on Bethania. If you have a mash for any of them, feel free to indulge on your time. You can have them in your room if you like. Just one thing, though. They are owned by me, and any offspring will be owned by me. Understood?"

"Yes, sir, Master McAllister."

"It's Master Sam, boy."

"Yes, sir, Master Sam." The brothers turned to leave.

"Hold on, boys. I don't even have your names."

"Jonathan Henry Hamilton, sir. And this is my older brother, Andrew."

"Glad to meet you, boys. There's still a job here for you, Andrew, if you want one."

"Thank you, sir, but I have my own farm to handle now, without my brother."

Master Samuel stood for the first time, and the Hamilton brothers almost broke out laughing again. The beard hung down to his crotch, and even Andrew was a head taller. The brothers had to turn away from this comical character.

"Mose!" The door quietly opened, and the huge servant stuck his head inside.

"Yassa, Massa Sam?"

"Take these boys to the master overseer. The tall one is Master Jon, our new overseer."

"Yassa, Massa Sam. This way, Massa Jon."

Jonathan felt a sudden sense of power, as he and his brother strutted behind the giant house servant. Outside, the three turned right, back under the covered walkway, toward another group of buildings.

"Mose, what is this big house here?"

"It has dem kitchen, Massa Jon."

"Wow, the kitchen is separated from the house."

"Yassa, Massa Jon. Long times ago, big fires in kitchen burns dem house. So's now kitchen away from dem house."

The first building was a long white house. Jon could see two rows of shacks behind. *Shanty row*, he thought. Mose stepped onto the porch of the long house and tapped on the door. An older man answered. He was thin, with wild reddish hair and a heavy moustache.

"Hello, Mose. What'll ye be a-bringin' here?"

"New overseer, sir, for gang twelff."

"That'll be fine, Mose."

"Yassa." Mose turned and headed back to the big house.

"Ye best be a-getting' in here, blokes."

"Yes, sir." The Hamilton brothers stepped into the long house. There was a big room with tables and benches in it to the left, and small desks and stuffed chairs to the right. A pot stove stood in the middle, directly in front of them, and a long hall behind.

"That'll be the dining, and that be the livin'," said the older man, "and I be Lentil McRae, the head overseer."

"Happy to meet you, Mister McRae. I'm Jonathan Henry Hamilton, and this is my brother Andrew."

"Jest be a-callin' me Jock, Jon Henry. Are ye both a-bein' overseers?"

"Just me, Jock. Andrew is headed back home in the morning."

"That'll be fine. I'll be a-havin' a room for ye and a guest room for Andy. I'll be a-showin' them now, then we'll be a-talkin'." Lentil started into the long hallway with the boys in pursuit. The first door to the right had a sign that read "Master Overseer." Lentil opened the first door on the left, showing a stark room with an oversized bed, table, and two chairs. A window looked back at the kitchen house and mansion.

"This is the guest room, Andy."

"Thank you, Jock. I'll be a-sleepin' here," said Andrew, to the frown of his taller brother.

"Your room'll be the last one on the left, Jon Henry. Your satchel's already a-bein' in there."

"Thank you, Jock. I'll settle in after we have that talk."

"Good. Let's be a-sittin' a spell in the living room."

The first thing Jock showed Jon was an overseer's report. There were forms in the small desks, and Jock had a sample to show, dated for a week in 1833 for gang seven. It listed fifteen bounders, six Toms, and nine Nans. It had a date for each paragraph of that week, and described the activities of that day and how many acres worked. At the end of the report was the number of acres assigned, the number of acres completed, and signed by the overseer.

"Be as accurate as ye can possibly be, Jon Henry. And be describin' all that happens. Ye kin?"

"Right. I can."

"Ye be a-fillin' each day's report, and be a-turnin' them in to me by Sunday evenin's. Ye kin?"

"Righto, Jocko."

"I denny kin that lingo, Jon Henry. Be a-speakin to me: Yes, Jock, or No, Jock."

"Okay, Jock. Anything else?"

"Yes. Ye be assigned gang twelve, and team fifteen, Jon Henry. Ye be a-takin' good care a them horses, hear?"

"Right, Jock. What about the gang twelve?"

"We'll be a-walkin' down bounder's row, and I'll be a lettin' ye meet them, the now."

"I would like to come along, Jock," said Andy.

"That'll be fine, Andy. One thing, Jon Henry, ye be stern with your bounders, hear? They be a-knowin' ye be new, and they be a-testin' ya."

"Okay, Jock."

"My brother can handle them."

"You'll be a-havin' trouble with 'em, Jon Henry, but ye be a-havin' Levi for your driver. He kin handle bad bounders. Toby kin give ye troubles. Ye be a-tellin' me when he does, hear?"

"Yes, sir, Jock."

"Jest be a-callin' me Jock," he said as he grabbed a whip.

The walk down bounder's row was an eye-opening experience for the Hamilton brothers. There were four long rows of shanty houses, all looking the same. Men, women, and children were crowded into them, most wearing very little or no clothing. The wide pathway between the second and third row was ablaze with activity and covered with mud.

"Where do these people wash, and clean their clothes, Jock?"

"They be wash houses by the creek."

"What about water closets, Jock?" asked Andy.

"They be a-dumpin' house at the enda each row."

"How many bounders live here?"

"They be more at harvest, but they be about two hundred the now."

"Why aren't they in the fields, Jock?"

"We're a-gettin' them ready, a-gettin' them clothes and tools, and assignin' them to gangs. Your gang twelve a-be at the ender row three."

Andy and Jon were in awe of the sight. A group of five males was fighting with each other. Jock let his whip crack above them three quick times.

"Any of ye be a-hurtin' and no kin work, I be a-whippin' ye all to the bone, hear?"

"Yassa, Massa Jock," came the responses.

Andy slapped at Jon, and pointed between two shanties, where a very black couple was mating while others stood around watching. Kids were running in all directions and playing games. At the far end of the row, a large bonfire flamed and several women were cooking. One had a furry animal speared over the fire, and Jon saw another couple playing bouncebutt in the dirt between shanties. Toward the end of row three, Jock started calling.

"Levi, gang twelve, be a-comin' out here." A few forms appeared. One black woman came out of her shanty nude.

"Lucee, ye be a-gettin' back in there, and be a-puttin' on some clothes."

"Yassa, Massa Jock." She turned back.

"She'll be a little trouble for ya, Jon Henry."

"Not for brother Jon," said Andy. "The trouble will be your overseer keeping his brain box on the job."

"Get stuffed, Andy."

"A few lashes wit this black snake will be a-keepin' her clothes on, Jon Henry."

Jonathan was becoming worried that he may have to use a whip. He wondered if he would be able to do it.

By now a couple of men and four women had gathered around the master overseer.

"Where's Toby, Wilma, an' Morna?"

"They's be comin', Massa Jock," said a male slave. "Skeets not backs yet."

"Wilma, Nell, Toby, be a-gettin' yer butts out here."

"Yassa, Massa Jock," came the reply from a nearby shanty. Soon others appeared.

"This be your new overseer, Master Jon. Ye be a-listenin' an' obeyin' him, ya hear?"

"Yassa," came from many lips.

"Master Jon, this be gang twelve. This be Levi, your head driver, and these be Jobia, Wilma, Dianna, Morna, Nell, Cora, Vera, an' Lucee." Lucee now had a sack, and nothing else, on.

"Where in damnation is Toby?" asked Jock.

"I's be here, Massa Jock," came the reply, as a strongly built slave ran out of a shanty.

"When I call, ye better be a-comin' runnin', hear?"

"Yassa, Massa Jock."

"Looks like ye'll be a-startin' wit 'leven, Jon Henry. Skeeter should be here by the 'morrow."

"Where is he now?" asked Andrew.

"He is a-farmed out. Lots a them be a-gone in the winter, and a-comin' back now."

"Good. When do we start, Jock?"

"If the weather be a good the now, we may be a-gettin' plantin' soon. I may be a-sendin' ye wit gang twelve to pull old cornstalks."

"Like the ones we saw sticking out of the ground on the way here?"

"Them'll be the ones, Andy."

"We were wondering why they were kept in the ground over winter, Jock," said Jonathan.

"Whar ye be a comin' from, Jon Henry?"

"Our farm is south of Salem."

"Then ye be a-kinnin' about the rains."

"Yes, sometimes it seems that our house will float away."

"Well then, Master Sam be a-thinkin' the cornstalks will be a-keepin' the soil from a-washin' away."

"That's a smashing idea," said Andrew.

"Tell Father about that, brother Drew."

"I will, Jonny Boy. I've learned something a-new here that we can be a-usin'."

"I'll see you all again tomorrow," said the frowning Jon as the brothers started back, behind Lentil McRae, toward the long overseer house.

"Goodbye, Massa Jon."

The boys turned back around and realized the goodbye had come from the prettiest of gang twelve, a tiny girl that Jon had judged to be still in her teens. She was wearing little more than a big smile and some cloth wrapped around her middle.

"Which one are you?"

"I be Cora, Massa Jon."

"Well, goodbye for now, Cora. I'll see you tomorrow."

Cora scooted back to one of the shanties, smiled, and waved at Jon. The three started back again toward the overseer house.

"Ye be a-takin' a likin' to that Nanny, Jon Henry?"

"Remember what the master said about having company in your room, Jonny Boy?"

"I remember. It wouldn't be a good idea to show favorites now, even before I've gotten to know my gang."

"Barmy! My little brother does have a little matter in the beanbox."

Master overseer Jock McRae led the brothers past the long house and behind the kitchen house. The boys saw a church in the open field.

"Wow," said Andy, "you even have your own church services here."

"That'll be a-fact, Andy. The whites have a meetin' every Sunday mornin' at ten o'clock, an' the bounders be the afternoon."

"What faith is preached here, Jock?"

"They be a-no special faith, Jon Henry. The Reverend Homster sorta mixes 'em around."

Now, before the wide-eyed brothers, stood a row of very large barns. There were four or five in a row, plus two long open barns, end to ends. The brothers knew them to be tobacco barns. The last two barns in the row, numbers three and four, were for animals. Barn one had two very large cotton gins and a small, older gin, a mechanism for bailing, and plenty of storage space for bales. There were several bounders scurrying about, even though the crop barns were mostly empty. One came over to Master Jock.

"Dan, this be Master Jon, the master of gang twelve. Ye'll be a-gettin' him team fifteen."

"Yassa."

"Hello, Dan."

"I's be Danny Doubleclutch, Massa Jon."

"Dan be a head barn bounder, Jon Henry. He be a-gettin' yer team handlin' done."

"Can I see team fifteen?"

"Surely ye kin. Ye be a-showin' team fifteen to Master Jon, Dan."

"Yassa, Master Jock."

Danny led the Hamilton brothers back into barn three. Jon noticed the large stalls housed two dobbins each, and Danny led them to stall fifteen. Two poorly matched red horses were busy eating hay. Danny patted the bigger red's rump. "This be Sloggy, an' this be Smutty, Massa Jon."

"They be a-gentle, hard-workin' pair, Jon Henry. Ye be a-hitchin' them to a-gang wagon tomorra."

"Yassa, Massa Jock," said Danny.

"Not too early though, Danny," quipped Andy.

"Ye be a-takin' gang twelve out tomorra after breakfast, Jon Henry. Jest ye getta know 'em a little better. A half-a day'll do, ye kin?"

"Okay, Jock. I'm looking forward to it."

"Let's be a-gettin' back ta the seer house and be a-havin' supper."

Jonathan woke with a start, and rubbed his eyes to clear them. He could hear dogs barking and people yelling outside. As he focused his eyes out his window, he could see men with long guns gathering behind the mansion. He made out Danny bringing several horses from barn row in the very early sunlight. Just then, his door burst open, and the thin form of Jock appeared.

"What happened, Jock?"

"They be a bunch a runaway bounders a-headed for da Smokies. They broke loose from their yokes an' ropes, an' Skeeter be a-one of 'em."

"You mean the Skeets in my gang?"

"That be a-what I mean, Jon Henry, an' you and me'll be a-goin' to find 'em."

"What about taking my gang out?"

"No time for that the now. Ye'll be a-ridin' yer horse Sloggy, an' I be a-takin' Smut."

Jon hurried into his clothes. Andy was already dressed and waiting.

"What, no breakfast?"

"They be a no time fer that the now, Andy. Will ye be a-comin' along?"

"No, thanks. I'll be a-goin' back home. So long, Jonny Boy. I'll be a-seein' ya."

Jon didn't much like it when his brother mocked the language of Jock McRae.

"Cheers, brother. Take care of the family."

"I will that, brother Jon. Don't kill any of those bounders."

Kill? Jon thought. "Will there be any shooting, Jock?"

"It'll be likely, Jon Henry. Once they be a-gettin' a taste a freedom, they no be a wantin' to come back. Too bad. Skeeter be a fast worker."

Jon now saw at least twenty mounted men and a team-drawn wagon with six or seven bloodhounds ready to go. As he and Jock were handed a musket, a powder horn, and a handful of flint and balls, he noted a bounder leading Andy to the kitchen house.

"Damn, he's going to get a breakfast. Beat me again," Jon mumbled.

"Ain't that crawdad goin' along?" one of the mounted men asked.

"Not the now, Mister Mullins. He be a-headed fer his farm," replied Jock.

"He's not a crawdad!" shouted Jon. "He's my brother, and he has a family to support!"

"Then let's be on our way. We have a lot of miles to cover. The Johnstones will have eats for us out of Salisbury."

The large posse headed around the mansion and out the iron gates of Bethania. Down the road and over the bridge they rode, and Jon soon saw they were headed back the way he had come the day before. When it came time to turn east, toward

Salem, they continued south instead. He stuck close to Jock McRae. This was easy, as Sloggy was much bigger than Smutty, and he had an easy canter. It appeared to be a half day of hard riding, when Jon saw another huge group of men camped by a large river. His posse pulled up, dismounted, and joined the larger group. They had a huge bonfire going, and were cooking and warming up. This was the first Jon realized just how cold and hungry he was. He and Jock dug in with the rest, to rest and chow down. No one seemed to do much talking.

"Thank you, men, for coming out. There were eight varmints that escaped, six of them bucks. Two belong to McAllister, four of 'em are mine, and we don't know who owns the other two. I don't give a damn if you shoot 'em," said Mister Mullins. "When we catch up to 'em, crack down on 'em and give 'em hell so's they'll never want to run again."

"Why ain't McAllister along with us?" someone asked the group.

"He be a-feelin' poorly," Jock replied. "He be a-sendin' nine o' us in his place."

"Good. That makes about thirty-five or so of us here. This is where they escaped last evenin', so they can't have gone too far. When we cross the river a ways, we'll split in groups of two or three. Most of you all have pocket watches. We'll fire every half hour, so's we don't stray too far apart, Okay? Let's get after 'em."

Jon slid his sore butt onto Slog's back, and the grand posse now waded into the river. Soon the horses had to swim, dumping some of the riders. Jon and Jock, along with several others, helped grab and catch those caught in the current. One of the two wagons full of dogs tipped over and finally broke apart from the team, pulling it, and floated down the river. It took a long struggle to get the men, horses, and dogs onto the opposite shore.

"We'll have to stop here boys, and build a fire," said Mister Mullins. He turned to three of his Salisbury men. "You three go back to Salisbury and get all the dry clothes you can."

"Yes, sir, Mister Mullins."

The three headed south along the river bank. There appeared to be an old road they followed.

"Won't they have to cross back over the river and get all wet again, Jock?" Jon asked.

"They be a ford crossing at Salisbury."

Many of the men had busied themselves gathering sticks and branches, and had a big fire roaring. Some had already peeled off their clothes and were holding them on sticks over the flames.

Someone asked if everyone was present and accounted for. Nobody answered, so a head count was taken.

"We're missing one!" a tall man shouted.

"Which one?" someone else asked.

"We're missing Sam Beatty, one of Mister Johnstone's overseers," the tall man said.

"Damnation!" yelled Mister Mullins. "Oliver, get on your horse, hustle down to Salisbury, and alert them. Those niggers will pay dearly for this!"

"Yes, sir, Mister Mullins."

"And stick with 'em till you find Beatty!" Mullins shouted after Oliver.

"Yes, sir!" Oliver shouted back at full gallop.

"Jacob, I'll cross back over, and you and I will search the banks for a mile or two."

"Yes, sir, Mister Mullins."

"The rest of you get dried off and head southwest after them varmints. We'll catch up later."

Okays and yes sirs came in response, as Mister Mullins headed back across the river. Jonathan was happy he had Jock McRae to stick close to.

"You alright, boy?" asked the tall man.

"Yes, sir. I'm Okay," was Jon's response. He noted that there were still a good thirty men to catch the running bounders. *That's still about four to one*, he thought. Those poor Negroes must be scared stiff.

Already some of the men started pulling clothes back on, while others were just stripping. Jock McRae never peeled any clothes off and was ready to go. Jon hurried back into his trousers.

"Mister Mullins is busy the now, so we'll be a-havin' a new leader till he be back," said Jock.

"You're the oldest and best known, Jock," said the tall man. "We'll follow you."

"Right then. When ye be dry, all but two o' ya be a-catchin' up to us. Ye two will be a-stayin', an' gatherin' up the rest to catch up."

"Okay, Jock," came the answer.

"The rest o' ye be a-followin' me. We'll be a-leavin' the wagon, an' be a-splittin' up the now."

As the group split, Jon stuck close to Jock. The dogs that came with Mister Mullins were released, and took off into the hills. The dogs from the Johnstone group seemed to be well trained, and started working in ever-widening circles. Some of the men who had started from Bethania now galloped away to catch up to their hounds. Jock stayed with the others, and Jon was content to bring up the rear.

What a beautiful country, Jon thought. The trees were presenting their new leaves, and wild flowers were blooming everywhere. Jon's mind and eyes continued to be consumed by the scenery, when suddenly a shot was heard in the distance, to the right. Jock pulled out his watch.

"Be that airhead a-signalin' the now, or be he a-findin' a bounder? It be close to three o'clock."

The pairs of hunters all seemed to sit in silence aboard their mounts. Only the sounds of the dogs, working their circles, was heard by Jon. Suddenly, another shot rang out in the distance, then two, three more.

"Ye all keep a-huntin'!" shouted Jock. "I'll be a-checkin' them shots out the now. Jon Henry will be a-comin' along, an' be reportin' back to ye." Jock already had Smutty at a gallop, and Jon dug into Sloggy's sides in an attempt to catch up. After a hard gallop of ten or so minutes, Jon heard the howls of the hounds. Another couple of minutes, and he saw the group gathered around a patch of underbrush. Jock jumped off a tired Smutty and ran to the scene. As Jon approached, he saw the black man lying still in the brush, dead.

"Any of ye be a-knowin' him?" asked Jock.

"Yes," came a reply.

"He was one of Mister Mullins's bucks, named Tate," said another man, cleaning the barrel of his gun.

"Too bad," said a short, heavy-set man. "He was always smilin' and happy. Wonder why he decided to run?"

"They all get that notion sooner or later," said the man, reaming his rifle. "That's why we have ta shoot 'em when they run."

Jon felt a sick feeling in his stomach. The dead Negro was bleeding heavily in a couple of places.

"Who is going to bury him?" asked the short, heavy man.

"Leave him for the bears and wolves," replied the shooter, his gun now cleaned.

"We'll be a-buryin' him the now!" yelled Jock. "Did any a ye see any others?"

"No, Jock, he was alone," came a reply.

"Okay then. Ye two be a-gatherin' up the dogs, an' we'll be a-startin' again as soon as he be buried. Jon Henry, ye be a-ridin' back ta the rest, an' a-tellin' them what happened. I'll be a-comin' back soon."

"Right, Jock." Jon was quickly on his way and feeling better about getting away from the scene of the killing. Soon he and Slog stumbled onto the other group, covering dirt over what looked like a grave. Jon saw Mister Mullins standing over the mound, hat in hand. He walked toward Jon.

"What did you find out, boy?"

"They shot a bounder named Tate. He was alone in the brush."

"Thank you, boy. He was one of my best bucks. What is your name, son?"

"Jon Henry Hamilton, sir."

"Thank you, Jon. You must be one of Sam's overseers."

"Yes, sir, I am. Did you find another bounder, Mister Mullins?"

"Yes, I found her in the river, drowned. Her name was Nelly. That's two of mine dead, and six more to find. You say that Tate was alone?"

"Yes, sir."

"Let's get back to the hunt."

"If it's alright with you, sir, I'll wait for Jock. He'll be back soon."

"That'll be fine, Jon. Let's get moving."

Jon thought of the dead bounders. *Two already*, he reflected. He wondered if all the bounders would be killed.

The group, now once again very large, headed into the forest; and Jon felt alone in his world. He hoped Jock would show up soon. "Nelly, her name was Nelly." A pang struck Jon again in the stomach. "One of my gang is named Nelly." Jonathan was thinking about his gang, and Skeeter, another of his gang, now out there in the woods. Mister Mullins was almost on top of him before Jon noticed him.

"Jon, I would like you to stay right here until the rest of my men get here from Salisbury, and have some word on Sam Beatty."

"Yes, sir, Mister Mullins, will do."

Jon felt relieved that he may not see another killing. He decided to go back to the river so the last of the men, back from Salisbury, would spot him. There he built the fire back up. He heard a shot in the far distance. Then he heard another, and one from the far right. He was really startled when he heard a fourth blast, very close. Jon jumped back on Sloggy and headed for that blast. It turned out to be Jock McRae looking for him.

"Where the tarnation ye be a-comin' from, Jon Henry?"

"Mister Mullins wants me to look out for the rest of the men from Salisbury. He found another bounder in the river, drowned."

"That be a-two the now, an' six ta go."

"Is there another bounder from Bethania out there, Jock?"

"Aye, there be another Tom named Rooker. He be a part o' gang seven last year. He be a-smooth talker. They be a-wantin' him fer other reasons down in Georgia, aside from hard work, Jon Henry."

"What other reasons, Jock?"

"He be a-breedin' their Nans."

"They buried the drowned Nan over there. Her name was Nelly, like the one in my gang."

"They ne'er be two alike, Jon Henry. Yer Nell be a quiet, hardworking Nan. She'd ne'er be a-runnin' off."

"I sure hope they don't kill Skeeter and Rooker."

"That be outta our hands the now, Jon Henry. Ye be a-gettin' back ta the river, an' I'll be a-bringin' up the rear, tryin' to keep 'em in earshot."

"Okay, Jock. What was all the shooting a few minutes ago?"

"It be four o'clock. Now be a-gettin'. When ye be a findin' out anything, be a-shootin' once, an' I'll hear. Here, be a-takin' a couple a corndodgers."

Jon swung back up on Sloggy and headed back to the bonfire. "I am a little hungry again," he said to himself. "These dodgers will taste good." Jon settled under a tree, warmed by the fire, and ate his corndodgers. Soon he dozed off, only to be stunned by the sudden appearance of four men, who rode up to the fire. They were the Salisbury men. Tied down on the horses were clothes.

"I've been waiting for you," Jon said.

"Who told you to?" asked one of them.

"Mister Mullins said to wait on you and find out if you found Mister Beatty."

"We found him. The Johnstones are burying him now in Salisbury."

"Okay. I'm to take that message to Mister Mullins." Jon grabbed his gun and shot into the air. As he was about to swing up on his horse, one of the men walked over to him.

"Which way ya all goin', boy?"

"Most of the men are hunting to the southwest, and some straight to the west."

"Have they had any luck?"

"They shot one, and one drowned. They're still looking for the other six."

"Okay, boy. We'll be along soon."

Jon rode west for a short ways and spotted Jock coming at a gallop. Smutty was huffing.

"The Salisbury men are back, and they found Mister Beatty drowned. He's being buried in Salisbury."

"Where they be the now?"

"Getting warmed up. They said they'd be along soon."

"Okay, Jon Henry. Let's be a-headin' west afore we be a-shootin', so's they be a-hearin'." Jock and Jon rode through a green forest for what seemed to Jon to be miles. They came to a clearing by a stream, and Jock jumped down. He poured powder and ball down the barrel of his gun and packed it in. He then blasted a shot into the air. Only a few seconds of waiting, before hell broke loose.

It sounded like a war, with all the shots being fired to the south and west. It seemed many minutes had passed before the noise stopped.

"Sounds like they caught up to them, Jock."

"Sho 'nuff, Jon Henry. They be a-findin' 'em."

"Why do they have to kill them?"

"They be a-gettin' the runnin' in their blood. All it be a-takin' is ta let 'em get by wit the runnin', an' they all will be a-scootin'."

Jon heard the dogs first, howling off to the west. They seemed to be getting louder.

"They be a-comin' this way, Jon Henry."

"What'll we do now?"

"Ye be a-waitin' here for them dogs an' men, an' I'll be a-headed for the shots. I'll be a-comin' back, so's ya keep 'em here, kin?"

"Righto, Jock. I'll let them know what's been happening, and wait until you get back."

There was a small clump of grass along the bank of the creek ahead, and Sloggy found it quickly. It felt good to Jon as well, and he stretched out on it and listened to the dogs coming his way. Their barks and howls seemed to have a rhythm to the tired overseer. He thought that someday he would like to own a hound or two. As they got closer, Jon could tell that the dogs were still off to the west a ways, and he would miss them. Jon decided to cross the creek and meet them. Sloggy didn't want to leave his patch of grass, but soon Jon had him headed west into the woods. A shot rang out close by, and Jon jumped down, capped his rifle, and fired a shot in response. The dogs were now just ahead of him in the brush. Jon reloaded his rifle and ran ahead a couple hundred yards. The dogs were all around him, but he couldn't see them. He decided to hide behind a large tree and wait. It didn't take long before he heard a rustling in the brush and trees ahead.

Suddenly, Jon spotted two dark forms running past him, about twenty-five or thirty yards ahead. They got close enough for Jon to see that they were two black slaves trying to elude the dogs, who had them circled. Jon wondered what he should do.

"Halt! Stop or I'll shoot!" Jon yelled.

The two male slaves turned and ran away from him, so Jon decided to fire over their heads. Bam! Jon felt a little pain in his right shoulder from the recoil, but the slaves stopped running and crouched down together. Jon ran to them and pointed his empty gun at them. They cowed down, whimpering and puffing. What clothes they had on were soaked, and they were covered with sweat.

"Please don' shoots me, Massa," one said.

"Just stay still, and I won't shoot."

"Yessa, Massa," said the other.

Suddenly, one of the dogs came out of the brush and attacked a bounder. It took only a couple of seconds amid the screams for Jon to realize that he had to stop the dog from killing. Other dogs were coming fast. Jon hit the dog, again and again, with his rifle butt. The hound had a hold on the slave's leg and held on, despite the pain from the butt of Jon's gun. He was yelping, growling and biting all at once. One last blow with all the strength Jon could muster, and the dog yelped, let go of the leg, and lay down, whining. Another hound was attacking the other slave, and Jon again started swinging his rifle at him. Other dogs appeared, and started in on the assault. Jon quickly grabbed his powder horn and poured a load down the barrel of his gun. He tapped it and a ball down, capped, and cocked the hammer. As fast as he could, he shot what seemed to be the most fierce of the dogs. The other dogs stopped attacking and gathered around the dead hound, sniffing and whining. One started growling, showing his teeth at Jon, and slowly stalked toward him. Jon again raised his rifle to defend himself.

In the brush, Jon heard the horses, and men whooping at their dogs. The stalking dog stopped in his tracks, still growling at Jon. Others howled in response, and the horses came fast. Jon felt relief that he would be spared the dog's attack. Several men and horses now popped out of the brush and jumped off their mounts.

"They're still alive!" shouted the first man.

"Just barely. The dogs did a good job on 'em," said another.

"This dog is dead," said the first man, as he picked up the shot hound.

"You bastard boy! You shot my dog!" Jon recognized the man on the horse as the shooter of the slave Tate. He was a stout man, with an unkempt, dark beard. His shirt was very dirty, with large spots of sweat. Jon couldn't help but notice the beady eyes and the dirty yellow teeth showing anger at him. In spite of himself, Jon had to grin at the thought of the dog's teeth looking much better than the shooter's.

"Had to, sir," Jon said. "The dog was about to kill the bounder."

"So what? He was just saving me the job!"

"Ya call 'em bounders?" asked another man from his horse. "Hell, they ain't nuttin' but niggers."

"Yeah. My dog's worth ten of 'em," said the shooter. "Guess I'll have to do the job myself."

"There ain't no use in killing them now, Jonas. They ain't going anywhere. They're through runnin'." Jon recognized the tall, friendly man from the first river crossing.

"Like hell they ain't," said the shooter, Jonas. He and his companion stepped down from their horses, guns in hand, and walked toward the two cowering slaves. The tall man stepped in front of the companion and grabbed hold of him. The shooter Jonas raised his rifle at the first bounder. Jon knew he had to act fast. With a running leap, he hit Jonas full force and knocked him off his underpins. The blast hit a tree, scattering its bark.

"Damn you, boy!" yelled Jonas, as he wrestled Jon on the ground. Jon tried to break free, but the stout man rolled him over onto his back and pinned him down. "I'm going to teach you a good lesson!" Jonas was yelling and punching Jon, who felt his blood running over his cut lip. Jonas continued striking him.

Not any too soon, a couple of men grabbed Jonas and lifted him off the young overseer. Jonas struggled with the two men, trying to get back at Jon. "He killed my dog, and deserves a good cobbing as much as them niggers!" Jonas shouted, still struggling. He finally gave out, and shrugged himself free of Jon's rescuers. He walked over to his dead dog, picked it up, and held it in his arms.

"Damn you, boy! Why'd you have to kill my dog?" Jon spotted tears running from those beady eyes.

"I'm sorry, sir, but why did you have to kill that slave, Tate?"

There was no answer from Jonas, as he hugged his limp hound. He stood and carried the dog off into the woods. The other dogs followed. Jon was happy to see the dog he wounded with his gun butt was up and following Jonas.

"Anyone know these two bucks?"

"One is a bounder named Skeeter," came a reply. Jon figured he was an overseer from Bethania, and walked over to the two slaves.

"Is one of you named Skeeter?"

"I's Skeets from Massa Sam's." He was the bounder Jonas was about to shoot.

"Good. I'm Jon Hamilton, your new overseer."

"So you're the new overseer Jock told me about," said the tall, friendly man. "My name is Charles Finley. I have gang eleven." They shook hands.

"A banger to meet you, Mister Finley."

"Just call me Charles. Okay, Jon?"

"Right, Charles, still a banger."

"Work hard for Master Jon, Skeets. He saved you."

"Yassa, Massa Charles. Thank you, Massa Jon."

"Who is the other one?" asked the short, heavy man. "He's not from Bethania."

Jon had hoped this bounder would be Rooker. *The short, heavy man must be from Bethania too*, he thought. "Are you an overseer from Bethania?"

"Yes, I am, Jon. My name is Wilbert Aims, and I have gang nine."

"Smashing to meet you too, Wilbert."

No one seemed to know who the second slave was.

"What's your name?" asked Wilbert. No answer.

"I said, what's your name?"

"O-Osari." The man was badly hurt.

"Sounded like 'Ursary,'" said Charles.

"Sounded like 'Osare' to me," said another.

"Tell me again!" Wilbert shouted. "Your name!"

"I's Osuree." His voice trailed off, and he suddenly became silent.

"Is he dead?"

"Close to it," said one of Mullins's men.

"Let's bundle them up," said another man.

"No need," said Charles. "They're so near dead, they won't go anywhere."

"Then we can leave 'em, and continue the hunt. There are still four out there," said Jonas's companion.

"Maybe not," said Charles. "Did you hear all the shooting to the south a while ago?"

"Yeah. It sounded like an army," said Wilbert.

"Alright then. One of us can go find the others and see what all that shootin' was about, and a couple stay here, and the rest of us hunt."

"I'll go find the others," said Charles.

"I'd like to stay with my bounder," said Jon.

"Yes, Martin, you stay with him. The rest of ya, get mounted." The companion of Jonas was good at giving orders.

A shot rang out, far away to the south.

"I think I'll stay here a while too, Les. It sounds like someone is looking for us," came the voice of a husky man. His shirt was open, and he sported a heavy coat of black hair on his chest. Jon now knew the order-giving companion of Jonas was named Les.

"You muddlehead, that's a time signal. Must be three o'clock," said Les. He fired in the air.

"Thunder, it's about six," said a man on his horse, watch in hand.

"Then let's get crackin!" hollered Jonas, now back with all but one of his dogs from the woods. Charles was on his way, and the group headed south as well, but a little to the east of Charles, behind the barking dogs.

"Whooee!" shouted Jonas, his horse at a full gallop.

"My name is Eli. I'm an overseer for Mister Mullins," said the hairy man.

"I'm Martin, and this is . . ."

"Jon Henry Hamilton, from Bethania."

"We need to care for these bucks," said Eli, "before they're gone coon."

"There was an opening by a creek, just a few yards back. We can get them cleaned up there. Where's your horse, Jon?"

"I left him a ways back there. I'll go get him."

"Good. We'll take the bucks over to the clearing," said Martin. "Meet us there."

"Okay. I'll be back in a few minutes." Jon took off, running east and calling his horse, Sloggy. To his surprise, he heard Sloggy answer. The animal had found another small patch of grass, and again was reluctant to leave. When they got back to the spot where Jon shot the dog, it was cleared. Jon turned north and soon caught up to Eli and Martin walking their horses.

To Jon's surprise, they had the bounders laid over their horses' backs. They found the clearing and laid the bounders in the soft grass. Martin peeled off his shirt and soaked in the creek, then tried to clean the wounds of the nameless slave. Jon did the same, and worked on Skeeter, who didn't seem to be as near death as the other.

"We've got to stop the bleeding from this buck's leg," said Martin.

"Do you have any rope and a knife?" asked Eli.

"Check my saddle," answered Martin.

Jon helped Eli cut a small length of rope and tied it around the slave's thigh.

"Pull it good and tight, Jon. We need to stop the flow of blood."

"Where did you learn that, Eli?"

"My grandfather was a surgeon at Cowpens. He saved my life doing this when I was young." The blood stopped running, and all three men breathed a sigh of relief.

"We must remember to loosen this rope every hour or so, and let it bleed just a bit."

A shot was heard fairly close, and Martin fired in response.

"Let's get our guns cleaned, Jon. We don't want that powder to cake up," said Martin. Jon and Martin were cleaning and reloading when the men from Salisbury pulled up. They had lots of clothes tied down behind their saddles, and Eli and Martin busied themselves making cloth wrapping for the slaves' wounds.

"Them two look dern near gone," said Oliver.

"They would have been, if Jon there hadn't stepped in and saved 'em," said Martin. "That one is his buck, but we don't know who the other is."

"I think he belongs to a farm over by Hillsboro," said another man, after looking closely.

"He probably won't make it that far," replied the first Salisbury man.

"Where have all the hunters gone?"

"They are all south of here now," answered Jon. "They've probably killed the rest."

"Yeah, all that shootin' musta gotten them. We heard the commotion from the river."

Suddenly, another shot rang out, this time close, and again Martin answered with his rifle. Jon heard the horse-breaking brush, and was happy to see Smutty under the slim frame of Jock McRae. Jon ran over to him, patted a worn-out Smutty, and grabbed his halter to lead the horse and master overseer into camp.

"We got Skeeter and one other here. They're both alive, but the one is near death."

"I be glad to be a-hearin' that, Jon Henry."

"Did you find out what all the shooting was about, Jock?"

"That I did, lad. They be a-buryin' two the now, an' Rooker be a one of 'em. He be shot a-coverin' Mullins's Nan. She be a lucky lass. They be all after the last bounder the now."

"Is he one of Mister Mullins's slaves?" asked Oliver.

"Denny kin. No ones be a-knowin' who he be, but he be a goner wit all them dogs and men a-chasin' him. What happened to yer face, Jon Henry?"

"He saved those bounders from getting shot," answered Charles," and he got Jessie for doing it."

"Ye be a-savin' Skeets, an' Rooker be a-savin' the Nan. It be a good day for Bethania, an' Master Sam will be hearing 'bout it."

"The other bounder is hurt bad, Jock, and we don't know who he belongs to," said Jon.

"Where is the wagon?" asked Martin.

"It be a-sittin' back at the Yadkin," answered Jock.

"We'll need it if we want to get this one back home alive," said Eli.

"I can bring it in at least as far as the last bonfire, maybe closer."

"Good. Ye be a-headin' back, an' be a-bringin' the wagon close as ye kin, Oliver, hear?"

"Right. I'm on my way," said Oliver, as he swung up on his horse and headed east.

"We be a-riggin' up two slings, an' be a-carryin' them bounders between horses."

As the men gathered poles and cut rope, forming two side slings, Jon thought he heard dogs in the distance. Now a couple other men heard them. The howls were getting closer. The men stopped to listen. Shots rang out, amazingly close.

"He be a goner the now."

"I'm afraid you're right, Jock," said Martin.

"Ye all be a-finishin' them slings, an' be a-headed fer the wagon. I'll be a-headed back, an' be a-tellin' the others where we be at."

"Is it alright if I come along with you?"

"Sho 'nuff, Jon Henry. We may be a-needin' someone to be a-ridin' back an' forth."

Team fifteen headed south, toward the noise, with the two Scotsmen aboard. The dog's rhythm now changed to a steady howl.

"It be a-soundin' like the bounder be treed."

The draft horses plowed on through the forest, for what seemed to Jon to be an eternity. Finally, in a small clearing, he saw a large group of men and hounds in a circle around a big tree. They pulled up just in time to see a man shoot up into the tree. It was Jonas, and Jon felt his spirits sink. The men started laughing.

"Hold it! Stop shooting!" Jon shouted several times. "Don't kill him!"

As Jon and Jock jumped off their mounts, Jon noticed Mister Mullins sitting on horseback. "Please, Mister Mullins, there's no need to kill that Negro."

"Why hello, Jon. The boys are just having some fun with the buck."

"It be alright ta be a-havin' some fun, lads, but don' be a-killin' him," replied Jock.

"Why not? He's a worthless nigger now." Jon recognized that voice as Les, Jonas's companion.

"He's not worthless!" shouted Jon.

"You may be right, Jon," said Mister Mullins. "Those bucks cost a lot of money nowadays."

"He's got running in his brain now, Mister Mullins. He ain't worth beans." It was Jonas speaking.

"Just the same, we'll save him and whip the running out of him."

"Call the dogs off, and I'll go up after him."

"Alright, Jon. Jonus, Bill, take your dogs back to the river and wait for us."

Yes, sir," came the response of Bill. From Jonas came the grumbles of discontent. Others helped round up the dogs. It was a tough chore, as the hounds were eager to get at the bounder in the tree. Jon looked up at the shaking, sweating bounder, clinging to the branches for his life.

"Come down. Climb down and you won't be hurt." Jon repeated these instructions several times, to no avail. Finally, the bounder turned his head from side to side in a no, which assured all that he understood Jon's orders.

"If you won't come down, I'm climbing up there and fix your flint." Again, Jon saw the head turning side to side, so he started up the tree. He was only ten or twelve feet up in the branches when the shot rang out. Jon looked out quickly and saw that Les had fired at the bounder, who was now falling toward him, bouncing off the branches. He flew past Jon, almost hitting him, and bounced once off the ground, then lay limp but still on the ground below. Rage flowed in Jon's veins as he heard Les's comment.

"Now he's a good nigger."

Jon leaped out of the tree, landing beside, and tripping over the limp body. He picked himself up and ran headlong at the mounted shooter. With all the force he could muster, he leaped at Les and knocked him off his horse. Both tumbled onto the ground. Jon got in the first blow to Les's jaw, but Les answered with a fierce swing of his own. Jon turned his head to one side, and the fist caught him on the ear. Les started to get up enough to pounce on Jon, but Jon quickly got a leg-lock around Les's waist and flipped him back over. Jon always knew his legs were strong, but he even surprised himself as he squeezed the midsection of the grunting Les, who tried to grab hold of Jon's feet to break them apart. Jon reared back and lifted Les straight up into the air. The momentum even lifted Jon up onto his own shoulders and upper back. Then he slammed the shooter down on his derriere with such force, that Jon himself came up off the ground.

"AAAH!" yelled Les, as he bounced and packed the soil under him. Jon never slackened his leg-hold, and lifted Les right back into the air and slammed him back to earth again. That second slam took the fight out of Les. Jon was determined not to let him go, and increased the pressure around Les's waist until Les was gasping for air intake. A couple of men rushed in and tried to pry Jon's legs apart. Jon just kept squeezing. Les had gone limp.

"Let him go, Jon, before you kill him!" shouted Mister Mullins, who had jumped down from his horse. Instead, Jon raised Les up again, and once again hammered the limp Les into the ground.

"Jon Henry! Be a-lettin' him go the now!" yelled Jock. More men grabbed Jon's legs and managed to pry them apart and hold him down.

"I want to kill him, Jock, like he just killed that bounder."

"He's not dead," came a voice from the tree. More men gathered around the limp slave, trying to revive him. He appeared dead to Jon.

"Anyone done any doctoring?"

"I do a little doctorin' on my animals," came a reply.

"Well, see what you can do for him."

"The shot opened a hole in his side. We gotta close it and stop the bleedin'," said another.

Jon couldn't see the bounder, since too many men were gathered around the tree. He looked over at Les. A couple of men had brought him back around.

"Anyone know this buck?" came a voice from the crowd. There were a lot of head-shaking no's and uh-uhs.

"He's probably from the Hillsboro area," said Mister Mullins.

"He looks like he will make it."

"You should take him, Mister Mullins. You lost three slaves."

"I'll take him for now, and try to heal him until someone claims him."

"Jest how'd he be a-gettin' this far away from ye?" asked Jock.

"He jumped one of my men and stole his horse. The dogs caught up to him here," answered Mister Mullins.

"That makes four out of the eight that are still alive," said Charles.

"Ye be a-forgettin' that a couple of 'em may not be a-livin' for long," answered Jock.

"Let's get him laid over a horse."

"Right, Mister Mullins. Some help here, men."

"The wagon be a-drivin' ta the second bonfire. We can be a-makin' it there the now."

"Good, Jock, get him loaded. Carefully," said Mister Mullins. "Les, come over here."

"Yes, sir, Mister Mullins?" he staggered to his feet.

"When we get back to the plantation, gather your stuff. You're through working for me."

"Just because I shot that nigger?"

"I told you to save him."

"Well, he ain't dead! You heard them say he'll make it."

"No, but you may be, if you don't get out of my sight. Be gone before I get home. Tell Amos I said to pay your time. If it's too much, I'll be coming after you, understand?"

"Yes, sir." Les headed for his horse.

"Remember, that's not your horse, either."

"Yes, sir." Les rode off toward the Yadkin.

"Jonas killed one bounder, and would have killed two more if Jon hadn't stopped him," said Charles.

"I'll take care of him later," replied Mister Mullins.

"Thank you, Mister Mullins."

"Thank you, Jon, for showing me the possibility that we may be able to get production out of these bucks again. If we don't, I'll be looking for you."

"It'll be a-gettin' dark soon. Let's be a-goin'."

"Right, Jock. What time is it now?"

"It's close to seven thirty," came the answer.

"We better get back across that river before dark, or more of us might drown," said Mister Mullins.

A man lifted the black Nan onto his horse and climbed up behind her. The group headed east.

The trip back through the woods took what seemed to Jon to be about an hour. Most of the original group of men from Bethania were there, mulling around the fire. Jonas was sitting in the wagon with his dogs.

"Is everyone here?" asked Mister Mullins.

"The men and dogs from Salisbury headed home. Les came by, crossed the river, and headed home. He said he got the last buck."

"He *shot* the last buck," replied Mister Mullins.

"Good for him!" shouted Jonas.

"Get your dogs out of the wagon, Jonas."

"What, so you can put these niggers in?"

"That's right. It's pretty dark, so you may want to swim the dogs at the trading ford at Salisbury. Either way, be on your way. You're fired."

"Fired! What am I fired for, Mister Mullins?"

"For the same reason I fired Les. On your way."

Jon was feeling pretty good about these firings. Jonas jumped down and called his dogs to him. Jon saw that same beady stare and dirty teeth.

"I'm coming after you, boy," he said.

"You do, and I'm coming after you, understand?"

The stare shifted from Jon to Mister Mullins, then back to Jon. He mounted his horse and called his dogs. "Come, Blue. Here, Don." They headed across the river. Jon lost sight of the menagerie in the darkness. Men were putting the slaves into the wagon.

"Drop my horse off at my place, and Amos will pay you for your time!" Mister Mullins yelled across the river. No answer, but barking continued well into the night.

"This buck is dead," said a man loading the slaves.

"Too bad no one knew his name," said someone.

"We'll bury him here by the river. Some of you men prepare a grave," Mister Mullins ordered.

"He tried to tell us his name," said Wilbert. "Sounded like Osurry."

"That's close enough. Can you make a cross?"

"Sure can, Mister Mullins."

"Good. You men want to cross the river in the dark, or wait till dawn?" There were answers back and forth, with nothing settled for sure. Mullins made the decision. "We'll camp here till dawn. It's safer than trying it in the dark, and it will only take a few hours to get home in the morning."

There was a nice patch of grass, but too many horses. Jon saw Sloggy pushing others out of his patch, so he and Smutty could get their fill. Jon had no food and felt the pangs as he drifted off to sleep, close to his friends from Bethania.

The "funeral" for "Osurry" included a few words on behalf of the overseer, Sam Beatty. When Jon awoke, some men had already shot and skinned two deer in the woods, and the meat was downed easily and quickly by the starved young man.

The young bounder, shot out of the tree by Les, was named Miles and turned out to be from a farm near Hillsboro. Mister Mullins's Nan was named Bess. Both Miles and Skeeter improved overnight, and were able to endure the wagon ride home. Jon felt very sad that only three out of eight escapees made it back alive. At the same time, he was proud of the fact that he had played a part in the saving of two of the three. The trip back to Bethania was without incident, and Jock had told Jon to take the rest of the day off.

It was still early, and Jon decided to take a well-earned nap. A knock at the door awoke him.

"Come in, Jock."

"How'd ye be a-knowin' it be me, Jon Henry?"

"I could tell by the knock."

"Denny ye be a-gettin' ta know me too well, hear?"

"I won't, Jock. What time is it?"

"It be a-closin' in on two o'clock, an' I be a-wantin' to show ye how to be a-fillin' a seer's report."

"I haven't taken my gang out yet, Jock."

"I kin, Jon Henry, but kin a report aboot the bounder hunt will be a good practice for ye."

"Okay, Jock, if you say so."

"I'll be a-waitin' for ye in the livin' room, then we be a-havin' some dinner."

Jon reported to Jock in minutes. Charles Finley was also filling out an overseer report.

"Hi, Jon. How you feeling now?" asked Charles.

"Great. Are you doing an overseer report?"

"Yes. I've got it about done. Want to see it?"

"Please. I'm new at this."

OVERSEER REPORT
2 MARCH – 7 MARCH 1835
GANG 11, TEAM
CHARLES FINLEY, OVERSEER

MONDAY, MARCH 2: LEFT EARLY WITH LGE GROUP FROM SEVEN OAKS TO FIND EIGHT RUNAWAY BOUNDERS, NORTH OF SALISBURY. HUNTED ALL DAY. FIVE BOUNDERS KILLED, ONE OVERSEER FROM JONESBORO DROWNED. ROOKER FROM GANG 7 KILLED. SKEETER FROM GANG 12

SAVED BY OVERSEER JON HAMILTON. STAYED OVERNIGHT BY YADKIN RIVER. BACK TO BETHANIA MARCH 3.

TUESDAY, MARCH 3: ORDERED TO REST BY JOCK MCRAE.

"That be a good report, Jon Henry. Ye be a-thinkin' ye can be a-writin' one the now?"

"Sure can, Jock. Not that good a penmanship."

"Ye be a-writin', Jon Henry. I will be a-watchin'."

OVERSEER REPORT
2 MRCH – 7 MRCH 1835
GANG 12, TEAM 15
JONATHAN HAMILTON

MNDY MRCH 2: HNTNG 8 BOUNDRS AL DAY, 50 MLS SOTH. MNY MAN FRM 7 OAK N DOGS. 2 BOUNDRS FRM BATHANA RUNING 1 KILED. SKETER ALIVE FRM GANG 12, ROKER KILED. ONLE 3 BOUNDRS ALIVE FRM 8. STA OFERNITE.

MRCH 3: DAY OF RSTE

"How's that, Jock?"

"It be a-leavin' a lot ta bein' desired."

"I can read it, Jock. He'll get better."

"I be a-hopin' so, Charles."

"I told you and Master Sam I couldn't write."

"What did Master Sam say to that?" asked Charles

"Neither can I."

All three got a big laugh out of that. Two more overseers came in the door and walked toward a dining table. They were both about five feet-seven or eight, medium-built, and middle-aged. One had long, jet-black hair tied back, and running halfway down his back. He had a beard to match. The other had curly salt and pepper hair, which covered his ears. The gray-haired man had been on the hunt, and recognized Jon. They waved at each other.

"Hello, Charles," said the black-haired man.

"Hello, Jerry and Fred," Charles answered.

"Hello, Jock." They both greeted the master overseer, who beckoned them over.

"Lads, this is Jon Henry, the new seer. Jon Henry, this be Fred Nichols, and this be Jeremiah Pierce, from gang 8." Jon shook hands with the black-haired man, Jeremiah, first.

"Glad to meet you, Mister Pierce."

"Just call me Jerry, Jon Henry."

"Righto. And I'm happy to meet you, Fred. I saw you all day yesterday."

"Did you enjoy the hunt, Jon?" asked Fred.

"The hunt was great, but I didn't like to see those bounders killed."

"You'll get used to it. You tried your best."

"Yeah, it's all over Bethania that you saved Skeeter. Good job, Jon Henry," said Jerry.

"I see a couple of bruises and a swollen lip on you, Jon. Are you alright?" asked Fred.

"Heck yes. The lip's a little sore, is all."

"Well, I hope it doesn't spoil your lunch."

"He'd be a-havin' to have the throat cut to be a-spoilin' his lunch," quipped Jock. All five seers laughed at that. They started across the room to the dining tables.

"Good luck with your new gang, Jon Henry."

"Thanks, Jerry. I'm going to need it."

"He just did his first report," said Charles.

"How did he do?" asked Fred.

"I be a-glad Jon Henry was a-huntin' yesterday. His report be a-lookin' like he jest be a-comin' out a the woods." More laughter.

The five seers had just sat down together, when, right on cue, several house bounders came in with plates, utensils, and dinner. It was pork and beans.

"A lot better than deer meat, right, Jon?"

"I don't know, Fred, I was *so* hungry this morning that deer tasted like Carolina beef."

"It did that," agreed Charles.

"What gang do you oversee, Fred?" asked Jon.

"Last year, I had gang 4."

"This year, he be a-steppin' up to gang 3."

"Thank you, Jock."

The overseers all joined in congratulating Fred, so Jon joined in, shaking his hand.

"It means a raise in pay, Jon." Charles had noticed the confused look on Jon's face. The five men settled down to heavy eating.

"Where's Wilbert, Jock?"

"He be home fer a couple days. He be a-livin' close by, in Bethabara."

"The lucky devil gets to go home to his family every week," said Jerry.

"Where do you all live?" asked Jon.

"I live down by Charlotte, and Fred here lives clear out at the coast, in New Bern," said Jerry.

"My home is east, by Raleigh," said Charles.

"An' I be a-livin' right here," added Jock.

"What about you, Jon?" asked Charles.

"My family has a small yeoman farm south of Salem."

"We all be a-livin' atlas a Carolina," quipped Jock, bean sauce spotting his red beard.

"These beans are delicious," said Jerry through a mouthful, and dipping more out of the pot. "I like that spicy taste in the molasses."

"That be the ketchup the cook be a-makin' the other day," answered Jock.

"Let us know where you're going to be this evening, so we won't be there!" More laughter.

"What are you doing this evening, Jon?" asked Charles.

"I thought I'd get to know my gang, and maybe take them out tomorrow."

"Want some company?"

"Sure thing, Charles."

"Sometimes it's best to have some company in Bounder Row. Besides, I need to check out my gang, too."

"That be a good idea, Jon Henry, an' be a-takin' a blacksnake wit ye," said Jock.

Fred saw reluctance in Jon's eyes, to take a snake. "It's mainly for show, Jon," he said. "If they see you have one, they'll keep clear of you."

"Thanks, Fred. I'm ready to go, Charles."

Jock handed Jon a whip off a shelf in the living area, which Jon hadn't noticed before. Jock also handed one to Charles, and out the door they went.

"Gang eleven is quartered just this side of your gang twelve, Jon."

As before, a blaze of activity stretched before the two tall overseers. Many bounders gathered in front of their shanties, in a row, along both sides of rows two and three, and Jon felt like he and Charles were the main attraction in a parade. Again, Jon saw a couple having a poke party between shanties in row two. Charles also saw them.

"Why do they boogy out on the ground?"

"It's the only place they have room, Jon. The shanties are all packed with bounders."

A chocolate-skinned Nan ran out of her shanty and up to Jon. "Is you Massa Jon?"

"Yes, I am."

"I's wanna thank you. You's saves my Skeets."

"How's he doing now?"

"He's be ins bad ways, Massa Jon."

"Where is he?"

"He's be ans rack. I's shows you." The Nan stepped quickly between shanties in row two, and Jon and Charles had to hustle to keep her in view. She sprang between the shacks of row one, and turned left, out of sight. As Jon cleared row one, he saw a terrible scene. A row of wooden racks stretched before him. The Nan was already standing in front of a Tom, his head and hands protruding through holes. When the bounder raised his head to look at the Nan, Jon recognized Skeeter.

As he approached, Jon saw the mud caked on Skeeter's back. The Nan was giving him water out of an old, rusty cup. Another Tom was mourning in a rack ahead. He too had mud piled on his back. The racks were waist high, so Skeets was in a crouch, knees bent, with nothing to sit on.

"What is the mud for, Charles?"

"To keep the whip wounds moist and to keep Master Sam from having salt rubbed in them."

"Can you hear me, Skeeter?"

"Yassa, Massa Jon."

"Are you in a lot of pain?"

"Yasaah, Massa Jon." It was very obvious Skeets was in much pain.

"That was a dumb question. Is there anything I can get you, Skeeter?"

"Nossa, Massa Jon."

"How long will he have to stay like this?"

"I've seen one, a couple of years ago, that was on the rack for over a month, and another who was cobbed so bad that he was only a couple of days on the rack. I heard he later died," said Charles.

"I'll see what I can do for you, Skeeter."

"Thank you's, Massa Jon."

"Why did you run, Skeets?"

"I's be whips an' maybes shot for breaks dem ropes, an' lettin' dems run nohow, Massa Charles."

As the two overseers were leaving, three Nans and a Tom were approaching the racks with food and water. Jon stopped and watched them wait on both bounders.

"Don't worry, Jon, Master Sam won't let them die."

"How do you know that?"

"There's a federal law that no bounders can be shipped in from Africa, and they are getting scarce and worth their weight in nob."

The two overseers headed back through rows one and two, and onto the fairway. They could hear drums at the row's end. They no sooner turned left amid the turmoil, when they spotted two bounders in a fight. Both were bloodied from the battle, and Jon decided to break it up.

"Hold it, Jon. This is the time to use your whip."

"I've never used one before, Charles, and I'm afraid I might hurt them."

"Don't worry about that. If they hurt each other, they'll both face the blacksnake on the racks, and you and I will get a reprimand for not stopping it." Jon uncoiled his snake and feebly waved it in the air a couple of times. The fight went on in the mud.

"It takes a quick snap of the wrist, like this." Charles twirled the lash in a circle behind his head and swung his arm in a quick, forward motion. It made a swooch, then a CRACK, and Jon saw the red line and beads of blood spring from the back of the bounder on top. They didn't stop. SWOOCH! CRACK! Jon's whip made the same sounds as the whip of Charles, but Jon tried to make sure that his crack didn't cut the bounder. It didn't appear to work. The fight continued.

"Again, Jon, before they kill each other!" This time, the business end of Jon's snake tip just barely caught skin. Jon saw a tiny bead of blood, and for a second, he was stunned. The bounder on top now had his hands around the other's neck, and he squeezed hard while shaking the head. The bounder on the bottom pounded on the sides of the choker's head, his eyes wide open.

Charles must have recognized those big black eyes. He let his whip go again. SWOOCH, CRACK, this time with all his might. A long, red welt appeared across the back of the top bounder, and blood squirted from it.

"Aaaghhh!" came the sound from the whipped man, as he released his grip on the nearly dead bounder under him and fell over on his side in the mud. The big-eyed bounder started coughing and trying to take deep breaths, which made a "hugh" sound.

"Are you alright, Tarr?" asked a concerned Charles.

"I's be fines, Massa Charles."

"Well, you won't be for long. Andy!"

"Yassa," came a voice from behind the shanties in row three. Row four, Jon judged in silence.

"Andy, get over here!" shouted Charles.

A large group of bounders of all shapes had now gathered at the scene, and Jon spotted two Toms pushing their way through the mob.

"I's here, Massa Charles," said the lanky, light-complected Andy Androsterone.

"Put these two bounders on the rack."

"Yassa, Massa Charles."

As Charles and Jon again walked down Bounder's Row, Charles guessed what Jon was thinking. "I'll make sure they don't taste the whip. I'll just leave them overnight on the rack for their fighting."

"You recognized the one on the bottom?"

"Yeah, he worked in my gang a few times last year. I think he belongs to Aims."

The overseers could now see the bounders pounding the drums. Some Toms had formed a wide circle and were clapping their hands and turning their waists left, then right, to the drum's beat. Inside their circle, Nans were dancing in rhythm while they circled left then right, counterclockwise, and then in the same direction as Jon's watch. The overseers walked to the end of Bounder's Row, and watched as the bounders continued their movements and clapping, then chanting sounds Jon had never heard.

"Damn, they sure do have rhythm."

"That they do, Jon. Whenever they dance like that, we call it the Juba. Your gang is in those shacks there. I'll be going back a ways to my gang. If you need me, just call my name. They'll let me know.

"Right, thanks, Charles." Jon was about to call his gang, when he noticed the pretty little Nan that said goodbye to him before. What was *her name? Oh yeah, Cora.*

"Hello, Cora," he said to the smiling Nan.

"Hello, Massa Jon," she replied, never losing the smile. "Is you's comes fo' me?"

"I came to see you and all my gang twelve."

"Oh." She seemed disappointed. "I's gets 'em." Cora scooted back into a shanty, a different one than she had entered on Sunday, Jon thought. He watched the dancing at the end of the row. He had never seen anything like it before; and he was entranced, for how long, he wasn't sure. Finally, he realized that none of his gang had come out of the shanties. He was wondering what he should do, when the cute little Cora reappeared from a different shack.

"Cora, where is my gang?"

"They's be here, Massa Jon, but they's don' comes out." The smile never left her face.

"Like hell they won't!" Jon could feel it when he got mad, and his face was heating up. "Levi! Get your keister out here!" he yelled, "Or I'll have you put on the rack!"

Still no movement, and Jon was boiling. He looked over at Cora, who was smiling and turning her little frame from side to side. Suddenly, she started to undress, still smiling at Jon.

"Keep your clothes on, Cora," he said. "Levi! Toby! You have one minute to get your butts out here!" Cora's smile disappeared as she slipped her arm back through the strap of her new cotton dress. Jon was waiting, arms folded and stewing, when he saw Charles and two bounders running his way. Relief came over Jon. Charles would know just what to do.

"I hear you yelling, Jon. What's up?"

"They won't come out, and they have twenty seconds left to do so."

"Then what?"

"I'm hoping you have the answer, Charles!"

"Levi! You get your gang out here now, or I'll get the Pattyrollers in here and sell Lizzy!"

"Yassa, Massa Charles." From the shanties, bounders poured out. Jon was amazed at the response. They gathered around the two overseers.

"We's comin', Massa Charles."

Jon turned and saw three Nans, who had been dancing, running toward them. They joined the group, huffing and puffing. Jon recognized two of them as being in his gang, but couldn't remember their names.

"Thanks, Charles. I didn't know what to do."

"You do now." Charles turned to the group. "Levi and the rest of you better listen and obey Master Jon. He has the power to bring in the Pattyrollers too, and he'll do it. Understand?"

"Yassa, Massa Charles," they responded.

"I think you should put this in your report, Jon."

"Oh no, Massa Jon. Please don' puts in reports," said Levi. "Please don' tell Massa Sam. We's be good boundas. Please, Massa Jon."

"We'll see how well you do the rest of the week."

"Thank you's, Massa Jon." Most of the bounders seemed content with Jon's answer.

"I'll take my leave again, Jon. I think they'll mind you now. If not, holler."

"Okay, thanks, Charles."

"You bet. Come on, Patience." One of the three dancers started to leave the group surrounding the overseer of gang twelve.

"Byes, Wilmas an' Vera," said Patience.

Jon picked up on these names as the two dancers of his gang answered Charles's Nan. He wondered which one was Vera and which was Wilma.

"Levi, introduce me to my gang again."

"Yassa, Massa Jon. This be Toby."

"Yes, I know Toby, and this one is Jobia.'

"Yassa."

"And I know which are Lucee and Cora."

"Yassa, Massa Jon." Cora was again smiling. "This be Wilmas, an' this be Vera."

Now Jon knew which was which. Wilma was tall and thin, with long, graceful legs. Vera was much older, with gray hair. *Both good dancers*, thought Jon. Wilma grabbed her dress with both hands and dipped at the knees in a curtsy.

"Which one of you is Nelly?" Jon remembered the drowned, escaped slave. *At least she died a free slave*, he thought.

"I's be Nell, Massa Jon," answered a very plain, very black woman, with only one distinguishing feature, her big brownish eyes protruding through long thick eyelashes.

Jon thought he must remember that Nell had big eyes. That left Dianna and Morna. Jon guessed that the slump-backed sickly Nan was Morna. He was wrong.

"This be Morna, Massa Jon." Levi grabbed hold of a heavy-set, happy-go-lucky Nan, who squealed and laughed when Levi grabbed her.

"Then you must be Dianna," said Jon to the slumped-over black woman.

"Yessir, I am Dianna, Master Jon."

Jon noticed Dianna's language was better than the rest of his gang, and he wondered where she acquired it. He also noticed that the other bounders had gathered, and were mingling with his gang.

"Is there someplace the gang can be alone, Levi?"

"Yassa, Massa Jon, outs pas' dem necessarys."

"Lead the way." Jon had never heard that word before, and wasn't sure what it was. They walked past the dancers, still dancing, drumming, clapping, and chattering in rhythm, minus three participants. They continued walking out into the field.

"Mays I's use dem necessary, Massa Jon?" Cora's smile was getting to Jon. Maybe the smile was only a part of what was getting to him, but this was his chance to find out what a "necessary" was.

"Yes, Cora, use the necessary."

"Thank you's, Massa Jon." The smile was broader than ever as she swayed her way to the outhouse, continually looking back at Jon and grinning.

"This be orites, Massa Jon?"

"Sure is, Levi. Let's stretch, gang." As the gang sat around Jon in the grass, he studied each one. "I know for sure now who the Toms are. You're Levi, Toby, and Jobia, right?" They all shook their heads yes. Jon noticed again those long shapely legs. "And you're Wilma, and you're Lucee." He had seen Lucee nude already. The big eyes caught Jon's attention. "You are Nell, right?" All of them shook their faces up and down. "Now let's see," he said, looking at the heavy-set Nan.

"I's be Morna, Massa Jon." She shook with laughter, and caused the others to laugh as well. Jon looked at the sickly Nan, then at the gray-haired woman. Jon knew one was Dianna and the other one was Vera. Oh yes, he remembered, Vera was older, and a good dancer.

"And you are Vera, and you are Dianna." They both nodded their heads in the affirmative, and Jon felt proud of his achievement.

"An' I's be Cora."

Jon looked behind him at the shapely smile that had taught him what was necessary.

"My name is Jonathan Henry Hamilton, and you already know that I am new at this job of overseer. I am happy that you are my gang, and I hope that we will all be friends and get on well together." He lifted his snake from his belt. "And I don't want to have to use this on any of you, but I will if you disobey me, Got it?"

"Yassa, Massa Jon," came many replies.

"Master Jon?" He knew now this was Dianna.

"Yes, Dianna."

"We all thank you for saving Skeeter."

"I'm going to try to get him off the rack as soon as possible. Where did you learn to speak?"

"I was a personal house servant years ago. My mistress learned me English."

"Where's you's be from, Massa Jon?"

"My family has a farm near Salem, Jobia."

"Thens you's has boundas befo'?"

"No, we had a small family farm."

"Why's you's comes here, Massa Jon?"

"Well, I wasn't going to—" Jon was interrupted by his name being called.

"Massa Jon, Massa Jon!" It was Andy.

"What is it?"

"Massa Jon, Massa Jock say he wan' you's now. Massa Sam wan's you's," puffed Andy.

"Okay, thanks. Is it Andy?"

"Yassa, Massa Jon. He's say hurry."

"Okay, tell Jock I'm on my way."

"Yassa, Massa Jon." Andy turned and ran.

"Well, gang twelve, I must leave. Tomorrow we'll try again to work in the fields. I think I have the best gang on Bethania, and we're all going to work together as one big family."

"Yassa, Massa Jon," was the reply.

"Goodbye for now. See you all tomorrow." Jon started back through the rows of shacks.

"Bye, Massa Jon."

He knew by the sweet-sounding voice who it was. "Goodbye, Cora." He also knew she was smiling.

"Are you going back to the seer house?"

"Yes, I am, Charles."

"Hold on a minute. I'll be right with you."

"Okay, but hurry. Master Sam wants to see me." Jon gazed up Bounder's Row toward the long house. It saddened him to see humans living in such poor conditions. It was difficult to walk this "fairway" without getting mud up the ankles, and yet it was full of people, as they had no place else to go.

"You say Master Sam wants to see you?"

"Yes. I don't know what it's about, but I'm going to try to get Skeeter off the rack."

"Good luck. Just don't push him too far."

"It's terrible they live in these conditions."

"Don't put all the plantation's problems on your shoulders, Jon. Most of them are content to live and work in these conditions, knowing that Master Sam will promote them someday to better jobs, like the barns or house bounders. He really likes it when a Nan has a pickaninny. Most of the kitchen and house servants have had two or three of these running around here. There is one house servant, Ella, who has thirteen toeheads, some by Master Sam himself. Andy here is one of them."

"Well, just the same, they shouldn't have to spend their days in this mud."

The two overseers were greeted by Jock McRae, who had started into the row, snake in hand. "It's aboot time ye be a-comin', Jon Henry. Masta Sam be a-lookin' for ye."

"What does he want, Jock?"

"I dinny kin what he be a-wantin, but ye best be a-movin' to thee house the now."

"Right, Jock, I'm scooting."

"Remember, Jon, don't push him too hard."

"Thanks, Charles. I'll dazzle him with charm and make him want to release Skeeter."

"Come in, boy. Don't stand out there pounding on the door."

Jon stepped into the master's study. He spotted him sitting behind his desk. As before, the sight of him caused Jon to grin. He noticed Master Sam's face getting a little red, and the stare-through him.

"What are you grinning about, boy?"

"I still think that's a funny-looking animal, Master Sam." Jon was again grateful for his brother's quick wit. "I guess it's those big teeth."

"Well, come and sit down, boy. Let's have a look at you."

Jon sat, and Sam stared. Jon grew uncomfortable.

"You wanted to see me, Master Sam?"

"Yes, boy. I wanted to ask you about the hunt."

"Yes, sir. It was very disappointing."

"Nonsense! What was disappointing about it?"

"Well, sir, only three bounders survived out of eight."

"I know, boy, and I hear there might have been only one if it hadn't been for you."

"There was no reason to kill them, Master Sam. They had given up. Besides, I hear it costs a lot of dibbs to replace them."

"It surely does, Jonathan."

"I just wish more of them could have lived, like Rooker. They were shot in cold blood."

"Did you see Rooker get shot, boy?"

"No, sir. I was in a different place, with Skeeter, when I heard all the firin'. I heard that Rooker got shot covering up the Nan. She lived."

"Yes, Jock told me that as well. Jonathan, I want you to know that I'm proud of you."

"Proud of me?" What for, sir?"

"For the way you conducted yourself, and represented Bethania during the hunt. And I want to thank you for saving Skeeter."

"Thank you, sir. I just feel these bounders didn't need to be shot."

"I feel the same way, and I want to reward you for your efforts."

"No need for that, sir. I was only doing what I thought was right."

"Nonsense, boy. When I give a reward, you better be taking it."

"Yes, sir, Master Sam."

"I'm raising your pay to fifteen dollars a month, same as the others get."

"Thank you, sir. Wow, I haven't even got my first twelve dollars yet."

"You're welcome, Jon. How are you getting on with gang twelve?"

"Fine, sir. I think I already know their names."

"That's good, boy. You'll be taking them out pretty soon. Is there anything else you need?"

"Yes, sir. There are one or two things, sir."

"Well, speak up, boy. Let's hear them."

"One is Skeeter, sir. He's being whipped on the rack unmercifully for something that's not his fault."

"Nonsense! He ran, didn't he?"

"Yes, sir, he did, because he was sure he'd be shot anyway for not stopping the other bounders."

"Is that what he said?"

"Yes, sir, it is, Master Sam."

Again, Jonathan felt uncomfortable, as Master Sam sat and stared at him in silence.

"Alright, Jon, I'll have him released tonight."

"Thank you, sir. He seems to recover quickly. I'll have him back to work in no time."

"Good. Skeets is a fast worker. Now, is there anything else?" The stare was back.

"Yes, sir, I have one more thing, sir." The stare grew more intense through the heavy brows. Jon felt he was pushing his luck, but he had to try for the sake of the bounders.

"What is it?"

"The pathway between Bounder rows two and three is covered with ankle-deep mud, sir. They have to play, cook, and all other sorts of things in that mud. Is there anything you can do for them, sir?"

The intense stare continued, but Jon thought he was seeing other changes in the small part of the face not hidden by the hair.

"What do you suggest, boy?"

"Well, sir, we had a big hole close to our house on the farm, and it was always muddy in the winter and spring. My father laid poles across it, like he was building a corduroy road. After he covered it with dirt, the hole never came back."

The stare lasted a long time. Suddenly, Jon thought he detected a grin on the master's face through the hair. "Can you keep a secret, boy?"

"Yes, sir, I can."

"How wide is that mud path?"

"A good twenty feet, sir."

"Okay, good. I have a patch of small trees up along my north line. I never cleared them, because the soil isn't much good for planting. I'll send a couple of gangs up there in the next few days to cut them in twenty-foot lengths. In the meantime, I'll have the forge make some shovels, and I can even borrow shovels from my neighbors.

Let's see . . . early Saturday morning, we'll build that corduroy road down that pathway."

"Smashing, sir. Thank you."

"Now keep it mum, boy. Don't even tell Jock."

"Yes, sir. Thank you, sir."

"Now on your way, boy. I've got work to do."

Jonathan thought he was on cloud nine as he strutted back to the overseer's house. He couldn't believe what he had just accomplished. "That old goat has a thin crust after all." He chuckled. He was whistling when he entered the seer's house, and was confronted by Master Jock, Jerry, and Charles.

"Well, ye gonna be a-standin' there, wit yer face a-puckered, or ye gonna be a-tellin' us what ye be so durn happy aboot?"

"Yeah, Jon, what happened?" asked Jerry.

"I got a raise," Jon said coyly.

"For what?"

"For saving Skeeter."

"What did he raise it to, Jon?" asked Charles.

"Fifteen dollars."

"Ha! That be the same as ye be a-gettin'."

"It sure is, Jock. Congratulations, Jon."

"Thank you, Charles."

"What else happened, Jon?"

"Master Sam is releasing Skeeter tonight."

"Wow, you really made out swell! What else?"

"That's it for now, boys." Jon walked to a desk.

"That be a great plenty, Jon Henry."

"I want to get it down in my report."

"That be a good idee, Jon Henry. The rest a-us be a-gettin' ready for supper."

MRCH 3: DAY OF RSTE. MEETE GANG TWELVE. MASTR SAM GEVE ME PAY RASE TO FIFTENE DOLARS, N FRE SKETS.

The pounding on the door wouldn't stop. Jon opened up one eye. It was very dark, and Jon was very sleepy. He covered his head with the blanket. It didn't work. "Go away, Jock!"

"Ye be a-gettin' your butt up the now, Jon Henry. Ye be a-havin' work to do this day."

"Not till after breakfast, you said."

"Breakfast be a-ready the now."

"What time is it, Jock?"

"It be a little after five, Jon Henry."

"Five? Why five? I'm only going half a day!"

"Yer day starts the now. Be a-gettin' up the now, Jon Henry. Jus' cuz ye be a-gettin' a raise in pay, don' be a-makin' ye plantation owna. I'll be a-gettin' the raise a-takin' back!"

"Okay, Okay, I'm up, Jock! I'll be right out."

Thus started Jonathan's first day in the field with his gang twelve. He no sooner came out of his room, and kitchen servants were setting his breakfast plate. He began to realize that this half-day work party wasn't really his idea. He looked out the window behind the kitchen, and saw bounder Danny Doubleclutch driving a wagon pulled by his team fifteen. Already his gang twelve was forming around the wagon. Jon could barely see them through the first rays of dawn. He guessed it was Levi who climbed up on the wagon's bench, and the others scrambled aboard.

"Where am I going, Jock?"

"Ye'll be a-workin' section twenty-six, Jon Henry. They be water holes a-settin' there the now. Ye be a-drainin' them an' be a-gettin' 'em ready fer plantin'."

"How do I find section twenty-six?"

"Levi be a-knowin' where it be. Be a-gettin' goin', before it be lunchin' time."

"I work them for about a half a day?"

"Aye, that be correct, Jon Henry. Don' be a-forgettin' yer blacksnake. Ye may be a-needin' it."

"Mornin', Massa Jon." It seemed they all greeted him at once.

"Good morning, gang. Are you all awake?"

"Yassa, Massa Jon," they answered.

Jon tried to count heads. He counted nine, including Levi on the bench. He could see the pretty smile, and knew Cora was there. He was sure Skeeter wouldn't be back just yet.

"Levi?"

"I's be here, Massa Jon."

"Yes, and Dianna?"

"I'm present, Master Jon."

"I's be here too, Massa Jon."

"I know, Cora. Holler out when I call your name. Lucee?"

"Here, Massa Jon."

"Nelly?"

"I's be here, Massa Jon."

Jon repeated the role call and still came up with nine. He wondered who was missing.

"Is there anyone I haven't called?"

"You's be missing Toby," came the smile.

"TOBY!" Jon screamed down Bounder Row. No answer came, and he called again. Still no answer. "What can I do now?" he quietly quizzed himself. "Should I go after him and tell him that I'm sending the Pattyrollers?" Jon was mad.

"I's be here to helps you's, Massa Jon."

"Is that you, Toby?"

"Nossa, Massa Jon. I's be Andy."

"Andy, get some help and put Toby on the rack. I'll deal with him when we get back."

"Yassa, Massa Jon."

Jon climbed up on the bench alongside Levi.

"Is everybody ready?"

"Yassa, Massa Jon."

"Then let's get moving, Levi. You know where we're heading?"

"Yassa, Massa Jon."

"Good. Get cracking."

"Yessa."

The wagon headed southward, until it clambered over the creek bridge, and then turned southeast. Soon the bounders of gang twelve were humming a tune. It broke out into a song, a church song, Jon reckoned. Over and over they sang it.

> *"Dere's a meetin' here tonight*
> *Steal away to Jesus.*
> *Comes from leff and comes from right*
> *Steal away to Jesus*
> *Steal away, steal away*
> *Steal away to Jesus."*

Jon's gang seemed to be enjoying the tune, and the way different bounders took the lead and others followed. The tune was catchy, and Jon thought about joining in, but thought better of it, for fear it might be resented by his gang.

"How is Skeeter this morning, Levi?"

The song ended abruptly when Jon spoke. He wished he hadn't spoken out. Dianna answered.

"Skeets be doing fine, Master Jon. We all want to thank you for doing what you promised, and getting him from the rack."

"I hear he's a good worker. We will need him."

"He be fas' worker, Massa Jon," said Levi.

"Can we's do fo' you's, Massa Jon?"

Jon was becoming too aware of that sweet voice.

"Well, I really liked the singing."

"We's sings more fo' you's, Massa Jon."

> *"Works da wheat*
> *Gets da corn*
> *Works da cotton*
> *From day you's born"*

> *"Plants tobacco*
> *All day you's try*
> *Gets da corn*
> *Till day you's die"*

The early spring sun felt warm to Jon, as the bounder wagon coasted over another of the rolling hills of the Piedmont. Jon saw the water holes ahead, among the year-old cornstalks, some of which were covered by the water.

"This must be section twenty-six!"

"Yassa, Massa Jock say so," answered Levi.

"Drive to the center of the holes, Levi, and we'll walk back and work toward the wagon."

"Yassa, Massa Jon."

Jon reckoned they were fairly close to Salem. *This must not be very good soil*, he thought. There had been a few heavy rains in the spring, but the water should have drained. Team fifteen skirted the holes easily, and when stopped, gang twelve exited the wagon. This was Jon's first chance to see what a bounder wagon looked like. Benches lined both sides, and a trough up the middle housed the tools. The gang each grabbed one, mostly hoes with a wide, flat bar. There were two flat boards attached to the ends of long poles.

"What are these?" asked Jon.

"Watta pussa, Massa Jon," came the reply from Wilma, the bounder with the nice legs.

"I'm sorry, Wilma. What are they?"

"They be water pushers, Master Jon." No mistaking the good English of Dianna.

"Thank you, Dianna. What other tools do we have, Levi?"

"We's has two plows, Massa Jon."

"Can we hook them up to the horses?"

"Yassa, Massa Jon. I's do's."

"Good. Let's all walk back to the first of the holes. Jobia, you help him."

"Yassa, Massa Jon. We's needs to takes dem wagon back to's firs' holes to hooks up plows, Massa Jon."

"Okay, Jobia, sorry. That would be much easier."

As they walked back to the first water holes, Jon surveyed his lot of Nans. There was Cora, with the cute shape and smile, and Wilma was easy to discern with long, shapely legs. Dianna, who spoke good grammar, and Lucee, who had a very unshapely body, and luckily hadn't yet attempted to remove her clothes. There was also Morna, plump and jolly. Jon guessed he could tell Nell pretty easily, because she had the eyes. That left only . . . only Vera.

"Have all of you worked together before?"

"Yassa, Massa Jon," came the replies.

"We works in pairs, Master Jon. Wilma an' Vera, and Lucee an' me have worked together, and Morna works with Toby, an' Nell with Skeets. Cora and Jobia be new to gang twelve." Dianna had read Jon's mind and answered his question before he had to ask.

"Thank you, Dianna. Do you feel alright?"

"Yes, sir, I'm alright, Master Jon."

"Let me know if you feel sick, Okay?"

"Yes, sir, I will, Master Jon."

"Nell, Cora, and Morna, all three of you work together behind Levi and Jobia."

"Yassa, Massa Jon."

"Wilma and Vera, you have the water pushers, so you take the bigger holes. The rest of you take the smaller holes with your hoes. The horses will plow up the cornstalks. Vera, your group will dig them up and make a big pile. We'll try to burn them later."

"Yassa, Massa Jon."

"Alright, get moving."

Jon was amazed at how easily and quickly his gang did their job. The water pushers worked well, and the two pushers, Wilma and Vera, pushed and spread the water onto the field. The others did the same with the flat hoes to the smaller holes. Sloggy and Smutty pulled the plows along the rows of short stalks of corn, and Levi and Jobia easily maneuvered the horses to plow up the wet spots where water holes had previously been. Soon they were far ahead of the wagon.

"Hold it right here! Levi and Jobe, unhook the plows, ride back, and bring the wagon up ahead of us. Let's take a rest."

"Yassa, Massa Jon."

Gang twelve sat down in a circle on the dirt. Jon judged it was still before noon, probably ten or half past ten. It was a warm North Carolina spring day, good to be alive. The bounders were passing around a canvas bag, and drinking from it. Jon was pretty sure it was water, but as Jock had said, "You ne'er kin tell. They be a-tryin' ta be a-makin' sport a ya, bein's yer new." Of course, it was Cora who sat next to him, and she ceased smiling only long enough to take a drink and hand it to Jon.

"Is it water?"

"Yassa, Massa Jon, fro' dem creek." She smiled.

He wondered what part of the creek as he took a drink. It tasted a little warm, but good.

Suddenly, Lucee stood up and started spinning back and forth as she removed her dress. The gang of Nans clapped and cheered her on. Jon wondered what he should do. The gang started singing.

> *"Dem sun be's hot*
> *Dem dress be clean*
> *Dem grouns be's dirty*
> *Massa Jon no be's mean*
> *Takes off dem clothes, Lucee*
> *Takes off dem clothes."*

Lucee wore nothing under her dress, and her appearance hadn't changed from when Jock had ordered her to put her clothes on. Long, flat breasts lay low to her stomach, which looked bloated. She was very heavy through the middle, with a heavy mat of black hair covering her private area. As soon as Jon spoke, the singing ended.

"Why did you peel off your dress, Lucee?"

"I's be's hot, Massa Jon."

"So am I, but I'm not going to shed my clothes."

> *"Dem sun be's hot*
> *Dem clothes be's clean*
> *Dem ground be's dirty*
> *Massa Jon no's be's mean*
> *Take off dem clothes, Massa Jon*
> *Take off dem clothes."*

Jon felt sure his face was beet red, and he turned his back away from his Nans. He noticed the two Toms had dropped the wagon ahead, and had rode team fifteen back to the gang.

"You better put your dress back on, Lucee."

"Yassa, Massa Jon."

Levi saw that Lucee was nude. He grabbed his whip, uncurled it, and raised it above his head to punish her.

"Hold it, Levi, what are you doing?"

"I's be cobbin' Lucee fo' undress, Massa Jon."

"Not unless I say so."

"Yassa, Massa Jon."

"Hook up those plows. Let's get cracking."

"Yassa, Massa Jon." The gang got up and back to work. Jon felt bad that he had not given his two Toms a break, but also relieved that they showed up when they did and got him out of an embarrassing situation. Gang twelve raced through the holes with ease, and before long had covered many acres. Jon was adept at judging the time from the angle of the sun, and judged it to be about one o'clock. He could see the end of the water holes ahead. He wondered if he should finish the job or just end it now, as his gang had worked the half day already. He chose the former.

"Let's take a break, gang."

"Yassa, Massa Jon."

"That be's ends of job, Massa Jon?"

"That's right, Levi. We can finish it in about an hour."

"We do it now, Master Jon?" asked Dianna.

"Do you want to finish now, or rest first?" Jon was surprised at his gang's answer.

"We's do it now, Massa Jon," they answered.

"Okay, hit the sod." Jon couldn't help but notice how sickly Dianna looked. "Vera, you team up with Lucee."

"Yassa, Massa Jon."

"Dianna, I want you to rest. Can you walk back to the wagon?"

"Yes, sir, Master Jon, but I am alright."

"Go to the wagon, Dianna. We'll be finished soon."

"Yes, sir."

The gang started singing another song as they worked, and Jon was amazed at how easily all picked up on the words. He wondered if they were made up or memorized.

> *"We's raise de cotton,*
> *Dey gib us de corn.*
> *We's bakes de breads,*
> *Dey gib us de cruss.*
> *We's siff de meals,*
> *Dey gib us de huss.*
> *We's peal de meats,*
> *Dey gib us de skin.*
> *An' dat's de ways*
> *Dey takes us in."*

The gang was finished, loaded, and on their way home in less than that hour. The singing continued all the way back to Bounder Row, where gang twelve continued singing as they walked down the pathway.

"Take the team and wagon to the barn, Levi. I want to check up on Toby."

"Yassa, Massa Jon."

When Jon saw Toby on the rack, his blood began to boil. The bounder had been beaten.

"Andy!" Jon heard the name echoed through the shanties. He wouldn't have to repeat it, or wait very long.

"Yassa, Massa Jon." Andy was running.

"Did you whip Toby?"

"Yassa, I's had to's whips 'em."

"I didn't order you to use the snake."

"Yassa, Massa Jon. Massa Jock say."

"Take him off the rack now, and help him back to the house," Jon said sternly. "And see to it he gets fed and rested."

"Yassa, Massa Jon."

Jon stormed back between Bounder rows one and two, and then turned toward the long house.

"Night, Massa Jon."

Jon stopped in his tracks. He knew who it was. He did an about face, to face the cute shape and smile. It took him a few seconds to calm down.

"Good night, Cora."

"You's wans me tonight, Massa Jon?"

Jon resisted a sudden urge to say yes. He stood there, purposely studying the figure before him, his mind recording every curve, oblivious to the many bounders gathered around him. A moistness formed at the corner of his mouth, and he quickly licked it away before he drooled. Cora seemed to sense her chance to become her master's mistress, and turned to the side to give him a better view of firm, small breasts, and a round, plump vestibule protruding out from the drilled cotton dress. Beads of sweat trickled from his hairline, down around his ears. She was probably a she-lion in the sheets, he thought, and he pictured the coal-black hair draped over the white pillowcase. Hell, he was drooling! So intense was his stare, that he did not notice Cora slipping a strap of her dress over her shoulders and freeing her arm from it. His mind was working overtime, imagining the coming view, and he unconsciously wiped away the saliva from his chin. Only the gasping of the surrounding bounders brought him partially back to his senses, as Cora dropped her dress to her waist, exposing two perfectly shaped mounds with long black nipples. Jon could only compare them to his sister's, which he had seen several times at home. These were smaller, but the long nipples made them wanted. Something suddenly jarred Jon back to reality. It was the tugging at his trousers. He glanced down at his prong-horn pushing against the buttons, and quickly turned away.

"No, I don't want you tonight, Cora. Please put your dress back up."

"Yassa." She turned sharply and ran down the fairway.

As Jon walked back to the seer house, he felt sorry that he had hurt Cora's feelings. "Damn, I've hurt my own feelings and chances," he mumbled. He couldn't stop thinking about that missed chance, and wondered if he would ever get another. He remembered the many times his brother had told him how great those Negro wenches were in bed. "How in the hell would he know? They don't have any Negroes in college," Jon told himself. He was having trouble walking straight with his bloated manhood. Jon was sure that his unmentionables were wet, as they got every time he had a blue-veiner. He hoped he could sneak into his room unobserved and change them, before they left a spot on the front of his Kentucky jeans. "Why does that always happen?" he asked out loud. He knew the answer. He was still a virgin.

Jonathan assaulted the front door of the overseer house and headed headlong toward his room. He wondered what the hell he was mad about. Jon then remembered it was Toby's whipping.

"Stop, Jon Henry. I be a-needin' to talk."

"I'll be out in a minute, Jock." Jon quickly dropped his kentucks, and sure enough, he had a large wet spot. He opened his trunk and took out another unmentionable. He wondered what he would do with the wet ones. He knew there would be a big spot when it dried. He decided that when the bounders came to pick up the dirty clothes, he would sneak it in with the others. Even if they saw it, they probably wouldn't say anything. At least Jon hoped not.

"Be a-gettin' yer buns out here the now."

"Okay, Jock." His kentucks back on, Jon strode out from his room. "Sorry, I was trying to cool down before I reported to you."

"It no be hot, Jon Henry, but I be! What be you an' Master Sam a-cookin' up?"

"What do you mean, Jock?"

"He be a-wantin' ta see ye again."

"Does it have anything to do with the scrubs we've been cuttin' down along the north line?" Jon looked into the living area at the questioner, Jeremiah Pierce.

"I'm not sure, Jerry. Maybe he'll tell me today. I'll let you know." Jon hated to lie.

"We all be a-wantin' to know how yer first day went, Jon Henry."

"It went very well, Jock. I have a good working gang. They got rid of all the water holes."

"Ye be a-foolin', Jon Henry. All of 'em?"

"That's right, Jock, and all the wet spots are turned under, and we have four big piles of last year's cornstalks to burn."

"Well, I'll be! I denny kin how ye do it, Jon Henry, an' ye be a missin' Toby."

"That's what I was mad about, Jock."

"He'll be a good worker the now, Jon Henry."

"I had him racked for not reporting for work, but I didn't want him whipped."

"Ye needn't be a-havin' him whipped, Jon Henry. I be a-havin' him whipped."

"For being late to work?" Jon felt his temperature going up, and he looked away from Jock.

"That be right, Jon Henry. He'll not be late tomorra, I'll be a-bettin'."

"He didn't need to be whipped, Jock."

"I'll be a-judgin' that, Jon Henry. Ye be a-overseein'. I be a-doin' the discipline, ye hear?"

Jon realized that he had overstepped his authority, and started for the front door. "I hear. I'm going to see the master."

"Ye be a-reportin' right back ta me, hear?"

"I hear!" Jon shouted from the porch.

"Come in, boy," came the call from the study.

Jon was apprehensive. *What does he want with me now?* he questioned himself. *As Andy would say, "Let's dozzle,"* he thought. Jon opened the heavy door and stepped in to the study.

"Don't waste my time star-gazing, boy. Come here and sit down."

"Yes, sir, Master Sam."

"You had a good day today, boy. Got all those water holes turned under."

"How did you know that, sir?" Jon was shocked.

"I have my ways of finding out things, boy. Do you think I'm muddleheaded?"

"No, sir, not a chance."

"Good."

That all-too-familiar stare was back, and Jon avoided it by clasping his hands and twiddling his thumbs. Damn, he hadn't had any lunch yet, and the master was wasting his time with eye games. *Let's get this over with*, he thought. "You wanted to see me, sir?"

"You also had Toby racked and cobbed."

"Racked, yes, sir, but cobbed, no, sir."

"Nonsense, boy. When they are racked, they must also be cobbed!"

"Why, sir?" He raised his voice to equal Sam's.

"So they learn the consequences of their bad behavior, boy!"

"I want to discipline my own gang."

"You will oversee your gang, and Jock McRae and I will worry about the discipline, understand?"

Jon's face was pulsating, and he tried to outstare the master, whose face was bright red. It didn't work. Master Sam was a master at many things, including the stare. Jon stood.

"If that's all, sir, I'd like to have lunch."

"Lunch can wait! Sit down, boy."

"Yes, sir." Jon sat. The stare returned.

"What all do we need besides poles to build that road in Bounder's Row?"

"We'll need lots of dirt, sir, and a lot of small rope."

"I can get the rope. We have that. But I'm not sure about the dirt."

"You said it was bad soil where the trees are, right, sir?"

"Right. It's on a rise, so there is a lot of dirt there."

"Good. Several gangs and their teams could pull the stumps and haul the dirt, sir."

"Then we can start Friday, instead of Saturday. I have the tools needed."

"Good, sir. My gang will start hauling trees. We'll need several long trees to anchor the poles first."

"I want this to remain a secret until we start. Don't worry about the trees, boy. You and your gang rest tomorrow, and Friday morning, you'll be in charge of building the road."

"Yes, sir, Master Sam."

"Is there anything else we need?"

"Well, we need to cut the ropes in about three-foot lengths, and I'll need my team fifteen with plows first thing. Then my driver Levi can hook up the wagon for hauling poles."

"Then we're all set, boy. Now get out of here and have some lunch, so I can get back to work."

"Yes, sir. Thank you, sir."

Jerry, Fred, Charles, and Jock were all waiting for Jon's return to the seer house. Even Will Aims was there, anxious to hear about the meeting.

"Well, denny be a-standin' there wit dat silly grin, Jon Henry. Be a-tellin' us about the meetin'."

"I can't, Jock."

"What ye be a-meanin' ye can't?"

"Master Sam made me promise to keep it a secret until Friday." Jon could see Jock's mustache twitching, which meant anger.

"No one be a-keepin' secrets from me this day or any other, ye kin?"

"I'm sorry, Jock. I don't know what to do."

"Ye be a-makin' the right choice today, Jon Henry."

Jon walked out of the house and over to the kitchen. As he sat chewing the beef dodgers and batter cake, he wondered what he should do. "I like Jock," he said, "and if I don't tell him, he will probably hate me. And he's my boss. I have to work for him and see him every day." Jon shuddered, and he put his half-eaten dodger back on the plate. He suddenly felt a throbbing at his right temple, and he brought his head to rest in the palm of his hand. "But the master pays my wages, and for these damn dodgers." He spoke out loud, and didn't even notice that the kitchen servants had stopped work to watch him. He was on edge with worry.

"Get your kazoos back to work, before I tell the master about your lazy bones!"

"Yassa, Massa Jon."

Jon decided he would have to tell Jock. Hell, Jock would be bossing the job anyway. Jon thought he would ask Jock to pretend to be surprised Friday morning. It was then that Jon envisioned another problem. Jon wondered how he would get Jock alone to tell him. He jumped up, leaving his lunch, and headed for the long house.

"Is you's finis' wit dinna, Massa Jon?"

Jon swung around and retraced a few steps, and yelled back at the kitchen servant. "Yes, I am finished. You can have the rest."

"Oh, thank you's, Massa Jon."

Several overseers were milling around the living and dining areas, and watched as Jon approached Jock.

"Well, what ye be a-decidin', Jon Henry?"

"I want you to walk with me, Jock. Maybe I can explain the secret without telling it."

"He thinks he's a magician," one of the overseers said, and several chuckled.

"One way or ta other, ye'll be a-tellin' me the now."

"Okay, Jock. Just walk with me."

Seers' eyes watched as Jon and Jock walked the worn path toward Bounder's Row.

"Be a-speakin' up the now, Jon Henry."

"Jock, you know you have me in a bind. The master ordered me not to tell anyone, and he pays my salary."

"Well, ye' be a-thinkin' I denny kin keep a secret, Jon Henry?"

"I'm hoping you can. I would like you to pretend it's a surprise to you Friday morning, Okay?"

"Okay, Jon Henry. Be a-tellin' me the now."

"I won't tell you, Jock, but I'll show you." Jock followed in silence until it was clear they were headed into Bounder's Row.

"Hold on the now, Jon Henry. I'll be a-needin' the snake."

"No, you don't, Jock. Look down the row and tell me what you see."

"Ye be a-funnin' me, Jon Henry?"

"No, I'm not. Tell me what you see, Jock."

"I be a-seein' bounders an' shacks."

"What else?"

"What ye be a-meanin', what else?"

"Don't you see what the bounders are walking in?"

"Ye be a-meanin' the mud?"

"That's it, Jock, the mud! It's unclean and unhealthy, and we need to cover it up."

"Aye, laddie, oh aye! We be a-coverin' it up wit poles an' dirt. That be the secret, Jon Henry?"

"I didn't tell you. You guessed it."

"Aye, that I did, Jon Henry." A grin gripped Jock's face.

Back at the long house, the overseers were anxious to hear the secret, and hounded Jock for it. "Ye all be a-figurin' it out fer yerselves. Be a-usin' yer brain box. Jon Henry and I will no be a-tellin'."

"I suppose you figured it out for yourself, Jock!"

"Aye, that I did. Jon Henry ne'er told me a thing."

The overseers ate supper bewildered and frustrated.

MRCH 4: FIRS DAY IN FELD. GANG TWELVE DRANE WATR HOLS IN SEK 26. TOBI NO SHO PUT N RAK N COBED. GANG TWELVE WERK GOOD.

MRCH 5: DAY OF RESTE WILE OTHR GANGS WERK.

"What happened to my night?" Jon asked himself. It was very early Friday morning when he abruptly awoke at four thirty. This was altogether different from yesterday morning, when he was able to sleep in.

"Yer breakfast be a-waitin', Jon Henry."

"Right. We'll be lucky to finish it today." Jon looked around and realized he didn't know most of the overseers. He only knew Jock, Charles, Wilbert Aims, Fred Nichols, Jerry Pierce, and B. J. Darby, who was part of the hunt. He hoped to meet the rest soon.

"What are ye all a-waitin' on? Gets yer buns outside an' to work the now. Yer gangs be a-waitin'."

"Okay, Jock, right," and "On our way, Jock" were some of the responses. Jock was right. There were wagons all around, hitched, and full of bounders. It was still dark, with only a tinge of light along the east horizon. Several bounders holding torches in a circle furnished the light source, and to Jon's surprise, Master Sam was in the circle's center.

"Listen up, men! We start in the fields Monday morning. In the meantime, we have a big project right here in Bounder's Row. We are going to build a corduroy road between rows two and three, to get our bounders out of the mud."

Chatter arose, and comments abounded about this being the big secret, and the reason for the pole cutting along the north line of Bethania. Jon noticed Jock's big grin.

"Quiet!" shouted Master Sam. "I'm not finished. As usual, Master Jock will direct the project, but Jon Hamilton will be in charge of building the road."

Jon again looked toward Jock. The grin was gone, and the overseers were all staring at him in disbelief, as if to say "How is it that this Johnny-come-lately is put in charge?" Jonathan felt embarrassed, and his eyes searched the dark ground.

"Congratulations, Jon," said Charles, standing next to him. Jon did not answer.

"Where do we start, Master Jon? Let's get to work," said the master of Bethania.

Jon was very conscious of the head overseer's glare, and tried to avoid stepping on any more of his toes. "With your permission, Master Jock, gangs eleven and twelve will work in Bounder's Row. The rest can start hauling dirt and the longest trees, and then the poles. Okay, Master Jock?" There was a pause, and all eyes were focused on Master Jock McRae.

"Aye, ye all heard Jon Henry. Get to crackin'!"

Jon felt relief, as the seers began searching for their gangs and started to move north. Jon had Levi harness plows on Sloggy and Smutty, and plow two parallel lines the length of Bounder's Row. The bounders converted these lines into trenches. Right on cue, Jock sent several wagons of dirt and the long trees, minus their limbs. Jon asked Charles to tie the three-foot length of rope around these trees, six inches apart. While gang eleven busied themselves with this project, gang twelve filled low spots with dirt, and all laid the trees end to end in the trenches, and then backfilled and tamped the trees into place. They were now ready to start laying the poles.

"Do you want my gang to tie down the poles?"

"That would be great, Charles. And my gang will use the shovels to fill the low spots." Jon was amazed how smooth the initial work had gone, and now looked forward to the laying of the road. The twenty-foot poles started arriving, and Jon decided to start at the far end and work toward the overseer house. Skeeter and Toby were flying, seemingly in a personal duel with each other. Charles's gang eleven were working hard, tying down the poles, trying to keep up with Toby and Skeets, who were laying the row of poles. In short order, they had the road started, and immediately Jon saw a problem. His gang was filling and packing dirt under the poles, but they were still bending, and giving, under the weight of the bounders. He called a halt to the project.

"What is the matter?" asked Charles.

"We need an anchor line down the middle. Twenty feet is too long a span."

"So what do we do now?"

"Untie the poles, and take them back up. Levi! Toby! Get a dobbin in here, and hitch the plow to him. We need a trench up the center."

"Yassa, Massa Jon."

"The rest of you take a break."

"Yassa, Massa Jon."

"Skeets, run to the barn and get a horse. Ride to Master Jock and tell him we need more trees if he has any."

"Yassa, Massa Jon."

When Levi had a plow hooked up, he ran a line straight down the middle of the pathway, and gang twelve quickly made it into a trench. They all waited for the delimbed trees. When they came, four trees total, Jock was in the wagon with them. Charles put his gang to work, tying the ropes around them. Jon got Levi and Toby busy strapping together several sets of three poles, to finish the full length of the middle trench.

"What be the holdup, Jon Henry?"

"I just found out we needed an anchor line down the middle, Jock. Twenty feet is too long a span for just two anchors."

"I coulda tolt ye that, Jon Henry. Ye be a-costin' us time."

"I'm sorry, Jock. We'll catch up in no time."

"Ye best be a-doin' jest that, Jon Henry."

"Yes, sir, Jock. By the time you get back, we'll be ready for more poles and dirt."

"Alright. Be a-takin' lunch break at noon, Jon Henry. The kitchen bounders be a-bringin' it out here."

"Right, thanks, Jock." Jon's gang sang as they worked. Gangs eleven and twelve quickly had the middle anchor packed and ready, and once again were tying down the twenty-foot poles, now in three places. That made the new road very sturdy, and by noon, the road builders had caught up and were waiting on the arrival of more poles and dirt.

"Time for lunch, Charles."

"Good. Both the gangs have earned it."

"Righto, that they have," Jon agreed. "Time for lunch!" he yelled at the bounders. "Let's all gather out there in the grass. You are all doing great!"

Jon and Charles walked over the poles. They were solid under the weight. Jon was proud of this.

"We're well over a third of the way, Jon."

"That we are, Charles. Time to start packing dirt over it."

"About how deep?"

"I would like it a foot deep, but they may not have that much dirt. Let's do eight or nine inches, and pack it good. Then, if we get more dirt, we can add a second layer."

"Sounds good. Let's eat."

As gangs eleven and twelve mingled and consumed their meager lunches, more wagons appeared with loads of poles and dirt. Jon ordered the drivers to join in the lunch, and ordered more food for all.

"Tell Master Jock to send the two drummers when you get back for another load," he told one driver.

"Yassa, Massa Jon."

Jon's gang struck up another song, and gang eleven joined in. Jon knew this one was made up.

> *"De rains dey comes,*
> *All de winner an' de spring*
> *Lets dem comes all de times*
> *An' Bounders, dey will sing.*

Fo Massa Jon, he builds de road,
Down de Bounder's Row
An' we's can cooks an' sings an' dance
An' plays in mud no mo'
Hallelujah, Massa Jon,
We's plays in mud no mo'."

As the bounders sang, Jon summed up the first half of the day. He was pleased. "We're over one-third of the way, and the toughest part is finished. Skeets and Toby do the work of two men each, and Lucee still has her clothes on! Cora is even smiling at me again!" Jon noticed Dianna bent over and holding her stomach. She was sick again.

"Dianna!"

"Yes, sir, Master Jon?"

"I want you to go to your house and rest."

"Yes, sir." There was no argument this time.

The second half day went even faster and smoother. The teams of horses refused to walk on the poles, so Jon had Levi, Toby, and Charles's driver turn them around and back up to empty the dirt wagons over the poles. The two drummers Jon had seen before appeared, and Jon had them go get their drums.

"Wilma, Vera! Get the sprouts out here. We're going to pack this dirt down with a dance!"

"Yassa, Massa Jon."

"Charles, we can spare a few dancers each without slowing down the building, can't we?"

"Sure can, Jon." Charles picked three rope-tiers.

"Morna, you and Cora dance the dirt down."

"Yassa, Massa Jon." The smile was back.

The pole laying and tying, and the dirt spreading and tamping continued all afternoon. Jon used small amounts of water from the creek to help pack down the dirt on the corduroy road. The bounders worked and sang their way to near dusk before Jon even realized that Jock had called a halt at the other end. It was about dark when all the bounders entered Bounder's Row. They yelled and clapped at the sight. The project was over three-quarters done, and more bounders gathered to dance on the solid-packed, damp dirt. They stopped as Jon spoke.

"What a wonderful job you have all done today. We will finish it early tomorrow morning. Thank you."

"We's thanks you's, Massa Jon." More clapping and dancing.

Master Sam appeared with Jock to survey the project. Jon watched them closely as they walked over the road. He could tell they were pleased as well.

"How thick is the layer of dirt, boy?"

"About eight inches, sir."

"Mmm. How much dirt do we have left, Jock?"

"There'll be a-plenty to finish, Master Sam."

"Is there enough left to put another layer on?"

"This here be enough, Jon Henry."

"Nonsense, Jock. If there's plenty of dirt, put another layer on tomorrow."

"Yes, sir, Master Sam." Jock's mustache twitched. No praises came forth that night.

MRCH 6: ALL HANS WERK ON BONDERS ROWD. GANG ELEVEN N 12 WERK HARDE N BILT THREE QARTRS ROWD. FINIS TOMAROW.

It wasn't quite as early Saturday morning as it had been Friday. It didn't need to be. The Bethania bounders took right up where they left off, and the road was finished by midmorning. The last couple of hours before lunch were spent tamping down a second layer of dirt over the new pathway. Jon made sure he thanked his bounders and the overseers. In the afternoons of both Saturday and Sunday, the bounders sang and danced on the road's surface. All the seers who had questioned Jon's right to head the project were now eager to congratulate him, including Jock.

SATERDAY MRCH 7: FINIS BONDER ROWD IN MRNING. GANG WERK GODE. NAN DINNA SIK N RSTE. HVE A NISE WEKEND.

Jonathan's first week as an overseer had been a plummy, the envy of the other seers. He had been on a slave hunt and saved two slaves from death, and he had taken his gang out into the field, and was very pleased at how well they worked as a team. As if that wasn't enough, he had suggested and led the building of a corduroy road to cover up the mud pathway in Bounder's Row.

It was Sunday afternoon. Jon had turned his first overseer's report in to Jock. It was sloppy, he realized, compared to others, but he was satisfied with his work. As he stood admiring the road, he didn't notice the Nan walk up to him.

"Massa Jon?"

"Yes," he said, as he whirled about. Before him stood a young Negro wench. Very white teeth accented the very black face.

"Thank you's fo de road, Massa Jon."

"You're very welcome. What is your name?"

"I's be Calley. My Massa be BJ."

"B. J. Darby?"

"Yassa, Massa Jon."

Jon noticed how thin Calley was. Not very tall, but so slender, only those shiny teeth stood out.

"Massa Jon, we's wans dem pole bark."

"Pole bark?"

"Yassa, Massa Jon."

"What pole bark are you talking about?"

"Dem poles bark un dem poles in road."

Jon was having difficulty understanding her. He tried to think of what she could mean. He wondered if he had heard her correctly. Nothing clicked in his mind.

"Show me the pole bark, Calley."

She walked to the side of the road, got down on her knees, and started digging with her hands. Soon she had exposed the ends of the base poles covering the mud. She wiped them clean with the palms of her hands. The poles were still shiny.

"Dem pole barks be off dem poles, Massa Jon."

In the two days of building the road, Jon had not noticed the poles had been debarked. "And you want the bark, Calley?"

"Yassa, Massa Jon. Deys be un dem place where dem poles cut."

"Then let's go get them."

"Yeehoo! Thank you's, Massa Jon! Yeehoo!"

From the near shanties came several bounders. Jon wondered what he had gotten himself into now.

"Andy!" The name echoed through the row.

"Yassa," came the answer within a minute.

"Andy, go to the horse barn, and tell Danny to hitch up a wagon for me."

"Yassa, Massa Jon." Andy was off and running. He soon was riding back with Danny, pulled by his own team fifteen. The bounders packed themselves into the wagon.

"I's be's you's driva, Massa Jon." Jon recognized Levi. More bounders were gathering, wanting to go along. He wondered what the hell they all wanted the bark for.

"Danny, hitch up another wagon."

"Yassa, Massa Jon."

In no time at all, two wagons were headed north, full of bounders. At the site, Jon found several large piles of fresh peeled bark in long strips. The bounders quickly stacked them high in the wagons. There was enough left for two more loads, and the bounders rode on top of the stacked bark. Back at the row, the bounders piled up the bark in one big stack at the beginning of the road, and went back for the rest. Upon returning, a large crowd had gathered around the bark pile.

"What ye be a-doin' wit the bark, Jon Henry?"

"I'm not sure, Jock."

"Ye be a-keepin' another secret?"

"Not a chance. Calley!"

"Yassa, Massa Jon?"

"What will you be using this bark for?"

"We's make mats, Massa Jon."

"Hear that, Jock? They're making mats."

"We's cova de road, Massa Jock."

Jon didn't need to look around. He knew that sweet, soft voice. His mind pictured the sexy little figure and the big smile. He also pictured the long, black nipples. Should he acknowledge?

"Thank you, Cora, that will be wonderful."

Many bounders were already cutting the bark into twenty-foot strips, less than half an inch wide. Over the next several weeks, the bounders covered a large portion of the pathway with a path of woven bark. Each evening, they would sweep and scrub it, as it represented a source of pride to them. The mats had heavy traffic on them every day, but still lasted most of the summer. The road lasted forever.

"'Leven twenty," the large clock on the living area shelf showed, "and I haven't finished this cussed overseer report. Badgerballs!" It was very late on a Saturday night, very late in March, and the lanky overseer of gang twelve had just been told that evening that his gang would be working Sunday. Gang twelve had worked all that Saturday, and they were visibly tired. Their week should have been completed at noon, but Master Samuel had sent down the word that the tobacco plants had to be weeded and thinned this weekend.

"Beaverballs! 'Saturday afternoons and Sundays off.' That's what Master Sam had said. I guess that's only if we're finished plowing, planting, hoeing, thinning, suckering, harvesting, grinding, ginning, baling, transporting, clearing, hewing, and building. Hell's bells, he might as well have said no days off, work your buns off all day every day, for that lousy fifteen dollars a month."

Jon was very tired as well, and he knew that bed-buster bell would ring at five o'clock sharp, even though it was Sabbath tomorrow, and he had to finish his report tonight. "Hell, I haven't even seen that first fifteen dollars yet!" Jon didn't realize his voice had risen steadily and he was practically shouting, until he saw Master Overseer Lentil McRae stick his head out the door of his room, and heard his groggy voice.

"Be a-turnin' off that bloody lantern, Jon Henry, an' be a-gettin' a bit a sleep. You'll be a-needin' it tomorra."

"Okay, Jock, just need to get this blasted overseer report finished. I may not get a chance to do it tomorrow."

"Denny kin ye can be a-doin' it in the bloody field, Jon Henry, an' ye denny be a-havin' to stay up all the bloody night!" The old Scot had been employed at Bethania for "nigh an' to thirty years," but still kept his brogue.

"Right, Jock. I'll do the Sunday report in the field tomorrow. It's this blasted summary that's giving me trouble. I never was much good at math."

"What be the count a bounders ye be a-havin' the now?"

"Eleven."

"Master McAllister'll be a-addin' to that soon, sonny. He be a-thinkin' highly a ye."

"I would like a day or two off, Jock."

"Ye'll be a-gettin' that too, Jon Henry. Jest be a-havin' a lil patience, and be a-gettin' a lil sleep. Jest be a-writin' nine sick, an' two pregnant. Master Sam'll ne'er kin the difference."

"Can't do that, Jock. I'll get fired, and never be saving enough for a farm."

"HA! Ye be a-funnin' yerself, ifin ye be a-thinkin' ye'll e'er be a-savin' enough booger fer a bloody farm a-werkin here, sonny. Be a-gettin' to yer room, an' be a-gettin' some sleep."

OVERSEAR REPORT
23 MRCH TOO 29 MRCH 1835
11 BONDRS 4 TOMS 7 NANS
GANG 12

MNDAY 23 MRCH: ALL HANS PLANTNG CORN N SEK 26 BEHIN TEEM 15 GANG 12. WERK GODE N PLT ES 15+ACRS AFOR LNCH. NAN DINNA TUK SIL N AFTERNUNE ES 35 ACRS PLNTD

24 MRCH: 11 HANS PLNTNG CORN SED BEHIN LEVI N TEEM 15. TOM TOBE FETHRBEDNG N MORNG LEVI GEV TOBE 8 LASHS N NO LUNCH. WERK GODE N AFTRNOONE. NAN DINNA SIK AGIN N AFTRNUNE. ES 40 ACRS PLNTD

25 MRCH: AL HANS PLNTNG CORN SED. WERK FASE N PLNT ES 20+ ACRS BI LNCH. NAN DINNA VERRY SIK SLEP N WAGN N AFTRNUN, SKEETS N TOBE RASE, ES 45 ACRS PLNTD

26 MRCH: 10 HANS PLNTNG CORN SED. NAN DINNA TO SIK TO WERK. TOMS TOBE N SKETS WERK FASE ES 20 ACRES N LNCH. TOM LEVI DU GODE WERK DRIVN ES 45 ACRES BI DRK

27 MRCH: 10 HANS PLNT CORN. BEHIN TEEM 15 NAN DINNA STY HOME VRY SIK. TOM TOBE FETHRBNDG. TOM LEVI GIV TOBE 6 LSHS N TOBE LAFE. TOBE FETERBEDNG N AFTRNOONE N GIT 10 LSHS. ES 35 ACRES PLNTD. TOM TOBE PUTE N RAK AT NITE.

28 MRCH: SATERDY: TOM TOBE GIT RAK N 12 LSHES LAS NITE. WERK LIK TO TOMES TODEY 10 HANS PLNT CORN NAN DINNA STIL SIK BUT BETRE ES 20 ACRES BY LUNSH. WERK N TABACKO SOT FILD HOENG N THINNG N AFTRNON ES 28 ACRES PLNTD.

29 MRCH: SUNDY: WERK N SOT WED . . .

Jon wasn't sure just how far he should go with his report. He had to tell about Toby, as Jock would have ordered the whipping. He also thought he had better tell about Dianna, for the same reason. Jock would know about it and observe the work of the bounder's medicine man. But should he tell about Lucee? Jon's mind raced back to last Tuesday, and he broke into a grin. A very strange thing had happened that morning. Right in the middle of planting a row of corn, Lucee dropped her bag of corn seed and started to take off her clothes. The gang immediately sang.

> *"Dem sun be's hot*
> *Dem dress be's clean*
> *Dem grouns be's dir-ty*
> *Massa Jon no be's mean*
> *Take off dem clothes, Lucee*
> *Take off dem clothes."*

Everything stopped when Jon yelled at Lucee. "Lucee! Put that dress back on!"
"Bu's, Massa Jon . . ." The singing restarted.
"I said put your clothes on."
"Yassa, Massa Jon, but I's be's hot."
"Everyone here is hot, Lucee, but they don't want to be looking at you, and neither do I."
"Yassa, Massa Jon."
How could Jon have noticed? One word of the song had changed, and kept changing at each rendition. The word was the bounder's name. It took three verses before Jon realized the change. He looked around, and saw all the Nans removing their clothes. They were at the last stage of the next verse.

> *"Take off dem clothes, Vera*
> *Take off dem clothes."*

Vera did a nude curtsy, and the song continued. Jon looked at Vera, who was now dancing. She had many wrinkles, and her breasts bounced. She was broad at the hips, and Jon figured she had contributed to the expanding of Master Sam's bounty. Sweat ran down Jon's face, but he knew it wasn't from the sun. His eyes shifted back and forth. Those long legs of Wilma's ran clear up to her vestibule! She had a nice figure, probably no wet-noses yet. He had trouble taking his eyes off Wilma, but he next studied Nell. Those big eyes signaled a pleasing circumstance; she was big all over! Jon's eyes next took in Morna, as did the song's words.

> *"Take off dem clothes, Morna,*
> *Take off dem clothes."*

Morna was well ahead of the song. She had rolls around her midsection, and for only a second, Jon wondered how she got them, considering the small amounts of food given to the bounders. His eyes next came to a screeching halt at Cora. Wow! She stood directly in front of him, hands on hips and twisting from side to side, to give Jon the best views. The saliva was back, and he didn't bother to lick it away. He didn't even bother to look up at the smile he knew she was flashing, but he had to turn away, for she was again affecting him. That's when Jon saw Toby removing his trousers. Things were out of hand, and he had to act fast.

"Toby! Put your trousers back on now!" Toby acted as though he hadn't heard his master. "TOBY!" Jon was screaming. "Levi, get that snake out."

"Yassa, Massa Jon."

"Use it on Toby!"

"Yassa." One crack of the whip, and Toby buckled at the knees, then quickly pulled his trousers back on. Jon turned back to Cora. She was still modeling for him, and he was still growing with appreciation. He tore his eyes away.

"Why are you still doing this?"

"We're doing it for Lucee, Master Jon."

Jon knew that was Dianna talking, and he gazed at her nude body slouched over in pain. Her arms were folded across her stomach, and she was so thin that her hands reached her back at both sides.

"For Lucee?"

"Ans fo' you's, Massa Jon." This time Jon noticed the big smile, which he matched.

"Yes, sir, Master Jon. Clothes bother Lucee, an' she works better out of them."

"Thank you, Dianna." Jon never took his eyes off Cora. He knew what he would like to do to wipe that smile away. He again tore his eyes from her, and tried to think about a response. He wished Jock were here. No. Jock would cob them and spoil the view.

"If I let Lucee keep her clothes off, will the rest of you put your clothes back on?"

"Yassa, Massa Jon," came the responses.

Jon wasn't sure he liked this solution, but maybe it was for the best so he could get his mind back to the job and calm himself back down. "Alright, then. Please get dressed and back to work."

Jon looked over at Dianna, still slumping. "Would you like to rest, Dianna?"

"Thank you, Master Jon. I'll be fine."

"Lucee, would you wear a dress out to the field and riding back to Bounder's Row?"

"Yassa, Massa Jon."

"Good. Let's all get cracking."

Jon had mixed emotions. He was happy to have found a solution, but at the same time mad at himself for letting the gang manipulate him. The gang went back to work, singing and planting. Now that Jon had seen his Nans nude, he wished he had not been so quick in finding a solution. He had a warm, glowing feeling all over as he watched them work, especially Cora. He wondered if somehow he could get Cora and Lucee to trade places. He thought maybe that afternoon he would demand that Lucee put her clothes back on, but decided against it, as no corn would get planted.

Jon glanced back at the clock. Eleven forty-nine. "Damn. I've got to get some sleep," he muttered. The rest of the week had gone well, and Lucee worked well without clothes. Jon added one more sentence to his report for Sunday.

OVER 225 ACRES PLNTD N CORN THES WEK.

The wagon behind team fifteen was loaded with hoes and bounders, as Levi headed them all east. A big welcome had been afforded Dianna when she showed up to work, but Jon was worried about her. As they rode past the church, gang twelve sang out in a mournful tune. Jon was amazed at how easily they picked up the words, and how easily the words fit the situation.

> *"A church wit no bounders*
> *Be a church wit no soul*
> *When we's meets on Canaan's shores*
> *Dey Lawd, he makes us whole*
> *There's a better day a-comin'*
> *Comes along an' you's will see*
> *There's a better day a-comin'*
> *Go souns de jubilee."*

Gang twelve took right up where they had left off the previous afternoon. It was much easier work, thinning and weeding, than planting corn, except that occasionally they would dig up the tobacco plant with their speedy hoes. Whenever this happened, Jon had Dianna follow up and replant them. He asked Vera to do the same, and to keep an eye on Dianna. She was right. Lucee did work faster with no clothes. Things were going too well to continue for long.

"Massa Jon! Massa Jon! Comes quick!"

Jon raced back down the row, trying not to step on the tiny, freshly thinned plants. He spotted the reason for Vera's frantic call. Dianna was on her knees, coughing up what looked like blood. Jon landed on his knees next to her, hugging the frail Nan, and helped her lay flat on the ground. Jon was scared, and his heart's pulse quickened.

"Dianna, can you hear me?" Jon could hear Vera crying behind him, as Dianna slowly opened the slits of her eyes.

"I'm so sorry, Master Jon," she said between coughs.

"It's not your fault, Dianna. I've got to get you to a doctor. Vera?"

"Ya, yassa, Mas—" She was bawling hysterically.

"Get Levi as close as possible with the wagon."

"Yassa, Massa Jon."

Jon held Dianna's hands, and tried to comfort her. She was laboring, trying to breathe. Big gasps and gurgling sounds came from her lungs.

"Hang on, Dianna. I'll get you to a doctor." Jon couldn't tell if she heard him. Her eyes remained closed as she continued the heavy breathing, but Jon thought he detected a slight smile wrapped around the open, gasping mouth. Vera came running back, and so did most of gang twelve.

"Will Dianna dies, Massa Jon?"

"I don't know, Vera. She is very sick."

Jon had a frightened, sinking feeling as team fifteen pulled up close, running over young sot weed.

"I's takes her to Bounder's Row, Massa Jon?"

"No, Levi. I'm taking her to the doctor in Salem."

"Salem, Massa Jon?"

"Right. You'll have to do the overseeing till I get back, Levi."

"Yassa, Massa Jon."

"Keep them busy, and give them rest and a long lunch. I'll be back as soon as I can."

"Yassa." Levi helped Jon place the tiny sick body into the wagon.

"Vera, you come along and ride with Dianna."

"Yassa, Massa Jon." Tears were still flowing down Vera's cheeks, as well as many others'. Jon wrapped a blanket around Dianna, tucked it under her for a bit of cushion, and jumped up onto the bench. Dianna was still gasping, as team fifteen tore through and over planted sot weed. He could scarcely hear the cries and well-wishers of his bounders.

Jon knew the direction, but didn't know how far he was from town. He just kept Sloggy and Smutty headed southeast, and hoped for the best. He wanted to race his team at full stride, but was concerned that they wouldn't last to Salem, so he held them to a steady gait. He worried that the bouncing would be unbearable for Dianna, and felt helpless to do anything about it.

"How is she doing, Vera?" he yelled over his shoulder, keeping the reins taut.

"She be breathin', Massa Jon. Please hurry."

It seemed hours before Jon saw a road running parallel to him, and he looked for an opening to it. He didn't recognize the road, but Jon was sure he was now close to Salem. He urged Sloggy forward. He heard Vera scream behind him, but couldn't turn around. The March wind hurt his face.

"What is it, Vera?" She continued to scream.

"Vera! Stop screaming! What is the matter?"

"She stops breathin', Massa Jon!" Vera stopped screaming, but started a loud cry. Jon urged his team on as tears now streamed down his cheeks. On they raced to the thunder of the hooves, and the even louder cries of Vera. Through his tears, Jon saw the town dead ahead. He slapped the reins across Sloggy's back. They entered the town at full speed, and Jon pulled back on those reins.

"Whoa! Whoa, Sloggy. Whoa, Smutty!" The team slowed to a trot, and Jon saw people standing, staring at him. He hollered at two standing together.

"Where's the doctor's office?" The couple continued to stare.

"Damn it! I said where is the doctor's office?"

"Around the next corner, and on the left."

Jon slapped the backs of team fifteen before they finished the sentence, and he didn't hear the rest.

"But he don't take niggers."

As team fifteen raced around the corner, the wagon skidded sideways to Vera's screams. Jon saw the big sign halfway down the block: NEWTON ROWDON, MD.

Jon dug his heels into the front board and stiffened up, pulling on the reins. "Whoa, Slog. Whoa there, Smut." The wagon skidded to a halt with such force that it appeared to bump the horses' rears. Jon glanced back at the sobbing Vera, and a very still Dianna. He noticed the blue tone on her dark lips as he jumped to the ground and ran into the office.

"Where is the doctor?" he yelled at the woman behind the desk.

"He's with a patient, sir. Do y'all have an appoint—"

Jon burst through the door into a small room. A lady sat on a chair in front of the doctor, her bodice off. Jon paid no attention to her.

"Sorry to bust in on you, doctor, but you must come now. I have an emergency."

"I'll be with you in a minute, sir."

"You'll be with me right now!" He grabbed the doctor's shirt and pulled him off his chair.

"How dare you interfere, young man!" snapped the woman, covering her bosom with her arms.

"See here, sir. I'll have you arrested."

Jon pulled the doctor through the door and out of the building, on the run. As they reached the wagon, Jon stretched the doctor over the side rails. "Help her, doctor. Don't let her die."

Jon loosened his grip on the shirt, and the doctor turned away toward his office.

"I don't treat niggers."

Jon grabbed him by the back of the collar, and yanked him backward. "You'll treat this one now, or I'll lay your back wide open." Jon unhooked his whip from the belt of his trousers. That was all the persuasion needed. The doctor leaned over the side board, and touched his new black patient.

"I can do nothing for her. The wench is dead." Vera screamed even louder than before, then laid her head and arms across the deceased body and cried very loudly. Jon leaned on the wagon and openly cried as well. The doctor looked disinterested, and even disgusted at the tear-shedding.

"That will be five dollars for the visit."

Jon looked at him with hatred in his wet eyes, and curled his face in a growl. The doctor backed off toward his office, his eyes large, round marbles.

"You'll get your money. I'll see to that. Send a request to the Bethania Plantation for Jon Hamilton. Now get out of my sight."

"Yes, sir, Mister Hamilton." Doctor Rowdon ran back into his office. Vera was still stretched over her bounder friend, crying loudly. Jon reached over and hugged her around her shoulders.

"I'm sorry, Vera. We tried."

"I's knows dat, Massa Jon. Thanks you's fo' tryin'."

"Sit up front on the bench with me."

"Yassa, Massa Jon."

Jon covered Dianna's head with the blanket, and walked upfront to his horses. They both were lathered around the shoulders and neck. Jon talked to them and patted them to settle them down. A thought struck him, and he pushed through the small crowd gathered around and marched back into the office of Doctor Newton Rowdon. He continued again through to the door of the examination room. The woman screamed and once again tried to cover herself, but not before Jon got a good look at her bosom. He grabbed the sheet off the examination table and started back out. He heard the lady speak.

"Can't you do anything?"

"Yes, he can, ma'am. He can add this sheet to his request for pay!" yelled Jon.

Jon walked back to his team and rubbed them down with the sheet. He knew they were thirsty, and probably hungry. He turned to the small crowd.

"Where are the stables?"

"The second block, turn right."

"Thank you, sir." Jon leaped up into the wagon, and headed for the stables. He was happy to see a Negro manning the shop.

"My horses need water."

"Yassa, dey be cool down now. I's get some." The buck ran to a big barrel of water and filled two buckets. He ran them back, and team fifteen drank heavily.

"How much do I owe you?"

"Oh, no charge, sir."

The buck again ran into the stable and came back with two canvas bags. "They be no charge, sir, as long as dem boss don' see." He waited until Sloggy and Smutty had their fill of water, then pushed the bags over their mouths and slipped the straps over their heads. The horses were in heaven, and ate heartily. Jon noticed the Negro eyeballing his whip. He unhooked it from his belt, and handed it to the buck.

"Is thanks yus, sir, a real black snake."

"Thank you for the grain and water."

The trip back to Bethania was a time for cogitation. Vera sat quietly, wiping tears from her face, and Jon thought about Dianna. She had been so afraid, and always sick. He remembered how she had explained what a water pusher was. "She spoke better English than me," he said out loud.

"Yassa, she be good speaka, Massa Jon."

"How long had she worked at Bethania, Vera?"

"I's no sure, Massa Jon. She be here when I's come."

"She always looked so sick, with those puffy eyes and shiny skin."

"Yassa, Massa Jon. She eats dirt."

"What? What did you say, Vera?"

"She eats dirt, Massa Jon, an' she be havin' worms. She ask me an' keep secrets."

"Didn't she get enough food to eat?"

"She be missus's servant a'for she comes here, an' she no like foods, Massa Jon."

"So she ate dirt instead."

"Yassa, Massa Jon."

"Do you get enough to eat, Vera?"

"I's be olt an' no need foods, Massa Jon, but's Tobs an' Skeets an' Levi no gets 'nuff."

Jon reflected on what he had just heard. He decided that Dianna's death would not be in vain. He would try to get his bounders more food.

"Well, her suffering is over, Vera."

"Yassa, Massa Jon. It be's ova."

The remainder of the journey back to Bethania was very quiet and quick. Team fifteen passed under the iron gates and around the mansion, to Bounder's Row before stopping. The row was even quiet.

"Andy!" He heard no echoes, and realized the bounders were all in the fields.

"Andy!" he yelled again.

"Yassa," came the reply, far down the row.

Jon spotted Bounder Andy Androsterone running toward him, alone. It took him just a minute.

"Yassa, Massa Jon?"

"Andy, my bounder Dianna has died. Where do I take her?"

"To's da church, Massa Jon. I's gets word to de preacha man."

"Okay. Climb up here and give me a hand."

"Yassa, Massa Jon." Vera climbed back with Dianna's body, and Andy scrambled next to Jon. At the church, Andy and Jon carried the body to the altar and laid her across three chairs, still wrapped in gang twelve's blanket.

"I's goes now, an' gets preacha man."

"Okay, thanks, Andy. Let's get back to the field, Vera. I hope they are doing alright."

"Yassa, Massa Jon. They be's doin' fines."

"Ye be a-waitin' jest a bloody minute, Jon Henry!" Jon was a couple minutes too late. "What the sam hell ye be a-doin', Jon Henry?"

"Dianna died in the field, Jock," he lied.

"Well, yer report be a-tellin' me she be sick, but no a-tellin' me she be that sick."

"It was a surprise to me too, Jock."

"What she be a-dyin' from, Jon Henry?"

"Vera says she ate dirt."

"Dirt, ye say? Why she be a-eatin' dirt?"

"We're not feeding the bounders well, Jock."

"Who be a-sayin' so, Jon Henry?"

"My gang says so, and I'm going to try to change that, Jock."

"Ye be a-gettin' yerself in hot water again, Jon Henry."

"Probably so, but I'm going to try. Got to get back to my gang right now, though."

"An' who be a-seein' them the now?"

"I left Levi in charge, while I took Dianna to a doctor in Salem."

"Ye what? Ye be crazy in the head, Jon Henry. Master Sam will be a-steamin' aboot that."

"Had to try to save her, Jock."

"Ye be a-puttin' that in yer report, Jon Henry. Now be a-gettin' back to work."

"Yes, sir, Master Jock. See you later."

The only sounds Jon heard until he saw his gang were a squeak in the front wheel, and the thumping of hooves. Gloom reigned supreme. Even gang twelve was very quiet going about their job. When they saw the wagon, they gathered for the bad news. Just looking into their faces told Jon they already knew.

"She be dead. Dianna be dead," cried Vera.

There was immediate shrieking and wailing, and then moaning, followed by tears and hugs.

Jon sat alone on the wagon's bench, watching the sad scene around him, tears running down his cheeks. He stepped behind the bench and rubbed his eyes with his shirt, hoping the sleeves would somehow stop the tears. It appeared as though his gang hadn't gotten too far with their thinning and weeding. *What the hell! It doesn't matter*, he thought. They were all too concerned to work, like him. Jon felt the wagon sway, and turned back to the scene of grief. There, standing in the wagon, was Cora. In place of the big smile, tears streamed down her face. She stepped around the bench and dashed into Jon's arms, her arms squeezing his waist and her voice emitting crying sounds. Jon let himself go, and pressed her body against his. This was not like the other times. Or was it? She was rubbing against him, and it was starting to feel good. He needed to break away from her.

To his rescue came Wilma. She pulled Cora from his grasp, and took her place in Jon's arms. This didn't help the situation much, as Wilma's great shape fit snugly against him. Nature was again asserting itself, and Jon pulled away from Wilma and jumped down into the waiting arms of Morna. Vera and Lucee were next, followed by manly hugs from all four Toms. Only those big, watery eyes were left. The relief Jon felt hugging the Toms quickly disappeared while he was holding Nell. He was glad she was the last. It was when Jon was free of the hugs that he noticed that Lucee was dressed.

"Maybe if we stay busy, it won't hurt as much, gang. Let's get back to work for a couple more hours." Moans replaced cries, and the bounders grabbed their hoes and reluctantly started jabbing the ground. Soon moans turned into a slow, sorrowful song.

> *"Sisters done gets weary,*
> *An' bruders sad no mo'*
> *We will see our sister Dianna*
> *When we gets to Canaan's shore.*
>
> *Ders a better day a-comin'*
> *Where no one's will be poor*
> *We will see our sister Dianna*
> *When we gets to Canaan's shore."*

The trip back to Bounder's Row was very quiet, until they reached the church. They knew Dianna was there, and they moaned and cried, and sang their song again.

SUNDY MRCH 29: WERK N SOT WED. OVERR 225 ACRES PLNTD N CORN THES WEK. DINNA SHOW UP FO WERK GIT SIK. TRI N GIT DINNA TA

DOkayTER BUTE DINNA DI IN SALUM. ES 40 ACRES THINND SOT WED.
DINNA IN CHURTS.

Master Samuel McAllister had given all bounders Monday morning off, until eleven o'clock, to attend the funeral, which started at nine. There was a special enclosed pew at the front side of the church, just to the right of the altar, and the McAllister family were all in attendance for appearances' sake. The master always hated it when one of his bounders died, because it meant time lost in the field. He hoped that these funeral "breaks" would endear him to his bounders, and that they would, in turn, fly through their tasks. The master planned to gain back a little of his loss by handing out a corn dodger to each bounder immediately after the service, which they could eat on the way back to the fields, thereby eliminating lunch break.

The overseers lined up in chairs along the entrance wall. Jon was sorry he had picked a chair in view of the master's row! Even at the entire length of the small church, he felt the hard stare. He was in trouble, as Jock said he would be. He was close to the entrance, and he hoped he could get his gang away in a hurry.

The church was packed with bounders, and Jon could see them gathered, many deep, all around the outside, hoping to hear and relate to the others, the happenings inside. The funeral "a be always the day afta the death," Jock had said, "so's they be a no stinkin' bodies a-layin' around." When he stood, Jon got a couple of glimpses of the box, below the altar, containing Dianna. The lid was leaning against it. Once Jon thought he saw the top of her head and some of her hair, all the way from the back of the church.

A field bounder, who Jon had seen before in Bounder's Row, turned out to be the "medicine man," and Jon was about to witness a spectacle he would not forget. He wished he could hear better. The screeches, chants, clapping, and "hallelujahs" all drowned out the shouts of the "Preacha Man" named Jimmy Withers.

"An' de Lawd will feeds her!"

"Hallelujah!" Screeches, applause, and shouts.

"An' de Lawd will clothe her!"

"Hallelujah!" Screeches, applause, and shouts.

"An' de Lawd will shelta her!"

"Hallelujah!" Screeches, applause, and shouts.

"An' de Lawd will heal an' loves her!"

The church shook with the stomping of the shoes, shouts, and screeches. The bounders were all standing, jumping, and applauding. They started hugging and dancing in place, with no let-up in the volume for a good half hour.

In the four corners, behind the altar, bounders stood and started singing. It took several verses before the noise had died down enough to hear the words. The audience hummed and clapped in rhythm. The chorus would sing a verse, then all the bounders would sing it. Jon thought he recognized one song, and part of another. The third song has been sung by his gang the day before.

"Sisters done gets weary,
An' bruders sad no mo'
We will see our sister Dianna
When we gets to Canaan's shore.

Ders a better day a-comin'
Comes along an' you's will see
Der's a better day a-comin'
Go sounds de jubilee."

The singing, stomping, and clapping grew steadily louder. The screeches were even in time with the verses. Outside, the bounders were dancing in tune.

"Quiet! Quiet! De Lawd be amongs us!"

"Praise de Lawd!"

"Hallelujah!"

Bounders fell to their knees amid the shouts.

"Lawdy, oh Lawdy, takes sista Dianna to's Canaan's shore!"

More "Praise de Lawds" and "Hallelujahs" followed, along with the screeches, stomps, and shouts.

"The Lawd, he takes her to's de Promise Lands."

With that, the screeches, shouts, and hugs quickly turned into holding hands in snakelike lines, winding up both sides of the building and making a circle around the box containing Dianna's remains.

Jon noticed each bounder placed little trinkets into the box as they snaked their way around it, then down the center aisle and out the door, through all the bounders from outside, joining the lines headed toward the deceased, inside. The screeches, shouts, and dancing never ended until the last bounders left the building. Jon made a dash for the door, behind the last of the bounders, and Preacher Withers placed the lid over the box.

Outside, the teams of horses, all hooked up to the wagons, were waiting for the workers. Jon spotted Sloggy and Smutty. His gang was already climbing aboard the wagon. Levi was seated on the bench and holding the reins. Jon tried to take a headcount. He got to nine. He counted again. Nine.

"Where's Toby? Toby! Get over here or I'll have you racked!"

"I's comin', Massa Jon." The overseer heard Toby's voice in the crowds of bounders. Quickly, Jon climbed up onto the bench, as Toby jumped into the wagon.

"Clear out, Levi."

"Yassa, Massa Jon." The wagon lurched ahead.

Jon stood and looked back toward the church. There was no mistaking Master Sam, and Jon even chuckled, seeing all that hair from a distance. Two tall women were beside him, dressed in black. *One must be the mistress of Bethania*, Jon thought. *But who was that beautiful redhead?*

"To de cornfields, Massa Jon?"

"To the cornfields, Levi. We should easily finish all the planting this week."

"Yassa, Massa Jon."

"Then I'm not sure what we'll be doing."

"Deys lots o' waterin' an' weedin' and sukin', Massa Jon, an' some boundas be sen' away."

"Sent away for the summer?"

"Yassa, Massa Jon. They be's back fo' harves'."

Jon thought on that. He wondered if he would lose any of his gang. He hoped not, as he had become fond of them. He thought about the life the bounders lived. He thought they would never be free or make money. Unfair, but there was nothing he could do about it, he reasoned.

"Let's have some lunch, gang."

There was not much response, and Jon remembered why. They were sad about the loss of one of their own, Dianna. The bag of dodgers was passed to the front. Only Toby and Jobia took one each. Jon held the bag for Levi.

"No, thank you's, Massa Jon."

Jon felt sorry for gang twelve, and his hunger also faded. He handed the bag back to Vera, who set it down beside her, in silence. Nothing had changed from where his gang left off Sunday, and the bounders quietly continued on. It was midafternoon when Jon called a break.

A few of the gang grabbed a dodger and nibbled on them in silence. Jon felt a need to get them talking, but wasn't sure how to do it.

"Her pain is over, and she is in peace."

"Yassa, Massa Jon, an' she be sick no mo'." It was that sweet voice of Cora.

"Hallelujah! Praise the Lawd."

"We's should do mo' fo' Dianna," said Skeeter.

"Can's we's puts cross in de field, Massa Jon?"

"As soon as you eat a corn dodger." That did the trick. The gang dove into the bag and quickly consumed the stale dodgers. They hurried back to work, and flew down the rows, just as Master Sam had wished. At the end of the rows stood a few small scrub trees. Toby and Skeets tackled one. There being no knives or axes did not bother them. They used the sharp edge of a plow to "worry" a small tree trunk into two lengths, and strapped them together into a cross.

"Wez plans corn in Dianna's name," said Nell. The matched teams of Sloggy and Levi, and Jobia and Smutty skillfully plowed up the ground into the letters *DINNA*, and the Nans placed corn seeds in the shapes of the letters. They were all happy with their little memorial.

"Can's we's come back tomorra, Massa Jon?"

"Yes, Vera, and we'll bring an axe to set the cross."

The rest of the day, and week, went well. The Tuesday lunchtime was spent cleaning and shaping the area, and the Nans brought necklaces and a wreath to decorate the cross. Singing again filled the air, as gang twelve got back to normal. The corn planting was finished on Thursday, and Master Sam gave gang twelve Sunday off, after the rain.

OVERSEAR REPORT
30 MRCH – 4 APRL
GANG 12 TEEM 15
10 BONDRS 4 TOM 6 NAN

MNDAY MRCH 30: FUNAREL OF DINNA, IN MORNIN PLNT CORN SED N AFTANOONE BEHIN LEVI N TEEM 15 ES 25 ACRS PLNTD

MRCH 31: 10 HANS PLNTD CORN SED. ES 25 ACRS PLNT BI LNCH. ES 50 ACRSPLNTD BI DRKE.

APRL 1: 10 HANS PLNT CORN SED. AL DEY ENDE OF CORN FELD NEER. NAN LUCEE TAK OF CLOS WERK GODE ES 45 ACRS PLNTD

APRL 2: AL HANS PLNT CORN SED NAN LUCEE WERK NUD N TOM TOBE FETHRBED. GIT 6 LASHS FRM LEVI. ES 20 ACRS AT NUN. FINIS PLNTD CORN N AFTANUN GO BAK N THINN N WED TIL DUSKE ES 30 ACRS CORN PLNTD FINIS ES 150 ACRS PLNTD N WEK.

APRL 3: 10 HANS PLNT WHETE AT NORH LIN GANG 12 WURK FASS ES 20 ACRES PLNTD BI LNCH. RANES COM N AFTRNUN RANE VERY HARDE AL DEY STRM WAST AWAY AL PLNTD WHETE. GANG HID UNDR WAGN. RANE AL AFTRNUN. NAN LUCEE PUTE CLOZ ON.

SATERDEY APRL 4: 7 HANS REPLT CORN ROS WAST AWAE FRM RANES N HO WATR FRUM ROS. FINIS IN DRKE TOM TOBE N NANS VERA N LUCEE SIK FROM WETE RANES

FINIS CORN PLNTD ES 150 ACRES PLNTD FORE WEKE. ES 35 ROS HAV DAMAG FRUM RANES. ES 20 ACRES WAST AWAY WEETE.

After church services Sunday, Master Sam sent for Jonathan. It was time to "face up" and defend his actions the day Dianna died. He tried to plan a strategy to get more food for his bounders.

"Come in!" shouted the master, in answer to the rap on the door. Jon hurriedly took a seat.

"You sent for me, sir?"

"You know I did, Jon Hamilton. I have here a statement from a Doctor Newton Rowdon, for six dollars. It's dated March twenty-nine. Do you know anything about it?"

Jon tried to equal the hard, hairy stare. He was certain the master knew about the statement, so he'd better not lie. *Compose yourself, Jonny, and give him back a shot of his own hardness*, he thought.

"Yes, sir. The statement is mine. I intend to pay it as soon as I get my first month's wages." When Jon admitted the statement was his, he noticed the heavy graying beard twitch, but the last part of his sentence caused face flesh to turn red.

"You haven't been paid yet?"

"No, sir, I haven't." A long stare ensued.

"March twenty-ninth was a work day. What was you doing in Salem?" Jon wondered if the master was playing a game. Jon was sure the master already knew the answer.

"My Nan Dianna was dying, and I had to try to save her, sir."

"Yes, I noticed in your report she was always sick. What did she die from?"

"Rickets or scurvy, sir."

"Wasn't she eating, boy?"

"Not enough, sir. She was eating dirt to get filled."

"Nonsense! I feed my bounders well."

"I'm sorry, sir, but your animals are fed better than your bounders."

"Nonsense!" The pits disappeared from the bright red face. "They get meat for every meal."

"Sir, they get corn pone, corn dodgers, and corn meal. Only occasionally do they get a scrap of bad meat, too rotten for the animals!" *If looks could kill*, thought Jon. He was the object of a hateful stare. *Just wait him out, Jonny Boy*, he thought. The long, silent stare continued, and Jon decided to speak.

"Master Sam, how many bounders have died here lately?" The stare continued.

"Two dozen last year, three this year, so far."

"That's a lot of plunder lost, sir."

"I suppose you're going to solve that."

"Well, sir, better and more food should help cut those deaths in half." Jon was feeling more at ease, despite the steady stare. "Wouldn't you save salt by feeding them better?" Jon had placed the ball right in Master Sam's court, and he felt good about it. He folded his arms, and waited for the starer to speak.

"This plantation doesn't make as much 'salt' as you may think, boy. Bounders are becoming harder to acquire. Most are purchased for the south and west. I even have to farm bounders out each year to help make ends meet. And on top of that, each year, the crops get smaller, and fertile soil diminishes."

"Have you ever heard of seven-year cycles, sir?"

"I've heard of it, but I'm not sure what it is."

"Well, sir, some religious farmers split their farms in seven sections, and each year, they give one section a rest, like the Bible says."

"Does it work, boy?"

"They say crops grow better, and produce better than ever before, sir."

"Mmmm." The pits were back, and the redness subsided. "All my ground is planted now, but I may try it next year."

"Maybe I can help you with it, sir. Do you have trees that shed leaves in the fall?"

"Yes. I have a large forest of them in the west, by the Yadkin. Why?"

"Well, sir, maybe this late fall, you could haul tree leaves, and store them by the barn. Mix in rotting food, hay, and manure. You have a lot of horse manure, sir."

"Yes, I spread horse manure over the north fields, where the soil is poor. It is too strong for the cotton and tobacco fields."

"I don't think it would be too strong, if it were allowed to rot for a year, and mixed with all those other things, sir."

"Mmmm. Maybe I'll put you in charge of the rotten manure gang."

"I'll help, sir, but please don't take me away from my gang."

"No, I can't do that. Your gang works better under you than they ever did before."

"Thank you, sir."

"You say you took your Nan to this Doctor Rowdon, and he actually treated a bounder?"

"Well, sir, I made sure he looked at Dianna long enough to pronounce her dead."

"How did you manage that?"

"I grabbed him and ran him out the door."

"Ho, ho! I would have liked to see that."

"And I took one of his table sheets to rub down my horses!"

"Ha, ha! Good for you, boy. Ho, ho! And you say he only looked at your Nan?"

"Yes, sir. She was already dead."

"Why that bamboozling bugger! He's trying to cheat you. I'll settle this hash. I'll take care of the debt, boy."

"Thank you, sir."

"Now get out of here, and get some rest."

"Yes, sir." Jon started to leave.

"Oh, one more thing, Jon Hamilton!"

"Yes, sir?"

"Who was watching your gang while you were in Salem?" The hard stare was back.

"The best driver, and most trustworthy bounder on Bethania, Levi Leglifter McAllister!"

"Mmmff."

Monday, April sixth, started like all the rest for Jonathan Hamilton and his gang twelve, but it didn't end like the rest. Oh sure, Cora smiled that cute smile, Lucee shed her clothes, Skeets raced over the cornfields replanting and thinning weeds, and Jon watched his bounders toil in the warm, spring sun. But this day was different. Master Sam had seen to it that the lunch gag bag was full of *pork* dodgers, and the gang related that they had a big breakfast. Their work showed it.

Early in the afternoon, Jon saw a horseman riding toward them at a fast speed. As the form grew near, Jon saw that it was Lenny Lightbark McAllister.

"Massa Jon! Massa Jon!"

Jon watched the very light mulatto man skillfully bring the horse to a halt and leap off in one swift motion. Lenny was a better rider than he was, thought Jon.

"Yes, boy, what is it?"

"Massa Jon, Massa Jock an' Massa Sam wan's you's as fas' an' dem horses cans run."

"Are you, Lenny, and what does Jock want?"

"Yassa, I's be Lenny, Massa Jon, an' Massa Jock sens boundas fo' all dem gangs."

"Okay, Lenny. You can tell them I'm on my way."

"Yassa, Massa Jon." Lenny leaped back onto the horse as easily as he had dismounted.

"Gather the tools, gang. We're headed back to Bounder's Row. Put your dress on, Lucee. Let's split, Levi."

"Yassa, Massa Jon."

Several overseers had already gathered outside the long house when gang twelve arrived. Jock was inspecting the plantation's only cuffee wagon. It was much like the other wagons, except it had chains and a collar to cuff around a slave's ankle. It also had a rumble seat at the rear of the wagon. It was all hitched and ready to travel along with another bounder wagon, loaded with field tools.

"What's burning, Jock?"

"If'n ye be a-meanin' what's be a-happenin', Jon Henry, jest be a-holdin' yer breeches an' ye'll be a-findin' out. Master Sam'll be a-tellin' us all."

In short order, Master Sam did come out of the mansion. Jon was amazed at how fast those short, fat legs were moving. He waved his arms, beckoning the overseers to gather around him.

"Boys, I have a problem down at Chic Wood. The rains we had Friday were from a big storm that hit the Georgetown area the day before. Chic Wood has a lot of damage, and the rice crops destroyed. I am sending some of my bounders down there to clean up and replant. Anyone want to go?" There was no answer. "That's what I thought. I'm sending Jon Hamilton and his gang twelve right away, and taking several more Toms down the Pee Dee in the morning. So all of you get your Toms ready to leave before dawn tomorrow morning. Keep your drivers. Any questions?" Still no answer. "Alright, boy, get your gang into the cuffee wagon, so they can get strapped up."

"Do they have to be chained, sir?"

"Yes, they do. You may trust them, but I can't afford to lose any of them. There is food and water in the bounder wagon. Just west of Salisbury, on the way to Cheraw, the Johnstones will have more food waiting. I am sending my son Sammy with you. He's an excellent shot, and knows the way. I suggest you put him in the rumble seat. He'll have the key to the cuffs. Any questions?"

"No, sir. We're on our way, Master Sam."

"Good. You can stay at the Johnstones tonight if you like, and you should reach Chic Wood sometime Wednesday. I'll be close behind, so have Allston pick me and about twenty bounders up on the Pee Dee."

"Yes, sir. All aboard, gang."

"Sammy has a rifle for you, Jon Hamilton. Don't be afraid to use it if needed."

"Yes, sir. Levi, you take the lead with the bounder wagon, and I'll follow and drive the cuffee."

"Yassa, Massa Jon."

As the two wagons lumbered away, the large group of bounders watching started to sing.

> *"Oh, bruders, hear our yearnin's*
> *an' sisters listen mo'*
> *We's prays de Lawd do's keeps you's safe*
> *Till we's all reach Canaan's sho*
> *Der's a-better days a-comin'*
> *When de Lawd take you's an' me*
> *Der's a better days a-comin'*
> *Go souns de jubilee."*

But gang twelve was silent as the mansion disappeared from view. Even Jon had a strange feeling gnawing at his stomach. He wondered what would happen to him and his gang, and when they would be returning to Bethania. He looked back at gang twelve, and saw young Samuel McAllister III sitting up very sternly in his rumble seat, rifle on his lap. Jon hoped his gang would toe the mark and produce like they were capable of doing. Jon thought young Samuel would probably shoot them if they didn't.

Cora had that big smile stamped on her face, and the thought of taking her, along the trail, flashed in his mind. He smiled back at her, and she ran her tongue around the outside of her mouth. "She could teach me all the tricks," he mumbled, as he turned back to the front. His team hadn't strayed one bit while he was viewing the scenery behind him. He wondered what team he had.

"What team is this, Levi?" Jon called.

"I's don' knows, Massa Jon. I's think this be's team nine, but don' knows dem horses."

"Well, they sure are old hands at pulling this load. Maybe we'll switch teams in the morning."

"Yassa, Massa Jon!" yelled Levi.

It was about dusk when the wagons crossed the Yadkin at Trading Ford, and completely dark as they trotted through the street lamps of Salisbury. They were flagged to a stop by two white men. Jon thought he recognized one of them from the slave hunt.

"We're going to escort you to Johnstone."

"Great! Lead the way."

About fifteen minutes east of Salisbury, the men pointed their torches to the right.

"It has to be right," said Jon to nobody. "I think we've been following the river on the left."

A couple of bounders screamed at the ghostlike figures on both sides of the wagon.

"We are passing through a forest of trees," said the leader. "The torches make them dance."

"Hear that gang? They're trees."

"Yassa, Massa Jon."

Ahead Jon saw an encampment light up with more torches. The wagons pulled up to it. There was a long, open-air tent and a big bonfire.

"The niggers can sleep under the tents."

"Thank you, sir, but these are Negroes! We call them bounders at Bethania."

"I don't give a damn what you call them! Here on Johnstone, we call them nigg—"

CLICK. The sound was the hammer on Sammy's rifle. He had it pointed at the leader. There was a pause.

"We call them Negroes too."

"Massa Jon, dem grass be wet."

"Thank you, Toby. If my gang is going to sleep out here, they need blankets to cover the ground."

"They should stay chained in the cuffee."

"I'm letting them sleep on blankets!" More stares were exchanged before the leader relented.

"Isaac, go get several blankets, and the chains. These Negroes are sleeping here!"

"Will do." Away Isaac went.

"I'll post several guards around for the night. In the meantime, we have lots of meat at the fire."

"We probably won't need the chains, or the guards. My gang is tired and hungry."

"Well, it's best to be safe."

"Suit yourself, but no chains. I'll be responsible."

"Okay. Are you one of Master Sam's sons?"

"Yes, I am his second son," said Sammy.

"Well, we have a place in the mansion for you and your overseer."

"Thank you. I'm ready for some sleep."

"I'll stay out here with my gang," said Jon.

"You'll catch your death of cold."

"Not if you have a lot of blankets."

"We'll get them. Now let's eat."

Servants served wooden plates full of meat and corn bread to the bounders in the cuffee. Jon was chomping away, when he noticed some of his gang coughing and spitting out the meat. It was then that Jon realized the meat did taste a little stale.

"How old is this meat?" he asked.

"Fresh from the cellar. It's good. I'm eating it. I hope your nigg . . . er, Negroes aren't fussy."

"Can we have more corn bread?"

"Sure can. We got plenty."

"Thank you." To the bounders, Jon said, "If you can't eat the meat, don't. Just fill up on corn bread."

"Yassa, Massa Jon."

It was a sleepless night at the Johnstone Plantation. Most of the gang, including Jon, had a churning stomach. Many were heaving and running to the edge of the woods, a guard watching them make messes. Vera got very sick.

"Isaac! Go get some calomel."

"Okay, Land." The assistant was again on his way.

"Hang on, Vera. Medicine is coming."

"What did your gang eat before they got here?"

"It was that sour meat you fed them!"

"Nonsense. Isaac and I ate it, and we're not sick."

That word "nonsense" struck a bad chord with Jon. Master Sam used it all the time, and Jon hated it.

"You and Isaac eat it all the time, and your stomachs are used to it, no nonsense to it."

Isaac came back at a gallop, and all the gang took large drinks of the calomel. At last, Vera went to sleep. She was about the only one. Jon stayed up with his gang, and freely gave out swigs of the medicine. In the first rays of sun, Wilma started screaming. Jon rushed to her side and hugged her.

"She be dead, Massa Jon! Vera be dead."

Screams, moans, and tears filled the camp. Lucee and Skeeter were running at both ends, and they were also moaning a different tune. That hopeless feeling came back to Jon. He wondered what he could do. As Jon was trying to answer himself, a bright flash of light struck close in the trees, followed by an ear-shattering boom of thunder.

"Levi, Toby, and Jobe, grab some shovels and dig a drainage ditch around the tents. Hurry!

"Yassa, Massa Jon."

"Nellie, you and Morna grab some shovels too, and bring them here. I'll put blankets over the horses and try to get them out of the rain."

"Yassa, Massa Jon."

In minutes, the jobs were done, and none too soon. The rains came so hard that Jon could barely see the bonfire. The servants of Johnstone pressed in under the tents, and Jon was amazed at the crowd.

"Push the tents up in the middle, so the water will run off the sides."

The lightning and thunder continued, as did the rain. Jon saw a bolt of lightning hit a tree. It fell and caught fire, but the heavy rain squelched the flames.

"I's be cold, Massa Jon," said Cora.

"Well, wrap that blanket tighter, and hug someone."

Uh-oh, thought Jon. Cora didn't need any more coaxing. She quickly walked over and squeezed Jon. He liked it. He needed to keep his mind on the storm, he thought.

At last the rains calmed down, and the thunder moved to the west. Jon tried to relax, but those black clouds were still there. Suddenly, hail started to fall. It quickly came down as hard as the rains. Jon watched the white pile up. The stones were the size of Jon's thumb. He heard the horses squealing.

"Levi! Let's get those teams under some trees for shelter!"

"Yassa, Massa Jon." They each grabbed a blanket and ran to the horses. They hustled them under some trees with heavy branches, and then ran back. Jon's hands were sore from the pounding. The hail had broken skin in a couple places. Cora tore the bottom of her dress and wrapped up the wounds.

"Thank you, Cora."

"Yassa, Massa Jon." The smile and hugs continued. The hail and rain also continued until midmorning. At last it stopped, and the dark clouds rolled west.

"Okay, gang. We're running late. Let's get started on the road. Isaac, can you get young Master McAllister?"

"Yes, I will. Sorry about the dead slave."

"Do you have someone who can bury her proper?"

"Yes. I'll bring him, and good food for your trip."

"Good. Let's dig a grave under those trees."

"Yassa, Massa Jon."

"How do you all feel now?'

"Skeets and Lucee be still sick."

"Well, we'll wrap them with blankets in the cuffee wagon, and feed them calomel and hope they get better."

"Yassa, Massa Jon."

The graveside service was quick, filled with tears and moans. No one knew much about Vera. Jon said that the first time he saw her, she was dancing. She was wrapped in a blanket and covered. Landon said he would get a marker for the site. Jon wished the medicine man of Bethania was there. That would get the gang singing.

"I'm really sorry you lost a gang member."

"Well, when Master Sam gets here today in a cuffee boat, I hope your food is better."

"I'll make certain of it. Good luck on the rest of the trip. I hear some roads are torn up."

"Just what we need! Goodbye for now. No cuffs on my gang. They're all too sick to run."

At last the wagons were on their way. They turned right on the highway to Cheraw. Jon was right; the road followed the river. For a time, the sun even came out and warmed the spirits of gang twelve. Despite the late start, Jon estimated the wagons traveled twenty-five to thirty miles without a hitch. By day's end, the bounders were singing, and even Skeeter and Lucee were better. Some of the gang stretched out in blankets on the still wet ground, but most slept in the two wagons. Sleep came easy to the tired gang, and when Levi woke them, all seemed in good spirits. Warmed by the bonfire and full of good food, the gang was headed east early.

At some point, the Yadkin River became the Pee Dee, but Jon wasn't sure just where. At midday, Jon stopped the wagons at a spot overlooking the river. After a good lunch, Jon walked down to the water, peeled off his shirt, and washed his face and upper body. This seemed like an invitation to his gang, as several pulled off their clothes and jumped into the river. The frolicking ended suddenly, with the roar of Sammy's rifle. He had missed, perhaps on purpose, Toby, who was running away. The shot stopped him in his tracks.

"Levi, Jobe, go get him."

"Yassa, Massa Jon."

It took all their might to subdue Toby and bring him back to the wagons.

"I am so disappointed in you, Toby. Where in the hell do you think you were going?"

No answer. Toby just hung his head on his chest.

"Cuff his arms and whip him, Levi."

"Yassa, Massa Jon."

Toby cringed with each snap of the whip, but made no sounds.

"That's enough, Levi. Keep him chained right there alongside the wagon. He can walk."

"Yassa, Massa Jon."

"Get your clothes on, gang. It's time to scoot."

After only a couple of miles at a very slow pace, Toby weakened and fell.

"Stretch him across the back of the wagon and cuff both his wrists and his ankles."

"Yassa, Massa Jon."

In the evening, the wagons rolled into the town of Cheraw, South Carolina. Jon felt like the Pied Piper, as the streets were crowded with people watching and following the two wagons. Jon was relieved to see the town and the bigoted crowd behind him, without any real damage. He had seen some damage to a few houses, and even heard one man yelling that the storm was "the fault of the niggers."

A short distance east of Cheraw, the road started to show damage. Deep puddles of water and holes greeted the wagons. Jon tried to skirt the worst parts, but soon even that didn't work. Places now showed the original corduroy road, and even that was damaged. Jon was happy that someone had thought of rope. He had the wagons unharnessed and walked the two teams ahead of the damage, then they pulled the wagons over the washed out areas. This took a lot of time, and before Jon knew it, it was very dark.

"Let's call it a day. Get a fire started, Levi."

"Yassa, Massa Jon."

Once again, the gang slept in wagons and on the ground, after a good dinner. They even sang around the bonfire, and Jon recognized the tune. The first line, however, was changed from wheat to rice.

"Works de rice
Gets de corn
Works de cotton
From day you's born

Plants tobacco
All dem days you's try
Gets de corn
Till day you's die."

The next morning, it was more of damaged road. The going was very slow, and Jon wondered if they would make Chic Wood by dark. Jon kept Toby in chains, arms and legs, all the way. At lunchtime, the gang ran out of food. Jon cut the break short.

"Let's get cracking, gang. We need to make Chic Wood by dark."

"Yassa, Massa Jon."

More damaged road, and more slow travel. About midafternoon, the gang heard shots to the north. The wagons kept rolling. Then more shots, very close. Jon had a strange feeling it was a slave hunt again.

"Get Lucee and Skeeter covered up with blankets. They have a strange disease, understand?"

"Yassa, Massa Jon."

They picked a spot where they could see across the Pee Dee River, and waited. They shortly spotted movement in the brush. It was a Negro slave, running toward the river and them. Jon could see he was worn out. He figured the slave was about to get shot.

"Get the rope, Levi."

"Yassa, Massa Jon."

"Heave it across the river. We'll try to fish him out."

"Yassa."

The gang started yelling at him, and Jon quieted them. "Just wave. The shooters can hear the hollering."

"Yassa, Massa Jon."

The Toms pulled the escapee across the river, and brought him to the wagons.

"Get those wet clothes off him. Do we have an extra set of clothes?"

"Yassa, Massa Jon,"

The Nans quickly peeled the slave's clothes off. That is when they saw the gunshot wound in his side. He also had a brand on his back.

"Ditch the wet clothes, and get him dressed quickly. Wrap him in a blanket alongside Lucee and Skeets."

"Yassa, Massa Jon."

The job was finished in just in time. The gang now saw a group of horsemen closing in. When they were close to the river, Jon saw the badges on their chests.

"Pattyrollers," he muttered. They were dragging something on a rope behind them. Gasps were emitted when the gang saw it was a slave being dragged by the neck. "I hope he's dead," Jon said. They pulled up and climbed down from their saddles.

"We're looking for an escaped nigger. We think he crossed the river close by here. Have you seen anything?"

"No, sir, we haven't. There are no niggers here. These are Negro servants, headed for the coast."

"What plantation are you headed for?"

"Chic Wood. Have you heard of it?"

"Yes, I have. Are you sure you haven't seen anyone cross the river? This nigger had a red bandana and a brand on his back. He may have been shot."

"Nobody came across here," said Jon.

"Why do you have one chained, and the rest free? And what is wrong with those three?"

"They have some kind of disease, and this one tried to escape the disease."

"Why didn't you shoot him?"

"Because slaves cost a lot of money. The rack at Chic Wood will cure him. He was just afraid he'd caught the disease. Not sure what it is, but I lost one to it yesterday."

"Do you mind if we look?"

A pang again hit Jon in the stomach. If he said yes, they could spot the wound and brand. "Go ahead, but you're taking a big chance."

"Why? What do you think the disease is?"

"The pox!" shouted Cora, and the rest joined in.

"The pox! Let's get out of here!" shouted another Pattyroller, and they scrambled for their horses.

"If you leave the dead slave, we'll bury him."

"Okay. Let him loose, and let's get. I suggest you camp away from the nigg . . . Negroes at Chic Wood until they get better. You don't want to give them all the pox." The Pattyrollers headed back across the Pee Dee.

"Good thinking, Cora." The smile was back. "Can some of you stop the bleeding while we bury this man?"

"Yassa, Massa Jon."

"We don't even know his name," said Sammy.

Jon walked up to the new member of his gang. "What is your name?" he asked. He had to repeat the question two more times.

"I's be Tad, and he be's Will."

"Welcome to my gang, Tad. You are now part of gang twelve of Bethania Plantation in North Carolina."

"Thank you's all fo' savin' dem life," he said.

Cora had now torn more off the bottom of her dress, to where it was above her knees. Jon tried to look away. The funeral for Will was quick. He had also been shot several times, and his neck was broken. Jon was relieved to think that he may not have suffered.

Late in the day, the wagons passed crews of slaves repairing the road. They stopped, and waved at the passers-by. The road suddenly became much easier to ride on, and Jon picked up the gait. It was well after dark when they reached Georgetown, on the coast. Of what Jon could see, it was a pretty town with big houses. The streets were well lit, and made of cobblestone.

"How far to Chic Wood, Sam?"

"It's Master Sam, Jon Hamilton! I think it's two or three hours by carriage."

"Then we'll camp just out of town. Is it north?"

"Yes, right up the coast."

Jon looked for a place to find food, but the stores were all closed and the town deserted.

"Looks like we go without any food tonight, gang. I'm sorry about that. We'll eat hearty tomorrow at Chic Wood. Let's get some sleep. Levi, clamp some chains around Tad's ankles."

"Yassa, Massa Jon."

"I's no leave's you's, Massa Jon. I's be shot, an' don' wants an' dies."

"We'll just play it safe, until I get to know you better, Tad."

"Yassa, Massa Jon."

Jon noticed how well Cora was taking care of Tad. She changed his dressing, and fed him some calomel. Was it jealousy, his sudden feeling? Jon wasn't dreaming. Cora wrapped Tad in the blanket and wiped his forehead. She sat squeezed against him, her dress now very short. They slept that way overnight, and in the early morning, Jon saw them hugging. Jon was certain he may have lost his chances with Cora.

The gang was headed north very early, and in no time, they reached Chic Wood. As they rode up the driveway, Jon studied the damage. The land had a gentle slope, away and below the level of a small, swift creek. Dirt banks divided very large areas of rich, dark soil, now full of pools of water and little else. On the upper side of the creek, even rows of plants were washed away. Jon decided that was cotton. The large house had part of its roof torn off on the seaward side, and boards covered widows, also on the seaward side. A young man stepped out onto the porch. Sammy had jumped down from his perch, and now ran to hug the host.

"My Lord, Sammy, you've really grown."

"It's good to see you again, brother Allston."

After a lot of idle conversation, Sammy turned to the wagons, and the tired, hungry gang.

"This is overseer Jon Hamilton, and his gang twelve. Papa is bringing a lot more Toms in the cuffee boat. They may be here tonight."

"Glad to meet you, Jon. As you can see, we took a direct, heavy hit last Thursday. Everything is damaged, and the crops are gone."

"Well, we'll see what we can do about that, but first my gang needs a break and some food."

"Coming right up, Jon. I notice you have only two of your gang chained. Why is that?"

"Well, one is a new member to the gang. He's been shot and needs attention. The other tried to escape, and I would like him racked."

"Alright. The racks are on the other side of the house."

"As soon as we eat, Levi, take Toby to the racks."

"Yassa, Massa Jon."

The food was good, and plentiful, and the gang filled their innards.

"Where do you want us to start, Master Allston?"

"I would like you to get as much water out of the rice fields as you can, and turn over the dirt so we can start replanting."

"Okay, let's get cracking gang. That's Toby on the racks. I don't want him whipped anymore."

"I hear you, Jon. No more whipping."

"Come-on. Levi, let's get the plows hooked up."

"Yassa, Massa Jon."

"How are you feeling, Skeeter?"

"I's try an' work, Massa Jon."

"No, you and Lucee just stay here. I'll check back with you at lunchtime."

"Yassa, Massa Jon."

"I's ready an' work, Massa Jon."

"Not today, Tad. Sammy, will you please free Tad of his cuff, so he can get his would dressed?"

"My name is Master Sam, and yes, I will."

"What are you master of?"

"Nothing yet, but I plan to be master of Bethania."

"I'll call you Master Sam when you are."

"Maggie may have something to say about that, Sammy. You know how she controls Papa," said Ally.

"Yes. But she will be married to Master Johnstone, which leaves me next in line."

"Do you have any water pushers here?" asked Jon.

"Yes, we do. I'll have them brought down."

Levi and Jobia skillfully manned the plows, turning over the wet soil. They were able to keep ahead of the gang. Wilma and Morna handled the water pushers, and soon they had a large portion of one field aired. That was when the rains came again.

"Let's get under the wagons, gang. Levi, help me get Toby out of the racks."

Some of the bounders of Chic Wood helped bring the horses into the barn. Skeets and Lucee had already climbed under the cuffee wagon with the blankets. The rains didn't last long, and soon the sun shone brightly, revealing water puddles over recently plowed soil.

"Looks like we start all over, gang."

"Before you do, we have some food coming."

"Thank you, Master Allston. We appreciate that."

Back to work, and the gang again worked the same soil, gaining back what they had already done. A bell rang at the house, and Jon called in the gang just as two cuffee wagons were pulling in. It was Master Sam and his boat bounders. Both

Master Allston and Sammy Jr. ran out to greet them. The bounders were in chains, and guarded by overseers Charles Findley and Jerry Pierce. Jon was happy to see his friend Charles. Everyone stood and gossiped as if they hadn't seen each other in years.

"Did you have any trouble on the way, Jon?"

"All kinds of trouble, Charles."

"I don't recognize that bounder over there."

"His name is Tad, and he joined my gang yesterday."

"When did you get in, boy?"

"Early this morning, Master Sam."

"Any problems on the way?"

"Yes, sir. We were fed bad meat at Johnstone, and my Nan Vera died from it. Skeeter and Lucee are still sick. We had lots of bad road, and bad weather. But I gained back one new bounder. This is Tad, Master Sam."

"How did you get him, boy?"

"I hid him from the Pattyrollers, sir. They had shot him, but he is going to be fine."

"I'll have to take one of Johnstone's bounders."

"Yes, sir. Vera was buried on Johnstone property."

It was completely dark when the conversation shifted to the house. The McAllisters walked and talked, leaving the bounders and overseers standing.

"Do you have any food for the bounders?"

"Oh, yes we do, Jon. Sorry. You can put your bounders in the barn, and we'll get them food and blankets. I've got an extra room for you overseers."

"I'll stay with my gang, Master Allston."

"And I think the overseers should stay with the other bounders, son, even though they're chained."

"Alright, Papa. Sorry, we have only a few shanties for the bounders."

"And I would like a report on your trip here."

"Yes, sir, Master Sam. Can I take a couple of days to get it to you?"

"Alright, boy."

"Do you have some papers and pen, Master Allston?"

"I'll get you some, Jon. I won't require any here."

"Thank you."

"I'll help you with your report, Jon."

"Great. Thanks, Charles."

Thanks to the help from Charles, Jon's overseer report was well printed. Charles also promised to help him with his reports when they got back to Bethania. The food was good, a dark rice with lots of pork. The bounders all ate well. Even Skeeter and Lucee ate well and looked much better. After eating, Jon's gang curled up at one end of the barn, and the chained bounders were at the other end. Jon's report was finished before they slept. He noticed Tad and Cora cuddled together.

OVERSEER REPRT
GANG TWELVE

MONDAY, APRIL 6: WORK IN FIELD IN AM. LEAVE FOR CHIC WOOD IN AFTRNOON. GET TO SALSBURY BY DARK. STAY AT JOHNSTON OVERNITE. FED BAD MEET, GANG GET SICK. VERA DIED.

TUSDAY, APRIL 7: BURY VERA. HIT BY HEAVY RAIN AN' HAIL. LEVE LATE. TOBY TRY TO RUN. WHIPED AND CHAINED BY LEVI. HIT BAD ROAD TOR UP. SLOW TRAVLE.

WEDNESDAY, APRIL 8: HARD TRAVEL ON DAMAGD ROAD. SEE ESCAPE SLAVE RUN FROM PATIROLLERS. HID TAD. BURYED ANOTHER DEAD SLAVE KILED BY PATTYROLLERS. TAD NOW IN GANG TWELVE. MAKE GERGETOWNE BY NIGHT. CAMP OUT.

THURSDAY, APRIL 9: REACH CHIC WOOD EARLY. WORK IN RICE FIELD. WASH AWAY. PLOW AGAIN. MEET MASTR SAM IN EVENING.

Friday morning, the sun shone brightly. After a generous meal, the gang got busy, this time using all four of the horses, two to plow, and two to drag level. They took the rice field they had started the day before. The Toms of overseers Finley and Pierce took another rice field a knee-high levee away. Each of the many rice patties seemed to Jon to be about half an acre. Toby was back, racing with Skeeter. The new hand, Tad, seemed to handle the reins well. He had to stop a couple of times to redress his wound, carefully taken care of by Cora.

By lunch, gang twelve had their patty a quarter planted, using a planting pole to punch seed holes two to three inches apart, between rows of levees. Two Nans dropped seeds in each hole, and two Nans lightly tamped the soil over the seed. Master Allston was amazed at the speed and unison of Jon's gang. They were far ahead of the large group of Toms in the next patty. Jon was interested in the planting process of rice.

"We generally grow seedlings in the early spring, and plant them instead of the seeds," said Allston, "but they were planted and washed away."

"Isn't the ground too wet for these seeds to pollinate?"

"No, we normally have to flood the field before we plant to get it moist. The storm solved that problem now. The ground is plenty wet."

"Well then, how do you keep it moist?"

"Did you notice the gates in the creek wall? We flood the fields."

"And that doesn't harm the plants?"

"No, it doesn't, Jon. Rice plants grow in water."

"That's really wild! I would like to know more about rice farming."

"Great. When you leave, I'll give you a booklet on rice growing. It even has drawings."

"Thank you, Master Allston."

"You're very welcome. Thank you for coming down here and helping me back on my feet."

The storms were over, and the planting went fast for gang twelve. They were so much faster than Charles's and Jerry's larger gangs, that Master Sam put that crew of Toms to repairing the house, leaving the rice fields to Jon. Two of the patties north of the big house were drying out fast, so Jon saw firsthand the gates opened, and the creek water flooding those fields until Jon's crew could get to them. And get to them they did!

In three days, the first patty was all planted, and Jon flooded the field two to three inches deep. The patty started by the Toms of Bethania was finished in two more days. By the end of April, gang twelve started on the sixth and final rice patty. Master Allston was very pleased, and fed Jon's bounders well.

Tad and Cora became increasingly close, and Jon overheard them at night, canoodling in the corner of the barn. At first Jon felt mad at himself for not acting early on his emotions and desires for Cora. But now he was glad in a way that she had found what she was looking for. The couple approached Jon on the first day of May, in the last rice patty.

"Massa Jon, we's wan's to marries."

"Are you sure, Cora."

"Yassa, I's sure, Massa Jon." The smiles were directed no longer at the overseer.

"Alright. I'll speak to Master Sam tonight."

"Thank you's, Massa Jon."

"He may want to split you up into separate gangs back in Bethania, but I'll try to keep you two in my gang."

"Thank you's, Massa Jon."

At the supper that Friday evening, Jon tried to ease the master into the subject, which happened to be about the losses of slaves to the west.

"You remember Lenny, don't you, Ally?"

"Yes, sir, Papa, I do."

"Well, I have him screwing Nans full time now, trying to replace sick and dying bounders. I may have to add Jon here, alongside of him." This drew a lot of laughter.

"How about that for a job, Jon? Talk about a dream duty," said Allston to more laughter.

"No thanks. Hell, I couldn't handle one of my Nans who wanted to be my mistress."

"Which one was that, boy?"

"Her name is Cora. Fabulous figure. She now wants to marry my Tom Tad."

"Nonsense. I can break that apart if you wish, boy. You can have her."

"Thank you, sir, but I would like to see them get married. They work great together."

"Mmmm! I generally separate married bounders. You say they work great together, huh?"

"Oh yes, sir," Jon lied, "much better than they do separated."

"That's nonsense, but I'll take your word for it. I'll be checking on them tomorrow myself."

"Yes, sir. We're on the final patty. We should be all finished planting rice by Monday or Tuesday."

"Good. Then we can put that excellent gang of yours to planting cotton," said Allston.

"Yes, sir, sounds good. Can we go ahead and get Tad and Cora married then?"

"We can do it Sunday, if it's alright with you, Papa. I can get a preacher man here in the afternoon."

"I think it would also really liven up the bounders, Master Sam," said Jon.

"Alright, boy. Sunday afternoon it is, and if they work together as well as you say, you can keep them both in your gang."

"Smashing! Thank you, Master Sam."

"You're very welcome, boy. Let's eat!"

True to his word, Master Sam and Allston were present on Saturday to watch gang twelve perform. And true to his word, Jon's gang whizzed through the rice-planting process. They were singing as they worked, all happy about the wedding, which would take place the next day. Jon was sure that the two masters were pleased. He was. They were over halfway done with the final patty by day's end.

Sunday services and wedding were held in the barn. The wedding was simple, but nice. Jon had mixed emotions of envy and happiness for Cora. He found himself dreaming about ways to sneak the bride into his room at Bethania, without Tad's knowledge. Jon thought maybe he could put Tad on the rack overnight. Cora would come to Jon's room if he asked her. Or maybe he could have Tad transferred to another gang for a day, and take her in the cornfield. He couldn't stop staring at those long nipples, covered only by the thin material of her clean, white cotton dress. The preacher quoted a few scriptures from his huge Bible, which blocked the view of his head for most of the ceremony.

"Do y'all want this woman?"

"Yassa, I's do."

"Do y'all want this boy?"

"Yassa, I's do," with that big smile.

"Old woman, go fetch the broom."

Tad and Cora jumped forward, then backward over the broom's handle. Somewhere they acquired a slave bracelet, which Tad put on Cora's wrist.

"I announce y'all husband and wife."

They kissed, and Jon watched the hugging and loving Cora was giving her new husband. The wedding was that simple and that quick. The gang had the rest of Sunday afternoon off, and the bounders enclosed a corner of the barn for the newlyweds to consummate their marriage.

On Monday, the entire gang was planting rice. By midday Tuesday, Jon flooded the last patty.

"What keeps the water a constant two or three inches, and keeps it from seeping into the soil?"

"There is a lot of clay underneath, but it does seep some. We just add more from the creek."

"And you keep the patties flooded all summer?"

"Yes, until two or three weeks before harvest."

"I can't believe how it grows in water!"

"Well, come look at the fruit of your labor."

The first two patties were already covered in bright green grass several inches above the water.

"So that's what rice looks like."

"Well, they will soon grow stems four to six feet tall, and flower in about four months."

"Super. Well, we're ready to plant cotton."

"That's up here, above the road."

"The soil has dried out a lot. Is it alright for planting?"

"Probably just right. We have trouble keeping the soil above the creek moist, but the cotton here is a long staple fiber that brings the highest prices."

Gang twelve broke out the plows and started tilling the soil. Jon was struck by the rich-looking soil here on the South Carolina coast. The cotton field was composed of about fifty acres. With all four horses pulling, the field was plowed by dark.

That night, after a good supper, gang twelve had a party of their own in the barn. A rhythm was beat out on the walls, and the gang danced into the night. Allston heard the clamor from the house and brought out a couple of bottles of rice wine, and the party raged on.

"I give you a toast, gang twelve. You are the best gang of bounders in the south. Thanks to you, we are going home early, probably by the end of this week. And here's to the newlyweds. Gang twelve is full of love and good will to all."

The gang cheered, and the dancing continued well into the night. Wednesday morning, May sixth, the gang doggingly got up a little after dawn. With a good breakfast, they were ready to plant "sea island" cotton. They had to prepare ridges a few inches above the level of the land to keep the plants from flooding, and also make a small ditch in the middle of the ridges to hold water. This confused Jon some, but he figured watering must be controlled to grow good cotton. This took an extra two days to prepare the ground. The seeds were planted on Friday and Saturday. By Saturday afternoon, everything was finished, and Jon walked the near three hundred acres of Chic Wood, admiring the work of gang twelve.

All six rice patties had plants growing above the water, the first two patties now between six inches and a foot high. Jon asked his gang if they wanted to rest on the Sunday before returning to Bethania, and they said no. They wished to return right away.

Another party was started that afternoon. Even Master Sam was in attendance. The master wanted to wait until Monday to return, as did Sammy Jr., so it was agreed that Charles Finley would ride the rumble seat of the cuffee wagon. All was set for the trip home. The bounders were anxious to leave.

"Massa Jon, we's wan's ta leaves now."

"We wouldn't get much further than Georgetown before dark, Skeeter. Wouldn't morning be better?"

"Nossa, Massa Jon. We's don' likes da hot an' sweat. We's starts ta gets sick again."

"Righto, Skeets. I'll ask Master Sam."

"Thank you's, Massa Jon."

Master Sam was cool to the idea, and asked why.

"The gang dislikes this hot, damp climate."

"Nonsense. One more night won't make any difference."

"No, sir, it probably wouldn't. But they are getting sick, and want to get away now, sir."

"Well, they've done an excellent job here, so you can get them started as soon as you and Charles like."

"Thank you, sir. See you on Bethania."

It took over an hour to get all the tools and wagons loaded, and ready and headed south toward Georgetown. The gang sang along the way, happy to be under way. Jon watched the rolling waves of the Atlantic. This trip was his first to see the Atlantic. Hell, his first trip east of Salem, he thought.

Jon wished he had a telescope when he saw a sailboat far in the distance. He and Levi were keeping a slow, steady pace. As Jon watched, the ship seemed to get closer. Soon he could see clearly the twin masts. It was headed in his direction. A few of the gang now noticed and watched it.

"That seems strange," said Charles. "There's no port here for it to dock, but it looks like that is what it intends to do."

"Orites, we's watch, Massa Jon?"

"We may not make it to Georgetown before dark if we do. Is that alright, gang?"

"Yassa, Massa Jon, we's watches."

"Alright. Levi, look for a spot to camp along these trees."

"Yassa, Massa Jon."

Gang twelve settled in the woods along the rocky edge of the ocean, ate cold dodgers, and waited and watched. The ship turned parallel to the coast, and dropped anchor about two hundred yards out, Jon judged. There it sat, seemingly waiting until dark. At dusk, Toby saw movement on board the ship.

"Dey's sumthin' happenin', Massa Jon."

From the ship came the flashes of a lantern. The gang could not see the answering flashes, but figured it happened, as much activity began occurring. It was getting dark and difficult to see, but the sounds of whips, screams, and chains were easy to decipher. Then came the splashes, as people were being shoved off the ship into the water. Charles and Jon knew what was happening.

"Those are slaves being brought in illegally."

"I think you're right, Charles."

"Dems how I's be brought in, Massa Jon."

Jon looked around, and saw it was Tad talking. "They shoved you overboard in chains, Tad?"

"Yassa, Massa Jon. Dey's sells me in Chawstown."

"Where was your boat from, Tad?" asked Charles.

"I's come from shuger mill in Jamaica."

"What should we do, Charles?"

"Well, it's a good thing they're behind us. I'd hate to try to pass by them in the morning."

"Levi, go unhitch one of the horses."

"Yassa, Massa Jon."

Gang twelve watched the commotion out in the water. One of the chained slaves was drowning. The other slaves tried to hold him above water, but he kept slipping under, making loud, strange noises. The men in the small keelboat were using the whip on the struggling slaves.

"Bring him up, boy. Pull, buck," the bounders heard clearly, as the whip cracked again and again.

"Charles, one of us is going to have to ride into Georgetown and alert the authorities."

"Will you be alright if I go?"

"Yes, it's best I stay with my gang."

"Alright, Jon. But get those wagons deeper into the trees, and keep them dead silent."

"I will, Charles. Good luck."

"Thanks. Same to you." Charles walked the horse down the road a good distance before he mounted him and rode away. The recent storms had a lot of branches on the ground, which helped camouflage and cover the wagons, and Jon had his gang get well hidden in the trees. Then they waited and watched.

The chained slaves struggled ashore, and were grabbed and hustled into the trees, dragging the one slave who appeared drowned. They were close enough that gang twelve could hear their voices. It was now very dark, and some of the bounders were getting cold. They broke out the blankets, and Jon had Levi and Jobia be lookouts, so the rest of the gang could get some rest. It was a long night for Jon, afraid he would miss some action if he slept.

The Sunday sun rose beautifully over the water, but gang twelve didn't pay much attention to it. The contraband slaves, and the smugglers controlling them, were already up and moving about. Jon and his gang could hear them a short distance away. Jon wondered where Charles was. The captors didn't seem too worried about being spotted, as they built a bonfire and made breakfast. Jon and his gang quietly ate cold corn bread.

After a long wait, Jon was sure the captors and contraband slaves were about to leave. Jon asked himself what he should do. The answer was nothing, just wait. At last, gang twelve heard horses. It was Charles, with several armed Pattyrollers, on a gallop toward the slave encampment.

A gun battle ensued. The horrified bounders remained hidden in the trees. The battle raged on for several minutes. Jon saw the smugglers' keelboat headed back out to sea, the men rowing as fast as they could. A shot from the shore hit one of them, but they managed to make it back to the ship. At last, Jon heard Charles calling, and a strong sense of relief came over him as he and his gang slowly emerged from the trees. The relief quickly turned to curiosity.

"What a battle," said Charles. "One Pattyroller and two smugglers are dead."

"And the slaves?"

"They seem to be alright, Jon. The captain of that ship and two other smugglers have been captured, and they're all going to Georgetown."

"On foot?"

"Yes. Maybe we can go ahead and send a couple wagons back for them."

"Good idea, Charles. Levi! Get Charles's horse hitched back up, and let's get on the road."

"Yes, Massa Jon."

The wagons came out, and gang twelve climbed aboard the cuffee wagon and headed south.

"Hold it! Stop!" came yells from behind.

"Get your slaves in that front wagon. We're taking the cuffee as far as Georgetown."

"I can't do that. The front wagon is full of tools."

"To hell with the tools! Throw them out. We're taking the cuffee," said the Pattyrollers' leader.

"To hell with you! Head out, Levi."

"Yes, Massa Jon."

Suddenly, half a dozen rifles were pointed at Jon and Charles. The bearers surrounded the wagons. Jon knew they were not taking no for an answer.

"Throw out the tools and climb aboard the front wagon, gang"

"Yassa, Massa Jon."

A lot of yelling took place, as Levi and Charles headed out. Jon, crammed in the back, watched the chained slaves being loaded into the cuffee wagon. They looked entirely different than his gang, hard and dangerous. The ship captain was cuffed, and snarled at the Pattyrollers, and then at Jon, who was seated with his gang ahead, pulling away.

"That wagon and team belong to the Bethania Plantation in North Carolina," Jon shouted back.

"Just wait for us in Georgetown, and you'll get it back," answered the leader.

"Y'all ain't heard the last o' this!" bellowed the ship captain. "Watch your back. I'm coming after ya!"

"Shut up, and get in the wagon!" Jon heard the leader yell at the captain, as Jon's wagon distanced itself from the cuffee.

Crowds were waiting, as gang twelve entered the town of King George. Another armed man approached and directed Jon's wagon where to park, and asked Jon what had happened. Jon told him the story of the smuggler's ship and the beaching of slaves, and of the gun battle early that morning.

"It was exciting, but a little scary too."

"It happens a lot around here."

"Even though it's against the law?"

"Yes. The plantations need the slaves, so the law turns its back," said the armed man. "Smugglers bring them up from the West Indies, and the buyers pay dearly for them at auction."

The midday sun made Jon both hot and wet, and he was glad to see his cuffee wagon pull into town fifteen or twenty minutes behind him.

"Take the prisoners to the courthouse, and the niggers to the stockade. We'll have an auction as soon as we can notify the league," ordered the leader of the Pattyrollers.

"Right, Chris," came the response of the armed man. The chained slaves were led away through the crowd by the Pattyrollers. As the captain and two smugglers were led past Jon, the captain spit at him. Jon jumped back to avoid the spit.

"I'll be lookin' for y'all. Enjoy your short lives while y'all can."

"What shall we do about the tools back there, Charles?"

"I'm not sure. We will need them back at Bethania."

"Right. It would be difficult to replace them."

"Yes, and difficult to explain to Master Sam."

"I'll go back and get them, Charles."

"Probably a good idea. Take as many as you need, and I'll take the rest and head north. We'll camp early and wait for you."

"Right!, Levi, Jobe, and Tad, come with me. The rest of you stay in the cuffee wagon with Charles."

"I's go too, Massa Jon."

"No, Cora, we'll catch back up to you tonight."

"I's be o-right, girl. I's be's back soon," said Tad.

Levi scrambled onto the bench and turned the team around. Charles headed for Cheraw, along the Pee Dee. It was now late afternoon. The tools had been retrieved, and Georgetown was close. Suddenly, Jon saw the slave ship making its way to Georgetown. "I wonder what they're up to now?" Jon said.

"Dems attack de town, Massa Jon."

"With one ship?"

"Yassa, Massa Jon. Dey's has big fire gun."

"Let's get in there and warn them."

"Yassa, Massa Jon."

Levi's team entered the town on the run. They spotted a couple of Pattyrollers immediately, and warned them of the possible attack. The Pattyrollers ran toward the courthouse. It was time to leave.

"Let's get out of here, Levi."

"Yassa, Massa Jon."

The bounder wagon left town at a run, heading north. Levi had to slow the team to a quick gait before they gave in. Jon figured it to be about a half hour, when they heard the boom of the ship's gun. He thought he heard rifle fire, but there was no mistaking the big gun when it fired. The road was now in good shape, and soon even the boom of the ship's gun grew faint. Jon was relieved, and had Levi slow the team to a steady trot. It was getting to be dusk when they caught up to the cuffee wagon parked along the road.

"We still have an hour or so to travel, Charles. Let's keep them going."

"Why? What happened back there?"

"The slave ship is attacking the town."

"Wow! We got ourselves involved in a slave war!"

"Well, let's get ourselves disinvolved. Get on board, gang. We're traveling until dark."

"Yassa, Massa Jon."

The wagons rolled well into the night. When they finally camped, they ate cold meat and bread, and Jon placed two Toms on night watch. Nothing happened.

The next morning, a sunny Monday, the bounders were on their way north bright and early. They were making good time when they spotted Pattyrollers. They looked like the same ones they had seen on the way south to Jon, the same ones he hid Tad from. The gang cringed in fear, and Jon didn't know what to do. He decided the only thing was just stay calm, as the Pattyrollers rode up to the wagon.

"You're the gang that went to Chic Wood."

"Yes, you have a fine memory."

"That's what we're paid for. Did you get all your replanting finished already?"

"Sure did, and we're headed back to North Carolina."

"Good for you. We're headed to Georgetown to guard some slaves," said the Pattyrollers' leader.

Another of those familiar pangs hit Jon in the stomach. He wondered what they knew.

"They wouldn't be just brought in on a ship, would they?"

"Why yes. Did you see them?"

Jon had that sweaty feeling. He may have spoken out of turn. *Why would they be headed to guard the illegal slaves? They were already in a stockade being guarded*, he thought. Something was weird. "They're already in a stockade in town," he said.

"What? How did they get there?"

Jon decided he would tell them the short story. He told the Pattyrollers about bringing the slaves ashore. He left out the fact that he knew the imports were illegal. He also related the story about the big battle with the smugglers, and how the Pattyrollers had taken the ship's captain and the two smugglers into Georgetown.

"Those weren't Pattyrollers, sir. They were government agents trying to stop the imports."

"Wow, this is really involved," said Charles.

The puzzle was now taking shape to Jon. He had made a big mistake thinking Chris and his men in town were Pattyrollers. They were government agents. These rollers were going to take the new slaves and auction them illegally. They were in cahoots with the ship's captain and his smugglers. Jon figured he'd better not tell these rollers about the captain's threat or the attack on Georgetown. The Pattyrollers headed for Georgetown at a gallop.

"Get these wagons rolling, Levi."

"Yassa, Massa Jon."

It was still a day and a half to Cheraw, but Jon had the feeling that this episode wasn't over, and wished he were in Cheraw now. He urged Levi to keep a quick pace. The road was now in good shape, and the teams were making good time, but not good enough for Jon.

Jon hoped those government agents were able to repel the attack. Otherwise, that captain and the rollers would be back, and after *him*.

"Why are you in such a hurry, Jon?"

"I'm worried those rollers will be back after us, Charles, for helping the government agents!" Jon shouted back over the noise of the heavy cuffee wagon.

"Maybe we should ditch one of these wagons."

"Yeah," yelled Jon, "I wish we had an extra horse."

"What for?" came the holler from the rumble seat.

"So one of us can watch for them and warn us when they appear."

"We don't want them to get that close! Let's ditch this wagon, Jon."

As the wagons rolled down the road, Jon thought about his predicament, and Charles's suggestion. He cracked his whip to try to get close enough to Levi and the lead wagon. Levi saw him, and slowed enough for Jon to pull alongside him.

"Can you harness both teams to that wagon, Levi?" shouted Jon.

"Yassa, I's can, Massa Jon."

"Good. When we get to those trees up there ahead, pull over."

"Yassa, Massa Jon."

Levi stopped at a large cluster of trees, which hid the Pee Dee River, and Jon pulled up behind.

"Jobe, help Levi hook this team up with the other. Toby! You, Skeets, and Tad pull this wagon through these trees down by the river."

"We don't have to go all the way down to the river, Jon," said Charles.

"Well, it will be good if Master Sam, in the cuffee boat, spots it tomorrow. He'll know then that we've had some trouble."

"Good idea. I'll help with the wagon."

"Thanks, Charles. Wilma, you women grab those tools and pile them in the cuffee wagon when the men get it down to the river."

"Yassa, Massa Jon."

The three bounders and Charles managed to push and pull the heavy cuffee wagon back and forth through the trees, and down to the river. The Nans were close behind with the tools, and piled them into the cuffee. Jon cleaned and covered tracks, so nothing would be noticed from the road.

"Hurry up, gang. Get into this wagon, and let's cut out. I'll ride back here with my gang."

"Right, Jon. I'll get up front with Levi."

Levi had cleverly used rope to hitch the cuffee team to the lead so they could pull evenly. The two teams easily opened up a quick gait.

"I think I know how to lose those Pattyrollers, Jon, if they are following," yelled Charles.

"How's that, Charles?"

"We can cross the river and head northeast to the town of Elizabethtown, in North Carolina."

"How far is that?"

"Oh, probably about forty to fifty miles. Then we could head west on the road to Charlotte."

"Sounds pretty good, Charles, but I would really like to know if they are following."

"Well then, we can still cross the river and continue northwest for a while. We can still head north later, and catch that Charlotte road."

"Okay. Levi, keep an eye out for a good spot to cross the river."

"Yassa, Massa Jon."

The bounder wagon rolled along for miles, along a swift, deep-looking river. At last they spotted a wide spot where the river looked much shallower, and rolled down the bank. The lead horses were soon up to their bellies in water.

"The river is deeper here than it looks."

"Right, and we would have a hell of a time getting back up the bank to the road."

"We have a couple of axes, Jon. Let's strap logs to the wheels."

"Okay. Toby, Skeeter, grab those axes, and let's cut a couple of logs."

"Yassa, Massa Jon."

Jon spotted a downed tree close by, and put the Toms to work, cutting two logs about eight feet long each. The logs were tied at the tops of the wagon wheels. The heavy load of bounders and overseers sank the logs, but they helped the wagon float, the water slopping at the wagon's rails, just enough for the bounders to get their feet wet. The two teams swam well together, and pulled the wagon across the Pee Dee. With the logs freed, the two teams faced heavy brush and spotty clumps of trees. Jon searched for a large clump, and Levi pulled behind it.

"Gather some branches and cover the wagon."

"Yassa, Massa Jon."

The bounders scattered and soon had the wagon hidden. Jon kept an eye on Toby, but he worked right along with the others with no escape attempt. The group was about one hundred yards from the river, and Jon hoped they were hidden enough from the road across the river.

"Okay, let's get behind the wagon and have lunch."

"Yassa, Massa Jon, we's hungry."

Again, nothing happened, and Jon began to wonder if he had ditched the cuffee and took all those precautions for nothing. It was late afternoon, and Jon decided to continue further, close to the river. It was rough travel, and Toby and Jobia walked ahead with axes and partially cleared roadway for the teams. Soon it was becoming dusk, and Jon found another good clump of trees and decided to camp for the night. Again, he instructed the gang to hide the wagon and themselves. This time, he was glad he had. The gang had just finished cold dodgers, when they heard the horses pounding up the road. Jon counted at least a dozen mounted men, galloping toward Cheraw. It was too dark to recognize any of them.

"Did you recognize any of them, Charles?"

"No, but you were right. I'm sure they are after us."

"Yes, and when they don't find us in Cheraw, they'll be back, searching the river."

"Well, we'll just have to be long gone. It's not too late for the border."

"They won't reach Cheraw until late tomorrow, so if we get an early start, we can get to the border ahead of them. But will they stop at the border?"

"I'm not sure, Jon, but we don't want to be that close to find out."

"Do you have a suggestion?"

"We can leave now and run all night, and head straight for Raleigh."

"Will we be safe in Raleigh? What's there?"

"The capital and the Carolina Militia, and my family and friends," answered Charles.

"Can we travel in this brush in the dark?"

"We can try. We should hit farms soon. I'm surprised this brush isn't farmland."

"Okay. Levi, harness up the horses again. Skeets, find some sticks for torches."

"Yassa, Massa Jon."

"I'm not sure torches are a good idea, Jon."

"Well, they're far enough away now that we can use them for a while. You women tear the bottoms of your dresses to make torches. Tad, you and Toby take each wheel off the wagon and take some grease. Jobe, you help Levi."

"Yassa, Massa Jon."

Charles found a heavy branch to jack each wheel off the ground, one at a time, so the Toms could get some grease from each wheel housing. The gang quickly and expertly made six torches.

"We're ready, gang. Levi, you drive. Women, man the torches, and Tad and Jobe, take the axes and clear the trail. The rest of us will walk."

"Yassa, Massa Jon."

The movement was very slow, but steady, in a northerly direction. A partial moon also helped, and soon, as Charles had predicted, the brush turned into farmland. Now the gang had to try to dodge rows of corn and, in several cases, fence lines. The torches burned out after a couple of hours, but the gang trudged on by the light of the moon.

It was difficult for Jon to judge, but he was sure that by the first rays of dawn, the gang had traveled between twenty and thirty miles. Everyone was exhausted, so Jon called a halt.

"We'll eat what's left of the dodgers, and try to nap for an hour or so."

"Yassa, Massa Jon."

The dodgers were gone and bounders sleeping in very short order, but Jon was worried and couldn't sleep. He walked a ways back, from whence he had just come, and found a place where he could see across a vast cornfield trampled by his gang. There he sat, and watched. No signs of life appeared, and Jon felt like letting his bounders sleep. But something told him to get moving, and he woke up his gang and got them staggering north again. The going was too slow to satisfy Jon, as Levi tried to dodge rows of corn. He kept a steady eye behind them. He spotted them coming over a long, sloping Piedmont hill, probably a couple miles away.

"Levi! Get them horses running!"

"Yassa, Massa Jon."

"They won't last long, Jon. Do you see them?"

"Yes, they're back there."

"Then they didn't go all the way to Cheraw."

"Brilliant! Hand me that extra rifle."

"I'm coming back with both rifles, Jon."

"I's can helps, Massa Jon?"

"Thanks, Tad, but we only have two rifles."

"Maybe he can help reload, Jon," said Charles, working his way to the back of the bouncing wagon. Over the next rolling hill, Jon could see them clearly. They were gaining fast. Another hill, and they would be in firing range.

"So will we," Jon mumbled. "Faster, Levi!"

"They're at a full gallop now, Jon. They won't last much longer."

"How close are we to the border?"

"We should be close, but I'm not sure."

As the bounder wagon crested the next Piedmont hill, Jon saw the puff of smoke, then another, as the Pattyrollers fired their rifles. He wasn't sure where the balls hit, and Jon was sure it would be just as difficult to hit a target while riding on horseback as it would be from a moving wagon. Jon decided he wouldn't waste any lead now and would wait until the Pattyrollers were closer.

Bam! The sound came from next to Jon.

"You're wasting balls, Charles. Wait."

"I think you're right, Jon."

The front wheel on the right started squealing as the wagon lost sight of the chasers, rolling recklessly down the long-sloping cornfield.

"What a time for a wheel to go out."

"Well, I guess we could expect it, Charles. We took a lot of grease out to make those torches."

"I suppose it doesn't matter. Our teams are tiring fast. They probably won't make that next hill."

As the Pattyrollers topped the hill behind the bounders, they again started shooting. *Bam!* Jon's rifle had a kick, he found out, as it thumped at his shoulder. His ball missed everything, but he felt the wood shavings hit him. One of the balls fired at him had hit the wagon's rail.

"That was close!" Jon yelled at Charles, who fired back at the horsemen, now about one hundred yards behind. The overseers quickly reloaded. The wagon started up the next hill, and Jon noticed it slowing. The horses were giving out. As they neared the top of the hill, the front wheel fell off, and the wagon dragged to a stop, almost spilling out the bounders and overseers, who all scrambled to the front of the teams. Jon tried to push the back of the wagon around, to use as a shelter from the coming rifle balls. Charles and Levi helped, and they laid the wagon on its side.

"Levi, Tad! I'm going to have to trust you. Take the gang over the hill and down the other side, and wait. When you see Charles and I coming, keep running north ahead of us."

"Yassa, Massa Jon."

"Can you take the horses too?"

"Yassa, Massa Jon."

As the bounders scrambled over the hill, the Pattyrollers reached the bottom of Jon's hill directly below them, and dismounted. There was no place for them to hide, so they spread out on the ground. Jon recognized the captain of the slave ship, along with a man wearing a blue-and-white striped short-sleeved shirt. *That man must be one of the ship's hands*, Jon thought. He recognized the leader of the Pattyrollers, who yelled out instructions.

"Throw out your rifles and come out. We won't fire at you."

"What do you want with us!"

"Y'all cost me three of my men!" hollered the captain. "And I aim to take y'all's niggers in return, and kill y'all too."

"And I lost one of my men too," said the leader of the Pattyrollers.

"You mean you lost three smugglers, Captain."

"That's none o' yer business, boy. I'd a lost none if'n ya'll hadn't butted in."

"I'm sorry about your losses, but you ain't getting any of my gang!" hollered Jon.

"We're in North Carolina. Leave us be!" shouted Charles, from behind the bounder wagon.

"Y'all don't know that. Yer justa hopin' we'll turn back."

During all the talking, most men on both sides had reloaded their rifles.

"Come on out, or we'll shoot," said the Pattyrollers' leader.

"Go to hell! We ain't givin' up, and you ain't gettin' our bounders!" answered Jon.

"What are you, a couple of abolitionists?" asked the captain.

"What the hell is a bounder?" asked another.

"Hell, they're doughfaces!" shouted yet another.

"They're probably quadroons. Shoot them!" yelled the leader of the Pattyrollers. Jon heard some laughter, as the shots rang out at him. He and Charles cowered low behind the wagon, as the balls tore through the planking.

"I'll fire first, then you shoot while I'm reloading, Jon."

"Right, go ahead."

Bam! Charles's rifle barked. Jon peeked around the corner of the wagon, and saw one man fall as others fired at the overseers. The balls smashed the wagon, and Jon heard his buddy yelp. He turned to see a ball had penetrated the wagon and had torn into Charles's thigh.

"Are you alright, Charles?"

"Yeah. I got one. Shoot the bastards!" Charles answered as he reloaded.

Jon peeked again, and saw a smuggler getting to his feet. Jon aimed and fired. The man went down in a heap. Jon ducked back behind the wagon. That pang came back, and Jon began to shake as he reloaded his rifle. "I killed a man," he muttered. He was having trouble ramming the powder and ball down the barrel, and his eyes teared up. He was breathing hard. Charles rose up on his knees and fired. He noticed Jon's shaking and tears.

"It was either him or you, Jon. You had to kill him. Don't stop now, or they'll kill us both."

Jon stretched back around the corner and fired again. He wasn't sure if he hit anything.

"Reload, Jon. They're starting to rush us." Charles fired again, and Jon saw a roller roll down the slight incline and lay still. "Come on, Jon," Charles said, "it's your turn."

Jon hoped he had the ball tamped hard enough, as his shaking hands placed the cap over the firing pin. He looked again, and six men were charging up the hill. He had to stop them, he thought. He aimed at the leader of the Pattyrollers and fired. The leader stopped his charge and fell backward down the hill. The others hit the ground and fired. As Jon was thinking that was two he killed, a sudden pain shot through his shoulder. He could still use it, and he temporarily ignored the blood and poured more powder down the barrel as Charles again rose up and fired. Jon replaced the cap and looked around the corner. The shaking and tears had ended, and Jon was determined to win this battle. Charles was right. If he didn't get them, they would get him, he reasoned. Jon then saw four men running back toward their horses. The captain was yelling at them, trying to stop them, to no avail.

Jon stood up from his shelter, and a sense of pride now flooded him. He hardly noticed the captain pull a pistol from his coat and aim it at him. It made a puff as the tiny ball tore into Jon's right side. Jon fell back to the ground, as Charles rose up to fire. "No, Charles. I want him."

Jon tried to get up, and found that he had to be helped by Charles. The captain was now running toward his horse. Jon took slow aim and fired. The captain landed on his face, slowly rolled over, and tried to sit up. The four mounted men headed south on the run, as the captain raised up on one arm, staring at the overseers.

"At least y'all lost yer niggers!" he yelled.

"We don't have any niggers, Captain," Jon answered. "My gang of bounders are just over this hill."

"Yeah, sure. Y'all ain't got them trained that well."

"Levi! Can you hear me?" Jon yelled up the hill.

"Yassa, Massa Jon!" came the answer.

"Did you hear that, Captain? They're just over the hill."

The captain didn't answer. He settled back down on his back. He saw the people running over the hill toward the two wounded overseers. They weren't slaves. They were North Carolina farmers, running toward the sounds of battle. A couple carried rifles.

"Help me!" called the captain, as the farmers reached the overseers. They were stunned at the scene. Five men lay at the bottom of the hill, and all looked dead except for the one hollering for help. Charles was helping to keep Jon propped up against the wagon with the broken wheel and rifle holes.

"What happened?" asked one.

"Those are slave smugglers and South Carolina Pattyrollers, aiming to kill us and steal our slaves," answered Charles.

"By the looks of you two, they almost succeeded," said another.

They all heard the commotion over the hill, and wondered what was happening.

"Joe, you and Walt go round up the slaves and bring them to the house. We'll feed them," said the leader. "The rest of you help these men to the house, and get them patched up. Jeff, give me a hand getting that wounded man down there to the house. Looks like your wagon is fixable, mister. We'll get it repaired tomorrow."

One man left on the run in the same direction he came from. "I'll get a wagon," he said.

Joe and Walt headed over the hill, rifles in hand.

"Thank you, sir. This is Charles, and I'm Jonathan. We're overseers for the Bethania Plantation by Salem."

"Salem? What the hell brings you all the way over here?"

"We were on a plantation close to Georgetown, replanting their rice and cotton crops," answered Charles.

"They were washed out by the storm," said Jon.

"Yes, we had a lot of damage to our corn crops here, mostly hail. Looks like we'll lose a lot."

"I'm sorry about all the damage we did to your corn crops, sir."

"Well, don't worry about it. We'll take care of it."

"Thank you, sir."

"The name is Samuel, and this is Jeff."

"Samuel? That's the name of the owner of Bethania, Samuel McAllister. Have you heard of him?"

"Yeah, I think everyone has heard of him! Come on, Jeff, let's go get that man."

"He is the captain of a smuggler ship," said Charles. "He brings slaves in from the West Indies, and auctions them in Georgetown and Charlestown."

"And you have some of his smuggled slaves?"

"Oh, no sir, Sam. These are all my gang from Bethania," answered Jon.

Just then, shots rang out from over the hill.

"My gang!" shouted Jon. He tried to walk but fell, and was grabbed by Charles. Levi came running over the hill.

"Massa Jon! Massa Jon!"

"What's happening, Levi?"

"Massa Jon. Toby runs again, an's those men shoots him."

"Oh no! Is he dead?"

"Yessa, I's thinks so, Massa Jon."

As three people tried to stop the bleeding of Charles and him, tears welled in Jon's eyes and ran down his cheeks. He thought about Toby, and if he had been fair with the bounder. *Toby was such a good worker and helper when he wanted to be*, Jon thought. Jon had been the overseer of gang twelve for only three months, and had already lost three of his gang. What was he doing wrong? Maybe he should have stayed home with Andy, and never applied for this job, he reflected. This thought brought more tears, and Jon tried to rub his eyes.

"Does it hurt a lot?" Jon looked up to at the only woman of the group that came running. She had a serious but pretty face, with brown hair and eyes. Jon saw tears welling in her eyes as well.

"No, ma'am, not much. I'm just worried about my gang. I've lost two on this trip."

"Well, don't worry about them, Jonathan. We'll take good care of them. Worry about yourself. This is a pretty deep wound on your side."

"What about my shoulder?"

"It's alright, only a surface wound."

"How is Charles doing?"

"He'll be fine," said another man, "but the ball is still in his leg and will need to be removed."

Before long, the wagon appeared, and the captain. Charles and Jon were carefully placed aboard. Jon finally got the chance to study the man who wanted to kill him. He had a tanned and weathered face, and gray hair. He was a stout man with large hands, and he looked more dead than alive except for occasional gasps of air. Jon wished that he would have let Charles shoot him, so he wouldn't feel guilty. Tears again ran down his cheeks. He had made a mess of things, and in so doing, he had killed for the first time, lost Toby, and gotten Charles and himself wounded.

"Everything will be alright, Jonathan," said the woman. "Just lay back and relax."

"Thank you, ma'am. I guess I'm worried about my gang. I'm to blame for Toby's death."

"No, you're not. He ran away."

"But he wouldn't have even been here if it weren't for me."

"Well, look at it this way, Jonathan. His days as a slave are over, and he is finally at peace."

As the wagon rounded the hill, Jon saw his gang being herded at rifle point toward the house. They were weeping and singing a familiar song.

> *"Sisters don' gets weary*
> *An' bruders sad no mo.*
> *We's will see our bruder Toby*
> *When we's gets to Canaan's shore*

Cora came running to the wagon. "Massa Jon, you's hurt," she said, teary eyed.

"I'll be fine, Cora. Tell the gang not to worry. The danger is over, and we'll be headed back home soon."

"I's tells 'em, Massa Jon."

"Thanks, Cora," Jon said. "You there!" he yelled. "You don't have to point the rifle at my gang. They won't run."

"One already has!" one of the men holding his gang at rifle point yelled back.

"We don't want to chase them all over the country," said the other rifle holder.

"I promise you won't have to."

The two men, Joe and Walt, lowered their rifles. Jon settled back. At the house, the bounders were led into a separate building.

"I'll stay in that building with my gang."

"No, you won't," said the woman. "You are badly injured, and I'm taking care of you. Your gang will be fine with our few slaves."

Indeed, they were fine. Charles and Jon were treated like kings. The woman spread a salve over their wounds and dressed them after skillfully cutting the ball out of Charles's leg. The salve stung like hell for a few minutes, and then all the pain disappeared.

"What is that stuff you're putting on our wounds?"

"It's a horse liniment, Jon."

"Horse liniment?" repeated Charles.

"That's right. We use it all the time on open wounds. It heals them up fast, you'll see."

Next came a large meal. The master and mistress, Sam and Amy Lowell, sat at the ends of the large dining table, which seated ten and was full. Next to Sam sat a young lady, very prim and proper. Jon later learned that she was the Lowells' daughter. Charles hobbled to the table next to the daughter. On the other side of Charles sat Joe and Walt. The other side of the table had Jeff and a man Jon didn't recognize, then the woman, who helped Jon eat. He sat next to the master.

"Don't worry about your gang, Jonathan. We feed them the same meal we eat," said Sam.

"Thank you, sir. I appreciate that."

"We can put you and Charles in our guest room."

"I'm going to sit with Jon overnight in my room, Sam," said the woman.

"Well, alright. You get the special treatment, Jon."

"Thanks, but I don't deserve it."

"Why not?"

"He feels he's to blame for his slave getting killed," the woman said.

"That's nonsense, Jon. If I know you, you did all you could to protect them."

There's that word again! He even sounds like my master, thought Jon. "Thank you, Sam."

The evening raced by quickly, as Sam's people were all ears listening to Jon's story. Charles turned in early, and by the time Jon got up the stairs, he was wishing he had been assigned the guest room too. He got lots of help climbing the stairs, and with the removal of his trousers, which embarrassed him to no end. The woman wasn't a bit ill-at-ease, Jon could see, as she poured some liquid down his throat that tasted bitter and bad. He had a tough time keeping it down.

"What is that?" he asked.

"Calomel. Want some more?"

"Not a chance. So that's what it tastes like."

"Well, here. Try some of this." This was a yellow-tinted, almost-clear, liquid, which burned all the way down. He had another tough time keeping it down.

"Wow, what was that?"

"You mean you've never tasted corn liquor?"

"Yes, I have, but it didn't taste like that!"

"It's good for you, Jon. It will take away all your pains and help you sleep."

"I'm too numb to be in pain."

"Good. Just rest a while. I'll get you another drink." The second drink went down the hatch a little better. Jon was feeling very light and lazy, and content. He thought he had never felt more comfortable. From the slave house, he heard his gang singing. It made him all warm and nice.

> "We's raise de cotton,
> Dey gib us de corn.
> We's bakes de breads,
> Dey gib us de cruss.
> We's siff de meals,
> Dey gib us de huss.
> We's peel de meats,
> Dey gib us de skin.
> An' dats de ways
> Dey take us in."

Jon was in a sort of peaceful rest, when he noticed the woman removing her clothes. His senses came alive in a hurry.

"What are you doing, ma'am?"

"I'm tired, Jon. There's room for both of us, and I want to take good care of you."

"You're taking too much care of me. Give me my trousers, and I'll let you have your bed back."

Jon found himself staring at her. He brown hair was curly, and hung almost to the very noticeable blades of her back, past small shoulders. She was thin to the waist, but wide at the hips. His eyes focused for a minute to the area between her legs, hidden from view by a thick patch of brown hair. She hadn't bothered to dim or extinguish the lantern, and Jon next gazed at her bosom, perfectly matched, and sagging just enough to be appealing to him. Hell, by now anything was appealing! He was horny.

"Don't worry about your trousers, Jonny. They'll be here for you in the morning. Just relax, and let yourself go." She was climbing in bed beside him, and Jon wasn't sure what to do.

"I'll let myself go, alright." He pushed the covers down a ways, but was afraid to expose his prong horn, which was now very stiff and uncomfortable. He stuck his leg out of the cover, and tried to get up. Too late!

"Please try to relax, Jonny." She reached across him and pulled his leg back. Her arm, then hand, touched him, and she reached under his unmentionables and took hold of his manhood. "Mmm. You're ready for me, Jonny."

She stretched her body gently across his, never taking her hand off him. She started kissing him, and Jon found himself kissing back. Now her hand let go of him just long enough for her to place his hand on her breast, and she quickly returned to rubbing, and then pumping his blue veiner. He quickly started feeling that same urge he'd felt before, with Cora, and he tried to hold back but couldn't. In a pistonlike fashion, he started shooting off. She cupped her hand, then the other over the head, and captured most of it. Nimbly, she jumped out of bed and walked to the pitcher set on her dresser. In a minute, she was back with a towel, wet on one end, and pulled the cover back. She washed, then wiped him dry, along with a couple of spots on the cover. She quickly disposed of the towel, and was back beside him, her hand back to pumping. He was still long and hard, and now he was doing his own exploring. She lay back and opened wide for him, not letting go of him. Jon started moaning and jerking, having trouble with his breathing.

"You just lay still, Jonny. I'll get on top."

"I don't even know your name," he said, as she expertly climbed over him and guided him into her. His words brought a chuckle from her.

"That's right. I'm Virginia, and not a virgin."

"Glad to meet you, Virginia. I'm Jonathan, and I am a virgin."

"Not for long, Jonny." She raised, then lowered herself onto him, muscles inside her clamping around him. It took only three or four of these exercises, and the urge was back. He wrapped his arms around her waist and pulled her down on him, and again unloaded. She kissed him and raised herself off him. He was still hard.

"I'll be right back," she whispered.

It was the same routine again, and the third time was a charm. They were both happy and satisfied, and kissed, hugged, and touched well into the night. Jon was sound asleep when Virginia snuffed out the lantern and dozed off, wrapped in his arms. Sometime in the middle of the night, Jon felt Ginny's hand playing with him again. He played back, and the two experts made love once more. Jon woke late in the morning, and a feeling of supremacy enveloped him. He had become a man. He tried to get up, but hurt too much in other places as well as his side. He lay there for what seemed a long time, before a knock came at the door. Jon made sure he was covered before he answered.

"Come in."

A house servant entered, carrying a pitcher set. She had a big smile on her face as she poured water into the bowl. "Good mornin', sir."

"Good morning," Jon replied, wondering how much she knew. As she left with her broad smile, Virginia appeared with breakfast and another smile.

"Good morning, lover. Hungry?"

"Bet your bustle I'm hungry."

"Haven't you noticed? I don't need a bustle."

"You don't need anything, baby. You've got it all."

"Thank you, Jonny."

"Thank *you*, my sweet nonvirgin."

"You're the nonvirgin now. I've been a nonvirgin for many years."

"How many?"

"Does it matter, Jonny?"

"Not really, baby, just wondering."

"Well, how old are you, Jonny?"

"I'll be twenty in July."

Ginny sat down on the side of the bed and laughed.

"What's funny?"

"I've been a nonvirgin since before you were born, lover." They both started laughing.

"Well, baby, experience is the best teacher."

She hugged and kissed him, and then helped prop him up for breakfast, after which she cleaned his right side. She was amazed at how quickly he healed.

"The shoulder is already scabbing, and the wound on the side has dried up."

"Good. Then I can leave for Salem soon."

"In a few days, maybe. Are you anxious?"

"Not to leave you, but I have an obligation to get my gang back to work."

"You go through that answer very smoothly."

"Thank you, baby. I wonder just what my gang is doing today."

"I think some of them went out to help replant corn with our servants."

"Smashing idea. How is Charles doing?"

"He is well. Probably out with your gang."

"Good. And the captain?"

"He died overnight. Jeff is taking his body to Raleigh today to turn him over to the authorities."

Strangely, Jon had no feelings about this. His mind turned to Toby, and another feeling of sorrow came over him. Ginny seemed to read his mind.

"Your gang buried him early this morning."

"I should have been there."

"It's alright, Jonny. They understood."

In place of remorse, Jon now had a feeling of not being needed. His bounders buried Toby, and were now planting corn without his direction. He finished his breakfast, and the two of them talked.

"Thank you for last night, Virginia."

"We'll have to do it again, lover."

"How about right now?"

Ginny laughed at this. "You are anxious."

"No hurry. You've got one minute to decide."

She laughed again, and lay down beside him. "We better not now, Jonny. Too many people running in and out. We'll do it again tonight."

"Smashing, baby. This time, I'm getting on top."

"I was surprised that you were still a virgin with all those wenches in your gang."

"Just bashful, I suppose."

"Oh sure, Jonny, you're really bashful."

They both laughed, and copped a few hugs and feels before Virginia left. He was alone again, with all his many mixed feelings, all day, but not all night.

The next morning, Jon was up early, and dressed all by himself. He descended the stairs slowly and joined the Lowell household for breakfast.

"Hello, everybody. Anything left to eat?"

"Well, hello, Jon. How are you feeling?"

"Very well, thank you, Master Sam."

"You look well. Ginny must be treating you well."

"Yes sir, she sure is. That horse liniment really works. I'm almost healed," Jon said sheepishly.

"Good. Come sit. There's plenty of food."

"Thank you, sir. I'm hungry as a bear."

"Well, thank you for your gang's help with replanting my cornfields."

"I hope it will at least partly pay you for all you're doing for Charles and me."

"Speaking of Charles, his leg is all scabbed over, and he is out overseeing your gang."

"That's where I'm headed too."

"Be careful with your side, Jon. I think you're pushing it too fast."

"Much too fast! Jonny, you'll open that would back up. Please get back to bed," Virginia said, entering the dining room.

"Yes, ma'am I will, for one more day. I want to finish this breakfast first."

"Good. I'll be up to redress your side when I finish my breakfast."

"Tomorrow I want to get out with my gang, and hopefully finish the replanting. I've got to get back to Salem."

"You're welcome to stay here as long as you like. It's important that you get well."

"Thank you, Master Sam, but I'm worried about how my Master Sam will take all the losses I've caused on this trip."

"You mean that slave that tried to escape?"

"Yes, and the other one who died of food poisoning, and the loss of the cuffee wagon and farm tools, and even the loss of several work days."

"I sent two men this morning to find your cuffee wagon, and try to get it to the Johnstone Plantation in Salisbury."

"Thank you, Master Sam. That will help relieve part of my worries."

"Good. Now get back to bed," ordered Virginia.

"Yes, ma'am. I'm on my way for one more day."

The next three days of sun-soaking, overseeing gang twelve, love and care from Ginny, and good food and rest worked wonders on Jonathan's health. He was thinking about starting back to Bethania by the weekend. The Lowells' corn had been replanted, holes plugged, and the wagon had new paint. Charles wanted to visit his family in Raleigh before the return to Salem.

"This is Friday, Jon. If I leave now, I can meet you late Monday in Fayetteville."

"Okay, Charles. Take one of team nine's horses. I'll bring the other, and meet you on Monday."

"Thanks. When you head north, you'll run into the road back to Cheraw. Turn right to Elizabethtown, then north to Fayetteville."

"How far is that from here?"

"Probably about two days."

"Okay, I'll need to leave here early Sunday to meet you in Fayetteville late Monday."

"Good. There's a good road from there, west to Salisbury. We'll take it Tuesday morning. See you Monday evening."

Charles thanked the Lowells and was on his way. Saturday night, Jonathan and Virginia made love for the last time. Jon didn't want it to end.

"I love you, Ginny. Come with me tomorrow. We can get married in Fayetteville, and live together at Bethania."

"Shhh, don't be silly, Jonny. It's not me you love. It's the lovemaking. If I know you, you won't be without it very long."

"Is that a no?"

"Yes, it's a no. I'm much too old for you, Jonny. You would tire of me soon, then I would be a burden for you. I'll never forget you, though."

"I'll never forget you either. I want to thank you for all you've taught me."

"Good, then lock the jaw and practice what you've learned."

"Alright, you asked for it."

Sunday morning, May seventeen, Jonathan and his gang twelve had breakfast before dawn and were ready to leave as the sun lit the Lowell farm. All the farm's hands lined up to say farewell. Jonathan thanked each one, and hugged Virginia closely.

"You sure you won't change your mind, darling?"

"Yes, Jonny. You made me feel young again when you asked, but this is where I want to stay."

"Then maybe I'll quit my job at Bethania and come back here to live."

"No, Jonny. I don't think that would be a very good idea. Just remember me as your first conquest."

"I'll always remember you. You taught me well. Thanks for all you've done for me."

"Bye, Jonny. Have a great life, lover."

With that, gang twelve was headed north. Before midday, they came upon east-west road. Jon was about to turn west, when Levi reminded him that it went back to South Carolina. They turned east, and eventually saw Elizabethtown, a pretty little town that still had several log homes. They camped there that night, along the Cape Fear River. Early Monday found gang twelve trudging north toward Fayetteville on good road. It was noontime when they saw some Pattyrollers. The gang was terrified, but Jon told them to keep calm.

"Hello there. Where are y'all headed?"

"To Fayetteville, then west to Salem."

"Well, you're a long ways from home. Did y'all come from Wilmington?"

"No, sir. We've been a month and a half replanting rice fields in South Carolina."

"You weren't in Georgetown, were you?"

Jon wondered just how to answer that question. "We passed through it."

"Did y'all see the damage?"

"Yes, we saw some. That storm really hit hard."

"I weren't talking about the storm. You must have seen the battle damage."

"What battle?" Jon asked timidly.

"Y'all ain't heard of the Battle of Georgetown?"

"No, sir. What battle was that?"

"Well, Jackson sent two frigates and militia from Washington, and they drove out the Pattyrollers who were smuggling in slaves from the West Indies."

"The hell! When did that happen?"

"A little less than a week ago. Are you sure you didn't see anything in Georgetown? How long ago did y'all pass through there?"

Jon had to think up an answer fast. The Pattyroller was getting suspicious. If gang twelve had come by road, they must have seen something. "A month and a half ago. We came back cross-country, and missed any towns," he lied.

"Oh, that answers it. Well, y'all would make a lot better time on the roads. At Fayetteville, y'all can catch a good road west to Charlotte."

"Thanks. We'll take that one."

"You're welcome. I notice you got no chains on your slaves. Ain't you worried about losing 'em?"

"No, sir. I have a happy gang that knows when they're well off."

"That's good. A lot of 'em escaped in South Carolina during that storm. Some were never caught."

"Huh! Didn't see any of them, or I'd have had me an addition to my gang."

"He wouldn't a been worth much, and you'd a had to use some chains and whips on him. Well, good luck to y'all. You're looking at four more days to Salem."

"Thanks, be seeing you."

Levi slapped the lead, and the wagon rolled north. Jon felt relief, as did his gang, who watched the Pattyrollers head south toward Elizabethtown. It was late afternoon when they reached the thriving town of Fayetteville, recently named after the French hero of the Revolution, Marquis DeLafayette. Charles was nowhere in sight, so gang twelve camped at the edge of town along the road to Charlotte.

Charles appeared late, accompanied by three men in a wagon. They were government agents from Raleigh, who were headed to the Lowell farm to collect evidence and bodies from the gunfight involving Jon and Charles. They seemed satisfied with Jon's answers to their questions, and headed south.

As he settled in for the night, Jon finally felt that the incidents of South Carolina were behind him. He thought about Vera and Toby. A pang of sadness hit him. His thoughts then went to Chic Wood, and he felt a little better. But the battle at the Lowell farm brought the pangs back, much stronger. Jon had never even shot at, let alone killed anyone before. But the pangs disappeared completely when his thoughts focused on Virginia. A smile crossed Jon's face as sleep overwhelmed him. This trip had made him a complete man.

The smiles and chipper attitude still existed Tuesday morning, as gang twelve raced west, toward home. The May sun felt warm, and the beauty of the low rolling hills of the Piedmont and miles of corn and tobacco stalks reminded the gang of what they were headed home to. In the early afternoon, they found a creek and stopped for lunch and rest. The Toms helped feed and water the two teams of horses. Levi grabbed a bucket and poured water over the wagon wheels. Jonathan had not seen this done before, but he was sure he knew what it was for.

"Were we close to losing a rim, Levi?"

"Yassa, Massa Jon. They's be loose."

"Well, thank you. Help yourself to some dodgers."

"Yassa. Thank you's, Massa Jon."

All seemed well with Jonathan's family. As they polished off some corn dodgers sent along by Master Sam Lowell, they gang broke into some songs, now familiar to Jon.

> *"Works de wheat*
> *Gets de corn . . ."*

"I hate to break up this party, but we need to split, blow away, gang."

"Yassa, Massa Jon."

Jon estimated that his two teams pulled them over fifty miles that day, and after a good sleep and some corn dodgers for breakfast, the two teams were at it again. About midday, they saw horses approaching at a rapid pace. Two pulled up next to the wagon.

"Are you Jon Hamilton and Charles Finley?"

"Yes, we are. Who are you?"

"We were sent by Master Samuel McAllister to find you and escort you to Bethania. We've been looking for you for several days."

"Is Master Sam worried?" asked Charles.

"More like mad, then worried. He thinks you may have disappeared with his slaves."

"He knows better than that," said Jon. "You can go back and tell him we're on our way."

"Can't do that, sir. We don't want him mad at us too. He ordered us not to come back without you."

"Alright. You can put your rifles away and fall in behind us. We don't have any food to spare."

"Amos, you go ahead and get some food, and notify the Johnstones. I'll stay with the gang."

"Right, see you there later." Amos was away.

"How far are we from the Johnstones?"

"About sixty miles or more."

"Good. We'll be there before dark tomorrow. Go, Levi."

"Where have you all been, and how did you get on this road?" asked the stranger.

"It's a long story. We'll explain it later," said Charles, yelling over the sounds of the wagon wheels. "I think maybe we should stop, and rest the horses before too long."

"Good idea. Find another creek if you can, Levi, and we'll wet down the wheels again and camp."

"Yassa, Massa Jon."

No creek was spotted, but Levi pulled off the road at a large patch of grass. The teams were happy. Back on the road about midafternoon, the gang found a river flowing west, and stopped again for a brief period to water the horses and wheels.

"We are close to the fork to Salisbury," said the stranger. "This little river empties into the Yadkin." Sure enough, the wagon soon reached a Y in the road, and a sign with an arrow on it pointed right to Salisbury. The Yadkin River soon appeared on the left, and Jon knew he would have to cross it to get to the Johnstones'. He worried about this for nearly an hour before he came up with a solution, just in time.

"The river looks swift here, Jon. We may have to go all the way to the Trading Ford and come back to Salisbury," said Charles.

"I have a better idea, Charles."

"Good. Let's hear it."

"Levi and I will take the lead team and cross the river here. You take the bounders and the wagon to the Ford, and wait there for me."

"Okay, but be careful. See you at the Trading Ford."

The wagon continued along the road. The bounders waved and yelled goodbye to Massa Jon and Levi, who had unhooked the lead team. They rode bareback along the river, until they spotted a likely spot to cross. Levi had brought along some rope, and cut a twenty-foot length. He then tied each end around a horse's neck.

"Tha's so's we don' get's too fa'apart."

"That's a great idea, Levi."

Levi then tied one end of the remaining fifty or so feet of the rope to a small tree nearby.

"We's use rope to anchor fo' mos' of river, Massa Jon, then we's swim de rest."

"Sounds good to me. Let's give it a go."

The two horses were soon swimming, with the riders hanging on. Levi released rope as they crossed. The hooves of the powerful horses churned forward, keeping ahead of the current, which grudgingly pushed them downstream. All too soon, Levi reached the end of the rope and let it go. The team swam hard. Levi grabbed the rope that connected the two horses, and slid off the dobbin's back. He tried to swim while keeping hold of the rope. This seemed to help his horse surge ahead toward shore, so

Jon did the same. Soon they touched ground under the water, and made their way to shore some seventy or eighty yards downriver from where they started.

"The horses be tired, Massa Jon."

"So am I, Levi, but let's walk them for a while. We should see the Johnstones' place soon."

"Yassa, Massa Jon."

They walked for several minutes. The horses seemed sound, so they rode for several minutes. Soon Jon recognized the forested road leading to the Johnstone Plantation. All were happy to see each other, and Jon asked that the horses be grained and that he and Levi be fed. The hosts had a bundle of questions, which Jon tried to briefly answer. They were amazed at his story, and each answer seemed to bring more questions. They had also heard of the Battle of Georgetown, but hadn't heard about the first battle with the slave ship, or the battle at the Lowell farm. Jon asked for enough food and grain to get his gang all back to Bethania.

"It's being put together right now," said Master Johnstone, "but you will stay the night."

"No, sir. Thanks, but I must get home."

"I understand, Jon Hamilton. Will you please tell Master Sam how sorry I am about the bad food and your slave's death? I will replace her with one of my own if he wishes."

"I'll tell him. Is the cuffee wagon here?"

"Oh, you haven't heard. Some South Carolina Pattyrollers found it, and burned it and the tools."

"Master Sam will be happy to hear that!"

"He probably knows by now. We have been sharing riders, searching for you."

"I wasn't lost, just delayed."

"And you were wounded? Are you alright?"

"Yes. That's what took some time. Both Charles Finley and I had to heal before traveling."

"Good. We're filling a buckboard with supplies, and will hitch your team up so you can be on your way. Anything else I can do for you?"

"You have done plenty. Thank you. My gang is waiting for me at the Trading Ford."

"Alright. There is a man here named Amos. Is he from Bethania?"

"I guess so, sir. He has orders to bring us back. Master Sam thinks we skipped out."

"Will he ever be shocked when he hears your story, Jon."

"Do you have a job for me here, if I get fired?"

"Sure do, Jon. But that won't happen, I'm sure."

"I'm glad you think not. I'm not so sure. I lost two bounders, a wagon and tools, and about a week's production."

"Well, good luck. If you ever need a job, come on back. You'll be welcome here. I heard about you during that hunt for the escaped slaves a couple months ago."

"Thank you, sir. I must be on my way now, but I might be back."

The buckboard was outside, full of provisions, and with Jon's team in harness. Levi and Jon climbed aboard and headed for Salisbury, and the Ford. It was close to total darkness when they, and Amos, crossed the Yadkin and regrouped with Charles and gang twelve. Over the campfire, they ate hearty. Dodgers were filled with meat for a change.

Bright and early Friday morning, they were on the road to Bethania. Levi had harnessed all four horses to the bounder's wagon, and tied the tongue of the buckboard to the rear. Everyone seemed happy to be close to home. Everyone, that was, except Jon. He was certain he would be facing the wrath of Master Samuel McAllister. How would he explain all his losses?

To hell with Master Sam! Jon would just tell it like it happened, he thought, and if he was fired, he'd head right back to the Johnstone Plantation. Jon now felt confident, and ready for the master.

Jonathan felt the wrath that same evening, after Bounder Row and the overseer house had welcomed the gang back home. Master Sam had sent Mose D. on the run to fetch Jon and Charles immediately.

"Start talking and don't leave out anything!"

"Are you going to fire us, sir?" asked Charles.

"I'm thinking about it!" shouted the master. "Unless you can convince me otherwise!"

"I wouldn't blame you if you did, Master Sam."

"What does that mean, boy?"

"I lost two bounders, the cuffee wagon—"

"What? You lost the cuffee wagon?"

"We had to leave it along the Pee Dee River."

"Nonsense! Why would you leave it there?"

That word again. Jon could feel the blood rushing to his face. If the master used that word again, Jon wouldn't wait to be fired, he promised himself. He was about to shout his answer, when Charles spoke up to answer the master's bellowing.

"We were being chased by Pattyrollers."

"That's nonsense!" roared Master Sam.

With that, Jonathan jumped up from his chair and headed for the door. "I quit! I'm tired of *your* nonsense!" he shouted as he exited.

Charles rose up to leave as well. He turned back to face Master Sam when he reached the door. "We'll draw our pay and leave in the morning."

"I haven't fired you yet. Get back here and tell me what happened."

"I'm as much to blame as Jon is. If he leaves, so do I, sir," answered Charles.

Samuel sat down behind his desk for the first time. "Please wait," he pleaded, "I can't afford to lose you both." The fire had left his voice, and the redness drained from his face. "Please come back and tell me what happened."

"I guess we owe you that much, sir. Did you hear about the battle of Georgetown?"

"Yes, I did. Don't tell me you were involved in that!"

"Yes, sir, we were. There were actually about four or five battles, and we were in two of them." Charles watched in amazement as the redness seemed to reappear, then again drain, pits reappearing in Sam's face.

"Start from the beginning, Charles."

Charles Finley proceeded to repeat the adventure. Samuel sat in astonishment as the story unfolded. The smuggled slaves and battle to claim them, the first gun battle in Georgetown, the chase into North Carolina and its ensuing battle, and the wounds he and Jon suffered. He ended with the shooting of Toby and the stay at the Lowell farm.

"Neither of us were able to travel for days."

"Are you both healed now?" asked Samuel.

"I think so, sir."

"If you had not stopped to watch the slaves being smuggled in, none of this would have happened, and you wouldn't have lost any time."

"I guess that's right, sir. Sorry, sir."

"Well, you can take the next few days off."

"I guess you didn't hear me, sir. When Jon quit, so did I."

"To hell with you both, then! You're both fired!"

Charles found Jonathan in his room in the overseer house. He was all packed.

"Did you tell him about our misadventure?"

"I sure did, Jon, and he fired us both."

"Hell, I already quit."

"So did I."

"Well, come along with me back to the Johnstone Plantation."

"The crops are all planted. I'm sure they wouldn't need two new overseers."

"Well, if they don't hire us both, they'll hire none of us."

"Then what?"

"Then we'll head for Mississippi or Alabama."

"You're forgetting that I'm married."

"Oh ya. Then we will go back to Raleigh."

"I told Master Sam we would leave in the morning."

"Good. We'll decide where to go tomorrow."

"Alright. See you in the morning, Jon."

Saturday morning brought more events strange to Jonathan. After saying their goodbyes to Jock McRae and the other overseers present, a commotion was overheard in Bounder's Row. Gangs eleven and twelve were refusing to work. Members of other gangs were also revolting. Fred Nichols had his gang rounded up and headed for the fields, as had B. J. Darby and his gang five. But the others were having trouble. Wilbert Aims was whipping a couple of bounders, as was Andy Androsterone and two other Negro servants. Jock grabbed his snake from his belt, and ran into the melee, shouting.

"Stop this bloody ruffle the now!" he bellowed.

Charles and Jonathan joined in, and the three managed to separate the gangs from the whips. Part of Jon's gang was missing, and he wondered where they were.

"What the bloody hell is a-goin' on?" asked Jock.

"Your gangs refuse to work!" hollered Wilbert at Charles and Jon. "They've even got some of my gang revolting!"

"You whipping them is revolting, Aims!"

"Master Sam say cobs dem tells dey works," said Andy.

"I'm a-sayin' stop the cobbin the now, kin?"

"Yassa, Massa Jock."

Jonathan and Charles started separating their gangs, as did the other overseers.

"Oh, Massa Jon. We's don' wans you's to leave," sobbed Cora, as the gang hugged and circled Jon.

"I don't want to leave, Cora, but I have to."

"But, Massa Jon, Tad an' Skeets, deys goin' ta runs away."

"Where are Tad and Skeets, Cora?"

"Deys un dem racks, Massa Jon. Deys won's work. Nell an' Lucee on dem racks too."

"Andy! Get my bounders off that rack *now*!"

"Yassa, Massa Jon."

"You be a-forgettin' I'm the boss, Jon Henry. I'll be a-doin' the orderin' the now."

"My gang is being punished for something I did, Jock. They had no choice."

"I be a-believin' ye, Jon Henry, but ye be a-lookin' afta a job, and be a-leavin' us soon, so I'll be a-givin' the orders, hear? Andy, be a-gettin' them bounders off the rack!"

"Yassa, but Massa Sam say cob until dey work."

"Will gangs eleven and twelve be a-goin' to work the now, Charles and Jon Henry?"

"We may be able to get them back," said Charles.

"But not until we are sure that they will be treated like humans," responded Jon.

"An' I be a-tellin' ye, they'll be a-treated like all the others be a-treated."

Andy had released the four bounders of gang twelve, and they joined the others beside Jon, when Master Sam came calling to Bounder's Row.

"Lentil! Why aren't these bounders working?"

"I be a-gettin' them out the now, Master Sam."

"Answer my question! They should have been out in the fields a long time ago."

"Yes, sir. They be a-goin' the now, Master Sam."

"And why are these two still here?"

"They be a-gettin' their gangs out to work."

"Nonsense. That's your job. These two aren't working for me, and neither will you if you don't get them moving. I ought to deduct your pay for the time they've missed already."

"Well, I'll be a bloody bugger!" said Lentil McRae, as he shook and lowered his head.

"Just what the hell does that mean?"

"It be a-meanin' that all the sudden I be a-tirin' of this job. Ye were just a boy when I started here, Master Sam, an' I helped yer father build it, an' now I be a-feelin' tired of it all."

"Nonsense! Now get these bounders working or whipped!"

"Yes, sir, I be a-gettin' them a-workin', then I'll be a-packin' my duds, Master Sam."

"What? What do you mean, packing your duds?"

"I be a-quittin'. I be a-havin' enough muck ta go back ta me home in the highlands the now."

"Nonsense. This is your home, Lentil. Why would you want to leave?"

"I'll be a-tellin' ye, Master Sam. In all them years a-workin' for yer father an' you, I ne'er have been a-talked ta like ye just talked ta me, an' I denny like it, and it'll ne'er happen again, hear? So I'm a-thinkin' I'll jest be a-headin' home."

Jonathan watched the master's face turn white, then red, and back again to white. His jaws dropped open as he searched for a response.

"And if Jock leaves, so do I, Master Sam." Jonathan whirled around to see Jerry Pierce, overseer of gang eight. Master Sam began to shake, and Jon wondered if the master might collapse.

"I guess that means me too," said Wilbert Aims.

Jon was sure the master would drop now, and he grabbed Master Sam's arm to steady the shaking. Up close, Jon now detected beads of sweat running through the hair, and tears flooding the eyes. He looked like a weary, defeated old man.

"Please don't leave me, Jock. I don't think Bethania could survive without you," sobbed Sam. Samuel McAllister was now openly sobbing and shaking, and began to buckle at the knees. Jon struggled to hold him upright. Jock seemed to be trying to decide what to do, as he ran his hand through his hair.

"I apologize to you, Jock, and I'll never get dandered at you again. I need you to stay."

"Well, Master Sam, maybe I'll be a-stayin' at least until the crops be a-harvested."

"Thank you, Lentil."

"But I'll be a-needin' all my overseers, an' that'll be includin' Charles and Jon Henry."

The master's face began to redden again, and he straightened himself back upright and pulled himself free of Jonathan's grip. "Charles and Jon? They cost me a lot of salt."

"They nearly a-got themselves killed protectin' yer gang from a-bein' stolen!"

The hair around Master Sam's face seemed to bristle, and Jon could see red in his eyes. "Alright. Charles, will you stay on as overseer to gang eleven?"

"I will, if Jonathan also stays."

"Jon Hamilton, will you stay on?"

"I don't know. Right now I am damned angry. I have another job waiting for me at the Johnstone Plantation."

"The Johnstones?"

"Yes, sir. And they will pay more."

"That backstabber is supposed to be a friend."

"He is that, sir. He wanted to hire me only if you fired me."

"Well, I take back firing you. All of those overseer jobs depend on you staying here. Will you? Please?"

"I don't like the way you have these bounders whipped for little or no reason."

That deep, heavy stare seemed to return, directed at Jonathan. It lasted an eternity. "Alright. I will ask you to cob your gang, or better yet, I will leave that to Lentil."

Another pause ensued, and Jonathan stared back at Sam. "And I hate the word 'nonsense.'"

"If you will stay, I will try not to use that word again in your presence."

Jonathan deliberately stared in silence at Master Sam. He had the master red-faced and fidgeting in discomfort. "Alright. I wills stay on for this season."

"Thank you. Now, can you please get your gangs out into the field?"

"Alright. Be a-gettin' yer gangs a-movin'," said Jock, with a big grin on his face.

Master Sam turned tail and headed at a torrid pace toward his mansion. The bounders cheered, and handshakes all around were in order.

Late in May, and summer had definitely come to North Carolina. As usual, Skeeter was blazing through rows of corn, and Lucee played hide and seek with her clothes. Cora and Tad worked close, but well together. Corn was already about four feet tall, and gang twelve busied themselves with weeding and thinning, and singing those tunes now familiar to Jon. It was a Tuesday, and about midmorning, the gang arrived at the memorial to Dianna. Levi almost ran Sloggy right over it, but Jobia, handling the reins of Smutty, first noticed it. The small stalks of corn showed no resemblance to the name Dianna, and the cross had been uprooted. Jobe called Master Jon to the site, and Jon called his gang to break. The work had gone slowly, as gang twelve only had two hoes to work with, and Jon had transferred them between his gang so all would get chances to work while standing.

"Levi, get the mall and plant the cross back into the ground."

"Yassa, Massa Jon."

"Pull up those cornstalks, and we'll try planting something else in its place."

"Yassa, Massa Jon."

"Der be un necklace. I's puts on cross, Massa Jon. Orites I puts back?"

"That would be nice, Nell."

"What's we's plants here, Massa Jon?"

"Let's see if we can find some flowers."

"Deys be lilies over by ovaseer house, Massa Jon."

"Yes, there are, Wilma, but they would spread all over, and we couldn't keep the name Dianna."

"Wha' kinds we's use, Massa Jon?"

"Maybe we can get some dwarf English roses."

"Dianna likes white roses, Massa Jon."

"Good. We would have to trim them back each year, and sneak back here to water them all summer."

"Andy gets horse. He sneaks watta, Massa Jon."

"Okay. I'll try to get some rose plants. It may take a couple weeks to get them.

All seemed happy with that, and gang twelve went back to work in a happy mood. By midafternoon, the sun was blinding. The rows of corn seemed to move in the distance. Jonathan rubbed his eyes, trying to focus on the red-and-white waves coming toward him. As the blur grew closer, Jon could see it was a horse and rider. Still closer, and the illusion became a beautiful red-haired woman on a pure white steed. Jon watched as the vision rode past, then returned minutes later, then disappeared in the same direction. He saw the same red-and-white waves in the heat, as the vision had first appeared. Jon thought she waved at him, but was not sure.

"Dem Massa Sam's daughter, Massa Jon."

"Yes, I know who she is, Levi."

The visits continued the rest of the week. Each day, the redhead came closer and became more friendly. The first couple of days, Jon was sure she was spying for her father, but by Saturday, she was stopping and spending time watching, smiling and waving, even blowing kisses. She made the tall overseer uneasy, but he looked forward to her return. Maybe he would attend church the next day, just to see her.

"Be a-gettin' yer drawers on, Jon Henry."

"Why are you waking me, Jock? This is Sunday."

"Aye, it be Sunday, alright, but ye be a-workin' today. Yer team an' gang be a-waitin' outdoors."

"Is everybody working today?"

"Ye be the only one, Jon Henry."

"Ah, so this is how that critter is going to get back at me, huh?"

"That critter ye be a-talkin' about be yer master, an' boss of us all, ye kin?"

"I kin, Jock, but I'll not take much of this."

"Yer breakfast be a-waitin' in yer wagon, Jon Henry. Ye'll not be a-needin' to put this on yer overseer report. I'll be a-tryin' to get ye off early."

"Thanks, Jock, but I plan to put this on my report, along with a few choice words."

"Jest be a-takin' it real easy on yer gang, hear?"

Jon listened to, and tried to answer the complaints of his gang, while trying to control his own anger.

"This is what you get for your loyalty to me, and what I get for threatening to quit."

"Bu', Massa Jon, gang eleven stop work too."

"I know, Morna. Maybe they will have to work next Sunday. Maybe Master Sam hates us more than gang eleven. We were the ones who lost all those days getting back home."

The one thing that cheered Jonathan up was the appearance, once again, of Margaret Rose McAllister. As she neared gang twelve, Jon sensed something wrong. She seemed to Jon to be having trouble controlling the beautiful white animal she was riding. Suddenly, the horse reared up high, kicked out his legs, then settled back, only to buck and lift his hind legs and kick them out. As he lifted his front legs again, the redhead screamed, and Jon ran to her aid. She was hanging on to the neck, screaming and begging the horse she called Pasha to stop, as Jon grabbed Pasha's bridle. The horse swung around to its right and lifted him off his feet.

"Whoa, boy. Whoa, Pasha," he said to the animal, who seemed not to hear and tried to rear up once again. Jon pulled down with all his weight to keep from being kicked. Pasha then kicked out his rear legs and spun around to the left, again swinging Jon, who grabbed an ear and yanked it down. "I said whoa, you ox-headed varmint."

The horse again swung the tall overseer around. He held on. Just then, the redheaded woman sat upright, and spoke to the horse as she pulled on the reins. "Whoa, Pasha."

The horse stopped abruptly and stood still in his tracks, almost throwing the tall overseer to the ground as he hung on to the ear and halter. He looked up at her, and she had a big smile on her lips. Jon got a feeling he had been bamboozled.

"Thank you, Mister Hamilton. Are you alright?"

"Of course, I'm alright. Why do you ask?"

"You haven't seemed to notice me. I'm been riding out here every day for a week."

"Well, I'm not blind. Certainly, I've noticed you." Maybe he was blind! He just then noticed the red dress hiked up almost to her waist. He thought he saw a fancy red undies, and he quickly shifted his eyes back up to a pretty, smiling face.

"Then why haven't you stopped me?"

"I'm afraid of white horses."

"Then you were so brave to rescue me."

"Brave? Maybe barmy."

"Are you afraid of me?"

"I'm afraid of your father."

"Good. Then help me down, Mister Hamilton. I promise my daddy will never know."

The master's daughter swung her leg over her saddle, brazenly giving Jon an eyeful of undies. Quickly, he stepped forward and lifted her off the saddle. Her arms circled his neck; and she pushed her body against him, making the lowering to the ground a slow, painful process. She clung to him, and Jon was getting very uncomfortable. He pushed her back at her waist, and she grudgingly gave ground.

"Please, ma'am. I'd like to keep my job."

"Don't worry about your job, Jonny. My name is Maggie, not ma'am, and I'll see to it you keep your job. Hold me closer, and I might even get you a promotion."

"Or get me fired."

"Nonsense. My father would be very unhappy if you rejected me." She locked her arms around him again. Jon felt a stirring in his loins, and struggled to free himself from her hold.

"Time to get back to work." Jon noticed that his gang had stopped work, and was staring at them. "Levi! I'll rack y'all if you don't get crackin'!"

"Yassa, Massa Jon."

In an instant, butts sprang into view, causing Maggie to giggle. "They're all fannies."

"Yes, ma'am. Well, if you'll excuse me, I'll give you a smashing view of *my* fanny."

Margaret clung to him, not letting him break free. "I suppose you'd rather see that black fanny out there in the field."

"Her name is Lucee, and she has been whipped for undressing, but she works a lot better nude."

"Does she excite you like I do?"

"What makes you think you excite me?" he asked, as he bent back a little at the waist.

"You're too late, Jonny," she smiled. "Don't be bashful."

"If I'm bashful, you're brazen."

"And you love it, you big beautiful lummox."

"I suppose I do. But this isn't the time or place for fritz in the field. So, if you'll excuse me, ma'am, I'll get my gang back to work."

"I'm not your ma'am! My name is Maggie, and I have a question to ask you."

"Well, fire up that pretty gummer, Maggie, then get out of here before your father misses you."

"Don't you like being stuck to me? I know you love being backed into a corner."

"Maybe so, but not in an open field with my job on the line. Now what is your question, Miss Margaret?"

"Will you have supper with me and my family this evening, Jonny?"

"Thanks, but no thanks. The farther the distance from your father, the better I like it. Besides, I'll be working here far past your supper."

"You don't need to. You can pack it in right now."

"I'm sure your daddy would like that."

"Daddy doesn't even know you're out here."

"What?"

"Don't get upset, Jonny. I ordered Lentil to send your gang out so I could see you alone."

"Of all the ox-headed, blunder-butted, tricks . . ."

"Please don't get your dander up, Jonny."

"Ma'am, you're a real rooker."

She pressed and rubbed herself against him, holding fast to his waist as he pushed away.

"Levi!"

"Yassa, Massa Jon."

"Load the gang up. We're through for the day."

"Yassa, Massa Jon."

"And be sure Lucee gets dressed."

"Yassa, Massa Jon."

The tall overseer grabbed Maggie's arm and walked her back to her white horse.

"I'd like one more big hug, Jonny, then I'll leave." Before Jon could resist, Maggie locked herself onto him. She could feel his response. "I'll see you at six o'clock for supper," she said.

"I don't think so, Maggie. I'm not ready for that yet. Maybe another four or five years."

"Very funny. Then I'll see you here tomorrow." She planted a quick kiss on Jonny's lips, and easily swung herself up onto the saddle. He knew he wanted to see her again.

"It wasn't a week, Maggie. This is the sixth day."

"Yippee!" she squealed, and slapped Pasha's rump.

Jon watched the beautiful red-on-white vanish in the haze.

The North Carolina sun was extremely hot, and so was Margaret. As for Jonathan Hamilton, he was having a lot of trouble keeping calm and collected, even when Maggie wasn't visiting him, and she was there every day. Their kissing and fondling became even more urgent, and Jon had trouble resisting. He wasn't sure he wanted to resist any longer, even though he knew the problems this would cause.

On Friday, June fifth, the tall stoker took the wagon with Maggie to a secluded area for lunch and munch, leaving Levi to oversee, and knowing this was against his principles. He was wearing two pairs of unmentionables, so he wouldn't make a stain on his kentucks. This had already happened the day before.

"Let's get in the bed. I have something to tell you."

"You mean the back of the wagon?" Jon quipped.

"For now, yes. It's the only bed in sight."

"You are a daring doucher, Maggie, but sorry, I can't accommodate you. I'm not ready to lose my job."

"I told you I can handle Daddy. Maybe you're afraid I'm just too much for you," she teased.

"Much too much, in my present state of hunger. All redheads do that to me."

"Your present state tells me your hunger isn't for these corn dodgers. I want you to take me, Jonny."

"Whoa! Your father would have me in chains."

'We're alone, Jonny. How would he find out? I'll never tell."

"Bethania is full of blabbers, Maggie. I'm afraid most of them already know what's happening."

"You've got nothing to be afraid of, Jonny."

"Like hell! I'm afraid of your daddy, Lentil McRae, my overseer job, and making a little boot in the kilter."

"You can't make me with child unless I want it, Jonny."

"And you're daffy enough to want it."

This entire conversation in the wagon bed had only taken a few minutes, but long enough for Jon to thank the Lord he had put on the second unmentionable that morning. Disgusted with himself, he jumped up and lifted Maggie out of the wagon and onto her steed.

"Please, Jonny, I need it now."

"Sorry, darlin', but I'm just not ready for that yet."

Margaret lowered herself to him and kissed him hard. "You're as ready as you'll ever be, big boy."

"And you're a real scrubber, Mag. Come on, you pretty plum, I must get back to work."

"Okay, Jonny, but I'll be in barn five tonight at seven thirty. Can you make it?"

"I can't make any promises, but I'll try."

"That's fair enough. See you then. Remember, barn five." With that, Maggie rode off to the west, and Jon hurried team fifteen back to his gang. He was relieved to find them all working hard together, weeding and thinning. It was well past lunchtime, and Jon was still hungry.

"Are there any corn dodgers left, Levi?"

"Yassa, Massa Jon. I gets some fo' you."

Levi ran to the wagon and pulled the lunches from under the seat. Jon realized then that he had taken gang twelve's lunch with him.

"I'm such a flunderhead, Levi. I'm so sorry. Have you had a break in the last couple hours?"

"Nosa, Massa Jon."

"Well, take one now, and everyone eat."

"Yassa, Massa Jon."

Jon didn't make it to barn five that night, but he certainly thought about, and lay awake that night thinking about it. She wanted it even more than he did, Jon thought, if that was possible. Jon smiled, as he pictured her legs wrapped around him. Maggie sure as hell was no virgin. "But neither am I," he mumbled, as his dream switched to Ginny and his trip to the Lowell farm from Chic Wood. He no longer really missed Ginny, but missed what she had given him. He realized that he had to get into those red undies. The next time she asked, he was going to have her, no matter who in the hell found out.

That opportunity came Sunday, the seventh of June, when Jon went to church and Maggie signaled him to meet her in barn five. It was still light outside when Jon walked from the overseer house, past the kitchen, and into Barn Row, whip in hand as if to punish a bounder. With an ever-expanding erection, he found barn five. He pulled open the door, and was excited to hear Margaret call his name from the darkness.

"Over here, Jonny," she said, and then he felt her body against his. Passions erupted as they rolled in the straw, and he fumbled with her riding breeches.

"You're late, Jonny," she whispered.

"It's still light out, Maggie."

"I know, but I can't wait any longer."

"Neither can I . . . aaah," she heard him say, as the member she had a hold of started to spasm. She felt wet spurts hit her belly. She tried to catch some of it in her hand and wipe it off on the straw, but it was sticky.

"I'm so sorry, Maggie."

"It's alright, Jonny. Just keep holding me close."

"I'll do better than that, my pretty plum," as he squirmed on top of her and plunged that member, still rock solid, into her body.

"Oh, Jonnyyy," she gasped, as they found a fast, torrid rhythm. He thought this one would last, but all too soon he was fighting the urge to release again. He tried to pull out and away from her, but she had arms and legs wrapping him, and wouldn't let go. When he heard her moan and quietly screech, he fired. They lay silent, bodies locked together for decades, before he finally started kissing her neck, ears, forehead, nose, hair, and eventually lips.

"You're beautiful. Thank you, thank you, thank you."

"Oh, Jonny, you are wonderful. Don't get off. Stay right where you are and do it again."

"With pleasure, my pretty plum."

To her amazement, he was ready, and a long third session ensued. Even when she was wrung out and wet, both inside and out, he was still prodding, wanting more. No rest for the drays that night!

"I wonder what time it is, Jonny."

"Time for some havoc in the hay!"

"You're not serious, Jonny. Do you wish to kill your bundle of fluff?"

"Oh, I'm sorry, Maggie. We had better put a cap on the canoodling for tonight."

"I hope you're as happy as I am, Jonny, even though I'm sore all over."

"Happy as a harlequin, and twice as jumpy."

"Then I'll meet you here again tomorrow?"

"Bet your babaloos I'll be here."

"Good. Do you need help getting dressed, Jonny?"

"I think so, or we will need to light a lantern. I would hate to have my unmentionables mentioned all over Bethania."

"Okay. You help me with my riders, and I'll help you with your unmentionables."

"You're getting the short end of the stick, baby."

"I'm sure I can make it long again, lover."

"You sure can, my pretty plum."

"What is this for, Jonny? Were you going to cob me?"

"Not in your lifetime, Maggie. It was for show. It was still daylight when I came, so I brought my snake."

"Well, take it back with you. I don't like them."

"And moonlight."

"What was that, Jonny?"

"Oh, nothing," he said with a smile. "Just gumming. I don't like them either, and I don't need two."

"Jonny, have you gone baffy?"

"Making love to redheads does that to me."

"And blondies, brownies, and blackies, and even grays too, I'll bet."

"From now on, it's only one redhead for me."

"I hope so, Jonny."

"For sure, my pretty plum. Be here tomorrow?"

"If I'm not too sore to walk."

"Good. I'll see you tomorrow night, darling, and thank you." As they felt their way out of barn five, they were shocked to walk into the early light of morning. They both had some trouble walking straight, but for different reasons.

It was work in the fields all day, futz in the barn all night. They barely even noticed June disappear, or that their activity was obvious to anyone who may be watching. They had both lost weight, and Jon's overseeing job was subpar. He knew he had to slack off one, or both, and he didn't like either option. They tried several gimmicks to hide what was very apparent to most, except the master and mistress of Bethania. Jon was warned of the consequences of his actions by fellow overseers, and even by Jock himself, but Jon would not, or could not stop. Something was bound to happen soon, and it did, in July.

One of the gimmicks Jon did was to tell his friends that his mother was sick, so he had to travel home to see her on July eleventh.

"I didn't expect you till next week, son," said Jon's father at the dinner table. "For your birthday."

"I did! Anytime after the crops were planted."

"Bite weasel, Andrew," answered Jon. "I may not make it next week, Father. Something has come up."

"Probably one of those black ginches in his gang. What do you call them? Bouncers?" quipped Andrew.

"They're bounders, you flunderhead."

"Now don't get all dandered, Jonny Boy. So you got one germinated. So what? Didn't your master say that all pickaninnies belonged to him?"

"You're not even close, brother. I haven't touched any Nans in my gang or any gang."

"Then what has happened that you won't be here for your birthday?" asked Jon's mother.

"I'll be working. The tobacco plants ain't doing too good. They have a lot of sot worms, and need suckering."

"I hope you can make it to my birthday, Jonny."

"I'll try to make it on the weekend of your birthday, Mary, but it's close to harvest time."

"Your sister's getting married pretty soon, son," said Jon's father, Alexander Hamilton.

"Buggers! My sister's marrying a dude from Savannah, and my brother's marrying a pullet from his gang. Guess I'll have to run up to the women's college and find me some fluff," said Andrew.

"Any educated fluff wouldn't have you! Have you set a date, sis?" asked Jon.

"Early in September, Jonny," answered Mary.

"We'll be in harvest then. I'm sure I won't be making that, but I'll try to be here around your birthday."

"Then we probably won't have you here for our harvest, will we, son?"

"Probably not, Father. How did you manage with the planting?" asked Jon.

"Can you quander? We had a Negro working on this farm! Doesn't that beat all?" chirped Andrew.

"We had to borrow a slave to help plant, son. We paid him and his owner wages," said Jon's father, Alexander.

"Looks like we'll have to rehire that black booger again at harvest," said Andrew.

"I'm sorry, Father. Maybe I can help pay the expenses."

"That's not necessary, son. I just wish you could come home more often on weekends. Are you sure you won't be here next week?"

"I'm sure, Father. I've been busy from dawn to after dark almost every day."

"Then this is as close to your birthday as we will get?" asked Jon's mother, Martha Hamilton.

"I'm afraid so, Mother."

"How can you work after dark, brother Jon? You must be picking a plum. Who is she?" asked Andrew.

"Do you have a lady, Jonny?" asked his sister, Mary.

"To be honest, yes, I do, sis. Her name is Margaret."

"Ah-ha! I knew it! My brother is playing futz-in-the-field!"

"Andrew! Stop that nasty talk!" yelled Martha. "Margaret is an unusual name for a slave, Jonathan."

"She's not a slave, Mother. She is the daughter of Bethania's owner."

"A McAllister?"

"Yes, Father. She is a tall redhead, and very nice."

"Gadzooks! You have really gone barmy," said Andy. "Somehow I knew you wanted to get more land than me."

"Do Samuel and his wife know about this, son?"

"I'm not sure, Father. They haven't said anything."

"My brother may end up back home for the harvest yet, if he don't get her germinated too."

"Bite bear, Andy! I know how you dislike the McAllisters, Father, but she is different from her father."

"Alright, son. I'll take your word on that. But be careful. McAllister is revengeful."

"Is she pretty, Jonny?" asked Mary.

"Like a beautiful portrait, sis."

"How is she in the sack, brother?"

"Andrew! I told you to stop that talk!" hollered Martha.

"It's none of your business, brother," answered Jon.

"Ah-ha! That means he is playing the slap and tickle with his master's ginch."

"I guess we should give you your birthday present now, Jon, being as you won't be here next Saturday," said Alex.

"I don't have a cake, Jonny, but I do have some goodies I made last week," said Jon's mother.

"That would be smashing, Mother. Thank you."

"I'll go get the birthday gift," stated Alexander.

"You purchased something for me?"

"It's something you always wanted, Jonny," said Martha.

"And it traveled across the country, Jonny Boy," quipped Andrew.

"Can you guess what it is, Jonny?" asked Mary.

"I don't have a clue, sis."

"Here's a clue for you, brother Jon. You powder it good, and it will ignite your balls."

"Andrew, please!" yelled Jon's mother, Martha, as she emerged from the kitchen with a plate of pastries.

"Here it is, son," said Jon's father, Alexander, as he entered the house from the barn. Alexander entered the house carrying a heavy, wooden crate, long and narrow.

"Now can you guess, Jonny?" asked Jon's sister, Mary.

"It's still a mystery to me."

"Then you had better open it, son," said Alexander.

Jon had trouble prying open the heavy wooden crate. The first thing he found in the straw packing was a beaded, hand-tuled leather pouch with a shoulder strap. Now he knew what the birthday present was.

"Oh, my gracious . . . my gracious family . . . now I know what it is! Wow! Thank you all!" Jon pulled out the remainder of the straw, and started wide-eyed at the long rifle. He picked it up and read the words stamped into the barrel, *J & S Hawken.* "A St. Louis Hawken!"

"Use it wisely, my son, and it will last you forever."

"I will, Father. And thanks to you and Mother."

"You're welcome. Happy birthday," was heard in response.

"Now, let's eat before these apple dumplings I made give us all a case of dyspepsia," said Martha.

"Andy and I will have a present for you when you come back next month, Jonny," said Mary.

"Thanks, sis."

It turned out that Martha had cooked a large dinner, called supper at the Plantation, and the Hamiltons ate hearty, with the birthday dumplings as dessert. Once again, the harvest came into discussion.

"How are the crops looking?" asked Jon.

"Not very good, brother. We have a lot of worms this year, both in the cotton and tobacco crops. And the leaves are not developing very fast," said Andrew.

"At the plantation, we rotated the crops to cut back on rot, but the worms still find the plants. I told Master Sam about the seven-year cycles, and he wants to try that next year."

"That's not even working well anymore, son. I think the soil is just getting too poor," said Jon's father.

"Maybe we should grow rice, Father. It takes a lot of prepping, but it sure is rewarding," said Jon.

"No, maybe Martha and I will just give the farm to Drew, here, and move to Arkansas," answered Alexander.

"Arkansas? Where is that?"

"At the end of the known world!" quipped Andrew.

"It's part of Missouri, on the western front," said Alex.

"It's in the wilderness, west of the Mississippi. If your father goes, he'll go alone," said Martha sternly.

"I got this ad in the Salem paper, son. It says that Arkansas is going to become a state, and has lots of river bottomland for the taking," said an excited Alexander.

"If you don't get scalped first," suggested Andy.

"Sounds interesting, Father."

"I'll show you the ad, son."

"Why would you be interested, bunko brother? All you need to do is marry that McAllister fluff, and have all the land you want," teased Andrew.

"Suck old croc eggs, Drew. Like Father says, the land here in Carolina is about worn out. Maybe Arkansas is the place to start anew."

"Here it is, son," said Alex, returning to the table.

Arkansas Needs YOU!

> *The next state in America, Arkansas, invites you to come plant your roots and seed into rich river bottomlands, ripe for the taking: 160-acre parcels, along the Arkansas and White rivers, are open to any white man or woman willing to take up the plow and become an Arkansawyer. Register in our new state capitol, Little Rock.*

"Take that ad with you, Jonathan. Your father is not going anywhere," said Martha.

"Wow! This sounds great!"

"You'll have to talk your mother into it, son. She is bound and determined to stay here forever."

"You bet I am. We're too old to start over again."

"Maybe after the crops are all in, Father, and I can start a farm in Arkansas, and send for the rest of you later, Mother."

"I'm staying right here, brother, and so is Mother. Mary will be living in Georgia, and I'll need Father for planting and harvest. So take your raggery and your piles, and go yourself, you lummox!" shouted Andy.

"Bleed out, brother . . ."

"And I'm staying here, like your father said, Jonathan," said Jon's mother, Martha.

"Yes, Yes. Consider the matter dropped for now, Okay?"

But all night long, Jon thought about a trip to Arkansas and the adventure of it all. He remembered hearing about the Cumberland Gap that Daniel Boone had made famous, and the mighty Mississippi. And what would he do about Maggie? He was pretty sure he loved her, but she would probably balk at traveling, just like his mother, Martha.

Sunday, July twelfth, Jon helped pull worms off the cotton and tobacco plants, thick as flies. He couldn't help noting the poor condition of the crops, and that made him want to move on all the more. Late that night, Jon went back to Bethania with the ad, and the St. Louis Hawken rifle.

The next week was a blur. Gang twelve worked late every night, and was back up ready to go again the next morning at dawn. Jon saw Maggie ride out on Tuesday, and they embraced and fondled a little, but he was just too tired to meet her in barn five. The next time he saw her was on his birthday. Gang twelve found themselves at the gravesite of Dianna, again in disrepair.

"Massa Jon, dis be Dinna's grave," said Nell.

"Yes, Nell, I know."

"Bu' it be's bad shape, Massa Jon," said Wilma.

"Levi, put the cross back up."

"Yassa, Massa Jon."

"You no brings dem flowas, Massa Jon." Jon had missed that sweet voice of Cora.

"We've all been very busy, Cora. I don't know when I will be able to buy some flowers."

"I's makes carve words, Massa Jon," said Jobia.

"Listen up, gang. Is it alright if Jobia here carves a nice, big cross for Dianna, and we all decorate it?"

"Yassa, Massa Jon," came the replies.

"Righto! Let's all break for lunch."

During the break, Jon saw the hazy red-on-white form heading their way. He was anxious to see her, and ran toward the ever-enlarging form. Kisses, hugs, feels, rubs, and squirms . . .

"Do you love me, Jonny?"

"Does a shark have teeth?"

"Please, Jonny. I need to know."

"Of course, I love you, and want you."

"Good. Then meet me tonight in barn five. I have something I need to tell you."

"Great! I have something to tell you, too."

Jon had longed for that smell, that feel of Maggie, and it was that first night all over again. Three, four, five times? Who was counting? A rest was finally needed.

"What did you need to tell me, Maggie?"

"I missed the curse."

"So did I. I hope we both keep missing the curse. Good luck awaits us, my pretty plum."

"No, Jonny, I mean my female curse."

"What do you mean, baby?"

"That's right! I'm going to have a baby!"

"Wow," said Jon, after a pause for thought.

"Wow what, Jonny?"

"Wow, I don't know what to say."

"Say you love me again, Jonny, and tell me how happy you are that you're going to be a father."

"Righto, I love you. I'm happy and I'm scared."

"I was scared too, but now I'm glad."

"Glad of what? That I'm about to be murdered, or torn apart by Mose?"

"Don't be worried, Jonny. I can handle my daddy and Mose, and anyone else."

"How, by gabble-gumming them to death?"

"I'll just tell them. They'll love being grandparents."

"Yeah, after they have my bones bleached. They are going to be double-dandered! How will we tell them?"

"I'll figure a way. But we won't tell them until we are sure."

"When will that be?"

"Maybe about a month from now."

"You mean I have to wait a month to find out if I'm going to be a father? How will you know?"

"When I miss my curse again."

There was a pause. "I thought you said I could never make you with child unless you wanted to."

"I might have lied, Jonny. I'm sorry."

"It's alright, Maggie darlin'. Wow! The father of a little munchkin."

"What did you want to tell me, Jonny?"

Jon stumbled about in the dark, trying to find the ad in his kentucks, and a lantern for Maggie to read. "I wish I were an owl!"

"I've got a lantern here, Jonny." She lit the lantern, and Jon handed the ad to her. "What is it, Jonny?"

"It's an ad in the Salem paper. Read it."

Maggie looked puzzled as she read about Arkansas. "What does this mean, Jonny?"

"I want to marry you and take you to Arkansas."

"What's in Arkansas?"

"Rich bottomland, and freedom."

"But, Jonny, we are free now."

"Not Mose, or Ella, or Levi, or Jock, or any of my gang. And I'm not free, working for your father."

"Now *I* don't know what to say."

"How about . . . *Yes,* I will marry you, and I will travel with you to Arkansas?" answered Jon.

"But, Jonny, I love Bethania."

"More than me?"

"Of course not, you big lummox. I want to marry you, Jonny, but Arkansas is so far away."

"Far enough to break clean of poor soil, working for others, and slavery."

"You mean we would be all by ourselves?"

"Just you and I, and three hundred twenty acres of bottomland."

"But, Jonny, how could we handle all that land?"

"With these, my pretty plum, our own two hands."

"Oh, Jonny, I'd miss Buelah, Nunky Mose, and Nanty Ella. Couldn't we bring them along?"

"Not as slaves, Maggie. Our land will be clean." A long silence ensued, and Jon felt her shaking.

"I'm so scared, Jonny. Would you still marry me and live in Bethania?"

"Yes . . . but I'd be unhappy living in the mansion."

"Daddy would build us a house, Jonny, and give us all the land and equipment we need."

"But that wouldn't be the same, Maggie. We would always be beholden to him, and under his influence. We'd probably need slaves to work this worn-out soil."

"But that's not bad, Jonny. We'll be close to our families."

"Too close for me, my pretty plum."

"Alright, Jonny. I promise I'll think about it."

"Good. That's all I can ask. I don't have any bands yet, but we can put a cap on our marriage vows."

"Mmm . . . Good idea, my husband-to-be."

The love session was long and furious. In the darkness of the barn, nothing was off-limits . . .

"You kept your promise."

"What promise, Jonny?"

"To give me something special for my birthday."

"Oh, Jonny, I'm so sorry. I forgot your birthday."

"I'd have never known that if you hadn't said it."

"That good, huh?"

"Best birthday present I've ever had."

"We had better leave now, Jonny. Thank you for asking me to marry you."

"Thank you for accepting, my pretty plum."

Where there's a will, there's a way, and somehow Jon managed to find the energy to rise before dawn, work his gang until dark, and meet Margaret in barn five for lovemaking sessions, lasting half the night. Bounder Levi had become something akin to an overseer, as the corn and tobacco plants were now tall enough to afford shade for Jon's ever-increasing nap times, and fellow overseer and friend Charles Finley was secretly doing most of Jon's overseer reports, trying to make them look as though they were from the hand of Hamilton.

AUGST 9: WORKE HAF DAY SUNDY. 9 HANDS PRESENT. HAF DAY WORMIN TOBACO PLNTS, HAF DAY SUCKERIN SAME PLNTS. 4 MALE BOUNDERS, 5 FEMALE WERK HARDE. EST. 15 ACRES KLEEND. TOBACCO LEFS SMAL.

THURSDAY, AUGUST 13: ALL HANS PRESNT, WORK IN CORN FIELDS. HAF DAY WEEDNG, CORNE REDDY FOR HARVEST. WERK HALF DAY WORMING COTTON PLNTS, EST. 25 ACRS.

"I'm sure, Jonny."

"Sure of what, my pretty plum?"

"Oh, Jonny . . . you forgot. You don't want it now."

"Forgot what? Won't what?"

"A baby, brainless!" shouted Maggie, eyes tearing up.

"Oh, are you sure yet, Maggie?"

"I just told you, Jonny. I'm sure."

"Wahoo! Wow! My own little sprout! Don't that just cap the climax?"

"Then you still want it?"

"Like a whale wants water! Let's see, how does David Drew sound?"

"Not very good for a girl," said a smiling Margaret. "We'll have a lot of time to think of a name, Jonny."

"How long, sugar?"

"Well, let's see . . . probably next March or April.

"That long? That's planting time."

"Is that all you farmers think about? Perhaps you should name it Sot or Corn Cob!"

"Righto! And if it's a girl, Cotton sounds pretty."

"Be serious, Jonny. We must figure a way to tell my mother and Daddy."

"Yeah. That'll be a smasher! Telling your father that you're engaged, and have a boot in the kilter."

"I'll work on Daddy. You have your family to tell."

"No problem. I'll tell them this weekend."

"You're going home this weekend?" asked Maggie.

"Sure am. I told you about my sister's twenty-second birthday next Tuesday."

"Oh, I forgot. What's her name, Jonny?

"Mary Jane. This may be the last time I see her. She's getting married next month and moving to Georgia."

"We should set a date too, Jonny."

"Alright. How about tomorrow, so I can beat my sister?"

"That's sweet, Jonny, but Daddy would disown me if I take you away before harvest."

"Alright again! Harvest should be over by late October."

"I'll be showing by then."

"You have a choice, my pretty plum. Either now when you ain't showing, or late October when you is."

"Then I have no choice, Jonny. Mother would be very upset if she didn't have time to make all the suits and dresses, and it will take time to bring Daddy around."

"Righto. So how about the last Saturday in October? I'm sure the crops will be all in by then."

"Can't we make it a little sooner, Jonny?"

"Not much sooner. Maybe the third Saturday?"

"I think I would like Friday better."

"Right. How about the first Friday . . . after the twentieth?"

"That will have to do, Jonny."

"Good. Now we should spread the happy news to our unhappy folks right away, so your father will have plenty of time to get used to our absence."

"What absence, Jonny?"

"Our living in Arkansas, of course."

"Oh, Jonny. I was hoping you had forgotten about that."

"Not in my lifetime, darling. Just think, our first son will be born in a new land."

"That scares me."

"It excites me, baby. Please, Maggie, come with me, and make our new home in Arkansas . . . please?"

"Alright, Jonny. I want to make you happy."

"You do, baby, and I'll make you happy in our new home. And I promise you'll come back to visit often."

"And I'll hold you to that promise, you big lummox."

"Thank you, darling. Now when can I talk to your parents?"

"I'll tell them, Jonny. I can handle Daddy."

"But I should be the one to ask for your hand."

"Alright. If you're going home Friday, how about asking them at supper on Thursday evening?"

"That's the day after tomorrow."

"I know, Jonny. You wanted to get it over with quickly."

"Righto. After this weekend, we won't have to sneak around anymore, my pretty plum."

"Slow down, Jonny. If he catches us doing this in the open, Daddy will fire you and kick me out of house and home."

"Great! Then we can head for Arkansas early."

"That's a long walk, big boy."

"Yeah . . . See how nice it will be getting away from him?"

"If you're that set on Arkansas, we are going to need some of Daddy's pile. So stay calm at supper Thursday. I'll do the screaming at him."

"Okay, darlin'. I'll just be glad when it's over."

"So will I. Come in around seven o'clock, Jonny. I'll sit you next to Mother. She likes you."

"She probably will hate me too, after we spill the beans."

"I'll make the first announcement at church on Sunday."

"Good, and I'll purchase bands in Salem this weekend."

"Can you afford them, Jonny?"

"Yes. I think my brother will have a late birthday present for me. I'll just exchange it for bands."

"Alright, Jonny. Let's seal it with a kiss."

"Like hell. Let's seal it with a poke!"

"Same old Jonny! By the way, how did you come up with the name David?"

"My grandfather. He was a colonel in the British Army during the War for Independence."

"Oh . . . traitor!"

"What a wonderful dinner, Missus McAllister. Thank you."

"You're welcome, Mister Hamilton. We call it supper here."

"Oh, I'm sorry. I'll remember that, ma'am."

What words could Jon use to describe the size if this dining hall? *Huge, enormous, gigantic, for starters*, thought Jon. *And that long, drawn-out table, red with white trim and oh-so-polished. Something like Maggie*, he reasoned with a broad smile. Jon liked the table's length, and the seating arrangement with Master Samuel at the distant end.

"What's so funny, boy?"

"Oh, nothing, sir. I was just thinking what a wonderful din . . . er, supper this is, and such a beautiful dining room."

"Dining room? This is McAllister Hall, where some of the finest concerts, recitals, caucuses, and confraternities in North Carolina have been held."

"I stand corrected, sir."

"How big is your farm, boy?"

"About eighty acres, sir, about five miles south of Salem."

"Tobacco, I assume?"

"Only about ten acres, mostly mundungus, but we do about fifty bales of cotton and some corn, sir."

"What's mundungus mean, Jonny?"

"It's discolored sot, Sissy. How many bounders?" asked Sam.

"No bounders, sir. My father doesn't believe in slaves."

"Nonsense! They were brought to this country to do work in the fields. That's where they belong." Samuel noticed the hard stare of his overseer, and remembered his promise not to use that word. *To hell with him*, thought the master. This was his house and he was the boss, and he would say what he damned well pleased.

"Do you have any brothers to help with your father's farm, Mister Hamilton?" asked Mistress Susan, breaking the lull.

"I have a brother and a sister, ma'am, but she is getting married soon, so this weekend may be the last time I see her for a long spell."

"What? You're going home when there's work to be done?"

"I have gone home only once since I started here, sir, and my sister has a birthday next Monday. Charles Finley said he would help oversee my gang on Saturday."

"I may also need them Sunday to pick sot worm before my crop turns to mundungus!" yelled Sam.

"Stay calm, Daddy. This may be the last time Jonny sees his family for several years," snapped Maggie.

"Why is that, Mister Hamilton?" asked Susan.

Jon knew that Maggie had let the cat out, and he felt her hand in his lap. He wasn't ready to pop the question. "Well, ma'am, my older brother will be getting the farm soon, so I'll be looking to farm some land of my own."

"Just how do you plan to do that, boy?"

Jon felt like this was the time to answer, but he had promised Maggie that she could bring up Arkansas last. "I'm not sure, Master Sam, but I don't plan to oversee all my life. Maybe I'll try searching for gold, like my father did." He pushed Maggie's hand away.

"Nonsense. There's no money in gold-digging. You should remain an overseer."

"Well, thanks to your nonsense, sir, my father got his farm from mining. You purchased his mine on the Yadkin."

"That was your father who bamboozled me?"

"No, sir. My father never bamboozled anyone."

"Well, boy, your father sold me a griefer!" yelled Sam.

"Well, sir, I'm sure my father would buy it back for the little nob you paid him for it!" hollered Jon.

"Your father will never get the chance to con me again!" shouted Sam, as both he and Jon jumped out of their chairs.

"Please, Samuel, Mister Hamilton is our company," said Susan. "Let's be civil in front of the children."

"Go to your rooms now, boys. You are excused."

"Yes, sir, Father," said the boys in unison. They kissed their mother and sister, shook hands with Jon, and left.

"And you, boy, if you're going to be sassy, you can leave too!"

"Not quite yet, *sir!* Not until I tell you why I came to dinner, or supper tonight."

"Maybe we ought to put it off right now, Jonny," said Maggie.

"Like hell, Maggie. There's no time like the present. Mister McAllister, I have asked for your daughter's hand in marriage, and she has accepted."

"You *what?*" The master came out of his chair again.

"I said I plan to marry Maggie, and take her away."

"Like hell you are! Get out of my house, before I have Mose throw you out!"

"Alright, I'm leaving, but that don't change a thing!" yelled Jon, as he left the big hall. Maggie followed him out.

Jon stomped through the passageway to the back entrance. He heard Master Sam yelling at Maggie, and she answering that she was not as ill-mannered as he. She caught Jon at the back door and hugged him tightly.

"I'm sorry, Jonny."

"Damn him for saying my father conned him!"

"It's alright, Jonny. He'll not stop us now."

"I didn't get a chance to tell him about the date, or the trip to Arkansas, or the baby in the basket."

"I'll tell him, Jonny, and I won't take no for an answer."

"I should be there with you, Sissy."

"I'm not Sissy! I'll meet you in barn five later."

"Are you daffy? We need to calm it down right now."

"Yes, my future husband. Wish me luck. I'm ready for the big blowout!"

"Good luck, darling, and please tell your mother thanks for the meal, and the apple pan-dowdy."

"I will, Jonny. I love you."

"And I love you, my pretty plum. By the way . . ."

"Yes, Jonny?"

"You look beautiful tonight."

"Thanks, Jonny," she replied.

"You bet. The flowers are all in the right places."

Margaret visited Jon in the tobacco field that Friday, to tell him of her success the night before. Jon then told his gang.

"We's happy fo' you's, Massa Jon," was their replies.

"You's still be's our ovaseer, Massa Jon?" asked Cora.

"Yes, until these crops are harvested."

"Then you's leaves us, Massa Jon?"

"Yes. I'll be going to Arkansas."

There was much sadness and questions about Arkansas for weeks.

"Thank you so much, Jonny." Mary had just opened her gift-wrapped birthday gift from Jon. He had stopped at a boutique shop in Salem on the way home and, luckily catching them still open, had purchased a turban of black and white, with fancy-colored feathers and gloves to match, on the promise to pay them that weekend. He had also had the boutique put away a set of wedding bands. Jon had persuaded his sister to open her gift early, and she looked smashing, modeling them.

"Happy birthday, sis. They look great on you."

"Drew and I have late birthday presents for you too." Jon was bewildered at the gifts he received from his siblings. From brother Andrew, he got powder and balls for his new St. Louis Hawken rifle, wool undergarments, a compass, and a hand-held sundial. From his sister Mary, Jon got an overcoat, called a frock, with gloves, a shirt and pantaloons, a scarf, and a pair of brogans.

"What are all these togs for?" asked Jon.

"For your excursion to Arkansas, brother," said Andrew.

"But . . . how did you know?"

"We could tell, Jonny, by the way you drooled over that ad in the newspaper last month," answered Mary.

"Well, you guessed it, at least part of it. Thanks bundles!"

"I think there is some rot in the brain box, though, brother. You have the monkey by the tail at the plantation. What happened? Did you get unearthed by the master?"

"Not exactly, Drew. I'll tell you all about it at dinner."

"Oh good! I can hardly wait!" said an excited Mary.

Jon knew he would need these presents for his trip, but how would he pay for the bands and Mary's birthday present? The answer came when Jon's parents entered the room with a small sack of coins, and handed it to Jon.

"It's not much, son, but Martha and I hope it helps."

"Thank you, Father, and thanks, Mother, but you've already given me the rifle. This is too much."

"It's alright, son. Use it in good stead on your trip. I only wish I were going along," said Alexander.

"We've already talked about this, Alex," said Martha to her husband. To Jon, he said, "Someday we may come out to visit."

"That would be wonderful, Mother."

Jon looked in the sack, and saw a few double Eagles, and a few Eagle coins. He figured he could pay for Mary's gift and a good portion of the bands. He better do the opposite, he thought, or he wouldn't be able to take the bands out.

"I'll need to make a quick trip into town tomorrow, then I can help some in the field."

"So you nab a little pile, and you forthwith go looking for some bunko bunny to spank it."

"Grab skunk, Andrew!" hollered Jon.

"What he does with the money is his business, Andrew," said mother Martha.

"Jonny has something important to tell us at the dinner table, Mother," informed Mary.

"Wonderful! Dinner is about ready. We have Mary's favorite dish, macaroni pie," said Martha to son Jon.

"Sounds good, Mother. Let's partake."

"Okay, Jonny, we're ready to hear your secret." With these words from Mary, the Hamilton family became quiet with anticipation.

"Well . . . Mag . . . Margaret said she will go with me to Arkansas." There was a long pause.

"Futz in the wild! Don't that beat all?" quipped Andrew. But the rest remained silent.

"That's fine, son, but you'll need more than just the two of you for that hard journey."

"I know, Father. We are taking a couple bounders with us," Jon saw the stare from his father, "It's Okay. I'm going to free them in Arkansas." This was met with more silence.

"Does this mean that you are marrying her, Jonathan?"

"Yes, Mother, the first Friday after the twentieth of October."

"I'll get the calendar," said Mary.

"Why so late, my bird-brained brother? It will be winter before you grace Arkansas."

"I know that, Drew, but I want to get all of Master Sam's crops in before we leave."

"It's the twenty-third of October, Mother." Mary had brought in a calendar. "And I can't be there."

"And you're leaving right after?" asked Martha.

"The day after, Mother."

After a long pause, Mary said, "Then this may be the last time we see each other, Jonny." Her eyes were starting to tear.

"I'm afraid so, sis, at least for a long time."

A tearful Mary hugged her tall kid brother.

"Don't cry, sis, this is your birthday."

"It's not till Monday, you cobble-head."

"Eat grasshoppers, Andrew!" yelled Jon.

"Why don't you wait until spring before you make that long trip, Jonathan?"

"Then we may not get any bottomland, Mother." This seemed to satisfy Martha for the present, but not Mary.

"I can't imagine that many people flocking to the wilderness, just for a piece of bottomland."

"Nor can I! There must be some other reason why you would leave a bundle and race to Arkansas," teased Andrew.

"Well, there is another reason." Jon paused.

"Tell us, son," said Alex.

"I . . . want my offspring born on free land."

"Well, wear a wizard wrap, flounderhead," harped Andy. There was another pause, as all waited for Jon to continue.

"Is there something else you wish to tell us, Jonathan?"

"Yes, Mother. Maggie missed her curse, and says she fell off the porch. That means I'm going to be a father."

"We know what it means," Martha quietly said.

"Well," said Mary, "I'm going to be an aunt before I'm a mother." There was another pause.

"If you wait until late October, she'll be showing."

"She knows that, Mother, but she wanted me to finish the crops, and her mother needs time to make the wedding togs."

"Gadzooks! I'll bet this wedding will be a barn-burner," said Andrew. "Stay home, boogie-boy. You'll have the whole boodle."

"It wouldn't be the same, Drew, and besides, Maggie's brothers will have a say about who gets Bethania."

"And the soil in this area is about played out," added Alex.

The dinner was finished in silence, as the Hamiltons ran out of comments and questions for Jon. They remained seated.

"I have a lot of home-spun material for your wedding, Mary. I guess we can use them for Jonathan's marriage too."

"Mistress McAllister is already making wedding togs for all of us, Mother. Maggie wants me to bring back a set of wear for each of you for her mother to size."

"That's a lot of work for her, Jonny," said Mary.

"She has a lot of help from the bounders. They're even going to be part of the wedding."

Andrew piped up. "Wow! This is even going to be a house-burner!"

"That's enough, son," said Father Alexander. "I guess I had better get busy writing a letter to Sam McAllister."

"About what, Father?" asked Jon.

"To demand horses, a wagon, food and grain, and a hundred other things you'll need for your trip, son."

"It's called a Dowry Demand, my barmy brother," said a sarcastic Andrew.

There was a long pause.

"Father, tell me about the mine on the Yadkin you sold to Master McAllister."

"What do you want to know, son?"

"Was it all pooped out?"

"Hell no! I have always regretted selling that mine to that rhino-grabber."

"He said you bamboozled him, sold him a griefer."

"Tell him I'll buy it back."

"That's exactly what I told him, Father."

"Now here's a smashing idea, blunder brother. Why don't you espouse your master's daughter, and ask for all the land along the river? Then Papa and I can help you mine for gold in the winter."

"Not a bad idea, brother Drew, but if we did find gold, Master McAllister would just take back the land and disown his daughter and I. I'll think about that in Arkansas."

Jon had just enough coinage to pay for the bands. He promised to send the money to the boutique shop for Mary's birthday gift. Jon worked like his bounders over the weekend, and late Sunday he kissed his sister goodbye for the last time.

Harvest was in full swing from July through October. First there was the topping of the tobacco plants, which led to controlled "suckering" of the new stems. Then the corn had to be picked and shipped to Salem, and the plants composted.

By August, the leaves of the tobacco plants were ready for "priming," and that lasted into October. Meanwhile, the cotton balls had opened, and the picking, ginning and baling, all by hand, lasted from late August to late October. Somehow, Jon even managed occasionally to find time for Maggie in barn five.

"Daddy was sure mad last night, Jonny."

"What about, my pretty plum?"

"He received a dowry demand letter from your father."

"I can just see that red face under all that hair!"

"Well, he gave in, and agreed to furnish our trip."

"Smashing! And we'll have some money, honey, with your birthday bundle and my wages, if your father ever pays me."

"How much does he owe you?"

"By the end of October, he will owe me one hundred twenty."

"I'll see to it he pays you, Jonny."

"Good, and just put it away for our trip, darling."

"Alright. You look tired, Jonny. Go get some sleep."

"Not until we boogie once more, my pretty plum."

"It's starting to get a little uncomfortable, Jonny."

"Righto. How about you staying on top from now on?"

"Alright, Jonny, but you need to slow down a little."

"Just because you're starting to show? I hope we won't have to stop the poke parties before spring in Arkansas."

"We won't, Jonny."

"Good. Tell me if I'm hurting you, my pretty plum."

The tobacco plants left to flower and grow for the prime cigar wrappings, were small and light, and the cotton balls and seeds for next year were small, which meant lower profits for Bethania, but no less work for the gangs and overseers. In seemingly no time, the crops were in, and it was time to say goodbye to Jon's gang twelve, the last day in the field, Thursday afternoon, October twenty-second. The gang already knew, and had been very quiet that morning, until the trip back to the barns.

"Do dis be you's las' day, Massa Jon?"

"Stop the wagon, Levi. Yes it is, Levi." Levi stopped team fifteen, and Jon stepped down to address his gang. He paused.

"I want to thank you all, and tell you all how much I care about you. You are the best gang in Carolina, and I'm going to miss you all. I wish I could take you all to Arkansas."

Jon couldn't help but notice the sad faces and even tears falling on some faces. Hell, he was tearing up too!

"We's be all o'side the big house, Massa Jon, fo's you's weds tomorrow," said Skeeter.

"An' I's wear's my besses dress fo' you's, Massa Jon."

"Thank you, Lucee. Just don't take it off!" All laughed or smiled between tears.

"We's miss you's too, Massa Jon," came the sweet voice of Cora.

"We's do dem jooba fo' you's tomorrow, Massa Jon."

"That would be wonderful, Wilma."

"We's be workin' in barns tomorra!" hollered Levi.

"I'll try to get you all off early tomorrow, gang."

"Thank you's, Massa Jon," said most of gang twelve.

"Den we's does dem jooba at dem marriage, Massa Jon," said Morna.

"You's be shakin' an' shimmin' Monas," teased Skeets, to much laughter.

There were handshakes for Jon from the Toms, and hugs from the Nans. Jon was rewarded with extra squeezes from Wilma and Cora. They then all climbed back into the wagon and were very quiet until the old church came into view. By some silent signal, they started singing. Jon recognized the tune.

> *"Sistas don' gets weary*
> *An' bruddas sad no mo*
> *We's will see our Massa Jon*
> *Wen we's gets to Canaan's shore*
> *Der's a betta days a-comin'*
> *Where we's be bounders no mo*
> *We's will see our Massa Jon*
> *Wen we's gets to Canaan's shore*
>
> *Ders a betta days a-comin'*
> *Massa Jon we's will see*
> *Der's a betta days a-comin'*
> *Go's sounds de jubilee."*

―――――――⁓⁓⁓⁓◦◦∽∽◦∽⁓∞◦◦⁓⁓⁓――――――――

FINEL OVERSEAR REPORT
18 OCTOBER – 22 OCTOBER
GANG TWELVE – TEEM 15
4 TOMS – 5 NANS

. . . THURSDAY, OCTOBER 22: CUT AN LOAD COTEN PLANTS FOR COMPOSTE. TILLE COTEN FEELDS, BERY COTEN TRASHE. LEEVE STEM ROOTE IN GROWNE. PIK LEEVES FRM LASTE TOBAKO PLNTS HANGING FROM POLS. HALL COTEN AN TOBACO STEMS FOR COMPOSTE. GANG

*WORK VERY HARD 11+ HOWRS. BEST GANG N CAROLINNA. NEDE HAF
DEY OF FRIDAY FORE MARIGE.*

Jonathan Hamilton

The wedding was the biggest affair that Jon would ever see. People came from everywhere. On the balcony, at the top of the grand staircase, Jon got a forbidden glimpse of Maggie, and knew why he wanted to marry her, and why he wanted to get this shindig over with in a hurry. She was breathtaking. Everyone in the ceremony looked great, especially Mose. It must have taken a ton of fabric to make his getup, but he looked like a king. And Esther Blowby . . . wow!

When Maggie came to the outdoor altar, Jon could see the swelling of her belly, and heard the whispers and gasps of the crowd, but she still was beautiful. Even the much shorter Master Sam looked sharp. His baraclave seemed to be curly.

The dragged-out ceremony finally ended, and Jon was allowed to plant a smacker on the now unveiled face of Margaret and pin a Hamilton tartan sash on her. Then it was off to the great hall, and a load of people. Jon was amazed at all the articles on the head table. There was a huge cake, a tall candle, a large bouquet of flowers, an object covered with a cloth, and strangely, a clump of dill. Jon couldn't believe it when Maggie took off her shoe and emptied it of pieces of cloth, wood, and coins, after they had jumped forward and back over a broomstick. He was happy over the large amount of money collected from the crowd, and the splendid meal, which included Jon's first taste of ice cream.

Much later, after Maggie had danced to jumpy Celtic music, had been dressed in a nightgown, and all the tricks had been played on him, Jon finally retired, with his bride, to Maggie's room. They were just about to consummate the vows, when a barrage of rifle fire sounded outside. The party continued most of the night. So did the cockelling! It was a "babbling bear garden."

CHAPTER IV

The Blues

It was daylight. It was cold. Jon knew these facts, because he could see as well as feel the soft, shivering form squeezing him into short, gasping breaths. Or it may have been the quilt, wrapped around his head, choking him at the neck. Either way, Jon was very uncomfortable, rammed against the wagon's railing, mashed by Maggie. She didn't even flinch when Jon gently lifted her up and over. That's when he felt the cold on his togless body. He scrambled into his unmentionables and his kentucks. He remembered that he had left his shoes and socks outside the wagon, and he knew it was cold when his feet hit the wet grass. Jon broke his record for fast dressing. Thank goodness for the huge bonfire and the smell of coffee. Thank goodness for Mose Dasilvalentis and Ellavated Ella McAllister. Or was it Hamilton now? *Guess they can decide that for themselves,* Jon thought.

Ella and her daughter, Buelah Botcherbuns, already had a stack of hotcakes, and were frying the few eggs left, after the "Hamilton Hill" mishap. Looking around, Jon could see that Mose and the boy, Chipper Cheechako, had already fed and watered the animals, and Chipper had a bucket of milkings.

"What a team I have," Jon declared. It was time to take stock, and get this strange show on the road. Jon figured about three days to Boone Town, and they would be getting a late start.

"Buelah, will you get Maggie up and dressed?"

"Yassa, Massa Jon, I sho will."

"Buelah! I am no longer Master Jon."

"Yessa," as she made tracks to the wagon.

"I's gots cakes an' eggs fo' you's," announced Ella.

"How many eggs do you have left, Ella?"

"Enoughs fo you's an' Sissy."

"Better call her Maggie from now on."

"Yassa Massa, er, Jonathan."

"Just call me Jon, Ella?"

"Yassa, Jon."

"Give the eggs to Mose and Chipper. They've earned them already this morning. How long have you all been up?"

"Since befo' dawn," answered Ella.

"Well, from now on, get Maggie and me up before dawn too, so we can be on the road by daylight."

"Yassa, Jon. I's gets all fed, an' we be off."

Buelah did a better job than Jon ever could getting Maggie up, dressed, made presentable, and fed. Jon helped Mose get the drays hitched to the wagons, and by midmorning all was ready for the journey to Arkansas.

"How much milk is left, Chipper?"

"'Bouts this much, Massa Jon," said Chipper, as he pointed to the bucket, less than a quarter full.

"Okay. I'll show you a little trick my father taught me. Find a short piece of rope."

Chipper ran to the buckboard and brought back a two-foot strand of rope, which Jon tied from the milk bucket to the back rib of the wagon's canvas cover. The bucket swung freely.

"Now, the more we bounce around, the more butter we should have for dinner."

"You mean for supper, Jonny," said Maggie.

"I mean for dinner, in the Hamilton household."

"You said that the majority will rule, and there are a lot of McAllisters here, to only one Hamilton."

"Me and my big mouth," quipped Jon, as he contemplated a defeat. "How about a compromise?"

"Like what, big boy?"

"Like supner or dinpur!"

Maggie laughed. "Alright, we'll settle on supner."

The Yadkin seemed lower this day than it was the day before, when Jon's gang struggled to cross it. The roadway ran in a northerly direction, and Jon felt compelled to leave it and turn west, but stayed instead, glued to the river. Early in the evening, the river did finally turn west, and Jon was thankful that he stayed with it. The afternoon was warm, and Jon felt content that his dream was happening. They found plenty of grass, and camped along the Yadkin River, pleased that they made between fifteen and twenty miles.

Diary of Margaret Hamilton

Monday, October 26, 1835

Happy, yet sad. Left my Bethania for the last time in many years, I'm afraid. Very cold this morning, but warm in the afternoon. Saw a flock of beautiful but noisy birds in the afternoon. Do not know what they were, but they looked like parrots, very colorful. Also saw a pack of four or five dogs. Jonny said they were wolves, but they were small. If only the entire trip was as easy and uneventful as today, the third day of travel. Many more to come . . .

Tuesday morning was again very cold. The grass was covered with frost. Once Jon had the quilt pulled off Margaret, she was dressed in a flash. What was once a road of sorts was now just a clearing, still following the river, with only a slight pull for the horses. It was still overcast and cool when the gang nooned, but the sun broke out in the early afternoon, around two o'clock, Jon reckoned, and confirmed the time with his sundial. By midafternoon, Jon was again beginning to worry. The trail was now taking them southwest. They were back due west of Bethania, he figured. Shortly thereafter, Chipper first spotted a small herd of animals. He shouted, and the wagons stopped. Jon jumped down, grabbed his Hawken, and frantically tried to load it. He was too late, as the beasts ran up the trail, then disappeared into the brush.

"Were they deer, Jonny?" asked Maggie.

"No, I think the damned things were antelope."

"Don't curse, Jonny. It's alright. There are more where they came from, and you'll get the next one."

"Righto. I'll keep my Hawken loaded from now on."

"Don' dat be dangerous?" asked Buelah.

"No, I'll keep the cap away from the hammer."

The wagons rolled a short ways around a corner, and low and behold, there they were again. This time Jon grabbed his rifle, inserted the cap, and *BOOM!* One antelope down.

"Got him!" yelled Jon as he jumped down from the wagon. Little Chipper ran past Jon, headed for the kill.

"You's got dem, alrights, Massa Jon!" hollered Chipper.

"Poor thing," said Maggie.

"Po' thing? We's needs dem meat, Mistress Maggie," said Ella, as she hurried past Maggie, knife in hand.

Mose and Jon quickly cleaned out the innards of the antelope and, with Ella's help, were in the process of skinning, when Chipper spotted them, Indians. He let out a shriek, and disappeared behind Mose. None of Jon's group had ever seen Indians before, and they stared for moments at the sight. Two men and a woman sat astride painted horses, all covered with beautiful blankets. The men wore shiny, silver-colored headbands and bracelets, looking very regal. In unison, they raised their right arms, having shifted rifles to their left hands. Jon took this as a sign of peace, and returned the arm gesture. As they climbed down off their steeds, Maggie saw the beautiful moccasins they wore, pure white with blue and green beads decorating the men's footwear.

"Those moccasins are lovely," she said.

"I's loves to has dem blankets," whispered a frightened Buelah, pushing close to Maggie.

"Shush, Buel." Maggie and Buelah hugged each other in fear, eyes glued to the three natives. They approached.

"I am Ned Steward," said the taller of the two men.

"And I am Will-See in Darkness," said the other.

"We are Cherokee from Georgia land," said Ned.

The squaw did not speak, and stood behind the men. Jon was relieved that they spoke English, and attempted to answer.

"Welcome. We are happy to meet you. Will you join us for a meal of fresh antelope?"

"We are grateful that you share Cherokee meat," said Will. "We shall join you, and smoke."

"Chipper, will you and Buelah please gather some branches for a fire, and Mose, you and Ella bring the wagons up, Okay?"

"Yassa, we's do, Jon," said Mose. They all left, while Maggie clung to Jon.

"These Negroes are your slaves," stated Ned.

"No, sir. They were the slaves of my wife's father, but they are free now and we are all going to Arkansas," answered Jon, as he hugged Maggie back.

"Arkansas! We have Cherokee who live in Arkansas for many winters!" exclaimed Will.

"They violate Cherokee Blood Law and maybe die, so they flee across Great River," explained Ned.

"What is Cherokee Blood Law?" asked Maggie, who had seemed to lose her fear.

"When Cherokee sell land to whites, must die." This time, the answer came from Will. The warriors seemed to take turns talking. A smiling Jonathan hoped Maggie noticed that, as well as the fact that the woman said nothing!

"But why would you kill each other, just because one sells some land to us?" Now Maggie was pushing things too far, thought an uncomfortable ex-overseer.

"Whites not keep promises, and take Cherokee land by force. They take sacred land and push all Cherokee on lands west of the Great River," said Ned.

"We are headed across the Mississippi River. I am being forced by my husband," said a smiling Maggie.

"This true?" asked Will, to Jon.

"No, not true, my wife is keeping her promise to me."

"Then she say these things in anger." This from Ned.

"No, sir. She says it in jest."

"What jest?" asked Will.

"Teasing . . . for fun," answered Jon.

The two natives shook their heads in unison. As if by signal, the woman got up and went to the pack horse and brought back a long-stemmed pipe and a small leather pouch. Meanwhile, Mose, Buelah, and Chipper had built a pile of wood for a fire, and Ella was busy cutting strips of meat from the hind quarters of the dead antelope. The Cherokee woman began to help. Jon could sense the uneasiness in Ella, next to a native woman with a knife, but they soon worked together.

Mose was having trouble getting a fire started with his friction matches. He was swiftly losing his patience, as well as wearing out the sandpaper. He finally got a flame on the little stick, and then on the twigs of the woodpile.

Jon turned his head back to the Indians. They had already started a fire on a small leaf from a carved wooden friction cup, and were applying this to the pipe, with a beautifully carved bowl in the shape of the head of a bear. Will took two or three deep puffs, sucking in hard on the long stem, which was carved in white pine to resemble a snake, with the snake's head in Will's mouth. Will then handed the pipe to Jon, who took two long drags, and ended up coughing hard. He took another drag after his coughing spell ended, and handed the pipe to Ned, who puffed contentedly. The three then stepped to the fire, where Mose was already sitting on a woven blanket, and other blankets were placed around the fire for the three "braves" by the native woman. Ned offered the pipe to Mose. All watched as Mose took a long, deep draw, and let out a burst of smoke the size of the bonfire's smoke in front of him.

"Big man make big smoke," said Will, laughing.

After a pause, Ned asked, "Why you go to Arkansas?"

"We are going to start a new life on new land," answered Jon.

"We start new life too," said Will, "in land of Great Smokies."

"You live in the Smokey Mountains?" asked Maggie.

"Yes. This secret," said Ned, finger to his lips.

"But you said you were from Georgia land."

"Yes, but Georgia militia force us off our land," said Will, "and try to capture Cherokee and send to new Indian lands."

"We have no farms now, in Georgia. Our land already auctioned to white farmers," continued Ned.

"Oh, how sad," said Maggie.

"About one hundred fifty Cherokee escape to mountains that smoke. We will shelter there in secret until new white president is elected," added Will.

"We go to Washington to try to help John Ross," said Ned.

"John Ross is chief of all Cherokee Nation," added Will.

Jon broke a long silence. "Then you will meet Andrew Jackson."

"Andrew Jackson traitor," answered a solemn Ned.

"Jackson traitor to Chickasaw, to Seminole, and to Cherokee," Will said.

"What has he done?" asked Maggie.

"Warriors from five great nations help Andrew Jackson fight Red Bowls in Bama, and Redcoats at Great River. He promise all nations can keep sacred lands," answered Ned.

"Now he stole all Creek and Chickasaw lands, and chase Seminole into swamps!" shouted Will.

"Jackson's army send Creek and Chickasaw to new Indian lands west of big river, and now pursue all Cherokee as well!" added a heated Ned Steward.

"Cherokee must never give up land to whites," said Will.

"Even as we speak, the traitor Jackson now dealing with Cherokee traitor, Jon Ridge, to sell Cherokee land."

"That's why we go to Washington to help Jon Ross fight such treaty," added Will.

"You say you already have your people in Arkansas?" asked Jon.

"Yes. They first Cherokee traitors," answered Ned.

"Then maybe you can get new lands in Arkansas."

"Maybe. Be we stay with our people in mountains that smoke, until new white president in power," said Will.

"I wish you luck," said Jon.

The men shook hands and puffed again on the pipe. The women had made fresh dodgers, and now served them, filled with the meat of the antelope. Before long, the natives and the strange band of travelers parted ways in friendship. The wagon looked as though it had a fringe decorating it, as strips of meat, dangling from rope, encircled the canvas covering.

Jon surmised that they still had three or four hours of daylight left, and he wanted to make enough mileage to ensure getting close to Boone by nightfall on Wednesday. So, on they trudged, through sometimes light, and sometimes dense thickets of pine. Once, upon reaching an open meadow, they spotted the dark, blue-colored mountain range that they must cross.

Late in the day, they passed a few scrub farms, and Jon wondered just how these people could make a living. The road became much better defined and easier to travel, so Jon pushed the now very tired animals on, ever in sight of the small, but still rapidly flowing Yadkin River. Darkness came swiftly, and Jon began looking for a grassy area to bed down in. Around a bend, and the group spotted lights.

"Is that Boone?" asked a very tired Maggie.

"I don't think so," answered Jon. "It can't be. I don't think we catch Boone until late tomorrow."

"It looks like a town, Jonny," she said.

"Righto, it sure does that. But I don't know what town it could be."

"Well, can we stop anyway? We're all tired, aren't we, Buelah?"

"Yes'm, we sho' is, Sissy."

"Okay, ladies. I'm looking for a grassy spot for the animals to feed."

"Maybe this town has a livery."

"Alas! There is a brain box under all those red curls."

"Quiet, you big lummox," said Maggie, as she punched his arm.

The main street was well lit by lanterns hanging from carved poles. There were several log homes, fancy storefronts, a doctor, apothecary, mercantile, clothier, hotel and boarding house, and even a bank. On back streets, they saw a church, a school, and what looked like a fire station. And, sure enough, a large livery barn at the end of the street. Nobody answered Jon's hollering, but the doors opened to several empty stalls, with plenty of hay and barrels of grain. The horses would eat well tonight! One corner of the barn had a stack of loose straw, so the group decided to sleep in comfort under a roof for a change. While the women busied themselves getting some supner, the men grabbed buckets and headed back through town to the river for water, some five or six blocks. Storefronts revealed the name of the town, as they passed by in the buckboard.

"Wilkesboro Hotel, the sign says," said Jon.

"Dat be town's name, Jon?" asked Mose.

"That it is, Mose. There's another sign on the general store, 'Wilkesboro Mercantile.' Never heard of it."

"Me needers," said Mose.

There were no signs of life anywhere on the street, except a few houses with lights. Jon felt that he should not bother them.

When Jon returned to the livery, he announced, "The name of the town is Wilkesboro. I've never heard of it before."

"I have. It's a county seat," answered Maggie, "but I thought it was more north, close to Virginia."

"We are close to Virginia, little missus smarty."

"No we're not, you dummy," said a grinning Maggie.

"I'll bet we're closer to Virginia than Tennessee."

"Okay, you've got a bet, Jonny. Now let's eat. Nanty Ella has fixed us something to eat."

After some cold antelope dodgers, the group hit the hay. Mose and Ella had everyone up and hungry before dawn. They started to prepare breakfast, when Jon suggested they see if they could eat at the hotel. The wagons rolled a couple blocks to the Blue Ridge Hotel and Boarding House. The noises coming from the side street proved to be the kitchen, and the Hamilton group entered and seated themselves.

"Can a band of wanderers find food here?" Jon asked the man working at the stove.

"You and the white lady can, mister, but not the Negroes," came the man's answer.

"They are free Negroes, and traveling with me."

"I ain't never seen no free Negroes before. What makes 'em free, stranger?"

"I made them free."

"Then they can feed themselves down at the livery."

"There ain't anyone there this morning, mister. I'd appreciate it if you would feed us all so we can be on our way. Our money is good," Jon angrily said.

"Well . . . if you eat quickly, before the guests start showing up."

"Good. We're in a hurry anyway."

"Susan!" the man yelled. To Jon, he asked, "Where are you folks headed?"

"We're on our way to new lands in Arkansas."

"Arkansas? Ain't that a way west a-here?"

"Sure is, and we're hoping to get there before dark," said Jon, trying to hold a straight face.

"You'll never make it, unless those Negroes can fly." Once again he hollered, "Susan!"

"Coming," answered a woman's voice, before Jon got a glimpse of the heavy, gray-haired lady. "What do you want now?"

"Fix these people some hotcakes and eggs, so they can get to Arkansas on a full stomach," he grinned. "That Okay with you-all?"

"Sounds wonderful," answered Jon.

Susan the cook had a way of making buckwheat flour taste sweet, and the group ate like there would be no tomorrow. Jon tried, but couldn't keep up with Mose.

"Okay, gang, let's get crackin'."

"We's be ready, Jon," said Ella.

"How much do we owe you, sir?" Jon asked.

"How about two bits?" said the man.

"Tell you what, here's half an Eagle. Take half a dollar for yourself, and give the rest to the owner of the livery. All of us and our animals bedded down there overnight, and we took some grain with us. Will you do that?"

"Yes, sir. Tom McGuire will be more than happy with this."

"Good. Oh, by the way, how far is it to Boone Town?"

"It's not much of a town. It's about forty miles. But you're not going there, are you?"

"We sure are. Why do you ask?"

"Well, sir, the only road over the Blues is north, through Abingdon, then down the Great Valley road to Knoxville, Tennessee."

"Thanks, but we're going to try to follow Daniel Boone's trail to Cumberland Gap," said Jon.

"Well, good luck. You're going to need it."

"Thanks again. But just in case, how far is it to Abingdon?"

"I'd say it's about sixty miles, more or less."

"See? You big lummox. I told you Virginia was farther away. You owe me now," teased Maggie, after they were back in the wagon and headed for Boone.

"That wasn't the bet, my pretty plum."

"It was too! Now you're trying to wiggle out of the bet, you big bunco."

"The bet was the distance to Tennessee."

"It was not, Jonny! Don't try to bamboozle me. You owe me a lot. Right, Buelah?"

"Yes'm. You's owes Sissy lots," answered Buelah.

"That's two against one. Pay up!" said Maggie.

"What do I owe you?"

"Let's see . . .," teased Maggie. "How about a new silk dress, a new house, and . . . a diamond birthstone ring, to match the wedding ring you didn't buy me."

"Whoa!" Sloggy and Smutty stopped abruptly. "Not you, Slog. Get up! Maybe your father will lend me enough for that too."

"You mean I'm following you to Arkansas for nothing?"

"I promise you, my pretty plum, you'll have all those things, as soon as my ship comes in."

"And where is your ship now?"

"It's working its way around the bottom of South America."

"It must be stuck in the sea!" said Maggie.

"But it will be on its way now. It's spring there."

"It's probably in dry dock, with a big hole in its side."

The band of travelers moved steadily west by southwest, ever watching the Yadkin River become a stream. About midmorning, they heard someone shouting behind them, so they stopped. A man was fast approaching on a horse.

"You just leave Wilkesboro this morning?"

"Yes, sir, we sure did," answered Jon.

"My name is Matthew McKnight, and I'm a deputy sheriff of Wilkes County."

"Glad to meet you, Mister McKnight."

"I'm afraid I'm going to have to take you back to Wilkesboro."

"Whatever for?" asked Maggie.

"Because you broke into the livery and stole a lot of grain," said Matthew.

"We paid him well for that grain, and the use of some stalls overnight."

"That's not what Mister McGuire says. Can you prove it?"

"There are six of us that saw us pay," declared Maggie.

"Yes, ma'am, but I can only believe you two whites."

"Then how would we prove it to you?" asked Jon.

"Can you describe Mister McGuire for me?"

After a pause Jon said, "Oh, we paid the man at the hotel kitchen."

"And what was his name?" asked Matthew.

Another pause ensued. "Do you remember the man's name, gang?" asked Jon.

"I don't think he ever told us his name," answered Maggie.

"Well, what did he look like?"

"He was slender, about fifty years old, and . . . and he had dark brown hair," said Jon.

"The hair had streaks of gray on the sides," added Maggie.

"Did he have a mustache?" asked the deputy.

"No, I don't think."

"Yes, he did," answered Maggie, about the same time as Jon.

"You're both giving me different answers." The deputy raised his rifle from its resting spot across the saddle. "You better turn the wagons around," he said.

"But we'd be wasting ten miles and a lot of time, sir. Maybe Susan can verify that I paid."

"Susan, you say? Where did you meet her, and what did she look like?"

"She cooked breakfast for us all, hotcakes and eggs, and she was heavy set with gray hair."

"Well, you got that one right, anyway."

"She fixed a ton of cakes and eggs," added Maggie. "Maybe she'll remember us paying."

"Well, it's about eight miles back to town. Can you pay for the grain again, and I'll make sure Tom gets it?"

Jon could feel the heat on the back of his neck, as he pondered paying twice for the grain.

"Oh, sure, we can do that, can't we, Jonny?" asked Maggie.

"How much will you take for the grain in that barrel?"

"Oh, I think Tom would be happy with an Eagle."

"I only have a quarter Eagle," said an angry Jon.

"Make it a half Eagle, and we'll call it square."

The fee paid and the "deputy" gone, Jon was cursing aloud as the wagons rolled again.

"Stop cussing, Jonny. It's only money."

"Only money? Only money! You think it grows on trees?"

"At least we saved going back eight miles," she said.

"And eight miles back here, and half a day's time. Damn it anyhow . . . Buggers!"

"Jonny! Stop it. Why are you so mad?"

"Because I'm not sure which one of them was the crook!"

Jon remained angry the rest of the day, as the wagons weaved in and out of pine trees. Not only was he mad at being conned out of money, he was also upset that he misjudged the distance to Boone by at least a half day.

Diary of Margaret Hamilton

Wednesday, October 28

. . . Made about thirty miles today through pine forests. Jonny was a bear all day, after being conned out of half an Eagle. Saw more wolves and a bear in the distance. A lovely day today, with lovely scenery, but cold already, at about seven and thirty tonight . . .

October 29

Day six started with the group awake early, shaking and shivering in the cold. As daylight loomed, frost was everywhere on the shrubs and trees. With all up, Mose put blankets on the animals, while the women cooked hot grub. Soon they were rolling west, and soon they were climbing steadily. About midmorning, the forests opened to brushy meadows with log cabins, "scrub farms," Jon called them, wondering what they could grow on these high plateaus.

"Will we's be livin' like dis in Arkansas?" asked Buelah. This was the first she spoke all morning.

"We better not, or I'm hiking back home," answered Maggie.

"Me toos."

"Now where is that frontier spirit? We will need to build a shelter of some kind to hold us all until we're able to put up something permanent," answered Jon.

"And just how long will that take?" asked Maggie.

"With good bottomland and a good market, it should only take a couple years."

"Two years? We squalor for two years?"

"Be brave, my pretty plum. I'll keep you *so* busy. You'll be in a new home in no time at all."

"Hmmph! I'll be busy enough with this little Jonny I'm carrying in my stomach."

"By the time he's a butt-biter, he'll be working in the cotton fields."

"I hope so."

"Along with all his brothers!"

"What? If that's what you married me for, you're cockamamie, Jonny."

"Cockamamie about cockelling."

Jon judged it was around noon when the rains came, still cold, and mixed with flakes of snow. Jon had never seen snow before, but Mose and Ella had. "'Bout eighteen-twelve, when dem grones shuck," they said. The group had stopped when Chipper spotted some bushes with reddish berries on them, and he was already eating them when the rest of the gang got to them. Mose brought a bucket.

"I wonder what kind of berry this is," said Maggie.

"Maybe they're mountain cranberry," answered Jon.

"I don't think so. Those are bitter, I think."

"Dees be tangleberry," said Mose.

"Yes'm, dey be's tangleberries," agreed Ella.

"How do you know that?" asked Maggie.

"We's had dem on plantation," answered Mose.

"Dem was long times ago," said Ella.

In a short time, two buckets of tangleberries were filled, and Chipper had eaten nearly another bucket full. The rain had now changed mostly to snow.

"Should we fix something to eat?" asked Maggie.

"Let's continue on. We should be close to Boone."

The wagons continued to climb west by southwest. There continued to be scrub farms, but no town. The snow was now sticking to the ground, and Jon was again getting worried. At last, a log-fenced farm appeared, with several long buildings. The Yadkin, now a creek, bordered the property on two sides. Above the gate hung a sign: *D. BOONE.* Jon reckoned the town was near, and that it was close to four o'clock by his dial, getting dark, and snow was now covering the ground. Another mile or so, and Boone appeared. It was just a small group of buildings.

"At last! Boone at last!" hollered Jon.

"I'm disappointed."

"What about, my pretty plum?"

"We're almost out of North Carolina," Maggie said.

"Not yet. You saw the mountains ahead?"

"I've been looking at them for two days."

"Well, darlin', we won't be out of North Carolina until we cross them, and that could take several days."

"I hope we're stopping. I'm cold and hungry."

"Me toos," said Buelah. "We stays overnight?"

"I wasn't planning on stopping, but it's almost dark and I want to getcha in this snow."

"Oh no, you don't, big boy. Buel and I want to eat and get warmed up."

"Okay, darlin'. I wonder if Boone has an eatery."

"That big building must be the mercantile, and there's a stable," said Maggie. "I wonder what that big log house is there?"

"Let's find out," answered Jon, as he leaped down from the wagon and headed for the structure. Jon's legs slipped out from under him, and he landed on the snow-covered ground. Maggie and Buelah both laughed at him, so he made and threw snowballs at them. The women's screaming only encouraged Jon.

"Stop it, Jonny!" yelled a laughing Maggie.

"Come on down and play, my pretty plum."

"Hand me that whip, Buel!"

"Yes'm," Buelah began searching for the snake.

"Chipper!" hollered Jon, as he tossed a snowball at the buckboard. "Come on down and join me!"

"Chips be very sick!" shouted Ella.

"He eats too many berries, Jon," said Mose.

"Poor boy. He did eat a lot of tangleberries," said Jon.

"We've got calomel, Jonny. I'll have Buelah take it back to them."

"Righto, and if I can manage to walk in this stuff, I'll get us some food."

Buelah climbed down very cautiously, but still slipped and fell in the snow. Like a cat, Mose walked forward and helped Buelah up and back to the buckboard with the calomel. Meanwhile, Jon slipped and slid his way to the two-story building, set back off the main street.

"Hello," said Jon to the lady answering the door-knocker. "We are traveling west and would like to eat and board overnight here in Boone Town."

"This is a boarding house," the lady answered. "How many of you are there?"

"My wife and I, and four Negroes."

"Sorry, I can feed and board you and your wife, but not the slaves."

"But they're not slaves, ma'am. They are free blacks."

"Free blacks are not welcome at all here."

"I'm sorry you feel that way, ma'am. They are just as good a-people as you or I am."

"Then you're not welcome, either. You can sleep in the livery," she answered, starting to close her door.

"Is there a place to eat in this town?" he asked, remembering the bamboozling he got in Wilkesboro.

"You might try the store, if they didn't close early."

Jon trudged carefully back to the wagons. He didn't want to display his anger toward the boarding house lady. "No room at the inn, but we can use the livery."

"Is there any place to eat a hot meal?" asked Maggie.

"Not unless the store is open. I'll go check. How is the Chipper?"

"Real sick, Jonny. If they're open, see if they have some laudanum or castor oil.'

"Will do," Jon answered, as he again trudged toward the long building across the snow-covered street. To his surprise, the door to the *Boone General Store* was unlocked.

"Hello! Is anyone here?"

"Yes, sir, come on in. Welcome, stranger." A small, gray-haired gentleman arrived behind a counter about the same time Jon got to the front of it. He was an elderly man with a beard, and a pipe dangled from his lips.

"Thank you. I have some tired and very hungry people outside, and one sick boy. Can you help us?"

"You betcha I can, mister. Bring them in."

Jon returned to the door, and yelled at his group. "Come on in, gang! It's warm in here!" He turned his attention to the elderly man. "I have some free blacks with me. Can they come inside? One of them is the sick boy."

"You are all welcome. I have a warm stove and some hot coffee in the back room."

"Thank you again, sir." Jon exited the store long enough to help his gang up the steps and into the store.

"Oh, Lawdy, it be's warm in here's!" exclaimed Ella.

"It's wonderful," agreed Maggie. She looked at Jon and the gray-haired man. "Do they have any laudanum?"

"I don't, but I have bottles of castor oil," said the store owner. "Go ahead into the back room, and I'll bring it."

"Righto. Thanks again. My name is Jonathan Hamilton, and this is my wife, Margaret."

"Pleased to meet you. My name is Duncan. Just call me Dunk, like they all do around here."

The back room had a long stove, fed by wood at both ends, with a long flat plate between, for cooking, and what looked like a homemade oven under the plate. It heated the room, and made the group warm for the first time all day. In one corner of the room were a line of small tables that folded, and chairs that stacked. Jon had not seen anything like them before.

Dunk began serving coffee to the travelers from a big pot on the stove plate, just as Chipper began throwing up his red berries onto the smooth, planked floor. "That's alright," said Duncan, as he grabbed a wet cloth and wooden-handled mop of sorts, with fur-skin strips at the business end. "Castor oil will do that every time," declared Dunk.

With the coffee served, the mess cleaned, and Chipper quickly feeling better, Dunk began mixing flour and other ingredients at a table next to the big stove. "I'll warm your innards with my favorite meal," he said. "Crapcakes."

The Hamilton group looked at each other in amazement.

"What are crapcakes?" asked Maggie, hoping not to get the answer they were thinking.

"Don't worry none, folks. It's not what ye be thinkin'."

"Tank de Lawd fo' dat," remarked Buelah, as she wandered over to Dunk's table to help.

"What's your name, Nan?" asked Dunk.

"I be's Buelah."

"Well, Buelah, if you stir this, I'll go out and get the other things I need."

"Orite, I's do."

Dunk was only gone a few minutes when he returned with a couple hand-carved wooden bowls full of strips of meat and churned butter. In a cupboard by his table, he grabbed another wooden bowl. The ingredient was red.

"Dem looks like dem berries we's pick," said Buelah.

"You picked some of these?" asked Duncan.

"Yassa, we's do. Dey makes Chips sick."

"Do you have any left?"

"Yassa, we's do."

"Would you like to sell some to me?" Dunk directed his question to Jon, across the room.

"Sure will," answered Jon. "How much do you need?"

"All the tangleberries you have. They make great jam."

The gang put their heads together, and all agreed to trade.

"We have two buckets of berries, Dunk. We'll trade them for a meal of crapcakes," said Jon, as Mose left to get them.

The cakes Dunk made actually rolled up. He put sweet butter, jam, and a strip of meat in each cake and, with the long, hot plate, soon had a large pile of rolled cakes. "Ta-da! I present to you . . . crapcakes!"

"Deys dee-licious!" exclaimed Buelah, the first to show bravery and eat one. She was on her second, when the rest scrambled across the room to partake. The pile was soon gone, despite Dunk's attempts to reload his hot plate with more.

"What kind of meat is this?" asked Jon, with a mouth full.

"The chewy meat is bear, and the white meat hare," answered Dunk. "I also got some wolf and deer."

"They're wonderful!" proclaimed Maggie.

"Dey is. Sho' wish Daddy wa' here to eats," said Ella.

"Where is Mose, anyway?" asked Maggie.

"Went out to get the buckets of berries."

"He's been gone a long time, Jonny."

"I know. I'll go find him." Jon headed back through the store and out the front door.

"I hope he's alright in all that snow," said Maggie.

"He be's fine, Sissy," answered Ella.

"Where are you folks from?" asked Dunk.

"A plantation close to Salem," answered Maggie.

"Oh? What plantation is that?"

"Bethania. Have you heard of it?"

"Isn't that a town?"

"Well, yes, it's a small village," said Maggie, "but it's also the name of my daddy's plantation."

"Are you Moravian?" asked Dunk.

"No, hardly. McAllister is Scotch and Irish."

"McAllister? Sam McAllister?"

"Yes. He's my daddy. Do you know him?"

"Not personally, but I've heard of him."

"Well, Mose and Ella here are like my uncle and aunt, and Buelah is my best friend."

"We's were house boundas," said Ella.

"What was that?" asked Dunk.

"They were house slaves, until my husband and I set them free and asked them to come with us," said Maggie.

"Oh! And where are you headed?"

"We's goes to Awkinsaw," answered Buelah.

The front door burst open, and through the store came the very cold Mose and Jonathan. They had the buckets of tangleberries, and headed straight for the replenished stack of crapcakes.

"Where did you find Nunky Mose?" asked Maggie.

"He had put the animals in the livery stables."

"Miss Buelah tells me you're a-headed for Arkansas."

"That's right, Mister Duncan," answered Jon. "It's going to be a state, and they are giving land to new settlers."

"Hmmm . . . are you sure they're *giving* land away?"

"Yes, sir. I have an ad they put in the Salem paper," said Jon, between gulps of crapcake.

"Well, what brings you to Boone?" asked Dunk.

"We're taking the old Boone Trail, so we can see Cumberland Gap."

"There hasn't been any Boone Trail for years," said Dunk. "Your best bet is to head north to Abingdon, then head back down to the Gap on the Valley road."

"Isn't there an old corduroy road going up to the Watauga River?" asked Jon.

"I haven't seen one in the thirty years I've lived here."

"See? We should have listened to Daddy," said Maggie, shaking a finger at Jon.

"Well, we want to follow Daniel Boone's trail, and see the gap the same way he did when he discovered it."

"You mean the Boone Gap, don't you?"

"No, sir, I mean the Cumberland Gap," said Jon.

"Well, I'm sorry to be the one to tell you this, but Boone didn't discover Cumberland Gap," said Dunk.

"He didn't? Who did, Mister Duncan?"

"That's hard to say, son. It was a Cherokee War path for probably centuries before the white man came along."

"Wow, that's interesting."

"Several white men had seen it before Boone, but he made it famous when he broke the trail from the gap into the heart of Kentuke," said Dunk.

"Oh. Well, thanks for that bit of history. We still want to see it. Did you say there was a Boone Gap?"

"Yes, I did. You can see it from here on a clear day," answered Dunk. "It goes up between two mountains."

"That's the way we want to go. How far is that from here?"

"'Bout fifteen miles or so."

"Good. We can start up it tomorrow."

"Well, I wish you luck. You're going to need it."

"About how high up is it?" asked Jon.

"Well, let's see . . . We're about thirty-three hundred . . ."

"This town is thirty-three hundred feet?" asked a surprised Jon, interrupting Dunk.

"That it is, son, so I'd say the gap goes another thousand or twelve hundred feet up."

"Wow! Hear that, gang? We're already more than halfway to the top of the Blues!" exclaimed an excited Jon.

"Oh, but the next half is the tough one. I still think you'd save a lot of days by going north to Abingdon."

"Thank you, Mister Duncan, but we have come this far, and we'll take our chances going due west."

"Looks like we get no say in the matter," said Maggie.

"Yes, we's wan's to votes," added Buelah.

"Alright, sorry, gang. I want to go west. How many of you will go with me?" asked Jon. No hands were raised.

"How many want to go north, like Mister Duncan suggests?" asked a confident Maggie. Only Buelah raised her hand, despite Maggie's urging.

"I's still wit, Jon. He makes us free," said Mose.

"An' I's sticks wit my husban'," said Ella.

"That looks like three-ta-two, my pretty plum."

"Not so fast, Jonny. Chipper gets to vote."

"He's not old enough to vote!" exclaimed Jon.

"Oh yes, he is. Don't try to con us, ya big lummox."

"How's you's votes, son?" asked Ella.

The poor boy's eyes sent from one face to another, and got wider with each glance. "I's votes wit my mom," he finally said.

"Ah-ha! Now it's four to two. That boy knows which side of the bread is buttered!" shouted Jon.

"Hush up, you big turkey," said Maggie, as she hugged Buelah. "I hope you're not making another error in judgment, like you did coming here!"

"This was no error, darlin'. If we hadn't a-come this way, we'd never have met Mister Duncan and his crapcakes."

"True. But we also would never have met Hamilton Hill, or nearly drowned in the Yadkin, or got conned in Wilkesboro."

"Why do you always have to win our arguments?"

"Why do you always have to win the votes?"

"Well, maybe you'll run into the people who came through here a couple days ago," said Dunk.

"So we're not the only ones going this way!"

"They say the world is full of them!" answered Dunk.

"Were they headed for Arkansas too?" asked Jon.

"Not sure. I don't think they'll make it anywhere."

"Why is that, Mister Duncan?"

"They were in an open wagon, with few provisions."

"Maybe we'll catch up with them tomorrow," said Jon.

"If they're still alive," answered Dunk.

That comment brought silence to the group for a spell.

"Have you learned a lot about Daniel Boone?" asked Dunk.

"Not really. Why do you ask?" asked Jon.

"Well, you're trying to follow his trail over the Blue Ridges, and through the gap. Seems like you'd want to end up in Kentucke. That's where he's buried."

"There's some question about that," said Maggie.

"What question?" asked Jon.

"He may be buried in Missouri."

"Missouri? Why would he want to be buried there?"

"And what's wrong with Missouri?" asked Maggie.

"I've heard the people there are stubborn and dumb."

"I've got some bad news for you, Jonny."

"What's that, my pretty plum?"

"Arkansas is part of Missouri!" She laughed.

"It is not! You're pulling my leg!"

"No, I'm not, Jonny. Arkansas is annexing from Missouri."

"Where'd you hear that?"

"In college, big boy!"

"And you say he might be buried in Missouri?" asked Dunk.

"Yes. He died in Missouri, and they say they sent someone else in a casket back to Kentucky," answered Maggie.

"Well, I do declare, that's news to me," said Dunk.

"Me too," said Jon.

"You know, I think he should be buried here in Boone. This is where he lived a lot of his life," reasoned Dunk.

"And raised his children," added Maggie.

"Right on his farm."

"And the town is even named for him," added Jon.

"Sure is. And that would bring the tourists," said Dunk.

"That is a nice farm he had. We went by it on the way here. Good-looking buildings."

"They're not the original buildings, Jonny."

"Sure they are, darling. Right, Mister Duncan?"

"Well, yes and no."

"Yes, I'm right, and no, you're wrong," said Maggie to Jon.

"Tell her it's the other way around, Mister Duncan."

"Most of the buildings are original, with a lot of upgradin' and remodelin' by the Boone Preservation Society."

"See?" said Maggie.

"See?" said Jon.

"Well, I guess we should be headed over to the stables, gang, so we can get an early start in the morning."

"But it's so nice and warm here, Jonny," said Maggie.

"We's tank you's Missa Duncan," said Ella.

"I insist you sleep right here in this room, folks. I've got some beddin' in my barn, and lots of blankets in the store."

"But they're new, Mister Duncan, and we can't pay for them. You may have a hard time selling them after we've used them."

"Have you seen any customers since you've been here, Missus Hamilton?" asked Dunk.

"Well, no, I haven't."

"We don't have many people come through this town, Missus Hamilton. Some of them blankets are five years old."

"Where do you sleep, Mister Duncan? In the boarding house?"

"No, Mister Hamilton, I'll sleep right here, with you all."

Thanks to Mister Duncan, the group had a warm and comfortable night. By the time Jonathan and Margaret awoke, Mose was away hitching the wagons, and Dunk, Ella, and Buelah were fixing breakfast.

"Good morning. Did you sleep well?"

"Like we were in hibernation," answered Jon. "You sure keep this room nice and warm."

"Got to. It's used a lot."

"For meetings of the Boone Preservation Society?" asked Maggie.

"That, and church, weddings, funerals, socials, some schoolin', and everything else."

The breakfast was oatmeal, with chunks of boiled venison. Mose came back wet from rain and confirmed that the temperature had warmed up overnight, and the snow was gone. The time was right to climb the Blue Ridge Mountains.

"How much do we owe you, Mister Duncan?" asked Jon.

"Nary a cent, and thank you all for the berries and milk. You have everything you need for your journey?"

"Well, I think we do."

"How many blankets do you have?" asked Dunk.

"I'm not sure. How many, Mose?"

"We's has six, Jon, and dey's all on dem horses."

"You can use a half dozen more, Jon," said Dunk. "How many guns and powder? And flour and grain?"

"Not enough of any of the above," answered Maggie.

"Well then, let me fix you all up."

"Thank you, sir, but we have all that we can afford."

"Bully for you! Are you going to let your group starve or freeze to death just because you're bull-headed?"

"No, sir, but we only have enough . . ."

"Tell you what, Mister Hamilton. I'll furnish the supplies you need for that cow you have."

"That wouldn't be fair to you, sir," said Jon.

"Let me worry about that. I need to turn some of this stuff over, anyway. Some of it has been here for years."

Jon turned to his group to decide. The women seemed to think it a good deal, except Ella, who was worried about milk for Chipper. Surprisingly, Mose was for the trade.

"You's gives my Abby aways," cried Chipper.

"You wouldn't want her to suffer, now would you, son?" asked Dunk to Chipper.

"No's, sir," answered the teary Chip.

"Well, she probably would suffer, trying to climb those mountains."

"And we can get another cow on the other side. How about that, Chipper?" asked Jon.

The boy wiped away his tears and shook his head yes.

"Good boy. We'll take your offer, Mister Duncan, and thanks."

"Alright. Let's get you packed in that big buckboard of mine. I'll trade for yours, and I can fix it back up like new," said Dunk.

The big wagon was still heavy with Maggie's dowry, so a lot of the new supplies had to go into Dunk's buckboard. There were small barrels of buckwheat and flour, large barrels of oats and grain, and blankets and wool clothing. Maggie balked at the suggestion of men's wool unmentionables for the women, but Mister Duncan convinced her that all the women would love them soon enough.

"Now here is something you're going to love," said Dunk, as he brought out an assortment of fur caps. "A couple years ago, all the people 'round here made these, but they never sold. We call them Booneskin hats."

"They are lovely," said Maggie, picking out a black-and-white hat.

"That's skunk," said Dunk, and Maggie quickly replaced it with another.

"That one is weasel." Maggie kept it.

"I's likes dis one," said Buelah. "What is it?"

"That's a pretty badger," answered Dunk.

There were hats made from every animal except one.

"Didn't Daniel Boone wear a beaver-skin hat?" asked Jon.

"Yes, sir, he did," answered Dunk, "but beavers have been trapped out of this area, and their pelts make a lot of money. How are y'all fixed for guns?"

"We have my Hawken."

"Is that all?"

"Yes, sir. It's the most advanced mountain gun there is, and it's been modified to a caplock," said Jon.

"That may be, son, but you're gonna need more than that to survive these mountains. There are Indians, billies, bears, and waymen you'll run up against."

"What are waymen?"

"They're skunks who'll rob and shoot ya."

"Well, thanks, but we'll have to do with this. I could use some more balls, though."

"Sure thing. Let me see . . . here are a couple old Kentucky flints. I can give them to you."

"You've done too much for us already," said Jon.

"Glad to do it, son. And here's a minibarrel of powder. I'd hide that Hawken if I were you."

"I don't think it will wear out, Mister Duncan."

"No, but it will probably get stolen if you don't."

"Oh! Thanks for the advice."

"Don't mention it. Keep those Kentuckies ready at all times. You may even run into the Boony."

"What is that?" asked Maggie.

"It's a big furry beast some folks say they've seen."

"We's go's back now, Massa Jon," said Buelah.

"Good idea, Buel, or at least head north to Abingdon," added Maggie. They were both turning pale.

"Nonsense. They ain't such a thing as beasts," said Jon. "We're headed due west, ladies."

"You sound like my daddy, Jonny."

"Oops, sorry. I see now why he was always using that word. Too much of you women!"

"Very funny! But if there's a beast here, I would just as soon go around."

"There's no beast, and we're not going around," answered Jon. "Just what does this thing look like, Mister Duncan?"

"I've never seen it, but they say it looks something like a big overgrown bear, only it's a reddish-brown color and walks on its hind legs."

"Okay. We'll keep a lookout for it," said Jon.

"Good. As I say, keep them guns ready. The winter a'fore last, they found the broken bones of a hunter who went lookin' for Boony with his brother."

"Did his brother say what got him?" asked Jon.

"Don't know for certain. They've never found the brother, I'm told."

"Jonny, let's go north," said a scared Maggie.

"Don't worry, my pretty plum. I think we're ready to tackle the beast of the Blues, gang. Let's get crackin'."

"Here's something I think you'll need. Keep it wrapped so it will stay warm," said Dunk, handing it to Jon.

"What is it, Jonny?"

"I'm not sure. What is it, Mister Duncan?"

"It's about half a pint of yeast."

"What would we do with that?" asked Maggie.

"You never know. You may need to bake bread, or celebrate by making ale," answered Dunk.

"Thank you," said Jon.

"Would you folks like to leave a letter? I can get it to Wilkesboro next week, I think, and it should get to Salem soon after."

"Could we, Jonny? I'll just write a note."

"Sure, but do it quick, so we can get scootin'."

"Good luck, my friends. I hope one day to see you all again, the good Lord willin', and the creek don't rise," said Dunk.

"Thank you, Mister Duncan. You are a true friend."

"Think nothing of it, Jon. Just keep your powder dry, and your noses pointed west, and you'll make it fine. By the way, here's something new that I think you're going to need." Mister Duncan handed a Jon a small barrel of nails.

"Thank you again," said Jon.

"You're welcome. I don't know how we ever lived without them. Now you're ready."

"If I follow the Yadkin, will I get to Boone Gap?"

"Not quite, but it will get you past the first mountain. You'll never make it up Boone Gap with them wagons. Just try to keep west. If you get stuck, go south, then west. You may have to go north a ways after you get over these Blues to find the Watauga River. About three or four days, I imagine."

"Thank you again, Mister Duncan," said Jon, as the group stepped out into the drizzly, cold rain.

"Just a minute," said Dunk. "Hand me those wet blankets you have on those horses. I'll get you some dry ones."

The trade was made, and Mister Duncan even brought out two tarps to put over the buckboard and Mose, Ella, and Chipper. The wagons rolled out of Boone amidst waves and shouts, and headed west along the tiny creek once called the Yadkin River, and into a bank of clouds.

"What time is it, Jonny?"

"I have no idea. It could be late afternoon."

"I'll bet it is. I'm really hungry."

"When we find an opening with grass, we'll stop."

The gang had been traveling for hours, through thick brush and large stands of trees. Visibility was only forty to fifty feet, and the creek had long ago disappeared from view. Mose had been clearing brush with his machete, and the climb became very slow. At least the rain had stopped. True to his word, Jon called a halt when a grassy clearing popped up in front of them.

"Let's build a big fire and get dried out!" he shouted.

"We's make bread fo' dodgas," said Ella.

"Righto. Maybe I can put up a stand for the Dutch oven."

After a hearty supner, the gang sat about, trying to get warm and dry. Each had jobs to do. Chipper was tending the horses, watering and securing them for the night. Ella and Buelah were making corn dodgers for the next several days. Mose was gathering limbs and wood to keep a big fire burning through the night, and Jon was constructing a hiding spot under the wagon to house his J & S Hawken. Mose was about to go find Chipper in the fog and help him finish bedding down the horses, when the boy let out a blood-curdling scream. Mose and Jon ran in that direction.

"I be comin', Chips!" yelled Mose.

"Are you alright, Chipper?" shouted Jon.

"Hurry, Massa Jon. Hurry! I's sees it!" shouted Chipper.

"What you's see's, boy?" asked Mose.

"I sees de Boone!" Chipper was pointing in the direction he had come from, and Jon could hear the horses snorting and squealing. He ran toward them. As the animals came into view, Jon tried to settle them down, but could not. Mose and Chipper were right behind to do that job.

"Whoa, boy. Whoa der, Slog. Whoa Jake." As the horses calmed, Jon thought he heard some thrashing in the fog, beyond eyesight.

"Let's bring the horses in, closer to the fire."

"Yassa. Dat be's good idea," said Mose.

"What was it, Jonny?" asked Maggie, as the men brought in the horses and tied them to trees close by.

"Don't know for sure, darl—"

"It's be's Boony!" shouted Chip, interrupting Jon.

"I couldn't see what was spooking the plowers."

"I's tell you's. It be's Boone!" said Chipper.

"Whas it looks like, son?" asked Ella.

"It be's big, Mamas, and runs fass."

"Time to runs back homes," said Buelah.

"No, it's not, Buelah. We don't know for sure just what it was that Chipper saw. It was just as scared of us as Chip was of it."

"How do you know that?" asked Maggie.

"Because it was running away from us," said Jon.

"Why are you so stubborn, Jonny?"

"It must be that marriage does that to a person."

"Very funny! If that beast . . . Boony . . . harms my Pasha, you won't live long enough to tell about it!"

"Why? What will you do, my pretty plum?"

"I'll get one of those guns out and shoot you!"

"Maybe I's learn ta shoots gun, Jon," said Mose.

"Not a bad idea, Mose. Have you ever shot a gun?"

"Are you joking again, Jonny?" asked Maggie.

"Why, yassa, Jonny. I's done shot Napoleon in der behinds, an' shoots Red Coats by George Washin'-ton's," chuckled Mose, and the laughs were on Jon.

"Sorry, Mose. I know. Ask a dumb question . . ."

"The only guns boundas sees is dem pointed at boundas."

"Well, you are no longer a bounder, Mose. You are my partner, and it's time you learned how to shoot."

"Yassa, Jon. We's needs mo' dan jus' you's ta shoots."

"I hope you never need to shoot me!"

Jon busied himself teaching Mose how to measure and pour the powder down the barrel of the Kentucky rifle, along with the ball and tamping them down. Jon explained the process of ignition of the powder, with sparks from the new flint. Then Jon inspected the touchhole and powder pan, and found them ready for the primer. The long rifle was now ready for Mose to fire. Jon took the axe to a nearby tree, delimbing and debarking a target area.

"Okay, Mose. Let's see you hit that target."

"I's do my bess, Jon." Mose was shown how to aim and shoot. Sparks and smoke blocked his view, and he lowered the kentuck down as it went off, scaring all.

"You've got to hold your rifle on the target until it fires, Mose!" yelled Jon.

"I's sorry, Jon."

"That's Okay. Let's try it again."

This time, Mose loaded the rifle with Jon's help, and Mose held the barrel straight and steady, and fired.

"Did you hold your aim steady, Mose?"

"I's thinks so. Do I's hits it?"

"No. You missed to the right, I think," answered Jon.

"Orites, I trys again, Jon?"

"Sure thing, Mose. This time, you load it yourself."

"Orites. I's do." As Mose was reloading, a distant shot was heard a long distance away, to the north.

"Did you hear that, Jonny?" asked Maggie.

"Yes, I did. It sounded a long ways off."

"Maybe not so far, Jonny. The fog can muffle sounds."

"Where did you learn that, my pretty plum?"

"Stick with me, lummox, and you will learn something yet."

"Like how to handle sassy women! How are you doing with the loading, Mose? I think we should answer . . ."

Just then, another shot was heard, much closer.

"I's ready, Jon," answered Mose.

"Okay. Go ahead and shoot at the target."

Mose's next shot hit a branch of the tree, just to the right of the target.

"You're getting better, Mose. Reload again."

Another shot was heard from the north, even closer.

"Whoever they are, they're coming closer, Jonny."

"Well, we agree on that, my pretty plum. Maybe it's the people Mister Duncan spoke about. I had better load my Hawken, just in case."

"Now you're scaring me again, Jonny."

"Me's too, Sissy," said Ella and Buelah.

"Well, at least it's not the beast, unless he can shot guns too!"

"Very funny. I'm scared."

"Well, busy yourselves building the fire, and find a hiding spot in those trees. How are you coming along with the reloading, Mose?"

"I's be ready, Jon."

"Alright. Fire at the target once more, then reload."

"I's do, Jon."

"Aim a little to the left, Mose."

Bam! The shot hit the target on the right side.

"Good shot, Mose. Now reload, and remember to shoot a little to the left. Move the buckboard closer to the fire, so they'll have trouble seeing you."

"I's be's ready, Jon. They's doun sees me in dem dark."

"Good. ladies, grab some blankets and find a spot in those trees. I'm going to load the other Kentucky rifle."

Just then, another shot rang out, this time close. Jon noticed some dirt on the powder pan, and found some clean patches in the patch box to clean the barrel and pan, and a thin wire to poke through the touch hole. He quickly started to load the second gun, when he heard them.

"Hello! Hello out there!"

"Can anybody hear us?" This sounded like another voice.

"There are at least two people," Jon said to Mose.

"Yassa, I's ready, Jon."

Jon had just snapped the frizzen down over the primer pan, when the strangers fired again, so close that Jon thought he saw the sparks.

"Hello out there! Where are you?" came voice number one.

"Right here, just ahead! Who are you?" shouted Jon.

"We're lost. Can we come in?"

"We can see your fire. We are cold, wet, and hungry." Jon couldn't tell which voice that was.

"How many are you?"

"Three of us, two men and a woman." This was from voice number one.

"The woman is suffering from the cold," said voice number two.

"Only shoot if I do, Mose," Jon softly said, as he readied himself behind the wagon.

"Yassa, Jon."

"Yes!" Jon yelled. "Come on in, slowly."

After two or three minutes, three forms appeared through the fog, followed by a team of worn horses pulling an open wagon. The two men were supporting the woman.

"Put the guns down and come to the fire."

"Yes, sir," came the answer from the taller man. "Our guns ain't loaded, and we're too tired to resist." The men dropped the weapons and advanced toward the bonfire, still helping the woman walk.

"Thank you for your hospitality, sir. Are you here alone?" asked the taller man.

"No, I'm not," said Jon, as he placed his two rifles on the wagon's bench. "Come on out, ladies. Chipper, go out and pick up those rifles."

"Yassa, Massa Jon," came the answer, as Chipper ran out of the trees toward the rifles.

The three women in Jon's charge came out and wrapped their blankets around the strangers.

"Thank you. Oh, that fire feels so good," said the woman, whose voice was barely audible, body shaking from the cold. She was tall, like Maggie, dark hair and fair complexioned. *Pretty*, thought Maggie.

The woman lay down on a blanket next to the fire.

"You're welcome, but we must get you out of those wet clothes before you catch your death," said Maggie.

"Thank you, but everything I have left is soaked."

"Don't worry about that. I have lots of clothes."

"She's worn my horses out, pulling all her clothes," quipped Jon.

"You better get some more horses, then," answered Maggie, as she helped the woman to the covered wagon.

"Thank you. My name is Liz, Elizabeth Chasney, and that's my husband, Davie, and his older brother Charles."

"Happy to meet you, Liz. I'm Margaret Hamilton, Maggie for short, and my husband there is Jon Hamilton. I'll introduce you to the rest of the family when you are changed."

"Where are you folks from?" Jon asked the two strangers now warming by the fire.

"Just a few miles west of Edenton," said the taller, bigger man. My name is Charles Chasney, and this is my younger brother, Dave."

"Glad to know you. I'm Jonathan Hamilton. Are you getting dried out?"

"Yes, we are. Thanks," said the smaller brother, Dave.

"And these are my partners, Ella and . . . Mose! Where are ya?"

"I's rights here, Jon," said Mose, by the buckboard.

"My god! Look at the size of that nigger!" exclaimed Dave. "He's a mountain on the mountain!"

"He's not a nigger!" shouted Jon. "He's a free black man, and my partner!"

"I apologize for my brother, Mister Hamilton," said Charles.

"I didn't mean to offend you," said Dave.

After a pause, Jon said, "Anyway, these are Ella's children, Buelah and Chipper, and my wife Maggie is in the wagon."

"Are you folks headed for Kentucky?" asked Charles.

"No, Arkansas."

"Arkansas! That's way out on the frontier," said Dave.

"Sure is. They're giving land to new settlers, so they can get enough people to be a state."

"Well, if we ever get over these mountains, we plan on taking the Wilderness Road to Blue Grass Country. We have some relatives already there," said Charles.

"Where are you from, Mister Hamilton?" asked Dave.

"From around Salem. We left from my father-in-law's plantation, Bethania. Ever heard of it?"

"No, can't say that I have. Who's the owner?" asked Charles.

"Samuel McAllister."

"I've heard of him," said Charles.

"We're going a ways up the Wilderness Road too. We want to see the Cumberland Gap, and then head down the river to Nashville."

"Do you know the way? Because we're lost," said Dave.

"We didn't find any place to take a wagon through, and we've been looking for the Great Warrior's Path for three days now," said Charles.

"Well, we are looking for Boone Gap. Mister Duncan, in Boone, says we can't get wagons through it, but he don't know the strength and mind of Mose here." Jon looked again for Mose. "Where are you, Mose?"

"I's fix line to drys clothes. Ella, you's fix food fo dem strangas, an's Chips feed dem horses," said Mose.

"We do's Daddy," answered Ella.

"Thanks, gang," said Jon.

"Thanks, Mose," said Dave.

"We met some Cherokee on the Yadkin a couple days ago. They were headed for Washington to try to save their lands in Georgia. They must have come down the Warrior's Path," said Jon. "Maybe if we find that, we can get across the Blues."

"Well, we ain't found nothing even resemblin' a path," said Dave. "Maybe if we travel together, we'd have better luck."

"We are going up north to Abingdon, remember?"

"I know, Charles, but this way's closer if we can just find a way, and maybe we can do that together," said Dave. "How about it, Mister Hamilton?"

"How about it, gang?" asked Jon to his group.

"I's likes dem, Jon. Makes clearin' trails fass," said Mose. "You's has axes in wagon?"

"What'd he say?" asked Dave.

"Do you have an axe in your wagon?"

"We do, but it's not very sharp," answered Charles.

"Don't worry about that. Mose can make it cut hair! How about you, ladies?" asked Jon.

"Less do's," declared Buelah.

"Fine wit me," said Ella, "but we's needs dem food."

"Looks like we just added three to the mix."

"Great! That's Okay with you, isn't it, Charles?"

"Sure. We'll give it another try, Davy."

"Hallelujah!" said Mose. "I's been practicing shootin'."

"Might as well shoot both the kentucks, Mose, and remember to aim left of the target."

"I's do, Jon."

Mose had finished with the hanging of all the wet clothes he could find in the Chasneys' wagon, and now grabbed both kentucks to fire at the target. Meanwhile, Jon was admiring the forms in the covered wagon. The lantern made the forms dance through the canvas, as the nicely shaped woman, Elizabeth Chasney, dressed.

"Our wives are good-looking wenches, ain't they?" The question came from Dave, and startled Jon.

"Why, yes, they are," answered Jon.

"I noticed your wife was PG. Congratulations."

"Thank you, Dave. Our first will be born in Arkansas, the good Lord willing."

"I've been trying to get mine pregnant for years. Not any luck, but sure fun tryin'," said Charles.

There was an awkward pause, finally broken by the blast of a Kentucky rifle, shot by Mose.

"Did ya hit it, Mose?

"Yassa, Jon. I's thinks so. I's look."

It was then Jon realized how dark it had become. Night had fallen fast. The ladies were emerging from the wagon, and now Jon had a good view of beauty.

"Yassa, Jon, I's hits dead center!" yelled Mose.

"Great! That gun is yours. Shoot the other one."

"Yassa . . ." *Bam!*

"Did you hit it?"

"I's don' tinks so, Jon. I's hears ball hits bushes. I's fires you's gun now, Jon?"

"No, Mose. I'll leave it loaded, but bring those guns over here, and we'll clean them."

"Yassa, I's do, Jon."

"Buelah an' I's has food fo' you's, dodgas an' coffee," said Ella. "I's suppose you's wan's some?"

"Sure do, Ella. Worked up another appetite scarin' away Boony."

"Hee, hee! You's floors me, sho 'nuff, Jon," laughed Ella.

"He's not a bit funny, Ella. Don't spoil him," said Maggie.

"Who's Boony?" asked Liz.

"He's some kind of beast. Mister Duncan in Boone told us about him, and Chipper there saw him when it spooked the horses," answered Maggie.

"Probably a field mouse that spooked Pasha."

"Like hell, you big lummox!" yelled Maggie. "All the horses were spooked, and you said it was crashing through trees running away."

"That could have been the wind."

"Wind, my derriere! You probably farted!" Maggie was red-faced, and everyone started laughing, especially Dave.

"Sure glad you two lovebirds get along so well, just like Davie and I," said Elizabeth.

There was a long silence, and each person looked at the others.

"I'm really tired. Guess I'll hit the sack," said Charles.

"This has been a long day for all of us," said Liz.

"I'll fix you a place to sleep by the fire."

"No need, Maggie. We sleep in the wagon," answered Liz.

"Alright. Nanty Ella, will you and Buel turn those clothes around, so the other sides dry? I'll fix the Chasneys a nice, warm bed in their wagon."

"I's do, Sissy. I's do."

Mose had brought the open wagon close to the fire and attached the ends of a makeshift "clothesline" rope to it. He grabbed a large cloth from the buckboard to rub down the two Chasney horses, and two blankets to warm those drays. Everyone in Jon's gang was busy again, with Ella and Buelah turning the wet-side clothes to the fire, and cleaning up the dutch oven. Chipper was helping Mose take the horses back out to good grass, and staking them to trees. Maggie was helping Liz make a bed, and Jon was cleaning the Kentucky rifles.

"I believe there's a tarp in the buckboard to put over your wagon, in case it rains again."

"Thank you, Mister Hamilton. I'll get it," said Charles.

"Just call me Jon, like everyone else."

"Okay, thanks again, Jon," Charles said, walking away.

"Do the three of you sleep together?" asked Jon, to Elizabeth.

"Yes, of course. We keep each other warm that way."

"Sounds like a good idea, but I'm sure Maggie wouldn't agree to it."

"Well, Jon, it's bound to get colder. Winter hasn't even started yet."

"I know. I'm hoping we get to Arkansas before it gets too bad."

"Good luck with that. These mountains are your worst part." There was a long pause.

"Where did you say you came from?" asked Jon.

"A few miles west of Edenton."

"Where is that?"

"Close to the Roanoke River. Edenton is on the old Main Post Road that runs along coast from Florida to Baltimore," answered Charles, with the tarp in hand.

"That's in Virginia, right?"

"No, we were in Carolina, close to Virginia."

"I guess we both would have been better off going to Abingdon first."

"S'pose so. We were going to take the old Jonesboro Road, but it's now called the old Western Road, what's left of it. Before we knew it, it became the Hillsboro-to-Salem Road, and goes nowhere near Jonesboro."

"Jonesboro's in Tennessee, right?" asked Jon.

"Right, but it's south of where we want to be. It's pretty close to Knoxville, I think," said Charles.

Jon's gang were finishing their chores, and once again gathered around the fire for one last warm-up.

"Elizabeth here suggested that, being nine of us, we sleep three together for warmth," said a smiling Jon. I don't think that's such a bad idea. How do you all feel?"

"Who sleeps wit whos?" asked Buelah.

"Oh, I don't know. Maybe we can take turns." Jon could feel those eyes staring at him, and the face was turning as red as the hair.

"You've got to be joking again," snapped Maggie.

"Whoever sleeps with Mose could get crushed," said Dave.

"No, I'm not joking. Just trying to be practical," said Jon.

"Hmmph! Well, you're practically sleeping alone!"

"Whoops! Sorry I asked! But we must find a way to get everybody up off the ground at night, so nobody catches their death of cold," said Jon.

"Maybe we can all think on that overnight. Right now I'm just too tired," said Charles.

Everyone thought that was a good idea, and all headed for the sack. Charles, Liz, and David went to their wagon, now warm with blankets and a tarp over them, and Jon and Maggie were in their covered wagon. Mose, Ella, Buelah, and Chipper slept on the ground, near the fire. It wasn't long before Jon heard the usual pounding and grunting of Mose and Ella, and some sobs from Buelah. There were also some new sounds, those of the Chasneys, having a party under the tarp, in their wagon. Maggie heard it as well.

"They're sort of strange, don't you think?" she asked.

"Yes, I guess, but like Mose said, we need them."

"She's pretty, isn't she?"

"Almost as pretty as you." Jon felt good about getting out from that entrapment.

"Sounds like they're making love."

"Yeah, it sure does, but who is making love to whom?"

"I suppose she's making love to her husband," said Maggie.

"They both are her husband!"

"Jonny! She said Davie was her husband."

"Yeah, and Charles said *he* was her husband, and Davie sat right there and didn't say a word."

"Oh, so that's why everyone clammed up when Liz mentioned about she and Dave being lovebirds."

"Well, she looks like she can handle both of them."

"And she said she was trying to get pregnant, like me."

"I hope she doesn't, for the sake of Charles and Dave."

"And what is that supposed to mean?" asked Maggie.

"Well, now that you're pregnant, I've been cut off!"

"Jonny, I'm sorry. It's just so uncomfortable."

"And *so* lonely!" Jon pressed his advantage.

"Poor baby. Is it really that bad?"

"Bad? I'm just about to jump in the covers with Buelah, or go kick Dave and Charles out!"

After a pause, Maggie asked, "Would it be alright if I got on top?"

"Over, under, around . . . any which way."

A little while later, Maggie questioned, "Feel better now?"

"I feel wonderful. Seven to one, I'm catching up."

"What does that mean, Jonny?"

"Mose is only six cockells ahead of me!"

Diary of Margaret Hamilton

Friday, October 30, 1835

Started in good season, wagons loaded with supplies, by way of trade for Abby the cow. Yesterday's snow was gone, replaced by rain and fog. Jonny doesn't believe in beasts, but Chipper saw Boony when it spooked the horses. We have three new traveling companions, Charles, David, and Elizabeth Chasney, headed for Kentucky. Miss my dear friends . . .

October 31

"MOSE! Where are you?" yelled Jon, as he sprang out of the wagon in just his unmentionables and stocking feet, Hawken in hand.

"Daddy be's wit horses aweady," said Ella, from her blankets by the embers.

Jon had awakened to the screams of the horses. It was still pitch black, very early, as Jon grabbed a gun and ran in the direction of the horses. At last he saw Mose's lantern, and could make out the forms of the drays, kicking and snorting.

The commotion was to his right, and Jon grabbed the lantern as he heard Mose cuss loudly for the very first time.

"Gets da blazes aways from dem horses, you's damn boots-lickin' bastads!" yelled Mose.

Wham! Jon heard the powerful sound, followed by the sounds of something hitting the ground hard. His lantern caught a form running toward the trees.

"Are you alright, Mose?"

"I be's O-'rite. Shoots dem blam devils!"

Jon was already pulling the plug and patch from the barrel and nipple of his Hawken. He opened his very ornate patch box and found a percussion cap, which he squeezed around the nipple. He could not see anything, but he fired in the direction of the familiar brush and limb snapping. *BAM!* There was a grunt in the dark.

"Do's you's hits 'em?" asked Mose.

"I don't know. Too dark to tell. We'll find out in the morning. Did you see it, Mose?"

"Nossa, Jon. It be's big. Attacks Corka, but Corka and I's gets 'em."

"You both got him? How?"

"I's thinks Corka kicks 'em, an' I hits 'em wit dem sticks. I's check Corka."

"Jonny, are you Okay?" came Maggie's voice.

Mose walked to where Jon had dropped the lantern and picked it up. It was still flickering. He walked over to Corker. "Whoas, Big Corka, whoas."

As the gang came running with lanterns glowing, Mose and Jon found blood on the flank of the giant white horse. There was a rounded wound and some bleeding scratches on the hind quarter of Corker. Jon had to smile when he saw Charles and Dave in their worn, holed unmentionables, but both wearing boots and carrying their rifles. Maggie and Ella were draped in blankets.

"What happened?" asked Dave.

"Something attacked the horses," answered Jon.

"It was the beast you say doesn't exist!" said Maggie.

"It was too dark to see what it was."

"Did you hit it when you fired, Jon?" asked Charles.

"Not sure. We'll have to wait until morning to find out. This almost looks like it bit Corker, Mose."

"Yassa, It do. Ella, you's gets clean rags, an' dem horse liniments."

"I do's, Daddy."

"If I did hit it, whatever it was will be back for revenge. Let's check the other horses, and bring them back in close to the camp."

"Yassa, Jon. I's stays up rest dem day."

"I can spell Mose in a couple hours," said Charles.

"That'll work. Chipper, can you and Buelah get wood, and build up the campfire?"

"Yassa, Massa Jon," said Chip, who ran to do his job.

"What can I do, Jonny?"

"Go get our bed warmed up again, my pretty plum."

"Are you joking? With Boony running around? I couldn't get back to sleep if I wanted to."

"Who said anything about sleep?"

"Don't push your luck, you big lummox! I'll help Liz gather up their clothes and help Ella with breakfast."

"Great idea, darlin'. All the other horses alright?"

"They look fine, Jon," said Dave. "Still shying some."

"Okay. Let's get them staked close to our wagons, then I think I'll get a couple more hours of sleep."

"I's gets dem guns loaded," said Mose.

By the time the men got the drays tied close to the fire, Maggie and Liz were gathering clothes off the lines. Jon couldn't help noticing that Liz had no clothes on under the blanket she had draped around her. He got some smashing glimpses of butt and breast. So did Maggie. When Jon noticed his wife looking at him, he quickly turned his eyes to the sky.

"Have you all noticed the fog has lifted?" he asked.

"Do you see any stars yet?" asked Maggie.

"There must still be heavy clouds. I see no stars."

"You will, if you don't go get that sleep you wanted."

It seemed that Jon had barely closed his eyes when he woke to the shaking of the wagon. Maggie had come in and was starting to get dressed. Jon's eyes focused fast on the view.

"What time is it, darlin'?"

"You can sleep for another hour or so, Jonny."

"Who can sleep, with you in Eve's togs? How about joining me for that hour or so?"

"No! I saw you staring," snapped Maggie.

"Staring? At what?"

"That pullet! See? You are a big lummox!"

"Shh, not so loud, my pretty plum. I was just doing what any American man would do."

"Not when you're married! And don't shush me. They went back to bed too."

"I live under the married man's code of conduct."

"And what is that?"

"Look, but don't touch," answered Jon.

"See to it you stick to that code, big boy. I'm going out to help Nanty Ella bake up more corn dodgers."

"Can you cool down by a fire?"

"Maybe I don't want to cool down just yet. Oh," as Maggie stepped out of the wagon," we've got more mouths to feed now. We're going to need more food."

"Okay, I'll go shoot that Boony, and we'll have food all the way to Arkansas!"

"Very funny! Go back to sleep."

No rest for the wicked! Jon could hear the talking by the fire, hear and feel its warmth, and smell coffee and food. He turned over, sore side up. That just brought back the soreness of this side. "Time to get dressed," he growled. Jon was surprised to find all hands up and eating.

"May I join you all?"

"Better hurry. It's about gone," said Dave.

"I's saves you's coffee an' dodgas," said Ella.

"Thank you, Ella. Everyone ready to travel?"

"We took a vote, Jonny, and decided to rest a day."

"We need to get over these Blues," pleaded Jon.

"Dem horses needs res', Jon," said Mose.

"How is Corker, Mose?"

"He be's fine, Jon. Jus' needs res'."

Jon was a little disappointed, as he drank his coffee and ate corn dodgers served by Ella.

"Dem horses o' Chasneys need res' too," said Mose.

After a pause, he said, "Alright, we rest today and start tomorrow."

"Good, Jonny. We need some fresh food," said Maggie.

"An' I's fixes beds fo' us," said Mose.

"We took another vote too, Jonny."

"Did you decide to divorce me, my pretty plum?"

"No such luck," said Elizabeth, looking good even under several layers of clothes.

"They decided that you will remain the leader of this group, and Charles will be second in command," said a stern-faced Maggie.

There was a pause. "Did everyone agree to that?"

"Everyone except me. I want to go back home."

"Okay. Charles will be in charge until I get back," said Jon. "See to the horses. There's plenty of grass yet, but your two leads will need extra grain. Keep them out there in the good grass. That means you will need to take turns guarding them. Mose, go ahead and see if you can build something attached to the buckboard that will get everyone off the ground at night."

"Why's dem bucksboard?" asked Buelah.

"There's no room to add anything to the wagon."

"Yassa, I's do, Jon. My Ellas tooks cold las' night."

"Where are you going, Jonny?" asked Maggie.

"I'm going to take Sloggy and do some scouting."

"Dats good idea, Massa Jon. We's needs food," said Ella, coughing.

"Righto. Did you find a pass anywhere north of here, Charles?"

"No, we didn't, Jon. It's hard to tell, just solid forest. How can you tell if you're looking at a pass?"

"I would say if the forest climbs steeply, it's not a pass, or if there's water running, that's probably a pass. Maybe a marshy area," answered Jon.

"Well, we saw none of those to the north," said Dave.

"Okay, well, I'll go west as far as I can, then turn to the south to try to find an opening, like Mister Duncan said."

"I'm scared, Jonny. How long will you be gone?"

"I hope to be back before dark. If I'm not back by then, fire three shots rapidly, and I'll know which way this camp is. As soon as it gets light, fire three again."

"We'll do that, Jon," said Charles. "You better take some food and blankets, and if you are in trouble, can you fire three shots too?"

"I'll try, but I can only carry a few balls and caps in my patch box, and I want to bag some game."

"Okay, and we'll hunt a little around camp," said Dave.

"Mose checked for blood where you fired at whatever was attacking your big white horse," said Charles.

"Oh? And what did you find, Mose?"

"I's fin' one reds spot, Jon."

"Then I wounded him. I want a guard on duty at all times, and the rest get some sleep. This is going to be a hard climb. Ella, take some calomel and some castor oil, and get some sleep."

"Yassa, Jonny, I's do," said Ella, between coughs.

"If you find a trail, how will you be able to locate it a second time with the wagons?" asked Maggie.

"Great question, my pretty plum. See, you're not a flounderhead! I'll have to mark my trail."

"With what, you big lummox?"

"Hmm, how about cutting up some of your clothes you don't need?"

"I have no clothes I don't need."

"I've got some pantalets I don't want. You can have them to rip up, Jonny," said a smiling Liz.

"So do I! Mine are red, so they can be spotted easily."

"Good. I can use both of them, and more."

"You's can use dem shulda bags I's gots," said Ella, her voice cracking.

"Okay. Will you put a bridle on Slog, Mose?"

"Sho 'nuff, Jon, I's do."

"Charles, please see to it that everyone gets rest and takes turns guarding. You are going to be amazed with Mose."

"Will do, Jon. Good luck." said Charles.

Buelah brought two blankets, which Mose draped over Sloggy, and Ella brought her shoulder bag, full of dodgers. Jon felt loaded down, with his heavy overcoat, pockets filled with torn strips of cloth from Maggie and Elizabeth, powder pouches, and Ella's large shoulder bag over the coat. He was ready, and Maggie rushed up to embrace him.

"Be careful, Jonny. I love you," Maggie said, kissing him.

"I love you too, both of you," he answered.

"I'll miss you. This will be our first time apart."

"I know, darlin'. I'll miss that beautiful body up against me. Keep it warm," he whispered back to her.

"I will. I liked it on top last night, Jonny."

"Well, get aboard again as soon as I return."

"I'll be waiting, Jonny."

With that, Jon jumped onto Sloggy and disappeared. Mose immediately grabbed a large and small axe and the toolbox, then headed for a group of small trees to cut. He would work all day on an ingenious plan to build a bed that he could attach under the buckboard that would raise for travel, or lower for sleep. It was just wide enough to squeeze Buelah and Chipper into, and extend about two feet out the sides of the wagon. Those extensions folded up under a small hinged porch roof, and all attached to the side railings of the buckboard.

The women also slept in shifts, two at a time, with the others keeping the fire stoked, coffee and dodgers available, and keeping Mose and Chipper company. By noon, Ella was very sick with fever and runny nose.

"Nanty Ella, please get to bed," pleaded Maggie.

"I's do, Sissy, soon as we's have's dinna."

"Please do it's now, Mama," said Buelah.

"Daddy fixes wagons now, Buelah."

"Then sleep in my wagon, Nanty Ella."

"Orights, Sissy, I's do." Ella's voice was very weak.

"Did you take some calomel, like Jonny said?"

"No's, Sissy. I's forgets."

"I'll get you some. Buel, will you help me get your mother in my wagon before she gets dyspepsia?"

"Sho 'nuff, Sissy, I's do," answered Buelah.

"I think we have some laudanum," said Dave, who was taking his turn at guarding.

"Oh, wonderful. Will you bring it to my wagon?"

"Sure thing, Missus Hamilton."

"Just call me Maggie, Davie," as she led Ella to her wagon. "Buel and I will make you better, Nanty Ella."

"Thank you's, Sissy."

"Chipper!" Maggie called. "Bring Mose in to eat."

"Yassum, missy," Chipper answered.

When Mose and Chipper reached the bonfire, only Dave was there eating. They each grabbed a couple of dodgers.

"Where's be's dem mammy?" asked Mose.

"What's that?"

"Where's be Ellas?"

"She is sick. She is in the big wagon with Missus Hamilton. I think she has catarrh," answered Dave.

"Wha's catarrhs?"

"It's fever and sick all over."

"I's look in," said Mose.

"She's in bed. Buelah is with her," said Maggie, as she stepped back out of the wagon.

"She be orights?"

"I hope so. She needs sleep."

A shot was heard from a long distance away.

"That be's Jon," said Mose.

"How do you know that, Nunky Mose?"

"His gun makes dem soun's."

"Do you think he's alright?"

"He's be's fine."

"Come on, Nunky. I'll fix you some more dodgers."

"Thank you's, missy."

As Mose and Chipper were getting fed, another shot rang out from afar.

"I's bets Jon gets food," said Mose.

"We sure need more food," said Maggie.

"He's gets 'em, missy."

"How is your project coming?"

"I's 'bouts ready to make dem bed," answered Mose.

"For the buckboard?" Maggie asked.

"Yassum. Fits under buckboard, der be no rooms, under you's wagons wit dem wheels."

Bam! The nearby shot startled Margaret and Chipper.

"What are you shooting at?" yelled Maggie.

"Just answering Jon's shots," said Dave.

"Well, we're trying to get Ella to sleep."

"Oh, sorry," answered Dave, who headed off toward the horses.

"Are you alright, Nanty Ella?" asked Maggie, through the wagon's canvas hood.

"Mama's be sleepin', Sissy," answered Buelah, from inside the wagon.

"I's gets back ta works," said Mose.

"Did you get enough to eat?"

"Yassum, missy. Thank you's."

"I's gets plenny too. Thank you's," said Chipper.

"You're welcome," answered Maggie, as father and son started toward the horses, and Mose's work area.

"How is Corker, Nunky Mose?" asked Maggie.

"He be's fine, missy," answered Mose. "I's walks him an' puts mo' liniment an Corka."

The next two to three hours were quiet in the camp. Maggie was on "watch," wrapped in blankets by the fire. Out along the edge of the grassy meadow, Mose was crafting the new bed to fit between the wheels under the buckboard. Chipper was playing close to Mose, who had his Kentucky rifle with him, as it was his turn at watch. Everyone else was sleeping the afternoon away in the two wagons. Late in the afternoon, it started to rain. Maggie sprang to her feet, and called Mose and Chipper.

"Nunky Mose! Chipper! Come in out of the rain!"

"I's bring horses, missy," came the reply.

"Do you need help?"

"No, I's do orights."

"I'll help him," said Dave, as he ran by Maggie in his unmentionables and boots.

"Here, take some blankets!" Maggie shouted.

Dave grabbed the blankets Maggie handed him, and ran for the meadow. Maggie hurried to help Elizabeth and Charles cover their wagon with tarp.

"You better climb under here with us, before you get soaked to the kazoo," said Charles.

"We have a lot of room. We can pass the time while it rains," added Liz.

"No thanks. I've got to get the buckboard covered and get more wood on the fire." Maggie moved quickly to get away from that "shameless" wagon.

"I can help. Just give me a minute," said Charles.

As Maggie hurried to the buckboard, she heard another shot. When she spread the tarp over the buckboard, a scream and loud crying came from the meadow.

"Mose! What happened?" she called.

"The boy just fell out of a tree," answered Dave.

Maggie ran toward them. She was met halfway by Dave, pulling horses, and Mose, carrying a sobbing Chipper.

"Is he hurt badly, Nunky Mose?"

"Dem leg be's broke, I thinks, missy."

"Oh dear. Bring him into my wagon."

In the covered wagon, Ella was sitting up in Maggie's bed, and Buelah was seated on her usual perch, just behind the bench. When Mose, Chipper, and Maggie entered, added to the stacks of supplies along the sides of the wagon, it was stuffed and overcrowded. Mose backed out into the rain, and only his head remained under the canvas hood.

"Where does it hurt, Chipper?"

"Rights here, Missa' Maggie."

Maggie felt the left leg below the knee, and the boy screamed and jerked away, hugging Ella.

"It must be broken, but it's not swelling yet."

"What we's do now, Sissy?" asked Ella.

"I'm not sure. I wonder if the liniment would help."

"Yassum, it helps, missy," said Mose. "I's gets dem horse liniments."

"Okay, and maybe we can brace the leg to keep it straight. I have some liniment."

"Yassum, I's brings stake an' rope." Mose left.

"How did this happen, Chipper?"

"I's be climin' in trees, an' falls to groun'," sobbed the boy.

Dave finished securing the animals, and Mose gathered a few straight sticks, and the ever-useful straps to bind Chipper's left leg, and hurried them back to Jon's wagon. The boy only cried a short while, when the brace was lashed to his leg and when the liniment was applied.

"I'll leave him here with you, Nanty Ella," said Maggie.

"Thank you's, Sissy, but where you's sleeps?"

"When Jonny gets back, we can sleep by the fire."

"I's sho' hopes Jon gets backs soon," said Ella.

"Me too. I don't want him sleeping in those woods."

"Jon be's fines, Sissy."

"Thank you, Nanty Ella. Your voice sounds better."

"Thanks you's, Sissy. I's uses dem liniment too."

"Good. Get some sleep now. You too, Chip. Call me if you need anything," Maggie said to Buelah.

"I's do, Sissy. Where you's be?"

"Thank you's, Sissy," said Ella quietly.

"You're welcome, Nanty Ella. I'll be just outside, Buelah."

Maggie wrapped herself in blankets, and crawled under her wagon to get out of the rain. She heard Mose working under the tarp in the buckboard. She missed her husband. She wondered if he would make it back tonight. It was almost dark, and Maggie remembered Jon's instructions.

"Mose!" she hollered. "Come here." She guessed that Mose hadn't heard her, so she ran to the buckboard through the steady rain.

"Mose?" she said, scooting under his tarp.

"Yassum, missy?"

"You were going to shoot three times for Jon."

"Yassum. I's forgets. I's do's now."

Mose grabbed the two Kentuckys, and started loading under the tarp. Maggie remembered that Jon wanted to hear three shots. She ventured over to Dave.

"Is your gun loaded, Dave?"

"Sure is, but I hope the powder isn't wet. I've been keeping it under my rain togs."

"Good. Mose is loading the two guns he has, so you can shoot three shots for Jonny to hear."

"Oh, that's right. We were going to signal him."

"Yes, and it's about dark."

In a few minutes, Mose came running to the fire with both rifles, and joined Dave and Maggie. Mose shot his Kentucky gun first. *Bam!* Dave had his rifle now primed, and fired. He got a lot of smoke, but no shot. The powder had become damp. Both men then started to reload. Dave had to try to quickly empty his barrel and add fresh powder. Mose fired the second Kentucky. *Bam!* Now it was a race to reload. Mose got his rifle loaded first, and refired. *Bam!*

"Sorry I couldn't get this all-fired contraption dried and reloaded in time," said Dave.

"Dat be's orights, Dave."

"Okay, let's all get out of the rain," said Maggie.

They scrambled under the tarps and wagon, just in time to hear the answer from Jon. *Bam! Bam!* The two shots came from a long way off, so Maggie sadly realized that her husband wouldn't be back tonight. Sitting on her haunches under her wagon, she began to softly cry. When she ran out of tears, she walked over to the buckboard and got under the tarp.

"Nunky Mose, you sleep in my wagon tonight, with Nanty Ella and Chipper. I'll sleep here, under the tarp with Buelah."

"Orights, missy, I's do. You's be orights?"

"I'll be fine. Tell Buel to bring my diary."

"Yessum, missy," answered Mose. "I's takes my turns on watch."

"No, you should be with Chipper and Nanty Ella. Ask Dave if he and Charles can take turns watching until morning."

"Yessum, I's do." Mose left, and Maggie climbed into the buckboard and started stacking supplies along both sides of the wagon under the tarp, so she and Buelah would have a place to sleep. Buelah arrived in a hurry, with the diary, and soon fell sound asleep.

Diary of Margaret Hamilton

Saturday, October 31

. . . Oh, how I miss my Jonny. He has been scouting a trail, so our wagons can scale this forested mountain. I will be spending my first married night without him. Dear me, this has been a trying day. Ella became quite sick from this wet, cold climate, and Chipper, our fine boy, fell from a tree and injured his left leg . . . Maybe November will be a better month for us all. Nunky Mose, Nanty Ella, and Chipper will sleep in my wagon tonight. I'll be resting here in the buckboard with Buelah.

Jon somehow knew, as he waved goodbye to his gang, that he wouldn't be returning this day to his wife, or encampment. Finding a trail through these Blues would be very difficult, if not impossible. He had decided that already, back in Boone, talking to Mister Duncan, but he wasn't about to "give in" to Maggie. He glanced back up to the sky for what probably would be the last time today. Heavy, dark clouds loomed overhead. He was now glad he had his heavy coat on, and some rain togs to boot. Rain was coming again soon. He hoped his group would be Okay.

Jon tied his first red cloth to a tree branch, just a short distance into the trees. He listened to the sounds of Mose chopping a tree. "Somehow that big wizard will come up with a bed that will travel, I'll bet your butt," he said to himself. All he had to do was find a direction to haul that bed and those wagons. Looking around, the only resemblance to a path was due north. He took it a short way, and spotted a narrow opening to the left. His compass showed it to be west, so he marked the spot with two cloths, and urged Sloggy through it. He came to a swampy area in thick pine. Now he had to turn either north or south again, so he turned south, through a thinner patch of pine. After what seemed like a couple hours of rough going, he came to a small opening with a tiny stream, coming from the northwest. He climbed down to give both Sloggy and himself a drink and rest. He was lost, yet knew he would follow the stream to who-knows-where.

"Poor fella," he said to Sloggy, patting him at the neck and shoulder. "All that brush and limbs are giving you a cobbing."

Jon found a rock big enough to sit on, and dug out a dodger from Ella's shoulder bag. Sloggy found some grass. "Must be about noon, at least," he said to himself, or to Sloggy. "We'll rest here for a few minutes. I wonder how far we've come from the camp. Only four or five miles at the most, I'll bet." Jon finished his dodger.

The soothing sound of the tiny, rushing brook made him sleepy, and he closed his eyes. He was about to fall off the rock when something startled him, a loud noise, coming from upstream and getting closer. Back to his senses, he grabbed Sloggy's halter and headed to the far side of the clearing and into the trees, where he wrapped the straps around a small tree. He popped the plug from the barrel, and the patch from the nipple of his Hawken, and dug out a cap from the patch box. What he saw next made him catch his breath. *BOONY!*

This huge, apelike creature reached the clearing and stopped abruptly, sniffing at the wind. He didn't seem to like what he smelled, Jon or Sloggy! He growled and beat his chest with his fists. The thump thump sound startled Sloggy, and he gave away their position by whinnying and pulling back hard on his halter straps. The beast gave a loud, growling noise, and headed toward Jon. He fired. *Bam!*

Jon could see where the ball tore into the chest of Boony, and he even thought he heard his rib crack. It skidded to its knees, and fell back into the creek and lay still. "What do I do now?" Jon asked himself. Reason seemed to tell him to reload, *fast.*

He tried to grab his powder flask and pour a measure down the barrel. He was having trouble getting the spout in the hole of the barrel. He could now see how scared he was, as his hand was shaking. When he jerked the flask back out, powder spilled down the outside of the barrel. He didn't even notice this, as he jerked the ramrod out of its "perch." He was concentrating on Boony, who was now attempting to get back up, blood running down the front of his body, soaking the reddish-brown hair. Jon again had trouble getting the ball and the tip of the rod down the barrel. "Blast it!" he said out loud. "Hamilton, settle down and get this damned rifle loaded!"

The beast was now back on his feet, staggering toward Jon. Sloggy was going wild behind him.

"Whoa, Slog. Whoa, damn it!" Jon yelled, as he tried to tamp what load he had down the barrel. He jerked the rod back out, and it went flying into the brush by his side. Now he had to dig another cap out from the rifle's patch box. He raised the Hawken up to his shoulder, pointing it in the direction of the beast, which was slowly approaching, now about ten yards away. Jon felt relief, as his fingers found a cap. Shaking profusely, he jabbed at the nipple several times until the cap finally fit over the nipple. He didn't have time, and didn't even think about squeezing it firmly around the nipple. "Lord, don't let me down now," he heard himself say. Boony was right above him as he fired. *Bam! Thud!* The beast fell backward and rolled away, blood everywhere.

Jon jumped up and sprang a short distance away, before he again reached for his powder flask. The beast still wasn't dead. He was getting up again, making gurgling sounds. It headed for the trees, as Jon frantically tried to reload. Jon couldn't stop shaking. The beast was getting away, bolting through brush and trees, falling, then staggering back up, and knocking down everything in its path. When Jon got the powder poured and the ball dropped into the barrel, he noticed that he had no ramrod. He felt soaked with sweat under his coat, and he was still shaking. He could still hear the branches and brush snapping, now a good distance away. He returned to his hiding spot to search for his ramrod. Then it struck him. Sloggy was missing!

Jon could see which way the dray had run, away from the beast, and he only had to trail the horse a short way before he spotted Slog, pacing and lifting.

"Whoa, Sloggy. Whoa, big fella," Jon coaxed, trying to sound reassuring like Mose. The blankets and bags had fallen off the horse's back, but he seemed alright other than that. Sloggy was reluctant to go back to the hiding spot, but soon Jon had him restrapped to a tree, and finally located his rod. He finished loading his Hawken and went back to his original rock perch by the stream. Jon was drained of energy. "Well," he said out loud, "I was surely wrong about beasts. Looks like I'll have to admit it to Maggie."

After a while, Jon replugged the barrel and repatched the nipple of the Hawken. He was ready again to trail hunt. He had settled down enough to travel. He wondered if he would ever see Boony again. He put enough lead in Boony to kill him twice over! Jon hoped Boony was laid out dead out there. He thought he heard a gunshot from his camp, to the east.

The stream became larger and turned slightly due north up ahead of him, so Jon concentrated on an opening to the left, which was west. He never realized that he was at the foot of Boone Gap. He found a narrow, brushy opening and plunged into it. This trail led him west by southwest, and took what seemed like hours to Jon before he came to a small clearing. He saw movement in the clearing, and readied his Hawken. Two does were feeding. He waited for several minutes, and was rewarded when a beautiful buck wandered into the clearing.

"Ella's going to be serving steaks tomorrow," Jon whispered, as he squeezed the trigger. *Bam!* The eight-point dropped in a heap. With the shot, the does scattered into the trees. Jon ran over and quickly slit the throat of the very dead buck, reloaded his Hawken, then opened the dead animal to bleed him out. He wanted to skin it out, but he had to do some more scouting. He wondered what he should do. He could hear water running just beyond the clearing, so he dragged the deer to it and cleared some rocks out of the water. He placed the buck in the waterhole, minus its head and entrails, which he had laid out in the clearing for predators. He covered the deer with stones as much as he could in the stream, and again marked the area and took to the trail.

The rains came, as he followed the new stream up a steep ravine to the northwest, for a long stretch, before finding a nice trail to the southwest. Jon followed this trail for what he thought was about three or four miles. He wanted to turn straight west, but couldn't find a suitable opening. It was time, once again, to stop and rest.

Jon figured it must be late afternoon or early evening, as he sat munching on a cold dodger in the steady rain. He wondered how close he was to the top of the Blues. Jon decided to try to find out. He spotted a large, very tall pine tree with branches all the way down to the ground. Jon shed his heavy coat and gear and started climbing the tree. Even in the rain, the climb was fairly easy. Soon he was high up above the neighboring forest, and felt like he was surveying the top of a jungle. With his compass, Jon plotted his next move. There were still some high forested peaks to his west, but he was past some tall mountains behind him to the east.

The trail he was on continued to the southwest for several more miles, but he could see what looked like a large opening about two or three miles further down this trail, and a possible pass around the mountain just to the west of the opening. He decided that was the only way to get out of the "jungle" he was in. It was getting dark very fast, and the rain was causing low clouds to form at the base of the tall mountains. He needed to hurry.

Jon scrambled down out of the tree and loaded himself with his gear again, and headed on down his fairly clear trail. He thought he heard a gunshot in the distance, to the east. Jon continued on for a few more minutes, and he was sure he heard a second shot. He stopped, climbed down off Sloggy, and readied his Hawken to answer what he was sure was Mose or Charles signaling him. He waited for several minutes before he heard the echo of the third shot. Jon raised his Hawken to the sky and fired. *Bam!* He then quickly reloaded and fired again, to the northeast. The shots from his group came from just about where he expected them, and Jon felt good about his sense of direction.

Back on Sloggy, he raced southwest down the trail to the opening he saw from the treetop. It was near complete darkness when he sensed he was in the clearing. There was plenty of grass for Sloggy to be in horse heaven. Jon made a shallow hole in the low hillside under the roots of a tree, and made a bed there. He gathered some twigs and sticks and found the flint he had placed in his patch box. After a brief struggle, he had a fire going in front of his "dugout." He was sheltered from the rain and cold, and soon he was fast asleep, dreaming of Maggie by his side.

Sunday, November 1

Jon was awake very early, almost dawn. He horsed down two cold dodgers, and even Sloggy ate one. He marked the area with his strips of cloth, and climbed up on Sloggy. He had hoped this would be a day of travel, but realized that he would not get back to camp before the afternoon, even if he tried to take a shortcut, which he didn't want to do. Jon needed to be sure he could spot the pieces of red-and-white cloth he had marked his trail with.

Jon found the opening where he had left his buck. The entrails and head had been scattered by some animal. As Jon hurriedly searched the stream for his buck, he heard three quick shots from his camp in the distance. He thankfully found his dead deer intact, and tried tying it to Sloggy's back, who shied away some. Jon had to decide how to get his prize back to camp. Sloggy was too skittish for Jon to load the entire buck, along with himself. He decided to take a hind quarter. After a lot of hard cutting and whacking, he freed a flank from the rest of the buck, and placed the remainder back into its "hole" in the water, and again covered it with rocks. Jon wished he had Mose along to expertly tie down the meat over Sloggy's flanks. He roped the leg of the deer and used his gear to balance the load hanging over Sloggy's hind end, and started back down the trail.

Luckily, it wasn't raining, but Jon was sure it was cold enough to draw complaints from the women. Continuing on his marked trail, he found the big turn to the southeast. After a while, Jon spotted the cloth in the dense brush and trees to the east. He and Sloggy struggled for a short distance, and Jon felt it took a long time to get nowhere. He retraced his steps back to the spot where he entered these dense thickets, and searched for a better trail. He heard another three quick rifle shots to the east. Jon thought he'd better answer them this time, so he readied his Hawken and fired. He reloaded with a steady hand, and fired again. He was now short of ammo, and was anxious to get back to the encampment.

Jon found a likely brushy opening that continued southeast, and pointed Sloggy into it, marking it well. It was hard work breaking through, but when Jon finally spotted his old clothes, he knew he was back close to his "family" and was happy he had taken the new path. He was sure that he had saved himself some time and miles. Jon had two balls and three caps left, but wanted to let his group know that he was finally close. It was well into the afternoon when he fired his Hawken. In just a few minutes, he heard the report of a Kentucky rifle in response, close by to his east. He knew exactly where he was, and felt relief.

Soon he was at the spot where the day before, he was obliged to go north. He was just a short distance from his group. Ahead was the first little clearing, where yesterday morning he had seen the dark clouds, and heard Mose chopping a tree down. He heard a movement to his right. He saw a doe, about the same time the doe saw him. He slowly pulled the plug and patch from his rifle, and fumbled for his percussion cap, fitting it over the nipple. He slowly raised his Hawken to his shoulder and fired. *Bam!* Down went the doe. He jumped off Sloggy and ran up to his second kill. He was cleaning it when he heard his group running through the trees toward him. He was thrilled that his lone excursion was over. Mose and Dave were the first in sight, but he could hear others coming as well.

"Hello, Mose. I have food for our dinner table."

"Yassa, you's sho'ly do's, Jon," came his reply.

The bear hug from Mose and the handshake from Dave felt good to Jon. It would be the beginning of many.

"You's gives me dem knife, Jon. I's cuts up meats."

"Righto, Mose. Be my guest."

Now Charles and Buelah emerged from the trees. A handshake and hug from Charles, and a full body hug from Buelah were in order. Jon saw Maggie next, trying to hurry in all her togs, and she looked beautiful to Jon.

"Oh, Jonny, I've missed you *so* much!" She gave Jon a long kiss.

"I've missed you too, darling."

"Are you alright, Jonny?" Maggie asked, as she held him tightly.

"Happy, hungry, and horny-brained!"

"Quiet, you big lummox. Just hold me tight, and we'll take care of the first two right now."

"But the third is more important than the others."

"Same old Jonny, I see. We'll take care of that little item later tonight in our wagon."

"Little? It's been two days in the making."

"Very funny. There's not much I could have done about it last night, in Mose's buckboard."

"Is that why it's a little item all of a sudden? What were you and Mose up to last night?"

"Really want to know, big boy?" Maggie teased. "I slept in the buckboard last night . . . with Buelah. Nunky Mose was in our wagon taking care of Nanty Ella and Chipper."

"Are they alright?"

"Well, Nanty Ella took sick with dyspepsia, and Chipper fell out of a tree. But they're both better today."

"Don't that cap the climax! I leave for one day, and my crew goes barmy!"

"We's all needs you's ta leads," quipped Buelah.

"Good. That's what I needed to hear."

"We's cuts dem strips back at camps," said Buelah.

"Not all of it, Buel," said Jon. "We need some big chunks and a good steak or two as well."

"Yassa, Jon, we's does dem too," answered Mose.

"See what Sloggy is carrying?"

The gang noticed the large hind section swinging from the side of the horse.

"Oh, Jonny! You got another one too?"

"Sure did, my pretty plum."

"But where's the rest of it?"

"I've got it hidden in a stream several miles from here."

"Oh good, Jonny! Now we'll have meat all the way over these hills."

"If nothing else finds it first."

"Did you find a good trail to follow?" asked Charles.

"Well, I found a trail. It has some good parts, and some parts that will be really tough to cross."

"How far did you get, Jon?" asked Dave, who was now helping Mose pick up the doe parts to carry back to camp.

"I think I was near the top. I camped overnight in a large clearing that looked to me like a dead end, except to climb straight up, about fifty yards, to a ledge."

"How are we going to do that?" questioned Charles.

"We have a block-and-tackle that we haven't used yet, and I've told you what a genius Mose is. I'm not worried."

"You were right about that," said Charles. "Wait until you see the bed he built. It fits under his wagon."

"I can hardly wait!" Jon patted a smiling Mose on the back. Everyone was ready to return to camp.

"I thought you'd be halfway up the mountain by now!" Jon teased. "What have you all been doing?"

"Getting healed," answered Dave.

"This is Sunday, you big lummox," said Maggie. "A day of rest and meditation."

"Good! Let's have a poke party tonight, and hit the brush tomorrow!" said Jon.

"Is that an order, boss?" asked a smiling Dave.

"The best one I've given yet."

"Let's see, we have four men and four women. This should be a blast!" quipped Dave.

"I hate to be a deadbeat or scallywag," said Maggie, "but I'm a one-man married woman, and there will be no butt-bartering around me."

So ended that baffy thought once and for all! The evening was spent by the fire, cutting and hanging strips of meat, making more dodgers, cleaning weapons, transferring supplies to the Chasney wagon to equalize the loads, and enjoying a large meal of venison steaks and beans. The blacks could now all sleep off the ground. Mose and Ella would be in the buckboard, and Buelah and Chipper would squeeze under the bed of the buckboard. Jon and Maggie, and Charles, Dave, and Elizabeth could all sleep in their wagons. It was now nighttime, and Jon was anxious to "rest."

"Everyone turn in early," said Jon. "We rise before dawn, and will leave at first light. Please try to get some rest. How are you feeling, Ella?"

"I's be fines, Jonny. We's be ready."

"I's take cares of dem horses, an' brings dem in."

"I'll help you, Mose," said Dave.

"Have you grained and watered them already, Mose?"

"Yassa, I's do already, Jon."

"That's good enough then. They'll be ready for the job ahead tomorrow."

"Don't you want to bring them closer in?" asked Maggie.

"Nah, there's still grass over there. They'll be alright. Let's turn in, Maggie."

"But what happens if Boony returns, Jonny?"

"Forget about Boony, my pretty plum. He doesn't exist." Jon wasn't ready to tell Maggie about his encounter with "Boony," and he figured that the beast was lying somewhere up in these hills dead anyway, so he would just tell Maggie a half-truth for now.

"That's what you said before," said Maggie.

"Yes, well, I mean it even more now."

Diary of Margaret Hamilton

Sunday, November 1

Jonny is finally sleeping, so I can write these notes. I was thrilled to see him, after nearly two days of loneliness . . . Thank goodness Nanty Ella and Chipper are better. They should be ready to travel in the morning. Chipper was hopping all over today in his leg brace. I suspect his leg is not really broken . . . Mose finished his project today, a wonderful, yet narrow bed that fits under the buckboard. Buelah and Chipper are sleeping in it now . . . That is, if Nunky Mose and Nanty Ella, or Jonny and I didn't keep them awake! . . . Jonny bagged two deer on his scouting trip. We had steaks from one tonight, and the other is hidden somewhere up the trail. I hope we'll find it when we get there, IF we ever get there . . . I remain your devoted daughter, and wife . . .

Margaret Rose Hamilton

Monday, November 2

All hands were awake and busy before dawn as promised, although they seemed tired and fatigued. A hearty meal of venison dodgers, and warmed beans were downed by all. As the teams were being harnessed to the wagons, Mose was already hacking away at brush and small trees at the trail's start.

"Okay, gang. I want all the men clearing trail. Ella, are you alright to drive the buckboard?"

"I's sho 'nuff is, Jonny."

"How about you, Buel? Can you handle a wagon?"

"I's neva do's befo', Jon," answered Buelah.

"Then, you take turns riding in each wagon, starting with Ella. Corker is real easy to handle. By day's end, I expect you to be an expert driver."

"Who's going to drive this wagon?" asked Elizabeth.

"You are! Can't you handle a team?" asked Jon.

"I've never done it before."

"Buggers!"

"I's do's it!" said an excited Chipper.

"Are you sure you can do it, Chip?"

"Yassa, Massa Jon. I's can."

"Alright, Chipper, you help Missus Chasney."

"Yassa, Massa Jon. I's do!"

"We'll start you behind the lead wagon, Liz, so Ella can keep an eye on ya. That Okay, Ella?"

"Yassa, Jonny, I's do."

"Alright, then. We're about ready to rumble. Ready with the lead, darlin'?"

"What are we waiting for? Let's roll!" she answered.

"Listen to you! I can't believe it!" smiled Jon.

A final check of the area revealed it in good shape. The fire was nearly out. Just some embers remained, well away from any grass, trees, or brush, all of which were wet. Mose already had several small trees and brush wacked down, using the big axe and the machete. Both Charles and Dave had small axes, and together they tried to keep up with Mose. No such luck! Jon pitched in and cleared the trail of the downed shrubbery. Chipper took a bucket of water and finished dousing the embers, then climbed back up with Liz.

"Don't do that, Chipper, or we'll be short of water!" yelled Maggie.

"Oh, I's sorry, missy," answered Chipper.

Jon heard the yell of his wife, and went back to check.

"What's the matter, darlin'?"

"Chipper used our last bucket of water to put out the fire."

"No problem. We'll hit a stream ahead."

The new trail zigzagged around larger trees like a snake. Jon and the Chasney brothers had to break from time to time, but Mose continued at a torrid pace. At last, they came to the spot where Jon had killed the doe and was first obliged to go north. Mose saw those pieces of cloth, and continued hacking to the north, past the turn.

"Whoa, Mose! We're not going that way now."

"But dem cloths come here."

"I know. That's the way I went Saturday. But I came back this way here, to the west."

"Orights, Jon. West we's go!"

"Let's all take a break right here in this clearing. It's close enough to noon, so let's have lunch. Chipper, fill up the water buckets in that stream."

"We need to block the wheels, Jonny," said Maggie.

"I's do!" hollered Chipper, jumping down from the Chasney wagon, bad leg and all.

"We's has deer dodgers fo' lunches," said Ella.

"With raw venison?" asked Charles.

"I's cooks sum strips wit breakfas'."

"Ella, you're a darlin'," said Jon.

"Hee, hee. You's embarrass me's, Jonny," laughed Ella.

"Now, Ella, we're all family. Nobody gets embarrassed."

"Yassa, I's rememba's, Jonny."

The dodgers were excellent, followed by a short rest period. Chipper grabbed the water buckets and headed for the stream. Mose started whacking brush again, this time heading west. The Chasneys just shook their heads.

"Better check out the sky," said Jon. "This is the last you'll see of it for days."

"Looks pretty bad, Jon. Do you think it will rain again?" asked Liz, in a soft, sweet voice.

"If it doesn't, it will miss a danged good chance."

"It's cold enough to snow again," observed Maggie.

"Don't even think of it, my pretty plum."

"How far have we come, Jonny?"

"You ought to know, darlin'. We just passed where I shot the doe, and you came running to greet me."

"Are you joking, Jonny?"

"No way. It was just back there a spell."

"Good Lord! We've been hours just getting this far?"

"That's right, Lizzy. Now you've got a good idea just how long it's going to take to put the Blues behind us."

"Please don't call me Lizzy, Jonny. Liz will do."

"Sorry, Liz."

"That's alright, Jonny," Liz said through a pretty smile.

"Has everything been fine with you ladies?"

"Smutty stepped on a cut tree that was sticking up from the ground. She was limping for a while," said Maggie.

"We need to cut the shrubs right to the ground, men, or place a rock over the tree stubs so the horses won't step on them. We can't afford to lose any animals."

"Otherwise, I think we did good, or Chipper did," said Liz.

"I hope he's teaching you to drive, Liz."

"He is! He's a talented little man," Liz answered.

"Righto. Well, let's get crackin'. I want to get through this heavy thicket area before dark."

"We're ready to hit the brush," said Charles.

"Yeah, we've got some catching up to do," added Dave, gesturing toward Mose, who was well ahead.

"The lunch was great. Thank you," said Charles to Ella.

"You's welcomes, sir," answered Ella.

"Is this the worst part, Jonny?"

"Well, it's one of the worst. Tomorrow we start up a long hill along a small river, to the northwest."

"How long will that take?" asked Maggie.

"It's steep for these wagons. Probably take at least four or five days."

"Is that the best trail you could find?" asked Liz.

"Yes, but after that, it's smooth sailing all the way to that cliff I was talking about."

"And Mister Duncan said it would take a couple of days."

"I know, my pretty plum, but he wasn't thinking of pulling wagons."

The crew worked hard all afternoon. They didn't notice when the rain returned, but kept working even when they did. The women brought the wagons forward every half hour or so, then sat in the covered wagon and chatted.

"Did you say that you came from Salem?" Liz asked Maggie.

"No, I came from my father's plantation, on this side of Salem. Jonny is from Salem."

"We's all come from dem Bethanias," said Buelah.

"Where's that?" asked Liz.

"Bethania. That's my plantation."

"Oh, I thought you said your father owned it."

"Yes, he does. I was born there."

"I's be born there too," said Buelah.

"Were you born there too, Ella?" asked Liz.

"No's, ma'am, I's be's from fa'ways ova wata's."

"Oh, you were slaves on Bethania?"

"Yassum, but we's be's frees now."

"My granddaddy didn't like the word 'slave,' so he called them bounders," said Maggie.

"We's all lives in dem bigs house," said Buelah.

"Well, I'm happy to know you all."

"We's happy's too," answered Ella.

"Guess we'd better bring the wagons back up, before Jonny has a fit," said Maggie.

"Your husband is a *fine* man."

"Yes, he is," affirmed Maggie, as the women scattered.

Darkness came before the men finished hacking their way to an opening. It was too dark to see anything, and Jon hoped that he would spot his markings in the morning. He was pretty sure he was at the foot of the long, steep wooded hill, running northwest, the one he knew would be trying on everyone.

"I hope by now we can set camp up in the dark."

"We's does fine, Jon," answered Mose.

"Good, Mose. You and Chipper have the job of feeding and bedding the horses. You women circle the wagons around this level area, and set up your beds, then help Ella with dinn . . . er, supner. Charles, will you help me gather firewood, and Dave, you help Mose, alright?"

The group all agreed, and in short order, the chores were completed; and all gathered around the fire in the circle.

"What do you have to eat, Ella?"

"We's has pemmican an' beans," said Buelah.

"An' I's cooks hotcakes, Jonny," answered Ella, "an' I's has hominys in dem pemmican."

"Sounds good, Ella. I'm hungry," said Dave.

"Can I say a prayer, Jonny?" asked Maggie.

"How about it, gang?"

"I haven't heard a prayer for ages," said Liz.

"That's because my family never said any," said Charles.

"But we did! A lot of the time, didn't we, Nanty Ella?"

"Yassum, Sissy, we's do's."

"Okay, you can say a small prayer now, and then only on the Sunday supners. That alright, darlin'?"

"Yes, Jonny."

"Then can we eat? I'm starved," said Dave.

"Oh, be quiet, Davy. This isn't going to hurt you. Go ahead, Maggie, please," snapped Liz.

Maggie bowed her head, and the rest of the group did the same. "Heavenly Father, thank you for delivering us into these mountains safely. Please bless my Jonny, and Nunky Mose, and Nanty Ella, and all the rest of this party gathered before you . . . and bless this food we share. Amen."

"Amen."

"Let's dig in," said Jon.

Jon's gang all ate heartily, after which they prepared for sleep. They had worked hard into the night, and were tired. Thankfully, the horses were inside the wagons' circle, which was connected by ropes.

"I'll take the first guard, and wake you in a couple hours, Charles. Then Dave and Mose early tomorrow."

"Sounds good, Jon," said Charles.

Diary of Margaret Hamilton

Monday, November 2, 1835

Started early, in good stead, after camping two days without Jonny . . . He says we only covered about six miles today, in very heavy brush and trees. We have a steep hill next . . . could take four to five days to its summit . . . Love to all, especially in Bethania.

———————— ∿∿⚬⚬✦⚬✦⚬✦⚬⚬∿∿ ————————

Tuesday, November 3

The routine was thus established. By the time all hands had risen, Mose had been up and on guard for two or three hours, had all the horses fed, watered, and harnessed and ready to hook up to the wagons, and Ella had breakfast ready. It was long, hard hours, little progress this day.

———————— ∿∿⚬⚬✦⚬✦⚬✦⚬⚬∿∿ ————————

Diary of Margaret Hamilton

Tuesday, November 3

What a terrible day! Heavy, very wet brush and rain, all day. Had to take frequent rests, both men and horses. Corker deserves praise. Each time the wagons were moved forward up, Corker was harnessed to each wagon, to help pull them to the next level. At each stop, the wagon wheels were blocked and chained, very scary! Mose worked nonstop with machete. Still in wet brush tonight, but Jonny says we'll break out early tomorrow, but with an even steeper climb! Only made about five miles today . . . Love to all.

Margaret Hamilton

———————— ∿∿⚬⚬✦⚬✦⚬✦⚬⚬∿∿ ————————

Wednesday, November 4

"Today we will be climbing that steep hill I was telling you about," said Jon, over breakfast. "We will need to break out our tackle, Mose. Our horses will have to do double duty, pulling the wagons up, with Corker pulling the tackle."

"Yassa, Jon, we's do," answered Mose.

"That Corker sure is powerful," said Dave.

"Daddy hated to give him to us. He said Corker could pull as much as two teams," said Maggie.

"We'll find out pretty soon, darlin'."

"He do's, Jon. You's see," said Mose.

"And you think that hill will take five days to climb, Jonny?" asked Elizabeth.

"Yes, if everything goes well."

"Will we be camping and sleeping on level spots?"

"Ever make love on a slanted bed, Maggie darlin'?"

"No, and I don't intend to!"

"Might be a blast!" exclaimed Dave.

About midmorning, the men reached the clearing at the bottom of the steep hill. Jon called for a break. It hadn't rained yet this day, but it was cool, just right for work. Ella gave out venison dodgers, and the men grained the horses.

"I'm not sure how to handle this hill," said Jon.

"It's going to need the block and tackle," said Charles.

"Righto! Got any ideas, Mose?"

"Yassa, Jon. I's takes Corka an' finds tree ta hooks dem tackles, and finds dem place fo' wagons."

"Okay, Mose. We'll work up toward you."

"Yassa, an' I's works down ta you's."

"Sounds good. Let's put down the hammer and give it a go. Everyone ready?"

The answer was affirmative, and Mose loaded Corker with the block and tackle, long rope, shovel, and axe, and headed up through the trees and brush to the northwest. The other men started hacking their way uphill. The agony had started. The women pitched in to remove brush, and even pull trees off the trail, using teams five and fifteen. The hill was a constant twenty- to thirty-degree slope, in Jon's estimation. At last, it was time to pull the wagons.

"Charles, let's put your team at the wheel of my wagon, with Jake and Red at the lead. We can add Sloggy and Smutty if needed."

"Sounds good, Jon," said Charles. "Then we bring them back down?"

"Yes, and hook up the buckboard, then your wagon."

"Alright. I can hook up Sloggy and . . . is it Smutty? To the buckboard, while your wagon is being pulled uphill."

"Better not do that, Charles. We may need to add them to get the wagon all the way up. Besides, I'll need you and Dave to stay with the wagon and block it if it starts to slip back down."

"Good idea. Let's get some blocking, Dave."

"Right, brother. Maybe a pole to stick in the wheels."

"Am I going to sit up here and drive, Jonny?"

"No, Maggie. I think you women, Pasha, and Chipper should all walk up the hill, away from the wagon, just in case."

"I's brings Slog an' Smutty behins, Jonny."

"Good idea, Ella. They can pull you women up the hill, and be close if we need them."

"Then I think we're all set, Jon," declared Charles.

"Good. Let's give it all hell. I'll walk the lead."

The Chasney brothers got on each side of the wagon with blocks, chains and pole at the ready. Ella had the reins of team fifteen with a rope leading Pasha that the women and Chipper could hang on to. Jon could see Mose up the hill ahead, ready with Corker. He had already brought the long rope down the hill, hitched it to the wagon, and had Corker ready to pull downhill from the other end. The procession started.

Crack, crack, crack, came the noise from above.

"Whoa, whoa, Red. Whoa! Block the wheels, men. What happened, Mose?" shouted Jon.

"I's be orights, Jon," answered Mose. "Dem ropes tights up an tree."

"Everything Okay there, Charles?"

"Yes. The pole and blocks worked well, Jon."

"Good. Let's start again."

Slowly but surely, with every animal straining, the wagon inched its way up the hill toward the level spot Mose had dug.

Everyone was amazed, watching the great white Corker go by them, exerting his power, pulling horses and wagon steadily uphill, to the fairly level spot cut out for them. There was some slipping from time to time, mostly by the two teams at the wagon, but Corker's rope kept the slipping in check. Everyone made it safely up the first leg of many. At the bottom of the hill, Mose and Corker brought the buckboard forward, and hooked it to Corker's end of the rope.

"Good job, gang. We'll rest for a couple minutes, then bring the horses back down the hill and hook up the buckboard. I think Sloggy and Smutty can do the pulling, with Corker working the tackle."

"What a job everyone did," said Maggie.

"Only ninety-nine more, and it's done," said Jon.

"You've got to be joking again, Jonny."

"Never joke on Tuesdays, my pretty plum."

"But this is Wednesday, you big lummox."

"Is it Wednesday?" Jon asked his group.

"Yes!" came the confirmation.

"Darn! I lost a day."

"You'd lose your head if it wasn't attached to your shoulders."

"I lost my head when I met you, darlin'."

"I knew it! But it's nice to hear you say it, Jonny."

Although the buckboard was close to the same dimensions as the covered wagon, it was lighter, and Sloggy and Smutty, with the power of Corker on the tackle, walked up the hill in an easier manner than wagon number one. Next came the Chasneys' wagon, already harnessed to Jake and Red at the lead, and the Chasneys' team, "Apple" and "Jack," at the wheel. The brothers had named their drays after their favorite drink. Their wagon also climbed easily, thanks to Corker. The same routine followed, and the second went better than the first.

"It's got to be close to noon, gang. Let's break here for lunch. Can you feed us all without a fire, Ella?"

"Yassa, Jonny. We's has pemmican dodgas."

"Good. I'm glad you came along, Ella. Please don't get sick again. I don't know what we'd do without you."

"I's tries not ta, Jonny."

"How far do you think we've come, Jon?" asked Dave.

"Well, about six hundred feet up this hill, and a couple miles in the brush this morning."

"And how many miles long is this hill?" asked Liz.

"If it were flat and clear, we could make it easily in a day, so it's probably three or four miles."

"My land!" exclaimed Liz. "At this rate, it could take us a week or ten days!"

"Did you blunder again, Jonny? It looks like it will take a lot longer than five days," quipped Maggie.

"No, I haven't blundered yet, Maggie. It depends on how many times we can make these legs each day."

"Hopefully, it will get easier each time," said Charles.

"How many can we do each day, Nunky Mose?" asked Margaret.

"We's see un afternoons, missy. Maybes six more."

"See, you big lummox? IT could take a month to get up this hill!" yelled Maggie.

"Don't get dandered, my pretty plum. However long it takes, it's the best way."

"The best way was to go to Abingdon!"

"Don't start that again, Maggie. Once we top this hill, it's fireball the rest of the way. And besides, we wouldn't have met the Chasneys if we'd gone to Abingdon."

"I's glads we do," said Mose.

"Thank you, Mose, you're a sweetheart," said Liz.

"Yeah? Well, what about that cliff you told us about?"

"We'll jump that hurdle when we get there, darlin'."

"Well, let's get crackin'," said Dave.

"Yes, I'm anxious to see how many times we can make these legs this afternoon," said Charles.

"Righto, gang. We'll do the same routine each leg, depending on how the horses hold up."

"It's how well *we* hold up, Jon. The horses get a long break between each pull," said Dave.

"So do us women," added Elizabeth.

"I guess you're right. Let's tackle this hill!"

The system was established, and the gang tackled each task that was to be their fate for days ahead. Mose found a spot to level for the next stop, but it turned out to be more than the length of his longest rope. That meant that Corker would do that much more work, hooked up to each wagon to help pull it far enough uphill, then block the wagon. Then Mose and Corker would have to hook up to the block and tackle, move and pull the wagons the rest of the way to the next level. The routine was accomplished four more times that afternoon. A very tired group sat around their fire on the mountainous hill that evening, eating venison and hotcakes. Eyelids were heavy, and muscles were sore.

Diary of Margaret Hamilton

Wednesday, November 4, 1835

. . . sSo tired I can hardly stay awake long enough to write . . . All are upset with my Jonny. He first thought it would be three days up this monster of a hill, then five days. Now it may be one to two weeks! Jonny says we only came two and a half, maybe three miles today, out of thirteen miles to the top . . . Chipper tossed away his leg braces today. The swelling is gone, and he has walked well since he injured it . . . We are sleeping on a slant. No matter, too tired . . .

MRH

Thursday, November 5

Started the day in good fashion. Jonny gave the men a good pep talk at breakfast, and the climb up this miserable hill continued. Five series of pulls, the length of the tackle rope, were accomplished by lunch. A strange happening at lunch. Nunky Mose was holding his Kentucky rifle, when a deer walked out on the hillside, very close above us. Nunky Mose shot it. It was hung from the back hoops of our wagon the rest of the day, and was partly used this evening in a soup made by Nanty Ella. She cooked beans and hominy with the venison. Very tasty. Jonny said we climbed only about a half mile today.

Margaret Hamilton

Friday, November 6

Same routine as yesterday. At least we've had no rain for the last two days. It looks like six "legs" before lunch is our very best limit. Jonny says that's less than half a mile! My poor Pasha! He is looking so raggedy. No one is paying any attention to him. Sloggy and Smutty have to pull him up the hill, along with us women and Chipper. I'm afraid that I will have to teach him his tricks all over again when (if) we get to Arkansas . . . We made ten levels this afternoon and finished in darkness. That makes close to a half mile for the day. Love to all.

Maggie H.

"How is everybody feeling this morning?"

"I's feels fine, Jon," said Mose.

"I be's tired," said Buelah.

"It looks like Maggie and I are the only mad ones," said Liz.

"I'm not even going to ask why," answered Jon.

"You know why!" shouted Maggie.

"How about you, Ella, and you two?" Jon asked of the Chasney brothers, ignoring the women.

"I's be fines, Jonny," said Ella.

"We're ready to tackle this big mound again, aren't we, Davy?" said Charles.

"Righto, brother. Let's get crackin'!" answered Dave.

A lot of the lower, brushy part of the hill had been disposed of, but that just meant more pine trees to dodge and cut through. Seven "levels" were reached before the gang broke for lunch in the early afternoon.

"That's the best we've done so far, gang. You're all doing great!"

"Only ninety-nine more pulls to go!" snarled Maggie.

"I think I've heard that before," answered Jon.

"Only about five days to the top," teased Liz.

"I deserve that. I apologize."

"Is orights, Jon. We's makes it," said Mose.

"Yes, we will, Mose. When we get to the spot where I got the buck, it should be easier and not as steep."

"Got a guess when that will happen?" asked Charles.

"Oh, about five days!" quipped Jon.

Everyone laughed at that. Even Liz, then Maggie broke into laughter. Jon decided to move out again, while all were in good humor. The first five afternoon pulls went fast. It was the sixth pull when the trouble began, with wagon number one.

SNAP!

"Whoa! Whoa!" cried Dave.

"Hold up, Mose! Block the wagon!" yelled Jon.

Charles and Dave rushed to get blocking behind each of the covered wagon's wheels, then stretched a chain between the wheels on both sides, and even shoved a pole between the spokes of the front wheels. Mose was next to a tree with Corker, so he tied the big white dray's halter straps to the tree, so Corker couldn't slack up much on his rope, holding the wagon steady. He hurried over to the covered wagon, where Jon was studying the damage.

"What's dem noise, Jon?" asked Mose.

"This wheel hit this tree, and it snapped two more spokes. It's the same wheel that we lost the spoke before."

"The one we lost on Hamilton Hill?" asked Maggie.

"The same! We may have damaged the hub as well, or the axle. The wheel looks bent."

"I's gets dem shovels, Jon, an' levels ground."

"Thanks. I think the blocking should hold the wagon steady. Let's get the other two wagons up this grade."

"We can handle that, Jon. While you two work on that wagon, we can get the others up," said Charles.

"Good. Maybe Ella can work Corker and the tackle."

"I's do, Jonny. I's do,' said Ella.

"Fine, Ella."

Most of the gang went back to work, pulling all but the covered wagon up to the next level, where Mose had found a level area. Meanwhile, Mose and Jon leveled a spot across the hill, just below the damaged wagon number one.

"When the wagons are up the trail, Jon," said Dave, "what can we do to help?"

"We'll need Corker to back this wagon back on to this level area, so we can work on it. Can you go ahead and clear another leg?"

"Will do. Sure you don't need help here?"

"We's needs Slogs and Smuts," said Mose.

"Okay. Leave that team, and Corker, and go ahead and clear another level. I don't know how long this will take, or if we can even fix it."

"If it can be fixed, Mose can do it," said Charles.

"You've got that right. I told you that before."

"And you were all-fired right. Come on, Dave, let's start clearing."

"Righto, brother."

While the Chasney brothers finished raising wagons two and three to the new level, and started clearing another "leg" of the hill, all the women except Ella sat in the wagons at the top of the cleared area. Mose harnessed Corker to the tongue of the disabled wagon, and Sloggy and Smutty to the backside of the wagon, uphill, so they could inch it back and turn it onto the level area, as well as help Corker with the drag. The wagon was thus guided onto the leveling and blocked. The bad wheel rubbed against the wagon rail, but stayed on. Jon and Mose then raised the corner up to take the wheel off. It was bent, and the hub was cracked.

"This wheel is deceased, Mose."

"Yassa, sho 'nuff is."

"I'm glad we have a spare one under here. I'll just roll this one over the edge."

"We's saves wheel, Jon. May needs banns an' spokes."

"Okay, we'll just switch."

"You's sees here, Jon? Axle be dry."

"Do we have any grease?"

"Nossa. Maybes makes grease."

"How do we do that, Mose?"

"We shoots deers, makes grease."

"Mose, you're a wiz—"

Before Jon could finish his sentence, the men heard a loud screeching, then growling noise, and the women screaming. Mose started running up the hill toward the women. Jon grabbed his Hawken and followed. Mose had reached the women, hunkered under the tarp in the Chasneys' wagon, still screaming. The high-pitched growl came again, close to them, and Mose grabbed a large branch he had cut before, and, before Jon's eyes, broke the end section off the branch to make a three-inch thick bat.

"What is it, Mose?" Jon shouted, now near.

"It be un panter."

"A panther?" Jon asked, as he fumbled for a cap in his Hawken's patch box.

"Yassa. He be's rights in dem trees."

As Mose beat the brush and pounded on a tree, the panther growled again. Jon spotted it as it was about to spring at Mose.

Bam! Jon fired the Hawken. The big cat sprang backward as the ball tore into its shoulder. It was flopping over and over, trying to get back up. Mose wacked him in the head with his heavy bat, and the cat lay silent.

"I don't think he's dead yet, Mose."

"Nossa, I's hit him again."

"Hold it, Mose!" Jon shouted, reloading. "I'll get him again."

Mose held his bat at ready, as Jon finished reloading. He snuck up behind the still cat, put the barrel to the back of its head, and fired. *Bam!*

"He be's dead nows," said Mose.

"Does he have any fat for grease?"

"Nossa, Jon. He be's lean and means."

By this time, Charles, Dave, and Ella had arrived. Chipper jumped out of the buckboard, where he had been hiding, and tried to calm down a wild, rearing Pasha.

The four drays, still hitched to the Chasney wagon, were upset but still standing in place. Mose calmed them all.

"Whoa, Red. Whoa, Jake. Whoa," he repeated.

"Wow! Will you look at that cat?" exclaimed Dave.

"He's a big one, alright," said Charles.

"We's saves dem hides, Daddy," said Ella.

"Yessum, we's do," agreed Mose, as he grabbed his knife from the buckboard.

"And I want the head," added Jon.

"What do you want with that, Jonny?" asked Maggie, as she, Buelah, and Elizabeth appeared from under the tarp.

"A souvenir, my pretty plum."

"I'll be your souvenir! I don't want any part of that thing close to me."

"I need all my souvenirs."

"You have a choice, Jonny. You keep that one, and you lose this one!"

"Not a fair choice, darlin'. You keep all your chemises. I keep my cat head."

"That's not a fair choice, you lummox! I'm keeping my chemises anyway."

"I's keep dem un dem buckboards," said Mose.

"Thanks, Mose. I'll put the new wheel on my wagon, while you skin the cat."

"Orights, Jon."

"While we're breaking, I'll help you, Jon," said Charles.

"Righto. We can all use a little break."

"Can we's has fire, Jonny?" asked Ella.

"Sure. Are you women cold?"

"Yes," said Maggie.

"You're always cold, my pretty plum."

"Well, then that means you're not doing your job!"

"Need more practice, Jonny?" quizzed Liz, smiling.

"I'll try to do a better job, darlin', if I can keep my cat head. Besides, I've never seen a panther before. I've got to have a keepsake."

"I've never seen one before either," said Charles.

"Nor I," said Dave. "Has anyone here seen one?" Everyone shook their heads no.

"Congratulations, Jonny," said the smiling Liz. "You look like you need a few souvenirs."

"Thanks," answered Jon, noting the angry look on Maggie's face. "I better get busy with that wheel. Dave, will you build a fire for Ella?"

"You bet. I can use a little catnap!" said Dave.

"You mean a little catnip," quipped Liz.

"I's cooks dem cat strips," said Ella.

"So's nows we's has cat dodgers," said Buelah.

"That would be a change," added Elizabeth.

Before long, Ella and the girls had a fire and were cooking the cat strips as Mose cut them. Charles came back up the hill, bringing Jake and Red back to help pull wagon number one, with its new wheel, up to the fire level.

Everyone ate a wild cat dodger. It had flavor, but was stringy and chewy. The group decided to finish cooking the strips and hang them off the Chasney wagon, just in case.

"We finished four pulls this afternoon. Can we do a couple more before dark?"

"We can and will," answered Charles.

"Good. That will put us over half a mile again today."

Diary of Margaret Hamilton

Saturday, November 7, 1835

. . . Climbed over another half mile today, but it was not "business as usual." We women may owe our lives to Nunky Mose and my husband. We were confronted by a huge panther. Nunky Mose hit it with a large stick, and Jonny shot and killed it. Now Jonny wants to save the panther's head! I don't understand that, and the sight of it still scares me. None of our group had ever seen or tasted panther before, but we had panther dodgers! I didn't like them either. Our wagon broke a wheel, the same one damaged on Hamilton Hill. I am very fortunate to have Nunky Mose, Nanty Ella, and Buelah along on this trip, but I still miss my family. It has now been two weeks since last seen.

Margaret R. Hamilton

Maggie was dreaming about being eaten by the monster, Boony, or by the panther. She wasn't sure which, as her demise kept changing back and forth from one scary creature to the other. One of them must have gotten Buelah too, because Maggie could hear her and feel her shaking . . .

"Wakes up, Sissy. Wakes up."

"Huh? Ooh . . . What?"

"Wakes up! You's misses breakfas'."

"Breakfast? I just got to . . ."

"Gets up, Sissy. You's sleeps all days?"

"Oooh, *yes!* It's Sunday!"

"I's knows. Bu' Jon's wan's to travels."

"What? He wants to travel on the Sabbath?"

"Yassum, Sissy, for half's day, maybes."

"Well, I'll straighten him out! Where is he?"

"He's goes scoutin' wit Papa Mose."

"Scouting? For what?"

"I's don' knows, Sissy, bu' you's bes' gets dressed, 'afore you's misses breakfas'."

"Alright, Buel, I'll be right out, as soon as—"

BAM!... BAM! BAM!

Jon had tossed and turned all night. First it was the wagon breaking down, then the panther about to attack Mose, then . . . then . . . the wagon again. He finally decided to get up. It was still very dark, but . . .

"Do you and Ella ever sleep, Mose?"

"Yassa, we's do, Jon."

"We's don' needs much sleeps," said Ella.

"I guess not! I do need it, and can't!"

"You's worries, Jonny?"

"Yes, Ella, but I'm not sure what was keeping me awake all night."

"I's knows, Jon," said Mose. "You's worries 'bout gets dem wagon ups dem hils, an' no grese."

"That's it, Mose. How'd you know?"

"'Cause I's worries too."

"What are we going to do about it?"

"Dis be's Sundays, Jon. We's hunts," said Mose.

"Righto. Which way do we go?"

"I's smells un, ups hill."

"Okay, let's try it, Mose. Got your Kentuck?"

"Yassa, I's be ready."

"You's gets some breakfas' first, Jonny."

"Thanks, Ella. I'm hungry."

Stomachs weighted with venison strips and coffee, Mose and Jon headed uphill, past strips of cloth marking Jon's trail. The going was easy without the wagons and horses. They quickly found a small, fairly level area, just a couple hundred yards above the wagons.

"Let's bring the wagons up to this level today, then we can break for the day."

"Yassa, Jon, bu' first we's go's up an' gets food an' grease."

"Alright. How far should we go?"

"Short ways, Jon. I's smells 'um."

"Okay, Mose, you follow my trail, and I'll go up a ways over here. When you get to a level area, where there's a stream, wait there for me, there?"

"Orights, Jon, we's do."

Jon plunged into the woods about a hundred feet to the right of Mose, and headed up the hill through brush and trees. The route was thicker and tougher than his marked trail, which Mose was using, so he was making a lot of noise, trying to keep up to where he thought Mose would be. The farther he went, the thicker the underbrush. But Jon trudged on for what seemed like hours. Suddenly, he spotted a red cloth. He couldn't believe he was at the spot where he and Sloggy and fought their way west after he had shot the creature called Boony. He took a left, toward Mose. He couldn't see but a few feet ahead through the heavy brush, but he was sure he was close to the clearing where Mose should be waiting.

BAM!

Jon could hear the commotion ahead, and tore his way through the brush. When he reached the clearing, he saw the black bear standing on hind legs and growling, massive arms waving, walking across the clearing. It looked like Boony, except it had black fur and coat.

"Bear!" Jon yelled. He quickly pulled the plug and patch, and squeezed a cap over the nipple of his Hawken. *BAM!* His shot hit the bear in the side, just below the arm. The bear went down, and immediately tried to get back up. Jon started to quickly reload. He managed to get the powder charge and had the ball down the barrel, followed by the tamping rod. The bear was now back on his feet, trying to rise back up on his hind legs. Jon was amazed that the bear had that much strength with the first ball in his body. He aimed his Hawken, and was about to fire, when, *BAM!* Another shot came from the brush in front of the bear, sending "blackie" back down for good.

"Mose? Is that you?"

"Yassa, Jon. We's gots grease now."

"Sure do," Jon agreed, as he ran over to the dead beast. "Nice shooting, Mose. You got him through the heart."

"I's aims ta lefts, like you's said, Jon, an' I's shoots him twice."

"Where did your first shot hit him?"

"In dem backs, ova der," said Mose, as he pointed across the clearing. Jon's eyes noticed something on the ground where Mose was pointing.

"There's something over there, Mose."

"I's see. Dem bear be killin' food whens I shoots 'em . . . it's be coons!"

Jon and Mose walked over to the raccoon. The bear had apparently killed it, but had not eaten any of it before Mose shot him. He started cleaning the coon.

"We can't eat coons, can we?"

"If you's hungry 'nuffs," answered Mose. "We's use dem fats an' skins."

"We shouldn't be that hungry, Mose, now that we have bear meat and venison."

"Yassa. I's gots ta gets dem bear cuts up fast, Jon, so's we can make grease."

"It's a big one, Mose. It's not going to be easy getting it back down the hill."

"I's stays here an' cuts, Jon. Maybes you's go gets Corka."

"Righto. That's a good idea, Mose. I can get the wagons up to that grassy area too."

"Yassa, buts we's needs Corka now, to make dem grease fast."

"Okay, Mose. Will you be alright?"

"Yassa. Brings ropes, Jon."

Jon headed back downhill in a hurry. It wasn't long before he came to that small grassy area just a short way above camp. This would be a great place to rest for the rest of the day. He quickly got back to camp.

"Where have you been, Jonny?"

"Mose and I went hunting this morning, my love."

"We heard the shots. What did you get?" asked Charles.

"Mose got a bear and a nice fat raccoon."

"Daddy needs me's," said Ella.

"What would anyone want a raccoon for?" asked Liz.

"You need a coon skin hat, don't you?"

"I don't think so," answered Liz.

"They're really warm," said Maggie.

"In that case, yes, I need a coon skin hat!"

"Well, maybe Ella will make one for you. In the meantime, I would like to get further up the hill."

"Today?" asked Buelah and Maggie.

"Righto. Today! There's a spot only a couple of pulls above us that is fairly level and has grass."

"This is Sunday, you big lummox, and we need a rest. I'm not going anywhere today," snapped Maggie.

"I think we should," said Charles.

"And you voted Charles and I as the captains, my pretty plum. It should only take about an hour. When you get there, build another fire so we can make grease."

"Where are you going now?" asked Maggie.

"I'm taking Corker back up to the hill, so he can pull boony bear down to that landing above us."

"An' you's takes Mama?" asked Buelah.

"Well, I don't think we'll need Ella until we get the kill down to the clearing up above."

"Orights, Jonny. I's helps wit wagons," said Ella.

"Thanks, Ella. I better get back up there with Corker. Mose and I will see you before noon."

"It will be tough work without both you and Mose . . . and Corker," said Charles.

"Oh, righto, Charles. Hmm . . . maybe I'll use Sloggy and take Ella up to help Mose, and I'll come back down."

"That sounds like a better idea, Jon," said Dave.

"Okay. Ready, Ella? We need to get going."

"I's ready, Jonny. Gets pole fo' fat."

"Why are you in such a hurry, Jonny?" asked Maggie.

"Fats needs ta boils fas', Sissy," answered Ella.

"And why do we need to boil fat?"

"We need grease for the wagons, darlin'," answered Jon.

"An' fats turns bad fas', Sissy," added Ella.

"Alright, Jonny. See you soon."

"I'll be back soon, gang. Meet you up above."

"Good," said Charles.

"Be careful, Jonny," said Maggie.

As Charles and Dave grabbed their axes to start clearing a trail above the camp, Jon, with Ella aboard Sloggy, headed up the marked trail toward Mose.

"Daddy shots bear, Jonny?"

"Twice. His second shot went right through the heart. He's getting to be a good shot."

"He's kill coons too?"

"No, the bear had killed the raccoon before Mose shot him."

"How's far ups dem hill?" Ella asked at the first clearing.

"About one-half mile, or a little more. It's where I came out from the heavy brush, that I change . . . oh darn!"

"Wha be, Jonny?"

"I just remembered. It's where I shot the buck."

"Goods! We's has meats orights, Jonny.

"I hope it's still there."

When Ella and Jon reached the landing where Mose was left alone, they found him cleaning out the bear. Jon hurried to the stream where he had left his deer. It was long gone. The stream was smaller from the days without rain.

"You's finds 'um, Jonny?" asked Ella.

"Nah, he's gone. Blast it!"

"Is alrights, Jonny. We's have pantha, deer, bear, and coons to eats," said Ella.

"We's goes, Jon. Needs ta get fats in fire, fast."

"Okay, Mose. I've got some rope."

"We's lashes 'em to Corka."

"I didn't bring Corker, Mose. They need him to pull the wagons. I brought Sloggy instead.

"Orights, Jon. We's goes downhill now.

Ella was cutting strips from the raccoon carcass. She cut away a large amount of fat and put it all in her small pail. Sloggy shied from the bear, but Mose calmed him down and harnessed the rope around him to pull the bear behind. He lashed the raccoon down on the dray, and put Ella on it. The trio headed back down the now-familiar hill. They reached the clearing and heard the gang working below. Buelah and Ella had gathered wood for a fire.

"You's can goes help dem wagons, Jonny. Daddy an' I works here."

"Okay, Ella. Slog and I will see you soon."

"Orights, Jonny."

The Chasneys were about to pull the covered wagon up the second leg. The block and tackle were not needed, and Corker was tied to the lead ahead of the Chasney team of Apple and Jack at the wheel. Jack and Red were at the lead. Smutty was pulling Pasha up, so Jon walked Corker and the teams up the hill.

"It's only a short way more to the next clearing where Mose and Ella are. We can do it with our eyes closed and our pantaloons down."

"I would love to see that," said Elizabeth.

"So would I," added Maggie.

"Jon meant pantalets," said Dave.

"Ha! We're ahead of your gummers. Our pantalets are already hanging in strips up the trail!" teased Liz.

"Yes! It's time for you boys to sacrifice too," said Maggie.

"Don't ever try to outgabble those women, Dave. They will have us in Adam's togs if you do."

"That would be interesting, right, Maggie?" asked Liz.

"Well, maybe. I'd hate to see them freeze their keisters."

"It is getting cold. Let's get going," said Charles.

Jon grabbed the third axe, and the men started clearing up the hill again. A couple more levels, and they reached the clearing where Mose and Ella were at work.

"Wow! That's some bear you got, Mose!" exclaimed Dave.

"Jon helped me."

"I just slowed him, so Mose could get a good shot."

"How big would you say he is?" asked Charles.

"I'd guess around five hundred pounds," said Jon.

"Nice shootin', Mose!" yelled Charles. "Let's get the women and wagons up here and get them warmed up."

"Good idea. See you two pretty soon," said Jon.

"We's be's here, Jon," answered Mose.

The last pulls of the day were pretty easy, and soon Jon's group was all together. *All this was done before noontime*, Jon thought.

"What's that terrible smell?" asked Maggie.

"Dat be's bear fats, Sissy," answered Ella.

"And you're using it on my wagon?"

"Maybe's all dem wagons," said Mose.

"I need to get by that fire, smell or not," said Liz.

"So do I. I'll put something over my nose," said Maggie.

"How are you two doing, Mose?"

"Orites, Jon. We's has grease for all dem wagons."

"An' we's has mo' ta boot," added Ella.

"Good. Maybe you can fry us some bear meat for our dodgers."

"You mean you use that smelly grease for cooking?"

"It makes great-tasting bacon, my pretty plum."

"No thanks. I'll use lard," said Elizabeth.

A large meal of bear dodgers and coffee. Now that's a lunch fit for a king, not a group of weary travelers. After lunch, there was plenty of work to do on this Sunday afternoon. The strips of meat had to be cooked and stored, or hung from the wagons to dry. The wagons had to be greased, and the axles of all four wheels of the covered wagon needed grease. The buckboard was low on grease as well. The Chasney wagon was fine, but the men greased it anyway. Mose made frames to stretch the animal skins, and the horses all needed tending to. There was not much time for rest. All this was accomplished in a cold rain, the first in over three days. The men stretched the extra canvas close to the fire, so the group could squeeze together for a hot supner under it.

"What's for supper, Ella?" asked Dave.

"We's has succotass."

"What was that?" asked Liz.

"We're having succotash soup," answered Maggie.

"Sounds good," said Jon, "but I thought succotash had pork and beans in it."

"It do," said Ella, "but we's has no powks."

"I's gots bears, an' pantha, an' coons," said Buelah.

"Okay, let's call it sufferin' succotash!" quipped Jon.

"Why call it that?" asked Elizabeth.

"What's suffering about it, Jonny?" asked Maggie.

"Well, we all suffered for it. We suffered getting up this hill. Ella and you women suffered cooking it. You suffered with the smells of making grease, and Mose and I suffered hunting the meat for succotash."

"You poor baby," said Maggie and Liz.

"Let's not suffer any longer. Let's eat!" said Dave.

"Good idea. Dig in, gang. Our suffering is over!"

"Hold it! Not so fast, big boy," said Maggie. "You're forgetting something."

"What's that, my love?"

"This is the Sabbath, you big lummox, and all decent people observe it with a prayer."

"All decent people?" asked Jon.

"All decent people?" Charles echoed.

"Oh, I'm sorry. I meant all religious people."

"*All* religious people?" asked Jon. "What about Jewish people? What about the Arabian people? I'll bet they don't only pray on Sundays."

"Help me out, Nanty Ella, Nunky Mose?"

"You's tells Sissy, Daddy," instructed Ella.

"Orites. When I's be a boy, dem families prays an' dances. Dey dances erry day. Dem buckra makes us prays on Sundays."

"Okay, Okay! I'm sorry I brought it up," snapped Maggie, as she stormed through the rain toward the wagon.

"Don't leave, Maggie! I want you to say a prayer," said Liz.

"So do I, my love. I was just teasing you. I'm sorry. Besides, I think I promised you could say a prayer on Sundays," said Jon.

"It do us alls good," added Buelah.

Maggie wiped the tears from her face and eyes, and said a quick prayer. After supper, the gang sang a few songs.

Diary of Margaret Rose Hamilton

Sunday, November 8

. . . Some Sabbath! Worked very hard all day climbing up this God-forsaken hill in the morning, and preparing for more climbing tomorrow in the afternoon, and in the first cold rain in three days. I'm beginning to think we may never reach the summit of the Blue Ridge Mountains! Nunky Mose killed a big bear and a raccoon. That makes three wild animals in two days. The panther kill by Jonny was yesterday. The bear fat made grease for the wagons, and the bear meat made tasty dodgers and succotash. Jonny almost refused to let me say a prayer at supper, but I did anyway, and I forgive my beautiful husband as he lay sleeping beside me . . . It's very cold.

MRH

Monday, November 9

Snow! Woke up to three plus inches this morning. The camp was a winter wonderland, but very cold. Nanty Ella was sick again with dyspepsia and ague. Poor Nanty. She and Nunky Mose are getting old. I would so hate to lose either of them. I love them so. Nanty Ella stayed in my wagon all day. It makes the pulls by Corker and the other horses harder, but we still did very well. Jonny said we made over a half mile uphill today, and Nanty Ella is better tonight . . . Snow in trees, but not much in path, and mostly gone tonight.

Margaret Hamilton

Tuesday, November 10

"Morning, gang," said Jon, tackling breakfast of bear bacon fried in bear grease, and coffee. "How are you feeling, Ella?"

"I's be fines, Jonny," she answered, voice cracking.

"Good, but I want you to get as much rest as you can today. Put more liniment on your chest."

"I's do."

"If we do as well as yesterday, we'll reach the clearing today where Mose shot the bear. From then on, the going gets easier."

"We've heard that line before, Jonathan," teased Liz.

"Yeah, about five days ago," quipped Maggie.

"Well, this time, it's for real," smiled Jon. "Let's get crackin' so we can make that clearing."

The gang had their jobs finely tuned, and by the time Jon called a stop for lunch, he reckoned they had gone over a half mile in brushless, easy ascent. Ella remained in the covered wagon most of the day, but came out to help fix lunch. It rained most of the afternoon, and late in the day, the team broke into the grassy clearing where Mose had dropped the bear.

"Nice work, gang. Let's get the camp set up so we can rest. Hear that creek? We have grass, water, food, shelter, and level ground. What else could we possibly ask for?"

"Food! Oysters," said Dave.

"An end to this hill," said Liz.

"Protection from this rain," added Maggie.

"Candy!" yelled Chipper.

"Sweets potater pies," said Mose.

"How about an end to this journey?" said Maggie.

"I'd like a long nine cigar or chewing tobacco," said Charles.

"Yeah, and some brandy," added Dave.

"I's likes dem chitlins, an' hogs, an' hominy," said Ella.

"I's wans moneys," added Buelah.

"And some love and romance," from Elizabeth.

"Hold it!" hollered Jon, hands waving. "I'm sorry I asked! Let's get set up for the night."

"You know, this really is a nice spot, even in the rain," said Charles, after a hot supper, under shelter of the tarp. "It's level, with lots of grass."

"Well then, why don't we just stay here and forget about Kentucky or Arkansas?" quipped Liz.

"It's too cold up here for me," answered Maggie.

"Just the same, Liz may be on to something. This place has water, and looks like a meeting place for wild game, what with the bear and raccoon, and the buck Jon got here," added Dave.

"I was only being sarcastic, you flunderhead!" exclaimed Liz.

"You can stay if you like, brother, but Liz and I are going to Kentucky," said Charles.

"So am I. Just thinking out loud," said Dave.

"I's be too tired ta thinks," said Mose.

"Me too, Mose. I think I'll turn in too. You go ahead and sleep in the covered wagon with Ella and Chipper, Mose. Maggie and I will take the buckboard."

"Good idea," said Maggie. "Nanty Ella still doesn't look that well. Put some more liniment on her."

"Orites, I's do. Thank you."

"I noticed you didn't say anything when staying here was discussed," said Maggie to her husband, after all had retired. "You wouldn't want to stay in a place like this, would you, Jonny?"

"Of course not, my pretty plum. You know how anxious I am to settle in Arkansas."

"Good. You had me worried. What were you thinking about then?"

"About maybe staying here."

"What? Are you going baffy? You just said you were anxious to get to Arkansas."

"I am. But what Dave said about this being a good place for wild game made me think about staying here for a day or two to stock up. What do you think about that?"

"Well, we could use more meat, but I would just as soon get off this cold mountain."

"We will soon, darlin'. But a day or two here would do wonders for the animals . . . and Ella."

"I hate to admit it, but I think you're right."

"Of course, I am! Put that in your journal."

"My journal is in the other wagon, you big lummox. In the morning, I'll write something in it about today."

Wednesday, November 11

Well before dawn, Jon quietly put his clothes on under the buckboard tarp and climbed out onto the wet grass. He was amazed that he didn't wake either Maggie, squeezed beside him, or Buelah, underneath the wagon. *They must be really tired*, he thought, *and a day's rest would do them good too.* The rains had temporarily stopped, but Jon felt they could start again at any time. He grabbed his Hawken and powder bag, and made his way to the stream, now running fast and high again from the rains, and found a place to sit. He had a lot of time to think about the many things that had happened to him this year.

Jon was sure he'd never forget this year as long as he would live. He thought about Cora and Wilma, and all the "chances" he'd missed with them. Then he thought about Ginny, and the "chance" he made good on there. He was sure that if he had the chance, he could make it with Liz. He fancied that she could teach him some new tricks. But with his mental deliberation, Jon decided that he could not be happier than he was right then. He had a beautiful wife, a son on the way, and soon would be enjoying both in a new land, a new beginning with no end in sight.

Jon's eyes were closed; and his mind was one track, so thank goodness his ears were alert, for they registered a noise behind him, which in turn alerted his mind. He quickly, but quietly removed the plug and patch from his Hawken and waited. Was Boony back? No, it turned out to be several white tails. Through the predawn light, Jon spotted a large rack on one of the deer. He took careful aim. *Bam!* Down went the buck, and Jon saw specks of white scattering in all directions and much commotion coming from the wagons.

"What was that?" he heard, coming from Liz, he thought.

"Jonny? Where are you, Jonny?" Jon knew that voice. Maggie.

"Somebody shot something," said either Charles or Dave.

"I's bets Jon gets deers again." That was Mose.

"Jonny? Answer me, Jonny," from Maggie.

"I'm over here, by the stream!" Jon hollered.

The first body in sight was the huge hulk of Mose, running toward him. "What you's gets, Jon?"

"I think I got a buck, up there by the stream."

"I's knowed it. Hee, hee! You's a good hunta, Jon."

"It's still too dark out to tell." Jon yelled toward the camp, "Could someone bring a lantern?"

"I'll bring one," came the reply from Dave.

"Oh, Jonny, you scared me," said Maggie, when she reached the others by the stream.

"I'm sorry I woke everyone up."

"That be's orites, Jonny," said Buelah. "We's needs dem venison."

"I thought Boony had come back," sighed Maggie.

"Not much chance of that," said Jon.

"I know you don't believe it exists, Jonny, but most of us do," said Elizabeth.

"Oh, I think it exists. Just not here, now."

"On some other planet?" asked a sarcastic Maggie.

"No, right here in these Blues."

"Will you stop talking in circles, you big bunco? You've been trying to convince me that it doesn't exist for the last two weeks."

"Well, I think I scared it away permanently when I wounded it, and when Mose knocked it down," said Jon, trying not to lie too much to Maggie.

"You're lying to me, Jonny."

"No, I'm not, my pretty plum. You saw what happened, when Boony tried to attack the horses."

"There's something more. I can see it in your face, you big lummox."

"I think I can too," added Liz. "Come on, Jonny, out with it."

"Well . . . Okay." Jon had everyone's attention now, even Dave's, who was back with a lantern. "I think I killed it when I was scouting the other day." A collective buzz came from the lips of the group.

"Are you still lying, Jonny?" asked Maggie.

"No, I'm not, darling. I shot him twice in the body. It had to have killed him."

"You don't know for sure?" asked Liz.

"I'm sure."

"Well, where is it then?" asked Dave.

"It's a short ways from here, actually, through that thick brush over there."

"Let's go see if we can find it," said Charles.

"Not in your lifetime!" yelled a scared Liz.

"I want to load up and leave here, Jonny," said Maggie.

"Don't you realize we can't leave here now?" asked Charles.

"And why can't we?" asked Liz.

"Yeah, just why can't we leave now?" asked Maggie.

"I's knows I's can leaves," said Buelah.

"Because if it is really Boony there, we are making history and changing science," answered Charles.

"He's right," said Jon.

"So what do we do, captain?" asked Dave of Jon.

"We's muss gets dem deer cut up," said Mose.

"Okay, Mose. Charles, will you and your brother take the women back to the camp, and one of you bring Corker back and the other stay with the ladies?"

"Sure thing, Jon," said Charles. "Let's go, ladies."

"Let's go find the buck, Mose," said Jon.

"Yassa, we's do."

Jon and Mose quickly found the huge ten-point buck right where Jon had dropped him. Mose grabbed the white-tailed deer by the antlers and started dragging him back to the clearing, when one of the antlers came off in Mose's hand. Mose handed it to Jon and continued pulling. Jon held the lantern for Mose, in amazement, as Mose easily pulled the two-hundred-pound animal toward camp. He didn't need Corker!

Back at camp, Mose started cleaning and stripping the animal, with the help of the women. The men started a fire, and Ella came out to make breakfast.

"Save some food for Charles and me, Ella."

"I's do, Jonny. Where's you's go?"

"We're going to find Boony. We won't be gone long. It's only a short ways."

"Are you sure you want to do this, Jonny?" asked Maggie.

"I'm sure. Make sure the rifles are all loaded, Dave."

"Righto. Take good care of my brother."

"Be careful, Jonny," said Maggie.

"Maybe we should take Corker along, Jon."

"Oh, that's a good idea! We also need rope."

Charles, Jon, and Corker plunged through the thick brush. The pieces of pantalets were still hanging, marking Jon's original trail. They soon reached the tiny clearing where Jon was sure he killed Boony. They searched, and finally found a few spots of blood that hadn't been washed away by the rain.

"He went down that way, through all those trees and brush," said Jon, pointing.

"Wow," said Charles, "look at that trampled brush! And those are some pretty good-sized trees he took out."

"He couldn't have gone too far. He had two heavy lead slugs in him."

"How are we going to get over there, through all that brush, and with Corker?" asked Charles.

"I don't think we can do it here. Let's see if we can find a way around this brush."

"Well, let's stick together, whichever way we go."

"Okay. We'll go on a ways further and look for an opening."

A short way further, along the original trail, the men spotted an area of lighter brush and decided to take it. It was miserable, very wet and slow going through the brush, but they finally found a way back to where Boony had disappeared. They found the torn-up brush and trees the beast had tumbled through, and even some blood spots in the brush, but no Boony. They spotted the place where Boony stopped tumbling, and a large blood spot where the beast must have lain for some time, but no Boony. They searched a wide-circled area, always trying to keep in sight of each other, but found nothing. They finally had to give up and again fight their way back to the camp, where the deer had been processed and breakfast eaten. Luckily, Ella saved some for them.

"What did you find, Jonny?" asked Maggie.

"We found the spot where Boony died."

"Well, where is it?" asked Liz.

"We couldn't find him," said Charles.

"Then he didn't die, you big lummox!"

"He had to have died."

"Why do you say that, Jonny?" asked Liz.

"Because nothing could have lived with all the lead this Hawken put in him, and there was enough blood around that he couldn't have survived without."

"Are you trying to con us again, Jonny? If it wasn't there, it had to have survived."

"Not necessarily, Maggie," said Charles.

"How so?" asked Elizabeth.

"Well," said Jon, "this mountain is full of animals, most of them scavengers. By now there could be parts of Boony scattered all over these hills."

"Somehow that's not very comforting," said Dave.

"I agree. Maybe we should hitch up and get going, and not stop until we get to Arkansas," said Maggie.

"What? With Charles and I getting no breakfast?"

"Would you rather be Boony's breakfast?" asked Liz.

"Not much chance of that," said Jon.

"I agree," said Maggie to a surprised Jon. "You're too thick-skinned, even for Boony!"

"These men would all be too bone-headed for Boony's taste," quipped Liz. "He would go for us women for sure."

"That's a smart beast," answered Jon.

"Somehow that's not very comforting either," said Dave.

"Well, beast or no beast, I'm hungry," said Charles.

"So am I," agreed Jon. "And we already agreed that we were staying here today to rest the horses and Ella."

"I would like a vote on that," said Liz.

"Are you sure about that, Liz?" asked Jon.

"It will do no good, Liz. He always wins the vote," said Maggie.

"I withdraw that request . . . for now."

"Good! Let's eat," said Charles.

Their stomachs full, the gang set about putting their wagons and belongings in order. Shortly before lunch, the rains came back, so the afternoon was spent mostly in the wagons, "resting." Jon and Maggie made love for the first time in daylight. They had no doubt that the Chasneys were doing the same, and maybe even Mose and Ella. Having Buelah and Chipper close by hadn't been a deterrent before. The experience was a little painful for Maggie, and Jon wondered just how much longer his wife was going to tolerate this activity. The two of them dozed off. Sometime later, Jon awoke. He looked around, spotting Maggie writing.

"Is it late?"

"Not too late. Why?"

"You're writing in your journal early?"

"No, Jonny. I'm writing a letter to Daddy and Mother."

"Oh, and you're sending it by pigeon?"

"No! I was feeling lonely, Okay? Hopefully, we won't be in these mountains forever, and I'll find a place to post it."

"I've got a better idea, my pretty plum. Let's do it."

"I thought that was what we just did."

"Once does not a lifetime make, my love."

"But once in a day or a week may!"

"Drat! Can I see what you have written?"

"When I finish."

Wednesday, November 11, 1835

My dearest Father, Mother, and Brothers:

We are parked in our wagon, in a steady rain, somewhere in the middle of the Blue Ridge Mountains, and I am so lonely. I cannot tell you how much I miss you all, and my beloved Bethania. I can hardly wait until the day when, once again, we will kiss and embrace.

We have had rain almost every day, and even snow twice. I cannot remember ever being so consistently cold. We have been climbing almost every day since leaving you. Only a few days more, and I swear we will reach heaven's pearly gates! If you received my previous letter, in which I told you about "Hamilton Hill," I can now tell you that we are on a hill that puts it to shame. The only thing good about it is that these forests have a lot of wild game, and a very scary giant, humanlike beast, which Jonny thinks he killed. Between Jonny and Nunky Mose, they have shot a bear, panther, raccoon, several deer, and what Jonny thought was an antelope. Good thing, as we have a lot of mouths to feed. We have three traveling companions, the Chasneys, on their way to Kentucky. Two brothers, who seem to share a wife! That makes nine people. We are all well, though Nanty Ella has been sick twice. Please tell all of her children that she is well now.

A day does not go by that I fail to think of all of you.

With fond memories and a heavy heart, I remain your loving daughter and sister,

Margaret Rose Hamilton

"Is it alright, Jonny?"

"No, I would like it changed."

"Why? What's wrong with it?"

"You make it sound like I mistreat you."

"What? Show me where it says that."

"Well, you sound so unhappy, darling."

"I'm not unhappy, Jonny, just lonely."

"How can anyone be lonely, married to me?"

"How can anyone stay sane, married to you?"

"That's a brilliant question, my pretty plum."

"When you find the answer, I'll change the letter."

"What a bargain."

After a fine supper of buck steak and beans, the gang retired early. They were well rested, and ready to climb again.

Diary of Margaret Hamilton

Wednesday, November 11

Had a day of rest in the same meadow where Jonny shot two deer. Nunky Mose bagged the bear and raccoon, and close to where Jonny shot Boony the Beast. I wrote to my family, but the Lord only knows when I'll post it.

MRH

Thursday, November 12

The gang was up early. The hill was still there, but the slope was less severe and everyone seemed eager to tackle it. Jon's path indicated a continuance in the same northwest direction, against the course of the raging stream, swollen by the constant rain. Jon wondered what river this stream eventually became, as he was sure he left the source of the Yadkin several days ago. The group worked hard in a steady drizzle. Jon decided to hitch all the drays to their original wagons, but have Corker pull the buckboard up first so he could be available to help the others if needed, and he was needed a couple of times to team up with Apple and Jack, pulling the Chasney wagon.

"Let's break for lunch, everyone. Block the wagons."

"Can we build a fire so we can dry out?" asked Liz.

"Certainly. And there are a few patches of grass around, so, Mose, will you and Chipper unhitch the horses to feed, while the rest of us build a fire?"

"Orites, Jon, we's do."

The group settled under the tarp for some bear dodgers.

"These dodgers are wonderful, ladies," said Charles.

"We's runs short dem flours, Jonny," said Buelah.

"Uh-oh . . . we are still several days from supplies."

"Only about five days now," quipped Maggie.

"We's has buckwheats flour, Jonny. We's be Orites."

"Thanks, Ella. I don't think it will be much more than five days, maybe six, before we summit," said Jon.

"Ha! We'll believe that when we see it," said Liz.

"These women have too much time on their hands for tongue-wagging, men. Let's get them back to work."

"I gets water for barrels, Jon," said Mose.

"Let the ladies do that, Mose, while we get the horses hitched back up. Maybe next time they won't be so cheeky."

"Now I want that vote, Jonny," said Liz.

"Righto! All those in favor of the ladies carrying water from that stream to put out this fire and fill barrels while we men hitch wagons and start clearing, raise their hand."

Jon, then Charles and Dave raised their hands, then Mose and Ella raised their hands. Liz stepped over to the Chasney brothers and angrily stared at them.

"That's five votes. Sorry, ladies," said Jon.

"Nanty Ella! Why are you voting with these men?"

"I's votes wit husban', Sissy," answered Ella.

"See, Liz, those men vote like sheep," snarled Maggie.

"Baa . . . Baa," said Dave, and Liz kicked him in the shin.

"Anyone have a couple extra blankets so these two don't get too cold and wet on the ground tonight?" asked Liz.

"That's our wagon. Nobody's sleeping on the ground," said Charles.

"Well then, you three men can sleep together, and Liz and I . . . and Buelah will sleep in *my* wagon," declared Maggie.

"Did you ever go teepee creepin', Jon?" asked Dave.

"No, and we're wasting time. Let's get crackin'."

The women all carried water, then climbed aboard the wagons and started back up the hill. There were places where the space between the stream and a drop over the side of the hill was narrow, but the team made great progress. When they made camp for the night, Jon was very pleased. The rain didn't even dampen his spirits.

"Great job, everyone."

"How far did we travel today, Jonny?" asked Maggie.

"I think we set a record today," added Liz.

"That we did, ladies. I'd guess close to a mile, in the rain!"

"Whooee! That calls for a celebration!" yelled Dave.

"We have nothing to celebrate with." Jon remembered the corn juice of Master Sam's that he had finished when he finally conquered Hamilton Hill.

"That don't stop us when we got my brother Charles around. He can make liquor out of looneys, I swear! He's a brewin' bugger!" answered Dave.

"How come you never told me that?" Liz asked Charles.

"Guess I never thought of it," answered Charles.

"How long does it take to make some joy juice, Charles?"

"That depends on the quality you want, Jon," answered Charles.

"Well, suppose we wanted to celebrate tomorrow, about this time?"

"Hmmm . . . about one day, huh? I might be able to make some spruce beer."

"What all would you need, Charles?" asked Maggie.

"Let's see . . . some spruce juice . . ."

"What's that?" asked Liz.

"We would have to cut a notch in a spruce tree and collect the sap," said Jon. "About how much?"

"Only about a large spoonful."

"Good. I think we can handle that. I thought I saw a small grove of spruce back down the trail."

"Yassa, it do be's red spruce, Jon," said Mose.

"Can you get some juice from them, Mose?"

"I's do, Jon. I's gets axe an' pan."

"I's goes to please?" asked Chipper.

"Orites, son. We's go now," said Mose.

"Better take your Kentucky rifle along, Mose, just in case. What else do we need, Charles?" asked Jon.

"Well, lots of molasses, or sugar."

"We has molasses. How's bouts ginga?" asked Ella.

"Yes, ginger," said Charles, "and maybe a couple tea leaves or spices to sweeten the brew."

"I's gets 'um," said Ella.

"And about a bucket of fresh water, heated, and I think that will do it," said Charles.

"Do you mind telling us what's so special about tomorrow?" asked Maggie.

"Yeah, I need to know what to wear," quipped Liz.

"Tomorrow we reach the top of this hill," answered Jon.

"Oh, sure . . . I should have guessed that!" mocked Maggie.

"Oh, please, no! Not the top of the hill!" teased Liz.

"And it only took five days," added Maggie.

"All but you two are going to celebrate!" snapped Jon.

David had taken a bucket to the stream, and placed it full next to the fire. Ella came back from the buckboard with a bucket of molasses, some ginger, and tea leaves. By the time the water heated, Mose and Chipper returned with some spruce juice. Anticipation was high, as Charles began mixing the brew. But something was missing.

"Don't you need some yeast, Charles?" asked Jon.

"Yeast! That's right! I'm sorry, but we need yeast."

Smiles turned to solemn faces and silence around the fire.

"How do you make yeast?" asked Jon.

"Well, it's a mixture of lemon juice and baking powder."

"And we don't have either of them," said Dave.

"Drat! After this hill, we need to celebrate," sighed Jon.

"What are you blunderheads worried about?" asked Maggie.

"Haven't you been listening? We need yeast," said Dave.

"Well, we have yeast!" Maggie announced.

"Where?" asked Jon.

"Don't you remember? Mister Duncan gave us some yeast when we were leaving Boone."

"Oh! That's right, Maggie darling. You are a jewel!"

"And you are a big lummox! It's wrapped in a bag under the bench. I better get it, since you would tear our wagon to pieces."

The gang watched as Charles broke down the molasses, and then added the spruce essence, tea leaves, and ginger. He let the mixture cool a little, then mixed in the yeast, in bits.

"Now, if we let this sit overnight, and maybe hang it from a wagon tomorrow so it doesn't get bounced around too much, it should be ready to down tomorrow evening."

"Yippee! See, I told you all my brother is a brewin' brain box," said Dave.

"You saved the day, Charles. Thanks," said Jon.

"You're welcome. It would be better if it were bottled and sat for a few days."

"Can't afford that luxury," said Jon, winking. "The six of us should have that gone by tomorrow night."

"Hold it, big boy. There are eight of us, not counting Chipper," corrected Maggie.

"But you two gum-grippers were going to kick the men out of your beds tonight," answered Dave.

"Oh, we were only fooling," said Maggie.

"Yes, we need you men to keep us warm," added Liz.

"Well then, maybe we should reconsider, men."

"Right, Jon. I think we can strike a deal," said Charles.

"They're a bunch of bunco artists, Liz," said Maggie.

"For sure, Maggie. But our turn is coming," answered Liz.

"We's has suppa 'bouts ready fo' now," said Ella.

Diary of Margaret Hamilton

Thursday, November 12

. . . Jonny was pleased at our progress today. He said we made over a mile, up a slight hill, and in a steady rain. Naturally, when the climbing stopped, so did the rain! My Jonny thinks we will top this hill tomorrow, so we brewed some "spruce beer" this evening for the occasion. The men think they will ban Elizabeth and me from the celebration, but we have news for them! Everyone in a good mood this evening. Love to all.

Maggie H.

"Today's the day we conquer this blamed hill, men."

"We'll believe that when we see it," said Maggie.

"Before breakfast, we must check the brew," said Jon.

"We already did that, captain," answered Dave.

"It's looking good enough to drink," added Charles.

"Righto! The most important job already accomplished, we can eat and be on our way. This is our lucky day."

"I'm going to miss this old hump," quipped Liz.

"I think we should stay camped here today," said Maggie.

"What? Now you are talking in circles," said Jon.

"Why you's say dat, Sissy?" asked Buelah.

"Do you know what day this is?"

"It's Friday, isn't it?" asked Charles.

"What day is it, my love?" asked Jon.

"It's Friday . . . the thirteenth."

"Oh, that is a bad omen. I agree. We should stay," said Liz.

"Nonsense. We mustn't keep our brew waiting," said Dave.

Jon and Maggie smiled at each other upon hearing that word.

"Do we's stays here, Jonny?" asked Ella.

"No. As soon as we eat, this hill we beat!"

"I guess there's no use calling for a vote," said Liz.

"No use," answered Maggie, "but if something bad happens, our resident poet is going to know it!"

"Ha! I guess that put him in his place," said Liz.

The day started out lucky, alright. It wasn't raining! With the beer pail swinging from under the Chasney wagon, it earned the honor of moving up to second in line behind the buckboard. More people could watch it that way. The ground seemed soft in some narrow places from all the rain. Twice Corker had to help pull the Chasney wagon, and the heavier covered wagon, through soft spots. The third time was not a charm! As the heavy wagon crossed a wet, treeless area already made softer by the other two wagons, the ground suddenly gave way, landsliding down the hill with the covered wagon's back wheels sliding with it. Corker was already pulling it in front of the regular pairs of teams five and fifteen, and he tried to hold fast while the other drays pawed at the dirt trying to find firm footing. Maggie, at the reins, started screaming. The wagon's back wheels were now free of ground, hanging over the edge.

"Block those front wheels!" yelled Jon.

"I've got 'em!" replied Dave.

"Stop screaming and come here, Mag."

Maggie stepped over to Jon, who lifted her off the wagon.

"Charles! Can you help Liz bring your team over?"

"Certainly, Jon." Charles ran to his wagon.

"We need rope. ELLA! Bring the rope!"

"I's do, Jonny," Ella loudly answered.

Mose and Jon tried to encourage the horses, while the Chasneys hooked rope from the slipping wagon to their team. With seven horses now pulling, the covered wagon stopped sliding backward down the open cavern of loose, slipping ground, but they still couldn't get the wagon moving forward.

"We're going to have to winch it up, Mose," said Jon.

"Orites, I gets block an' tackle, Jon."

"If we unhitch Corker, we may lose the wagon."

"I know, Charles. I'm not sure what to do," answered Jon.

The group then witnessed an unbelievable feat. As the Chasney brothers and Jon continued pressuring the seven drays to pull, pull, pull, Mose hooked the block and tackle to a large pine and one rope end to Corker. Mose then wrapped the open rope end to *his* waist, and started pulling downhill. At the same time, he called to Corker.

"Come, Corka. Here, Corka," Mose yelled, and the two giants started toward each other. The wagon shook, slowly slid, then rolled up onto solid ground.

Hurrahs, hoorays, and yippee were heard, as the relieved group hugged and shook hands all around.

"Great job, everyone. What all did we lose?"

"I'll check, Jonny," answered Maggie.

"See, I told you it was a bad omen to travel on Friday the thirteenth," said Liz.

"It could have been a lot worse," answered Charles.

"Yeah, we could have lost the beer," added Dave.

"Can you tell what's lost, Maggie darlin'?"

"My clothes," said Maggie, tears starting. "We lost some of my clothes!"

"Sorry . . . Anything else?"

"Anything else! What else is there?"

"Well, we had some extra grain for the animals, and that short barrel of gun powder."

"Oh . . . I guess they're gone too."

"Damn! We needed that powder."

"Powder? I needed my clothes!" Tears were running down Maggie's cheeks.

"It's Alright, honey. I've got some extra clothes," said Liz.

"I want my own clothes!"

"You've still got piles of clothes, darlin'."

"That's easy for you to say, you big lummox. You didn't lose anything!"

"I lost my rifle powder!"

"We have some powder in our wagon, Jon," said Charles.

"See? You have powder! I need my clothes!"

"Alright! Ella, bring me a basket, please. Mose, will you hitch that rope to the wagon? I'm going down."

"Dat be's dangerous, Jon," cautioned Mose.

"I'll be careful. I've got to see if I can salvage anything for my wife."

"Orites, Jon. I's hooks ta Corka."

"Thanks, Mose. Charles, will you check ahead and see if there's a spot to noon?"

"Sure thing, Jon. Be careful," said Charles.

Charles and Dave left to scout ahead. Liz hugged Maggie, as Jon tied the rope around his waist. The other end had Corker and Mose at the drag. Maggie started to have misgivings, as Jon hopped over the edge, causing another minilandslide. Liz held Maggie closer.

"Come back up, Jonny! I'm sorry. I can do without those clothes!" yelled Maggie.

"Too late. I'm down here now!" hollered Jon. "Must be a lot buried under all this mud. Here's something . . ."

"What is it, Jonny?" asked Maggie.

"Looks like a shirt, or a blouse, I guess."

"I can wash it!" yelled Maggie.

"And here's a boot. It's got a fur top!"

"Oh dear, that would be my Adelaide boot."

"It's scraped up, and full of mud. Do you want it?"

"Can you find the other boot?" hollered Maggie.

"No, I don't see it. It's no good with just one. Oh, and here's that thing you wore after our weddin'. What did you call it? A chemise?"

"My chemise. Can it be salvaged?"

"No. I'd rather see you in Eve's togs!" yelled Jon.

"Even with my big belly?" smiled Maggie.

"Even with my son in your belly," answered Jon.

"We would like to see you in Adam's togs!" shouted Liz.

"Do you see anything else, Jonny?"

"Not much. I'll send up what I have. Oh look, I think I see my powder barrel, if I can get to it."

"Be careful, Jonny. I want you safely back up here."

"Now's a fine time to say that! Don't worry, my pretty plum. I intend to make it back up, mud and all."

"Can you reach it, Jonny?"

"Yeah, I think I have it, and it doesn't look too bad."

"That's enough, Jonny. Come back up."

"I've just got to tie these things to the rope. There, tell Mose to pull me up, darlin'."

Mose heard that, and started backing Corker. Up came what must have been Jonathan, caked in mud, behind the basket and barrel.

"Eek! That must be the beast, Boony!" teased Liz.

"Come kiss me quick, ladies."

"Not in your wildest dreams," answered Liz.

"Let's get you to the stream, and get those clothes off you. I'll wash these things too," said Maggie.

"Did I hear you correctly? You want me to peel off my togs in front of the whole world?"

"Well, I remember you once saying that we were all family, and we should not be embarrassed."

"Righto! Let's get to that stream. But first I want to hug you two."

"No! Get away from us!" Liz jumped away from Jon.

"You'll get your hugs when you get clean and dried."

With these final words from Maggie, they went to the stream, where Jon lay out in the water. After he shed the outer layer of mud, he shed his shirt, pants, and brogans, and handed them to Maggie. His unmentionables even had mud on them, but Jon washed it off with the cold water. Liz was taking it all in, and Maggie didn't seem to mind. *Surprise!*

"If that's all you're taking off, I'll get a blanket," said Liz.

"I thought we were all going to wash."

"I'm willing, but I didn't get muddy," smiled Liz.

"I'm not! Get up out of there, Jonny."

"Righto, my love. I'd like that blanket, Liz."

"I'll be right back," said Liz.

"Good," said Jon. "Ella, will you bring me a cloth?"

"Orites, I's do!" shouted Ella in return.

Quick to respond for her elder age, Ella brought a rag in short order. Jon started cleaning the barrel of gun powder, as Liz arrived with a blanket. He didn't stop cleaning.

"You better put this around you, before you get sick."

"Thanks, Liz. I'll be just a minute here."

"It's winter, Jonny, in case you forgot. Better put the blanket over your shoulders," ordered Maggie.

"Do dem powda stay dry, Jon?" It was Mose, who had hitched the horses back up to the wagons.

"There's a hole in the barrel, but I think we can save most of it. How are the horses?"

"Dem's orites, need rest."

"Well, if the Chasneys don't find a place to lunch, we could rest them here and have lunch. We're not far from the end of this hill, where I turned southwest."

"About how far, Jonny?"

"Well, we came close to a quarter mile, before we almost lost the wagon, so I'd guess less than half a mile to go."

"Then what? You said something about a shelf?"

"Yes. We turn southwest to a spot where we will have to winch the wagons up to a shelf. That will take us over the top and into Tennessee."

"Hmm, sounds like extra work to me," said Liz.

"And extra time," added Maggie.

"Well, you'll see why when we get there. Meanwhile, I need to get some clothes on."

"I'll get you a dry shirt and jeans, but you will have to wear those wet brogans," said Maggie.

"Thanks, darlin'."

Just then, the Chasney brothers popped out of the trees.

"What did you find?" asked Jon.

"Nothing real close, but the clearing where you turned left is just a short way up," said Charles.

"It's a little steep just before it, but it shouldn't take long to make that clearing," added Dave.

"Can the horses make it there, Mose?"

"I's thinks dey makes it orites," answered Mose.

"*See?* I told you lasses! Alright. Let's get crackin'." Jon thought Liz might call for a vote, so he asked, "How many think we should get to the top before breaking for lunch?"

All raised their hands, except Maggie and Liz.

"Okay, it's nonstop to the top."

It was midafternoon when Corker pulled the covered wagon over the crest and onto flat ground. Jon's trail now turned southwest on a wide, open path. Jon, with his brogans now dry, was the last to step up onto the clearing amidst much cheering and hugging.

"Let's break out the spruce!" shouted Dave.

"Not yet, Dave. We lunch here, get rested, and we can celebrate when we reach the wall."

"We're driving wagons to a wall?" asked Liz.

"It's the best way to get over this last hurdle."

"Why can't we just continue straight?" asked Maggie.

"Take a look, my pretty plum. It's just a rocky crevice through there. We would never make it."

"How far is it to that wall?" asked Charles.

"About four or five miles of open road, just like you see there. We could make it by nightfall."

"Then it would be too late to celebrate. I say we camp right here and party," said Dave.

"I think we should try to go straight through this crevice and over the top," said Maggie.

"What do you say, Mose? Do you think the horses and wagons could make it through there?"

"Nossa, Jon. Dat kills dem horses."

"Well, we have a couple things to vote on," said Jon.

"You's gets dem votes ova, Jon, while I's makes lunch."

"Okay, Ella. Those who want to try making it up through this crevice, raise your hand."

Only Maggie, then Liz, raised their hands.

"Those who want to camp here and go southwest to the wall tomorrow morning, raise your hands."

"Is there any place less than five miles down this road that we can cross over?" asked Maggie, interrupting the vote.

"Nope! It's a trail straight through tall mountains on both sides."

"How do you know that, you big lummox? We can't see the mountains, for the trees," snapped Maggie.

"I'll show you how I know when we get a ways down the trail," answered Jon. "Now again, all those who want to camp here for the night, raise your hands."

This time, Liz and Maggie joined Dave in the hand raising.

"Looks like we're never going to win a vote, Mag," said Liz.

"Depends on what we're voting on," quipped Dave.

"Well, let's get a lunch under our belts, so we can race down that path."

"I's take care dem horses, Jon," said Mose.

"Thanks, Mose. There's no time to graze them. Do we have enough grain for them?"

"Yassa, we's do, Jon."

"Good, and we need to fill our buckets with water from what's left of this stream."

"I's do!" said an excited Chipper.

"Why don't you help your dad, Chipper, and the rest of us can get the water."

"My brother and I will get the water, Jon. You go finish getting dried out by the fire," said Charles.

"Thanks. But we don't have much time to rest."

"What's for lunch, Aunty?" asked Dave.

"We's has buckwheats flapjacks," answered Buelah.

"Good! No beer. Jacks will have to do."

"We'll put that beer to good use tonight, brother," said Charles.

"It'll be dark before we make three miles," said Dave.

"Then I promise we will party in the dark," said Jon.

"There's another reason I'm glad you all voted to take the trail southwest before trying to summit," said Jon, as the gang downed flapjacks.

"I know, you love these blamed mountains," teased Maggie.

"He wants to be sure he got Boony," added Liz.

"What is your reason, Jon?" asked Charles, after the giggles.

"Well, for the last few days all the way up the hill, we have come northwest, even a little more north, and I'd guess we are a lot north of the Watauga River, where we need to be. By going southwest a ways now, we should find the river, and the settlers there, pretty easily."

"The last *few* days, he says," quipped Liz.

"Only five! It just seems longer," said Maggie.

"That is a nice-looking trail there. It seems strange, way up here on the mountain," observed Charles.

"I would say it's a Cherokee trading or war trail."

"If it leads to a dead end, it *will* be a war trail."

"Atta girl, Mag. I want the spoils," said Liz.

"Well, let's get on the road, gang. The party is waiting at the foot of the wall."

With only a slight incline and no obstacles, the group raced southwest. After about three hours of travel, Jon called a stop for a break. The horses were winded.

"Why are we stopping? It will be dark soon," said Dave.

"We need to rest and water these animals," answered Jon.

"I's do, Jon," said Mose.

"We'll help you," said Charles.

"See that really tall tree back there, Maggie?"

"Yes. What about it?"

"I climbed it. I could see for miles to the south, and the wall with the ledge above it," said Jon.

"So now he's part monkey," quipped Liz.

"More like a baboon, but I love him," laughed Maggie.

"That's how I saw that we are in the midst of some tall mountains, and the ledge is the only way through."

"Well, it's getting dark. Let's get going," snapped Dave.

"Horses needs rest, Jon," said Mose.

"I know, Mose. I'd like to make the wall tonight before we camp. It will be dark soon. Do we have any of that grease left?"

"Yassa, we do's, Jon."

"Well, while we're resting the horses, let's make some torches." Jon remembered his escape from the Pattyrollers and Ginny. "We may still have an hour of daylight, then we'll finish by torchlight."

"Orites, Jon. Dem horses be plum tuckered."

"I know, Mose. They'll get plenty of rest and good grass at the wall."

With half a dozen torches ready, the group continued southwest for over an hour before stopping to light the torches. From then on, it was slow going, with Mose and Corker leading the way. Ella and Chipper were at the reins of the buckboard behind Mose, then Dave and Charles were guiding the Chasney wagon with Liz at the helm. Finally, Maggie was at the rear, driving the covered wagon, with Buelah walking at one side and Jon walking on the other. After a while, Jon and Mose traded places so Jon could spot the wall.

It had been dark for nearly two hours before Jon's gang reached what may have been the clearing. He wasn't sure until he walked around the area and spotted the wall.

"This is it, gang. We are at the wall. Tomorrow you will see the job we face, lifting horses, wagons, and all of us up onto a shelf above us."

"Good. Let's break out the spruce juice!" said Dave.

"Not quite yet, Dave. Mose and I will get these wagons parked in a circle and tend to the horses. Dave, will you and Charles gather wood for a fire?"

"Right away," said Charles.

"We need to dry our clothes, Jonny. Can we stretch ropes between the wagons again, like we did at the foot of that dreadful hill?" asked Maggie, parking the wagon.

"Sure thing, my love."

"Was that five days ago, already?" asked a sarcastic Liz.

"He only misguessed by two weeks! That's good for a man," answered Maggie. "Mister Duncan, in Boone, said it would take about three days!"

"It take nine day, is awl," said Ella.

The camp was all set up, and most of the gang had a bite to eat before the party. Dave and Liz skipped eating, and brought out some mugs and started drinking spruce beer. Soon everyone had a mug of beer, and the party was on. About four gallons of beer made a half gallon for each, but Mose and Ella only drank two cups. Dave and Liz drank the rest of their shares and got loaded. Maggie sipped some beer; while Jon, Buelah, and Charles drank enough to get very happy! Singing around the fire soon turned to dancing, with plenty of hugs and kisses. To everyone's surprise, Mose came up with a harmonica, and Ella provided a beat for the dancing. The party raged on and on.

"Having a good time, Maggie darlin'?"

"Sure am," she answered, "but stop shpinning me 'round. I'm gettin' dizzy!"

"Then sit for a spell."

"No! I wanna dance with Charles. He's a good dancer."

"Okay, honey, go to it."

Maggie strode a little unevenly over to Charles, and they began to dance. Charles was a good dancer, Jon could see, so he sat down with his beer. Not for long, however.

"Come on, Jonny, you gotta dance with me."

"Righto, Lizzy. But I'm not very good."

"Who cares? Grab onto me and swing, big boy."

Jon and Liz turned round and round several times, then Mose started blowing a much slower tune. Soon Jon was getting that almost forgotten rubbing up against him. He tried to pull back some, but Liz kept up the pressure. It was having an effect on Jon.

"Are you getting horny, Jonny?"

"Why, no, why do you ask that?"

"Just guessin', Jonny. It must be getting difficult for Maggie to take care of you proper."

"She does just fine, Liz."

"Hmm, I'll bet! Well, big boy," Liz whispered, "if you ever need it, you know where to look."

"I'm sure your husband would like that."

"What husband?" She tongued his ear.

This revelation and the rubbing were too much for Jon. "Can we sit a spell, Liz?"

"Sure thing, Jonny. Too much for you, huh?"

"Yes. I'm sorry. This is embarrassing."

"It's alright, Jonny. We can sneak behind that wagon, and I'll take care of you."

"Thanks, but no thanks."

"Alright. I'll take care of you here. Nobody's looking." Jon felt her hand in his crotch, fumbling with the buttons of his jeans. He grabbed her hand and looked around the area. Maggie and Charles were still dancing, in a tight embrace. Mose and Ella were still making music by the fire, but Mose was straining his eyes, peering into the darkness. Jon looked in the same direction toward the Chasney wagon.

"Come with me, Liz," he said, taking her hand.

"With pleasure, honey," Liz answered, thinking she was about to score behind the wagon.

What Jon, then Liz, saw behind the Chasney wagon was a shocker. Buelah was laid out on the ground, her cotton-drill dress above her waist, and naked. Dave, in all his drunkenness, had his jeans down around his knees, and was trying to crawl on top of the waiting Buelah. Jon grabbed him by the back of the neck and yanked him off Buelah, onto his back.

"Hey, what do you think you're doin'?" yelled Dave.

"Quiet, you blunderhead! Act like you're passed out!"

"Go ta blazes, you bast—" Jon hit him hard on the jaw, and Dave slammed back on the ground, out cold.

"Help me get his jeans back on, Liz, quick! Pull your dress back down, Buelah!" This was done just in time.

"What's going on back there?" asked Maggie, approaching.

"Dave is passed out, and Buelah was trying to help him," answered Jon.

"I's helps 'em," said Mose, first on the scene. He picked Dave up like he was made of balsa, and placed him in his wagon.

"It's late. Think I'll join him," said Charles.

"It is late. I think it's time for all of us to turn in."

"Good idea. I'm really tired," said Maggie. "Will you help me to our wagon, Jonny?"

"Sure thing, my darlin'."

"I's picks up, Jon."

"Thanks, Mose." Jon had Maggie propped in his arms.

"Chicken!" said Liz, as Jon, with Maggie, passed by her.

Saturday, November 14

The sun shone through the canvas of the covered wagon, blinding Jon, as he tried to rouse from his deep sleep. He looked around, spotting Maggie sitting on the bench, journal in hand. He had some pain at his temples.

"What time is it?" he asked.

"I don't know, probably midmorning."

"Damn! I wanted to get an early start on that wall."

"Nunky Mose is doing it for you."

"What's he doing?"

"He's gone, trying to make it up to that landing."

"Double damn! How long ago did he leave?"

"Nanty Ella said he left at dawn. He took Corker and Sloggy. I hope we'll spot him up on the ledge."

"What's he going to do up there?"

"I don't know, Jonny. Nanty Ella says he packed a lot of stuff on the horses."

"I hope he took the block and tackle with him."

"Well, you know Nunky Mose. He doesn't forget."

"True enough . . . Doing your journal?"

"Just finished."

"Can I read it?" Jon asked.

"I guess, but this time, no criticism!"

"I hardly ever criticize."

"Only when you're alone, or with someone!"

Diary of Margaret Hamilton

Friday the Thirteenth
November 13, 1835

A long, but exciting day! After a very scary episode, in which we almost lost horses and wagon, we reached the top of the long, dreadful hill that I have written about for many days. I am writing this on Saturday morning, because of the party we had last night, which lasted until early this lovely morning, the start of our fourth week of travel. With only a couple miles to go to reach the summit of this nine-day climb, the rain-soaked hill collapsed, with the loss, thanks to Nunky Mose, of only several items of my clothing. Upon turning southwest and traveling well into the night, we reached the wall we now face. We must lift ourselves, and all we bring, to a ledge, some one hundred fifty feet above us. Jonny says it is now the only escape through these Blue Ridge Mountains into Tennessee. At least we had no rain, and Friday the Thirteenth gave us a new closeness. I believe Jonny now realizes we should have traveled north into Virginia, as you suggested, Father, to cross these "Blues," although he would never admit it.

Much love, Maggie H.

P.S. I didn't know Nunky Mose played the harmonica.

Love, Mag

"I would too admit it . . . if I was wrong."

"You heard me, no criticism," said Maggie.

"I'm only statin' a fact."

"Sure you are!" Maggie paused. "Are you hungry, Jonny?"

"I could eat the kazoo of a cottontail!"

"Nanty Ella made breakfast, but not many ate."

"Where is everybody?"

"Well, she is working around here, with her two offspring, and Nunky Mose is gone, and the Chasneys are still asleep in their wagon."

"So much for all my plans!"

"Nunky Mose thinks the horses need rest anyway."

"I suppose that's true."

"It would have been difficult to get any work from David or Liz today."

"I suppose that's true too."

After a pause, Maggie said, "I don't know what to think of these Chasneys."

"What do you mean, darlin'?"

"Don't act stupid, Jonny. I saw how Liz was trying to play roger with you, and Charles was trying to do the same thing with me. He wanted to take me into this wagon! I think they are all sex-crazed!"

"What a life that must be!"

"Don't be cute! She did make a play for you, didn't she?"

"Well, yes. But I refused it."

"Sure you did! And I was beginning to like her."

"They are likeable," agreed Jon, "and they're not even married, none of them."

"What? Did she tell you that?"

"She did indeed. And I'll tell you something else."

"What now? She's a he, and he's a . . ."

"No, nothing like that, but you know when I went behind their wagon, just before we hit the sack?"

"Yes, I saw you taking Liz back there."

"Well, Davy and Buelah were back there naked, and they were about to play bouncebutt."

"Oh my god! Jonny, are you sure?"

"Yes, I'm sure, my love. Liz and I got them dressed just in time. Mose would have killed him."

"But he was passed out, Jonny, I saw him."

"I put him out, my pretty plum."

"Oh my god! Poor Buelah. She's still a virgin, I'm sure, and she wants *so* to be with child, like me. She just doesn't realize the problems that entails."

"Hey! What problems? You're not sorry you got knocked up and married, are you?"

"No, Jonny, I'm not a bit sorry."

"Good. Neither am I. It's your own fault you got knocked up, you know."

"My own fault?"

"Sure. You shouldn't have taken me seriously, when I was only poking fun at you!"

"Very funny! Anyway, I'm glad you're my husband, and I'm having your child."

"He's going to be tall with a dark complexion, just like me. If he's a red-head, like you, that's Okay too."

"What if he's a she?"

"Well, that would be alright too."

"Good. Just so it's healthy, and a pretty baby."

"No problem there, just look at his parents!"

Jon felt all the sore spots as he attempted to dress. The once-muddy clothes of his and Maggie's were neatly folded, and Ella had food ready for him. The forgotten sun felt good, but bothered his vision. He squinted as he looked up.

"Any signs of him, Ella?"

"Nossa. I's be lookin', Jonny."

"We should be seeing him up there. Looks like it's around eleven, so he's been about four hours."

"How can you tell it's eleven?" asked Maggie, her head sticking out of the wagon.

"It's where the sun is in the sky."

"You're conning us again, Jonny. You can't see the sun because of the trees, and we've all forgotten what the sun looks like! And besides, you're always telling us the time, even in the rain, you big bunco."

"And I'm always right, right?"

"No, you're not! I'll bet it's closer to twelve."

With that, Jon started digging into items in the covered wagon. He finally found the little sundial, the present from his brother Andrew. Using his compass to position the dial, he showed Maggie the time of approximately 10:50 a.m.

"See? What did I tell you?"

"You said it was noon," said Maggie, winking at Ella.

"I did not. I said it was eleven."

"You big lummox, why did you ask me the question when you already knew the answer?"

"Drat!" Jon was bewildered. He was suckered in again. "You lost the bet."

"What did I bet, Jonny?"

Suckered again? "I'll think of something," he answered in frustration. Just then the sound of chopping with an axe was clearly heard from above them.

"Mose! Mose!" Jon shouted, through the chopping noise.

"Glory be! Daddy makes it!" said Ella.

"He sure did, and he's already clearing a landing."

"How is he going to get back down, Jonny?"

"He's not. We're all going up there."

"Don't be a dullard! You're not going to make Nunky Mose sit up there alone for two days."

"Two days? In two days, we'll be in Tennessee."

"Want to bet on that too?" asked Maggie.

"Bet your butt I do! But this time, we need something to bet on, my love."

"What do you suggest, big boy?"

"Hmm . . . How about the winner gets to name anything he wants from the loser?"

"Alright! You've got a bet, Jonny. Shake hands on it?"

Maggie was so quick to extend her hand, that Jon was sure she was about to pull another fast one. Jon was positive Tennessee was just around the side of the hill on that ledge, so he wondered why Maggie was in such a hurry to shake hands. He mustn't let her win the bet.

"Come on, chicken!" said Maggie. "I'm betting that two days from now, we still won't be in Tennessee."

"I'm a witness," said Liz, who had been awakened by the shouting and had emerged from her wagon. "He is a chicken, alright."

"Okay . . . but it has to be anything within reason."

"See? He is a chicken," announced Liz.

"It's a bet, Jonny." And the Hamiltons shook hands.

"Congratulations, Maggie! You got him," chuckled Liz.

"Thanks." Maggie had a big grin.

"What do you mean, you got me?"

"Tomorrow is Sunday, you big lummox!"

"Ha! What did you win, Maggie?" asked Liz.

"Oh, I'll think of something!"

"What if I call for working starting right now, and going all day tomorrow and Monday?"

"That's a vote you would lose," said Liz.

"And if you happen to win the vote, it's going to take you days to get us all up to that ledge, Jonny."

"Failed again! I'm not betting with you anymore."

"Don't be too hasty, Jonny. She may demand something really interesting," said Liz. "I would!"

"We know what you would demand," retorted Maggie.

Jon was relieved when the ladies started laughing over that remark. His attention returned to the work above the camp, and he hoped Maggie would forget about the bet.

"Can you hear me, Mose?" Jon shouted.

"Yassa, Jon, I hears ya," answered Mose, as he appeared at the edge of the ledge above them.

"How does it look for a road?"

"It be's good road. I's clear path."

"Good. Did you take the tackle?"

"Sho 'nuff, Jon," answered Mose. "I's got big pines fo' liftin' wagons."

"How can I get up there to help, Mose?"

"I's do, Jon. You's rest."

"Do you have a lunch? Send down a rope."

"Yassa, I's has food, horses has food, you's has food. You's rest an' eats, Jon."

"Okay, Mose. After you have lunch, lower a rope so I can come up and help."

"Yassa, I's do, Jon."

"We're ready to help too," said Charles, as the two Chasneys, finally up and hungry, appeared at the fire.

Ella had food ready for the suddenly hungry gang.

"It's about time," snapped Elizabeth to Dave.

"What time is it?" asked Dave, sheepishly.

"It's close to noon," answered Maggie.

"Don't give these two any more beer, Jonny. They can't take it," said Liz.

"What happened to the beer?" asked Charles.

"It be's gone," said Ella.

"Thank God for that," remarked Maggie, as she angrily stared at Dave.

"Yeah, you owe everybody an apology, you prick," said Liz to Dave, "and especially to Buelah."

"Where is Buel?" asked Maggie, shocked at the language.

"She be's sick, stays in buckboard," answered Ella.

"I'll go see her and take some food to her."

"Thank you's, Sissy," said Ella. "She be's cryin'."

"I'm sorry, everyone, for the way I acted last night," said Dave. "Especially to you, Jon. And Buelah."

"I think we all had plenty of juice to last us for a good, long spell," said Jon. "But thank you, Charles, for making the brew. It had a great taste, and a greater kick!"

Attention now turned back to Mose, chopping away above them. As they listened and watched, Mose fell a very tall pine. Jon could see the top as it fell.

"I'm ready, Mose!" he shouted.

"Orites, Jon. I's sends rope. You's brings axst."

"What can we do?" asked Charles.

"Well, maybe you could clear and level this area at the base, so we can start lifting this afternoon."

"Will do. What are we lifting first?"

"How about the buckboard, so Mose and Ella can sleep together up there?"

"They might start another landslide!" quipped Liz.

That broke the ice, as everyone present, even Ella, started laughing. Nobody noticed the rope dangling at the base of the wall. Maggie, still consoling Buelah, spotted it from the buckboard.

"You be careful climbing up that hill, Jonny."

"I will, my pretty plum."

"You's comin', Jon?" Mose yelled down at him.

"Righto, Mose." Jon made a loop at the end of the dangling rope, and stepped into it. "Haul me up!"

Mose had rigged a pulley to a tree, very close to the stump of the pine Jon had seen fall from below. Corker easily hoisted the "captain" up to the ledge. Mose already had a large area cleared, and was cutting branches off the tall pine he had just fallen. Jon noticed a tree in the center of the landing that Mose had cut about six feet off the ground, above the split in its trunk, forming a cradle to nestle the pine he was trimming. *What a genius he is*, Jon thought. The long pine would be the arm that would jut out over the ledge. At the base of the "arm," Mose had cut a groove around the pine and had fitted a length of rope in the groove. This baffled Jon.

"What is that rope for at the base of this arm?"

"We's ties dem ropes 'round dem stumps, so's dem arm don't move," answered Mose. "We's needs ta makes holes unda dem stump."

"Okay, Mose, I'll do that."

Jon found the shovel Mose had brought, and dug a hole in the hillside under the newly cut stump. Mose hitched Corker to the arm's trunk, and Corker pulled the butt of the arm into the hole. He wedged a large rock into the hole so the arm could not move in the hole. Mose then tied that length of rope around the stump.

"Now, how are we going to get this heavy tree into that cradle, Mose?"

"We's trys liftin'."

"We might strain our keisters."

"Well, we's use dem pulley an' tree," said Mose, pointing to the tree used to hoist Jon up to the landing.

"Alright, Mose, you know what you're doing."

"Yassa. We's gets tackle tied ta tree, Jon."

"It's still a good six inches thick where it hangs over the edge."

"Tha' be's 'nuff, Jon."

"Right, let's give it a try."

The trunk of the tall pine was still eight or nine inches thick where it was to fit into the "cradle" of the "post" tree. Jon could hardly budge it. Mose wrapped his long, powerful arms around it and lifted it waist high. The "arm" still expanded twenty-plus feet beyond him out over the ledge, and was awkward and very heavy.

"Forget this, Mose. Let's use the pulley."

"Orites, Jon. You's climbs tree an' raise dem pulley."

"Sure thing. More leverage that way."

One end of the pulley rope was still attached to Corker. Mose wrapped the loop end around the trunk of the tackle arm again, several feet beyond the cradle area. He also used another length of rope to attach the trunk to Sloggy. When Jon finished roping the pulley about thirty feet up his tree, Corker lifted the arm into the air, and then Sloggy pulled it over the cradle. All Corker had to do was back up a little, and the pine arm was cradled with the tackle swinging out over the ledge. A roar of approval was heard from below.

"Good job, Mose!" Jon had handled Sloggy.

"We's do's good work, Jon. I's hooks Corker ta dem tackle, an' we's lifts wagons."

"Hello. Are you ready down there?" shouted Jon.

"Yes!" came the reply from Charles. "Ella wants to come up in the buckboard."

"Not a good idea until we see how it works."

"We're ready," answered Charles, "send down the hook!"

"Here it comes. Tie on a six- or eight-foot length of rope to this wall side of the buckboard, so we can yank the wagon in, up here."

"Okay, Jon. We've looped all four corners of the buckboard with four lengths of rope. We'll put the loop ends in the hook of your tackle. Is that alright?"

"Sounds good," Jon shouted back. "Stand clear just in case, but keep an eye on it."

"We're ready. Raise her up!" yelled Dave.

Mose walked Corker forward, and the rope tightened at the tackle. Both he and Jon could see that Corker would have to pull a long way into the trees, so they stopped the process and again used the pulley to take up rope. Ready again, Corker easily lifted the buckboard below. Up it came, slowly but steadily. It was now forty feet up.

"Hold it! Jon! Let it down, quick!"

"Back it up, Mose!" Jon yelled. "What's wrong?"

"A corner's coming loose!" answered Charles from below. "Bring it down, fast!"

Mose walked Corker back fast, but it was too late. Jon heard the screams as the rope went slack, and the crashing sound could be heard clear back to Boone. He peered over the edge at the wreckage. Destruction.

"What do we do now?" he heard either Maggie or Elizabeth ask. Ella and Maggie were hugging and weeping.

"Can anything be saved?" Jon heard himself call out.

"The wagon's all torn apart," answered Charles. "The bed can be saved, and maybe a couple wheels."

"Ella's kitchen and Buelah's bed are gone!" yelled Liz.

"Alright. Start picking up. We'll be right down."

"The buckboard's gone," Jon said to Mose. "I'm going back down to help."

"Orites, Jon. I's stake dem horses, an' be's down."

"Will they be Okay?"

"Yassa. They's be fine."

"Alright. I'll see you down there."

Jon wrapped the hook end of the rope around his leg, and started shimmying down. As soon as he was safely down, Mose unhitched the other end from Corker and staked the two horses to a grassy area. With both ends of the tackle rope now extended down to camp, Mose scampered down. The cleanup was well in progress.

"What all did we lose besides the buckboard?"

"The last of the flour and buckwheat, all the barrels, some meat, coffee, water, a couple buckets, and I'm not sure what all else, Jonny," answered Maggie.

"At least nobody got hurt or killed," said Liz.

"There's a town called Sycamore Shoals on the Watauga River, where we can replace our raggery, hopefully."

"How far is that?" asked Liz.

"If I've guessed correctly, it should be just ahead of us, in Tennessee."

"Only five days ahead," snapped Maggie.

"Whas we's eats till then?" asked Buelah.

"We still have meat," said Jon.

"And we have some flour left," added Liz.

"We makes it, somehow," said Mose.

"And Dave and I can sleep up above and do a little hunting," added Charles.

"That's the spirit! We still have a few hours left of light. Let's get as much lifted as we can."

"How?" asked Maggie. "One piece at a time?"

"We'll use the bed of the buckboard and pull it up and down with our supplies and animals."

"We's ties dem betta."

"Yes, you tie the corners, Mose."

"Orites, Jon. I's do."

"Good. Can we use any more of the buckboard?"

"Yassa, Jon. I's makes trailer from dem buckboard," answered Mose.

"Righto. Let's get a bite to eat and haul until dark."

Singed meat on a stick was the supner special, after which the men loaded an axle, two wheels in fair shape, and supplies on the bed of the broken buckboard.

"I's goes up an' sorts dem pots an' foods," said Ella.

"Sure you want to try it, Ella?"

"I's gots to, Jon, an' works up there."

"Okay. Mose, take blankets. It's going to be cold tonight. Maybe you can ride the bed for a few lifts."

"I's do, Jon."

"Can I's go's too?" asked the silent Chipper.

"Maybe you should stay . . ."

"Please, Massa Jon?"

"Is it alright, Ella?" asked Jon.

"It's be's fines, Jonny."

"Alright, Chip. Do you want to go too, Buelah?"

"I's skeered, Jonny," she answered.

The first load, with Mose, Ella, and Chipper left, raised up by Jake and Red, pulling the tackle from below. Soon Mose came back down on the platform, which had been the bed of the buckboard. It went smoothly.

"Let's try lifting Pasha this time. You are really good with him, Mose."

"Orites, Jon, we's do," said Mose.

"I'm going with my Pasha, Jonny."

"I think you should stay here, Maggie. Mose can handle him well."

"No! I'm going too! I can help Nanty Ella up there."

"Yes, darlin', get aboard. Hang on tight, my love."

"We's blind Pasha, Sissy," said Mose.

"Should I ride him, Nunky Mose?"

"No, Sissy. We's puts hobbles under Pasha, so he don' move."

"Let's get crackin'. Hang on, my pretty plum."

As soon as the platform moved, so did Pasha. Mose and Maggie both kept a constant chatter at him. Maggie was holding on to a corner hook rope and Pasha's halter. It was a battle keeping him calm, but they made it. Next it was Smutty, a calm, easy lift.

"What should we try next, Mose?"

"We's tries wagon, Jon, froms above."

Apple and Jack pulled the Chasney wagon onto the platform. It was then tied down solid at the wheels and corners.

"Do you want to go up with your wagon, Liz?"

"No thanks. This time, I'm the chicken."

"How about you, Buelah? Most of your blankets and clothes are already up there, and it's getting late."

"Orites, Jonny, but I's still skeered."

"Just climb in the wagon and cover up."

"It be's heavy loads fo' teams five, Jon. I's helps hitch Chasney horses."

"Good, Mose. It's getting dark pretty fast. This may be our last lift."

"Yassa. We's finish in mornings."

"Anybody else want to take this last ride?"

"No thanks, Jon," said Charles. "I think the hunting's better down here."

"And you'll need help with the horses," added Dave.

Jon sensed that the Chasney brothers didn't trust him with Liz—or Liz, period! He was glad they were staying. He didn't trust himself! He wished Maggie had stayed.

"The hunting is much better down here," he said.

"I'll get some wood on the fire. It's getting cold."

"Good idea, Chucky. I'll take care of the horses," said Dave.

The four drays leaned into the pull, and the Chasney wagon slowly rose up the wall. Jon held his breath until it reached the ledge and was pulled onto the landing. Jon was fully aware that he was momentarily alone with Liz.

"Only one wagon, and some horses to go tomorrow," said Liz.

"Yes, we can get that done early."

"Looks like you might win your bet yet, Jonny."

"Not much chance. It is Sunday, and Maggie would be snarly. Besides, there's a lot of work to be done up there before we can continue on."

"Don't you want to win, Jonny?"

"Of course I do, but I'm not lucky betting with Maggie."

"You could be the luckiest man alive if you really wanted to, Jonny," teased Liz, smiling.

"I already am," Jon replied.

"Ooh, that was cold," she coyly said.

"Cold? I'll get you a blanket."

"Thanks," Liz said, as the Chasneys returned.

Jon headed for his wagon as the brothers tended the fire.

"Oh, that fire feels good," said Dave.

"That it does. I can see stars, so it's going to get really cold tonight," added Charles.

"I wish we had some hot tea," said Liz.

"The sassafras was in Mose's buckboard that got smashed all to tarnation," said Charles.

"Maybe there's some still lying around," said Dave. "Hand me that lantern and I'll go look."

"Would you go look too, Chuck? I really need something hot to drink."

"Sure, Liz, anything you ask."

"Thanks, I appreciate that."

"Looks like you have them trained well," said Jon, as he draped a blanket over Liz's shoulders.

"Are you jealous, big boy?"

"Now why would I be jealous of your husbands?"

"Maybe because I'm jealous of your wife."

"She has me trained pretty well too," quipped Jon.

"Well, tonight you can put some of that training into action. I can handle three men," smiled Liz.

"I'm afraid it will have to be just two."

"We could make it just one, you." Liz was enjoying this game of words.

"And leave your husbands in the cold?"

"They're not my husbands, you know."

"They're more like your slaves."

"True. They're my body servants, keep me warm."

"We'll keep you warm tonight," said Dave, hearing that last part of Liz's statement.

"Thanks, Davy. I'm going to need it." Liz stared at Jon.

"We found some tea bark, Liz," said Charles.

"Wonderful! I need something to warm my insides."

"You'll have to try something else," said Jon, "no water."

"Goodness," said Liz, "where can we find water?"

"I'll pee in your mug," said Dave.

"Now that's loyalty!" smirked Jon.

"It's uncouth! Would there be water down this trail, Jonny?" asked Liz.

"The way it's rained lately, there could be."

"Good. You boys wanted to do some hunting. Now's your chance. Take something to carry water."

"It's getting pretty late, Liz," said Charles.

"Then you better hurry! We need meat . . . and water."

"What do we have to carry water?" asked Dave.

"Your hat? Anything," answered Liz. "Maybe Jonny has a bucket in his wagon."

"Maybe. I've got a lot of things in my wagon," Jon said, staring back at Liz. "I'll go look."

"I'll go with you," said Dave. "Have any extra gun powder?"

Jon knew the game Liz was playing, but seemed powerless to stop it. Maybe he didn't want to stop it! His searching uncovered a small bucket, which he handed to Dave.

"It's nice and cozy in Jon's wagon," said Dave, back by the fire. "Nice for sleeping."

"It's only lacking one thing," quipped Liz.

"And what would that be?" asked Jon.

"Why, Maggie, of course! Someone to comfort you."

"What are the sleeping arrangements tonight?" asked Charles.

"I'll stay by the fire. You three can use my wagon."

"But, Jonny, it's so cold out. Maybe all four of us can cram in your wagon."

"I guess we can worry about that later," said Dave.

"Yeah. We'll be back soon," added Charles.

"Come back with water . . . and a deer," said Liz.

"We need to talk, Liz," said Jon, after the Chasney brothers had left.

"We need to do a lot of things quickly, Jonny, and talking's not one of them."

"I'm married, Liz, and I love my wife."

"Good for you! And I love my husbands, as you call them. The Lord gave us the ability and need to love more than one. 'Love thy neighbor,' the good book says."

"Please keep the Lord and good book out of this."

"Alright, Jonny. I'm really cold. Please come over here and at least warm me up."

Jon knew he shouldn't but did anyway.

"That's better." She hugged him close, and he hugged back.

"Better for you, maybe. Agony for me." He looked up, and thought it impossible for anyone to see from above.

"It doesn't have to be, Jonny. You want to please Maggie?"

"Of course, I do. Why?"

"Well, I can show you some things that you can try on her later. She'll love them, and you, for doing them to her."

"I swear. You are a little strumpet, Liz."

"Hmm . . . strumpets need it a lot, Jonny. You know you want it. Why fight it?" She grabbed his free hand and placed it on her breasts. They felt good to Jon, even through her clothing. Her hand went to his crotch.

"Oh, Jonny," she whispered, "you need it as badly as I do." She tried to unbutton his jeans, but they were stretched to the limit. "Kiss me, Jonny." He did, as his hand tried to find the flesh of her breast.

"Let's go in your wagon, Jonny. I promise you won't regret it."

"I'm already regretting it," he said as he stood and pulled her to him. They kissed passionately, and Jon felt her tongue probing.

"Let's hurry, Jonny."

"JONNY? What are you doing down there?"

"Nothing, my love," he lied.

"I miss you, Jonny. I wish you were up here."

"I miss you too, till I see you first thing tomorrow."

"Are you there, Liz?"

"Yes, Maggie, I'm right by the fire," Liz answered.

"I'm going to give the Chasneys our wagon tonight, and sleep here by the fire!" shouted Jon.

"Where are Davy and Charles?"

"They're hunting and looking for water." There was a long pause.

"I'm going down," Jon and Liz heard her say.

"Don't come down, Maggie darlin', you'll get hurt."

Jon wasn't certain that Maggie even heard that last remark. All they heard was commotion from above.

"Those two alone," Jon and Liz heard.

"I don't care, I'm doing it!"

"If I have to jump!"

"My husband . . . murder!"

"What's going on up there?"

"Sissy wans ta comes down." That sounded like Buelah.

"Well, tell her to stay put. Everything is fine."

"She won' listen, Jonny." It was Buelah.

"Well, tell Mose to take this slack-end rope, and send down the platform. I'm coming up."

"Orites, Jonny." There was more commotion.

"I'm sorry, Jonny. We strumpets cause trouble!" said Liz.

"It's not your fault, Liz. It's not meant to be right now. Will you be alright until Charles and Dave get back?"

"Sure, Jonny. You don't hate me for trying, do you?"

"I thank you for trying."

"Well then, maybe I'll try again sometime."

"Go ahead and use the wagon tonight. I'll see you in the morning." The platform was on its way down.

"Jonny, I have something to tell you," said Liz.

"What is it?" asked Jon.

"My real name is Elizabeth Engels, and we're headed for a town called Frankfort, on the Kentucky River. You can send a letter to that town, and I'll get it."

"Don't bank on me sending any letters, the way I write."

"Just in case you need me, Jonny, I'll come."

"Thanks, Liz. I'll remember."

"I'll write it down for you, so you don't forget."

"Good, I'll keep it. And Liz, you're not a strumpet."

"Thanks, Jonny. See you in the morning."

Jon climbed aboard the platform and yelled for Mose to "haul her up." As he gained altitude, he saw Liz blow him a kiss, and he blew one back. When he reached the landing, Maggie was waiting. She ran up and hugged Jon.

"Sorry I'm so spoiled, Jonny, but I just couldn't be without you all night."

"That's a banger, darlin'. I'm glad we're together."

"So am I. You'll see how much in a while."

"I can hardly wait, my pretty plum." They hugged tightly.

"Jonny!" whispered Maggie. "You're already horny!"

"I know. I'm anticipating what will happen later."

"Let's go cuddle by the fire."

"Good idea, darlin'. I see Ella has food cooked."

"Braised meat."

"Can we send some down to Liz . . . and Charles and Dave?"

"Sho 'nuff, Jonny. I's has plenty," said Ella.

"No matter what they say about you, Ella, you're wonderful."

Ella, Mose, and Buelah were not sure they understood what Jon had just said, but when Maggie grinned, so did they.

"Can you hear me, Liz?" Jon shouted.

"Sure can, Jonny," came Liz's answer.

"Ella sends some meat. And her love."

"Tell her thanks, Jonny. See you tomorrow."

Diary of Margaret Hamilton

Saturday, November 14, 1835

. . . Disaster struck today. Everyone slept in today after the big party. Everyone except Nunky Mose. He took Sloggy and Corker, and made his way to the landing above. He worked all morning and made a sling to raise us up. The first was the buckboard. NO MORE. The corner rope came loose, and it plunged back to the ground and broke in pieces. Buelah, Chipper, Jon, and I are sleeping on the ground tonight. We are up on the landing, and still have our wagon and four horses to lift in the morning.

With love, Margaret H.

Sunday, November 15

Mose and Ella were up early, and their banging of pans and talk woke up the neighborhood. They had a big fire going, and "bear bacon" ready to consume. Mose had hooked up Corker and team fifteen to the tackle, waiting for Jon.

"Are you awake, my pretty plum?"

"Yes, I am, my wonderful husband."

"Thanks for last night, darlin'."

"Hmm, thank you, Jonny. It was like the old times in barn five, remember?"

"Old times? That was just this last summer!"

"But they were good. Weren't they, Jonny?"

"You bet! That's when we made our son!"

"Or our daughter. I want a Sunday kiss."

"You got it, darlin'. I hope I didn't hurt you last night."

"Not a bit, Jonny. You were so careful, and good."

"Good. We'll do it again soon, I hope. Let's get dressed."

"Are you awake down there?"

"Yes we are, Jon. What's first this morning?" asked Charles.

"Are you dressed and ready for breakfast?"

"Almost! Hope you have lots of meat!"

"Did you get anything last night?" asked Jon.

"That's a loaded question!" shouted Dave. "If you mean deer, no! But we found a little stream a couple miles south."

"Good, then you have water?"

"Only enough to fill that little bucket you gave us."

"Hmm . . . I'll come down with a couple buckets, and Mose will haul you up to eat, and I'll get water."

"Sounds good, Jon. Have you eaten?"

"I'll grab a few strips and be right down."

"Good."

"Good morning, Jonny." That was Liz calling.

"Morning. Are you decent?"

"If I'm not, you can help me get decent."

"I have to pass on that. Thank you."

"You should have stayed down here, Jonny, and brought Maggie down. We had a blast!"

"I had a blast up here too, with Maggie."

"That's good, Jonny. That makes everybody happy this Sunday morning. Let's do it more often," said Liz.

"I'll vote for that! I'm on my way down."

"Come-on. Your greeting committee is ready."

Jon grabbed a handful of bear bacon and the two buckets left from the buckboard mishap. Mose had Corker lower him down the wall for what Jon hoped was the last time. When he reached the bottom, Liz was waiting with a hug and kiss. Jon felt that stirring again, and gently backed Liz to arm's length. He had a feeling he might be watched from above.

"Good morning . . . Captain, at your service," said Liz.

"Morning." Jon shook hands with the Chasney brothers. "First order of business is to get my crew fed."

"We're all for that, Captain," said Dave.

"Good. Climb aboard that ship and rise to breakfast."

"Aye, aye, Captain."

"Do you want me to wait for you, Jonny?"

"No, go eat, and stay up there, Liz."

"What about these horses?" asked Charles.

"They'll be alright until you eat and come back down."

"Everything looks white this morning," said Liz.

"I know. It got really cold last night."

"Didn't even notice," smiled Liz.

"You were just too busy," quipped Jon.

It was a pretty Sunday, but cold. Jon walked briskly along the open trail, feeling good about his lot, even though he had lost the buckboard. If they were to travel today, he could still win his bet with Maggie, he thought. Nah, he better not do that, now that he was on the good side of her.

Jon had walked a good mile, when he heard noises in the trees to his left. He ducked behind a tree and waited. Soon a doe popped out onto the trail, then another. They seemed to be waiting. So did Jon. In just minutes, out strutted a nice buck with a pretty rack. Just when he didn't have his Hawken with him! Jon wondered how he could down that beauty. He was determined to try. He had a couple of nice rocks near him, as well as a heavy branch. If Jon could get close enough to the buck, he could hit him with a rock, then with the branch, then cut the buck's throat with his trusty knife.

Jon had a rock in his pocket, one in his right hand, and the branch in his left. He ran as fast as he could toward the buck. He closed the gap between them to about twenty feet when the buck bolted up in the air. Jon threw the rock, and hit the buck in the shoulder. He grabbed the other rock out of his pocket, and was about to throw it at the retreating whitetail, when he almost ran into another deer that had sprung onto the trail. Jon's arm came down as he tried to avoid running the deer down. He hit the spike with the rock. It stunned him, and Jon quickly slugged him with the branch. The spike went down to his knees, and Jon drew his knife and slit its throat in one swift stroke. The spike lay kicking, as the blood and life gushed out of him. Jon grabbed a flaying leg, and sunk the knife into the spike's chest where he thought the heart would be. The spike died instantly. Jon cut a line down the spike's belly so he would bleed out. He pulled it off the trail and hid the spike in some brush.

Jon went back, grabbed his buckets, and headed for the little stream of water to fill them. On his way back, he double-checked to be sure the deer was still there, and he wasn't dreaming. It was there. When he finally reached the old campsite, Dave and Charles were there, the two teams remaining pulling his wagon to the lift.

"Hold it there, Charles!" Jon yelled. "I've got another job for your first."

"What job is that, Jon?"

"Grab a horse. We've got a deer to haul."

"You got a deer?" asked Dave. "We heard no shots."

"He don't have a gun, Dave," said Charles.

"Believe it or not, I got a spike by clubbing it and slitting its throat."

"My god, what a stroke of luck!" exclaimed Dave.

"I'd say it's a lot of skill," said Charles.

"What be happenin'?" Mose shouted down.

"Jon got a spike, and we're going to get it," said Charles.

"What's a spike?" asked Liz.

"It's some kind of deer," said Maggie.

"I'm sending up this water, Mose."

"Orites, Jon. We's watch fo' you's."

Jon, aboard Jake, and Charles, aboard Red, raced to the site of the dead spike and quickly field-dressed it and brought it back to camp. There was cheering from above.

"Glory be! We's has plenty meats," said Ella.

"Pull it up, Mose. The women can work on it while we get these horses and wagon up there."

"Orites, Jon," answered Mose, as he led Corker forward.

"Should we lift the horses first, Jon?" asked Charles.

"I think it would be best to get the wagon up, so we have the horses available down here if anything goes wrong."

"Yessir, Captain, let's get your team hitched back up."

"When did this Captain thing start, Dave? I prefer Jon."

"Jon it is, then," said Dave, as the brothers prepared to pull the covered wagon onto the platform.

"Pull it forward. I'll holler when to stop," said Jon.

The wagon inched up onto the buckboard's bed, now the platform. The men could tell it was heavy. The platform settled down into the earth.

"Hold it! Back it up just a tiny bit . . . Whoa! That's just right. Let's get it roped down tight."

"That's heavy! Maybe we should unload some of the stuff and left them separate," said Charles.

"Well, we'll try it this way and just raise it a little, and see how the tackle holds it."

"Is you's ready down there?" hollered Mose from above.

"Just about, Mose," came Jon's answer. "Double-check everything, men." All three checked and rechecked.

"I think it's ready, Jon," said Dave.

"Mose will need some help pulling it in when it reaches the top, so I'll go up with my wagon."

"Okay, Jon. We can handle the horses," said Dave.

"Pull it up a couple of feet and hold it, Mose."

"Orites, Jon." Mose could be heard from below, urging Corker forward. Jon felt the lurch as the platform below him slowly lifted off the ground. He could hear the tackle and rope straining above him. Then he heard Mose stop Corker.

"Whoa, Corka. Whoa! Stay, Corka. Whoa, Big Corka."

"How does it look up there?" Jon hollered. No response. "Hello up there! Can anyone hear me?" Jon yelled.

"We hear you, Jonny!" shouted Maggie. "It's too heavy for Corker to hold it still."

"It's amazing Corker can even lift it off the ground," said Jon. "Tell Mose to back it down."

As Maggie disappeared from view, Jon heard a creaking noise. All of a sudden. *CRACK!* The platform under Jon and the wagon shuddered and dropped a little. Jon leaped to the ground, as the platform and wagon dropped back slowly to the earth.

"What happened up there?" Jon shouted. He received no response. "Hey! What's going on up there?" Jon repeated.

"Nunky Mose is looking, Jonny. Hold on."

"Damn!" Jon paced the ground around the wagon.

"Orites, Jon, dem tackle arm be's crooked. Dem wagon be's too heavy!" shouted Mose.

"Okay," Jon said to Dave and Charles. "We need to go up there and try to repair the tackle arm. Let's unhook the platform, and I'll go first. When you've unloaded some of the stuff from the wagon, come on up."

"Will do," said Dave.

"Back Corker a little, Mose, so I can get a foot in the hook." The tackle rope came down to ground level, and Jon stepped into the hook and grabbed the rope. "Raise me up, Mose!" Jon shouted.

The tackle had no trouble lifting Jon. At the top, Maggie was concerned about the arm breaking with Jon's weight and was relieved to see him at the landing.

"You shouldn't scare me like that, Jonny."

"Sorry, darlin'. It's just the wagon that's too heavy for the tackle. I don't think it will even lift the horses the way it is now. We've got to figure out how to get our wagon up here . . . Any ideas, Mose?"

"Yassa. We's builds posts ta cradle arm un edge."

"You mean a support for the arm at the edge?"

"Yassa. We's makes teepee cradle," said Mose.

"Let's do it. Where do we start?"

"We's cuts dem legs." Mose motioned with three fingers.

"Oh, you mean like a three-legged support."

"Yassa. We's cuts tree."

"Righto, Mose. Ella, can you handle Corker and bring up Charles and Dave?"

"I's do, Jonny."

While the other women were cutting deer, and Ella was bringing up the Chasney brothers, Jon and Mose were cutting three trees to length and delimbing them. Soon Charles and Dave were helping, and a sturdy tripod was formed. It was fastened at the top with spike and rope. Next, the three legs were braced to each other in several places, so the tripod could not collapse either in or out.

"Now how will we get this tripod under the tackle arm?"

"And why does this tripod have to be so big and heavy?" These questions came from Charles and Dave.

"It's big and heavy so it can lift that wagon, and then pull the wagon in between its legs," answered Jon.

"We's uses horses ta walk tripod unda arm. Firs' we's raises arm."

"That means I have to climb that tree again, Mose."

"Yassa, you's do, Jon. Lifts dem arm."

With the pulley back up the tree, Sloggy lifted the arm up just a little, and Maggie held him steady. Dave and Charles were lifted up to the landing, and all helped Corker "walk" the tripod to the edge of the wall, directly under the arm of the tackle. It was then braced and counterbraced until nothing moved. Holes were dug around the base of the three legs, setting them in the ground so they wouldn't slide or skid. The arm was braced at the crack, and then secured at the top of the tripod. All seemed ready to lift.

"I'll go back down and hook up the wagon and platform," said Charles. "Good luck."

"Thanks. Tie a short rope to the sideboard again, and one to the tongue. It should be turned out."

"It is, Jon. Lower me down, Mose."

Everything was a "go." It was silent prayer and lip-biting time, as Mose started Corker forward. Creaking and straining noises were heard as the tackle rope tightened. Slowly, the platform with its heavy cargo rose up. The only sounds were the straining tackle. The whole gang were holding their breaths. There was a cracking sound, and Jon was sure it was at the same place on the arm that had cracked before. He was about to call a halt when the cracking noises stopped. At long last, the canvas top appeared, then the sideboard of the wagon, then the wheels. Finally, the entire wagon was visible, swinging in the air under the block. Cheers came from the group.

"Thank the Lord!" said Ella.

"I'll hook Sloggy up to that sideboard rope and pull her in," said a relieved Jon.

"It won't fit!" yelled Dave.

"Uh-oh," said Charles, "we forgot something."

"I see," answered Jon. "I forgot to take off some hoops, so the wagon can fit inside the tripod."

"So what do we do now?" asked Dave.

"I'll have to climb aboard and take off two hoops from each end. Can Corker hold it, Mose?" shouted Jon.

"Sho 'nuff, Jon, but we's lowas dem back down."

"Good, Nunky Mose. That's too dangerous to climb into while in the air, Jonny," said Maggie.

"No, I can do it. Lower it just a little, Mose."

"Orites, Jon. Back, Corka. Back, Big Corka."

"That's good, Mose." Jon jumped onto the platform and grabbed hold of the wagon. The arm creaked again and the platform banged against the cliff, but held.

Jon scrambled into the wagon and began pulling the two hoops at each end, so the wagon top would fit into the triangular space of the tripod. Mose had Corker now pulled the wagon back up to clear the landing.

"That's good! hook Sloggy up to this rope, Charles, and pull this crate into the tripod."

"Right, Jon." Charles and Dave hooked Sloggy to the rope attached to the wagon's sideboard, and the big dray pulled the wagon in, between the tripod's legs.

"Lower it down, Mose." The two giants backed a little, and the wagon and platform settled onto earth, finally conquering the wall. There were cheers and hugs.

"Now we must tear down this tripod so we can get the wagon out from under it."

"Then how are we going to get my horses up here?"

"They're *our* horses, Dave," snapped Liz.

"Hopefully, the arm will be strong enough to lift the horses and supplies up without the tripod."

"Did you blunder again, Jonny?" asked Maggie.

"You are a blunderbutt, Jonny," said Liz.

"What do you mean, ladies?"

"If you had brought the horses and supplies up first, *then* the wagon, you would be all through," said Maggie.

"And we wouldn't have to worry now about getting them up here with no tripod," added Liz.

"Wouldn't have worked," said Jon.

"You're trying to con us again, you big lummox."

"Would you ladies have pulled the wagon back onto the platform down there?" asked a smiling Jon.

"Certainly not," answered Liz.

"That's why the Lord made men with strong backs . . . should I say the rest, Liz?"

"Nah, Maggie, let them spend the rest of the day trying to figure out the rest."

"I know the rest," said Jon. "Now will you ladies please help Ella fix lunch, while we strong minds get the rest of the horses up here?"

It turned out that the arm was still strong enough to lift the platform five more times to get cargo up, then Dave or Charles with a horse. At last, the group was all at the same upper level. After a meaty lunch, repairs, cutting and drying meat, reloading, and a little rest made up the afternoon and evening. Mose made a two-wheel trailer out of the remains of the buckboard and attached it to the covered wagon to carry some supplies, and sleep Mose and Ella.

Diary of Margaret Hamilton

Sunday, November 15

. . . Some Sunday! The arm of the tackle broke under the weight of our wagon, and we almost lost it too! Most of our Sunday was spent repairing the lift, and getting our wagon and remaining horses up to this level. Jonny did get another deer, though, a "spike." It had two little horns sticking out of its cute little head. Jonny says we will be out of these mountains and into Tennessee tomorrow. He is always the optimist. We shall see! Hope my family is well.

Love, Maggie

Monday, November 16

"Early to bed and early to rise" didn't fit with Jon's group. They were only fairly healthy, not wealthy for sure, and not wise! Monday morning was cold again, but up on the "ledge," the sun felt wonderful. For once, everything went like clockwork with an early start. As Jon predicted, the easy inclining, lightly timbered shelf made a sweeping turn to the west. The gang was a couple hours into clearing and moving forward when they encountered another hazard.

"What is it, Mose?"

"We's has dem landslide," answered Mose.

What Jon saw caused him to curse his luck. A V-shaped portion of the shelf had collapsed down the hillside.

"Buggers! What else can go wrong?"

"We're very near the summit too, I can tell," said Charles.

"What the blazes we do now?" asked Dave.

"I'll be damned if I know," answered Jon. "I guess we can go back to the wall, lower ourselves back down, continue southwest, and hope to find the road that connects Charlotte with Knoxville . . ."

"After all that work getting up here?" asked Liz.

"That would be like giving up, Jonny. There must be some way to cross this gap."

"What do you think, Mose?"

"I's think we's cross here, like Sissy say."

"Just how do we do that?" asked Dave.

"We's build bridges."

"Can we do that, Mose? This gap must be fifteen feet or more where we would need to cross."

"We's do, Jon. We's cuts dem trees, an' dig troughs."

"Righto, Mose. Charles and Dave, can you cut one thick pine, about thirty feet long? And we'll need one about twelve feet long, and a bundle of ten-footers."

"Okay, let's get started, Davy," said Charles.

"Right, brother."

The women watched the men busy themselves cutting and trimming timber and digging troughs. They gasped when Mose leaped the gap at the narrowest spot next to the hillside, a jump of about six feet. He started digging the trough on the west side. When the Chasney brothers finished the long pole, they slid it across the gap at the narrow, hillside opening. They then rolled it into the trough, about ten feet out, and filled back dirt around it, holding it in place.

"It fits like a glove, Mose."

"Yassa, it do. We's ready fo' dem short 'un too."

"Yup! I sure hope more of this ground doesn't decide to give way down the hill."

"Yassa. It looked solid, Jon."

Jon helped the Chasneys finish the shorter log and place it in the trough next to the hillside.

"Good job, men. Now all we need are boards to athwart these beams," said Jon.

"What does that mean, Chuck?" asked Dave.

"He means pieces to lay across the poles."

"That's a pretty fancy word, Jonny," said Liz.

"I'll bet you don't even know what it means," added Maggie.

"Yes, I do, my pretty plum."

"Let's hear it in another sentence, you big lummox."

"Right. You two thwart me all the time. When we athwart into Tennessee, I'm trading you in for a pair of mules!"

"Ha, ha, that's funny, but you'll lose in the end," teased Liz.

"Right, mules don't produce sons," added Maggie.

"And they're much more difficult to sleep with," smiled Liz.

"Thwarted again!" said Jon. "Let's get our bridge finished, and noon on the other side."

"We's splits dem boards, Jon."

"Alright, Mose. This will be a good solid bridge."

As fast as the Chasneys could cut logs about ten feet in length, Mose and Jon had them split and laid out across the gap. To tie them down, Mose laid a solid strip along the length of the bridge at the outside edges. He then had the Chasneys fill the cracks, uneven spots, and approaches with dirt from the troughs.

"Hurrah, gang, we're ready. Let's each bring the women over first, then Mose and I will walk Pasha and Corker across. Dave and Chuck, drive the wagons."

Again, Pasha shied when his hooves hit planks, but Mose had a firm grip on him and talked him across.

"Now, Charles, bring the heavy wagon across first."

Mose walked back out on the bridge to help walk teams five and fifteen across. The bridge shook and settled a little, but the wagon with trailer spanned the bridge with ease. Mose backed Corker onto the bridge to help pull the Chasney wagon across, with little difficulty. Just after it reached solid ground on the west side of the bridge, a large section of the shelf along the hill gave way and plunged downward, creating a wider gap and exposing the beam bridging the gap. The bridge held, but no longer could have held the weight of the wagons.

"Wow! That was close!" exclaimed Dave.

"I'll bet that bridge is gone before dark," said Charles.

"Don't anyone take that bet!" warned Liz. "That skinflint only bets on sure things."

"Daddy, you's gets fire goin' an' we's has lunch," said Ella.

"Orites, missy, I's do."

"I guess we have some meat, right, Ella?"

"Yassa, Jon. I's makes jumbalies."

"What's that, Nanty Ella?"

"It be's some of all we's has."

"We still have close to half a day yet, gang. Let's make our camp in Tennessee!" said Jon. He was answered with "Hurrah!" "Yeah!" and smiles.

The all-too-familiar cutting and advancing continued for a couple hours. Mose was in front, chopping the trail clear, when Jon noticed something different. The ground seemed to level. He didn't say anything until he was sure, a couple miles further, when the group came upon a small stream.

"Stop the wagons, ladies. Gather around, everybody."

"What is it now, Jonny?" asked Maggie.

"We must be going the wrong way," quipped Liz.

"What is the matter, Jonny?" asked Maggie.

"Does anyone notice anything strange?" asked Jon.

"Strange?" "No" and "What?" were the responses, except the smile on Mose's face, which told Jon that he knew.

"Don't say anything, Mose."

"Yassa, I's very still, Jon."

"Come on, Nunky Mose, what's strange?"

"I's don't tells you's, Sissy."

"Don't keep us guessing, you big lummox!"

"Alright! Please tell us your little secret," said Liz.

"Look at that stream, everyone."

"So it's a little babbling brook, so what?" asked Dave.

"What about it?" asked Maggie.

"Looks wet," said Liz.

"Look at the direction it's flowing." There was a long pause.

"By darn, it's flowing west!" exclaimed Charles.

"Damned if it ain't!" added Dave.

"What's that mean, Jonny?"

"We're in Tennessee!" shouted Jon.

"Damned if we ain't!" said Dave.

"Yippy!" yelled Liz, and the hugging and dancing started on the spot. Buelah led a version of the Juba.

"Congratulations, Jon!" said Charles, shaking hands.

"Where's that beer when we need it?" asked Dave.

"We could use some of it now," agreed Liz.

"It be's all gone," said Ella.

"It about got us all in trouble before, and Jonny said no more beer."

"Did I say that, Maggie?" asked Jon.

"You bet your buns you did!"

"We don't have any yeast anyway, so forget it," said Liz.

"Righto! Let's see if we can find civilization," said Jon. "We still have a couple hours of light left."

"Yeah, let's get out of these Blues!" agreed Charles.

"Straight ahead, Captain?"

"Straight ahead, Dave. Follow this stream. It may be the start of the Watauga River."

It was dark when Jon called a stop in an open area lacking timber. He would determine the location tomorrow.

Diary of Margaret Hamilton

Monday, November 16, 1835

Tennessee! After twenty-four terrible days! Rain, snow, freezing, and struggling over the Blue Ridge Mountains. What awaits us ahead? Time will tell. I sooo wish we could have talked Jonny out of this journey. I love and miss my family.

Margaret Hamilton

CHAPTER V

———ɷ———

Appalachia

Tuesday, November 17

"Wow! Will you look at that?"

David Chasney's exclamation, late as it came, was on the minds of the entire group as they gazed below them. As far as the eyes could see in the early morning sunlight lay a vast prairie, wide open, save the occasional cluster of trees and bodies of water from excess rain.

"Looks like pretty good land from here," said Charles.

"Yeah, I wonder why nobody's farming it," added Dave.

"Maybe we should forget about Kentucky and Arkansas, and just settle here," said Liz.

"What do you think of that idea, Jonny?"

"Not much, my pretty plum. This plateau is pretty darn high up, and that would make a short growing season. Besides, if the land were any good, you'd see farms spread out all across it already."

"It probably belongs to the Indians anyway," said Charles.

"Yes, I believe it does," answered Jon.

"Where's that river you were talking about?" asked Liz.

"Yeah, big boy, where is that river we were supposed to run right into, Jonny?"

"It's called the Watauga, and I don't know where it is!"

"So, you bamboozled us again!" exclaimed Elizabeth.

"No, I didn't. It's got to be close."

"It probably was right on the other side of that crevice we didn't take, at the top of that long hill."

"I don't think so, Maggie."

"We's no gets dem wagons up dar, Sissy," said Mose.

"But you didn't try, Nunky Mose. Jonny could have at least scouted up through the crevice."

"Well, it's too late to worry about that now," said Liz.

"Yes, but we must find that river, right, Jonny?"

"Right, my pretty plum. Mose, where did that stream end last night?"

"It turn leffs, Jon."

"I thought so. I think we're north of the Watauga."

"Why do you think that, Jon?" asked Charles.

"Well, all those days we climbed that hill, we were climbing northwest, and we ended up way north and east of our goal."

"Yes, but then we went a good distance southwest, and probably ended up due west of our starting point."

"Maybe, Charles, but I think we need to go a little further south."

"It was probably somewhere halfway down that Warrior's Trail," chirped Liz.

"Or right up that crevice," added Maggie.

"Well, I've got an idea."

"What is it, Jonny?" asked Maggie.

"Charles, you take the wagons straight out onto that plateau, and I'll take Corker south for a few miles, and catch backup with you later."

"That's dangerous, Jonny."

"Don't look very dangerous from here, darlin'."

"Alright, Jon. If we find anything unusual, should we stop?"

"Unusual, like what?" asked Jon.

"Oh, like a river . . . or a farm," answered Charles.

"Yeah, maybe you should wait there, but be sure to mark your trail so I can find you."

"Be careful, Jonny," said Maggie, hugging and kissing him.

With that, Jon grabbed his Hawken, some dried meat, a blanket, and the giant white dray and rode out. The remainder of the group started down onto the plateau.

Little puffs of breath clouds emitted from Jon and Corker as they headed southwest along the tree line of the Blues, but it didn't feel that cold in the Tennessee sun. The scenery changed from the pine to a variety of trees. There seemed to be an abundance of food, as Jon saw cottontails, squirrels, and what he thought was a gray fox. He figured he had traveled three or four miles when he spotted an old cabin. A closer look concluded that it had been abandoned for many years. Another half mile found another cabin in similar condition. *There must be a river close by*, Jon thought, but he found none. Another rundown cabin and more miles traveled, and Jon hit it, a nice, large river, running west.

"The Watauga! I was right!" he said. "Guess I'll have a bite to eat and go find my gang." Jon found a spot along the river with grass for Corker. He sat down with his strips of meat.

He noticed several fox squirrels playing in a tree, and decided to try his luck at hitting one with his Hawken. He took careful aim and fired at one. *BAM!* His target leaped up into the air and landed several feet from the tree. The others just scurried around the trunk of the same tree. Jon loaded again from his sitting position and fired again. *BAM!* Pieces of red squirrel splattered around the tree.

It was now time to find his gang. Jon headed Corker due north, hoping to intersect their trail. It was early afternoon, and he was in a hurry to spread the good news that he had found the Watauga River. He spotted another abandoned cabin near the river, and wondered just what had caused the widespread desertion. The ground was soft under Corker's weight, so Jon was sure he could find the tracks of the wagons. In short time, he had covered eight or nine miles of open plateau and began to wonder if he had actually found the Watauga. "I couldn't have been that far off in guessing its location, could I?" he asked himself. "Must be getting old!"

Just then, Jon spotted a pony grazing near a cluster of trees. He jumped down, Hawken in hand, and cautiously advanced on the cluster. He saw nothing at first, but then he suddenly spotted parts of two human legs jutting from behind a tree. It was not moving, and Jon wondered if it was a dead man. He took aim and called.

"Hello? . . . Hello?" he called again. There was no movement or response."

"Are you alive?" he shouted. The leg finally moved.

"Help!" Jon barely heard from ten feet away.

"Are you sick?"

"I am shot."

"Can you move?"

"No . . . Please . . . Help."

"Don't move." Jon circled around to his left, until he could get a better view. It was a young Cherokee man, lying on his side, his rifle a short distance away. Jon raised him to a sitting position. It was easy to tell that a ball had hit him in the chest on the right side. The man had large pools of blood in front of him on the ground, and on the rag he held to his chest. He had also been bleeding from the mouth and nose, and was very nearly dead.

"Who shot you?"

"Mont-an persons kill Chero-kee."

"Well, they danged near killed you," Jon said, as he propped the man against the tree. A large lump projected from his upper back, where the ball had shattered his shoulder blade. The ball was probably still lodged there.

"I am John Naa-shun."

"I too am Jon . . . Hamilton. I must get you some help . . . and stop your bleeding."

"I am dying. You tell . . . my father."

"Yes, but I will get the bleeding stopped, and get you some help first. I will be back as soon as I can."

"No, you stay. Tell my father . . . I die."

"Where is your father?"

"In ref-ugee town . . . two days south, in place . . . of Blue Smokes."

"I will find it. Is it close to the Watauga River?" asked Jon, as he wrapped the Cherokee's chest.

"No, no . . . it is south . . . past Noli . . . chuk . . . ee."

"I will find it, John. You rest. I'll get help."

Jon used his belt to hold his wrapping in place, then covered the man with his blanket and raced Corker north. In just a short distance, Jon spotted the wagon tracks running in a westerly direction. As he rushed along the tracks, he pulled the patches from his Hawken, found a cap to fit over its nipple, and fired into the air. Another couple miles further, and Jon found the wagons waiting.

"Mose! Ella! Bring the wagon back around. Hurry! We may be able save a man's life!"

"Yassa!" shouted Mose, as he and Ella jumped down from the flatbed trailer and hurried to climb aboard the covered wagon. Maggie was driving, along with Buelah and Chipper, who scrambled behind the bench so Mose could turn the wagon around.

"Is the horse liniment in the wagon?"

"Nosa! It is in the trailer, Jon."

"Mose, you unhitch the trailer. We'll put the liniment in the wagon. Leave the trailer here for now."

"Yassa, Jon, I's do."

"What about us?" shouted Liz, who was in the Chasney wagon with the brothers.

"See if you can pull the trailer with that wagon, and follow our tracks. We'll be about two miles back, and less than a mile south. You can't miss it."

"Okay, Jon, we'll see you there," said Charles.

"Why don't we take the Chasney wagon, and have our wagon and trailer follow?" asked Maggie.

"That's a much better idea," said Liz.

"Is that alright with you, Charles?"

"Sure is, Jon. Go ahead and take our wagon. We'll catch up to your with yours."

"Thanks. Sorry, Mose. Put the liniment in that wagon, and you and Ella follow me."

"I want to come along with you, Jonny."

"We can't, darlin'. We're in a hurry. I'll see you there."

"Go take care of that man, then. We'll catch up," said Maggie.

With Mose and Ella aboard the Chasney wagon, and Jon leading on Corker, the three took off, leaving the rest to get things in order and follow the tracks. When Jon reached the wounded Cherokee, John Nation, he had fallen over sideways and lay still on his side.

"He be's dead, Jon?" asked Mose, climbing down from the wagon.

"He still has a pulse, I think."

"I's takes him," said Ella. "We's needs hot wata an' clean rags, Daddy."

"Orites, missy. I's gets fire."

"Good. If I can find a bucket, I'll find some water."

When the covered wagon rolled up, Mose had a fire started, and Ella was tending to the motionless man.

"He looks like an Indian," said Dave.

"He be's Cherokee," answered Ella.

"Do we have any water?" asked Charles, helping Ella.

"They's be's wata in dem wagon," answered Buelah.

"Heat some up, Dave."

"Alright, brother," said Dave, heading for the wagon.

"Where is Jonny?" asked Maggie.

"He be's lookin' fo' wata," said Ella.

"He knew we had water in the wagon," said Maggie.

"He probably didn't know we were right behind them, Maggie," said Charles. "He should be right back."

In short order, Ella had the wound cleaned, liniment applied, wound bandaged, and the patient bundled up. That was when Jon appeared with water.

"Looks like I made a wasted trip."

"So what's new?" asked Liz.

"Your record is still intact," added Maggie.

"Is orites, Jon. We's uses dem wata fo' horses?" asked Mose.

"Thanks, Mose. At least I have one friend."

"So, what are our plans now, big boy?" asked Liz.

"Looks like we camp here tonight."

"Yes, but what about tomorrow, Jonny?"

"I'm not sure. Ask the doctor," he answered, pointing at Ella.

"He can't be's moved," said Ella.

"How long before he can, Nanty Ella?"

"Dun knows, Sissy. When's hole close."

"That could be a month!" said Liz.

"Are we going to have to wait here that long, Jonny?"

"I don't know, Maggie. It didn't take very long for my wounds to scab over when I was shot."

"Jonny! You never told me that you were shot!"

"Yes, I did, didn't I?"

"No, you didn't! When did that happen?"

"It was when I went down to your brother's plantation to help put his crops back in." Jon had spilled the beans.

"Who shot you, Jonny?"

"I don't know, Maggie."

"You do too, Jonny. You're lying."

"Look, Maggie, darlin', I don't want to talk about it now."

"He's keeping secrets from you already, Mag," said Liz.

"Jonny, please don't keep secrets from me. I'm your wife."

"I won't, darlin'. I thought you knew."

"Well, I don't, and I want to!"

"Okay, I'll tell you all about it soon."

"You'll tell me tonight!"

"Alright, my pretty plum, tonight. Now let's make camp. It will be getting dark pretty soon."

"It's time, Jonny. Tell me about your trip to Chic Wood," said Maggie, after the group had supper and retired. Jon and Maggie now shared their wagon with Buelah, while Chipper shared the trailer with Mose and Ella. The wounded Cherokee, John Nation, never regained consciousness that evening, and remained bundled on the ground by the fire.

"Well, honey, a group of men tried to steal my gang in South Carolina, and Charles Finley and I had a shootout with them. We both got wounded. That's why it took longer than expected to get back to Bethania."

"Oh, Jonny, why didn't you tell me?"

"I thought I did. Anyway, I wanted to forget about it."

"Did you kill anyone, Jonny?"

"Honey, I'm trying to forget."

"Please, Jonny. Tell me."

"Yes . . . Charles and I had to kill them, or they would have killed us."

"Oh, Jonny, I'm so scared."

"Why? It's over and done with."

"But some relatives may still come after you."

"Not likely now, after all this time." There was a pause.

"Where's your wound, Jonny?"

"Maggie, it's right here, in my side."

"Huh. I never even noticed it before."

"Yeah, that horse liniment really does a good job."

"Yes, just a funny-looking scar." There was another pause. "What's this, Jonny?"

"What's what, Maggie?"

"What's this scar on your shoulder?"

"Oh, it's just a spot where I got nicked."

"From a bullet?"

"Yes, darlin' . . . Can I go to sleep now? Please?"

"Don't you like talking to me, Jonny?"

"Yes, Maggie, during the day, when I'm not so tired."

"But you're always busy during the day."

After a pause, Jon said, "Well, my pretty plum, we may have a few days of rest now, while that Cherokee heals . . . or dies."

"Are we going to stay here all that time?"

"Well, we can't move him, and we can't just leave him and let him die out here all by himself."

A few moments passed. "You're right, Jonny. I guess we're stuck here for a couple days," said Maggie.

Diary of Margaret Hamilton

Tuesday, November 17, 1835

Tennessee! Jonny's five-day journey over the Blues took over three weeks, but we are here. I love my parents, but I'm mad at them for not telling me about my husband getting shot in South Carolina. I just found it out by accident when Jonny found a Cherokee shot through the chest, but alive . . . We only made around ten miles today and even backtracked to help the Indian. We may be here several days while he heals.

Love to all,
Margaret Rose Hamilton

Wednesday, November 18

Spent the day in camp tending to the wounded Cherokee named John Nation, alias "Son of the Sun!" He opened his eyes only once or twice today. Nanty Ella dressed his two wounds three times today. Nunky Mose cut an opening in the Cherokee's back to get the ball, and a lot of pieces of bone, out. Jonny says he was shot by some "Mountain People." The gang busied themselves cutting and gathering wood to burn. Jonny went hunting this morning, and brought back a rabbit and several squirrels. It made a good, big stew. This evening, Nunky Mose played his harmonica, and we had an old-fashioned sing-along. I have a wonderful, caring husband, and will follow him to the ends of the earth. But I miss Bethania, and my family.

Margaret Rose

Friday, November 20, 1835

The patient is now awake, talking, and ate a little food. Nanty Ella has done a brilliant job of nursing this John Nation, who is the son of the chief of a splinter group of Cherokees who escaped from captivity in Georgia. They have been robbed of their homes and possessions, and President Jackson wants to ship or herd them to Indian territories even west of Arkansas. The patient's wounds have stopped bleeding, and look like they are about to start healing. He is very grateful to us, and says he will "reward" us when he returns to his family. He has much difficulty at all times breathing. Jonny says it's because he now has only one lung. We have had very cold nights, but sunny days. Tomorrow starts our fifth week of this journey, and I still have to get used to it! I have a patient husband.

Much love,
Maggie

Saturday, November 21

"Jon! Wakes up, Jon!" shouted Mose, from outside the covered wagon.

"What is it, Mose?"

"Dem Cherokee be's dead!"

"Oh no," said Maggie. "Nunky Mose and Nanty Ella tried so hard to save him."

"I'll be right out, Mose."

"Orites, Jon. I's be comfort Ella."

"I better go comfort Nanty Ella too."

"Right, darlin'. Not sure what I can do now."

"Bury him, of course."

"What? And have the whole Cherokee nation after us?"

"You big lummox, why would they be after us? We tried to save his life."

"Yes, but they don't know that."

"Oh, so what do we do, Jonny?"

"I'll have to take the body to his father."

"Oh no, I don't want to be a widow . . . with child."

"That shouldn't happen if I bring the body to them, my darlin'. Then they would know I'm not the killer."

"How would they know that, Jonny?"

"Because the killer would just leave the body and run, or bury it out of sight."

"Okay, but this time, send Dave or Charles with the body."

"I can't ask them to do my job, Maggie darlin'. I'm the one who found him. I have to deliver him."

"Oh, damn! You're always the one to leave us . . . me!"

"I know, darlin'. When we get to Arkansas, I promise I'll never leave you. So come on, my pretty plum, let's have some breakfast."

"Mose, can you wrap the body in a blanket, and rope him down on his pony?"

"Yassa, I's do, Jon."

"Where are you taking him, Jonny?" asked Liz.

"He has to take the body to his father, so the whole Cherokee tribe won't be after us," answered Maggie.

"How long do you think that will take, Jon?" asked Charles.

"Well, he said his group lives two days south of here, past a place called Nolchukee."

"He probably meant the Nolichucky River," said Maggie.

"How do you know that, Maggie?" asked Elizabeth.

"In school, we had a boring class on the Appalachians."

"Then the river I found wasn't the Watauga."

"And it wasn't the Mississippi or Amazon," teased Liz.

"It was the Nolichucky, Jonny. The Watauga is north of here, just like I said it was," said Maggie.

"I didn't think I was that far off. The Watauga must be just a little ways ahead. That river I found is ten miles south of here."

"Well, you were that far off, Jonny. The Watauga is probably ten miles to the north."

"Or more," added Liz.

"I'll find out while you're gone, Jon," said Charles.

"Good. Be sure it's the Watauga River."

"What are we supposed to do for four or five days?"

"If Charles finds the Watauga, there should be folks living along it. Maybe you should go there and wait for me."

"Hallelujah! We may find civilization!" exclaimed Dave.

"Maybe we should stay here until you get back, Jonny."

"Yeah, we'd hate to lose you!" added Liz.

"You won't. Just mark your trail."

"We can decide that when I get back," said Charles.

"Be careful, Jonny. I'll miss you."

"I'll miss you too, my love. I'll be back as quick as I can." With that, Jon, on Corker, and the pony carrying John Nation, left.

The afternoon sun was sinking to the west when Charles returned. He had a large cloth bag hanging from the shoulder of his horse, Jack, and a smile on his face.

"What did you find, Chucky?" asked Liz.

"I found the Watauga and civilization."

"Were they friendly?" asked Dave.

"Very friendly. They sent this, full of food!" Charles handed the sack to Mose and Ella. It had vegetables, bread, beans, pork, and some beef.

"We eat tonight!" exclaimed Dave.

"An' fo' nights ta come!" added Ella.

A supper of hog and hominy was enjoyed by all, followed by talk.

"I wish Jonny were here to enjoy this supper."

"It be's supna, Sissy," said Buelah.

"Oh, that's right. I forgot," smiled Maggie. "Anyway, I wonder what he's eating tonight."

"I's puts meat in dem carry bags," answered Ella.

"Thank you, Nanty Ella. Too bad he has to eat cold venison, while we eat this hot pork."

"Poor fellow. Maybe he'll find a squaw to cook and take care of him on his way," retorted Liz.

"Jonny would never be unfaithful to me."

"You've got that right, Mag," said Liz. There was a pause.

"Should we move our camp to the Watauga?" asked Charles.

"How far is it?" asked Maggie.

"It's only five or six miles," answered Charles.

"I's waits for Jon," said Mose.

"I's do too," said Ella.

"But it's only five miles more, and there is good food and water," pleaded Liz.

"And civilization," added Dave.

"We's do's need wata, Daddy," said Ella.

"Alright, all those who think we should move on to the Watauga tomorrow, raise your hand," directed Charles. Dave, Liz, and Buelah raised their hands. "All who think we should stay here and wait for Jon, raise your hand." Mose, Ella, and Chipper raised their hands.

"You're not voting, Maggie?" asked Charles.

"I don't know how to vote. Jonny suggested we move if Charles found the Watauga . . ."

"Un we's needs wata," added Ella.

"I'll settle this and cast the tie-breaker," said Charles. "I vote we wait for Jon at the Watauga."

"Do any of you realize tomorrow is Sunday?" asked Maggie.

"Uh-oh! What do we do about that?" asked Charles.

"It's only a couple hours. I think we should do it, and observe the Sabbath the rest of the day," said Liz.

"I agree," said Dave. "Sunday is supposed to be the day of rest, but it seems like we've been resting all week."

"Then, we move to the Watauga tomorrow, and wait there," Charles said.

Diary of Margaret Hamilton

Saturday, November 21

John Nation died sometime in the early morning hours. Jonny is taking the body to their village. I am afraid they will kill him in revenge. Jonny says he will be gone four days. I will not sleep until he returns.

Love to all, Maggie

Saturday, November 21

Jon could not travel anywhere near the pace he liked, with the body draped over the pony. It was midafternoon when he reached what he now knew to be the Nolichucky River. Jon wondered how the river got that name. Riding past the old, half-rotten cabins gave Jon a creepy feeling. They had been abandoned a long time. *Maybe those people were killed by Cherokee*, he thought. He again saw a lot of squirrels running around, and thought about bagging a few for lunch and dinner. He reasoned that he was a little hungry, but killing and skinning those little devils would be a lot of work. Jon hoped Ella put some food in his bag.

Jon crossed the river with ease, and dug into Ella's bag. There were cold strips of venison. "Remind me to make a fire and kill a couple of you varmints for dinner . . . or supner," he said to the busy little squirrels. Jon then thought maybe he should kill them now. He only saw lots of the squirrels close to the river. He readied his Hawken. *BAM!* He got one, but couldn't be sure if there would be any meat left. He reloaded and fired again, and again, a third time. Jon walked over and skinned two squirrels. The other one was only bits and pieces. He cut off the heads, cleaned them in the river, and put them in Ella's bag.

Jon was about to mount Corker, when he spotted a cottontail on the riverbank. He reloaded. The cottontail spotted Jon and began to run. Jon fired, and the rabbit did a flip in the air. It then started running in a circle, and as soon as Jon reloaded again, *BAM!* He dropped the rabbit. Jon also skinned and beheaded the cottontail and was off again.

He headed due south, toward the forest, which was no longer the dark blue pines that his group had crossed, but lots of deciduous trees, bare of leaves, mixed with lighter pine and spruce. Jon decided he was entering the Smoky Mountains, and began to look for a place to build a fire and camp for the night. He found a small opening with a tiny brook flowing through it, and figured it was a good spot. It wasn't really dark yet, and Jon gathered and rustled twigs and branches for a fire. Just then, he thought he heard a noise from his left. He crouched down and listened. There it was again! Damn, the Hawken was with Corker, Jon thought. He decided to sneak back, very slowly, to get it. Suddenly, he thought he heard a noise to his right. Whatever it was, it had him surrounded. He had to make it back to the horses. Then the noise was upon him.

"Stop there!" a voice shouted. Jon froze for a moment. It was dark enough so that Jon couldn't see him. "I will shoot! Stand very tall, do not move."

"Are you mountain person?" came another voice from Jon's other side.

He did hear them both, thought Jon, as he stood straight up and extended his arms out. "I am unarmed."

"Tell us who you are," came the first voice.

"I am Jon Hamilton. I am not a mountain person."

"You journey alone?" from the second voice.

"I bring the dead body of Cherokee John Nation to his father and family."

"That John Nation? How you know?"

"He told me before he died."

"How he die?" asked the second voice.

"He was shot and left for dead by mountain people."

"He tell you it was mountain person?"

"Yes. We kept him alive for four days."

"He not look like mountain person," said the second voice.

"Where Princess Etowah?"

"Princess Etowah?" asked Jon.

"Yes," said the first voice, "Princess Etowah, Pure as Rushing Water. She journey with John Nation."

"She married to Son of Sun," said the second voice.

"I found only John Nation, not his wife."

"Then mountain persons kill Son of Sun, and capture Pure as Rushing Water."

The second voice said, "We must tell Ustanali Nation."

"Yes, we go now."

"Wait! I go with you to refugee place," said Jon.

"You know of refugee place?"

"Yes. John Nation told me. I go there now to bring him home."

"We tell Ustanali Nation of son's death. He wait for you."

"But I do not know the way," said Jon.

After a pause, the second voice said, "I go now. You bring John Nation and Jon Hamilton."

"Yes. We will be at refuge place when sun is high."

With that, the Cherokee to Jon's right vanished.

"I am Elizah Sands of Coosa Nation."

"I am glad to know you, Elizah Sands."

"We go now, Jon, much light still in sky."

Jon thought, *What light?*

The man, Elizah Sands, was tall and lean. Everything he wore was crafted from skins of animals, except a red band around his head that held in place a full head of hair. He also had a couple of pouches, also of leather, hanging from his waist. Jon now noticed that he had been facing the point of an arrow.

Elizah seemed annoyed that, even on foot, he practically leaped through the forest, and then would have to wait for Jon and the body on horseback. After his fourth or fifth "leap," he was astride a pony when Jon again saw him. Silence seemed beautiful to Elizah. Not more than two words were spoken as the Cherokee led the way to a cleared campsite, as the last rays of sun poked through the leafless forest. Jon again gathered and rustled branches for a campfire.

Jon started digging through his patch box on his Hawken for a flint to set off some gun powder. When he turned around, Elizah already had the fire started.

"How did you do that?"

"How I do what, Jon?"

"Start the fire so quickly."

"Start fire with slow water from tree with cones," Elizah said, as he patted a small leather pouch hanging from his waist.

"I would like to see your slow water."

Elizah hesitated for a moment, then poured a few drops of heavy liquid from one pouch onto a twig. From a second pouch, he dug out a small cup with a metal piece attached. He struck the metal to the cup, and sparks immediately set off the twig, which was coated with the liquid. It looked like sap to Jon, who felt like a sap!

"This is friction cup, makes sparks for fire."

"So I see."

"And slow water make fast fire."

"I see that too. Do you have slow water at refuge place?"

"Yes, much slow water at refuge place." After a pause, Elizah asked, "Where you from, Jon Hamilton?"

"A farm, close to Salem, North Carolina."

"Why you here in mountains that smoke?"

"I am going to Arkansas," answered Jon, chewing on a seared rabbit leg.

"Arkansas two moons, over Great River."

"Yes, have you been there?"

"No, but Cherokee there. They break Blood Law and sell land, and flee west."

"Yes, I've heard of them," said Jon.

"Now Georgia and traitor Jackson want all Cherokee to leave homeland of our fathers."

"And you have left your homeland to live here?"

"I never leave homeland! We are forced out of Georgia homeland, but mountains that smoke still home."

"Will you live here forever?"

"Until White Congress pass law that give Cherokee lands back to Cherokee people, or new president elected."

"I wish you well, Elizah Sands. Have another piece of rabbit."

"Thank you," said Elizah. "We sleep now. Leave for refugee place at first light."

"Good night, Elizah."

Two men sleeping by a dying fire, with a wrapped body draped over one of three horses. Together, but far apart.

Sunday, November 22

The morning sun finally appeared over the Blues, and its rays seemed to direct themselves at Maggie's eyes as she lay in her traveling bed. The sun's rays pierced the canvas overhead. She heard the noises outside, and knew breakfast was ready. There was food left from the bag that Charles had brought from a farm near the Watauga River, and Maggie could almost taste it. "Get up, lazy bones," she said to herself.

"We's has hotcakes an' real bacons," said Buelah.

"We's saves some fo' you's, Sissy," added Ella.

"Thanks, Nanty Ella. Smells delicious. I wish Jonny was here to enjoy it too."

"He'll probably get some squaw-cookin' today," said Dave.

"I hope he'll be alright, and these Indians realize that he didn't shoot that Son of the Sun!"

"Don't worry, Maggie," said Liz. "He probably has them all bamboozled by now."

"Where is Charles?" asked Maggie, as she worked on her hotcakes and bacon of real pork.

"He hopes you don't mind, Maggie," answered Liz, "but he took Pasha out for a ride in the sun. He said he might meet us along the way."

"He took my horse out?"

"Da horse needs exercise, Sissy," said Mose. "I's hitches dem wagons up now."

"Good idea. I'll help, so we can be on our way," said Dave.

"Yippee! We's go's ta see's civilization," said Buelah.

"But why did he take my Pasha?"

"Daddy say to, Sissy," said Ella. "Say Pasha need exercise bad."

"He wanted to find a good spot to camp for a few days, and thank the people for this food," added Liz, "and he wanted to do a little hunting along the way."

"An' we's needs dem big horses to pulls wagons, Sissy," said Ella.

"I know, Nanty Ella. I just wish he'd ask."

"It's be's good fo' Pasha. You's worry too much, Sissy."

"Let's get loaded and on our way," said Dave.

Mose had the wagons and horses ready to travel. The camp belongings were thrown into the wagons. Mose and Ella took the lead wagon, with Buelah and Maggie under the canvas. Chipper rode on the trailer, and Liz and Dave followed in the Chasney wagon. As they ambled north, retracing their own tracks, Maggie gazed behind, hoping to see her husband.

"He's a long way away by now!" shouted Liz.

"I know. I just hope he'll be able to find us."

"Don't you worry about him. He's a good tracker," said Dave.

"As long as we're making tracks, anyone should be able to follow, Mag, even Jonny."

And then it happened. As the wagons neared the spot where the tracks turned east and west, Mose spotted several men, with long rifles pointed at them. Three were on horseback, and at least three were on foot. They looked shaggy, with hair covering most of their faces, ragged clothes, with suspenders holding them together. Mose stopped the wagons and raised his arms.

"That'll be downright common a-ya," said a tall, slim man, with an unkempt beard hanging close to his waist.

"A-rightly coobratin' fella," said a shorter, white-bearded man, who had an old hat down to his eyes.

"Man-person's black as Coaly's tail," said a high-pitched voice to Mose's side.

"Big as a b'ar, all get out," came another scratchy voice.

"What's y'all wants?" asked Mose.

"What-all ye gats?" said the man with the big hat.

These strange-looking men kept a steady aim at Mose. He tried to lean forward, and in front of Ella.

"Ye may-could hand down yer guns," said Long Beard.

"Watch 'em close, Jeb," said Big Hat.

"I watch 'em," said the high-pitched voice by the wagon, as Mose reached behind him for his worst Kentucky rifle.

While these people were watching Mose, Dave, in the second wagon, reached behind into his wagon and grabbed his flintlock rifle. Before he could swing back around, he felt a gun barrel in his back.

"Ye shouldn't oughta do that, Jasper," said a low, deep voice. "I plum should oughta shoot ya."

"I was just going to hand it over," lied Dave.

"Fittin'!" said the deep voice, as he reached up and grabbed the rifle. "I like ta blowed ye abroad."

"Are you-uns alright, Cole?" shouted Big Hat.

"Just nighly shot this here, fella," said deep-voiced Cole.

"What right have you got, treating us this way?" asked Liz.

"Hesh up, rat now, afor I bile over," ordered Cole.

"What did he say?" whispered Dave.

"I think he told me to shut up," said Liz.

"Climb down, here all you'uns!" hollered Long Beard, with Mose's second Kentucky rifle in hand.

"He wants us all to climb out of the wagons," said Liz.

Dave and Liz climbed down from the Chasney wagon. Mose was helping Ella step down from the covered wagon. He noticed all eyes seemed to be on Liz, and he sprang out of the wagon onto Jeb, crushing him into the ground. He next jumped up at the scratchy-voiced man, and hoisted him into the air by the neck, squeezing the life out of him. *BAM!* Mose and the scratchy-voiced man went down, and Mose lay motionless. Ella screamed.

"Daddy! Daddy!" she yelled, and went to her knees, trying to hold the big, bloodied head of her husband. "Oh, Lawd, please don' takes my Daddy," she sobbed.

Jeb lay holding his chest, and the other man lay choking and trying to get air. Mose's head was cradled in Ella's arms.

"Are ya alive, Jeb an' Winiferd?" asked Long Beard.

"My ribs . . . be . . . a bursted," said Jeb, while Wineferd was still trying to take deep breaths.

"I gats that nigger right good," said Big Hat.

"Ye sure 'nuff did, Aden," said Long Beard.

"Jist like I gats dat Injun."

"Blowed 'im clear ta Glory!" exclaimed Cole.

"A-body may o' heard the sound o' that shootin' iron."

"Yer right, Zake. We best be a-goin'," said Long Beard.

"We gets what we're after, Aden," said Cole.

"That, an' exter! Zake, you'n Cole gets them horses. Wini, you'n take in after them shootin' irons, an' climb up there ta see if there might could be more."

"You're not taking our horses!" exclaimed Maggie.

"We won't be able to travel anywhere," added Liz.

"Shut up! You'ns travelins' are ova," said Long Beard.

The group of "mountain persons" all laughed at that, which scared Liz and Maggie. None had noticed that Mose had started to move, and come around. Ella, with the help of Buelah, tried to hide his movements so these people wouldn't shoot him again.

"You'ns get on up the horses," said Aden, pointing at Liz and Maggie.

"We will not!" said Liz.

"Zake, you'n Cole put them females on them horses right now," said Aden.

The struggle was on. The two women proved good fighters, kicking and clawing. Long Beard finally stopped the battles with blows to the heads of Liz and Maggie. Mose struggled to his feet to take on the intruders, but was hit over the head by Winiferd, who clubbed him over and over again. Ella tried to cover Mose with her body, and also received a blow.

"That's 'nuff, Wini. You'n clew him good," said Aden.

"Should we take in them female niggers?" asked Jeb, now up, but still holding his chest.

"Not nohow. The oldin female cain't make no new generations," answered Long Beard.

"But ye know'd we're a-needin' females."

"You'n might could take in the young nigger, Jeb," said Aden.

"David Chasney! Are you going to just stand there and let these ugly bastards take me away?" Liz had come around from her semiconsciousness.

"There's not much I can do right now, Lizzie," said Dave, looking at a barrel pointed at him. "But we'll be coming after ya, count on that."

"And you's gets jist what that nigger's a-gotten," said Cole, rifle pointed at Dave.

"Chipper!" yelled Maggie. "Tell Jonny what has happened when he gets back . . . hear me?"

"Yes, ma'am," cried Chipper, running to his mother, Ella.

"Let's be a-gittin' outta here."

"Tie down them feisty females," ordered Aden.

As the "mountain persons" gathered up the six drays plus their three captives, Cole helped the injured Jeb onto a horse, then climbed behind Buelah.

"I'll take this purty one," said Long Beard, as he climbed onto Sloggy behind Liz. "Sorry I had ta hit ya."

"You're going to be a hell of a lot sorrier, if I ever get free of this rope," hissed Liz.

"Zake, get on up a-hind that red-haired female."

"But she's about ta pop a-pickanniny, Aden."

"Then ya has a new generation aready started."

"Goodbye, Nanty Ella. I love you!" cried Maggie.

"I's love you's too, Sissy."

"I hope Nunky Mose is alright."

Tears flooded the cheeks of Maggie, Buelah, Ella, and even Chipper, as the caravan started in a southwest direction. Liz stared angrily at Dave.

"If'n you hurry on that-a-ways, ye might could be a-findin' country folk ta take you'ns in!" yelled Aden.

Six men, three women, and nine horses disappeared.

Sunday's first light filtered through the forest and onto Jon. He was very warm, and opening his eyes, he noted that Elizah Sands had the fire going and, on sticks, was cooking the squirrels he killed yesterday.

"You eat now and we go," Elizah said.

"Did you start this fire with slow water?"

"Yes, very easy, Jon. Harder to put out fire."

"I'll bet. Nice day, isn't it?"

"Yes, a good day to travel."

"Is the refugee place very far?"

"Slow travel with John Nation, maybe high sun."

"Okay, I'm ready."

As if to prove its namesake, the two men saw small meadows and mountains that had a blue-colored "smoke" rising into the sky. Jon was captivated by the beauty. It was slow going, but around midday, Elizah suddenly made a sharp left and began to climb. Jon knew they had turned east. The trail had ended, and the climb was especially difficult for Corker. The forest was now very thick, with a large assortment of trees. Elizah jumped down and led his horse up the steep incline. Jon followed suit. At the top of the incline, Jon found himself surrounded by Cherokee warriors, seemingly behind every tree.

"This man is Jon Hamilton. He brings the dead Cherokee, John Nation, Son of Sun, to his father."

"Do we allow white man in place of refuge?"

"Yes, we do." It was the other Cherokee who, with Elizah, had first stopped Jon yesterday evening. The "second voice" said, "Ustanali Nation awaits Jon Hamilton."

"Then go inside place of refuge."

Elizah mounted his pony. Jon mounted Corker, and the three horses, laden with bodies, descended into a small meadow full of campfires, teepees, and roughly built cabins. There were busy women and children, doing chores and playing games. They all stopped and watched, as Elizah led the way through a group of trees and into a second meadow, with more of the same. The path led again through the center of the meadow to a larger log building. There, standing with ribbons around each folded arm and heavily beaded headdress, and in the middle of several sitting Cherokee, was Ustanali Nation. After a long, silent stare, the chief stepped to the pony and pulled the blanket back enough to see the head of his son. He touched the face and hair, then covered the head again and stared at the sky. With a wave of his arm, a young warrior stepped forward.

"Take your brother to place of burial and rest."

The young Cherokee took the reins of the pony, and led it away. The chief's eyes followed the procession, as it headed back to the trees separating the meadows.

"I am Jon Hamilton."

"I know who you are. I thank you for bringing my son home to rest, Jon Hamilton."

"I am sorry for your loss, Chief Nation."

"Step down from your great white horse."

"Thank you," said Jon, as he jumped to the ground. "I found him shot in the chest, about five miles north of the Nolichucky River. He was shot by mountain persons."

"I know this too. He alive when you see him."

"Yes, but he had lost a lot of blood. We kept him alive for four days, and he told us much about you. He was very proud of his father."

"I am proud of Son of Sun," said the chief. "I must send son to final place of rest. You wait here?"

"Do you want me to stay?"

"Yes. We must talk. You rest in house. I will send food and happy water."

Inside the log house, Jon noted the luxury. The floor was carpeted, with elaborate furniture and décor. Jon was jolted again, when he saw that the woman bringing food was not Cherokee. She was black. The food was a kettle of wild game stew, and the black servant dished it into a bone china bowl with silver utensils. *Wow*, Jon thought.

"Is there anything else I may do for you?" she asked, in better English than Jon could speak.

"Who are you, and why are you here?"

"I am Winnie, house servant for Chief Nation."

"Did the chief name you Winnie?"

"Yes. He thinks that I bring him good luck."

"I once knew a man who gave his servants unusual names. Most of the time, the names fit!"

"Mine doesn't fit."

"Why do you say that?"

"Because my master lost his beautiful home."

"Yes, I heard about that."

"He has hopes of getting it back, but there is really no hope. His land has been sold to whites."

"This stew is delicious, Winnie. Did you make it?"

"Yes, thank you. I'm glad you like it, Jon."

Drums started beating loudly, and sounds of women screeching to the beat filled the room.

"This is a hiding place, isn't it?"

"Yes, it is. Why do you ask, Jon?"

"Those drums can probably be heard all the way to Salem."

"Yes, you're right," laughed Winnie, "but this is a very special occasion."

"A very *sober* occasion."

"To you, that would mean silence and solitude, but the Cherokee feel each happening has a reason, a meaning."

"So they celebrate a death?"

"No, they are awakening the heavens, preparing them to welcome a new being," answered Winnie.

"What will Chief Nation do about the death?"

"I think he would like to fight the mountain persons. That is what the Cherokee would have done in the past, but now they are farmers with no weapons."

"They have one great weapon."

"And what would that be, righteousness?"

"You call it slow water."

The drums were still beating when Chief Ustanali Nation returned. Winnie quickly left, and the chief lit a pipe and sat in a finely stuffed chair.

"I am very sorry for what happened to your son."

"I wish for revenge, but we could not win a battle. Many my people would die."

"Do these mountain people live in a village?"

"Some live on farms close to river, but most live in small village, guarded."

"Where is this village, Chief?"

"On Cherokee land, by river Nolichucky."

"I crossed the Nolichucky yesterday."

"I know that. Village of mountain persons west and south of place where you cross."

"You know where I crossed?"

"Yes, by very old farms."

"What happened with those old farms?"

"They on Cherokee land. Whites afraid of Cherokee then, and flee to Watauga. That over sixty winters ago. Cherokee warriors then, like Seminole."

"Like Seminole?"

"Yes. They fight against forced move to west."

"And you want to fight against mountain people."

"Yes, but they have guns."

"And you have slow water."

"Slow water? How slow water help?"

"By burning them out of homes, Chief."

"Burn mountain persons from homes," said a thoughtful chief, with a broad smile.

"How many people live in village?"

The chief motioned for Jon to come outside, where he grabbed a stick and made an egg-shaped circle in the dirt.

"Village long circle. River on end, houses on both sides. Church and stores in middle. Maybe twenty homes."

"Hmm, about fifty or sixty people."

"They kidnap two Cherokee women, Laurel and now my Princess Etowah."

"Pure as Rushing Waters."

"Yes, Jon, and Sweet Blossoms of Laurel."

"What are these things here outside the village?"

"They . . . how you say? . . . Outhouses. Some say they use person and horse piles in field."

"Where do they keep the horses?"

"They have barns on sides."

"Good. We can take their horses right off."

"You help Cherokee fight?"

"I don't know. I will ask my men when I get back to my wagons," said Jon, as they walked back in the house.

"How many men? How many rifles?"

"Four men . . . five rifles."

"You help, Ustanali very grateful, Jon Hamilton."

"Are there trees around the village?"

"Not sure, maybe some with no leaves."

"You must find these things out before you attack."

"What we find out, Jon Hamilton?"

"Where there are trees, how many buildings, how many men, how many guards, and where they guard."

"I find these things out. You help?"

"I will try to help you, Chief. I will talk to my men just as soon as I get back to my people."

"Thank you, Jon. You have more questions?"

"Hmm . . . Yes, where is the happy water?"

"You did not get happy water?" The chief clapped his hands, and almost immediately a head poked in the door. "Bring happy water!"

Two, maybe three minutes, and the Cherokee had a large leather pouch that looked a lot like a large gun powder pouch, and cups. The chief poured two cups full of liquid. Jon tasted his. It had a familiar taste.

"This tastes a lot like spruce beer."

"You stay here this night, Jon Hamilton. We empty pouch, get drunk. Maybe get happy."

The "happy water" did just that. Before he knew what hit him, Jon hit the floor and was out like a light. He wasn't sure, but he thought he saw the chief and a naked female together before the lights went out.

Monday, November 23

Something was wrong! He felt crowded. The air was filled with smoke, and he needed to cough. Something started crackling. Was he by a campfire? His head was throbbing. What was happening to him? He tried to turn over in his sleep but couldn't. He was up against something. He reached out to feel . . . soft, warm. Suddenly, his eyes opened wide. He had a hold of a breast! She was in Eve's togs. He felt himself . . . in Adam's togs. His eyes were finally focusing. He was under a blanket with Winnie. How did this happen? "My god, what did I . . ."

"Just in time for breakfast, Jon Hamilton. How long it been since you have hot cakes, real pork loins, and hot, black coffee?"

"Let me see," his mind wasn't clear. "Two months, two weeks, two days . . . Two . . . two . . . two."

"Oh, damn," said the chief. "I burn them. How long since you have *black* pork loins?"

"Two, two hours . . ., two . . . minutes?"

The chief had two Cherokee women helping him at the stove. "You come have breakfast, Jon Hamilton."

"I can't, Chief. I have no clothes."

"Where you put clothes?"

"I don't remember anything about . . ."

"They are here, beside me, with mine." It was Winnie. She was awake!

"Put on clothes, Jon Hamilton."

"Would you hand them to me, please?" Jon asked Winnie sheepishly.

It was awkward trying to grab his togs from Winnie and still remain covered under the blanket.

"He, he, he . . . Be careful you don't get wrong clothes, Jon Hamilton," Winnie laughed.

As Jon attempted to get his feet into his Kentucky jeans, Winnie threw back the blanket and got up to get dressed, a la natural.

"He, he. You look pale, Jon Hamilton. You need sun, make dark skin like Winnie. He, he, he."

The Cherokee women, Chief Nation, and even Winnie were all laughing, so Jon started laughing with them as he continued dressing. He scooted over to finish dressing beside Winnie.

"Did . . . did we do anything last night, Winnie?"

"No, you were too drunk."

Jon felt a sense of relief equaling his sense of guilt.

"We can do something tonight, if you wish."

"Thank you, Winnie, but I'm married."

"You women go now. Leave Jon Hamilton and Ustanali. We eat and talk," said the chief. "What you think, Jon Hamilton? Ustanali has three wives and one house servant, Winnie."

"The chief is rich."

"Ustanali don't feel rich, lose Son of Sun, home, and farm in Georgia. Three nights, and Ustanali have answers to your questions, Jon Hamilton, and plenty slow water."

"Do you have any weapons, Chief?"

"Many arrows and bows and knives."

"How about guns?"

"Cherokee farmers. Had guns taken by Georgia whites. Maybe have two guns."

"Pick two Cherokee and have them practice shooting their rifles. I have some powder for you. Have the rest practice shooting bow and arrows, both men and women. Have two practice shooting arrows that are on fire, at long-distance targets."

"This, Ustanali do also in three days, but need help from Jon Hamilton."

"Okay, Chief. I will help you, and bring three more men to help."

"Thank you, Jon Hamilton. Ustanali very grateful."

"I must go back to my wagons now."

"It take you two days to wagons, and two days back. Just right for Ustanali."

"But I will need to find a place for food and shelter for my women."

"Still just right, Jon Hamilton. Five days just right before fight with mountain persons."

"I will try to be back in five days, Chief."

"Ustanali go in morning for Son of Sun for four days. On day five, Ustanali call Council of War."

"How long will that take?" asked Jon.

"War party all here. Council very short. We move down to Nolichucky on day five, and camp west of old farms where river turns south."

"How far is that from the mountain people, Chief?"

"About half day past farms to village."

"Good. We will meet you at your camp, and make our final plans there."

"Yes, Jon Hamilton. We will make camp there, wait for you. Ustanali Nation very grateful."

"Goodbye, Chief. Goodbye, Winnie."

"Until day five. Ustanali send Elizah Sand with you to Nolichucky. How much you want for great white horse you ride?"

"Not for sale, Chief. Corker is a special wedding present from my father-in-law."

"He pull wagon by himself."

"Yes. He was, but we lost a wagon coming over the Blue Ridge Mountains."

"You help Ustanali, you get wagon."

"Thank you, Chief. See you in five days."

Monday, November 23

A quiet, despondent camp watched the sun break over the Blues that Monday morning. Mose was moving about early, tending campfire. There were no horses to tend. There was only one woman, his beloved wife Ella, who was making breakfast. He missed the work, the sounds of laughter, and the constant chatter and complaints of Liz and Sissy. He missed Buelah, who he now considered his daughter. At least they hadn't taken Ella and Chipper, who he thought of as his son. Mose had a constant headache all night and morning. As he felt the wrap around his head and the large welts on his head and body, Mose was thankful that he was even alive.

"You's wakes up Davy an' Chips, Daddy. I's has breakfass ready," said Ella.

"I's thinks dey awake already, but I's look."

"What we's do, Daddy? I misses dem so."

"We's waits, Mamas. Charles an' Jon be's here soon."

"Yes, Daddy. Deys knows what to do."

"Where you goes, Daddy?"

"I's goes find wata. Be's back soon."

"Orites. Be's careful."

Ella was worried, being there alone with just her ten-year-old son. What if those demons reappeared? Then she thought about what they would want that they hadn't already taken. "Us old niggers and a young boy! They would hardly come back for that," she said to herself. Ella started picking up the breakfast remains, when she heard someone approaching.

"Where is everybody?" asked Charles, jumping down off Pasha.

"Dey's all gones," cried Ella.

"Gone? Gone where, Ella?"

"Bad mens comes an' takes Sissy an' Liz, an' Buelah an' horses."

"Why didn't someone go after them?"

"With what?" asked a quiet Dave, awake from a short, early-morning nap. "They took the horses and guns, along with the women."

"Did Mose go after them?"

"Nosa," answered Ella. "Daddy gets wata."

"Well, that will make three of us. How many were there and which way did they go?"

"They go's dat ways, Charles." Ella pointed south.

"There were six of them, Chuck, and they took the horses and our guns. It would be barmy to follow them."

"Well, we can't just sit here and do nothing, Dave. They have our Liz!"

"We best sit and wait for Jon, brother."

"How long will that be?"

"He thought four days. He should be back tomorrow."

"Then. We'll wait until tomorrow."

"Comes has some breakfass. It's gets cold," said Ella.

"I found a good place to camp along the Watauga River, close to Elizabethton and the Stones," said Charles.

"Elizabethton! We can't go there without Elizabeth."

"I'm sorry, David. I wasn't thinking when I said that."

"It's alright, brother. I miss her, is all."

"So do I. I should have called the town by its old name, Sycamore Shoals."

"Wha' be dem Stones, Charles?" asked Mose, who had just returned to camp with water.

"They're a nice family that will help us."

"Will they help raise an army?" asked Dave.

"No, but maybe we should go there now, and wait for Jon there. I think they will give us a couple of horses and guns."

"We's waits fo' Jon," said Mose.

"We will need to find a place for Ella and the boy anyway, and Jon mentioned about us waiting there."

"We's waits here!" repeated Mose.

"How much of a walk is it?" asked Dave.

"About six or seven miles, I guess."

"I think we should wait, brother."

"Okay. I'll wait until tomorrow. If he's not here by midday, I go back to Eliz . . . I mean Sycamore Shoals, and get things we'll need to get Liz back."

"And Maggie and Buelah," added Dave.

"Yes, and pay them back for the trouble."

"Hot dang! I'm ready to kill me some thieves!"

The rest of the day, through lunch and supper, the small group rested, cleaned their two rifles, one of Charles's and the favorite one of Mose, and moped about the camp. As daylight fell, Mose got out his harmonica and tried to cheer up the group, to no avail. Finally, everyone shuffled off to bed.

Tuesday, November 24

Sometime during the night, it started to rain. Jon had made his camp by the Nolichucky, and now woke up getting drenched. It was still dark as he grabbed his belongings, found Corker, and crossed the river. He spotted the old farm cabin and entered after he found an evergreen to shelter Corker.

The cabin leaked almost like the outside, but Jon found a dry corner and bundled back up in his wet blanket. He couldn't sleep, just doze. When daylight came, he left early, heading north. Jon thought perhaps he could get some shuteye at his camp before his men started back to join up with Ustanali.

It was an hour or so past midmorning, sloshing along in a steady rain, when he spotted the place where he thought he had found the Cherokee John Nation. Something was wrong. The wagons had to be close, but he heard nothing. *Maybe they're all resting under canvas*, he thought. Then Jon spotted the wagons, about a mile further north, where the tracks north crossed the east-west tracks. Strange, no activity. Mose had stretched the extra canvas, and Jon saw him, Ella, and Chipper, he thought, close to the fire, under the tarp. They didn't seem to hear him as he neared the camp.

"Hello, Mose, Ella." They turned and walked into the rain, toward Jon.

"We's glad you's back, Jon," said Mose.

"Where is everyone?"

"They's all be's kidnap, Jon," answered Ella.

"Kidnapped? By who? When?"

"Day afo' yesterday," said Mose.

"By who?" asked Jon, as he pushed them back under the tarp.

"By bad mens. They takes Buelah an' Sissy, Liz an' horses," answered Ella.

"It was those damn mountain people," said Charles, who had left his tarp-covered wagon to join them.

"And those dirty bastards took the women?" asked Jon.

"Yassa, Jon, dey takes dem, an' shoots me," said Mose.

"Are you alright, Mose?"

"Yassa. Dey leaves cut ova ear. See, Jon?"

"It's a channel all along your head, Mose."

"Yassa. I's gets back at dem, Jon."

"I was about to take Pasha and get help. There is . . . a town, and friends at the Watauga," said Charles.

"You found Sycamore Shoals?"

"Yes, but it has a different name now."

"What name, Charles?"

Charles looked around and noted that Dave was still under the tarp in their wagon, so he said softly, "Elizabethton."

"Then I think we should go there now," said Jon. "Maybe we can find help there to get our women back."

"Right now, in this rain?"

"Yes. Do we have our guns and some powder left?"

"Dey take two guns," said Mose.

"But we still have two, and your Hawken, and I met a family named Stone who I know will help," said Charles.

"Good. Mose, can you hook up Corker to the Chasney wagon, so we can head for the Watauga?"

"Sho 'nuff, Jon."

"In this rain?" asked Charles again.

"Right. We have three days to get supplies and meet the Cherokee at the Nolichucky."

"Dem Cherokee help us, Jon?" asked Mose.

"We help each other, Mose. When the crapheads killed John Nation, they took his wife, a princess. And now they've taken our women as well."

"And now we join forces and kill them bastards. Dave will be happy to hear this," said Charles. "I'll help you hitch up Corker, Mose."

"Wha's we do wit dem wagon, Jon?" asked Ella.

"We take only what we need, and leave the wagon and trailer."

"Orites, Jon. I's gets Chips an' blankets."

"Charles, saddle up Pasha and go ahead and tell those people we're coming."

"Right, Jon. I'm on my way."

"Ask them if we can borrow a couple horses, guns, and some powder."

"Will do, Jon. See you there," said Charles, as he saddled Pasha, grabbed his raincoat and hat, and left.

"Dis be's awful heavy load fo' Corka, Jon."

"I know, Ella. Corker's the only horse that can handle it, I think.

"Yas, Corka strong horse."

"Let's get everyone in the wagon and under the tarp."

As they were climbing aboard the Chasney wagon, Jon searched his own wagon for a small pouch in a hidden spot. He found it, and tied it to his waist under his jeans.

Corker had little trouble pulling the Chasney wagon in the steady rain the nine miles to the Stone farm. It was a little past noon, Jon guessed, when they pulled up to the farm along the Watauga River.

"This is our leader, Jon Hamilton," said Charles.

"Hello, Jon. Welcome to our home. My name is Jess Stone, and this is my wife, Victoria."

"Very glad to meet you. Charles said that you were fine people and would help us."

"Come in out of the rain. We are so sorry to hear about your women," said Victoria Stone.

"Yes, come in and get dried out. You must be hungry."

"Thank you again, Mister Stone," said Charles. "Can you help us with horses and a gun?"

"I can do better than that," said Jess. "I'll help you get your women and horses back."

"Great! These are my partners, Mose and Ella, and her son Chipper, and Charles's brother Dave."

"Are you free Negroes?" asked Victoria.

"Yassum, we is," said Ella.

"Well, welcome to our farm."

"Thank you, missus. We's lose my Buelah too."

"We'll get them back. My next-door neighbor will help too, but first you need to get into some dry clothes and eat a hot meal," said Jess. "Do we have anything to fit this giant, Vic?"

"Not unless he can wear the garb I made for the scarecrow. We can just wrap him in a blanket, and I'll dry his things out by the fire," said Victoria.

"He looks like he can just about wipe out them hillbillies on his own! Vic, you take . . . is it Mose? And Ella to the stockroom and get their clothes, and I'll find these three some dry clothes," said Jess.

"Alright, Jessie, then I got some good, hot meat stew for y'all."

"As soon as y'all finish eating, I can head over to Hugh's place and get him, so we can be off after them damned skunk-asses that took your women," said Jess.

"Well, we can't go after them just yet, Mister Stone."

"Why the hell not? They got your women," said Jess.

"We are going to meet up with some Indians in a couple of days, Mister Stone, and attack them together," answered Charles.

"Indians? Cherokee Indians?"

"Yes, sir, Mister Stone. They killed the chief's son and kidnapped a princess too. We meet them in a couple days."

"Hmm . . . I didn't even know they were around here."

"There's a small band of them that escaped from Georgia and are living in the Smokies," said Jon.

"Escaped? From their own land?"

"Yes, sir. The Georgians took their lands illegally, and now want to force them to lands west of the Mississippi, where we're going."

"I thought y'all were headed for Kentucky."

"We are, but the Hamiltons are on their way to Arkansas," answered Charles. "We go through the Cumberland gap together."

"But not before we get our women back," said Jon.

"When do you meet the Cherokee?"

"In five days, at the Nolichucky."

"Five days from when?"

"From yesterday. Let's see, that's Friday," said Jon. "That gives us time to prepare."

"Well, I got guns and horses," said Jess.

"What about powder and rope?"

"Some powder, maybe not enough, but Hugh would have some."

"Hugh?" asked Dave.

"Yeah. My neighbor. He'll want to come along."

"We's has ropes on dem wagons, Jon," said Mose.

"Oh yeah, we do. Tomorrow I'll go into Sycamore Shoals and pick up powder and anything else we'll need," said Jon.

"Ma, bring out some of our corn, so's we can rightly prepare for the comin' battle."

"Alright, Jessie. Good thing y'all have a couple days to sober up afterward," said Victoria.

"When you's gets dem clothes dries, we's go's sleep in dem barn," said Ella.

"We have an extra bed," said Jess.

"The barn will be great for us, thanks," answered Jon.

"Well, Then you, Charles, and your brother can use the bed."

"Now that we have that settled, Ma, bring the corn," said Jess.

With that, the group had some snorts of the sweetest and strongest corn whiskey that Jon had ever tasted. Mose brought out his harmonica, and each took turns swinging Victoria and Ella around. Mose and Ella put most of the drunks to bed.

Tuesday, November 24

It was midmorning Tuesday, when church bells began ringing. Slowly, the plaza in front filled with bodies, some still in their nether garments. Despite the steady rain, there was an air of excitement.

"What is the ringin' abouten, Granville?"

"I heard tell that Aden an' them other men persons are a-comin'."

"I should oughta be a-getting' me a wife then."

"If'n they brought any, it nigh be your turn, Hummer."

"Yeah, but CT be a-takin' first choice."

"I figured he done took up that princess," said Granville.

"Well, we can should wait in the church house."

"If'n we don't, we'll be a-drenched."

Cheers broke out, as some weary riders on horseback sauntered onto the plaza. The men had three women with them, and they were soaked. At the lead was Aden, with his big hat pulled down over his ears, followed by Cole, then the women, one with CT, a red-haired female person with Zake, and a young black female with Zeb. Winifred brought up the rear. The women were pulled off the horses, kicking and hollering, and the people noted that they had their hands tied with ropes, and the redhead was swollen at the belly. They were led into the church.

"Eddie, you an' Bixie go out ta storehouse, an' brang some blankets and clothes fer the women folk."

"Good idee, Aden, will fetch 'em."

"I'd rather wear what I got on, soaked and all," said Liz.

"Hush up, woman! Ye been a-gibberin' for two days."

"When our men get here, you're all going to die," said Maggie.

"Shut up! You shouldn't talk about death."

"Looks like Humma gets his choice," said a voice.

"I'll be a-takin' the feisty doney gal for meself," said CT.

"No, CT, it ain't right fer you to have two females, when thar's some that ain't got none."

"Yeah, what about that, Aden? CT shouldn't oughta gets two female persons when some got none."

"I'm a-deservin' two, ain't I, Aden?" said Long Beard, now known as CT.

"Ye kin one er the other, CT," answered Aden.

"Well, this un's a she-panther," said CT. "Reckin' I'll be a takin' me a princess then."

"Right fair o' ye, CT. Thar be a-more-some comin' I reckin', an' we'll all be a-havin' two."

"Then you's gets ta pick one-a these 'uns, Hummer."

"Well, I might should oughta take that nigger woman," said Hummer.

"Yeah, Hummer. She'd produce lotsa generations."

"Took the redhair, Hummer. She's awready started a new generation." This teasing statement was met with a lot of laughter.

"One-a ta-other, Hummer," said Aden.

"Well, I allow ta take me the black-haired feisty female."

"Yeah, you do that, Hummer, and I'll have your hummer broke off at the root!" sneered Liz.

"I jist 'bout had me 'nough a-yer sass," said Aden.

"Then untie us, and we'll leave," said Maggie.

"Imagine that. She wans ta leave," said a voice in the crowd.

"You wan 'er, Hiram?"

"Rekin' I do, watermelon seeds an' all," said Hiram.

"At be a-leavin' that nigger."

"Lookit at plush black body. She throw lotsa generations."

"Ye wan' her, Zeb? Ye brung her," said Aden.

"Yep, I wan 'er. We make lotsa leg biters."

Wednesday, November 25

Wednesday was a day to relax, but who could relax with the women missing? So Jon's men busied themselves preparing for the showdown with the "Mountain Persons." Jess Stone had three flintlocks, but not much powder, so Jon rode Corker into Elizabethton. It was a good-sized town, close to the size of Wilkesboro. Jon noticed the road lead northwest, with a sign that read *Kingsport, thirty miles.* He thought that must be close to Fort Patrick Henry, where he was headed. With a good road like that, he should be able to make Kingsport in a day, he thought, but not without his horses and women. Jon found a busy little gun shop, and purchased two ten-pound barrels of gunpowder, some flints, balls, and even found some caps for his Hawken. He decided he liked this busy town set on the Watauga River.

"Haven't seen you around before. Live around here?" asked the shop owner.

"No, sir. I'm just passing through," answered Jon.

"Don't get many passers-through around here off the beaten trails. From where did you come?"

"From Salem, North Carolina."

"Salem! You are off the beaten trail. Come down from Virginia?"

"No, sir. I came over the Blues."

"The hell! Musta been tough, with all the rains. Right up Boone Gap, hey?"

"I couldn't find Boone Gap."

"The hell! A natural draw, straight up through the ridge. Comes out right at the head of this river."

Jon wondered if he was talking about the draw Maggie wanted to take at the top of the long hill. He hoped not, he thought. "We did see a draw, but didn't think our wagons and horses could make it up through it."

"The hell! Yep, that was it, where Boony has been seen a lot."

"Boony?" Jon asked innocently.

"Big, hairy creature, like a gorilla. The gap has a few rough spots, but mostly easy goin' for a wagon."

"I sure didn't see anything like that."

"About three days from the Yadkin River to here, through the gap," said the storekeeper.

"The hell!"

The men had three wonderful meals that day, thanks to Victoria Stone, but they had trouble eating from thinking of the women, and what they might be forced to do. In the evening, the Butler brothers appeared, Hugh and Henry, all ready for the battle, with sleeping gear and three rifles.

"Sure glad to meet you, Hugh and Hank. Thanks ever so much for your help," said Jon, shaking hands.

"Wouldn'ta missed it fer the world," said Hugh. "Think they done took our prize bull about a year ago."

"If they done it, they're a-payin' dearly," said Hank.

"When and if I see 'Govner,' four thieves are a-gettin' it," said Hugh, pointing to his rifle.

"What kind of gun is that?" asked Dave.

"I've never seen anything like it," added Charles.

"It is an Ellees Jennings flintlock," answered Hugh.

"And it shoots out four shots in a row," said Hank.

"Where did you get a gun like that?" asked Jon.

"Our family expressed it to us from upstate New York."

"And Hugh can shoot out a duck's eyes with it," exclaimed Jess, "in flight!"

"That there's a pretty nice gun y'all got there, Jon," said Hugh.

"Yeah, thanks. It's a converted Hawken."

"Let's see who can get the most of them bastards on Friday."

"I'm not aimin' to kill them all, Dave. I just want to teach them a lesson and get our women back."

"'Un dem horses too, Jon," added Mose.

"I agree with Jon, Davy. We don't want to be murderers like they are, just make sure they don't ever do it again," said Charles.

"You might have trouble convincin' Mose of that. They tried to kill him. Or that Cherokee chief, since they killed his son."

"Or my brother Hugh, if they be havin' Govner," added Hank.

"I's don' wans to kill, Jon, jus' gets my Buelah back."

"Good, Mose. That's what we're going to do."

"Well, it be's a good day's drive to the Nolichucky, where we meet them Cherokee. I suggest we get some sleep," said Jess.

Thursday, November 26

Not much sleep overnight, but when Jon woke, he noticed through the open barn window that the rain had stopped. It was just getting light, and the sky was filled with heavy dark clouds. Mose and Ella had been awake for a spell. Mose had three horses saddled, and a matched team of dark horses hitched to a two-seat light wagon with a canvas canopy. The bed behind the seats had blankets, guns, rope, and the two powder kegs that Jon had purchased in Elizabethton.

"Mamy an' Missus Stone has breakfass ready," said Mose.

"Today's the big day, Mose. Are you ready?"

"Yes, I's ready, Jon. I's gets Chasneys up."

"Good. I think I can smell the bacon clear out here," said Jon. "That sure is a nifty-looking wagon."

"They call it a carryall," said Charles, buttoning his jeans.

"Why ain't we takin' our own wagon, Chuck?" asked Dave.

"I'm not sure, Davy. I guess it's 'cause this has two seats."

"It be dem one Mista Stone wans hitched," answered Mose.

"Well, let's get us some of that food I smell," said Jon.

What a breakfast! Hot cakes with sweet syrup, real chicken eggs over chopped and fried potatoes, milk, coffee, and bread! Wow! The women also had a large bag of food to take along. Everyone ate their fill.

"This is about the best breakfast I ever ate," said Dave.

"Yes, thank ye a lot, Victoria," said Hugh.

"Ella here helped a lot. Too bad your womenfolk ain't here to enjoy it too," said Victoria.

"We are about to correct that, Missus Stone," said Jon.

"Yes, we are," said Jess. "Are y'all the leader, Jon?"

"He is," said Charles. "We all voted for him on the trail."

"That be good enough for us, right, Hugh?"

"Sho 'nuff is, Jess. We're ready, Jon, anytime y'all are."

"Those women will want some fresh clothes when you rescue them," said Victoria. "Let me see what I can—"

"Don't bother, Missus Stone. The women all have clothes in our other wagon. We can grab some on the way, right, Jon?"

"Right, Chuck. I have just the one to take to Maggie."

"Alright then, but take this here reticule to carry them in."

"Brings Sissy an' Buelah an' Liz home, Daddy," said Ella. "I's be waitin'."

"Let's do it, gang. Let's get crackin'."

"Good luck. See y'all back here," said Victoria.

The carryall bed was full of provisions, Mose and Jess were in the front bench, the Butler brothers were on the bench behind, and it was off to the races. The Chasney brothers rode horses borrowed from Jess Stone, and Jon was astride Pasha. Pasha was not so white and beautiful now, but spirited. The eight or so miles back to the covered wagon was made in a breeze. The men and horses rested there and gathered dresses and other items they felt the rescued women would need.

"We should get some clothes for the princess too, Jon."

"Oh, that's right, Chuck. And Chief Ustanali said they kidnapped another of his women too."

"Usta-who?" asked Jess.

"The chief's name is Ustanali Nation."

"So they done took two of his women too, huh?" asked Hugh.

"Yep, and maybe one other that the chief said turned up missing sometime ago."

"Maybe we pick up a woman for you, Hank."

"Oh sure, brother, that's just what I need, a warmin' squaw!"

"Ya need somethin'. I was dodgin' yer advances all night!"

"I'm hungry," said Dave. "Let's get something to eat."

"You just had a huge breakfast, brother. Ya can't be hungry!"

"Here, take a dodger, Dave, and make do with that. We have to make sure that bag of food lasts for two or three meals."

"I'll try, Jon. It's just that the bag smells *so* good!"

"By the way, where do we spend the night?" asked Jess.

"I told the chief we would meet west of the old abandoned farms, where the Nolichucky turns south."

"Then we wouldn't a needed to leave the Stones' place till tomorrow," said Hugh.

"I guess not. I'm sorry, men. Guess I'm just too anxious to get them women back."

"Well, so are we, Jon, so's it be alright," said Jess. "But if'n yer meetin' them Injuns west of those old homesteads, then there's no need ta go there yet."

"But we might get rained on. We've been lucky so far today," said Charles.

"Ha! Them thar old log houses don't have much for roofs anyhow," said Jesse. "Right, Jon?"

"That's true. Maybe we should just head southwest to where we're meeting the Cherokee."

"Sounds like that would save some time," said Dave.

"We have lotsa time, and thar would be better feed for them horses around the homesteads," said Jess.

"Okay, that settles it. We spend the night at the farms."

"What do we do in the meantime? It only be ten or eleven miles more to the Nolichucky," said Hugh.

"There be good fishin' on that Nolichucky, and there's lotsa boomers," said Hank.

"What are boomers?" asked Charles.

"Red squirrels," answered Jess.

"That's true. I shot several squirrels and a cottontail there, but we don't have any poles for fishing."

"No bother about that. We can put Hank midstream, an' the fish jump right up on the banks!" said Hugh.

"Very funny! I can make us some poles," said Hank.

Hugh seemed to enjoy making fun of his younger brother Hank, who wasn't too happy about the inference of his looks. He wasn't what one would call handsome, thought Jon, as the men saddled up and again headed south.

Shortly after midday, it started raining again. The canopy helped some, but the passengers were still getting wet. They were thankful that Mose had thought to bring the extra tarp from the covered wagon. They stopped and threw a tarp over the canopy so that the carryall was completely covered. Jon and the Chasney brothers wrapped themselves in blankets, and the procession continued south. They were even more thankful for Mose and the tarp when they reached the old log farmhouse Jon had stayed in. They stretched the tarp over the leaky roof, giving them refuge from the rain. There was lots of grass for the animals, and the men stretched ropes inside the cabin to hang wet blankets and clothes. Jon judged it to be late afternoon. The men dug into some great beef dodgers.

"How old ya be, Jon, if ya don't mind my askin'," asked Jesse.

"Twenty and a half, why?"

"This be the first time I ever been bossed by a young'un."

"I don't mean to be bossy."

"Oh, you ain't bossy, Jon. Yer a leader."

"My brother Hank's a contrary leader," said Hugh.

"Thar he goes again," sighed Hank.

"What do you mean, contrary leader?" asked Dave.

"Right now we'd be attackin' them Injuns!" This statement was followed by laughter.

Jon wanted to change the subject and said, "I wonder if that old stone fireplace still works."

"Can't do no more'n burn this place down," said Jess.

"And it sure is a pretty place!" smiled Jon.

"I's go's an' gets wood," said Mose.

"I'll go with you, Mose," said Charles.

"Did y'all say you were headed to Arkansas?"

"Yes."

"What's in Arkansas?" asked Hugh.

"Good, rich bottomland for the taking."

"Where'd y'all heard that?" asked Jess.

"I saw it in a paper in Salem."

"An' yer headed for Kentucky."

"Yes, sir. We got some land waitin' on the Kentucky River," said Dave.

"Ya know, we shore could use some good ole people like'n y'all around here. I'll bet you could pick up some of this here land fer little or nothin'," said Jess. "We could help y'all get started."

"Well, thanks, Mister Stone, but I have a promise with my wife to go to Arkansas."

"And we got family already in Kentuck," said Dave.

"Well, think about it afore ya go a-traipsin' off over more mountains an' rivers. You'd be welcome here."

"Thanks. You all lived here all your lives?"

"Yep. My grandpappy settled our land over sixty-odd years ago, from Pennsylvania," said Jess. "We got kinfolk all 'round."

"My brother and I come from Albany 'bout twelve years ago. Paid a hundred for ova two-hundred acres, cleared," said Hugh.

"Whar did ya pick up them niggers?" asked Hank.

Jon thought about getting after Hank, but Jess grabbed his arm to settle him back down. "These are free Negroes, sir. They come from a big plantation by the Yadkin where I was an overseer, but now they're my partners, going with me to Arkansas."

"Didn't mean to insult y'all. Sorry. I'd rather have that big man on my side."

"Best keep yer mouth shut, brother. That black man cold whip alla us at once!" said Hugh.

As if on cue, Mose entered the cabin with a huge armload of branches and some moss to start a fire. It took some doing, but the men finally had a hot fire. Now warm, the men settled in to tell jokes and tall tales, and drink Jess's sweet corn juice. Jess told about his grandpappy fighting the British at cowpens and Kings Mountain, and down the Catawba and Broad rivers. "Chased 'em right outta them mountains, down into Carolina." Jon was coerced into telling about the battle of Georgetown and his escape from the South Carolina Pattyrollers. Later, Mose brought out his harmonica, and Hank did a jig. The cabin started filling with smoke from the fireplace, so Jess went outside and knocked a hole in the stone chimney. Smoke then poured out of that hole, instead of the room inside. The whisky finally gone, the men stretched out by the fire and slept.

Friday, November 27

Once again, the rains had stopped very early, leaving dark ominous clouds. Mose had been up early, tending the horses and stoking the fire back up. Now he mixed up some batter to make hotcakes. The men were stirring.

"Don't y'all make much hotcakes, Mose," said Hugh.

"Why not?" asked Dave.

"'Cause Hank's a-goin' ta show us how to fish with no pole nor hooks!" The men laughed at this.

"I'll bet Mose can do it," said Dave.

"His hand would have to be quicker than the eye," said Jess.

"Mose here is amazing. I believe he can find solutions to any problem," said Charles.

"Well, Mose, will ya help me prove ta my brother that we kin catch fish without no pole?" asked Hank.

"Does we's have time, Jon?"

"Sure, Mose. We only have a few miles to go to the place we meet the Cherokee."

"Orites. I helps ya, Hanks. Does you's have dem tools?"

"What did he say?" asked Hank.

"Do you have any tools in your wagon?"

"Oh, sho 'nuff we do, in a box under the front bench. I'll be a-gettin' 'em fer ya."

Mose and Hank went to work. Mose found a file in the toolbox, and began searching the banks of the Nolichucky. Mose drew the attention and interest of the others. He picked up some small bones, probably from squirrels that Jon had shot, and began filing them into hooks with a "knob" on top to attach a string, which they didn't have. Next, Mose cut a four- or five-foot length of rope off the end of his roll of rope, and began taking it apart so he had several strands of thin rope. He then attached one end of a strand to the squirrel bone he had filed, thus hook and line.

"You's goes an' find worms in ground by horses," Mose directed Hank. "I's goes an' makes poles."

"Amazing!" exclaimed Hugh. "I'd a-never thought he'd a-done it!"

"He's what I call a genius," answered Jon.

Mose broke a couple branches off a tree and attached the hooked lines to each pole. Hank dug up some fat worms, and the two of them went fishing, to the amazement of the others.

"The laugh's on y'all, brother!" shouted Hank.

"Guess it be at that," answered Hugh.

"Look, there are tons-o fish in that river!" exclaimed Dave.

"Sets hook hards, Hank, an' toss fishes on banks."

"Okay, Mose. Get ta guttin' them trout, brother!"

In near record time, Mose and Hank had a pile of fish slung up on the bank, and the others had them cleaned. Hotcakes and fish were the breakfast menu, and the men filled themselves "almost to glory."

Soon it was time to pack up and move west along the Nolichucky. They found a good place to cross the river, and soon sighted small groups of Indians, also heading west. They waved to each other.

"They look meaner'n all get out," said Hugh.

"I ain't ne'er seen 'em in war paint afore," said Jess.

Jon spotted Elizah Sands in a small group of three warriors, and rode Pasha over to greet him.

"Jon bring many white warriors," said Elizah.

"Yes, there are seven of us ready for action."

"We ready too, Jon Hamilton."

"Have you scouted the village?"

"Yes, I scout four days in hiding."

"Do they know we're coming?"

"Don't think so, Jon Hamilton. Guard in tower during day, when not rain."

"Good. We'll catch them by surprise."

"They have twenty-two houses and twenty-five men."

"How many women?"

"Seventeen women, thirteen young."

"Including our women?"

"Yes, I see Sweet Blossoms of Laurel, and young black woman, and three Cherokee women."

"Did you see my wife?"

"What she look like?"

"Tall, red hair, and with child."

"Yes, I see her, Jon Hamilton. She alright."

"Thank God."

More abandoned farms greeted the men on their way west. Soon the group had reached the spot where the Nolichucky made a sharp left turn, and they made camp. *It was about midday*, Jon thought. It was difficult to tell with the heavy, dark clouds overhead. If it rained again that night, Jon thought, they might be able to take the Mountain persons without firing a shot. He sat down close to the campfire and drew the layout in the dirt of the village he was about to attack. Elizah joined him.

"That good, like village," said Elizah.

"Where are the barns?"

"Barns outside of circle, where road to fields start."

"We can put two rifles in the barns then. Jess, will you take one of the barns, and Hank the other? With Hugh and his four shots in the church tower, we'll have good coverage."

"We have two good Cherokee with guns, Jon Hamilton."

"Are there trees outside the village, Elizah?"

"Yes. Many trees on west by river, and three trees together on east side to climb."

"Great, Elizah. We'll put one in a tree on each side."

"That will make full coverage, right?" asked Charles.

"Yes. Did you have two practice with fired arrows?"

"Yes. One is woman. That good, Jon Hamilton?"

"That's fine. How many warriors do you have?"

"We have thirteen man warriors and ten woman warriors."

"That is great, Elizah. We outnumber them."

All the Cherokee suddenly stood, and Jon saw why. The chief, Ustanali Nation, approached in full head gear and paint.

"Greetings, Chief Nation. These are my friends I brought along. This is Jess. This is Hugh and his brother Hank Butler. These are my traveling companions, Charles and Dave Chasney, and my partner, Mose. Men, this is the chief of the Smoky Mountain Cherokees, Ustanali Nation."

There were greetings all around the campfire.

"Greetings, Jon Hamilton, friend of Cherokee, and greetings to all white fighters. Ustanali very grateful."

"We have been planning our attack. We outnumber the enemy, Chief. With rain, we will surround the village of mountain persons, and win with few or no shots."

"That is good, Jon Hamilton. I bring my second son, Coosastan Nation, Son of Moon, and ten brave women, three my wives. Shoot better than Ustanali! This is Josiah Sands, brother of Elizah. Best hunter."

"Did you bring the slow water, Chief?"

"Yes. Bring six pots full to heat, and four brooms."

"You have good tree climbers and rope climbers, Chief?"

"Yes, Jon Hamilton, and good with bow and arrow."

"Then we attack at first light. By tomorrow, the mountain persons will be our prisoners."

"Ustanali like that talk, Jon Hamilton."

"Okay. We split into two groups. My group will attack from the west side, from the river. The chief will lead the other group, attacking from the east, after we have seized the farms, and take the farm people into the village. We will put prisoners in the church. Chief Nation, you will have two of my best men on your team, Mose and Charles?"

"That good, Jon Hamilton. You take my son on your team."

"Thank you, Chief. I will take the woman who shoots the fire arrow, and one warrior with gun."

"That be Taliwa, Pleasing to All Senses, and Nathan Hall."

"And you have the other shooter of fire arrows and gun warrior, Chief. We still have two extra guns."

"Wives all shoot guns good, Jon Hamilton."

"Great, Chief. We'll put one at the church, and one at the storehouse to guard from the ground."

"Let me see," said Charles. "Two guns in the barns, two in the trees, one in the tower, two in each of the groups, and two on the ground in the village. That's eleven guns."

"Righto, and they're all spaced out to cover all angles."

"I counted thirty people," said Jess, "with five in each group, four on each side by the fires and in two trees, five guarding the prisoners, and the three of us in the barns and tower. That don't leave much left."

"And we have two of the chief's wives with guns on the ground. That leaves two to run around and help where they're needed. Everyone has a job to do," answered Jon.

"I think maybe one guard in church should have a gun," said Hugh.

"Good idea. We'll put one of your wives in the church with one of the guns, Chief."

"Maybe both wives with guns in church, Jon Hamilton."

"Okay, Chief, that's better. Now let's spread out here and take positions, so we'll all know where to go."

Jon and Elizah drew the village to scale on the ground, with the barns, houses, church, outbuildings, and river all in their approximate location.

"Now, Jess and Hank are at the barns, and Hugh is in the tower. My team, Nathan and, is it Taliwa, are in the river, and the two warriors will tend fire and shoot arrows if needed. So, I have nine in the water that will slip past the village to the west on river side. Chief Nation, you should have nine in your group as well."

"That right, Jon Hamilton. I have nine."

"Then we have Jess, Hank, Hugh, five church guards, two ground guards—one of them your wife, Chief—and two extra on the ground to help where needed."

"Both my wives should be in the church, Jon Hamilton."

"That makes thirty, alright," said Jess, "but ya have four females guardin' the church."

"Yeah, maybe ya needs more men there, case some prisoners want ta fight back," said Hugh.

"Right you are, Hugh. Let's spread these women around here, by the fire, and put three warriors in the church, along with the chief's wives. Yo, that's better. Now, does everyone know their jobs? Any questions?"

"Who do the slow water brushes, Jon Hamilton?"

"Good question, Chief. The two extra men on the ground can help spread the slow water along with the church guards, before we take too many prisoners."

"Slow water needs to be heated," said the chief's son, Coosastan. "Spread better that way."

"So we each need to take three pots to our bonfires to heat. When we control the grounds, before we take many prisoners, each team will take two hot pots down to the guards. We must sneak them past the houses. Then anyone available spread the slow water on the sides of the church and storehouse, and the buildings in the middle."

"What about other two pots, Jon Hamilton?"

"When that is done, we will each take a pot with our group and quietly go from house to house and take prisoners to the church, one house at a time. If they resist, we use the slow water to burn their houses after we take the others."

"Good plan, Jon Hamilton. We ready."

"The first thing we all do together is take over the farms and take prisoners, so we have no enemy behind us."

"When dark comes, we take farms then surround village, all very quiet. At first light, two groups take houses, one at a time, north to south. Right, Jon Hamilton?"

"Right, Chief Nation. Everything is ready."

Mose broke open the gun powder keg and helped fill the powder bag of each gun holder. The raiding party of thirty men and women rested and chatted. A few even tried to sleep. As if in answer to prayers, it started to rain again in the evening. Everyone seemed to have blankets, and the three wives of Chief Nation kept their husband warm. At last it started getting dark, and with little fanfare, the militia moved southwest along the Nolichucky River in a light, steady rain toward the village of the mountain persons, about ten miles from the river bend. Their first encounter was a farm that was a little over halfway to their goal. All was dark, as Mose drove the carryall right to the door. The raiders quickly surrounded the log house, as Jon and the chief knocked on the door once, twice, and a third time.

"Who's thar a-knockin' at my door?"

"I'm lost, a-lookin' for Knoxville," answered Jon.

"Well, yer a long ways off. You'n too far off ta be a-tellin' the truth. Now gedaddle on outta here!"

"But I'm all wet . . . and hungry. Ken you's help me?"

"Ye kin use me barn ta dry yerself off."

"I'll pay ya fer some vittles."

There was a pause. "Oh, ah-ret. Stand back from da door."

"A-ret! I's a back in the rain!" yelled Jon.

The farmer cracked open the door just enough to see a huddled white man crouched in the rain. Just as the farmer started to open the door wider, he heard a noise at the back of his cabin. He turned his lantern back in that direction, and something grabbed the gun he held in his other hand. He spun back around and stood face-to-face with an Indian chief in war paint.

"Ahh . . . what ye want? I ain't got no money."

"We kidnap white farmer off Cherokee land."

"I'm jist aimin' to leave."

"You sure are, mister," said Jon. "Get a heavy coat and a hat and come with us."

"But it's a-night out there. I's be a-leavin' in the mornin'."

"You'll be a-leavin' right now or dyin'," mocked Jon.

"He has a mule in his barn, Jon!" shouted Charles.

"Good. Tie his hands and put him on it. Rope the mule to the carryall. We got another rifle, men."

The next farm, about a mile further, had lantern light in the window. The men surrounded the house, as a dog started barking from the inside. A face appeared in the window.

"What's these people's names, mister?" asked Jon, his Hawken aimed at the captured farmer.

"McDaniels. Jobe an' Ann."

"And your name?"

"Bill, ah . . . William Rush."

"Right. Keep quiet, and you'll live."

"Who's out there?" came a female voice.

"William Rush, Missus McDaniels," answered Jon.

"Oh, ye skeered me, William. Come in." To the dog, she ordered, "Quiet, Boomer."

Jon, Hank, and Dave rushed into the cabin, guns shouldered, followed by the chief and others. The woman, Ann, screamed.

"Drop that rifle or die!" shouted Dave.

"What do ye wan'?" asked the farmer, Jobe.

"We kidnap you off Cherokee lands," said Ustanali.

"Ah . . . we'll pays ye fer the land."

"Too late . . . you make good farm. We take back."

"They have a buggy and three drays, Jon," said Charles.

Just then, a baby started whining in another room, and the dog, Boomer, growled, as if to guard the child.

"Who you have in that room?" asked the Chief.

"A son, and a baby girl," answered Jobe McDaniels.

"Please don't harm them," begged a frightened Ann McDaniels.

"Can you keep them quiet?"

"Oh, yes. I might could even keep them asleep."

"Even in the rain?" asked Jon.

"Where ye a-takin' us?" asked Jobe.

"Where I come from, we don't answer a question with another question," mocked Jon.

"I promise to keep 'em quiet," said Ann.

"Hitch up their buggy and put them all in it. Rope it to the carryall too."

"Where we a-goin'?"

"Those are the last words any of you speak again until I tell you that you can talk. Hear?"

"Yes, sir," answered Ann.

Roped and "buggied," the McDaniels family were quiet as a mouse. The raiders collected two more guns, including an over-and-under twelve-gauge shotgun. Hank thought he would like to use it in the barn, so he gave his flint to a Cherokee.

The next farm was a couple miles closer to the village. Jon was sure they were close to it, so he rode about, telling all to stop all talk. The farm was dark and quiet, almost as if nobody was home. But smoke was billowing out of the chimney. Again, the house was surrounded and a group stepped to the door. Jon tried the latch, and the door started to open. He waited until rifles were ready before we swung the door open. Good thing he did, as the door made a big squeaking sound as it opened. This awakened the couple in bed, and the man started to jump up for his rifle on the wall.

"I wouldn't do that, were I you," said Hugh.

"What the hellfire . . .," the young man said.

"Shut up, an' get yer hands outta them covers so's I can see 'em," said Jess. "Who are ya?"

"We Cherokee come to take back our land," answered Ustanali.

"Ha! Ye's funnin'. They ain't no Cherokee aboutin' here."

"Setcha Egett! I are richer, an' I aim ta get back what I own, one way or nuther," said the chief sarcastically, amid chuckles, giggles, and laughter.

Jon shushed the men with a "Shh!" He turned to the chief and said, "That was good, Chief. You fit right in here."

"What all you'ns want anyways?"

"We want you and yer wife, and any other persons ya got here to come wit us," said Hugh.

"We ain't goin' nowhere nohow," said the man.

"Then ya dies right here in bed," said Jess.

"Ye shouldn't oughta come a-bargin' in here like this. We's civilized persons," said the young woman in bed.

"Then get yer hinders outta that bed, afore we pulls ye out!"

"Cain't, sir, we gots no clothes on."

"Don'cha thank we's seen naked persons afore?" asked Jess.

Two Cherokee women were watching through the window, as the man jumped out of bed. They giggled, and were shushed by others. The man then threw on some trousers and held a blanket over the bed so the lady could get up. The men still had a pretty good view, as she threw on a long cotton dress that made her look like a granny.

"Where youn's a-takin' us?" asked the man.

"Ret straight ta glory, if'n ye make a peep," answered Hugh.

"They have several animals, Jon," said Charles. "They must be doin' pretty good."

"Well, saddle up a couple horses for them."

"Yeah, I know, tie them up and rope the horses to the carryall," said Charles.

"What your names?" asked Ustanali.

"Shelton an' Liddie . . . Jennings."

"No more talk all night, Shelton and Liddie, or I cut out your tongues. Understand?"

"That's the Cherokee chief talkin'. Ya better listen," said Dave.

"We all understand."

"I have one more question, Jennings," said Jon, "and you better answer truthfully, hear?" Shelton shook his head yes. "Are there any other farms close to your village?" Shelton shook his head no . . . then yes.

"You play a game of headshake with Jon Hamilton?"

"N-n-n-nosa . . . There's a farm two miles south a-the town, sir, out whar we farm."

"You think we should take it too, Jon?" asked Charles.

"I suppose we should. It's probably around midnight now, so why don't you take the chief's group and bring them to your meeting place, where we have the others."

"What others you's have?" asked Shelton Jennings.

"Ustanali cut tongues out now."

"No, please, we ain't sayin' a word."

"See that you don't the rest of the night. Let's get them on their horses and collect their guns," said Jon.

The chief's team, minus the chief, headed south to take the last outlying farm. The rest continued toward the village, which turned out to be about a mile and a half away. They very quietly assembled at the grouping of three leafless trees. As Elizah had stated, the rain kept the church tower empty. Everything had gone well so far. Jon was sure it was time for some "hitches."

Mose stretched the tarp between the carryall, the captured buggy, and the group of trees to get some protection.

"We have more guns now, Jon Hamilton."

"Yes, Chief, at least five more, and Charles will probably bring one or two more from that last farm."

"I think we ought to arm everyone in our two groups," said Dave.

"See to it, Dave. Chief Nation, you decide who gets the other three or four captured guns."

"Okay, Jon Hamilton, Ustanali decide. Your big black man give them gun powder for guards in church."

"Righto! Mose will take care of that when he returns."

"What be the first order-a-business, Jon?" asked Jess.

"Let's see . . . Do we have extra flints?"

"Yep, I brung some extra flints with me," said Hugh.

"Good. Hugh here will be our signaler. Each of you three, and the chief and I will have an extra flint. When you, Jess, and you, Hank, get into position in the barns, you signal Hugh that you are ready by shootin' some sparks on your gun barrel. Hugh will answer and let us know by throwing a few sparks."

"Got it," said Hugh, "careful you don't burn the barn down."

"I be careful, brother," said Hank.

"Then go to it. Remember, you only shoot at them if necessary. Try to stop them by wounding them in the leg. Don't kill anyone unless you think they are about to kill. Okay?"

"Okay, Jon. Lets us indulge," said Jess.

"Good luck, men. Real quiet. Good luck," said Jon.

"What Ustanali do now, Jon Hamilton?"

"You are in charge here, Chief Nation. You find good spots in the trees for your rifle shooter and for your shooter of fire arrows so they can see the buildings. When Hugh signals, start your fire and melt the fire water. Send two wives and three man guards into the church."

"Ustanali ready."

"Good. Send two or three other guards to other areas outside the church and by the storehouse."

"One be my other wife. All with guns, Jon Hamilton?"

"Yes, if possible, Chief. Wait until your team gets back, so you'll know how many guns you have."

"Ustanali know. All guards need guns. Outside guards need guns too."

"My team will take four guns to start, Chief. Be sure that your outside guards, your wives, and one or two other guards have guns. We will get more guns when we raid each house."

"That be at first light, Jon Hamilton."

"Yes, Chief. Just as the sky starts to light, we set our fires. Have them ready, so we can heat the slow water. We will signal Hugh in the tower, and sneak two pots of hot slow water into the village and paint the walls of all the buildings. Then we sneak back and signal again for our teams to start from house to house. Take the prisoners to the church, give out guns, and go to the next house, Okay?"

"Okay, Jon Hamilton. When Ustanali send guards to church and outside, we take farm prisoners to church."

"Yes, very quietly, and very quiet painters of slow water."

"You go now, Jon Hamilton. We get very wet, but we teach lesson and get women back."

"That's our main goal, Chief. Good luck."

The rain wasn't very comforting to the nine people of Jon's team, but the swift current of the river and the noise it and the rain caused helped the team slip easily past the north side of the village, and into position along the village's west side. Jon put his team right to work collecting wood for a fire.

Jon strained to see in the dark. He thought he could see bodies moving about the church, and he wondered what was happening. He grew anxious, worrying that something was going wrong. He motioned for Elizah to accompany him down to and between the dark houses. After what seemed to be a long, agonizing period, Jon and Elizah saw some sparks from the church tower. *Relief!*

They waited and watched. Jon and Elizah finally saw movement between houses, across the compound. It was the guards ushering the prisoners to the church. Suddenly, a scuffle broke out close to the church. Jon and Elizah heard *'Help!'* shouted by one of the farm prisoners. Jon thought it was probably Shelton Jennings. Jon and Elizah ran across the plaza in front of the church to help. They saw a light go on in one of the houses right beside the path that the prisoners and guards had just used. They raced by the chief and Mose and the rest of their group to the now lit-up log house, just as the front door opened. Jon and Elizah hit the man head on before he could react, and knocked him back into his house. Elizah had a knife out, about to stab the man, but Jon stopped him. Together they punched the man out. They then blew out the two lanterns in the house and carried the man to the church.

"That was close, Jon Hamilton," whispered Ustanali.

"I's don' see any lights in dem houses, Jon."

"Good, Mose," whispered Jon. "Then this man is the only one we woke. Where is he? You got him tied up good?"

"He over there, on bench, Jon Hamilton. He quiet now."

"Good, Chief. That's one less house you have to raid."

"That good, Jon Hamilton. Plenty dark in here."

"Yes, Chief. There are two lanterns in that open house if your guards need them. I hope they don't. The darker, the better until daylight."

Saturday, November 28

Jon and Elizah crept back between the row of houses to their team and waited. Jon figured they still had two or three hours before the first rays of light. All they had to do now is wait. It seemed nobody could sleep, so they just rested. Sometime very early, the rain slowed, then stopped, as it had the previous two mornings.

Lights suddenly came on in the church, alarming Jon's team. They started to walk again toward the houses in their charge. Just as quickly, the church lights went back off, temporarily giving Jon's team a sigh of relief. Just as suddenly, a light appeared in a house in Jon's row. He quickly signaled his team, and they rushed to the house, two cabins to the south of his team's position. They surrounded it and waited.

A young mountain person opened his door and stepped outside. He found himself staring at two gun barrels pointed at him. His eyes became very large.

"Get back in that cabin. Now!" whispered Jon. The young man quickly reversed his steps. Jon, Elizah, and Dave followed him back into his cabin.

"Whaddya you'ns want?" he asked quietly.

"We want you to be very quiet. Not a word, hear?"

"We's might should oughta be able ta talk in our own home, be goddamitty."

Whop! Dave hit the man in the side of his head with the butt of his rifle. "The man says to be very quiet," ordered Dave.

Jon noticed movement under the covers of the bed. "Who have you got in that bed?"

"My bespoken. We are a-gettin' married."

"Congratulations. No more talking, or you'll die still single! Take him over to the church, Dave and Elizah. And get some clothes on him."

"He looks familiar, Jon. He may be a kidnapper," said Dave, as he and Elizah left with the prisoner.

"I find out!" said Elizah, as he carried the man's rifle.

Jon walked over to the bed and grabbed the covers. They were held tightly by the person under them. Jon pulled them off, and then stared in shock. It was Buelah!

"Please don' hurt me, Jonny."

"Hurt you? I came to get you and Maggie!"

"An' please don' hurt Zeb."

"Zeb? Who is Zeb, Buelah?"

"He be's dem man you's just took. I's gonna marries him."

"Marry him? He took you prisoner, Buelah."

"I's knows, Jon, but I's loves him. He's treat's me likes a queen, an' makes me happy."

"What about your mother and Mose, and Chipper and Maggie? Where's Maggie?"

"She be's in house across dere. I's don' care, Jon. I's wan's ta marries Zeb."

"Well, we'll talk about it later, Buelah. Where do they have Liz?"

"Liz be's close ta church, in dis row. She be's fine."

"Alright. I want you to stay right here, in bed, until I call for you. Understand? And put some clothes on."

"Yassa, Jon. I's do."

Jon stepped back outside. He noticed that the chief's team had already started their fire. He saw Dave and Elizah coming, and waved for them to get back to the team's meeting spot. Jon's men were starting their fire. Jon grabbed his flint and helped. They were a little behind the Chief's group, so he tried to hurry his crew.

"Let's get the pots of slow water boiling," he said.

Jon fudged a little. He poured a little slow water on the fire and it flared up, catching him up with the chief's group. He sent the first sparks, signaling that his pots were ready. In a few minutes, the return signal came from Hugh. It was time to paint some walls. Jon had Nathan and Taliwa guarding from the trees, and he sent Dave and Elizah in close for protection. That left himself, Coosastan, and the other female in his group, Estelle, Flower of Tulip Tree, to help the "painters."

They quietly stole past the houses to the church, and brushed a wide area with the pitch. They next brushed the west side of two small buildings and a small storage building next to the big storehouse. The brushers didn't see the mountain person sneaking across the open area from his cabin toward them, but Jon did, and Hank saw him as well from the barn. *BAM!* Hank's shot sent the attacker sprawling on the ground. He quickly got back up and continued toward Jon and the brushers. Jon aimed his Hawken at the man's legs, but before he could fire, he again heard *BAM!* This shot came from the church tower, and the man went down again and stayed down.

The damage had been done. Lanterns were lighting up most of the houses. Jon cursed under his breath.

"Get in the church and bring out some prisoners as shields," he told the ground guards. "Go with them!" he hollered at the brushers.

"I get wounded man's gun," said Estelle.

"Okay. Take over a couple houses!" Jon yelled to the chief. Jon then raced across the open area toward his row of houses. He grabbed Estelle's hand as he ran by.

"Take over that house!" he shouted to Dave and Elizah, pointing at the house next to them. With Estella at his side, he hit the door of the house he had left Buelah in. *BAM! BAM!* Shots came from next door.

"Can you shoot that flint rifle, Estelle?"

"Estelle shoot good as man."

"Good. You take over here. Get under the bed, Buelah!"

All hell had broken loose now. A war was going on. Jon raced next door and found Dave and Elizah with guns ready. The house owner was lying on the floor, his shirt bloody.

"I'm not sure if he's dead," said Dave, "but he ain't movin'."

"Nothing we can do for him right now. Are you two alright?"

"We Okay, Jon Hamilton. Worried about brothers."

"Yes, I know. Dave, can you hold down this spot?"

"Sure. I ain't seen nothin' to shoot at yet."

"Good. Elizah and I will try to make it to the other side."

"Elizah ready, Jon."

"I'll go first to the storehouse. Then you follow."

Shots were ringing out from all directions, as Jon made a dash for the storehouse. He then waved at Elizah, who raced toward him. A man stepped out of the cabin close to Dave's, and Jon fired. The man fell back into his home. Jon reloaded and peered out at the houses. There was a Cherokee lying dead on the ground in front of the "empty" house that he and Elizah had taken earlier. They saw a mountain person come out of his house and drop dead from a shot from somewhere. Just then, a group of men and women, hands tied, came out of the church and onto the plaza in front. The chief's armed guards had brought them out. The shooting slowed to a stop.

"Stop shootin'! Stop firing!" yelled a man, waving a white rag. "Put yer shootin' arms down."

A strange silence gripped the compound for a few seconds.

"Who all's in charge, an' whaddya wants?"

"You steal women and horses. We take back," said Ustanali.

"What if'n we all keep them women?"

"Cherokee has place surrounded. Kill all persons."

"Let's make widderers outta 'em!" shouted someone in a cabin.

"Is'n the preachman here?" asked the man with the white rag. "We'uns has needments fer womens."

"Then you ask for them, or advertise, or barter for them!" yelled Jon. "You don't steal and kill for them."

"We all er askin' then fer them womens," said the preach.

"No!" answered Ustanali. "You steal Cherokee women. Ustanali take back!"

"They all ain't a-gettin' my woman," said the man who had yelled earlier from his cabin. He stepped out from his front door and shot at Hugh in the church tower. *BAM! BAM!* The man was hit twice by shots from the Cherokee in the tree and one of the chief's wives. Jon saw that Hugh also had a bead on him.

Another shot rang out from Jon's side at someone on the west side of the church. Jon thought it was probably Nathan.

"Ahh! Help! I's hit!" came that someone's yell.

"Stop firin'!" shouted the preachman. "Get back on yer horse, fer you'uns all get kilt!"

"Put prisoners back in church, tie up," said Ustanali. "We burn them alive. You help tie." Mose and some others ran into the church with rope.

"That thar's our Sunday goin' ta meetin' place," said the preach. "You cain't burn it."

"The chief has something to show you, Preach," shouted Jon. "Don't you, Chief?"

"Ustanali show mountain persons magic."

"Anybody poke a gun out their door, shoot them!" yelled Jon.

Ustanali strode boldly over to one of the smaller buildings between the church and large storehouse. He waved his arms and pointed to the small building. A few seconds passed. *Swooch, thud! Swooch, thud!* Fire arrows hit both sides of the building. It exploded into a ball of fire, and was consumed in minutes. Ustanali strode toward the church.

"The church is next!" shouted Jon. "Come down out of the tower, Hugh, and bring out the guards."

"Stop! Stop!" yelled the preach. "I reckin' we're whupped. We give out! Please don' burnt the church."

"Did you all hear that? They surrender!" yelled Jon. Cheers rang out from all sides, and Jess fired into the air.

"Keep your positions. Keep on guard!" shouted Jon.

The cheers continued.

The preachman and two others walked to the center of the plaza. They had produced a sword. One "aide" had a rifle held above his head. They stood in front of Ustanali.

"Get back in the church!" shouted Jon to the guards, who had started to bring out the prisoners. "Back to the tower, Hugh, until we clean out the houses."

"We all surrender this here sword," said the preach. "You's take yer womens and horses an' leave please."

"Ustanali accept sword as sign of peace, but no peace until Ustanali revenge dead son."

"You'ns done took yer revenge. You's kilt my pardners."

"We'll talk about that after we clear out these houses," said Jon. "Right, Chief?"

"That right, Jon Hamilton."

"Okay then. We need to get our groups back together."

"Put wife number two in tower with Hugh, guard both sides."

"Which one is wife number two, Chief?"

"She Polly, Sweet as Molasses, shoot straight."

"Good idea, Chief. You got company coming, Hugh?"

"Who's a-comin', Jon?"

"The chief's wife. She'll help guard one side."

"Alrights. Send her up."

"Mose, stay at church, tie up prisoners."

"That will make your group short, Chief."

"Ustanali send wife number one to my group. Rebecca Bright as Stars in Sky, mother of Son of Sun, first love of Ustanali."

"Okay, Chief. We'll start at the north end, one at a time, and take the prisoners to Mose at the church. Preach, you tell all your people to stay in their house until we come for them."

"What all a-happin's if'in them won't come out?"

"We'll burn them out, Preachman. Ya better make sure they do come out. We'll stop when we reach the front of the church, Chief, and make sure we have the first four houses cleared out, alright?"

"Yes, Jon Hamilton. We go now."

The preacher man ran, tied at the hands, from house to house, shouting to the inhabitants to stay put and come out when they were told to. Elizah and Dave ran to the back side of Jon's row of houses to surround each from behind. Jon, Estelle, and Coosastan started around the corner of the church, and almost walked into trouble. The hillbilly that Nathan had shot from the tree was lying wounded on the ground beside the church, tended to by a woman. When he saw Jon, he reached for his rifle. The woman told him no, and tried to wrestle the rifle from the man.

"Hold it! Don't touch that gun!" shouted Jon.

"When a you'ns shot me down, an' this here is yer comeuppance!"

"No, Junar, we'all had 'nuff killin's!" said the woman.

Coosastan raced forward and helped the woman take the rifle away from Junar. Jon had a bead on him.

"Might could die from this here wound," said Junar. "I ain't ne'er done you'uns no harm."

"Mose!" yelled Jon. In a minute, Mose was there.

"Yassa, Jon."

"Take this wounded man and his woman into the church, and see if there is anything you can do for him. And take his gun."

"I's do, Jon. I's takes care o' him."

Jon, Coosastan, and Estelle continued on to the northernmost house and rapped on the door.

"Who-alls a-knockin'?" came the voice from inside.

"Come out with your hands up, now," said Jon.

"We alls want no part a-all this," said a woman from inside.

"Just come out here, and you won't get hurt."

"We'uns might could get kilt out thar."

"Get your asses out here now, and you won't die," said Jon.

"We all ain't done nuttin' to you'uns," said a heavy-bearded man, as he stepped outside, hands in the air. He was followed by his woman, dressed like a granny, with a long dull dress, apron and all.

"That's why we're not going to kill you. Head for the church."

The couple made their way to the church, where two Cherokee tied them up and ushered them inside. The chief and his group were also bringing in their first prisoners.

"So far, so good, everybody. Are there enough guards inside to handle all these prisoners?" asked Jon.

"I think so, Jon," said Charles. "This may be the first time this place will be full."

"We pack them like fish in barrel, Jon Hamilton."

"Okay, Chief. Let's bring in our guests from house number two."

Jon, Estelle, and the chief's second son now headed back around the church to another big surprise.

"Anyone home?" asked Jon, knocking on the second door. "I say again, anyone home? Open this door." After a couple poundings on the door, Estelle stepped forward and tried the latch. The door opened, and she shoved it wide. Empty.

"Hello, where are you? Look around."

As Jon's group was looking, two shots were fired from the other side of the church.

"Stay here. I'll be right back," said Jon. He stepped out the door, as Dave and Elizah raced past, and around the back of the church. Jon followed to the other side of house number two.

"What happened?" Dave asked Charles.

"Someone in there fired through the door and hit Josiah."

"Where my brother?" asked Elizah.

"He went over to the church," answered Charles.

Eliza ran to the church. Ustanali had sent the female from his original team, Heidi, back to his campfire.

"Ustanali burn mountain person from home."

"Right, Chief. But we finish the first four houses first."

"We finish first four houses, then burn, Jon Hamilton. Ustanali send Heidi for slow water."

"Good. When Heidi returns, have her guard this house until we have finished the first four. Alright, Chief?"

"That good, Jon Hamilton. Heidi and Polly guard house."

"You in this house!" shouted Jon. "You have a few minutes to decide. Surrender or die."

"You'ns go ta blazes! *BAM!* His shot hit the door, almost in the same spot that splinters showed he had hit before.

"See to it he doesn't come out!" Jon yelled to Polly and High, then started for the front of the church. He met Elizah there.

"How is your brother, Elizah?"

"Josiah fine. Splints from door stick in arm."

"Good. Let's get back to our side and see how Coosastan and Estelle are doing. Dave, stay here with your brother."

When Jon and Elizah got back to house their number two in their row, they found Coosastan and Estelle waiting in front of the third cabin.

"Are we ready to tackle this place?"

"What tackle mean?" asked Coosastan.

"To invade, or raid, I guess. To clean it out," said Jon.

"Coosastan ready."

Jon walked to the door and knocked. The door flew open, and Jon saw a blur, then arms grabbing him and holding on.

"Oh, thank you. Thank you! I thought you would never get here!"

Jon pulled the body away from him, just far enough to get a look at who was holding him so tightly. It was Elizabeth Engels Chasney, hanging onto him, hugging and kissing.

"Liz, are you alright?"

"Yes, now I am. Thank you. You saved me."

"You'ns done saved me!" said the man in the cabin.

"Get yer hands up, mister! Elizah—"

Elizah stepped around the couple and into the cabin.

"Did ye come for this she-panther? Ye can half 'er!"

"Tie him up, Elizah. Did he harm you, Liz?"

"Harm her? Jist look here!" The man had cuts and bruises on his face and hands. "I kin barely walk jist 'cause a her."

"Gave him Jesse, huh, Liz?"

"She kicked me at ma pride an' cods," said the man, Hummer.

"Were you mean to her?"

"Nary a bit, but I shoulda oughta been."

"Here I go, being truthful again, Jonny. He treated me well."

"Looks like he was the prisoner!"

"Yeah, well, get me out of here, Jonny."

"Liz, have you seen Maggie? Do you know if she is alright?"

"Yes, I saw her. She is somewhere on the other side. When I saw her briefly, she seemed fine."

"Good. Elizah, this is one of my women. Her name is Liz."

"Elizah, see Liz no enemy."

"Are Charles and Davy here?" asked Liz.

"Yes. They're working the other side of the church."

"I guess you better take me to them."

"They've been worried about you . . . So have I."

"I'm happy to hear that. Davy stood there and let them take me away."

"He didn't try to stop them?"

"I'm being truthful again. He had guns pointed at him."

Jon dropped Hummer and his gun off with Mose, just as the chief's team was bringing in a family with children. Dave was the first to spot Liz, and ran toward her.

"Chuck, look what I found!" He wrapped Liz in his arms and twirled her around. She allowed Dave to kiss her on the cheek before she broke loose from his grip and into the arms of Charles. Soon the three were in a bear hug.

"I hate to break this up, but we still have a lot of work to do," said Jon. "Would you like to wait in the buggy behind the houses where those trees are?"

"Best place for pretty woman," said Ustanali.

"What have we got here, a pow-wow?" asked Liz. A smile crossed Jon's face. Nothing could change Liz's disposition.

"I'll take her to the buggy," said Dave.

"I'm the oldest. I'll take her," answered Charles.

"Never mind," said Liz. "I'll find the way alone."

"We'll send some others to join you soon," said Jon.

The next house for Ustanali was the one in which the man died in a hail of gunfire, and the cabin was empty. Not so on Jon's side. He was at the house he had fired at in the heat of battle, where the man fell back in.

"Come out with your hands up," he said.

The door opened, and another "granny" stuck her head out. "My man husban' cain't come out. He done got shot."

"How badly is he hurt?"

"It might coulda been worser, reckon he'll live."

"Mose! I have another wounded man!" Jon yelled, and Mose came running. "Anyone else in your home?"

"Jist our son, an' he ain't right," said the woman.

"Bring him over to the church. Hurry, ma'am."

Mose picked up the man to carry to the church. Jon watched the woman help her son, fully grown, out the door. It was sadly obvious that he was retarded. Jon wondered if it was from inbreeding.

The next house was where Buelah was.

"Okay, Chief. We have your second house to deal with."

"We burn house now, Jon Hamilton."

"Yes, if he refuses to come out."

"Inside, ya coming out now?" asked Jon, rapping on the door. "Ya only got a couple minutes to decide."

"Here's my answer!" *BAM!* The door now had many splinters.

"Burn it!" shouted Jon.

Out came the brushes and pot. In minutes, the walls were coated with the slow water. One of the chief's extra men climbed up on the roof and was handed the pot. He poured some pitch on the roof's south side. *BAM!* The man shot through his roof, striking the Cherokee. He rolled over the edge and hit the ground. He was helped to the church with a leg wound. *Swooch, thud!* The first fire arrow hit the south side of the building, as fire flared up fast. *Swooch, thud!* The second fire arrow hit the poured pitch on the roof, causing an instant blaze. The next fire arrow hit the south side of the cabin again, but missed the painted area, already heavily ablaze. A Cherokee grabbed the fire arrow, ran around the cabin, and set the north side on fire. Jon knew it would take some time to penetrate the logs, but the smoke should get the man first.

In the church, Mose could hear the prisoners talking.

"They's done set Aden's house afire."

"Aden's? Why's they done 'at fer?"

"Guess they done knowed he kilt the Injun. He said he done also kilt a nigger."

Mose finished taping the leg of the wounded Cherokee.

"Jon!" he yelled, as he ran to the fire.

"Yeah, Mose, what is it?"

"Dem man in der cabins be's shootin' John Nation."

"Are you sure, Mose?"

"Yassa, day talks un dem church."

"Well then, good riddance. We'll just let him burn."

"He shot my son? Ustanali want him." He had heard Mose.

"I's wans 'im too!" shouted Mose, as he raced for the burning cabin's front door. He hit the heavy, thick door at full speed and force, and the door collapsed inward. Smoke billowed out. Mose disappeared inside.

"Mose! Come back! Mose!" yelled Jon, eyes blinded and lungs filling with smoke. "Where are you, Mose?"

Jon didn't see anything, but he felt it! He was almost knocked back out of the cabin by Mose, who had Aden by an arm, pulling him, and now Jon, out to fresh air. Aden was coughing loudly and hard, trying to breathe, his big hat down over his eyes and ears. His shirt was on fire. Mose dropped him and rolled him in the dirt, snuffing it out.

As he raised his head, still coughing, Aden saw pants of animal hide, decorated with beads and fringes. Looking up, he saw a Cherokee chief in full headdress, arms folded, hate in his eyes. Aden's cough ended, and his eyes widened. Terror gripped him when he saw the huge black man he thought he had killed.

"Dat man shoots me, Jon," said Mose.

"You kill my son, next chief of Smoking Mountain Cherokee. You steal princess Etowah, wife of Son of Sun."

"I . . . I . . . I had to. He were gonna kill me."

"Now Ustanali kill white savage."

"Let's finish the houses first, Chief, Okay?"

After a pause, Ustanali answered, "Okay, Jon Hamilton, give killer time to think before death."

The next set of four houses on Jon's side had the house that Buelah was in. She was dressed when he returned.

"Come with me now, Buelah."

"I's wans to be's wit Zeb. He be orites?"

"Yes, he's fine. I want you to be with Liz for now."

"Orites, Jon. Bu' I's marry Zeb."

"Talk to Liz about that. I'll talk to Mose if you'd like."

"Oh, thank you's, Jonny. Tells ta Mose I's loves Zeb."

"I will, Buelah, but first I find Maggie, Okay?"

"Orites. Sissy be's ova dem houses."

When Mose saw his stepdaughter, he engulfed her in his huge arms.

"You's Orites, Buelah?"

"Yassa, I's fines, maybe's a bit tired."

"We'll put her in a wagon with Liz. Okay, Mose?"

"Orites. Yer motha be's happy un see's you's, Buelah."

Jon's second house was a family of five, who gave up without an argument. Jon's group now numbered four, Coosastan, Elizah, Estelle, and himself. They started for the church.

"May could we'uns take out blankets fer childrens?"

"Yes, ma'am. Where are they? Estelle will get them."

"You's best go show 'em whar they are, Wini," said the woman.

"Ah reckon I had better," said Wini, turning back to the cabin.

"His name is Wini, huh? I know a lady named Winnie."

"His'n name's Winifred, a might good father."

Blankets in hand, they all marched to the church.

"Here are your next tie-ups, Mose. You probably don't have to tie up the children. Just Win—" *WHAM! Crack!*

Mose had hit the man so hard, that Jon was sure the cracking sound was Wini's jaw. He was out cold.

"Why did you do that, Mose?"

"You's see dem bruises, Jon?" Mose pointed at the marks on his arm and shoulder. "Dey comes from dis man an' club. He hits my Ellas."

"Well, it looks like you got even."

The third house of Jon's charge wasn't as easy as the last two. Jon knocked on the door.

"Come out with your hands up."

"You's come an' get me, wit them redskin bastads!"

"You don't come out, we'll burn you out."

"Like ya done to Aden, huh?"

"Yeah, like we done to Aden."

"Well, this'un here might could be a bit different. You'd be a-burnin' a princess!"

"Princess Etowah!"

"Pure as Rushing Waters," added Coosastan.

"Let the princess go, and the chief will let you go."

"I done gone too long a-time without no womenfolk that I cain't a-let her go."

"Maybe we can find a woman for you, but you have to let the princess go first!" shouted Jon.

"Really? You'ns ain't just a-funnin' me?"

"If you don't let her go, you won't have to worry about any woman. You'll be dead."

"You'ns promise?"

"Yes, now come on out!"

"Well, knowin' as how I wanna live, here her be!" With that, out came the beautiful princess Etowah, followed by the ugly, long, dirty-bearded C. T. Redlegg. Jon's group walked them over to the church. CT's cabin was filthy, but he had rifles, knives, bows, arrows, and spears of all kinds. The princess wept as she hugged Jon's group, including her brother-in-law, Coosastan. When they got to the church, they waited for the chief's group.

"Der be's Sissy, Jon," said Mose.

Jon saw the red hair and ran toward it, catching Maggie with a hug, then kisses. He lifted her off her feet and slowly twirled her around.

"Oh, Jonny, I thought I'd never see you again."

"You'll see me the rest of your life, my darlin'."

"Promise, Jonny?"

"Promise, my pretty plum," said Jon. "Did they hurt you at all?"

"No, Jonny. They saw my belly and didn't want to hurt me."

"Thank God for that."

At the same time, Maggie and Jon were embracing, so were the princess, her father-in-law, and brother-in-law.

"Let's get them to the carryall with Liz and Buelah."

"I don't want to let go of you, Jonny."

"I don't either, darlin', but we still have work to do."

Maggie and the princess eventually joined Buelah and Liz at the buggy, and Jon reformed his group for house number four.

"Come out with your hands up!" ordered Jon.

"We're a-comin'," came the reply.

Out came a spry old man, followed by a middle-aged woman dressed like the other grannies, but Jon could tell she was an Indian squaw.

"You speak English?" Jon asked.

"Yep, you'ns here to steal women too?"

"No, just to get our women back."

"Huh! Ne'er a-thought 'at would happen," said the squaw.

"Are you Cherokee?"

"Nah, I were Chickasaw, ne'er had a nary a one come after me!"

"Well, I did! You are free now, back to your people."

"My man is my people," she said, "an' besides, I hear tell Chickasaw done sold out an' left their homes."

"Then you're free to come with me and my group."

"Where ta?"

"Arkansas."

"Arkansas! 'At's where I hear tell them Chickasaw done gone!"

"Then I'll take you back to them."

"Plum neighborly a you'd, but I reckon I'll be a-stayin' here wit ma man."

"Okay. If you change your mind, let me know."

The fourth cabin on Jon's side housed a shaggy mountain person and two children, but no woman. Jon promised no harm to the children, and they all came out and walked to the church. This left three houses to go for each team. No women were found in any of Jon's last houses, but he had to threaten the "bachelors" in each that he would burn them out, before they surrendered themselves and their guns. Ustanali had it easier, finding a family in one of the last three cabins, and Laurel in another. The job was done.

"This is the last of them, Mose."

"Orites, Jon. It be's good thing. Dem church be's full!"

"I'm glad we didn't have to burn it down with all these people in it."

"I's don't think you's do that, Jon."

"But the chief might have. I'm happy we don't have to find out."

"I's goes gets dem horses, an' we leaves now, Jon?"

"You can bring the horses, Mose, be we still have a couple things to do before we leave."

"Wha they be's, Jon?"

"Some punishment for the ones who took our women."

"We's gets dem all back, Jon, un' kills un' wounds dem mans. We's punish dem already."

"I'm glad you feel that way too, Mose. You don't hate them, then?"

"Nosa, I's don' hates dem. I's don' hates nobodys."

"Good. 'Cause Buelah wants to stay."

"Buelah . . . what's, Jon?"

"Buelah wants to marry her kidnapper."

"Nosa, Jon. Nosa! I's take Buelah wit me."

"Think about that, Mose. She has found someone she loves and is very happy." There was a pause.

"I's goes gets horses, Jon."

"Okay. I'll talk to the preacherman and chief, while you're doing that. Tell Jess and Hank to come on in."

"Yassa, I's do."

Jon now wondered where the preacher was. He found the man speaking to his people in the church.

"Thank the Lawd we'uns still got our homes, an' we ain't deader den doornails."

"Thank the Lawd!" agreed several people.

"We alls might coulda gone got kilt."

"Praise da Lawd!"

"We alls make peace wit dem Injuns. We alls whupped."

"We didn't want to kill anyone!" shouted Jon. "But all of a sudden we were spotted and all hell broke loose."

"We alls wans you'ns to leave now,' said the preacher.

"We are not quite finished here."

"You'ns have took our women, our guns, an' kilt our men folks. What more'n ye wans?"

"We want your promise that you will never steal anything from anyone again."

"We alls kin promise 'at."

"Good. My wife can write up an agreement for you all and the chief to sign."

"How'er we all gonna get women?" someone asked.

"You and the chief, you trade something valuable. What town do you trade with?"

"Knoksvill," said someone in the crowd.

"If Knoxville has a newspaper, advertise for a wife."

"We alls aim ta do jist 'at," said the preacher.

"Good, I'll have my wife write up your promise . . . Oh, do you marry couples?"

"Shorely do. Youn's ain't married?"

"I'm married, but my black woman, Buelah, wants to stay and marry Zeb.

"Well, glory be! A black wife will be welcome."

"You can't be serious!" said a tearful Maggie.

"Yes, Sissy, I's be serious," answered Buelah.

"But how can I get along without you?"

"You's has husband, an' I's wans husband."

"Oh, please, Buel, don't leave us!"

"Bu' I's loves Zeb, Sissy. I's be happys here."

"But I'll never see you again . . . What about Nunky Mose, and Nanty Ella? What would she say?"

"My momma be's happys un I's happys."

"Maybe they could get married in Elizabethton."

"You're a lot of help!" said Maggie.

"Elizabethton? Where is that?" asked Liz.

"On the Watauga River, where we're going," said Charles.

"I'm famous already!"

"And there's a Charlestown. I wonder if there's a Davestown?"

"I've never heard of one, brother. Maybe you can start one in Kentucky," said Charles.

"Is there be's a preecha un Lizabethton, Jonny?"

"I think so, Buelah. I saw a church there, but I already asked this preacher if he would marry you."

"You really are a big help," said Liz.

"I only want Buelah to be happy. I promised I would help her persuade you all."

"Thank you's, Jonny. I be's happys wit Zeb."

"For the rest of your life, Buel?"

"Yassum, Sissy, fo' rest a my lifes." There was a pause.

"Then I have a wedding present for you," said Maggie.

"He, he, oh, Sissy, wha' it be's?"

Maggie reached into the back of the carryall and brought out the red dress that Jon loved and had brought along. "Your wedding dress. You always liked it," said Maggie.

"Oh, thank you's, Sissy. I's do loves it!"

"So do I, Buelah. Look out. I might marry you in that!"

Buelah laughed. "You's already marrys, Sissy . . . Jonny!"

"I know," smiled Jonny. To Maggie, he said, "I need you to write up an agreement, Maggie, between these people and the Cherokee."

"Alright, Jonny. What do you want it to say?"

"I'll tell you, as you write it. I got this paper and pen from the preacher man."

"What day is it, Jonny?"

"Mmm, I don't know. It's a Saturday."

"We were kidnapped last Sunday," said Liz.

"Yeah, and that was the twenty-second, I think, so tomorrow would be the twenty-ninth. Today is the twenty-eighth."

"Time sure flies when you're having fun," quipped Liz.

Saturday, November 28, 1835

This agreement, signed and witnessed below, between the Smoky Mountain Cherokee Nation and all settlers on Cherokee lands on the plateau within fifty miles on either side of the Nolichucky River, shall last as long as both parties reside on the above-mentioned lands.

To wit: The first party (Cherokee) grants the second party (settlers) the right to live and prosper, without interference, on said lands bordering the Nolichucky River. The second party (settlers) agrees to honor and respect the property rights of the first party (Cherokee), never to steal from them, and never to engage in conflict of any type with the first party, and, further, to help prevent any suffering or starvation of the Smoky Mountain Cherokee.

Signed and witnessed on this 28th day of November, in the year of our Lord, 1835.

Maggie had provided places for party and witness signatures at the bottom of the page. She showed it to Jon.

"That is very good, my pretty plum. We need two copies, one for each party."

"You will be a witness, won't you, Jonny?"

"Yes, I think so."

"Well then, you have three parchments. I'll make three copes, so you'll have one."

"Thank you, darlin'. I knew there was a reason I needed you back so desperately."

"Jonny! That's not funny!"

"Let's stay here with Buelah, where we're appreciated," said Liz.

"I'm sorry, darlin', that wasn't funny. Forgive me?"

"You've got one up on him, Maggie. Don't forgive him," warned Liz.

"Hmm . . . promise never to let anyone kidnap me again?"

"I promise."

"Then I forgive you."

"Ah, true love must be grand," sighed Liz.

It was late afternoon when the kidnappers were lined up to be judged by Ustanali. Maggie, Liz, Dave, and Mose were able to identify the six kidnappers.

"You judge all five these men, Jon Hamilton. Ustanali kill this man who kill Son of Sun and steal Princess Etowah."

"We have already forgiven these men, Chief."

"You show mercy, Jon Hamilton? They steal your women and horses."

"Yes, but they promise never to steal again from Cherokee."

"What promise they give, Jon Hamilton?"

"I have promises in writing, Chief. They will sign it for you, and you sign for Cherokee."

"What I promise, Jon Hamilton?"

"That they can live on this land forever."

"Hmm . . . and they sign not to steal Cherokee women?"

"Yes, and they promise never to kill or fight Cherokee, and to help Cherokee live in peace."

"Ustanali sign paper, but want reward."

"What reward, Chief?"

"Want guns for protection and wagon for Jon Hamilton."

"You should get some guns, Chief, but a wagon . . ."

"You say you lose wagon in blue-colored mountains?"

"Yes, but I . . ."

"Then Ustanali say you take wagon from mountain persons."

"We'll see what they say to that at signing of papers, Chief."

"Ustanali say! Still kill this man!"

"P-please don't kill me. I be done sorry I shoot yer son. Promise I would ne'er done it again," said Aden.

"My son dead. Ustanali sure you never do it again." The chief pulled a knife from his belt. Jon saw the hate in his eyes, and the fright on Aden's face.

"Chief! I ask you to spare his life."

"But he wound my Cherokee, Run Like Wind, and he steal Princess Pure as Rushing Waters, and he kill my son, Son of Sun. Ustanali must show strength and revenge."

"Ustanali already show strength and revenge," said Jon. "Now you must show mercy."

"Mercy? Ustanali let mountain persons live. Let live on Cherokee land. That is mercy, Jon Hamilton."

"Yes, Chief, that is mercy. But a chief who replaces hate with love and kindness is the greatest chief of all."

"John Ross is greatest chief of all, Jon Hamilton, but your words have meaning to Ustanali."

"Good, Chief. We have already killed four of their men and wounded many more. We have lost only one. We have a great victory!"

"You are right, Jon Hamilton. I not kill this person."

"Oh, thanky, you'ns great Chief," said Aden, relieved.

"You are a great chief," agreed Jon.

"Ustanali give this person chance to live."

"Chance? What chance, Chief?"

"All Cherokee in mountains that smoke want revenge. Ustanali make killer run for life, ancient Cherokee custom. Take shoes off."

Aden sat on the ground and took off his shoes, exposing bare, dirty feet.

"Put shoes back on, feet smell, better chance to live. What town you know?"

"Knoxville," said several people.

"How far Knoxville?" asked the chief.

"Nigh onta ninety mile by river," said a mountain person.

"Yeah, but might should outta be sixty a-goin' straight west," said another person.

Ustanali threw his knife, sticking it in the ground.

"You savage, now run like savage! Run for life. You get to Knoxville, you live. Never come back, or Ustanali kill. Take knife and run. One hour start, and Coosastan follow to kill you. Run for Knoxville and live. Go now!"

"Please, Chief. I cain't run 'at far," begged Aden.

"Ustanali give one hour and half, send two Cherokee to kill, Son of Moon and Swift as River. Go now, or Ustanali change his mind and kill."

Aden grabbed the knife and ran west, between the row of houses that Jon had cleared. He ran through the trees and into the Nolichucky River, where he disappeared from view.

"You never come back!" yelled the chief. "Son of Moon, you take Swift as River in one and half hours, and kill mountain person who kill your brother."

"Coosastan kill man who murder Son of Sun."

"But only if you catch him before he reaches Knoxville, right, Chief?"

"That right, Jon Hamilton. You keep track of time for Coosastan?"

"Yes, Chief. I will tell Coosastan in one and a half hours."

"Ustanali grateful."

"But first we must sign the agreement of peace and friendship. No more fighting and killing!" shouted Jon. A wave of cheers sprang from those gathered around the plaza.

"Mose! Can you find a table and chairs?"

"I's do, Jon."

"Good. Bring them out, and bring out the mountain persons to witness the agreement."

"I's bring dem, Jon."

In minutes, the prisoners and guards started pouring out of the church, followed by Mose, who was carrying the pulpit in one massive arm and a stack of chairs in the other. He sat them in the middle of the plaza, and the chief and preacher man sat across from each other. Jon read the proclamation out loud, so all could hear. He then asked if anyone had any questions.

"How long ever-body hafter live wit this here promise?"

"As long as you live on these lands," answered Jon.

"Do that means we alls cain't steal from whites?" asked another person.

"Yes, you don't steal from anyone anymore."

"Will we alls git our guns back?"

"Most of them," answered Jon. "The Cherokee will take a few to protect themselves and hunt for food."

"Jon Hamilton take one wagon," added Ustanali.

"Why fer you'ns do that?" asked yet another voice.

"You call . . . spoils?" asked the chief.

"Spoils of war!" yelled Dave.

"Whut all yer tooks?" said that voice, to Dave.

"We don't want anything else," answered Charles.

"Maybe one of your women," said Dave, "to replace Buelah."

"We'uns are short a-women a-ready," said the preacher man.

"We won't take any of your women," said Charles.

"Are there any other questions?" asked Jon.

"Thar be a coupla towns in fifty mile a this here river."

"Hmm . . . well, I guess they will be included in this agreement. I'm sure the Chief won't bother them, as long as they leave the Cherokee alone. Where are these towns?"

"Thar be Jonesboro . . . an' Grenville north un west a-here."

"Ustanali not bother white man's towns."

"Good! Will some of you go to those towns and tell them of this agreement?"

Responses such as "Yep," "We all will," and "Should outta do that" were heard.

"Good. Any other questions?" There was a long pause. No questions. "Good, let's get the signing over with. Who will sign for the parties?"

"I will," said the preacher.

"We need two people, and a witness for each side."

"Ustanali sign. Coosastan not here."

"How about the princess, Chief?"

"Yes. Good choice, Jon Hamilton. Ustanali hope she marry Son of Moon now. Stay in family."

"Aden were liketa ours leader, but he be a-goner now. Maybe we-alls has CT, er, Granvell a-signin'," said the preacher.

"Okay, one can sign, and one a witness."

"You put on paper Ustanali take six guns and wagon. Spoils, Jon Hamilton."

"An' Hank and I be likin' these here guns we took from them farmers," said Hugh.

"Good. We will leave the rest of the rifles at one of the farms east of here," said Jon. "Maggie, will you please add to this agreement that the first party is taking from the second party eight rifles and one wagon?"

"Yes. There's room enough for that between the main agreement and the signatures, Jonny."

"Good. Let's get those signatures."

The chief signed first, in both English and Cherokee. The preacher signed his name, Robert Ralley, in uneven letters. Next, the princess Etowah signed "Etowah of Oostanaula Cherokee." The second signer for the villagers was Granville Weatherbe, in readable English. C. T. Redlegg signed as witness for the first party, and Jon was witness to the second. Cheers erupted with the signing, and someone even climbed up into the church tower and rang the bell.

"Mose!" Jon yelled, as the crowd cheered.

"Yassa, I's here, Jon."

"Take a team of horses and go pick out a wagon that can make it to Arkansas. Bring it over with the carryall."

"Orites, Jon. I's do."

"Let me do that, Jon," said Charles. "Mose has to give the bride away."

"That's right! Thanks, Charles."

"Our'ns groomer are a-gittin' ready ta be wed," said the preacher, Robert Ralley. "How's 'bout the bride?"

"She be's gettin' ready," said Mose.

"This here huge black person done aim ta give-out the bride aways?" asked Robert.

"Yes," said Jon. "He is the stepfather."

"Then let's git 'er done wit!"

It had been heard before, that the wedding was another "babbling bear garden," according to Jon. The wedding "lineup" was interesting. The groom, Zebriel Castrum, and best man, Zakiah Pickney, both kidnappers, looked very much alike with a black dress coat over their coveralls. The bride, Buelah, dressed in Maggie's short, sexy bright red dress, and matron of honor, Maggie, in an ordinary dress that Jon had brought along on the raid. The preacher was still dressed in his coveralls, with a long, white scarf and a Bible, the only items to show his status. The church was packed, and all went well.

"We-uns are gather-alled ta watch see the weddin' a'tween Zabriel Castrum an' Buler . . . what's you'ns last name, honey?"

"Hamitons."

"'An Buler Hamiton. Who giv'n this here bride aways?"

"I's do," said Mose.

"'At's fittin'. Buler . . . a . . . Hamiton, does ya takes up this here man, Zabriel Castrum, to be you'ns husband fer generations?"

"I's do," answered Buelah.

"An' ta obeys him?"

"I's do."

"Reckin' I'll allow that. An' young Zabriel Castrum, does ya takes this here woman, Buler Hamiton, ta be you'ns broomstick wife fer generations?"

"Reckin' I do."

"What all you'ns gots fer a ring?"

"I's made 'em," said Zeb, "outta wood."

"Reckin' I'll allow that. I hereby pernunce you'ns man an' woman fer generations. Kiss da bride. Edie! Whar's da broom?"

"Right 'ere, Preachman!"

"I guess all weddings have the broom to jump," said Jon.

"Anybody tries to marry me, and I'll jump his bones," added Liz.

"Guess you would at that!"

The broom jumping brought on the cheers. It was party time.

"Edie! Whar are da shine?"

"We are a-gittin' it, Preachman."

The moonshine flowed like the river! And just as quickly, there came the music. A lot of strange-looking instruments produced some fine music, and the church became the dance hall. The party lasted through much of the night. Jon and Maggie finally snuck away. He wondered if he was "feeling the corn," when he saw two carryalls, almost exactly alike.

"One of these is ours, replacing the buckboard."

"Must be this one, Jonny. It's got Sloggy and Smutty hitched to it."

"It's a nice one, darlin'. Let's try it out!"

The "bed" was longer than the other carryall belonging to the Stones, and the Hamiltons fit in it well. They started the hot and heavy lovemaking, when suddenly Maggie froze and caught her breath.

"What is it, darlin'?"

"There's something in the trees."

Jon turned and looked up. He couldn't believe what he saw. The Cherokee guard on the chief's team was still up in the tree!

"Come down and rest!" shouted Jon. "We have food."

"Ustanali say not come down," the Cherokee answered.

"The chief forgot. He is in the church partying."

"This I know, Jon Hamilton. You party and forget too."

"What did I forget?"

"You forget to tell Son of Mon and Swift as River to run after killer of Son of Sun."

"Damn! I did forget! I'd better go tell them now."

"Not to worry, Jon Hamilton. They leave long ago. Not tell Chief Ustanali," said the guard.

"That's good. Come down now."

"That's good? Another killing is good?" asked Maggie.

"The one they're after killed John Nation, Maggie. He was the chief's son, you know, and all the Cherokee need revenge. Besides, he just might make it to Knoxville."

"I hope so, Jonny."

"Now, where were we?"

"You can't mean that, Jonny."

The lovemaking started quickly, as soon as the Cherokee left to join the party in the church. It was unfulfilling for Jon, and uncomfortable for Maggie. There were no seconds.

"Did you miss me, Jonny?"

"Does a mule have an ass?"

"I'm serious, Jonny. I missed you *so* much."

"I am serious too, my pretty plum. I just about went crazy without you. I was so worried!"

"Jonny, you became close to crazy when you decided to move to Arkansas!"

"How about when I decided to marry you?"

"You didn't decide. This is what made you decide," she said, patting her large tummy, "and I decided that for you."

"Guess you're right, darlin', but I'm happy I decided."

After a few moments, Maggie said, "I'm going to miss Buelah."

"I know, darlin'. I'll try to keep you occupied."

"I'm sure you will, you big lummox." Maggie paused. "Jonny, are we staying here the rest of the night?"

"Certainly we are. It's only a few hours until morning. Why?"

"These people can be mean. They frighten me."

"Why? They signed the agreement."

"I know, Jonny, but I don't trust them."

"Okay, my pretty plum. We'll post guards until morning."

"Thank you." Maggie paused again. "You know what we missed while we were apart?"

"Each other."

"I mean, besides that."

"No, what?"

"Thanksgiving was last Thursday."

"Really? Does your family celebrate that?"

"Of course, they do. Ally would have come home from Georgetown, and my uncle might have come down from Baltimore."

"It's just to remember those who got away from the British, isn't it?"

"Well, I suppose that's one way to look at it, Jonny."

"Well, my grandfather *was* British!"

"Someday, when we're in our home in Arkansas . . ."

"And all our rugrats are asleep . . ."

"I would like you to tell me about your grandfather."

"Will do, my pretty plum. Just remind me."

After a few moments of silence, Maggie said, "Jonny . . . can we take Buelah and her new husband with us tomorrow to see Nanty Ella one last time?"

"I suppose so, darlin'. We'll see what they say. We just can't bring them back. We've already lost a week."

The party finally started breaking up in the early hours of Sunday morning. Jon found a couple Cherokee willing to stand guard for those few hours. All the hill-folk were too drunk to break the agreement even if they wanted to!

Sunday, November 29

It was pure luck that no more damage or killings occurred that night, as some of the Cherokee had some of the corn whiskey. They were still out cold and were tied to their ponies as the invaders prepared to leave. Jobe and Ann McDaniel and their children climbed into their buggy. Farmer William Rush rode his mule, and the Sheltons rode their horses. The Chasney brothers were back on the horses they had borrowed from Jess Stone. Maggie wanted to ride her Arabian horse, Pasha, for a while, but Jon said no and tied Pasha to the wagon. Maggie instead rode with Jess Stone, and Mose drove the new carryall that was taken from the mountain persons. That left Jess Stone to drive his carryall with Maggie, and Liz decided to ride along with Jess and Maggie for a ways, so that the newlyweds could ride with Mose. The Butlers, Hugh and Hank, agreed to help Jon herd all the other animals: Jake and Red, Apple and Jack, and the Butlers' prize bull, Gov'nor. An extra horse was also taken so that Buelah and her new husband, Zeb, could get back to their home. It was close to midmorning, and all were ready.

"You'ns all come back," said Preacher Robert Ralley.

"We'uns come back in two or three day," said Zeb.

"Ustanali come back, make trade."

"You'ns will be welcome," said Robert.

"What 'bout our guns?" asked Granville Weatherbe, who must not have drank too much "shine."

Jon looked at the chief, and they seemed to silently agree. "Ustanali leave few guns here, some at farm, take some," said the chief.

"We must go now, Chief. Goodbye, Preacher Ralley," said Jon.

It was early evening when the victors reached the same abandoned farmhouse where Jon's men had stayed before the raid. Mose again stretched the tarp over the roof, so the crowd could stay dry under the threatening sky. The men also started a fire in the old fireplace. The Cherokee had a large bonfire on the south side of the Nolichucky River, but the chief, his three wives, and the Princess Etowah were invited to spend the night in the old farmhouse. That made sixteen people snuggled together in the little log cabin.

"As we are all packed together for the night, I think we should introduce ourselves. Charles, will you start?"

"I will, Jon. I am Charles Chasney. This is my brother Dave, and my wife Elizabeth."

"Okay, I be a-livin' on the Watauga River, an' my name be Jess Stone. My wife's name be Victoria, and them are my neighbors, Hugh an' Hank Butler."

"I'll go next. My name is Jonathan Hamilton, and I thank you all for rescuing my wife, Margaret. My partner's name is Mose, and his stepdaughter is Buelah."

"I's Buelah Castrum, an' des be's my husban', Zeb."

"Your turn, Chief."

"I Chief Ustanali Nation. This Princess Etowah Nation, wife of dead son, John Nation. These my three wives, Rebecca Bright as Stars in Sky, Polly Sweet as Molasses, and Lilly Lovely as Spring Lilly."

"You Cherokee women have beautiful names," said Maggie.

"The description of each woman is lovely," added Liz. "What is the princess's full name?"

"Etowah Nation, Pure as Rushing Water," said the chief.

"That is delightful," said Maggie.

"I wonder what phrase they would have for me," said Liz.

"Mine might be 'Too Big for Clothes,'" quipped Maggie.

"Or Done Got Pizened, Has Big Pod!" said Liz, and she and Maggie got a laugh out of that.

"What does that mean?" asked Jon.

"That's our secret, Jonny," answered Maggie.

"We have no secrets from each other, my love. Zeb, what did she say?"

"Don't you say a word, Zebriel!" shouted Liz and Maggie.

"Do you know, Buelah?"

"I's no sures, Jonny."

"You want to see your mother, don't you?"

"That's bribery, Jonny!" said Maggie.

"Dishonest!" added Liz.

"Yassa. I's wans ta see my momma."

"Then you better tell me what they said, Buelah."

"Don't do it, Buel."

"I's sorry, Sissy. I's wans ta see Momma. It be's somethin' 'bout pregnant un big bellies, Jonny."

"We'll never tell you any more secrets, Buelah," said Liz.

"I's be sorry."

"I can guess what a phrase for you would be, Liz."

"Let's hear it, big boy."

"Let me see . . . how about 'Will Cut You to Pieces?'"

"That's too mild for me. More like 'Will Cut It Off and Feed It to the Alligators'!" There was laughter after Liz's comment.

When the laughter had quieted down, the chief said, "Ustanali show how grateful for help." He then untied a pouch from his waist and opened it. "This for you, Hugh. This for you, Hank. This for you, Charles. This for Davy, and this for Jess."

The chief was giving out chunks of gold, sizing bigger than a man's thumb. Next he handed one to Mose. The men were all speechless. The women were squealing.

"I's be grateful to you's, Chief, very gratsfuls," said Mose.

"Where did you get those rocks, Chief?" asked Jon.

"White Georgians take land from Cherokee for gold, but Ustanali take gold and leave."

"Good for you, Chief. Hide it from the whites."

"Ustanali know white man's greed for gold. Have few yellow stones in secret place many days ride away."

"No one knows where?"

"Only Ustanali knows. If whites kill Ustanali, no one ever find gold."

"Ustanali, you are a great chief. Thank you for helping me take back my wife and friends."

"Ustanali not finish with Jon Hamilton, friend of Cherokee for life." The chief reached into the pouch again. "This is for best friend, Jon Hamilton." The chief brought out a gold stone almost as big as two long fingers of his hand and handed it to Jon.

"This is too much, Chief. I cannot take . . ."

"You take, Jon Hamilton. Use in Arkansas. Buy big land. Maybe Ustanali live there someday."

"You will always be welcome on my land, Chief."

"Thank you, Jon Hamilton. Ustanali very grateful to all white men in this cabin, share wives two and three." The men all looked around at each other.

"Look at them drool," said Liz.

"I don't think that's . . .," said Maggie.

"Now, Maggie," interrupted Jon, "the chief is showing his gratitude. It would be insulting to turn him down."

"Not much damage can be done in this crowded little cabin, anyway," said Liz. "But it might be fun watching."

"You take Polly, Jess?" asked the chief.

"I thank ya, Chief, but I has a wife that I'll be a-seein' tomorrow evenin', and I'll be true ta her."

"I'll be twat-tied!" quipped Liz. "Never thought I'd ever hear that from any man. I volunteer Chuck and Davy."

"I've always been true to you, Liz," said Charles.

"So have I," added Dave.

Liz looked at Dave with disdain. She didn't need to answer.

"Ustanali call for two more Cherokee female persons from camp across river. Cannot give Princess Etowah, and don't have Winnie for Big Black Brother."

"Mose has a wife too, Chief. We have enough women now. One for Hugh, and one for Hank."

"They keep you warm tonight, Hugh and Hank."

Jon signaled Hugh with eyes and head to accept.

"Thank you, Great Chief. My brother an' me accept," said Hugh.

It was very cozy and warm in that small cabin. Mose got out his harmonica, and the cabin rocked with singing, clapping, hugs, and kisses. Silence soon overtook the crowd, as some very tired bodies were soon asleep.

Monday, November 30

Sometime in the wee hours, the cold rains came back. As usual, Mose was up early. He fed and watered the horses and Gov'nor, and got the wagons ready. He built a bonfire, and soon some others were up to help with a breakfast from all the food Victoria Stone had sent. There was a sadness in the air, as Jon knew this would be the last he would see of the Cherokee chief, Ustanali.

"You come back someday, Jon Hamilton, when Ustanali have white hair. We get drunk, tell lies, love woman." Jon noticed the eyes of the great chief were tearing up.

"Yes, Chief. Someday we will meet again."

"You must cross river once more, say goodbye to my people."

"Yes, Chief. I'll be right back, darlin'," Jon said to Maggie. Jon hopped on Pasha and started across the Nolichucky. Maggie felt a sense of pride, as the Cherokee men and women surrounded her husband with screeches and cheers. Soon they were dispersing and heading east into the Smokies, and Jon was back across the river. The two carryalls turned north, and for the last time, Jon looked back and saw the chief with his three wives standing at the bank of the river waving goodbye. He blew them a kiss. It was early afternoon when they reached the covered wagon and a happy reunion with Ella and Chipper.

"This is where all our troubles started," said Jon.

"What!" exclaimed Liz. "We've had troubles ever since we met up on the other side of those mountains!"

"Yeah, what do you call trouble, Jonny?"

"I guess it's when we lost our women, my love."

"Great answer, Jon," said Charles.

"You really wormed your way outta that one," said Liz.

"What do you call all the other troubles we've had since we left Bethania, Jonny?"

"Adventures, my pretty plum."

"Do we have any food left around here?" asked Dave.

"Yes, there is still a little left," said Liz.

"Jess's wife sure can cook, can't she?" asked Charles.

"As good as Nanty Ella?"

"I didn't get like this any other way," said Jess, patting his stomach.

"Wow, that's as big as Maggie's," said Liz.

"But I think Maggie got her stomach in a different way," said Charles.

"Maybe we can talk Jess and his wife into coming along with us to Arkansas," said Jon.

"Or Kentucky," said Liz. "We'll need a cook after we split."

"I's sorry, folks," said Jess. "Vic be stayin' here wit me. Now if ya'll want to stay here, I promise a lot more a-her cookin'."

"I know a great bribe when I hear one," said Liz.

"Very tempting, thanks, but we must be moving on," said Jon.

"We's takes Buel wit us ta Arkansas, Jon?" asked Ella.

"I's stays wit Zeb, Mama. I's be happier here."

"Stays wit Zeb? You's come to Arkansas."

"But, Mama, I's his wife. I's stays wit my husban'."

"Ella, once we are settled in Arkansas, maybe we can come back to see Buelah," suggested Jon.

"Yassa, Jon, thank you's. I be missin' my Buel."

"I know, Ella, let's get crackin'."

"I's gets wagon an' trailer hooked up, Jon," said Mose, hurrying away.

"Thanks, Mose, hitch teams five and fifteen back up to the covered wagon, so they can get used to it again."

"I guess Apple and Jack won't need to get used to our wagon."

"No, brother, that's the only one they ever pulled," said Charles.

"Guess that leaves Corker to pull this big carryall, doesn't it, Jonny?"

"Sure does, my pretty plum. It's bigger and heavier than the buckboard was, but Corker can handle it fine."

"Do we need another pair, Jonny?"

"Might not be a bad idea, darlin'. That way we can free up Corker again, in case we have some trouble."

"You mean in case of another adventure," joked Liz.

"What would another pair of horses cost?" asked Maggie.

"I ain't certain you'd even be a-findin' a pair fer sale," said Jess.

"That's true," said Hugh. "They'd sure be a-high priced grass guzzlers! Ye'd probably use up that gold stone."

"In that case, we'd have to use Corker, my love. I don't have a lot of money besides this gold nugget."

"Huuh!" said Maggie, catching her breath and running to the covered wagon.

"What's wrong, darlin'?"

Maggie climbed into the wagon and started digging through the supplies and clothes. "Oh please, be here," she said.

"What are you looking for, Maggie?"

"Thank God!" Maggie exclaimed, lifting her porcelain horse. "It's still here!"

"I could have told you that, my love."

"So now you're a sorcerer," said Liz.

"That horse will never pull a wagon!" quipped Dave.

"No, but the money in it will," answered Jon. With that, the two carryalls and covered wagon with trailer rolled on north, reaching the Stones' farm in the late afternoon.

"Welcome home!" said Victoria, rushing to her husband.

"We got our Gov'nor back," said Hugh.

"Did you have to use that gun ta get him?"

"We did, Vic. Couldn'ta be helped," said Jess.

"We's gets bak my Buelah, tank do Lawd," said Ella.

"Dear Lord, you even brought a prisoner!" said Victoria.

"Dis be's my husband, Zeb Castrum," said Buelah.

"Husband?" asked Victoria.

"Yassum, I's marrys dis man. He's makes me happies."

Ella stood in silence as a tear rolled down her cheek. Mose had snuck back and now wrapped his huge arm around Ella. Buelah then advanced to hug both her parents and brother Chipper, who had joined them.

"I's be happies now, Mama," said Buelah, as Maggie joined the huddle, tears flowing down her face. Buelah motioned to her husband Zeb to join the huddle.

"You's come wit us to Arkansas?" asked Ella.

"Where's dat at?" asked Zeb.

"It be's long ways ova Mississippi Riva, Daddy," answered Buelah.

"Daddy? He be's no daddy, be's he?"

"No, Mama. Bu' we's wans lotsa pickaninnies, like you's."

"An' we has a farm here abouts, Mama," said Zeb. "We should outta has our wee'uns right here."

After a pause, "Don' worries, Mama. We's be happy," said Buelah.

"You's happy, we's happy," said Ella. "Bu' you's stays dem nites an' leave tomorra, Buel."

"Orites, Mama."

"Ya-all come inside now a while. The food's hot," said Victoria.

A big dinner, cooked by Victoria, Ella, and Buelah, was followed by drinking and a rundown of the last five or six days. Then it was time for dancing, singing, and hugging until late into the night. Hugh and Hank left for their home long before the party ended, among hugs, kisses, and handshakes. They took their bull, Gov'nor, with them. The party finally ended after midnight, and the newlyweds got the extra bed. The rest went to the barn with all the animals.

Tuesday, December 1

Sometime in the very early hours of December first, it started to snow. By the time Mose woke, there were several inches on the ground; and it was still snowing hard, causing a new dilemma, or new "adventure." Should Jon take a chance on making it to Fort Patrick Henry, some twenty miles northwest?

"Should we try it, gang?"

"Not in your life," answered Liz.

"I think we should wait until this snow melts, Jonny."

"That could be next spring, my pretty plum."

"Let's give it a day or two before we decide, Jon," said Charles.

"Okay, but I was hoping to make it to Arkansas before the winter really sets in."

"Then you should have started in July," said Liz.

"My pappy used to say, 'Ya wish in one hand and spit in the other and see which hand fills first,'" said Dave.

"That isn't quite how he said it," said Charles.

"I didn't know you had a father," quipped Liz.

"I'll bet Victoria and Nanty Ella have breakfast ready," said Maggie.

"I know they do, darlin'. I can smell it," answered Jon.

"Well, what are we waiting for? I'm starvin'!" yelled Dave. He ran out into the snow and hit the ground hard.

"Your stomach is going to break your neck!" yelled Charles.

"We're all safe. Only the good die young," answered Liz.

"We'll all starve if we wait for the snow to melt," said Jon, "so let's walk to the house, slow and easy."

"I'm afraid of falling, Jonny, like Dave did."

"Hold onto me, my love, and you'll be fine."

"Yeah, what could possibly go wrong when we have Jonny as our anchor?" quipped Liz.

A large breakfast of pork and corn cakes, covered with a type of pork gravy, really hit the spot. Jesse and Victoria Stone graciously invited the Hamilton travelers to stay with them until it was safe to travel.

"If the snow lets up tomorrow, I want to go into town."

"You mean Elizabethton?" asked Liz.

"Yes. It's a nice town."

"Well, I'd like to go along to see the town named after me."

"What do we need, Jonny?" asked Maggie.

"Lots of blankets, I think, and maybe I can find a team of horses to pull our new carryall."

"How are you going to pay for that?"

"Well, I have over a hundred dollars from your father from the overseer pay, my pretty plum."

"How did you manage to get that, Jonny?"

"I just told him he'd never see his daughter again if he didn't pay, and he handed me a hundred fifty dollars!"

"But you promised I would get to go home, Jonny."

"I did, but it still worked. Besides, I have the gold piece the chief gave me."

"You promised to spend that on land in Arkansas."

"I did that too, but that land is free, my pretty plum."

"I hope you're right about that, Jonny. But you'll still need that gold for improvements and shelter."

"I know, darlin'. I won't cash it in."

"Maybe I should go with you."

"And take a chance on losing the baby?" asked Liz.

"She's right, my love. It could be stressful for you."

"Stressful? What do you think this whole trip has been? Besides, this baby isn't due until next spring. You said you would never leave me again, Jonny."

"I did that too. I'm sorry, darlin'. You can come along if you wish."

"That's better! In that case, I think I'll stay here and get caught up on my diary. But you two better behave."

"I promise we will, my pretty plum."

"It wouldn't be much fun in a snow bank," said Liz.

"That's what I'm counting on!" said Maggie.

Wednesday, December 2

The next morning, the snow had stopped. The cold made a crust on top of the nine or ten inches of snow. Jon had a quick breakfast and tried to sneak out to the barn, where Mose had hitched Corker to the carryall.

"You're not thinking of leaving without me, are you, Jonny?"

"Of course not, Elizabeth. Just getting Corker ready."

"Oh, Mose didn't do his job? You'll have to speak to him."

"What didn't I's do, Jon?" asked Mose, who had entered the barn from the house.

"You forgot to hitch Corker to this wagon, Mose. Least that's what Jonny says."

"No, I didn't say that, Mose. You had it ready. Liz is just trying to give me a hard time."

"That's easy to do, even in this cold weather, Mose. I'm going to give him a real hard time on the way to town."

"He's maybe leaves you's in town," smiled Mose.

"He wouldn't dare! While we're gone, could you do me a big favor, Mose?" asked Liz.

"Sure, I's do. Wha' you's needs?"

"Will you make some walls so we all can have some privacy tonight?"

"Yassum, ma'am, I's do."

"Thank you, Mose. I promise not to give you a hard time."

"An' please don' gives Jon hard times."

"Oh, he likes it, Mose."

"And you might give Pasha a rubdown with liniment, Mose. He's looking pretty bad. This trip has been hard for him."

"Yassa, I's do. He be weezin' ova nites, Jon."

"Well, he's in good hands now. See ya later today, Mose."

"Orites, Jon. If'n you's don' gets back in aftanoons, I's come lookin' for you's."

Out the barn, down the driveway and right onto the main road trudged Corker, having no trouble. He seemed to enjoy it, like he was used to snow. Out of sight of the Stone house, Liz cuddled up to Jon.

"Wow, that breeze is cold," she said.

"There are blankets behind the bench."

"I know. It's my face and hands that are cold."

"Use my scarf to wrap your face, Liz."

"Alright. And I know how to warm up my hands."

"Didn't you bring some gloves?"

"Didn't think I would need them."

"Well, here, I'll share mine with you."

"Thanks, but I have another idea."

Liz reached under Jon's blanket and coat, and started working on the buttons of his Kentucky jeans.

"Now don't start that again, Liz."

"Why not, Jonny? I know you want me, and this may be our last chance before we split."

"You want to freeze that ass of yours off?"

"It's my ass, Jonny, and I want to share it with you."

"Please, Liz, I'm trying to be faithful to my wife."

"She will never know, Jonny."

"I said please! I want to be faithful."

"Oh, alright, Jonny. Be a chicken. But I still need to warm my hands." With that, Liz grabbed Jon's gloves, as Jon buttoned his kentucks.

Jon handed Liz a blanket. "This blanket and the gloves should warm you up enough."

The rest of the journey into the town of Elizabethton was quiet. Not a word was spoken.

"So this is Elizabethton."

"Yes. It was called Sycamore Shoals."

"But when they heard I was coming, they changed it."

"I guess so. What do you have to get here?"

"Not much, loverboy. Just wanted to see it."

"So where should I drop you off?"

"Maybe at a beauty salon."

"You'd be a hit at a saloon."

"Would that make you jealous, Jonny?"

"Of course. I don't want anyone else getting what I can't have."

"What you refuse to take. Find me a saloon."

"Well, what do you know, here's a salon. I'll let you off here."

"How long are you going to be, Jonny?"

"I want to go to the gun shop, then the general store."

"Alright. Where's a mercantile?"

"I saw one a couple blocks down this street."

"I'll meet you there in an hour or so."

"Okay. Wait for me if I'm not there. See ya there, Liz."

"Aren't you forgetting something, Jonny?"

"What am I forgetting?"

"To thank me . . . for joining you," said a smiling Liz. There was a pause.

"You really mean that?" After a moment with no answer, Jon added, "I guess you meant it when you said you were going to give me a bad time."

"I said a hard time, Jonny."

"Oh, . . . thanks. See you in an hour or so."

Jon drove Corker and the carryall down the street to the gun shop he had been to before, where the same owner was waiting to serve him.

"Well, well, you're still here! Decided to stay here?"

"No, sir, I just got sidetracked. I'm about to be on my way again, and need a few items."

"Where ya headed, Mister . . . I don't believe I know yer name."

"Hamilton, Jon Hamilton, headed for Arkansas."

"The hell! That's a long ways to travel in the middle a winter!"

"Well, I was hoping to get there before winter sets in."

"The hell! Shoulda left in July! What can I get ya?"

"Let's see . . . I'll need a barrel of gunpowder, and . . ."

"Gunpowder? The hell! I just sold ya two barrels a week ago. Been shootin' squirrels?"

"No, just practicin' firin' my Hawken."

"Say . . . you weren't one a them men that had yer womenfolk stolen, are ya?"

"Well, yes. How did you hear about that?"

"Glory be! I heered ya whooped them good, killed every one a them bastards."

"Nah. Had to kill a few. Didn't want to, though."

"The hell! I'da killed them all, an' took their women."

"Well, we got our women back, and a couple Cherokee women too."

"An' the Butlers' bull. Hell, the powder's on me!"

"Thanks, but that's not necessary."

"The hell! It's about time someone taught them bastards a lesson. What else you need, Jon?"

"Some caps and balls, and some fine, startin' powder."

"Okay. I only got a few a them caps left. They're only testin' caps, ya know. Not many cap locks around, but I have some odd-lookin' pellet caps that oughtta work on yer gun. Do ya have it wit ya?" asked the storekeep.

"Yes, I do, out in the carryall. I'll get it."

Jon went out and came back in with his Hawken.

"Say, that's a pretty fancy gun ya have there, Jon. Bring it out the back a the store, an' we'll see if these pellets work."

"It's a J. and S. Hawken, made in St. Louis, and converted to a cap lock."

"The hell! Well, put one a these pellet caps on the nipple, an' let's see if'in it fires. Shoot thataways, so you'll only hit ole' Boony, down that gap."

"Not much chance of that happenin', sir."

"The hell! He was just spotted again the other day."

"The hell! I heard he'd been killed," Jon said casually.

"Na, nobody here wants ta kill him. He's harmless."

"The hell!" said Jon, as he placed the pellet on the nipple. The Hawken fired with a swift, clean charge, which Jon liked. "I'll take that box of pellets too, and some balls and fine ignition powder."

"Ya got it, Jon, on the house."

"Thank you, sir. You don't know if anyone has a team of work horses for sale, do you?"

"No, but ya might check at the stables down the street."

"Thanks. I'll do that. I need grain for my animals too."

"The hell. By the looks of that big beautiful horse ya got out there, he could eat bear, or elk, or Boony all by hisself. What do you need more horses for? He can pull a train a wagons."

"Thanks again. You're right. Corker can pull anything."

"Corker? He should be called Goliath or Hercules."

"Well, Corker means remarkable and clever, and Corker is both of them."

"The hell! I reckon you've got a good name for him then. How about . . . Corkules?"

"I'll take that name under consideration, sir."

"You going down ta Knoxville an' across to Nashville?"

"No, sir, I have a family with me going to Kentucky, so I'm takin' them through Cumberland Pass, then following the river to Nashville."

"The hell! Yer takin' the long, hard way. Ya might be till July just a-gettin' to Arkansas!"

"I sure hope not. I plan on plantin' a crop come spring."

"The hell! Well, take my advice, then, an' don't follow the river, 'cause it winds up an' down, north an' south, on its way west."

"The hell! Then I should just go straight west?"

"Right as rain. When ya reach the river, about ten miles northa the gap, just head due west. Ya might even do a degree or two south of west for a hundred miles or more, an' you'll run smack inta the river headed south and west for Nashville."

"Thanks a lot, Mr . . . I don't know your name, sir."

"My name is Thomas Clark, son of George Rogers Clark, and nephew of William Clark."

"The hell!"

Jonathan climbed aboard the carryall and pointed Corker's nose north, up the main drag of Elizabethton. He was thinking about Thomas Clark, son of George Rogers Clark, who was the man who captured Jon's grandfather at Vincennes. "WOW!" Jon almost didn't hear the screams and shouts, coming from a saloon across the street. Those screams and shouts sounded like . . .

"Get your hands off me! Help! Take that, you prick! Arrgh! Let go of me, you bastard!"

It was Liz! Jon pulled on the reins to stop Corker and jumped out of the carryall. He raced across the street and through the swinging door of the pub. There was Liz, and a group of men looking at him, smiling, then laughing.

"This is him, Jon Hamilton, come to rescue me again." Everyone laughed even harder and louder. The joke was on Jon.

"Glad ta meet ya, Jon," said one of the hyenas, reaching out his hand to shake. Jon, red-faced, ignored him.

"Don't be mad at me, Jonny," said Liz.

"Yeah, don't be mad, Jon. You're a hero 'round here."

"Yeah, we wanna buy ya a drink, Jon."

"Don't blame ya fer wantin' to rescue this puss, Jon." This from another jackass.

"Thank you, lover. This really means something to me," said Liz.

Jon was now shaking with anger. He pushed Liz's outstretched arms away and walked back out to his carryall and drove on down the street. He passed the general store, still shaking. It occurred to him that he had missed the store, but didn't turn around. He needed to go to the stables anyway. It was another five or six blocks, enough for Jon to cool down considerably.

"Howdy. That's a big, beautiful animal ya got there."

"Thanks. Got any food for him?" asked Jon.

"You bet. I'll fix you right up."

"I could use some liniment and a set of shoes as well."

"Right. Anything else, sir?"

"What do you have for a sick horse, dyspepsia in lungs?"

"Quinine, potassium, castor oil. He don't look sick to me."

"No, this if for another horse."

"Well, I'd give him some quinine, then castor oil about an hour later, and keep him warm."

"I've got a blanket around him," said Jon.

"You need one of these." The man showed Jon a leather wraparound for a horse with a thick, wool insert.

"How much is that?"

"Sell it to you for three dollars, sir."

"Sold! I think that's all I need. You don't have a team of horses for sale, do you?"

"No, sir, but unless you're pullin' a whorehouse full of customers up a steep, slippery hill, you have all you need right here in this monster of a horse. I never seen one this big and powerful."

"Thanks. How much for two sacks of grain, the wrap, castor oil, quinine, shoes, and liniment?"

"All together, with nails, is about ten dollars."

"Fair price. Thank you, and here you are," said Jon.

"Great doing business with ya. Come back again."

The next stop was the general store. When Jon pulled Corker to a stop in front, there was Liz, waiting.

"I thought you had left me."

"That's what you get for doing your own thinking! You can wait in the wagon, or help me with supplies."

"It's too cold out here. I'll help. Please don't be mad at me, Jonny."

"Mad? Who's mad? You would drive any man cockamamie and baffy in the brain box, but never mad!"

"Do I drive you cockamamie, Jonny?"

"Only when I'm alone, or with somebody! Come on in and help me resupply our wagons."

"Okay, love. What do we need?"

"Everything that carryall can carry."

"Good morning, sir. If you don't mind me a-sayin', ya got a purty wife there."

"Thanks, but she's not my wife," said Jon.

"Then ye must be daffy to let a purty thing like that get away."

Jon looked at Liz, who had a grin from ear to ear.

"I have a wife who is just . . . is pretty too."

"Well, sir, ya either gotta pile, or yer the luckiest critter in the Cumberlands! What can I get ya?"

"I need to restock my wagons for a long trip."

"In the middle a winter?"

"I didn't plan for winter to come so early."

"Probably shoudda started in July! How many persons, an' how many miles?"

"Ah . . . eight persons, and Kentucky and Arkansas."

"Whoa! That's some serious travelin'. Gotta couple wagons just to haul food?"

"Well, we have three wagons, but we sleep in them too."

"I gotta big tent you kin sleep in. You gonna need lotsa food for that long a trip."

"No, thanks. We have some tarps, and a trailer to haul most of the food."

"Yes, sir. Ya goin' all the way up to Boonesborough?"

"Well, three are going up the Kentucky River. We split when we reach the Cumberland."

"Pass, mountains, or river?" asked the clerk.

"I didn't know I had a choice! River, I guess."

"Well then, ye'll hit all three to Pinevull. Ye'all can regrub there. Lessee, three from 'at are five, so five goin' to Nashvull, then?"

"That's right. We'll just follow the river due west."

"If ye'all faller the river, ye'll be a-goin' north, south, an' even some east, every which way."

"I know. Mister Clark down at the gun shop told me that, so I'm goin' due west."

"Well, I'm tellin' ye ta go more southwest, laddie, an' ye'll even save more miles. Now, from Pinevull to where ye'all hit the Cumberland again is over hundred miles, so ye'll hafta regrub down heavy there. So, ta Pinevull, ye'll need hundred pound flour."

"Yes, and I want some bacon, potatoes, corn meal, salted pork . . ."

"Hold on ta yerself, yer gettin' ahead a me," said the clerk. "'Bout thirty pound taters, a small barrel a pork, and ye'll need twenty pound or more corn meal, ah, two barrels."

"Righto! And I want bacon, beans, and blankets."

"Barrel a bacon, barrel a beans, an' barrela . . . blankets?"

"Yes, sir, lots of blankets. Six or eight, at least," answered Jon. "What else do we need, Liz?"

"How about sugar, coffee, and . . . salt?"

"Oh yeah . . . some sugar and molasses, coffee, salt, ginger root, yeast, and hops."

ARTHUR HAMILTON

"Are ye gonna drink an' travel?"

"No, but we need to party before we split."

"Well, don't tell nobody, but I gotta few bottles a good corn juice. I'll throw one in for yer party."

"Great! Thank you . . . but please throw in enough of those other things to make a good batch of spruce juice too."

"Alrighty. Anything else, sir?"

"Can you think of anything else, Liz?"

"Hmm . . . maybe some spices? And tea leaves? And maybe some rice?"

"Rice!" said Jon. "I shoulda thought of that. And how about some dried beef?"

"Yep, we has some-a that too. A barrel a beef, an' barrel a rice, a box of spices, an' tea leaves."

"Is that everything, Liz?"

"I think so . . . for food, at least."

"Do ye have the kitchen pots an' pans? An' maybe a Dutch oven? Where ye be a-storin' an' cookin' an' servin' from?"

"Yes, Jonny, Ella lost her kitchen when we lost the buckboard, remember?" asked Liz.

"I got jist the ticket fer ye'all. Looky here, it's a built-in kitchen that ye attach to the back a the wagon, an' it comes wit pans, knives and forks, and cookin' tools."

"I'll take it! How much does this all come to?"

"Hold on jista gol-durn minute! How about cards, er, games? An' lanterns an' candles . . . and' bedpans?"

"Bedpans!" said Liz. "I can use one of those, and I think Ella may need some vinegar."

"Okay, throw in a bottle of vinegar, oil for four lanterns, candles, and a couple of bedpans. Now how much?"

"Lessee, addin' vinegar, two bedpans, oil fer lanterns, grease fer wheels and throwing in some cards and three, er, four extra barrels . . . ye probably has hundred fifty or more."

"I have about a hundred twenty dollars. I'll have to bring . . ."

"That'll be jist fine. Call it square."

"Here, I have a few dollars to add to it," said Liz.

"Jist right. I hope ye'all have a safe trip. I'll get ye some help to carry all that out."

"Thank you, sir. We appreciate this."

Early afternoon at the Stone farm found a powerful white horse pulling a wagon loaded with supplies. They headed for the barn, where an afternoon of work was started. Jon and Liz walked into the farmhouse to tell most of their story to the Stones, and to Margaret Rose. So many things needed to get done to be ready to travel in the morning. The three wagons needed to be greased, and lanterns filled with oil. Mose started attaching Ella's new "kitchen" to the back of the carryall, so she could arrange the dishes, tools, food, spices, etc., the way she wanted. The men also hitched the trailer to the back of the covered wagon, and started loading it. Duplicated and slow-moving items were loaded first. They built a railing around the trailer to hold items in. The Chasney wagon would hold the food items needed first, and could be quickly restocked, with most of the bed open to hold the crammed three Chasneys. The carryall would hold feed and supplies for the animals, Mose's tools and supplies, the immediate items needed for Ella to cook, and a cramped space for Mose and Ella to sleep, with Chipper on the benches. The covered wagon would now be entered and exited at the front, with the stocked trailer behind. The one side, and behind the bench were again loaded to the limit.

Everything was then roped down and covered with canvas.

"How does it look to you, Jonny?"

"Crammed, and be damned, my pretty plum."

"How much did all of this cost?"

"Everything Liz and I had, except for my gold stone." Jon's attention now shifted to Pasha. "How's our prize horse doing, Mose?"

"He be's bedder than dem mornin's, but stills no good."

"That box has quinine. Give him some of it now, rub him down with liniment, then put this wrap on him. In an hour, give the poor devil some castor oil. Okay, Mose?"

"Orites, Jon. I's do, an' somethin' un night an' mornin'."

"That wrap is beautiful, Jonny. It must have cost a lot."

"It's probably worth over ten dollars, but cost three, darlin'."

"Thanks for thinking about him, Jonny. I'm worried."

"Don't worry yourself, honey. If anyone can cure him, it's Mose. That castor oil will either cure him or kill him."

"Don't say that, Jonny. We should have left him at Bethania. This trip is so hard on him."

"That's true, darlin', but you would have been unhappy without him this last month."

"It's been forty days now, Jonny."

"Once we get on level ground, through most of Tennessee, we should make much better time."

"Don't believe him, Maggie. He's given us that line before," joked Liz.

"Well, I have to be right sometime! Maybe this will be it."

"I believe him," said Maggie, "right or wrong. Someday he'll be right."

"Oh, brother! Love must be grand," sighed Liz.

With all the preparations finished, it was time for a big supper, which Victoria Stone, Ella, and Buelah cooked. The party followed. Everyone danced to Mose's harmonica music and Ella's spoons.

"We owe you so much. How can we ever thank you for putting us up and feeding us?"

"You don't owe us a thing. It's been our pleasure," said Victoria.

"We got a lot outta it, Jon. A rifle, a gold stone, and an adventure we'll ne'er forget," said Jess.

"And we made some good friends," added Victoria.

"I've got something for Vicki, Jonny," said Maggie. "Would you go get my little red chest, under the bench of our wagon?"

"Sure thing, my pretty plum." Jon hurried out the door to the barn, and was back quickly. Maggie unlocked the ornate box and brought out a beautiful brooch with a large blue stone surrounded by diamonds.

"This is for you, Vicki, from all of us."

"Oh, Maggie! It's lovely . . . but too expensive."

"Nothing is too expensive for all you've done for us."

"Thank you so much. I'll treasure it forever."

"Y'all be sure ta write ta us, Jon, so's we're aware a yer trip an' life in Arkansas," said Jess. "An' that goes fer y'all too, Chuck an' Dave."

"Maggie here is the writer of our family, but I'll be sure to remind her."

"We're sure glad you came by, Charles, and asked for help."

"We're glad too, Missus Stone," answered Charles.

"Yer welcome to stay a few more days until this here snow is melted."

"Thanks, Jess, but we'd really like to get started again. We'd be grateful if you kept Buelah and Zeb a day or two more."

"We would be happy to," said Victoria.

"We's thanks you's. Good nights," said Ella.

"Yes, good night. See you early in the morning," said Jon.

Back in the barn in their divided stalls, Maggie took out her diary and started writing by the light of the lantern. "Tell me about your day in town," she whispered to Jon.

"What do you want to know?" Jon whispered back.

"Everything!"

"Well, I dropped Liz off at a salon, and she went to a saloon while I was at the gun shop. Oh, have you heard of George Rogers Clark?"

"Yes," Maggie whispered. "What about him?"

"His son owns the gun shop."

"Shh! I want to hear about you and Elizabeth Engels."

"George Rogers Clark is the man that captured my grandfather."

"Really? You promised you would tell me about your grandfather someday."

"That's right, I did. Well, my grandfather was a British colonel, who came down out of Canada to Detroit."

"Jonny . . . I want to hear about today!"

"Well, I went to the gun shop, then the stables, where I got that wool wrap for Pasha, then to the general store."

"And where was Liz all that time?"

"In the saloon! She met me at the—"

"Shh . . . and nothing else happened?"

"Nothing . . . at all," he lied.

"Alright, Jonny, go to sleep."

Diary of Margaret Hamilton

Wednesday, December 2

. . . Nothing else happened while Liz and my Jonny were in Elizabethton. The afternoon was spent preparing for our continued trip tomorrow. The Stones have been so nice to us, and we will miss them terribly. Jonny and I both like this area, and the people, but he won't live here. He says the seasons are too short this high in altitude for good crops, so it's off again tomorrow for Kentucky and Arkansas. What an adventure this is!

Love to all,
Maggie

Thursday, December 3

Daylight brought a beehive of activity, as Jon's group prepared for the journey ahead. Ella wanted to try out her new kitchen, so Mose drove Corker, pulling the carryall, out of the barn and started a campfire. Ella quickly whipped up some buckwheat cakes with real maple syrup. The sun was just exposing its full roundness as the group sat on the ground, on blankets and ate. Everything was ready for travel.

"What's our first stop?" asked Charles.

"Fort Patrick Henry by this evening."

"If we're lucky," quipped Liz.

"How far is it to the fort, Jon?" asked Charles.

"Close to thirty miles, but it's all road."

"Covered with snow," added Liz. "You won't make thirty miles."

Victoria Stone stuck her head out her door and shouted, "Breakfast is ready! Come on in!"

"We're having breakfast cakes out here," answered Maggie.

"Whatcha got in there?" asked Dave.

"I have rice cakes and chicken eggs. Buelah cooked them."

"Rice cakes . . . we have to try them, gang."

"I's stays an' cleans up," said Mose.

"Thanks, Mose. Let's taste them quickly, and get started."

"Good," said Maggie. "I've not tasted Buelah's cooking."

"The rice cakes are delicious," said Liz.

"And the eggs were wonderful," added Maggie.

"I think Buelah will make a good wife, Zeb," said Charles.

"I's knows my Buelah be good wife. I's hopes you's has good life, child," said Ella.

"Thank you, Mama. I's do." Buelah and Ella hugged for the last time. Then, as Maggie hugged Buelah, Ella hugged Zeb.

"Thanks again for your kindness, Jess and Victoria."

"Yer welcome, Jon. Y'all come back anytime, an' write."

"And thank you again for the brooch," added Victoria.

"Goodbye, Vicki and Jess. Goodbye, Zeb." Maggie hugged Zeb and Buelah. "I'll miss you *so* much, Buel!"

"I's miss you's too, Sissy. Has a good life."

"Ella, you take the lead in the carryall with Chipper, then Liz will take her wagon second, and Maggie, darlin', you bring up the rear. Tie Pasha behind the Chasney wagon, Mose."

"Yassa, Jon, I's do."

"May I ask where you men are riding?" asked Liz.

"We'll walk a while and see how the horses take to the loads."

To waves and shouts, the wagons pulled out of the Stones' driveway, turned west, and started toward Fort Patrick Henry over a snow-covered roadway. Mose walked in the lead, close to his wife and stepson. The Chasney brothers walked close to their wagon, and Jon brought up the rear, close to Maggie.

"Keep an eye on your horse, darlin'. If he starts slowing down, let me know. By the way, where did you get that brooch?"

"It was a birthday present from my little brother, Miles. I won't need jewelry for a long time, and Victoria will take good care of it."

"I thought I recognized it."

The Chasney brothers were having trouble walking in the snow, especially Dave, who fell several times, to the delight and laughter of Liz. After a couple hours, Jon had a sore, tired Dave climb up on his wagon. He noticed that Charles, and even Mose, were tiring, so he called a stop.

"We's has lots a food. Missus Stones send bag 'un foods."

"Great, Ella, give each a little food. We'll stop again for lunch after a couple more hours of travel."

"How far have we gone, Jonny?"

"About five or six miles, my love."

"Where did Mose go, Ella?"

"Daddy makes snow shoes fo' Davy."

With knife and axe and a little time, Mose cut two lengths of thin boards, drove some nails through each, and attached them to the bottom of Dave's shoes with some of the leather straps he had had, and used, since they left Bethania.

"Hey," said Dave, "they work real good!"

"When we stop for lunch, will you make me a pair, Mose?" asked Charles.

"Yassa, I's do fo' you's, Charles."

"Thank you . . . from my brother and me."

"You's welcome."

"Time to get rollin' again, gang," said Jon.

Jon estimated that it was between one and two in the afternoon when he called a halt for lunch. Ella dug into the large bag of food that Victoria had sent along. Mose grabbed his knife and axe again so he could make spike shoes for Charles.

"I'll get some water for the horses," said Jon.

"I'll go with you, Jon," said Charles.

"Good. And, Dave, will you and Chipper feed the horses a bit of grain? You'll have to break one of the sacks."

"We's has grain!" yelled Chipper.

"From before?"

"Yassa, Massa Jon," answered Chipper.

"Good. Use that up first."

"How many miles have we gone now, big boy," asked Liz.

"A good twelve, probably thirteen or fourteen miles."

"Not even halfway. Give up?"

"Not a chance."

"Silly question, Liz. He never quits a challenge," said Maggie.

"Oh, I think he does."

Victoria had cooked beans in a pot the day before, and Ella got them out, along with some pork and real bread, also baked by Missus Stone. Dave put them all together on a slice of bread. When the juice started seeping through the bread, he grabbed another slice and folded it around the pork and beans.

"How does that taste, Davy?" asked Maggie.

"Better'n a dodger."

"Then I'm going to try one." Before long, they were all eating a "sandwich" of cold pork and beans, and liking it.

"How is Pasha doing?" asked Jon.

"He seemed to be keeping up," answered Maggie.

"He be's breathin' hard, Massa Jon," said Chipper.

"Will he make this journey alive, Jonny?"

"I don't know, my love. Will you look at him, Mose?"

"Orites. I's do, Jon."

"Thanks, Mose. Do what you can for him."

Back on the ever-improving road, the group settled into the task and made headway. Soon the Chasney brothers were discarding their "snow shoes," as sunshine peeked through the clouds. As they made their way west along the Watauga River, and toward Fort Patrick Henry, they passed many farms. Sometimes people would wave to them, and Jon's group would return the wave. They finally came to what looked like the ruins of an old fort, and the Watauga River seemed to empty into another larger river, running northwest. Jon's gang was mystified.

"Is this Fort Henry?" quizzed a sarcastic Liz.

"I hope not," said Maggie.

"So do I," answered Jon. "We've only gone less than twenty miles, and the sign at Elizabethton said the fort was thirty."

"So what do we do now, oh fearless leader?"

"Yes, Jon," said Charles, "it looks like it's getting late."

"Let's make camp here, and I'll take Corker back to that last farmhouse a couple miles back, and find out for sure."

"I's get's Corka readys fo' you's, Jon."

"Thanks, Mose. We'll start again early tomorrow morning."

The group got busy making camp. Jon took Corker back to the farm.

"Hello," Jon said to the man coming out the door.

"Hello. What can I do for you?"

"I'm just traveling through, and I'm looking for Fort Henry."

"It be nine to dozen miles down that there river."

"Thank you, sir. I saw the ruins of a fort a couple miles down there, and was sure it wasn't Fort Henry."

"Yer right. That be old Fort Watauga."

"Thanks again. Let's go, Corker," said Jon.

"How much you wan's for that horse?"

"Not for sale, sir. Thanks for the information."

"Ye bet. I be a-givin' ye a fair price for him."

"Sorry, sir. Goodbye."

Jon hurried back to his camp, and found his group in turmoil. "What's happening?"

"Maggie's horse collapsed," said Charles, standing back from the group surrounding the horse.

Jon spotted Maggie standing alone, crying. He went to her side. "I'm sorry, darling," he said, as he hugged her.

"Oh, why did I bring him along?" she asked through sobs.

"Because he's your horse, darlin'."

"But he would be well at Bethania."

"Maybe. But if he died there, you wouldn't be with him." Jon could hear Pasha wheezing and struggling for breath, even over Maggie's sobs. He could also hear Mose talking to Pasha.

"Easy, Pasha. Easy, boy," soothed Mose.

"He needs to be put out of his misery, Jon," said Charles.

Jon shook his head in agreement. "Can he make it, Mose?" he asked.

"Nossa, Jon. He be's bad. Bad. Sick, Jon."

"Pasha is in a lot of pain, darlin'. It's better if we end it." Maggie was sobbing hysterically.

"Did you hear me, Maggie? We can't let him suffer like this."

Maggie nodded her head yes. It was buried in Jon's chest.

"Okay, Mose. Will you do it?"

"I'll do it, Jon," said Charles. "Mose is attached to him too."

"Thanks, Charles. Come on, honey, let's go in our wagon." Jon and the sobbing Maggie lay in the covered wagon for what seemed to be an eternity. Suddenly, they were shook by the sound. *BANG!* They stayed in their wagon the rest of the night, while the remainder of the group had supner, buried the Arabian horse, and turned in.

Chapter VI

———∞∞———

The Cumberlands

Fort Patrick Henry was a big, busy town. There were several stores with the name "Kingsport" on them, such as Kingsport Cemetery, Kingsport Building Supplies, Kingsport Day School, and "Welcome to Kingsport, Tennessee, Population 745, -800 DOGS."

Jon Hamilton was certain this was Fort Henry, with another name change, just like Sycamore Shoals was now Elizabethton. That is, he was certain until about two blocks into Kingsport, where he saw a sign reading "Fort Patrick Henry" with an arrow pointing to the right, along a busy street. Jon headed his group down that road. Five busy blocks later, they came to the Holston River, and the Old Fort on its bank.

"So, the town must be inside those log walls," quipped Liz.

"Yes, and Kingsport has its citizens surrounded," added Maggie.

"All six of them," said Liz, and the two women laughed.

Jon was willing to take the banter in silence, as it had brought Maggie out of her sad state.

"We're all very tired, Jon. Let's lunch here," said Charles.

"Yeah, I'm hungry," added Dave.

"Okay, gang, we'll rest and have lunch here."

"We's can builds a fire un dis park, Jon," said Mose.

"That be's Orites, Jonny. We's has corn dodgas," said Ella.

"Good. Let's eat."

"We's still eats on, Missy Vicky," added Ella.

"It was sure nice of the Stones to help us the way they did."

"Yes, Victoria made enough food to last us another couple days yet, Jonny," said Maggie.

"Looks like we won't need all these supplies for a while," said Charles.

"Maybe we didn't need this much all at once, Jonny."

"We never have enough supplies, my pretty plum."

"Yeah, well none of us could get any sleep last night with all those supplies," said Liz.

"That's true, Jon. There wasn't room to stretch," added Charles.

"So what do we do about that, big boy?" asked Liz.

"I guess I shoulda bought that tent we saw in Elizabethton."

"Maybe we'll send you back to get it."

"Well, if they had one there, perhaps we can find one here."

"Good thought, my darlin'. We'll check at the mercantile."

There were three mercantiles in Kingsport, and in the second, Jon spotted what he was looking for.

"Hello there, Jasper," said the clerk. "Gonna do some huntin'?"

"No, sir, travelin'," answered Jon.

"Oh? Where to?"

"Arkansas."

"Arkansas? In the middle a winter? You must be part Eskimo."

"No, just North Carolinian," answered Jon.

"Well, it can get plenty cold here in Tennessee and Missouri this time a year. Shoulda started in July!"

Jon could feel the heat under his collar rising. "I ain't goin' go Missouri!" he yelled. "I'm going to Arkansas, and I need a big tent. Are you going to sell one to me, or do I go to another store?"

"Okay, Okay. Don't get all snarly, Jasper. I's just tryin' to make conversation."

"Skip the tongue-waggin', Nancy boy. I'm in a hurry."

"I'm not a Nancy boy!" shouted the clerk.

"And I'm not a Jasper."

"Oh, sorry . . . ah . . . sir. You say you need a big tent? Well, this is our best one. Sleeps eight, and even has a metal stove to heat and cook on."

"How many have burned the tent down, and the people?"

"Why, none that I know of."

"Well, it looks dangerous, but I'll take it. How much?"

"Twenty dollars." Jon turned to leave. "Make it ten."

"I'll take it," said Jon.

"Cheap at half the price. Ya got a bargain, mister."

"Only if it doesn't kill us."

"Hope not. Good luck on your trip ta Arkansas."

"Thanks. I'm sorry I got dandered."

There was suddenly some room now in the wagons, as the tent came equipped with eight small, feathered mattresses and a metal plate for the stove to sit on. The lengths of stove pipe also served as the center pole of the tent. The group could sleep in the tent, making room in the wagons. They headed north, on the Great Valley Road, and soon came to the famous Blockhouse, used as protection from a once-hostile group of Cherokee. That is where the Wilderness Road, blazed by Daniel Boone himself, started west to the Cumberland Gap, and Kentucky. These were the best roads Jon's group had traveled on, and they made a good twenty miles on a fairly busy road, to a river running southwest along the base of the mountain range. Jon learned that they were on the Clinch River, and the range was called Powell Mountain. The Wilderness Road cut right through it. Jon was glad he had stopped while there was still daylight, as it took some time to get the tent pitched. Maggie wanted to sleep in the covered wagon, in the cold, so Mose was able to use the extra mattress under his huge body. The tent stayed warm.

"Is anything the matter, Jonny?"

"No. Why do you ask, darlin'?"

"You haven't spoken two words all afternoon."

"Just extra tired, like everyone else, I guess."

"Nonsense. You always talk when you're tired."

"Don't use that word, please, Papa Sam."

"Whoops, sorry, but something is bothering you, Jonny." There was a pause.

"Well, yes there is . . . sorta."

"Well, let's hear it."

"Maggie, darlin', if anyone else says to me, 'you should have started in July,' I think I will choke him to death."

"Why would they say that? They know you promised to help get the harvest finished before you left, and I wouldn't be with you if you hadn't married me first. Who has been saying that, Jonny?"

"Almost everyone I've met on this trip."

Maggie paused. "If we had left in July, would we be all settled in by now?"

"Of course, my pretty plum."

"What would we have for shelter . . . and warmth?"

"We'd have our tent, and maybe a building."

"Nonsense again, Jonny! You only just bought the tent because we were crowded, and there wouldn't have been enough time to build a building."

"Well, if you know the answer, why the question?"

"Because I wanted to know what we're going to do when we get this land in Arkansas."

"Maybe it will be spring, and we can all sleep on the ground."

"On our *bottomland!* And I can have my baby in the mud!"

"Now, darlin', don't get dandered. When our baby is due, we'll have shelter for you both. Are you forgetting what a genius your Nunky Mose is? Besides, it might be nice, having a mud rat!"

"And a mud-mudda." Maggie and Jon laughed.

"Wasn't that sign at Kingsport funny?"

"What sign?"

"Population seven hundred, Dogs eight hundred?"

"Yeah, it was. I wish they'd stop changing names, though."

"What's our next town's name, Jonny?"

"Pineville, in Kentucky, if they haven't changed it too!"

"Is that where we split with the Chasneys?"

"Yes, it is. I'll miss them."

"You'll miss *her*, Jonny."

Diary of Margaret Hamilton

Friday, December 4, 1835

. . . And I'm finally caught back up with this diary. Today we passed through the town of Kingsport, formerly Fort Patrick Henry, and the famous Blockhouse, once used to protect from the hostiles, both on the Great Valley Road. We are now on the Wilderness Road, headed for Cumberland Gap. We now own a large tent, and everyone is sleeping in it except Jonny and me. After we pass through the Cumberland Mountains and Gap and reach the Cumberland River, we will be leaving the Chasneys and heading west for Nashville, Tennessee. I am still scared of kidnappers, but my husband is my hero and will always protect me. Love to all my family.

Margaret Rose Hamilton

Saturday, December 5

In the morning, Mose put the covered wagon in the lead. Snow flurries and cold temperatures greeted the group as they crossed the Powell Mountain range on good road, and in light-to-moderate traffic of families looking to settle in Kentucky. Midafternoon they saw a wagon train of six or seven wagons trying to pass a very slow moving wagon. They seemed to be shouting at the draggers, and even using a whip on them as they passed by. Mose called Jon up to the front.

"Deys cob dem wagon wit black snake, Jon. We's should helps them."

"We can't race our horses, Mose, but let's pick up the pace some. I'll let them know we're here behind."

Jon placed a cap on his Hawken and fired into the air. *BAM!*

"That scared them, Mose. Look at them run! Ella, lead them a little faster until we catch up with that wagon."

"Yassir, Jonny, I's do."

"They're probably a little over a mile ahead."

"I's thinks close to two, Jon."

"Maybe so, Mose. We'll try to keep up with you."

"You trying to kill my horses?" asked Liz.

"This is too much for Apple and Jack, Jon," said Charles.

"Okay, Chuck, you and Dave tie our wagon ahead of yours, so Corker can help pull them both. I'll go on ahead with the carryall. We'll wait for y'all a mile or two ahead, when we get to that slow wagon. If you hear shooting, come running."

"Can Corker pull two wagons and a loaded trailer?" asked Dave, jokingly.

"You bet your bloomers he can, Dave," Jon joked back.

"What are bloomers, Jonathan?" asked Liz.

"They're pants the ladies are starting to wear under their dresses," said Maggie. "Sounds horrible to me."

"Well, that might help keep our legs warm. The men are falling down on the job."

"They're busy right now, Liz. Besides, it's supposed to be a new fashion, not a warmer," said Maggie.

"Are they worn over or under the bustle?"

"Not sure. Maybe over to protect us from bustle-grabbers."

"Who needs protection?" asked a laughing Liz.

Jon was on the run during this conversation, trying to catch up to the carryall. Mose and the carryall had just about reached the slow-moving wagon when Jon caught up to them. Both Jon and Mose noticed how deep the wagon's wheels were sinking in the road.

"Dey's carries heavy loads, Jon."

"Yes, but I don't see anything stacked in the wagon," huffed Jon.

"See how highs dem bed is, Jon? Dey has two beds."

"You're right, Mose. Wonder what they're carrying."

"Hello the wagon."

"Hello. Thanks for the help," said the elderly man, who sat on his wagon bench beside an elderly woman. There were two black men, a woman carrying a baby, and three other black children, all walking beside the wagon.

"Are you all headed for Kentucky?"

"Yes, sir, up the Kentucky River."

"Well, you're not going much farther with just those two horses pulling. They're worn out."

"Yes, sir, I know. I'm hoping they can get us to Boonesborough."

"Then we can ferry to Indiana," said the elderly woman.

Jon noticed the angry stare the man gave his wife.

"Oh? You're going that far north?"

"Well, maybe," said the man. "Depends on how they treat us, ah, slave owners, in Kentucky. What part of the state are you headed for?"

"I'm headed for Arkansas, but I have some people with me who are going to Frankfort. Maybe we can help you get to Pineville, and then with the Chasneys to Boonesborough."

"That would be wonderful . . .," said the lady, who stopped her sentence when the man again stared at her. "Except we ain't a-goin' through the gap." Another angry stare.

"You ain't?" asked Jon. "I think it's the only way to get a wagon through these mountains." Jon's statement was met with silence. "How do you plan to get into Kentucky?"

After a pause, the elderly man said, "Guess I better tell ya. These ain't our slaves. We are a-sneakin' them ta freedom."

"Dem escaped bounders?" asked Mose.

"Yes, they are, Mose." To the elderly man, Jon said, "You have more of them in your wagon, don't you?"

"Yes, sir, I do. They don't deserve to be treated like animals."

"My husband didn't mean that you treat your slaves that way."

"I don't have slaves, ma'am. These are my partners, Mose and Ella, and they are free blacks going to Arkansas with me."

"Glad ta meet ya. I hope you make it. People down south a-here don't take too kindly ta free blacks."

"We helped them escape from Georgia ta freedom in Indiana," said the woman. "So far, we've escaped the bounty hunters too."

"We've had to pretend they're our slaves," added the man.

"Yeah, I know. We had to do that once in North Carolina."

"We believe bounty hunters from Virginia, and maybe even Tennessee, will be waiting for us at the gap."

"We's helps dem, Jon."

"Okay, Mose. Let's make camp right here for a few hours, while we rest and grain the horses. Then we'll all go through the gap together tomorrow, with all our slaves . . .

"Orites, Jon. Ella's an' me be's you's slaves again."

"Just until we get through the Cumberland Gap, Mose."

Mose unhitched the horses and led them to grass before grabbing the grain and feeders from the carryall. The old man opened the back of his wagon, and another black couple crawled out. That made nine slaves the elderly couple were sneaking to Indiana. Jon wondered what would happen to them when they reached their goal.

Mose had fed and watered the six horses and had helped Jon build a fire, when the rest of the group arrived. Mose grained and watered those three drays as well, while Ella started to warm the last of the food sent along by Victoria Stone.

"How were you planning to feed all of those people?"

"We've had some stops along the way, people who believe the same as us, who have hidden us along the way," answered the old man.

"They've had food waiting for us," added the wife.

"By the way," said the old man, "I'm Adam Schinland, and this is my wife Amelia. We're from Huntsville."

"Glad to know you. That's my wife, Mag . . . Margaret, and I'm Jon Hamilton. These are my partners, Mose and Ella, and her son Chipper. And these are my friends, Charles and Dave Chasney, and Elizabeth."

"Thank you all for helping us," said Adam Schinland.

"More company? You're a real charmer," Liz said to Jon.

"They would like to go with you up the Kentucky River."

"Just what we need. The more the merrier," said Liz.

"Can those women cook?" asked Dave.

"Yes, sir," answered Adam. "We've had lots of grits and hominy."

"Just what we need," repeated Liz. "Any meat with that?"

"Oh yes, ma'am. Lots of meat and food waiting for us along the way."

"Along the way? That sounds interesting," said Charles.

"Sure does," retorted Liz. "You *are* just what we need."

"I'm hungry just a-thinkin' about it," said Dave.

"It's a problem from here on, though. There ain't no more rest stops 'tween here an' Boonesborough. Wish there were," said Adam.

"I said it before . . . Grits! Just what we need," moaned Liz.

"Let's worry about that when we get there. We've got lots to worry about before then."

"Like what, Jonny?" asked Maggie.

"Like getting these escaped slaves to Boonesborough."

"Escaped? You didn't tell us they were escaped, Jonny."

"I haven't been able to get a word in the last ten minutes, my pretty plum. We're helping them get through the gap."

"And I have to help them get to Boonesborough?" quizzed Liz.

"Only if you want to make it there yourself. They can cook, remember?"

"Who knows, Dave and I just might help you along the way if you're good to us," cracked Charles.

"I get the picture," snapped Liz. "I'm always good to you."

"Before this goes any further, let's eat, everybody."

Ella had heated enough food to feed Jon's group, plus the eleven others who now joined them.

"There is only one or two hours of daylight left, so let's just spend the night here. Maybe we will reach the gap tomorrow."

"Alright, Jon. Let's get the tents pitched up," said Charles.

"Horses needs rest, Jon. We's all rests," said Mose.

"Good. Let's brew some beer. We'll have a party in a couple days."

"What happens in a couple days, Jonny?"

"We reach the Cumberland, my pretty plum."

"You just said we reach the gap tomorrow, big boy."

"I'm talking about the river. Ha! I fooled you."

"Oh, so you want to party, getting rid of us."

"Yeah . . . ah, no! I want to celebrate our time together."

"You got out of that one nicely, Jonny."

"He's getting to be a charmer, Mag," said Liz.

"Well, we have to figure out how to charm our way through the Cumberland Gap."

"Charm who, Jonny?"

"Possibly some bounty hunters, darlin'."

"Are you getting us into trouble again, Jonny?"

"I hope not, Maggie."

"You better not be, big boy. Maybe we should just leave them here, on their own," said Liz.

"We's helps dem," said a stern Mose.

"We help them, Liz."

"I understand. So let's make some beer."

"And everyone check and clean your rifles. We'll turn in early and be back on the road at first light."

Diary of Margaret Hamilton

December 5, 1835

. . . And we had snow again this morning. In the afternoon, we caught up to a wagon full of bounders, nine of them. They had escaped from a plantation in Alabama, and an elderly white couple are trying to sneak them through Kentucky to Indiana. Jonny thinks we may have trouble getting them through Cumberland Gap. If we get through the gap alright, we are planning a celebration at the town of Pineville, Kentucky, where we split with the Chasneys. The Schinlands and the nine bounders are going to continue with the Chasneys. I miss you all, and Buelah.

Love, Maggie Rose

Sunday, December 6

At first light, they were all back on the Wilderness Road, thanks to Mose and Ella, who made the fire, cooked breakfast, and hitched up all the wagons in the dark! Mose attached a rope line from the carryall to the Schinland's "slave wagon," so Corker's power could help pull them along when the team pulling the Schinlands, the two slave women and the baby, got tired. There were now nine horses pulling four wagons and a loaded trailer over good road. The Schinlands and their slaves were very apprehensive because they were nearing the gap, where they expected trouble.

"Don't worry, Adam. We'll get you through the gap."

"Thank you, Mister Hamilton, but until we get through that gap, and even through Kentucky, we are very worried."

"Well, we won't reach the gap until late tonight or tomorrow, so try to relax today."

"No, sir, we can't do that. Right now we're in Virginia."

"An' they could mean trouble," said Missus Amelia Schinland.

"We're in Virginia?"

"Yes, sir. The road went north, across the state line, when we crossed the Powell Mountain."

"I'll be damned . . . you're right! But we are going a little south now, but mostly west."

"Yes, sir. But we'll still be in Virginia until we pass through the gap, where the corners of Kentucky and Virginia meet Tennessee."

"You sound pretty sure of this."

"Yes, sir. I've studied our escape route thoroughly. This road was once an Indian trade route and warrior's path."

The sun was high overhead when Jon's group came to a settlement along the Wilderness Road. There was a general store, a barn, and a long log building. Jon stopped his group and went into the store.

"Is this a town?" he asked, in the store.

"Nah, just a rest stop. I can rest ya, sleep ya, feed ya, marry ya, or fleece ya, all for a price."

"I guess rest is all we need. Does this place have a name?"

"Well, I guess Martin's Station is as good as any, but we ain't had no Martins here fer thirty years or more."

"Are we still in Virginia?"

"I guess we are, ain't for sure, though. The border here is kinda foggy. If'n ya wanna be in Virginny, you's here."

"I wanna be in Arkansas, mister . . . And no, I shouldn't have left Carolina any sooner!" There was a pause.

"I guess I just don't understand ya, stranger, but what can I get ya?"

"How far are we to the gap?" asked Jon.

"'Bout twenty miles or so, but with that bunch a people ya got there, it just might take ya a long time to get there."

"What do you mean by that?" asked Jon.

"I'd guess ya be walkin' wit dat many people, on dat few horses, and looks like they got a hellava load to pull."

"Not much I can do about that."

"Ya kin buy some more horses from me."

"That I can do. What do you have?"

"I got a matched pair a Conestogas, like that big beauty ya got out there, a set a roans, an' an extra mare and foal I ain't a-sellin'."

"Let's have a look. Mose! Come with me." The men of Jon's group and Adam Schinland all fell in behind Jon and the store owner, headed for the barn. Jon spotted the big white pair. They looked like Corker, but not quite as big. There was a third white dray, very young, but as big as the pair. Jon thought it was probably a yearling Conestoga.

"Take a look at those two roans, Mose."

"Orites, Jon." Mose talked to the animals, as he carefully examined them, front to rear. "Dey's needs work, Jon. Dey's be four or five years old, an' fine."

"How much for the pair?" asked Jon.

"I'll trade straight across for your Conestoga."

"I'm buying, not swapping."

"Hmmm, well, hows 'bout ya have yer big horse bang my mare a couple a times fer one a them roans? She's ready."

"Fair offer, but we haven't the time, and I want both of those roans. How much?"

"Hmm . . . I'd really like ta have a foal from yer Conestoga. Hows 'bout ya take my two mares, Dolly and Betsy, wit ya, get 'em knocked up, an' leave 'em in Pinevull, an' I'll a-give ya the pair of them roans fer . . . a double Eagle?"

"That sounds like a good deal, Jon," said Charles.

"It does indeed. Mose, can you handle the breeding of Corker to these mares while we travel?"

"Yassa, Jon, I's do."

"That extra team of roans would really help my Apple and Jack."

"It would help us all, Charles, but I was thinking of adding them to Mister Schinland's wagon. That way you would have six horses to pull two wagons."

"And then they'd be yours," said Adam. "Amelia and I have a boat waiting at Boonesborough ta take us all the way to Indiana."

"Okay, you have a deal, mister," Jon said to the owner.

"I'll pay the double Eagle," said Adam. "They're to help my wagon to get to freedom."

"Freedom?" asked the owner. "Are them escaped niggers?"

"Yes," answered Jon. "They are escaped slaves from Alabama."

"Alabammy! Well, maybe I'll call our deal off."

"Why? They won't harm you."

"But them bounty hunters will."

"What bounty hunters?"

"They's come through here two days ago. Said they were from Alabammy. They kill niggers fer money."

"We'll make sure your mares won't get hurt, mister. How many of them were there?"

"Six or seven, maybe. They're stayin' at the gap, least that's what they say. Niggers gotta come through there."

"Are you paying the double Eagle, Adam?"

"Yes, sir. Here you are, sir," said Adam to the owner.

"I's likes dem Conestoga, Jon," said Mose.

"How much for the Conestoga, mister?"

"I ain't a-sellin' no Conestogas."

"Then I ain't breedin' my horse with your mares."

"Hmm . . . you's hard to please."

"It wouldn't last that long, Mose. Besides, there's no river close by here that's navigable."

"But that gives me an idea," said the owner. "I know a way ta hike over this here mountain. I'll just close up me shop, an' meet ya in Pinevull in a coupla days."

"Then you'll sell me the Conestoga?"

"Shur will."

"How much?"

"Hmm . . . How 'bout two double Eagles?"

"That's forty dollars!" exclaimed Dave. "Too much!"

"Allrite . . . one Eagle and a double Eagle."

"Sold," said Jon. "Let's get them hooked up and get hoppin', so we make the gap by nightfall."

"Now that's the deal. You take Dolly an' Betsy an' breed 'em before Pinevull, an' I bring 'em back."

"Sounds like you're namin' mares after presidents' wives."

"Now that's an idea. Anyone knows Jackson's wife's name?"

"Not offhand. See you in Pineville. Oh, do you have lanterns?"

"Sure do. I'll give you a couple."

"Thanks. We'll be camping along the Cumberland River, just west of town. Let's get crackin', gang."

"I think I found out what breed of horse Corker is," Jon said to Maggie, as the wagons rolled toward the sunset.

"What kind is he?"

"The same as those mares that Corker is going to mate with."

"And what kind is that?"

"They're called Conestogas."

"Don't be barmy, Jonny. The Conestoga is a wagon."

"I know, darling, a big wagon. So they had to breed a big horse to pull them. They named the horse after the wagon."

"Are you trying to bamboozle me again, Jonny?"

"Not at all, my love, unless that store owner is bamboozling me."

"Okay, gang, it's dark enough now to try traveling by lanterns. We are going through the gap by lantern, Adam. Put two of your slaves walking along the sides of the road with lanterns. You ladies keep your teams between those lanterns. Ella, you take the lead in the carryall, then Adam and Amelia next, then Liz and Maggie. Charles, hang a lantern on the back of each wagon so the ladies can keep in a straight line. Will you be alright, darlin'?"

"I think so, Jonny, but I'm scared."

"Dave, will you follow up and help Maggie if she needs it?"

"Sure thing, Jon. Where will you be?"

"Mose and I are going to scout ahead for a ways."

"We'll keep going slowly until you stop us or we see the gap."

"Good, Charles. We'll be back soon."

"Be careful, Jonny."

"There's the gap, Mose. That must be the bounty hunters around that campfire."

"I's be black, Jon. I's gets close look."

"Okay, Mose. I'll get a little closer, so I can guard you."

Mose and Jon were well ahead of their wagons, and it took Mose only a few minutes to investigate.

"Dey's has one guard, six sleeps 'round fire," Mose whispered.

"Good. Where are their horses?"

"Horses be saddled. Dey's graze close. I's gets guard."

"Right, Mose. Don't kill him, but put him out and bring him here."

"I's do, Jon," Mose whispered. He was gone again and returned a few minutes later with the man over his shoulder.

"Where are their guns, Mose?"

"Dey be's on saddles, Jon. I's hide guard's gun."

"Good, let's quietly try to sneak the horses back here."

One at a time, Mose used his special way with horses to untie each one and lead a horse away, while Jon stood guard. Mose had just led the third horse away, when one of the men started to waken. He rolled onto his back and opened his eyes.

"What the—" Jon hit him over the head with the butt of his Hawken. The man had raised almost to a sitting position, but now hit the ground hard on his back. The *thud* of the rifle butt against the head caused stirring by some others, but thankfully, they all continued sleeping. Jon quietly dragged the butthead away from the fire. When Mose returned, they laid him over the saddle of the next horse.

"Mose," Jon whispered, "leave the last two horses, and take the rest to our wagons. Tie up the two bounty hunters and take them into the woods with their coats on so they don't freeze. Then bring all our men here, guns loaded, on the horses we just took. Hurry, and have the women keep the wagons rolling."

"I's do, Jon. What if dem bad men wakes up?"

"I'll try to keep them asleep until you all get here."

"Orites, Jon. I's hurry."

Now Jon was alone with five sleeping "bad men." What would he do if they all started waking up? He tried to dream up a scenario of what would happen, and it turned out badly. Then he remembered the guard's rifle Mose had left, and the rifles still in the saddles of the two remaining horses. Jon looked around, and finally found the guard's rifle and quietly gathered the other two from the horses. They shied some from Jon, causing the sleeping men to stir. Jon hurried back to his position, now with four guns. Three were flintlocks, and the barrels loaded, so Jon poured some primer powder on the pans very quickly, hoping they would fire. He laid each on the ground so he could grab them easily. The men were waking up.

"Hey, John . . . are y'all still awake?" one said. "John?"

"Get back to sleep!" Jon said, hoping that the sleeper was calling the guard, and hoping the guard was named John.

"Go to blazes! I can't sleep nohow. I'll spell y'all."

"I said, get back to sleep, fart head." Jon crept up on him.

"Hey! Y'all ain't John. Who the blazes are ya?" *Wham!* Jon hit him hard with the butt of his Hawken.

"What the fuck is goin'—" Jon hit the man lying next to the one he had just thumped, and ran to his guns.

"Stay where you are! Don't move a lick, or I'll splatter your guts all over Sam Hill!" Jon's adrenaline was flowing.

"Who are you?" asked a white-haired man, sitting up.

"I'm the one you meet just before the Devil."

"What y'all want wit us?"

"I want you to sit there quietly, and don't move a hair!"

"Hey," said another, "our horses have done disappeared!"

"Did y'all have anythin' ta do with that?"

"There are still two of them there. One for me and one for my friend hiding in the trees," answered Jon.

Two men looked around. One man with bloody hair that Jon had hit was awake, and the fifth man was still asleep.

"There ain't no other friend out there," said a bald man.

"What ya'll did wit, Jon?" asked a face full of hair.

"Harper's gone too," said baldy.

"They made the mistake of waking up," said Jon, "and my friend and I had to dispose of them."

"You ain't got no friend," said baldy. "What's say we rush the bastard? He only got one shot."

"That one shot will split you right in half, baldy."

"You're a-gonna be damned sorry ya fucked wit us," said the one Jon had hit, holding his head. "Y'all's time on earth be 'bout ova."

"That bump on the head didn't seem to help your thinking, Nanny boy. Guess I'll have to use the first ball on you."

"He can't use it on us all. Spread out, an' give 'im Jesse," said the hairy face.

"Jesse hell! I wanna kill da bastard," said Baldy.

"You get my friend's ball, Baldy."

"Ya ain't got no friends, bugger!" hollered the hairy-faced man, jumping up and charging. "Umma gonna braa—" *BAM!* Jon put the ball from his Hawken right into the mass of hair coming at him. Parts of hair and bone shot out the back of his head, and he flew backward, hitting the ground close to the fire. The three other talkers sprang to their feet, ready to charge Jon, who quickly dropped the Hawkin and grabbed one of the flintlocks. The men froze.

"Hold it! I'll put this ball into the next one of you who takes another step closer. Now get back to the fire."

"He's got another gun! Ya bastard, where'd you get that gun?" asked baldy.

"From the John! Now sit back down."

"That's only one more shot," said the fifth man, who had awakened with Jon's shot. "Let's get the shithead!"

"How much is your life worth to you? Or your families down in Alabama?" There was a pause.

"How'd ye knowd we're from Bamy?" asked the fifth man. "Any you varmints tell 'im?"

"Nosa, Neil, nunn us tolt 'im."

"How'd ye knowd we're from Bamy, friend?" asked Neil.

"I'm not your friend, Neil, but I know about you attempting to kill some slaves trying to escape to freedom."

"So? What's it ta you?"

"Me and my friends are seeing to it that they make it."

"Why, you's a Nigga lova," said Baldy.

"Are you one a them abolitionists?" asked White Hair.

"When my friend walks out of those trees, you'll see he is a free Negro, smarter than all of you put together."

"Well, he ain'ts gonna live any longer'n you anyways," said the leader, Neil.

"Just another fuckin' ear ta add unta the collection," said the man with the bloody head. They all laughed at that.

"Rightcha are, Billy," said Baldy, laughing.

"You seem to like to use that word, don't you, Billy? Before I leave, I'm going to cut out that tongue of yours and add it to *my* collection."

"You's ain't a-gonna get the chance, friend. 'Cause we're gonna add your ear to our collection," replied Neil.

"We kin paint it black an' sell it too," said Whitey.

"I said I'm not your friend, and I intend to keep my ears intact. Now sit back down and be quiet."

"You's don't understand, friend. We makes our livin' collecting left ears o' niggas, an' yer ear will pay good."

"Nigga lova's ears jest may pay more," said Baldy.

"We're gonna have ta kill ya, young man. Why don't you's tell us where Jon and Harper are?" asked Whitey.

"You can look for them on your way back to Alabama."

"We ain't goin' back without our friends and horses." As Whitey talked, the four bounty hunters slowly spread out, inching their way toward Jon, who cocked the flintlock.

"I told you to sit back down by the fire."

"But we can't do that, young man. You'll kill one more of us, but ya know we're gonna have ta kill you," said Whitey.

"If you don't get back, I'll kill all of you!" shouted Jon.

"Dat'd be a bit hard ta do wit one ball," said Baldy. As the four men charged Jon from all sides in the dark, they appeared as shadows coming toward him. He took careful aim. *BAM!* A flash and a little cloud of gun smoke, and Billy went down with a thud. Jon dropped that gun and grabbed the next flintlock. The men were on him as he raised the gun, pulled back the hammer, and fired. A fizz and a sputter of sparks was all he got. Neil swung at Jon as he tried to bend down and grab the last gun. No use. They hit him from all sides. Somehow, before he went down, Jon grabbed the barrel of his misfired flintlock and swung it around. *CRACK!* Jon was sure he'd broken Baldy's jaw, but that didn't stop him. The three were now on top of Jon, hitting and spitting.

"Kill da bastard," said Neil, between huffs and blows. "Do unta him what he dunta Billy and Clyde."

"And Harper . . . John," added Whitey.

Jon was squirming, kicking, and trying to block blows from the three, but was losing ground and taking a beating. His nose and lip were bleeding, and his arms and left shoulder were getting numb and sore. A heavy blow caught him on the side of his head, and he felt a little dizzy from it. Suddenly, Jon saw Neil get up and step over to the last loaded flintlock. Neil picked it up slowly and stepped back toward Jon and the other two attackers. Oh no! Neil was going to shoot him, thought Jon. Neil brought the gun to his shoulder and aimed.

Jon was the victim of a headlock from Baldy. He closed his eyes amidst the punishment. Instantly, a picture of Maggie came before him. So beautiful. "I love you, my pretty plum," he thought he said through sore, bleeding lips. Who was that coming up behind Maggie? It is Elizabeth! "I love you," he may have said aloud, but unsure to whom it was said. Jon shook his head, and that vision vanished and was instantly replaced by his family. There was mother and father. Mother was crying . . . for him? Brother Drew was astride Jon's horse, Dandy, laughing and joking like he always does. Then there was Mary, Jon's loving sister. She was dressed in a wedding gown, getting married! Jon thought he'd never see his sis again. What's that? His sister had a bulging belly? No, not Mary! The belly got bigger and bigger, and the face suddenly changed back to Maggie. Jon thought he'd never get to see his son. *BAM! BAM!* Was that two shots? Was he dead? Jon didn't feel anything. Ahhh . . . he was shot . . . a lifting of weight . . . Was he ascending? Descending? He must be dead. There was Finley . . . and Jock! Gang twelve, Toby! Dianna, Vera . . . all dead . . . like Jon. Maybe he'd see them again. There was Levi, Jobe, and Skeets . . . and . . . Tad! That's Morna . . . look at that body shake! She was laughing again. There was Lucee with no clothes! Nell, pretty eyes . . . and Wilma, what a body. Cora! Beautiful little Cora, and who was coming next? Ginny! . . . His first. What? Who . . . Sam McAllister! Nonsense! Change the view! There was Buelah, and Esther . . . wow! Ella . . . and Mose . . . Jon's good friend Mose . . . bumps . . . murder . . .

"You's kills Massa Jon! I's kills you!"

Jon opened his eyes. "Mose! You're here!" There was screaming above him.

Mose had Neil, one arm dangling and a bloody mess at his elbow, raised off the ground with one huge hand around Neil's neck. Mose looked down at Jon, eyes as big as double Eagles, and hurled Neil through the air. Jon sat up. Whitey was on his knees, fear on his face, watching Mose's power. Jon hit him as hard as he could in the face, and sent Whitey sprawling backward. Jon felt a sudden burst of pain in his hand. He had feeling! He was alive!

"Massa Jon! Massa Jon! You's orites?"

"'Course I'm alright . . . and it's just Jon, my friend."

"I's thoughts you's dead, Massa . . . Jon."

"Takes more than this bunch of scalawags to kill me! I want you all to meet the friend I was telling you about . . . Mose."

"That's the biggest nig—" said Baldy, with a bloody shoulder.

"Ah, ah, ah, be careful what you call my friend. He may get mad. He likes to pick up people the way he picked up Neil, and then pull their limbs off. One arm, one leg . . . arm, leg, poke-stick, nose, ears . . . ears! I'll show you something, Mose." Jon looked around the campfire, checked the bodies, and found it. A bag tied to Billy's belt. He yanked it loose and brought it back to Mose. It had an odor. Jon opened it. Ears!

"This is what they do for a living, Mose. They kill slaves and take their ear back to Alabama for money."

Mose's face hardened and he gnashed his teeth. The Chasney brothers appeared, rifles ready.

"I was just showing Mose this bag of ears. They cut them off the slaves they kill, and sell them back in Alabama."

"Shall we just kill them and be done with it?" asked Dave.

"No, not yet. That's what they deserve, though." Jon turned to the remaining bounty hunters. "Recognize your horses? We're going to be using them for a while."

"Fer how long?" asked Whitey.

"Until my gang gets rested from all their walking. When we find someone traveling this way, we'll send them back. You turn their noses southeast back to Alabama, hear? You won't get another chance if we spot you again."

"I think we should keep one horse for each of us when we split up," said Charles. "They won't need the extras."

"Good idea. While you wait for your horses, you can bury your dead. The exercise will keep you warm."

"What about John and Harper?" asked Whitey, now recovered.

"Tell them where to find their friends, Mose."

"They be two miles back. You's sees dead trees an' woods, on both sides dem road. You's sees friends tied to dead trees."

"You can pick them up on the way back to Alabama."

"What if'n we decide ta keep hoggin' yer tail?" asked Neil, holding his severed arm to his bloody body with his good arm.

"You don't learn lessons very well. Your lives will end, that's what's if'n!"

The sounds of wagons and the sight of lanterns told Jon's men that his group was nearing the gap.

"Tell them to keep going, Dave. We'll catch up to them."

"Righto. I'll be back in a few."

"I want you slimy slave killers to see our wagons pass by into Kentucky with the escaped slaves you've been hunting."

"They's purty slow," huffed Neil, holding his arm in agony.

"We can catch them easily," said Whitey.

"You'll freeze your keisters off first. Take off your coats and brogans."

"What?"

"You heard me. Take off the coats and brogans. Charles, will you collect them all? Even off the dead."

"Sure will, Jon. Do you want to burn them?"

"No, the slaves will need them."

"Slaves? Ye ain't gonna give my sit-down-upons ta no niggas, not while I'm alive!"

"I guess you should have killed him outright, Mose, instead of just taking his arm nearly off."

"Maybe's I's do him now, Jon. I wan's dem ears."

"If we don't do something, they will bleed to death. Do you have them covered, Charles?"

"I do. I don't think they'll try anything, though."

"Okay. Let's get their coats and brogans off, and stop their bleeding. When Dave returns, send him back to the wagons. We need Ella here to help. And bring back their horses."

"Going soft-hearted again, Jon?"

"Maybe so, but they need a doctor badly, or they may die too."

Jon and Mose found rags to tie around Neil's arm and Baldy's head and shoulder. Jon was now worried they may not make it.

"It's seventy-five miles back to Kingsport and a doctor."

"You're not planning for us to go back there, are you?"

"No, Charles, but Whitey here is going to have to do it if he wants his friends to live."

"I can't do it without coats and brogans . . . and horses."

"I know. Guess we'll give them all back, except the guns."

After a while, the men heard the horses returning. Ella was on one of them, and Dave was herding the rest. Ella went to work, cleaning and bandaging wounds, and removing Neil's left arm that Mose had shot nearly off. Then she insisted on doing the same with Jon, who had a broken nose and split lip. She expertly yanked the nose back in line, and applied horse liniment to the lip. Ella opened Jon's shirt and saw many bruises, but nothing else.

"Can we bring the wagons back here for the night?" asked Jon.

"Good idea. The women are probably having fits by now," answered Charles.

"We's do, Jon," said Mose. "I's go helps bring dem backs."

"Dave and I will get more wood for the fire," said Charles.

"Good, but let's tie these three together first, and I'll stand guard until Mose gets us up in the morning."

"Least it ain't freezing," remarked Dave. "I wonder what time it is."

"I'd say between one and two in the morning," answered Jon.

"Doesn't seem to matter with Mose or Ella," said Charles. "They are up before dawn every morning."

"We better get those two buried before the women get here."

"Dave and I will do that as soon as we have the wood gathered."

"Thanks, Charles. Just take them into the brush for now. I've got one more thing to do first." Jon pulled out his knife and pried open Billy's mouth, which was now pretty stiff. He yanked the dead man's tongue out as far as he could and cut it off. He then dropped the tongue into the "ear bag" and tied it to his belt.

"What was that all about?" asked Charles.

"A little promise I made to a filthy tongue."

When four wagons pulled up to the fire, everything looked ship-shape. Mose laid out blankets for sleeping on the ground.

"What happened, Jonny? We heard shots, and I was so worried! Are you alright?"

"Yes, yes, and yes! There was a battle, and the bounty hunters got the worst of it."

"Didn't you say we would never go backward?" asked Liz.

"I may have said that. We're not going backward. We have just made a circle. We have to help these men."

"Aren't these the bad guys?" asked Maggie.

"Yes, they were. They're not so bad now."

"Then why are we helping them?" asked Liz. "You gone barmy?"

"We're helping them because we're not bad!"

"You make as much sense as a rotten turnip!" snapped Liz.

"Taste better, I'll bet, and not as hard to cook."

"Hmm, I'll buy that," said Liz.

"Jonny, let's sleep in our wagon again tonight."

"I am not sleeping tonight, my pretty plum. Someone has to keep an eye on our prisoners."

"Then I'll stay up too. I've got to finish my diary for today."

"Please get some sleep, darlin'. You need some rest for my son, and you have to drive tomorrow. I'll spell you tomorrow, long enough for you to catch up."

"Alright. Good night, Jonny. I love you. You do know what day it was today, don't you?"

"No . . . don't tell me it was Sunday."

"Yes, it was. You owe me another one."

"I can hardly wait for you to collect!"

Monday, December 7

As usual, Mose and Ella were up before dawn, getting things ready to eat and travel. They fed the three bounty hunters and Jon early, and sent the three on their way, with five horses.

"Now you know where to find your friends?"

"Yep, we do," said Whitey.

"If you hurry, you can make Kingsport in two days. Good luck, and don't come back, or you'll wish you hadn't." Jon turned to Mose. "It's still early, Mose. Let's bury those two ear collectors!"

"Orites, Jon. I's gets a shovel an' pick."

With Mose's strength, a hole big enough for two was dug. Billy and Clyde, minus their coats and shoes, were buried.

"Do you want to say a prayer over them, Mose?"

"Yessa, I's do . . . Lawd, may dey souls rest in hell. Amen."

"Mose, will you breed Corker to Dolly? I'll handle the questions."

"Where have you two been? You promised that you would never leave me alone again, Jonny."

"You were all asleep when we went for a walk, a little scouting, and a little bear hunting."

"Were you going to beat the bears over their heads with your shovel?" asked Liz.

"No, Liz. I guess if we saw something, we would come back and get your help. Thankfully, we didn't see a thing."

"Did those men get buried alright, Jonny?"

Jon paused. "Yes, they did, my pretty plum . . . sorry."

"Why are you lying to me all of a sudden, Jonny?"

"It's not all of a sudden, I just . . ."

"A-ha! He's been lying to you all along, Maggie," accused Liz.

"You just what, Jonny?"

"You're carrying our son, darlin', and I didn't want you upset."

"Watch out, Mag. He's becoming a con-man."

"What did you do that would upset me, Jonny?"

"I had to shoot those men, and almost got shot myself."

"Jonny, you didn't tell me that."

"Mose here saved my life."

"Now I am upset."

"See? That's why I tried to keep it from you, my love."

"Oh, what a smoothy you're getting to be," quipped Liz.

The group was back on the Wilderness Road early, and the extra team of horses pulling the "slave wagon" allowed the two slave women and two youngest children to ride in the wagon. The group made much better time. They reached Pineville well before noon.

"Let's make camp on down the river, gang."

"I guess this is where we part company, huh?" asked Liz.

"Not for a couple of days. This is where we celebrate for now."

"The mighty Cumberland doesn't look mighty to me, Jonny."

"Well, it just starts a little ways up in these mountains we just crossed, darlin'. The next time we see it, it will be big."

"The next time? You said we would follow this river all the way to Nashville. Were you lying again, Jonny?"

"No, my love. We're just going straight, where the river zigs and zags. Saves a lot of time that way."

"Like you saved time going straight over the Blues?" asked Liz.

"That was different. I had two women to argue with until now."

"Can you double your efforts from now on, Maggie?"

"You bet I can, Liz. It's not going to be any easier for him from here to Nashville."

"Good girl," said Liz. "He loves all the attention."

"Here, gang. This looks like a good spot to make camp."

Everyone went to work, pitching tent, gathering wood, building a fire, washing clothes, making and eating lunch, cleaning guns, etc. Maggie updated her diary, and Mose again bred Corker to Dolly and Betsy. They had just settled in for supner, when the owner of Martin's Station, who had sold the pair of roans to Adam, showed up.

"Howdy! Looks like ye made it here alrights."

"Yes, we've been here all afternoon," said Charles.

"Well, I guess I could've rode wit you 'uns. Had a thundera time gettin' ova dat mountain."

"It's a good thing you didn't come with us," said Maggie.

"Yeah, our fearless leader here took on some devils," added Liz.

"See, I's told you's dem bounty hunters was awaitin'."

"My Jonny and Nunky Mose took care of them," said Maggie.

"They's kilt all six a-dem?"

"No, just two, and wounded two others," said Charles.

"Den dey be back . . . you'll see."

"I don't think so, sir," said Jon. "We sent all five of them back to Kingsport with only one gun and a warning."

"Well, they's looked awfully mean an' determined. Didya gets my mares bred?"

"Yessa," answered Mose. "I's sure dey be's fertilized."

"Good. I thank the good Lord above they's both ready at the same time."

"Well, come on over to the fire, and get something to eat. We'll put you up with us for the night."

"Thank ye. I'lla be dinged if'n I knows yer names. I'm Connestoga Joe. Everybody calls me Conn."

"I can see why," retorted Liz. "I'm Liz, and these two are Chuck and Davie."

"And I'm Margaret, my husband Jon, Nunky Mose and Nanty Ella, and Chip."

"I'm Adam Schinland, and my wife Amelia."

"An' alla these, these escaped slaves is yers?"

"Yes, they are our responsibility," answered Adam.

"Glory be! Never thought I'da see da day!"

"It's startin' ta happen all across the south," said Amelia.

"What's the people up north gonna do wit 'em?"

"Give 'em jobs, so's they can make a livin'," answered Adam.

"Glory be! Neva thought I'da seen da day!"

"You said that already," smiled Liz.

"It's time to celebrate. Break out the spruce juice, Chuck!"

"Right, Jon. It should be good and skookum by now," answered Charles.

"I've got some good corn whisky to go with it."

"Where did you get that, Jonny?"

"In Elizabethtown, my love, and no, I didn't tell you!"

What a party! Another "babbling bear garden"! Maggie was feeling happy, and Jon was feeling loaded, mixing whisky and beer. So were Charles and Connestoga Joe. Dave was passed out. The three slave men were high, before Adam and Amelia herded all the slaves into their wagon and the tent with Chipper. Mose and Ella played music, both a little tipsy. Liz was dancing, and doing her best to get the men all horny. She sat on the prostrate Dave, bouncing up and down on him, laughing and screaming. What a party!

"Wheeee . . . C'mon, Davy! Get up! Ha, ha!"

"He's too fart gone," laughed Charles. "Come on, baby, let's you and I get it on."

Charles and Liz hopped and twirled around the fire, and fell in a heap, laughing. Liz crawled on top of Charles, squirming and laughing. She planted kisses all over his face as she squirmed.

"Hell's fire, you ain't no better'n Davy. Where's Jonny?" Liz staggered to her feet and swayed and weaved her way around the camp, until she spotted Maggie and Jon sharing a pitcher.

"Come on and dance with me, big boy."

"Ish it Okay, Mag?" Jon asked, handing Maggie the pitcher.

"Is what Okay?"

"Ta dance wit Lish?"

"I thought you made alla da decisions," slurred Liz.

"You sip da brew, an' I's dances wit Lish, darlin' . . . I'll be right back," said a very drunk Jon.

"Ah . . . alright, Jonny," said Maggie.

Jon worked his way to his feet; and Liz was on him, kissing, hugging, and rubbing Jon. Jon felt the tightening of his kentucks.

"Hmm . . . Least ya ain't dead yet," said Liz.

"C'mon, Lish, let go . . . let's dance."

"Hookay, lovas . . . Hold on tight."

Jon and Liz hopped, turned, swaggered, and stumbled their way around the campfire and fell in the dark, near the tent.

"Whoops . . . hold on yourself," slobbered Jon, as he laughed.

"I am holdin', Jonny."

As they rolled and laughed, Liz worked a hand down Jon's jeans.

"Whatcha doin', Lish?"

"I's fishin'," laughed Liz, "for worms!"

"Uh . . . uh . . . whatcha doin', Lish? Ahh . . ."

"C'mon, Jonny . . . this is our las' chance."

"No, Lish . . . I told ya no."

"Jonny, I needs you . . . oh, you needs me."

"No, Lish . . . stop."

Liz slid down his body, fumbling with the buttons, her lips devouring him. Jon was trying to push her away. "Please, Lish . . . Please, nooo, aaagh."

"Wasn't tha' good, Jonny?" Again, Liz kissed him all over. "Jonny . . . do me. Please."

"Nooo, Lish. Nooo. I's love Maggie."

"Please, Jonny . . . ya love me too." Liz grabbed his hand, placing it under her redingote.

"I said no! I loves Maggie. I'm goin' back to Mag . . . I's wants Mag . . . Let me up!"

"Hokay, Jonny. Better button up," Liz laughed.

Jon tried to button his Kentucky jeans, as he fumbled and shook.

"I'll help, Jonny," Liz said, as she fumbled with his buttons, laughing. "There," she laughed again. "Remember me, Jonny," she whispered. "Lish Ingals, Frankfurt."

"I remember. How can I forget?"

"Write ta me, Jonny, when ya get to Arkansas."

"Alright. Wurs Mag?" asked Jon, as he stumbled back around the campfire, past many sets of eyes. "Maggie!"

"Where you been, Jonny?" Maggie had tears in her eyes.

"Dunno . . . 'round there." He pointed to the fire.

"Tell me, Jonny," cried Maggie. "I've got to know."

"Teel ya what, my purty plump?"

"What you and Liz did, you bastard!"

"Are you crying, Mag?" Jon was sobering up fast.

"Did you and Liz have sex?"

"Sex? No, I didn't. Why're ya cryin', Mag?"

"'Cause you're lying to me, Jonny!"

"No, I ain't! Darlin' . . . I want you!"

"You're lying!" Tears were running down Maggie's cheeks. "I hate you, Jonny! You cockelled Liz!" Maggie staggered to her feet and ran toward the covered wagon.

"No . . . Maggie! I swear I didn't! Mag, wait!" Jon tried to follow, but fell. By the time he was able to stand again, Maggie was at the wagon, stopped by Liz.

"Wait, Maggie." Liz tried to grab Maggie's arm, but Maggie shoved her to the ground and climbed shakily into the wagon. "Mag, you're wrong 'bout Jonny. He loves you," said Liz. "Lawd knows I tried to trifle with him, but he loves you."

There was a long silence from inside the wagon, as Liz and Jon waited outside.

"Mag? I'm a-comin' in," said Liz.

"Really?" asked Maggie, as the two women stared at each other.

"True, Mag. Every time I tried ta roger with him, he pushed me away and told me he loves you."

Maggie sat down on a box, her crying out of control. Liz sat beside her and hugged Maggie. "He's true blue, honey. Your man."

"Oh, thank you, Liz. Good night," Maggie said tearfully.

"Jonny's right outside, honey. I'll send him in."

"Thanks, Liz. Good night again."

Liz staggered out, and Jon had to catch her from falling to the ground.

"She's all yours, lova boy."

"An' I'm all hers. Thanks, Lish."

"Oh, Jonny, I'm sorry I mistrusted you. I love you."

"I love you too, my purty plum."

The kisses and hugs turned to fumbling with clothes, and eventually wagon-shaking love.

"Oh, I'm sorry, darlin'. I'm too heavy on you."

"No, you're not, Jonny. Don't stop."

The young couple never came outside again that night.

Tuesday, December 8

The noises Mose and Ella heard early the next morning were the Schinlands scurrying about, trying to get on the trail back to Pineville, then north. The male slaves were moving very slowly, and Adam was trying to push them along.

"Hurry, hurry, Tommy. You too, Tech. We's gotta get rollin' fer Boonesborough an' freedom."

"We's got no breakfass, boss," said Tech.

"Say, why's you's leave, Mister Shnland?" asked Ella.

"We're wantin' to leave this den of iniquity," said Amelia.

"Whats 'at means, Daddy?"

"I's dunno," answered Mose. "But you's stays fo' breakfass."

"We're appalled by what we seen last night," said Adam.

"Whats 'at means, Daddy?"

"Means day don' likes our party, Mutta."

"You's be goin' with dem Chasneys, ain'tcha?" asked Ella.

"We was, but we ain't now," answered Adam.

"Well, Ella's gonna cook breakfass, fo' you's go," said Mose.

"We's stays fo' breakfass, boss?"

"Yes, Tech, we's stay, then we leave," answered Adam.

"Amunno! Stays fo' breakfass," said Tech to Tommy and the others, pointing to his mouth and rubbing his stomach.

"Good," said Ella, getting out food and fixings, as Mose busied himself building up the fire.

When nobody was watching, Mose woke Charles, then Jon. They were very slow getting dressed and out to the fire.

"What's goin' on?" asked Charles, the first out.

"Dem Schilans be's goin' on der way," answered Ella.

"So soon?" asked Charles, holding his head.

"Yes," said Amelia. "We want's to be leavin' now."

"But why? Our animals . . . and I need a rest," said Charles.

"Ya should! The ways ye acted last night!" retorted Adam.

"We acted like anyone would who was about to leave friends," said Jon, who had finally appeared from his wagon.

"Wit someone else's wife?"

"With my wife and friends. Be very careful what you say, Mister Schinland. We're trying to help you."

"What do you think you saw?" asked Charles to Adam.

Adam saw the glares from Jon, Mose, and even Charles.

"Uh, nothin'," stammered Adam, "just thought I'd heard voices."

"Voices saying what?"

"Uh, I couldn't hear what they said," answered Adam.

"Then keep your mouth shut," stated a relieved Jon.

"Yes, sir. We's wants to leave now."

"What are you going to use for food to feed all these people?"

"We's planned ta buy food in Pinevull," answered Amelia.

"Well, if ya leave today, we won't be with ya," said Charles.

"After breakfast, we'll do a little hunting. It's a long ways to Boonesborough, probably over a hundred miles," said Jon.

"So ya better not run off half-cocked," said Charles. "Wait until tomorrow, and we'll all go together, at least as far as the fork to Harrodsburg that's closer to Frankfort, I think."

"Oh, alright, tomorrow we's go then," stammered Adam.

The slave women and Ella made breakfast. Jon and Charles had the task of getting the partygoers up and fed.

"I thank thee all fer da hospitality. I'll be a-headin' back," said Conestoga Joe.

"By the way, Joe, is there any good hunting around here?"

"Right there, on that mountain. Whitetails er like flies!"

"Good. As soon as you're back, Mose, we're all going hunting."

"I can't see," said Dave, as Mose and Joe left.

"Ya know what makes ya blind, brother?"

"Yeah . . . whiskey an' spruce juice, not what Pa said."

"It had to have been the drink," said Liz. "He was too drunk to do anything else."

"We have enough rifles to take two each. Let's hope we can restock all our wagons with venison."

"Those bounty hunters are probably wishin' they had these guns by now," said Charles.

"Yeah, with one gun, they might get a little hungry before they get back ta Alabama," said Dave.

"Let's get ready. Load your rifles, and dress warm."

"Where's Maggie?" asked Liz.

"She wasn't hungry. She's catching up on her diary again."

"I can imagine what she's writing!"

"I can't."

Conestoga Joe came back to the campfire with Mose and a smile on his face. He climbed up on Dolly and rode around the fire, shaking hands with everyone. Ella gave him some dodgers.

"Good luck ta ye-all a yer trips, an' thanks fer breakfast."

"Thank you for the horses," said Charles.

"By the next time ye-all pass through 'ere, I'll have a stable full o' Conestogas."

"Dey's be fine horses if Corka da father," said Mose.

"Keep a watch fer dem bounty huntas," said Joe.

"Okay, we will. So long, Joe."

The hunting trip was a blast! The men followed the stream, called Cumberland River, a few miles past Pineville, and found a clearing on the Cumberland Mountains. Mose and Jon circled up the mountain and drove deer back down to the clearing, where Charles and Dave were waiting. The first drive bagged two bucks, but Jon wanted more. They hiked a short distance further, and Jon and Mose each shot a whitetail, one a doe.

On one occasion, Jon heard some noises a short distance ahead. Safety off his Hawken, he crept forward until he saw a pack of dogs feasting on a large whitetail.

They had made a fresh kill by the looks of the blood. The dogs growled, and even started to spread out and stalk Jon. He retreated, and the red-colored dogs went back to their kill. Jon realized he had just had a brush with red wolves.

"Now to get these deer back to the horses," said Dave.

"When we get back down to the river, we can field-clean them, and tie them down on Corker. Right, Mose?"

"Yassa, Jon. Corka's packs dem all."

"Good thing we brought him along," said Charles.

"Yassa, Corka be's worn out from lovin's," said Mose.

"Ha! Right. He's getting more than all of us," added Dave.

"Drag him by the horns, Dave," said Charles.

The men dragged and carried their game back down the mountain, to the stream and horses. They cleaned the game, loaded it onto Corker, and then headed back through Pineville to their camp.

"Wow, you drunks did good," said Liz.

"We saved the sex bones for you, Liz," said Dave.

"Good, then I won't need you two anymore!"

"Okay, ladies, now you can all go to work. Let's chunk out and cook two of them, and hang strips from two on Adam and Charles's wagons. We'll take what's left."

This took the rest of the day, and into the night, with only a break for supner. All the wagons now had fresh venison hanging from them, and packed inside them, except the carryall.

"Is everyone as tired as I am?" asked Charles. This was met with several yes answers.

"I'm turning in, and sleeping alone all night," said Liz.

"Big day tomorrow. Good night, all," said Jon.

"We's needs guards, so dem meats don' get stolen," said Mose.

"Oh, drat! You're right, Mose. I'll go first."

"Wake me in a couple hours, Jon. I'll take second," said Charles.

"I'll do my diary and wait up for you, Jonny."

"I wish you would get some rest, darlin'."

"I will, Jonny, but I must keep my log up."

Diary of Margaret Hamilton

Tuesday, December 8, 1835

. . . And the weather was good, no sign of rain or snow. We didn't get much rest, though. We were all nursing headaches and cutting up deer meat most of the day. The Schinlands,

with all their escaped slaves, will be leaving tomorrow morning with the Chasneys. I will miss them like I miss my monthly cycle. I'll always miss my family, but I will always have my Jonny. No one will ever take him away from me.

Hugs and kisses
Maggie Hamilton

Wednesday, December 9

The Schinlands were again up very early, along with the ex-slaves, wanting to get started. It took half the morning to get the Chasneys ready. They seemed to be reluctant to leave the Hamiltons, as much as the Hamiltons were reluctant and sad to see them go. Maggie was trying to hold back tears.

"Are you's Chasneys ready?" asked Adam. "We's wants ta gets a-goin' afor dark! We'll be a-gettin' more supplies in Pinevull to last ta Boonesborough."

"Good. I like lots of batter cakes and beans," said Dave.

"Ye'll be lucky if'in ya gets hogs an' hominy," said Amelia.

"We'll be a-buyin' brine pork in Pinevull."

"We must be careful not to overload the wagons," said Charles. "We have only Apple and Jack pulling our wagon."

"Lessee if'in we can buy another team fer you's in Pinevull, so's we can load 'em up. It's a long ways ta da river."

"That would be nice, Mister Schinland, but what will we do with all the animals when we split up?"

"Well, we'll sell ours in Boonesborough," answered Adam.

"Alright, but we don't have money to buy more horses," said Charles.

"We got them gold stones we got fr—"

"Quiet, Dave! We will need them later."

"Oh, ya has gold wit ya's," said Adam.

"Just a couple small rocks we'll need in Frankfort," said Charles.

"We maybe need them rocks ta get ta Indiana," said Amelia.

"Well, ye ain't a-gettin' 'em!" snapped Dave.

"We're a-buyin' all da supplies. What are ya a-buyin'?" asked Amelia.

"They're furnishing the venison and the safety," answered Jon, overhearing the conversation, "and powder and grain, an' them two roans."

"Thanks, Jon," said Charles. "Maybe we should let them try to make it through the wilderness alone."

"Yeah, there may be a few hostiles ta face, before we get ta the Kentucky River," added Dave.

"Please, Ma, I'll be a-handlin' this," said Adam. "Pay no attention ta Amelia. We needs ye along."

"Good," answered Charles. "Now we need time to say goodbye to our good friends before we leave."

"Yes, sir, we'll wait," said Adam. "We should say our byes ta de Hamiltons too, Ma."

"Ya go ahead, Adam. I'll wait."

It was time for parting. Maggie and Liz were exchanging goodbyes. Adam climbed down from his wagon and shook hands with Jon, thanking him for helping get everyone through the gap. Liz and Maggie both shed tears, as Liz hugged Mose, Ella, and even Chipper. Maggie walked to Charles and Dave, who were hugging Jon, and began hugging and kissing them. An embarrassed Jon hugged Liz goodbye.

"Remember, Jonny," Liz whispered, "it's Elizabeth Engels, Frankfort. Please write."

"Okay. Maybe when we get settled."

"What about . . . when we get settled?" Maggie had overheard.

"I was telling Jonny to write us when you get settled," answered Liz.

"Oh, yes. We must do that, Jonny," said a sarcastic Maggie.

"Well, you're the one who writes well, darlin'."

"I'm going to teach you to write better on the way to Arkansas, Jonny, so we both can write to our friends."

"I'm not sure how much writing time we'll have, my pretty plum, but I'd like to write better."

"Good. Then we'll be looking for a letter soon. Just Frankfort should get to us eventually," said Liz, finally letting go of Jon. "Who knows, maybe we'll see each other again someday."

"I'm sure we will . . . someday," responded Maggie.

"Here's to that someday," said Charles, who had been saying goodbye with Dave to Mose, Ella, and Chip.

Another round of hugs and smooches followed, under the watchful eyes of the Schinlands and nine ex-slaves. Liz then climbed aboard her wagon, blew all kisses, and snapped the reins of Apple and Jack. Tears were on her face.

"Goodbye," Liz said. "I love you all."

"Goodbye and have a good life!" shouted Maggie, as the wagons headed upriver toward Pineville for the last time.

"Charles!" shouted Jon. "Do you need another rifle?"

"No, Jon!" Charles yelled. "We have four already. That's enough."

"Alright, then. Good luck!"

"Same to you, Jon, and thanks for everything!"

Crying, Maggie hugged Jon, who comforted her. "Will we ever see them again?"

"Yes, I promise, darlin'."

"When should we start our journey to Nashville?"

"How long is that going to take, Jonny?"

"I'm not sure, my love," said Jon, as his small group sat around the campfire, whiling the day away.

"I would like to stay here and rest another day, Jonny."

"How do you feel about that, Mose and Ella?"

"We's needs rest, Jon."

"Okay, Mose, let's take a day off tomorrow and relax. Maybe we can go into town and just look around."

"Dat cheers up Sissy. She be tired, carryin' dem babies 'round."

"Yes, I am a little tired, Nanty Ella."

"That settles it, then. We'll see if we feel better tomorrow night, and start this leg the day after."

"That would be Friday, Jonny."

"We needs mo' grains, Jon. We's has seven horses now."

"Yeah, Mose, and only five of us."

"What are the names of our two new horses?" asked Maggie.

"I don't know, my love, that Conestoga Joe and the bounty hunters never said."

"Then let's have a naming contest."

"How we's do dat?" asked Mose.

"Well, we'll all give a name for the bounty hunter's horse, and draw the name from a hat."

"Okay, my pretty plum, my pick is Chasney."

Maggie brought out her diary and tore out a back page. *Jonny says Chasney*, she wrote. "How about you, Nunky Mose and Nanty Ella?"

"I's say Sam, fo' our forma owna," said Mose.

"I's say Susan, fo' mistress," said Ella.

"You's can't names 'em Susan, Mama. He's be a man horse," Chipper chimed in.

"Orites. Den I's names 'im Jonny."

Nanty Ella says Jonny, wrote Maggie. "How about you, Chip?" she asked.

"I's dunno, Missy Maggie. I's calls dem Abby."

"I think that's a female name too."

"Bu' I's wans dem name, Missy Maggie, fo' dem cow," Chipper said.

"We's gets nuther cows, boy, whens we gets ta dem Arkansas."

"Bu' I's wans horse be Abby, Mama."

"Abby is part of a church, and that can be male."

"When did you get so smart?" asked Maggie. "Okay, Chip, we'll put your choice down as Abby."

"Thank you's, Missy Maggie. It be's you's turn."

"Alright, Chipper. How about Boony?" There was a pause.

"How did you ever come up with a name like that, darlin'?"

"Well, you're supposed to have killed the beast, right? It's only fitting that another beast take its place."

"I never told you that. There is no beast," said Jon. "How do you know what I'm supposed to have done?"

"You talk in your sleep, Jonny. I've got all the names you picked. I need a hat."

"You's use my hat, Sissy."

"Thank you, Nunky Mose. Chipper, do you want to draw?"

"Yassum, Missy Maggie." Chipper drew out a piece of paper.

"It's Abby! Yay! You won, Chip! That horse's name is Abby."

"Thank you's. I's loves dem horse!" exclaimed Chipper.

"Then I think the horse should be yours, boy," said Jon.

"Oh, Mama. Mama! Is dem horse be mine?"

"Yassum, son, if'in Massa Jon say so, it be," answered Ella.

"Yippee!" said an excited Chipper. "Abby be's mine! Yippee! Thank you's, Massa Jon!"

"You're welcome, boy." Maggie gave Jon a hug.

"You made a good choice for a change! Alright, now we draw for a name for the white colt. Nanty Ella, you go first."

"Oh, deerie me's . . . I's picks Jonny again."

"Jonny it is. Your turn, Nunky Mose."

"Orites . . . I's picks Sam again."

"Thank you, Nunky Mose. How about you, Chipper?"

"I's don' know, Missy Maggie."

"Well, how about something that matches or rhymes with your Abby, boy?" asked Jon.

"Likes dem Crabby?" Chipper was laughing with that.

"That's funny, Chip," laughed Maggie. "Do you pick Crabby?"

"Yassum, Missy Maggie."

"Okay. It's your turn, Jonny."

"Hmm, I think something that will match with Corker."

"Why, Jonny?"

"Because I plan on matching him with Corker."

"Corka has no match, Jon," said Mose.

"That's true, Mose, but I think he'll end up being big and strong, like Corker. How about Corking?"

"Corking? Is that a word?"

"You should know, my love, you went to college."

"Well, I never have heard the word before. What does it mean? Are you making it up, Jonny?"

"No, I'm not. Haven't you heard 'that's a corking good horse ya got there?' my pretty plum?"

"No, I haven't, and besides, it's too close to Corker."

"Is it too close, Mose?"

"It be's close, Jon, but dat orites."

"Corker and Corking, I like that."

"I don't! Can't you come up with something else, Jonny?"

"I could, but I like Corking. It means 'excellent!'"

"Alright, Jonny, have it your way. It's my turn now, and I choose the name . . . Conqueror."

"Corker and Conqueror . . . I like that too."

"You're too late, Jonny, that's my pick. Now let's see, Chipper drew last time. You pick, Nanty Ella."

"Orites, Sissy. Here goes," she laughed.

"Good! You picked Conqueror, Nanty Ella.

Ella laughed again. "Dat be's whatcha wans, Sissy!"

"Chipper, will you please stake Abby and Conqueror with the rest of the horses for the night, and give them all food and water?"

"Yassa, Massa Jon."

Diary of Margaret Hamilton

Wednesday, December 9

. . . A very sad day indeed. I shall truly miss the company of the Chasneys, despite Liz's behavior . . . I hope the Schinlands and the slaves make it alright to Indiana . . . We had a horse naming contest, and the horse taken from the bounty hunters was named Abby, and the big, white Conestoga colt we got from "Conestoga Joe" was named Conqueror. I picked that name. He is pretty, all white, like Pasha was, and he is already bigger than Pasha . . . and only two years old. Guess I'll close for now. If any of my family ever reads my diary, you will know that I love and miss you all . . .

PS. The weather has been good for December.

Love, Maggie H.

Thursday, December 10

Mose and Ella were up early as usual, stoking a fire and preparing breakfast. Later in the morning, a young male deer wandered into the clearing, and Mose shot him with the flintlock rifle with which had become a good marksman. The shot woke Jon and Maggie, who were for the first time sleeping on mattresses together in the tent.

"What was that, Mose?" Jon only had his unmentionables on.

"I's practice, Jon." Mose had his cleaning knife.

Ella was laughing. "He's be funnin' you, Jonny," she said, pointing. "We's has meats now."

"What did you get, Mose?"

"I's gets un small whitetail, Jon."

"Good. I'll be right out."

"Yassa, Jonny, you's and Sissy comes fo' breakfass," said Ella.

"Anyone want to come along to town?" All answered yes.

"What do we need, Jonny?"

"Lots of blankets. We gave a lot of them to those slaves, and now we're short. We also need more grain for the horses, and a couple more barrels for water. No telling what we will find for water the next few days."

"Days? You think it's only days to Nashville?"

"I don't know, my love, but we best be prepared."

"Was that Washington or Jackson?"

"It was me, my pretty plum."

Diary of Margaret Hamilton

Thursday, December 10, 1835

. . . It was a day of rest. Jonny will now probably want to start moving again, through Sunday. Nunky Mose shot another deer, so we now have plenty of venison for a while . . . Had fun in the town of Pineville. Found a beauty store, and had my hair washed and made into an earlock. My face was burned by the hot curling tongs, and I worried that the long side curls would bother the sore. It didn't. Jonny says it's pretty, though. He may be prejudiced, or lying! Hope not. It looks like we travel west tomorrow. This afternoon, Jonny taught Nanty Ella and I how to load and shoot a rifle. We have several now, and Jonny thinks we may need to know how to use them before this journey ends. I hope not, again! Love to all.

Margaret Hamilton

Friday, December 11

Mose and Ella had breakfast made, and the wagons all hitched and ready early. But it was not to be! Maggie got sick and heaved. This was the first of her pregnancy, and Jon didn't know what to do. Thank goodness for Ella.

"Will she be alright, Ella?"

"Yassa, Sissy be's fine soon, Jon."

"I wonder what made her sick all of a sudden."

"Sissy be's wit child, Jonny."

"I know. I hope she'll be alright."

"Sissy be's fine till next time."

"Next time? I hope this is the last time."

"Maybe's, Jonny, bu' wit child, dun knows."

"You mean she's sick because of being with child?"

"Yassa. Bu' Sissy be's fine."

"Did you ever get sick when you had a kid in the kiln, Ella?"

"Yassa, Jonny. First babies makes me sick fo' long time, bu' last babies I be's fine."

"Well, what was the difference?"

"I's thinks maybes foods, Jonny."

"Food! You mean if she starves, she'll be fine?"

"Maybe's some foods make Sissy sick, Jonny."

"Hmm . . . I wonder what foods make Maggie sick."

"Dun knows, Jonny," answered Ella.

Jon went back to Maggie.

"Hi, love. I'll be ready to go in a minute," said Maggie.

"You're feeling better, that quick?"

"I feel pretty good now, Jonny."

"Good, then maybe we can get started."

"I smelled something that made me sick."

"Have any idea what it was, darlin'?"

"I'm not sure, but I'll know next time."

"I hope there is no next time."

"Oh, I'm sure there will be, Jonny."

"I was really worried about you, my pretty plum."

"I know you were, Jonny, but don't be. It happens all the time in pregnancy, usually sooner though."

"You mean you have to suffer, just because you're fertilized?"

"I prefer you call it pregnant, Jonny, and yes, I think most pregnant women have sick spells."

"I'll be damned! It ain't hardly fair."

"Don't swear, Jonny. I'm alright."

"Good, then you can take the reins again, my love."

It was late morning when the group got started west by southwest. The terrain was flat, with groupings of trees, sometimes three or four, and other times there was a large patch of woods. They had eaten a late breakfast, so Jon pressed on.

"When are we going to eat, Jonny?" yelled Maggie.

"You must be feeling better, my love."

"Yes, I am, and now I'm hungry."

"Okay, darlin, we'll look for a good spot, a clearing."

A good spot was found about midafternoon, and the men built a fire so Ella could serve hot food. As she fried some venison strips, Maggie again got sick. Ella gave her some laudanum, and she lay down in the covered wagon . . . and fell asleep.

"I guess we'll pitch the tent and stay here tonight."

"How's many dem miles we's travel, Jon?"

"I would say about seven or eight."

"We's done better un morrow, Jon."

"I hope so, Mose. Is she going to keep getting sick, Ella?"

"No, Jonny, shes be fine soon."

"I hope so. Let's get the tent up, and rest some more. Maybe a nap and a late supner will help us all."

"I's will, Jonny."

After lunch, and animals taken care of, Jon lay down with Maggie in the wagon and dozed.

"Jonny? Are you awake?"

"I am now, darlin? How do you feel?"

"Better now. I'm sorry you had to stop.

"That's Okay, my love. Get some sleep if you can." There was a pause.

"Jonny? Are you awake?"

"What is it, darling?

"I know what it is that's making me sick."

"You do? What is it?"

"I think it's venison."

"Venison? Venison? It can't be!"

"Why not, Jonny?"

"Because we've been eating venison this whole trip, and you're just now getting sick?"

"I know, Jonny, that's barmy, but just when I got a good whiff of it, I got sick."

"Oh my Lord . . . we'll starve!"

"I can put something over my nose to block the smell."

"What, and hide that pretty face from me?"

"You timed that one just right."

"Do you really think it's venison, Mag?"

"Yes, Jonny. What will you do about it?"

"Not sure yet. Get some sleep, my pretty plum. I'll think of something."

"You're so smart, Jonny. Good night."

"Good night, baby. We'll all get a good sleep."

"She's better now, asleep." Jon was back in the tent.

"Sissy say un makes her sick?"

"Yes, she says it's the venison, Ella, but how can that be? We've been eating it this whole trip."

"I's knows, Jonny, Lawd acts in strange ways."

"What can we do about it?"

"Big wagon carrys meats, Jon. We's puts Sissy in carryall in front, an' Mama drives big wagon behin's."

"Good idea, Mose, and if that doesn't work, maybe we can put Maggie on Abby."

"An' I's gets hanky fo' ova Sissy's mouth."

"Right. Let's all turn in, and get an early start tomorrow."

"You's puts Sissy in tent, aways from meats, Jonny."

"Okay, Ella, and Maggie can drive the carryall tomorrow."

"Yassa, Jon, you's an' Sissy gets rest. Good nights."

Saturday, December 12

Mose had wagons hitched, and Ella had breakfast ready at the break of a cold dawn. Maggie took the news well that she would be handling Corker and Conqueror in the lead. Once the venison was cooked, it didn't seem to bother Maggie.

"How are you doing, my love?"

"Fine, Jonny. How far have we traveled this morning?"

"I would guess about five miles."

"Well, let's get our keisters moving!"

About midmorning, the group entered a large opening with only a few clusters of trees. It was over a mile in length, and one hundred yards wide. They were two-thirds through the clearing, when Mose spotted men on horses entering the opening behind them.

"Looks, Jon! Horses comes fast!"

"Let's head for those trees ahead. I'll take the carryall, and you get the wagon and trailer on the run, Mose."

Mose ran and jumped aboard the covered wagon with Ella.

"Chipper! Head for those trees ahead! Hurry!"

"Yassa, Massa Jon, I's runs Abbys fast!"

"Good. Slide over, darling. I'm coming aboard."

"What's happening, Jonny?"

"We have company coming fast behind us. It may be those bounty hunters again."

"Oh no! What are we going to do, Jonny?"

"We're going to run up into those trees ahead and wait for them. Ho! Get up, Corker, Haa!"

"How many of them are there?"

"I didn't stop to count, my pretty plum, but if it is those bounty hunters, there would be five of them."

"I'm scared, Jonny."

"Don't worry, darlin'. We'll have those trees to hide us. They will be out in the open. Maybe you'll get a chance to use those gun-loading skills early. Haa! Get up, Corker!"

Jon was well ahead of Mose in the covered wagon. He looked back and saw Mose driving the wagon as hard as he could. The trailer was bouncing around behind, and the chasers seemed to be gaining a little. Jon and Maggie reached the trees behind Chipper, who was still on Abby.

"Whoa, Corker. Whoa . . . Whoa, Conqueror. Chipper, you get the wagons back in the trees, out of sight."

"Yassa, Massa Jon. Comes on, Corker un Conkers."

"Come down, darling. Hand me all those guns. One minute, Chipper." Jon helped Maggie down after collecting four rifles from the carryall. Mose and Ella finally caught up, and into the trees. The trailer carried six more rifles, making ten total. The chasers were now over halfway across the clearing.

"Get them all loaded and lined up here, gang."

"Orites, Jon. Chips, you's stays hidden wit horses."

"Yassa, Papa."

BAM! Jon fired his Hawken in the direction of the oncoming horsemen. Jon spotted the white hair, Whitey! "Stop right there!" Jon yelled. They kept coming. Jon quickly reloaded. The chasers were now one hundred yards away.

BAM! Jon fired again, and Whitey fell off his horse. The other three stopped and hugged the ground by Whitey.

"What do you bastards want now?"

"We wans you!" Sounded like Whitey hollering.

"Jonny, you swore!" said Maggie.

"Keep loading, my love. I'll probably swear a lot more, trying to stall them." Jon turned back to the group of men. "You ain't getting us, so get your asses back to Bama!" he yelled.

"We're a-gonna kill ya bastards!" That was Baldy.

"Like hellfire you are! I got the drop on you again!"

BAM! A ball struck the tree Jon was behind.

"Now who's got da drops?" Jon wasn't sure who that was.

BAM! Jon had reloaded and fired again. He saw where his ball had hit the ground between Baldy and one other.

"I do!" Jon yelled. "I'm giving you one last chance to leave."

"Go ta hell! Is where ye are a-goin'!" This from another voice.

Jon saw the loaded flintlock rifles lined up beside him, and another tree to his left, which Mose was now behind. "I got ten rifles all loaded and aimed at you."

"Ye'r a liar! There be only two a-you's!" Yelled another man.

"You remember, Whitey? I had extra guns loaded, back at the gap."

"I rememba."

"Well, now I've got all your guns too . . . all loaded."

"Dats what we be afta! Guns and ears!" someone yelled.

"Who was that talking?" yelled Jon.

"I be John," came the answer. "An' I am Harper, come ta kill ye'all fer tyin' me ups, an' left me ta die."

"And Whitey and Baldy. What happened to Neil?"

"Bled to death. Died from his arm." That was John.

"And you want to join him!" hollered Jon.

"Not hardly," answered Whitey. "We aim ta kill you's."

"Whitey! One of you stand, and take your horses off to the side so I won't shoot them too!" Jon yelled.

There was a pause before a heavy-bearded man stood. Jon fired in his direction, and the man hit the ground.

"Reload this, honey," Jon said to Maggie.

"I heard ya say ya wouldn't shoot!" This sounded like John.

"Leave your rifle on the ground, and I won't shoot!"

The bearded man again stood, both hands in the air.

"That's better! Now remove the horses, John."

"I ain't John. I be Harper."

"Okay, Harper, get your nuts swinging, before I shoot them off!"

Maggie gasped. "Jonny!" She had never heard Jon talk like that before.

"See that Harper run? It's the only language they understand." Harper ran the horses off, then ran back to his buddies.

"Now ya got one more chance to leave! Get, or come shooting!"

"We ain't a-leavin' afore we kill all ya bastards!" yelled Baldy.

"Then bring it on, bitches. Come and meet your maker!"

BAM! Maggie had reloaded Jon's Hawken. Jon grabbed it again and saw Whitey bounce on the ground when his latest ball hit him. Jon grabbed the closest flintlock and fired again. *BAM!* Again, Whitey jumped, then lay still. Shots came at Jon, striking the tree, and the brush he was lying in. As Jon reached for another flintlock rifle, Mose fired and reached for another rifle, as Ella took his favorite to reload. Thinking that Jon and Mose now had empty guns, two men ran off to Mose's left. Mose fired, and Baldy screamed and fell in a heap.

"Ahh! Dat bastard gots me in the other shoulder!" was heard from Baldy.

The other man, John, who was ahead of Baldy, kept running, reaching some trees to Mose's left. Mose's second shot had missed him. As Jon watched this action, and the women kept busy reloading, the other hunter, Harper, raced off to Jon's right. He was now in the same cluster of trees that Jon's group was in, and Jon perceived a threat to Chipper and the horses.

"I'm going after that Harper. Stay down."

"Be careful, Jonny."

"I will, darlin'. Be back as quick as I can." Jon grabbed his now reloaded Hawken and a flintlock, and headed into the woods to his right. He tried to be quiet as he crept through the trees, but the brush was making a lot of cracking noises. Suddenly, he heard the blast, and felt the ball whizz past his head. He strained to see Harper through the trees. He heard Harper trying to reload, but couldn't see him. Jon wondered if he should charge Harper while he was loading. He heard Harper tamping his load down the barrel of his gun, and decided it was too late to charge now, so he waited. Now all was quiet, as the two waited each other out. Jon put down his Hawken and made a noise in the brush with the flintlock. *BAM!* Jon saw the flash. The ball hit the tree next to Jon's hand, and he fired the flintlock where the flash had been. He heard a grunt from Harper and saw him take off running back toward his horses. Jon picked up his Hawken. *BAM!* Jon shot Harper in the legs, and he crashed into the brush.

"I'd better go down there and make sure he's dead," Jon whispered to himself. He reloaded his Hawken and started toward the brush where Harper lay. *BAM!* A scream. *BAM!* This came from Jon's gang, and he raced back to them. He saw the three hugging in a huddle, and Ella was shaking and crying.

"What happened?"

"Nanty Ella shot the bad man," said Maggie, pointing to the trees behind their huddle.

"Must be John," said Jon, as he ran past his group. "Yep, it is John, deader than a doornail. Ella shot him?"

"Yes, he appeared out of nowhere, and was about to shoot Nunky Mose, so Nanty Ella shot him."

"Wow! Good shot! Looks like you got him in the heart."

"We's hears you's shootin' too, Jon. You's orites?"

"Yes, but I got to go check on Harper and make sure he's dead."

"We's wait's here, Jon. Baldy not dead yet," said Mose.

"Where is he?"

"He be's down, shot bu' not dead."

"Why don't you check on him, and I'll check out Harper?"

"And leave Nanty Ella and I alone?"

"They're all dead or wounded, my love. And besides, you have Ella to guard you and Chip."

"Chipper! Oh my god! Is Chipper alright? Chipper!"

"Yessum, missy, I be's here."

"Oh, good. I had forgotten about you," sighed Maggie.

"Why don't you bring the wagons back out here, Chipper?"

"I do's, Massa Jon."

"You're not going to travel now, Jonny?"

"Certainly, my pretty plum. Why not?"

"Jonny, we just had a lot of trauma."

"Tell you what, we'll have lunch first, then travel. How's that?"

"How's that? Heartless."

"I prefer to be heartless rather than having cheeks frozen off!"

Jon found Harper with a severe leg wound. He took Harper's rifle and tied Harper's shirt around his leg. "Hold on, I'll get you a horse, and bring you to my expert nurse."

"I curses dat day I met ya!" said Harper.

"So do I! And I hope I'll never see you again."

"I'll be a-seein' ya in hell!"

"That's where you're headed, if we don't get this bleeding stopped. Now just lay still until I get back." Jon ran with Harper's rifle into the clearing, past Whitey's dead body, and toward their horses. He saw Mose tending to the wounded Baldy.

"How's he doing, Mose?" Jon yelled.

"He be's having two shoulders shots, Jon."

"Dat be's a-nunya yer business, ye bastard!" screamed Baldy.

"I'll get their horses, Mose. Stop his bleeding if you can."

"Orites, Jon, I's do," said Mose.

Jon ran to the horses, and brought all four over to Mose. "Put him on a horse, Mose, and take him to Ella to be patched up again."

"Orites, Jon."

"Patched up by a nigger?"

"Don't hit the dummy, Mose. You'll kill him. And you, dummy, would you rather just lay here and die?"

"Ya bastards shoot me twice, an' now you's gonna has some nigger patch me up?"

"You's own man shoots you's," said Mose, "an' I's shoots you's too." Mose easily and gently lifted Baldy onto a horse.

"If he don't straighten up, shoot him again, Mose, right between his wounds! I'm going to get Harper. I'll meet you at the wagons."

Jon took two horses across the clearing and into the trees.

"It's about time ye got here."

"Would you like me to leave again, or do you want to live?"

"If'in I's can't walk, maybe I's wants ta die!"

"If you can't walk, maybe you'll stay home in Alabama!"

"Maybe I will. Am I's the only one left?"

"Baldy is alive and jaw-jackin'."

"He's dang good at dat!" smirked Harper.

"Well, if he wants to live, he better hush his black hatred." Jon struggled to get Harper onto a horse. He led him back into the clearing and over to the wagons.

"Here's another patient, Ella."

"Orites, Jonny, I's fix 'im."

"I don't know why. They hate colored folk."

"Dey be's the Lawd's cree-tions, Jonny."

Ella expertly patched Baldy's shoulders and Harper's leg. Mose put horse liniment on all the wounds, then Maggie and Ella fed everyone. Baldy cursed, but Harper seemed grateful.

"I'm going to keep your guns, and two more horses."

"That be stealin'," said Baldy.

"I call it payment for all the grief you've caused!"

"I be a-findin' ya's again, an' kill all ya bastards."

"Put him on a horse, Mose, and get him out of my sight."

"Put me on dat horse right there," said Baldy.

"Who's horse was that, Harper?"

"It were John's horse," Harper answered.

"Then we'll keep it. Put him on that horse, Mose."

"Orites, Jon, I's do dat gladlys."

"Ya bastards! I wan's on dat horse!

Mose picked Baldy straight up into the air, and slammed him into a saddle.

"Ahh! My shoulders! You's bastards!" yelled Baldy.

"Your shoulders are going to heal, thanks to these blacks!"

"I'm appreciatin' yer help. Thanks be to ya all," said Harper.

"That's more like it. Now be gone, and don't come back."

"See ye all in hell!" shouted Baldy.

"Not if I see you first!" answered Jon.

The two bounty hunters headed east for Pineville.

"Whew. I'm glad to see them go. They're creepy," said Maggie.

"Well, I don't think we'll see them again, darlin'."

"I sure hope not, Jonny."

"Well, gang, we can still get in a few hours of travel."

"It's still heartless, Jonny. We would only have two hours before it gets dark, and we need the rest."

"And what about tomorrow?"

"Tomorrow we travel, Jonny."

"Ah-ha! Got ya! Tomorrow is Sunday, my pretty plum."

"Oh my gosh! I forgot!"

"Too late! Tomorrow we travel!"

"You win this one, but I want a stop to rest and pray."

"Okay, darlin', we camp here tonight."

"Yes, Jon. An' we bury dem dead mans," said Mose.

"Oh, yeah. I almost forgot that."

"See, I'm not the only one who forgets, Jonny."

Diary of Margaret Hamilton

Saturday, December 12, 1835

. . . And we have only traveled about fifteen miles in two days since splitting from the Chasneys. This was a scary day. Those bad bounty hunters returned, four of them. It was scary! Jonny and Mose killed one, and believe it or not, Nanty Ella killed one man who was about to shoot us. Then she bandaged the two wounded men and sent them back east once again. She is a wonder! The weather has been freezing at night, but no rain . . . Tomorrow is Sunday again, but we have lost a lot of time, and Jonny wants to press on. We have now been traveling for eight weeks.

Love, Margaret H.

Sunday, December 13

Ella had breakfast cooked early, so the smell of venison wouldn't bother Maggie. Mose now had nine horses and fourteen rifles to take care of. He would need grassy spots and streams of water to keep the horses content. He told this to Jon when the newlyweds woke. Hot dodgers, filled with pemmican of venison, was the breakfast waiting for the Hamiltons. Maggie just ate corn dodgers and no meat.

After breakfast, it was an early start with no stopping until a stream was found. It was late morning when such a stream appeared, and Jon called a break in the journey.

"We'll rest here and take a lunch later. Let's get the horses watered in that stream, then let them graze for a while on that grass."

"Where does this stream go, Jonny?"

"Hmm, it's running northwest. It probably runs into the Cumberland River. Nice, clean little stream."

"Yes, it's so inviting. If I were alone right now, I would take a cold dip, maybe a bath. I need one."

"Go ahead, darlin'. You are alone, with only our family."

"I'd be too embarrassed, Jonny."

"Then I'll take a bath with you, my love."

"I's takes bath wit you's too, Sissy," said Ella.

"Let's all take a bath! Do you have some of your mother's soap, my pretty plum?"

"Yes, if I can find it, Jonny."

"I's has soaps too, Sissy," said Ella.

"I's gets dem fire big, so's we's gets warm," said Mose.

Maggie was hesitant to take her clothes off. "Is it alright, Jonny?"

"It's alright, my love. We are all family."

"Alright, Jonny, but I will leave this little bit on."

"That's fine, my pretty plum."

"Eeek! Th-the w-water's c-c-cold!" chattered Maggie.

"Sure it is, darlin'. It'll put hair on your chest!"

"Jonny! I d-don't want hair on m-my chest!"

"I guess not, my love. You are beautiful just the way you are!"

"I am not, Jonny. I'm f-fat!"

"Our son is getting fat. You are beautiful."

Jon noticed Ella and Mose were washing each other.

"Here, my darlin', soap up briskly, like this." Jon rubbed the soap briskly over his body, while Maggie shivered. "I'll warm you up, my pretty plum." Jon soaped Maggie.

"Jonny . . . don't rub there so much," Maggie whispered.

"Why not, darling? It gets dirty too!"

"Jonny, you're embarrassing me again."

"Sorry, honey. Here, sit in the water, and I'll rinse you off."

"It's too c-cold, Jonny."

"Honey, look . . ."

What they saw was Mose and Ella hugging in the stream.

"Does that give you any ideas, darling?"

"No, it doesn't, Jonny. Come on, let's get to that f-fire."

With clean clothes on, and dirty clothes washed and hanging close to the fire to dry, it was time for lunch.

"Wasn't that a great bath, gang?"

"No, it wasn't, Jonny. Too cold!"

"Well now, let's take a vote on that! I liked it, and I know Mose and Ella liked it. How about you, Chipper?"

"You're not funny, Jonny," said Maggie.

"I's likes it toos, Massa Jon," answered Chipper.

"You're outnumbered, my pretty plum. It's going to smell a lot better in that tent tonight, too."

"It does make my skin feel a lot cleaner," said Maggie.

"How can your skin feel cleaner? Your skin doesn't feel anything, does it?"

"Of course, it does, you big lummox! Here, feel! Not there, Jonny!"

"It feels soft, smooth, and clean, my love."

"See? My skin feels soft and clean."

"Yes, but it feels that way to me, not itself."

"You blunderhead! When you got out of that water and dried off, wasn't your skin tingling?"

"Why, yes it was, darlin', from the brisk rubdown."

"Your skin was sending a message to your brain that it feels clean, Jonny."

"I think my brain was sending a message to tingle!"

"What brain?"

Everyone and everything watered and fed, it was west-southwest again. The atmosphere seemed much better, and the gang made good time that Sunday afternoon, only slowed by an occasional small forest needing some hand clearing. Dark came early in these winter months, so even in the best conditions traveling every daylight hour, Jon figured it would be difficult making twenty miles. Today they made about fifteen, and were close to the Tennessee border. They found no other stream, but as darkness settled in, they came upon another grassy area and pitched their tent. The only meat left was venison, and Maggie got sick again when Ella cooked it.

"How be's Sissy now, Jonny?" asked Ella, as Jon stepped out of his covered wagon.

"Her stomach is still a little upset, but she's better. I think she wants something to eat. She lost her lunch."

"I's takes Sissy food, Jonny," said Ella.

"Thanks, Ella. I think she can eat venison that's cooked."

"Yassa, she sho 'nuff can."

"What can we do about these sick spells, Ella?"

"I's don' knows, Jonny. We's keeps Sissy aways from cooks."

"Okay. What do you think, Mose?"

"Maybe's Sissy can eats horse meats."

"Hey, that's an idea, Mose. We have too many horses, and a change in meat might do her good."

"An' cuts down on grains, Jon."

"We'll keep that in mind, in case she can't eat venison at all."

"Orites, Jon. I's go stakes horses for the nights."

"Thank you, Mose. You too, Chip."

"Jon . . . Jon, is you's up?" Mose could be heard, not seen.

"I'm here, Mose. Where are you?"

"I's be comin', Jon. I's has sometin' ta shows you's."

"I'm right here, by the fire, Mose. What's wrong?"

"Looks what I's finds, Jon."

"What is it, Mose?"

"Ears, Jon. I's find ears on saddle, on dem horse Baldy wans ta rides."

"No wonder he wanted that horse, I kept some, from the pass."

"Yassa. Wez burns dem now."

"Let's hide them from Chip and the women, and hold on to them for a few days."

"Why's we's do dat, Jon?"

"I'm not sure, Mose, but we are about to cross back into Tennessee, a slave state."

"So's be Arkansas, Jon?"

"Yes, I think it will be a slave state too."

"Maybe's we's stays in dem Kentucky, Jon."

"You are free, Mose. Are you worried?"

"Fo' missus and Chips, Jon."

"I've heard that there are free Negroes already in Arkansas, Mose, and we can't get free land in Kentucky."

"Orites, Jon, we's go ta Arkansas, an' we's hides ears!"

"Good. I'm sure Ella, Chip, and you will be Okay."

"I's sures too, Jon."

Monday, December 14

A very cold and threatening morning greeted Mose and Ella as they scrambled to build up the fire.

"Brrr," said Jon, as he exited the wagon. "It looks like snow again, doesn't it, Mose?"

"Sho 'nuff do's, Jon. I's hitches dem wagons."

"Have you had breakfast already?"

"Yassa. How be's Sissy dem mornin', Jonny?"

"Just fine, Ella. She'll be out in a few minutes."

"I's has hot cakes readys fo you's . . . warms up stomachs."

"Thanks, Ella. You know the way to a man's heart."

Ella laughed. "Gots dem gets stomach full first!" she said, still laughing.

"My stomach needs filling," said Maggie, from the wagon.

"Well, get that nice round stomach out here."

"Dress warm, Sissy. It be's cold," said Ella.

"Put on my frock coat, darlin'."

"Thanks, Jonny," came Maggie's reply.

The wagons got an early start, and had no slow-ups all forenoon. They found a good grassy spot to lunch, and ate cold dodgers that Ella had made Sunday evening. The barrels of water were getting low, so they pressed on.

"How many miles did we make this morning, Jonny?"

"A good ten, darlin'. If we do this well this afternoon, we should be in Tennessee again sometime tomorrow."

"Is that when we see the Cumberland River again?"

"No, we'll be in Tennessee a long time before we see the river again."

"We're not going to get lost again, are we?"

"No . . . again? We've never been lost, my love."

"Ha! You were lost several times in the Blues, Jonny."

"I was not!"

"Then why did it take so long to get over them?"

"Because I had two women giving me trouble."

"Now you have one, huh? Be careful how you answer!"

"Why, you are no trouble at all, my pretty plum."

"Good. Now don't get us lost again, Jonny."

"I won't, my darlin'."

Another four or five easy miles were made in the afternoon before the problems started. They were hit by strong wind.

"Jonny! I can't see ahead! That wind! I'm freezing!"

"I know, darlin'!" Jon shouted. "It's coming right at us. Put a blanket over you. I'll be right back."

"What? I can't hear you. Where are you?" asked Maggie.

"I said wrap in a blanket. I'll be right back."

Jon turned his horse back to the big wagon and Ella. "Where is Mose?"

"He be's off dat ways, Jonny!" yelled Ella.

"Can you see the carryall?"

"I's sees, den I's don' sees."

"I'll stop her. Stay with her, Okay?"

"You's stops, Sissy?"

"Yes! And I'll go find Mose!" Jon yelled.

"Orites, Jonny. We's wait."

Jon rode back to the front and found Maggie trying to drive Corker and Conqueror straight ahead.

"Hold it, Maggie!" Jon shouted.

"Is that you, Jonny?"

"It's me! Hold on. I'll get Corker."

"Jonny, where are we going?" asked Maggie.

"Right here." Maggie heard that loud and clear, as Jon was now in front, shouting back toward her. "Come on, Corker, let's get you out of the wind."

Jon grabbed Corker's halter and turned him, Conqueror, and the carryall around, so their backs were to the wind. He saw the covered wagon approaching, and signaled Maggie to do the same.

"Where are you going, Jonny?"

"What?"

"I said, where are you going?" screamed Maggie.

"To find Mose. I'll be back."

"Jonny, I'm scared!"

"You and Chipper stay with Ella."

"What if you get lost?"

"I'll be alright. Be back soon." Jon disappeared.

"Mose! Mose!" Jon hollered. No answer. Jon slipped a cap on his Hawken and fired. *BAM!* "Mose!" Jon screamed. "Where are you, Mose?"

"I's here, Jon." Mose was right behind Jon.

"Where did you go, Mose?"

"I's finds trees fo dem horses and wagons."

"Where, Mose?

"Ova there, Jon." Mose pointed the direction.

"If we can find the wagons, we'll head there."

"I's fire guns, Jon." Mose shot his flintlock.

There was no response, so Mose and Jon reloaded. Jon fired. In a couple minutes, they heard the return shot.

"Dey be ova der, Jon."

"Yes, that's where I thought I'd left them. I'll go get them, and you wait here for my shot, Okay?"

"Orites, Jon. I's waits."

Jon reloaded his Hawken, and headed back toward the wagons in heavy wind. He was having problems seeing, and the cold was making his face and hands hurt.

After a while, he fired his Hawken again, and heard the women screaming at him. They were very close. He also heard Mose's responding shot.

"Over here, Jonny!" he heard Maggie yell, and he rode right up to them, huddled together.

"Is Daddy be's orites?" asked Ella.

"Yes, he's fine. Did you hear him shoot his rifle?"

"We didn't know who was shooting," said Maggie.

"Okay. Let's tie a rope between the carryall and Ella's team, and head over to Mose. He found some trees."

"I'm scared, Jonny."

"We're fine, honey. Chipper, will you ride with Maggie?"

"Yassa, I's do," he answered.

"Good. Will you be alright behind, Ella?"

"Yassa, long as you's gets ropes tied, I's fine."

"Good. Let's get started." Jon reloaded his Hawken, loaded an extra gun, and fired. They heard Mose's response.

Jon tied a short rope to Corker's halter, and led the group in Mose's direction. When he thought he had led about the correct distance, he fired his Hawken. Mose's return shot was just a short distance away, and he came right up to where Mose was waiting. Mose grabbed Conqueror's halter and led the group a short distance into some dense woods. Mose and Jon worked the wagons into the middle of the trees.

"We've got a lot of blankets. Let's put one on each horse, and bundle up ourselves, gang."

"Can we build a fire, Jonny?"

"No fire, darlin'. Too windy."

"How will we keep warm?"

"We can all climb in the covered wagon and huddle!"

"That would be really crowded, Jonny."

"That's what we need to keep each other warm, my love."

Somehow, they all got into the covered wagon among all the boxes and stacks, and huddled together.

"Jonny, I'm too cramped."

"A-ha! You can't get away from me now!"

"Be's good wagons heavy loads, so's dem don' blows ova."

"That's right, Mose. We're lucky at that."

"How far have we traveled today, Jonny?"

"I'd say about fifteen miles."

"Is that enough to get back to Tennessee tomorrow?"

"Yes. We should be close right now. Why do you ask?"

"I'm afraid of those bad men, Jonny."

"Nothing to be afraid of now, darlin'. They're either dead or wounded, thanks to Ella."

Ella laughed. "You's funnin' wit me's, Jonny! Hee, hee!"

"You're going to be the best shot in Arkansas, Ella, *and* the best cook!"

"Thank you's, Jonny. Hee, hee!"

"Jonny . . . I'm getting sick again."

"Oh no, the venison! Find a pail."

"There's one behind the bench, Jonny . . . oops, arrghh!"

Jon grabbed the pail just in time to catch Maggie's retching.

"I's gets sometin' fo' cova Sissy's mouth," said Ella.

"There should be some cloth pieces around here, Ella."

"Here, I's finds, Jonny."

Maggie's mouth and nose were covered, and four downcast adults and a boy, were now huddled together to ward off cold and despair.

"We's lucky we's don' gets cova blown aways from wagon."

"We sure are, Mose. You've got those hoops good and secure to the sideboards. How about the canvasses on the trailer?"

"Dey be's fines, Jon."

"So you think we're in Tennessee, Jonny?"

"If not, we're pretty close, my love."

"Good. I'll be glad when we get to Nashville."

"I'll be glad when we get to Arkansas!"

"We's be safe un Arkansas, Jonny?" asked Ella.

"I hope so, Ella. It will probably be a slave state too, but you will have papers to show that you're free."

"At least we'll be far away from those bounty hunters."

"Don't worry, darlin'. Those bounty hunters are dead and gone for good."

"When we's in Arkansas, we's pretends we's you's slaves."

"If anyone questions us about it, we can say that, Mose."

"Orites, we's pretends, Jonny."

"We've never thought of you as slaves, Nanty Ella."

"I's knows, Sissy. You's my babys."

"I love you and Nunky Mose . . . and Chipper."

"An' we's loves you's, Sissy."

"Well, now that love is in the air, let's celebrate our good fortune. Mose, do you have your harmonica?"

"Sho 'nuff do's, Jon."

"Then cheer us up with some mountain music."

"Yassa, I's do."

Despite the conditions Jon's group found themselves in, an old-fashioned sing-along ensued for hours.

"Jonny, I don't hear the wind anymore."

"Well, let's look, my pretty plum." Jon opened the laces at the bench and peered out. Darkness was settling in, but he could hear the winds in the distance. His eyes found a small opening through the trees and . . . "Snow! It's snowing, gang!"

"Just what we need," said Maggie.

"Keep up the good spirits, gang. All of us will find freedom and a new life in Arkansas."

"How long will that take?" asked Maggie.

"Well, we're probably a good third of the way already."

"Already? Jonny, we've been traveling two months. We should be there by now."

"No, we shouldn't, my love. I told you we would be there by spring."

"At the rate we're going, it will be spring of thirty-nine!"

"No, darlin', I meant this coming spring. We'll make good time once we get to the river again."

"What river? The Missouri?"

"The Cumberland, once we reach the Cumberland."

"Jonny, how many times have you said that? Once we get over the hill, over the Blues, reach the Watauga, get through the gap . . . now it's reach the Cumberland." There was a pause.

"I'm sorry, Maggie . . . and Mose, and Ella . . . and Chip . . ."

"It be's orites, Jon. We's makes it orites," said Mose.

"It be's fines, Jonny. We's be free!" added Ella.

"I know you're trying, Jonny. I just want to have our first child in a home."

"We will, darlin'. First, last, and all between."

"Goodness, how many children you's all plans ta have?"

"One or tw—," said Maggie.

"Dozen!" interrupted Jon.

Laughter spread through the covered wagon.

"I's go feeds horses."

"I's helps," said Chipper.

"Thanks, Mose . . . and Chip. What's our sleeping arrangement for the night?"

"In the tent, Jonny."

"I don't think we can pitch the tent, darlin'."

"Too much snow, Jonny?"

"Too much brush and trees."

"I's clears spot, Jon."

"I'll get the axe, Mose, while you tend the horses."

"Orites, Jon. Gets lights fo' Jon, Mama."

"I's do, Daddy," said Ella.

Jon found a brushy spot right next to the wagons, and began clearing a large spot for the tent. Only light snow was falling through the trees, but Jon was sure it was snowing hard.

"What about supper, Jonny?" asked Maggie.

"Well, the wind has died down a lot. Maybe we can use this brush for a small fire."

"Thanks, honey. Nanty Ella and I will make supper."

"It's supner, my pretty plum."

Diary of Margaret Hamilton

Monday, December 14, 1835

. . . And we traveled about fifteen miles before we were struck by a fierce wind. Jonny and Nunky Mose found a small forest for camping out of the wind. Then it started snowing! I think it still is. I hope the snow doesn't stop us from making it back into Tennessee tomorrow. I'm still afraid of those bad bounty hunters. Jonny says they won't return. There are only two left alive, but I'm still worried. I'm being silly, I know. They have already crossed two states. I hope Jonny's right. I miss my parents and my brothers, and hope they are safe.

Love, Maggie

Tuesday, December 15

Jon woke to the sound of chopping. *Good Lord, what was Mose doing now?* he thought. The sounds seemed far away, and Jon sensed a strange silence and aloneness. Maggie was up already, but Jon couldn't hear her.

"Maggie?" No answer. "Maggie!" Jon shouted.

"I'm out here, Jonny, by the fire."

It was cold in the tent, and Jon jumped into his kentucks. "What's happening?" he asked, head out of the tent.

"We have nice warm venison dodgers, Jonny, and I didn't get sick helping Nanty Ella make them."

"Good! What's Mose . . . Hell, the wagons are gone!"

"Over there, Jonny. Nunky Mose found grass under the snow just past the trees, so he's taking the horses to it."

Mose was only about fifty yards away, but sounded further.

"Isn't it strange how the snow deafens the sound?"

"It sure is, my love. Look at the snow!"

"It's only three or four inches here, but look at the trees, Jonny. Nunky Mose says there is over a foot of snow where the grass is. Thank goodness it has finally stopped."

"That looks like it's just ahead of him. I'll get a shovel."

"You's eats some hot dodgers, firs', Jonny," said Ella.

"Okay, Ella, sounds good. Thanks!"

Breakfast was good, and soon Jon was helping Mose and Chipper clear a path, through well over a foot of snow, to grass.

"How manys snow we's shovels, Massa Jon?" asked Chip.

"Enough to feed nine horses, Chipper."

"That be's lots!"

"Sure is, boy. We may need more of those dodgers before we get through here."

"Yassa, we's do."

"You bring the wagons up here, Chipper, and unhitch them. Mose and I will keep shoveling."

"Yassa, Massa Jon, I's do."

The snow was light and powdery, and easy to shovel. Soon the horses were busy grazing. The sun was bright, but not producing warmth. Another fire was started at the open field, and Jon's group closed ranks around it. It was now midmorning.

"Jonny, are we going to try traveling today?"

"I don't know. What do you think, Mose?"

"Maybe's we's shovel paths fo' wheels, Jon."

"That sounds like a lot of work. How many would like to try traveling in this snow?"

"Are we going to get to vote on something?"

"That sounded like Liz talking," said Jon.

"In your dreams! Anyway, I vote yes," said Maggie.

"See's dem trees long way ova wit dem bare trees? We's tries an' makes it dat far, Jon."

There were many snow-laden trees and tree groups ahead, but Jon could see the cluster Mose was referring to over a mile away.

"I see them, Mose. Okay, we'll try for them, and see how we do. You and Chip hitch the wagons, and I'll get some water."

"Water? What water? And you didn't let Nanty Ella or Chipper vote, Jonny."

"We already have a majority, darling, and I'm packing snow into the barrels to make water."

"You're counting on it melting in this cold weather? And I still think they should get to vote!"

"Alright! I'm really surprised that my little scarypants wants to try fighting this snow, but how do you vote, Ella and Chip?"

"We's votes ta stays . . . wit Daddy," said Ella.

"See? I knew it, my love. Hope you can keep Corker headed in the path that Mose and I cut out."

"Don't you worry about that. Just get us back to Tennessee."

"What? And miss all those bad bounty hunters?"

"Cut out the tongue-wagging, you big lummox!"

"Let's get crackin', Mose."

Amazingly, the snow-covered mile was covered quickly and easily, so the journey continued. Mose was like a giant steam shovel, and was doing more and more of the work as Jon tired. It was well past noon, and Jon called a break.

"Let's stay here for a rest, Mose."

"Orites, Jon. We's rest."

"How far have we traveled today, Jonny?" asked Maggie.

"I would say about two or three miles."

"It be's gets easier," said Mose.

"Easier? Why do you say that, Mose?"

"Snow gets less."

Jon cut a line into the fresh snow, and looked.

"Durned if you aren't right, Mose. It's less than a foot deep here. Maybe we'll run out of snow ahead."

"I be's hungry," said Chipper.

"So am I. Can we have some dinner?"

"Dinner? We haven't had lunch yet, my love."

"You call it lunch. I call it dinner, Jonny."

"Oh no! Do we have to rename it too?"

"Not if you weren't so stubborn."

"How about dinnunch? No, lunner."

"Eder ways, you's get dodgers," said Ella. "Cold 'uns!"

"That was good, Ella. Thanks. We still have two or three hours of daylight left. Let's travel."

"Sounds wonderful, Jonny."

"You're too agreeable, darlin'."

"And you're stubborn, so let's get going!"

Go they did. Another mile, and the snow was less than six inches deep.

"We's stops shovelin' now, Jon."

"Do you want to make camp here, Mose?"

"Wagons rolls fine in snows now, Jon."

"Good, Mose. I'm ready to ride a spell."

"I's be ready toos," said Mose.

The two men climbed onto the extra horses, and the group moved on. Corker and Conqueror broke trail easily. All too soon the darkness came, and the men started camp along a small creek.

"The moon and snow makes it still light out, Jonny. We can still make a couple more miles."

"This is a perfect spot to camp, darlin', with a stream and grass for the horses. Stop your worrying. Nobody's going to get us."

"I'm sorry, Jonny, but I can't help it."

"It's Okay, honey. We may be in Tennessee right now. Besides, if there was someone after us, it wouldn't matter if we were in Arkansas. They would still keep coming."

After a pause, Maggie asked, "We might be in Tennessee right now? How many miles did we make today, Jonny?"

"Lord help me! Let's see . . . about six or seven, I guess."

"Why don't you talk to someone who knows you, Jonny?"

"Very funny! You're sounding more like Liz every day."

"You're never going to forget her, are you?"

"Probably not. Are you?"

"Probably not."

A hot meal on a cold night, then some cuddling under the blankets made a perfect evening.

Wednesday, December 16

The overnight freeze made a crust of ice over the snow. That was what woke Jon, Mose walking around the tent.

"Wake up, my pretty plum. The sun is shining."

"How do you know that? Ooh, Jonny, it's cooold out!"

"A nice hot breakfast will warm you up, my love."

"I'll need more than that, Jonny."

"Good. Let's get back under those blankets."

"Hold it! Nice try. I'll just wear your frock coat today."

"You are a joy, darlin'."

"Let's get dressed and get an early start, Jonny."

"You are a killjoy, darlin'."

"Get dressed, you big lummox."

"That was a wonderful breakfast, Ella. Thank you."

"You's welcome, Jonny."

"Can I help break the tent down, Nunky Mose?"

"No's, Sissy. I's do."

"You's sho in a hurrys, Sissy," said Ella.

"She wants to get into Tennessee, before the bad men get us."

"Orites, Sissy, you's helps me picks up, an' puts out fires."

"Sure will, Nanty Ella. Jonny thinks I'm barmy, but I think those bad men will come back."

"Orites, Sissy, we's hurries."

"Thanks, Nanty Ella. I'll feel better once I know we are in Tennessee."

After a couple hours of traveling, the snow was mostly gone, except for mounds of drifted snow. The temperature was above freezing.

"We are in Tennessee for sure, darlin'!" shouted Jon from his horse. "And no bad men!"

"Good. I feel better now, but how can you tell?"

"We were never more than about twelve miles into Kentucky at Pineville, my love, and we've traveled well over fifty miles in a southwest direction. We have to be in Tennessee."

"You said we were going in a west by southwest direction."

"That was brilliant, darlin'. You surprise me!"

"You think I'm stupid! I know what you said!"

"You're not stupid at all, my pretty plum. Now, if we traveled west by southwest, we should have been in Tennessee after about thirty-five miles or so . . ."

"And we've traveled over fifty. Yeah! They can't get us now, can they, Jonny?"

"No, my pretty plum, they can't get us now."

But they could, and did! Jon's group started up a small rise, when they saw a group of several riders coming after them.

"Hurry, ladies, get those wagons up this hill, and into those trees. I'll try to hold them off."

"I knew they would come again!" Maggie shouted to no one.

"Get then into those trees, Mose."

Jon saw Mose guiding the wagons into the trees at the top of the rise, and found a tree to protect himself, jumping off his horse. The chasers were less than one hundred yards away, coming fast. Jon had to stop them to give Mose time to set a defense in the trees. *BAM!* Jon fired his Hawken, and shot a horse out from under the falling rider. The other riders scattered for cover, so Jon sprinted up into the trees where his gang had found a small trench in the middle, and were lining up the extra rifles. Mose fired his favorite rifle, and Ella and Maggie started to reload for the men. Two shots came whizzing through the trees, then silence.

"Who are you, and what do you want?" shouted Jon.

"We are the Pineville posse, and we want you!" came the response from behind a tree halfway up the hill.

"Leave us be. We have done nothing to you."

"You murdered five men and wounded two others, and we aim to take you back to Pineville."

"We didn't murder anyone! You're mistaken."

"You'll have a chance to prove that. Now, are you coming out, or do we have to kill you?"

"I's count seven, Jon, an' dat one be's Harper, I's thinks."

"Harper! I might have known. I'm worried for Chipper and the ladies, or I'd fight it out. I don't want to go back."

"Don' you's worries 'bout Sissy an' me's, Jonny. We's shoots too, don' we, Sissy?" asked Ella.

"Yes. I want to stay with you, Jonny. Tell them we are in Tennessee and going west."

"Are you coming out or not?" came the leader's voice.

"You are in Tennessee now, and not legal!" shouted Jon.

After a pause, "How do you know that?" asked the voice.

"I can prove it, if you'll let me. Besides, those two wounded men are lying to you. They attacked us, and we had to kill or be killed."

"Don' listen ta dem bastards!" came a shout. "Thems lied! See dem horses, they's are the horses they stole!"

"That was Baldy, no doubt about that," said Jon to Mose.

"An' he can't shoots wit shoudas hurts," said Mose.

"That makes six we have to shoot."

"We's shoots dem, Jonny," said Ella.

"I can prove those two wounded men are killers, and lying to you, sir!" shouted Jon.

BAM! The shot just missed Maggie and the group, and dug into the side of the covered wagon.

"Don't ya believe them, Ron. They can't prove nothin'." Jon thought that sounded like Harper.

"I said, don't shoot!" yelled the leader, Ron, to Jon. "If you can prove what you're sayin', I'll listen."

"Okay. Walk toward me, alone, and I'll come out alone," said Jon.

"The bastards be lying! Kill them all!" shouted Baldy.

BAM! A ball tore into Mose's calico coatee at the shoulder.

"I told ya to stop shootin'!" screamed the leader, Ron. "Get his gun and tie him up!"

"How bad are you hit, Mose?" Jon quietly asked.

"I's be fine, Jon. Mama takes care o' me's."

"Where are those ears, Mose?"

"Dey be's in dem saddle bags, Jon."

"Are you Okay up there?" shouted Ron. "I'm coming out."

"Ya," Jon returned the shout. "Are you unarmed?"

"Yes. Are you?"

"Yes. I'm coming out." Jon grabbed the ear bag.

The two men stepped out from behind trees, about fifty or sixty yards apart, and stepped toward each other.

"Be careful, Jonny . . . I'm scared."

"It's alright, darlin'. Keep a watch for them."

Jon veered to the side, to keep out of gun sight of Mose, as he walked down the hill. He still had his knife in its sheath on his belt, if he could get close enough to use it. He hoped he wouldn't need to. He was soon halfway, and stopped. Out of the corner of his eye, he saw Baldy jump from behind a tree, rifle in his hands. Jon dove for the ground. *BAM!* The shot came from behind Jon. Baldy fell backward, as Mose's shot hit him in the chest. Baldy's shot went astray as he fell. Jon noticed that Ron had also hit the ground close to him.

"Is he dead?" asked Ron to the others.

"I'm sure he is," answered Jon. "My man Mose is a crack shot."

"He deserved it. I told him to hold his fire."

"He didn't want me to prove that he's a liar and killer."

"Can you prove that?"

"I sure can. You heard him say that those two horses over there are theirs?"

"Yes, I did."

"Well, this is what they were carrying on their horses." Jon showed Ron the sack.

"What the sam hell is . . ."

"They are ears, sir, left ears to be exact. They take them off Negroes they kill, and sell them in Alabama."

"Bounty hunters! We don't like them in Kentucky."

"We don't like them anywhere! And we're in Tennessee, sir."

"I'm Ron. You said you could prove that?"

"I can, Ron." Jon squatted to the ground and found a stick. He drew a triangle, the long side east and west, a short side due north, and the connecting line west southwest. "Now, how far north of the gap is Pineville?"

"About twelve miles due north," answered Ron.

"Right. This north line is twelve miles from the gap to your town of Pineville. Then this line east and west is the border, and this line running west southwest is the direction, by my compass, that we have been traveling."

"Okay, so what?" asked Ron.

"Well, if this direction is twelve miles from the gap to Pineville, watch this."

Jon took his stick and measured the north line. Then he laid that length along the west southwest line. It took a little more than three lengths to reach the east-west line. "Three lengths is thirty six miles, and we are back to the border, and well into Tennessee."

"We have chased you for at least fifty miles."

"Yes, you have. Four lengths is forty eight miles, so we are probably about seven or eight miles into Tennessee."

"At least. There's no doubt we're in Tennessee, Mister ah . . ."

"Jon. I'm Jonathan Hamilton, and we are headed for Nashville."

"That's a long way to travel in the winter."

"I know. We're actually going to Arkansas, and couldn't leave until the crops were all in."

"That's been two months ago, uh, Jon."

"I know that too. It's taken that long to get here."

"From Virginia?"

"No, from North Carolina, over the Blue Ridge Mountains."

"I'll be damned! You took a long way to get here."

"I know that too."

"Well, Nashville is probably two hundred miles yet, but you should hit the Nashville road in another seventy-five miles."

"Don't tell my wife, but that's the way I should have gone."

"Yeah, the road runs through the Blues to Knoxville."

"Yeah, I know."

"Ya know a lot, Jon, but ya gotta use that know-how! In two months you could have been to Nashville and past."

"I know, I know, Ron."

"Hey, Al!" shouted Ron. "Bring up that wounded man."

The man named Al ran over to where Harper was tied up, got him on a horse, and they rode up the incline to Ron.

"Here he be's, name's Harper," said Al.

"What ya wants?" asked Harper.

"Were those horses over there yours?"

"Danged rights they were ours," answered Harper.

"Then what are these things in this bag?"

"Oh . . . I, ah . . . don' know . . . Uh, where'd ya get that?"

"It was on the horse you said was yours."

"I, uh . . . ne'er seen it afor," stammered Harper.

"Oh, I think you have. You're going back to Pineville with us to stand trial for murder."

"We didn't kill no niggers in Kentucky," pleaded Harper.

"You were a-tryin' to. That's attempted murder."

"That other guys shot 'em, not me!"

"But they're all dead. You're the only one we can try."

"Looks like you're the only one going to hell, Harper," said Jon.

"I'll be a-seein' ya there," replied Harper.

"Not if I see you first."

"Take him away, Al. I guess we have enough horses without the one your slave shot. You can take Baldy's horse too."

"He's my partner, not a slave."

"Oh, well, good luck the rest of the way."

"Thanks, we'll need it."

The two leaders shook hands and parted. Jon walked back up the hill to his group with a feeling of triumph.

"See, I told you we would be safe in Tennessee," said Maggie.

"I know you did, darlin'. How's your shoulder, Mose?"

"It be's orites, Jon. Mama fixed good."

"Good, then we can make a lot of miles yet today."

"Jonny! We just went through a battle, and Nunky Mose got shot. We need a rest. Don't you have a heart?"

"Ah-ha! My wife is back to normal! We still have a good half day of light, and Mose says he's alright. We travel."

"Well, at least we can get some rest while we lunch."

"Ah-ha! You said it! It's lunch, not dinner, my love."

"Alright, you big lummox. Can we have lunch before we go?"

"Sure thing. Let's build a fire and rest a spell."

"You're the one back to normal, Jonny."

"I know, my pretty plum. We all need a rest and some food."

"I couldn't believe it when I saw that Baldy jump out and try to shoot at us. Both of his shoulders have wounds."

"Yassa, buts he's don' shoots nowhere, Jon," said Mose.

"He must have had a powerful hate for us."

"Yassa, Jon, he do that orites."

"That dinner was so good, Nanty Ella. It warmed me up," said Maggie.

"Now it's dinner again! It was a great lunner, Ella."

"It warms us alls, an' fills us alls. Dat's alls," said Ella.

"I calls it good foods!" exclaimed Mose.

"Righto, Mose. Now can we get back on the road, gang?"

"What road are you referring to, Jonny?"

"The road to paradise, my darlin'."

"Oh? There are two paradises?"

"No, my pretty plum, just the one we find in Arkansas."

"That's strange. I'm sure we left paradise in Bethania."

"It were no's paradise ta me," said Ella.

"Oh, I'm sorry, Nanty Ella. We'll make it up to you."

"You's alredy has, Sissy . . . an' Jonny."

"We will always try to make all people we meet free from now on, starting with you all. Now, let's get crackin'," said Jon.

"Thank you's, Jon. We's gets crackin'," said Mose.

Diary of Margaret Hamilton

Wednesday, December 16

. . . And I was right. They did come back a third time. This time, they had vigilantes with them. But Jonny proved to them that we were in Tennessee, and they let us go. Nunky Mose got wounded slightly in the shoulder, but he shot the one who did it. Traveled about ten miles today in the cold!

Love and miss my family,
MRH

Thursday, December 17, 1835

. . . Jonny assures us that we're not lost. He uses his compass all the time, and says we should reach the Nashville Road in three more days. The country looks the same, mile after mile. This afternoon Nunky Mose spotted movement in a large snowbank. It was rabbits, as white as the snow. We all had fun trying to catch them. We trapped one, and Jonny shot another, so we had a wonderful hot stew for supper. But that's where the fun ended. We made about twelve or thirteen miles under ugly, black skies to the north, then the storm hit us. Strong winds first, then hail covered the ground with ice, and finally a blinding snow storm. We found shelter in a thick forest, and we may be stuck here in our tent for a long time.

Miss you all, Maggie

Friday, December 18, 1835

. . . And the winds are still howling! I felt so sorry for the men, who had to feed and water the horses. They are down to the last barrel of grain, and any grass is covered with ice and

snow. Jonny got the water barrels filled with snow again. They are inside our tent, so the snow will melt. We are protected by the trees, but Jonny says the snow is getting deep in the open . . . I miss the warmth of Bethania.

Love to all, Maggie

Saturday, December 19, 1835

. . . But I can tell he's worried that we may be stuck here and die of starvation. We are about sixty-five miles either way to civilization, and running out of food. Jonny says we can always eat horse meat. I hope he's joking. The winds have finally stopped this afternoon, and it is very quiet and cold tonight. We have been traveling for eight weeks now, and it may end here . . .

Love, Margaret H.

Sunday, December 20, 1835

. . . And woke up to a sunny day, above freezing, as the snow was melting. The men got us up early, and made a big fire close to our tent. I don't know why, but we ate the last of the food, venison, for breakfast this morning. Then the men waded through the snow to a clearing and shoveled snow and ice to find grass for our ten horses. They were nearly frozen to death, and used that fire to thaw out. We had no food to warm them, but the animals were happy! Jonny thought that we should try to travel in the afternoon, hoping to find food, but we voted to stay the rest of today and try in the morning. The snow is about two feet deep in places where it drifted and piled up, but it is still melting this evening. Nanty Ella and I both prayed for deliverance, or rescue. Nunky Mose and Jonny made skis and strapped them to the wheels of both wagons for better traveling tomorrow . . .

Lord, help us. Margaret H.

Monday, December 21

"You didn't build the campfire back up, Mose. You're asleep at the job. Are you alright?"

"I be's fine, Jon. They be no foods ta cooks."

"Yeah, I know. Let's hope we can find some game to shoot."

"Is Sissy be's orites, Jonny?" asked Ella.

"The first thing she said when she woke up was 'I'm hungry.'"

"We's hungrys too, Jon," said Mose. "You's too?"

"Yes, me too. My stomach thinks my throat has been cut!"

"Sissy's be comin', Jonny?"

"Yes, she's putting on lots of clothes. How does it look to you, Mose? Are we ready to give it a go?"

"Yassa, I's grease dem rails good, an' horses readys."

"We's just waits fo' Sissy," said Ella.

"Good. I'll do some scouting ahead, looking for food. You follow my tracks with the wagons, ?"

"Orites, Jon. I's shoots when we's needs you's."

"At least it's not too cold. I'll see you up ahead."

"Orites, Jon. We's readys."

Jon swung up on his adopted horse, which was reluctant to move, and gingerly "felt" his way into the snow. Jon waved to Mose and Ella as he headed his horse west southwest, around the dense group of trees that had saved their lives.

"Just where do you think you're going, Jonathan Hamilton?"

"If I do, or if I don't change my ways?" Jon shouted back.

Maggie had her head out of the tent. Jon saw the pretty red hair.

"Stop joking, Jonny. Where are you going?"

"I'll be just ahead of you, looking for food. Get crackin'."

"Yes, master, we'll be right behind you!" Maggie yelled. "Don't you get lost now!"

Jon's horse seemed to prance through the snow, and perked his ears when Jon called him Prancer. He looked back and saw the wagons sliding through the snow. "That man is a genius," he muttered. Mose had smoothed the bottoms of the rails, then greased them heavy with horse liniment and some wagon wheel grease. They seemed to glide over the snow. He waved back at Maggie, in the lead carryall, and urged Prancer forward. "Let's find some game, Prancer," he said, "or find Nashville." The sun was bright behind him, but not very warm yet. Jon thought it was right around freezing. *Crunch, crunch.* Jon thought the sound of Prancer's hoofs cracking the ice under the snow, along with the other horses and wagons must sound like thunder! On and on he went, checking the wagons' progress at times, but saw no game. Everything was very quiet, and Jon was getting very hungry and discouraged. He came upon a grouping of trees with an ice-covered little stream, and waited for the wagons. He thought this looked like a good place to lunch, and there may even be some grass. He kicked and foot-shoveled. There was grass! "Lunch? What do we eat? Each other? Right now I'm thinking the other horse those bounty hunters left," he said to himself.

"Where's the food?" Maggie called, as her team of Corker and Conqueror pulled up to the grassy area Jon had cleared.

"I didn't see a thing to shoot at."

"What are we going to do, Jonny? I'm starving."

"So am I! I'm thinking of horse steak and coffee."

"Horse steak? We can't do that, Jonny."

"Just how hungry are you, my love?"

"I said I'm starving, but I could eat no horse."

"Why not? It's one less animal to feed, and a nice, full stomach for a few days."

"We would never talk Nanty Ella into cooking it, and what about Chipper? We shouldn't let him see that, Jonny."

"Mose? I didn't see anything to kill."

"I's knows, Jon." Mose was climbing down from his newly acquired horse. I's didn't hears no shots."

"I think it's time we killed a horse. We all need food."

"Yassa, it be's almost two days since we's eats."

"No! No! Don' kills horses, Massa Jon!" shouted Chipper.

"Hush, son. We's has ta eats," answered Mose.

"Please, Massa Jon. Please don' kill horses," cried Chip.

"Aren't you hungry, Chipper?" asked Jon.

"Yassa, but's we's gets deer an' eats. Please, Papa?"

"Maybe we can hold off a little longer, Jonny," said Maggie.

"How can we, darlin'? We're all getting weak from no food."

"We's waits one mo' day, Jonny. Please?" pleaded Ella.

"Hmmm . . . One more day, Mose?"

"Orites, Jon, we's waits on mo' day." Mose pointed one finger.

"At lunch break tomorrow, if we haven't found any food, we eat horse meat, gang."

"Which horse, Jonny? The one you're riding?"

"I don't know. We'll think about that. We have ten to choose from."

"I's sho hopes we's find dem deer afo' then," said Ella.

"So do I, Nanty Ella, for Chipper's sake."

"For everyone's sake, my pretty plum. I guess we might as well get traveling again."

"How many miles did we travel this morning, Jonny?"

"Thanks to Mose and his rails, we did very well. I'd guess over ten miles, maybe twelve."

"Whoopee! And all on an empty stomach."

"It won't be empty after tomorrow noon."

"I think we'll find food today, Jonny, so keep your eyes open and your rifle ready."

"I will, my love, so let's move our keisters!"

"Where did you learn that gabble?"

"From you, my pretty plum. Your college gummin'."

"Get on those steaks and roast and ride, you big lummox!"

"His name is Prancer, my love," Jonny said as he rode away. Out ahead of his gang again, Jon could feel the sun, now a little ahead of him. Still no sign of wildlife, though. "Excuse me for thinking this, Prancer, but horse steak is going to taste great!" Jon said to his horse. Prancer's ears perked up. "I'm sorry, boy. I hope it's not you. I'm beginning to like you." Prancer's ears moved again. Jon could see the gang and wagons far behind, and could see a dot of red hair. He decided to wait, and let them close the distance. Suddenly, Jon heard some yipping noises in the trees to his left. He watched and listened. Squirrels were chasing each other around a tree. Jon slowly capped his Hawken. *BAM!* Pieces of flesh and fur splattered in all directions. So did squirrels. Jon rode the twenty or so yards to the tree. "Damn," he said out loud. "There's nothing left of him to eat!" Jon saw two others scrambling over the snow to a heavy stand of trees. "Double damn. They can hide in the trees!" He quickly reloaded and rode Prancer into the trees, but saw nothing. They had escaped.

"What did you get, Jonny? I'm starved."

"A gray squirrel, but there's nothing left of him."

"You ate, him, you big pig!"

"No, I didn't, my love. He splattered into tiny pieces."

"Are you sure there were none big enough to eat?"

"I'm positive, darlin', or he'd be roasting on the fire."

"Sure! You probably ate him raw!"

"Ugh . . . no chance of that. Sorry, he was the starting of a tasty stew. At least I finally found something to shoot at!"

"Lot of good that did. He shot a squirrel, Nunky Mose, and splattered it into pieces."

"They must be mo' o' 'em arounds," said Mose.

"There were, but I couldn't find them in those trees."

"We's looks, Jon. Chips, you's rides Abby 'round trees, an' makes noise. Jon an' me's shoots 'em from dis side."

"Yes, Papa. Comes on, Abby. We's scare 'em squirrels."

"Okay, Mose. I'll take the far corner of those trees."

"Orites, Jon, let's do's."

Jon could hear them chattering in the thick stand of trees, but couldn't see them. *BAM!* Mose fired to Jon's right. The chatter ceased. Jon couldn't see Mose, so he called to him.

"Get one, Mose?"

"Nosa, guns fires ta left. Miss 'em."

"Now they've stopped all that yipping. Smart little devils."

"Sho 'nuff has, Jon. Don' sees dem."

"Yes. We could look the rest of the day, and not see them now."

"You's rights, Jon. Douns finds now. Dey's knows we's here."

"Well, we still have light. Let's roll."

No other signs of life. The terrain looked all the same, so Jon kept a steady eye on his compass, on the wagons behind, and on the surroundings for wildlife. "Three eyes, I have." He smiled thoughtfully. Ahead was another large stand of trees, and Jon wondered if he should wait for the wagons before he entered the stand. *No*, he thought. He would just go slow, and mark his trail well. "We may have to go around," he said to himself.

The stand was very dense. They would just have to take the time to go around. Jon wondered how deep the stand was. He had to walk and pull Prancer through the thick brush. Suddenly, he came upon a large open field in the middle of the stand. There were old, dried cornstalks still in the ground, and signs of plowing the field. *Who would plant this field so far from nowhere?* he questioned silently. He had to find out, but he decided to go back and let the others know where he was first. Back through the brush and trees he trudged, and found the wagons close.

"You don't expect us to drive through those trees, do you?"

"No, darling. We'll have to go around tomorrow, but first I want to camp here."

"Here? Why here? No grass or shelter. We still have daylight."

"Yes, darlin', but I found signs of life."

"In those trees? Good! We won't have to kill a horse."

"I mean human life, my love."

"Human? Way out here? You're joking again, Jonny."

"Never kid a redhead. Mose, I found a cornfield in those trees! An old garden. Let's camp here and investigate."

"Orites, Jon. I gets tent up, close to trees."

"Good. Let's get a fire started, ladies."

"What do we feed the horses, Jonny? Why don't we start around these trees while there's still light, and find a better place to camp? We have to go around anyway, right?"

"Yes, my love, it's much too brushy and dense to try to get the wagons through here. But I want to end up on the other side west by southwest of this point."

"That's easy, Jonny. One of you go through the woods in the same direction, and the rest of us go around and meet him on the other side."

"Where and when did you get so smart?"

"In college. I'll show you how to do it, Jonny."

"I don't need any showing! Let's get crackin'!" Jon yelled.

"Well, you don't have to take my head off, Jonny. I'm only trying to help. Maybe we'll spot a deer on the way."

"Sorry, darling. You're right. Maybe we'll spot a deer. Let's put the tent back in the wagon, Mose. I'm sorry."

"It's orites, Jon. We's gets crackin'. I's goes through dem trees."

"Thanks. Thanks, Mose. We'll see you on the other side."

An hour later, the group reached a spot where the forest turned, or dipped to the west for a distance, before again driving south. Jon was reluctant to turn with the trees.

"Let's keep going south, gang."

"Why, Jonny? That's a waste of time, and extra traveling."

"Perhaps you would like to become the captain, darling?"

"Don't get snarly, Jonny. I just want to help."

"I'm just very hungry, darlin', sorry."

"We's goes 'bouts . . . some'un ova mile, Jon?" asked Ella.

"Yes, not quite a mile and a half. Let's go a little further south, then head west."

"Alright, lover, south it is. Go, Corker. Up, Conqueror," said Maggie.

"We's all hungas too, Jonny," Ella said, passing by Jon.

"I know, Ella. Sorry!"

Jon rode ahead of the wagons and marked a spot that seemed to be about one and a half miles of traveling south. He then turned the wagons west, back toward the forest.

"Whoa, Corker. Whoa! Okay, gang, this is about a mile due west. Mose should be close."

"It's getting dark, Jonny, and I'm getting cold."

"Orites. We's mark dis place, Jon, an' we's goes ta trees an' camps?"

"Good idea, Ella. Head for the trees, Maggie, right where Mose is coming from."

"See, I told you! We are right in line with the other side."

"Well, get that wagon over there, smarty! This is a good spot. There's grass for the animals, and some shelter from the wind. Welcome back, Mose," said Jon.

"I wonder what grass tastes like?" said Maggie.

Ella laughed. "I bets it don' cooks verra well," she said.

"I really want to find out about that old cornfield."

"We's do dat in dem mornin', Jon."

"Corn would taste real good about now," said Maggie.

"I's even eats dem cobs!" quipped Mose.

"Play us a tune, Mose. That might help us think of something else besides our stomachs."

A very tired, confused, and hungry group of five people turned in early that night, and slept soundly. No diary written by Maggie!

Tuesday, December 22

"Wakes up. Wakes, Jon."

"Huh? What is it, Mose?"

"We's scouts dem cornfields, Jon."

"Oh yeah. What time is it?"

"Don' knows, Jon. Sun comes up."

"Shhh, don't wake the ladies."

"Ella be sick. She be by's fire."

"Sick? I'll be right out," Jon whispered.

"What is it, Ella?" asked Jon, when he reached the fire.

"I's don' knows, Jonny. I's be bads."

"Mama throws up dis mornin', Jon."

"I'll bet it's from hunger. You're not pregnant, are you, Ella?"

"Nosa! I's jus' sick."

"Whew! That's good. I'm going to kill a horse while Mag and Chipper are asleep."

"No, Jon, we's promise Chipper."

"I know, Mose, but we can't starve ourselves to death."

"We's waits, Jon. Fo' noons."

"Okay. Let's check out the cornfield."

"Orites, Jon. We's checks cornfield."

Bundled and armed, the two tall men started north, into the forest. They quickly found a path, which seemed to head right back to camp and the cornfield.

"I's don' sees dem paths ta camps."

"Neither did I. It was hidden. Goes straight to the field."

Just about a mile more, and the men smelled something foul in a small opening. They checked the brush. Mose took a stick and pushed some brush away. *Wham!* A trap slammed shut with great force.

"Wow, that could have taken your foot, Mose."

"Yassa, it sho 'nuff could."

"Someone wants nobody to find this place."

"Toos' bad dem trap don' have deer caught."

"Yeah, something edible. There are probably more traps ahead."

The two men continued north on the trail. Soon they spotted the cornfield ahead. They stayed in the trees, and continued just to the left of it. They spotted another trap, just as the path came to another opening. There was a group of run-down sod and log buildings. No signs of life.

"I'll bet there's a still around here. I smell it."

"I's smells it too. I's checks first house."

"Okay, Mose. I'll stand guard."

Mose crept up to and around the closest building, a shack that looked like it was ready to fall down. Mose popped open an opening, and disappeared inside. He soon poked his head back out, and waved to Jon to come in.

"Wow! Will you look at that," said Jon.

It had been a barn, of sorts, as it had a couple bundles of old straw, and what appeared to be stalls. But one wall had stacks of homemade wooden crates, full of corn liquor. The smell alone had Jon reeling. There was also a barrel, half full of corn, ground into a meal, or mash. They quickly exited. The next building smelled so bad, Jon felt a little nauseated. When they lifted the latch, they both fell over! Neither wanted to investigate, but they soon found the reason for the smell. A dead horse!

"Oh my god! All that corn, and that horse starved!"

"Dis place smell worse in firs' place."

"Yes, no telling what we'll find in the next shack!"

"We's finds out, Jon."

The next building looked like it was the home. It had a dirty window and porch. They crept up and tried to look into the window, but it was too dirty to see in. All of a sudden, they heard growling and saw a large, big-headed dog showing his fangs, about to attack.

"Hellos, big boys. Down, big boys. We's don' harms you's."

The dog stood still and growled, while Mose continued to talk to him. Jon noticed the reason for what seemed to be a big head. The dog was skin and bones, starving.

"I left the door open to that second building. Maybe this poor thing can get past the smell and eat what's left of that horse. Let's back up and get out of his way, Mose."

"Orites, Jon. Comes on, big boys. Comes eat horse."

Still growling, the dog carefully edged his way to the smelly building, and inside. Jon motioned to Mose to check out the house again. They reached the porch, and the dog came running out in attack mode. The men quickly got back off the porch, and the dog returned to the horse meat.

"Maybe we can lock him in that building, Mose."

"I try's, Jon."

"Let's walk to the door and you talk to him again."

"Orites, I's do."

They approached the second building again. The dog was just inside the door, and growled loudly. The men stopped, and Mose started talking to him again. Slowly, the dog turned around, and around again to the meat, his back to the door. Eventually, with Mose's soothing voice, he stayed at the horse's hind section, where he had found some meat. *Slam!* The men had the door shut and bolted. The dog lunged at the door, barking and growling, but the door held.

"Okay, Mose, let's check out the house."

"Orites, Jon, we's do."

The dog was going nuts in the second building, as Mose and Jon stepped back on the porch and tried the door. Another terrible smell! The door was unlocked, but Jon was reluctant to enter. He had a strange feeling about the cause of the smell. He swung the door wide open.

"Dey's a dead mans in der, Jon."

"Is that what's making the smell?"

"Yassa, I's smells dem smell afore."

"Take a deep breath and hold it, Mose."

"Orites, we's do."

They entered the shack, full of cobwebs, dirt, and little else. Mose pointed to the bed, where the remains of a body lay, partly beneath a very old blanket. It was an old, white-haired man, eyes and mouth wide open. The skin was drawn tight over his cheekbones, and a hand protruded from under the blanket. The men ran back outside and released the air they had been holding, and gasped new air.

"That man has been dead a long time, Mose."

"Yassa. You's sho he's be a man?"

"Well, I think so. He had all that hair."

"Yassa, but not an dem face, Jon."

"You're right, Mose. I don't care to find out for sure."

"Maybe's he starves, Jon."

"Yeah, no blood anywhere. I just don't understand it. It looked like he had a corn crop."

"I's wonders what else dem has."

"You mean valuables?"

"Yassa. I's very hungrys, Jon."

"And maybe he had food somewhere, huh? But if he had food, he sure wouldn't have starved."

"Maybe's we's finds out fo sho, Jon."

"Okay. Let's cover our faces with a cloth, Mose."

"Orites."

Just then, there was a crash and the dog lunged out of the second building. He headed straight for Mose and Jon.

"Hurry . . . inside, Mose."

"I's be rights behinds you's, Jon."

They jumped inside and slammed the door. It had a latch, and Jon locked it, as the dog hit the door with its body.

"I'm not sure which is worse, the dog or the smell."

"I's gots dem rags on mouth, so's dog be's worse."

"We might as well look around. Not much here."

"Looks at dem rifle, Jon."

"Yeah, that's an old Brown Bess. Look how long it is. I'll bet it's five feet long."

"You's takes rifle, Jon. I's don' wants."

"As if we need another gun! Do you think it's stealing, Mose?"

"I's don' knows, Jon. Maybe's we finds families."

"I have to look, Mose, to see if it's a . . ." Jon pulled the blanket back. The body was clothed in rags. Jon wasn't about to look any further, and covered the body up. "He . . . it won't need the gun anymore."

"Looks, Jon, it be's a man. Says Misser." Mose had found a small dresser, made out of the same crates used to box the corn whiskey. It had a drawer, and Mose had found a handwritten slip of paper in it.

"It's a sales slip, Mose. No, looks like a trade."

"Fo's what, Jon?"

"It's hard to read. It's pretty old. Says Fren . . . Lick, in May, eighteen something two. Oh two, or twenty-two."

"I's be bounders then."

"Yes, and I, or my brother or sister, weren't even born in 1802. Says Mister Isaak Dre . . . something field, traded two cra . . . something juice for something, watch."

"He dun trades fo' watch," said Mose.

"I'd say this man, Isaak Dreadfield, traded his corn juice for a watch."

"Dredfiel'?"

"Well, something field. I don't see a watch on him."

"Maybe's in dem box."

"It's the right size. Open it up, Mose."

"Orites, Jon, I's do."

Inside the little box was a beautiful pocket watch. It was gold with a figurine of a man and dog on the back.

"I can't read the name of the person who signed. He must have really needed to get drunk to trade a beautiful timepiece like that! His first name is Ivan or Ian."

"We's takes dem watch too, Jon?"

"For now. Maybe the ladies can figure out his name, and we can get his gun and watch to his family."

"What's if'n he has no's family?"

"Then the watch will be yours, Mose. Let's get out of this stinkin' place."

"Orites. Bu' we's kills dog?"

"The dog! I haven't heard him lately."

"He's maybe's back un dem horse."

"If that dog can eat on that horse, maybe we can too."

"Him look likes dog an dem watch."

"Yes, you're right, Mose. That could be Isaak and his dog.

"We's leaves door opens, Jon. Maybe dog wans in."

"Okay, Mose, you talk to the dog, and I'll shoot him if I have to. I'll bet he wants to see Isaak."

"Orites, Jon. We's gets aways fro' dem door."

The men crept away from the porch, but the dog heard them and appeared again, baring teeth. Mose talked to him, and the dog slowly made his way into the house. In a short time, the dog was heard whining by his dead master.

"Let's check out the horse, Mose."

"Orites, Jon, maybe's mama cooks aways smells."

"This side is pretty bad. Can we turn it over, Mose?"

"Yassa, I's do."

The powerful black man grabbed the hind legs of the dead horse and flipped it over easily. It looked a little better.

"I'm hungry enough to eat that hind end, skin and all!"

"I's be's too, Jon. We's takes dem rears, an' Mama cooks."

"That's pretty heavy, Mose."

Mose grabbed the hind leg and yanked it back. The bone broke free, and Mose grabbed his knife, cut away the skin and hide, and tossed the hind quarter on his shoulder.

"I'll go shoot the dog," said Jon.

"No, Jon! We's comes back afta we's eats."

"Okay, Mose, let's head for the wagons. I'll bring the mash."

The lunch was superb! Mose had to cut away bad spots, but there was still enough meat for three or four meals, maybe two, the way the gang was eating!

"Try not to eat too fast. It may make you sick," said Maggie.

"We were already sick, my love, from hunger."

"Feeling better, Nanty Ella?"

"Yes, yes, Sissy. I's feels great."

"We have that dead man to thank for saving us from starving. I just don't understand how he could starve, with the corn and mash he grew."

"Maybe selling the liquor was more important than feeding himself or his horse," said Maggie.

"That would be barmy, darlin'."

"An' he starved dem dog, toos."

"Dog? Dem man has dog toos, Papa?" asked Chip.

"Yes, son, dem man has dem dog," answered Mose.

"Oh, boys! I's go's back an' gets dog, Papa?"

"No, son, dem dog be wild, an' 'tacks us."

"Bu' dog don' 'tack Chips . . . Massa Jon?"

"It's up to your mother and dad, Chipper."

"Please, Papa? Please, Mama?"

"We's sees un we's go back," answered Mose.

"Do we need to go back, Mose?"

"I's thinks so, Jon, an' burys man Isaaks."

"Was that his name, Jonny?"

"Yes, darlin', Isaak Dredfield, or something field."

"Well, Nunky Mose is right, Jonny. You can't just let him rot there in his bed. You must bury him."

"Guess you're right, honey. Besides, I want to get some of that corn juice to take with us."

"You didn't tell us about that, Jonny."

"He had big crates of it, darlin', and still starved to death! He had an old Brown Bess rifle, and a beautiful gold pocket watch, too. Mose has that. That's about all the old man owned. He traded corn liquor for the watch."

"How do you know that, Jonny?"

"Here, look at this old slip. It was with the watch."

"Fre-French Lick! One . . . around the middle of May 1802," said Maggie. "You're right. It's Isaak D-r-e . . . field. Drewfield, I bet."

"What is French Lick? Sounds naughty."

"That's Nashville, Jonny."

"Nashville! Tennessee?"

"Yes. French Lick was Nashville's early name."

"Strange name. You learned that in college?"

"Yes. Tennessee was a territory of North Carolina's before the War of Independence."

"Brain Bunny! Have you all had enough horse for now? Let's go back and bury the old man."

"An' we's brings horses, Jon."

"To carry the corn drippins?"

"Yassa, Jon, an' maybes other things toos."

"I's stays an' cooks horse meats, Daddy," said Ella.

"Then I should stay with Nanty Ella, Jonny."

"That's up to you, darlin'."

"I's be orites, Sissy. You's goes."

"No, Nanty Ella, I need to get caught up on my diary."

"I's goes gets dog," said Chipper. "Please, Papa?"

"That dog might attack us, Chipper."

"Dog don' 'tacks Chips, Massa Jon."

"Orites, son, you's stays on Abbys."

"Orites, Papa, I's do."

"Sure is quiet," said Jon, back at the clearing with the three run-down buildings. "Let's check them all real good again, after we bury this Isaak fellow."

"Where be's un dog?" asked Chipper.

"Not sure, Chipper. Stay up on that horse, and yell to us if you see him."

"I's starts digs grave, Jon."

"Right, Mose. That leaves me to check the buildings and bring out the body. Good thing we brought these old blankets."

"An' ropes ta ties corn liquas ta horses."

Mose grabbed a pick and shovel, and headed for some trees behind the clearing. Jon made his way into the first building and carried out three crates of corn liquor. He tried to figure out how to stack them on Corker's back. "I'll leave it to Mose to figure that out," Jon said to himself, as he headed for the second building.

"I's come wit you's, Massa Jon?"

"No, Chipper, you stay on Abby and keep a lookout."

"Yassa. Sho bad smells in there."

"Sure does, Chip, bad smells from all the buildings."

"Maybe's you's burns 'um, Massa Jon." There was a pause.

"Chipper, you're going to be as smart as your papa!"

"I's smarts toos, Massa Jon."

"You sure are, boy. That old man would probably want to have his home burned down around him."

"Wow, thems be's big fires!"

"Go get your papa, Chip."

"Yassa, Massa Jon." Chipper rode off to find Mose.

Jon wondered why he didn't think of that.

"You's wans ta burns Isaak, Jon?"

"Sure, why not, Mose?" Jon was checking the second building.

"Orites, Jon. Maybe's we's has trouble startin' dem fire."

"Maybe. They probably have had a lot of rain here too."

"We's burns firs' buildin' an' sees."

"Okay, Mose. I'll check out the main house with the body one last time, while you see if you can burn that first shack."

"Orites, Jon, I's do."

Jon tied a rag over his mouth and nose, and entered the home of the squatter, Isaak D-field. He heard the dog before he saw him. It was by his master and sprang at Jon, who blocked the dog with his Hawken and yelled. He tried to ward off the dog with his rifle, when he heard Chipper.

"Dog! Whoa, doggies. Whoa. Here, boy . . . here."

"Get back on your horse, Chip."

"Here, boy. Here, dogs, here."

A very strange thing happened right in front of Jon. The dog became quiet and still. He seemed to study Chipper for a minute, as Chipper continued to talk to him. Suddenly, Jon noticed the dog's tail wagging, and he walked over to Chipper. Jon quickly capped his Hawken, ready to shoot the dog if he attacked Chipper, but instead the boy began petting him. Jon was amazed.

"See's, Massa, Jon, dem dog don' 'tack Chips."

"He sure didn't, Chipper. Don't that beat all?"

"Can I's keeps 'im, Massa Jon?"

"If it's Okay with your papa."

"Papa, Papa, please can I's keeps dem dog?"

"The boy deserves that dog, Mose," said Jon.

"Orites, boy, you's takes care of 'im."

"Yes, Papa, I's do. Than' yuz!"

"That's unreal, how the dog took to the boy."

"Yassa, it be's unreals, Jon."

"Whas be's his name, son?" asked Mose.

"Why don't you name him Isaak, Chip, after his dead master?"

"Orites, Massa Jon. I's names dog Isaak. Comes, Isaak." The dog ran out with the boy.

"Don' go near dem fires, boy!" yelled Mose.

"Orites, Papa."

"You got that building burning, Mose?"

"Yessa. It be's burns good, Jon."

"Great. I'll finish looking in here, then we can burn it too."

"Orites, I's gets middle house ready fo' fires."

Jon pushed the bed containing the body to the center of the room, and continued searching. A few old clothes, boots, and rotting blankets were all Jon found. He wrapped the blankets around the body. He noticed a skeleton key on the crate dresser. He wondered what that key was for. Probably nothing around here. Maybe the man owned something in Nashville . . . French Lick!

"Jon? Do's we's needs dem tools?" yelled Mose.

"What tools, Mose?" Jon walked out onto the porch.

"Dems garden tools. Axe, ropes . . ."

"Set them out on the ground, Mose." The first building was now a mass of flames. "Maybe we can use them."

"Orites, Jon. I's fires dem middle house."

"Right. This place is ready too. All I found was this key."

"Wha' too, Jon?"

"I don't know. I wonder if the old man had something hidden away somewhere."

"Maybe by dem creek."

"What creek, Mose?"

"In dem trees, hear wata runs."

"Huh! Better take a look." Jon walked into the woods behind the buildings and spotted a rapid little creek. He noticed another crate in the water, with the stream flowing over it. It had a lock! Jon pulled it out of the water and tried the key he had found. It fit!

Inside the crate, wrapped in very wet, cold cloth, was more meat! There was venison and some other meat from some animal that Isaak had probably trapped. It seemed fresh. Jon locked the crate back up, and carried it back to the clearing.

By now, Mose had the second building aflame. *BAM! BAM! BAM!* Sounds came from the first building, now a mass of flames.

"What was that?" Jon asked, as more explosions occurred.

"Dems bottles o' corn liqua breaks," answered Mose.

"Look what I found, Mose! More meat! Isaak must have died from something else besides hunger."

"Maybe's hims heart stops, Jon."

"I guess that's possible, Mose. He was an elderly man."

"We gets dem crates on dem horses, Jon."

"Righto! Can we rope them on Corker?"

"We's gets two dem crates an Corka, an' rest on Sloggy an' Smutty's Jon. I's do."

"Okay, Mose. I'll try to start the main house on fire." Jon grabbed a couple of long sticks and wrapped the ends with old cloth. He approached the middle building to set the sticks ablaze. He took those to the house, set blankets and the crate on fire, and watched them flame up.

"Goodbye, old man Isaak. Rest in peace." Jon walked back outside and joined Mose and Chipper in a prayer for the old man. Jon had never heard Mose pray before. He sounded like the preacher at the little church on Bethania when Dianna died. Memories! A lot had happened since then.

Mose had roped two crates on Corker, a crate and tools on Sloggy, and the meat cage on Smutty, team fifteen! Jon grabbed a bottle of whiskey and put it in the burning house. The first building had collapsed, the second starting to, and the house was now a ball of flame. Mose and Jon walked out of the clearing, followed by the three drays and Chipper riding Abby, and calling the dog Isaak, who had whimpered some as his old master's house burned, but now followed his new master down the trail, south.

"Jonny! You burned the house down around the old man instead of burying him?"

"Yes, we did. That is the way he would have wanted it."

"Oh, so you are a dead mind reader?"

"No, my love, but that's how I would have wanted it."

"Well, don't count on me burning down our house in Arkansas when you die. I'll still need a place to live!"

"You and I are never going to die, my pretty plum."

"You better include Nunky Mose and Nanty Ella, and even Chipper in that forecast, Jonny."

"All of us are going to have long, successful lives. Now, we have full stomachs again, and meat for a few more days. Let's get some sleep and an early start tomorrow."

Diary of Margaret Hamilton

Tuesday, December 22, 1835

. . . And Ella and I stayed at the camp as Jonny and Nunky Mose went into the forest to check on the cornfield. They came back with a smelly hind quarter of horse meat and corn meal, and we all had our first big meal in days. Both Nanty Ella and I had been sick from lack of food, and Jonny was about to kill one of the horses for food, but the meat they brought was from a dead horse at the cornfield. They found a dead man in his bed. He had been growing the corn and making whiskey to trade for a gold watch and long rifle. The men went back after dinner with Chipper, and burned the old squatter's buildings, with him inside. We now have food, corn whiskey, and the old man's dog. The man's name was Isaak D.

Love, Maggie

Wednesday, December 23

"That was the best breakfast I've ever had, ladies."

"Dat's 'cause you's has no breakfass fo' days," said Ella.

"Today is Wednesday, right?"

"Yes, Jonny. December twenty-third, eighteen thirty-five."

"Well, the last meal we had was Sunday. Breakfast, December 20! Eight in the morning!"

"Well, you're not entirely baffy in the brain box, Jonny."

"No, I'm not. Now let's get crackin', gang."

"Do we go back the way we came?"

"No, my love, we head south until we reach the end of this group of trees."

"Then you're going to get lost! We won't be headed due west by southwest, and we'll miss the Cumberland River, Jonny."

"You watch me, my pretty plum. We'll be in Nashville for Christmas."

"Your predictions haven't come true yet, so I don't believe you."

"Oh yeah? You've already lost a couple bets to me, but I'll still bet you again, my love."

"That's big of you! I'll take that bet."

"Ah-ha! I've got you again. We could go straight south from here, and hit the Nashville Road, and make it easy to . . . French Lick by Christmas."

"Then why don't you, if you're so smart?"

"Because I've got to prove to you that I'm right! We go my way, and we'll find the Cumberland River in two more days."

"You'd better be right, Jonny!"

"Or what, my pretty plum?"

"Or this will be the first, and last child you'll ever have!"

"But when we reach the river, we're still a ways to Nashville."

"About how far?"

"I don't know, my love. Shouldn't be far."

"You'd better pray we get there by Christmas."

"Then let's make tracks."

The group headed south at a good clip. Mose had the "skis" greased, and they soon found the end of the large forest.

"Whoa! This looks like the end of these woods."

"Now which way do we go, you big lummox?"

"We go due west, my love."

"Why not south, and find the road?"

"I've already told you why. Besides, the shortest distance between two points is a straight line. Didn't you learn that in college, my pretty plum?"

"You just lead the way, Jonny, and get there in two more days."

"Bring them on, Mose. I'll scout ahead again."

"Orites, Jon, I's do."

Using his trusted compass, Jon struck out on Prancer and headed west. The wagons glided smoothly behind. He came to a spot he judged to be about one mile. Jon jumped down and made a big "1" in the snow, then continued on. The forest, to his right, finally ended at about one and three quarters miles from where Jon had started west. The line of trees seemed to line up straight to the north. Mile number two came quickly, and Jon again marked the snow, making a big "2" with a stick. Jon thought the snow was getting shallow, so he used the stick to determine that the snow was only about four or five inches deep, and thawing. Another half mile or so, and Jon ran into a large group of whitetail deer.

"Sure, now you show yourselves after you nearly let us starve!" he said to them, as he capped the nipple on his Hawken. He wondered which one was the buck. Jon picked out a large, well-built deer and took aim, as the herd scattered. *BAM!* The deer went down, thrashed his legs a few times, then lay still. Jon thought he hit the deer just below the head, in the neck. He rode Prancer over to the kill. Jon took out his knife, slit the deer's throat, then its belly to let it bleed out. It wasn't the buck. It was a nice doe, though. By damn, they wouldn't starve again this journey! Jon tied a rope around the doe's neck, and Prancer pulled it back to the westward trail he was making.

"We heard your shot. That's a nice big deer, Jonny."

"Yes, it is. I was hoping it was the buck, but no such luck. There were nine or ten of them all together."

"That's funny. We went days looking for one, and now that we have some food, they jump out, ten at a time!"

"Got a little work for you, Ella," Jon said, as she pulled up in the covered wagon. "Can we just skin and chunk her for now?"

"Sho 'nuff can, Jonny. Papa's alredys doin'," said Ella.

"Good. I want to get as much travel time as we can."

"We's puts chunks in trailer wit booze."

"Thanks, Ella." Jon turned to Maggie. "What was that word Ella used? Sounded like boose."

"It was booze, Jonny, a slang word for liquor."

"Huh! I thought I knew all the slang words."

"I did too . . . and the swear words."

"I'll help carry the chunks of venison to the trailer."

"Jonny? Why were you hoping it was a buck?"

"Because does reproduce and fill the forests, so people like us won't starve to death."

"It takes two to tangle, Jonny. But you mean to tell me you can't tell the difference?"

"Not in the winter, my love, until they grow new horns."

"Oh, will you be growing horns, so I can tell you apart?"

"One big one, my darling."

Mile four came up soon, and Jon waited for the wagons.

"We now have completed our triangle, gang."

"So what? I don't see Nashville anywhere! It looks like we're going in circles."

"Great things take time, my pretty plum. If we could have gone straight through that forest, this is about where we would have ended up, heading west by southwest."

"Hoop-de-doo! Where's the river?"

"Believe it or not, I think we're close to the river."

"Only three more days! At least we have food now."

"Righto, darlin'. Next stop, Nashville."

"At the rate we're going . . . how many days has it taken to get past that forest, Jonny? And how many miles?"

"I'm not telling you, Maggie."

"Yu don't have to, Jonny. Let's see . . . five miles in nine days."

"Dat canno' be's right, be's it, Jon?" asked Mose.

"I'm afraid she's right, Mose. But that includes the snow storm, Isaak the squatter, and going around the woods."

"At that rate, only three more years to Nashville!"

"Well, we better get started. West by southwest, Mose."

"Orites, Jon. We's gets crackins."

"When is dinner . . . or lunch?"

"I'll find a spot up ahead, darlin'."

"You better! I'm not letting you starve me again."

Jon found a good spot with grass and water, and all ate well. "This must be like heaven, lots of food and drink," he said.

"More like hell, Jonny. Too much food, all meat and no potatoes, feel dirty all the time, sore and uncomfortable, and too cold for me."

"It's anything but cold in hell, my love."

"I suppose you've been there too, Jonny?"

"Not lately, my darlin', plenty of time for that."

"It's probably where we are headed."

"What, Arkansas? Our own bottomland? Space to grow? Why, Arkansas is a little bit of heaven."

"A very little bit!"

"Well, let's be crackin', so we can find that little bit."

"How far did we travel this morning, Jonny?"

"Oh, about seven or eight miles, I reckon. We need to do a lot better this afternoon."

"We do's, Jon. We's get's crackin'," said Mose.

By midafternoon, there was little snow left on the ground, mainly in pockets, so the wagons stopped and the rails were removed from the wagon wheels. Up ahead, Jon saw several signs and sightings of wild game. The group was making very good time. Late in the afternoon, Jon saw the first signs of life—cleared land, and cabin! Then another.

"We must be close to Nashville, Jonny."

"I'm not sure, my love. We haven't seen the river, or the Nashville Road yet."

"You didn't expect to, did you?"

"Of course, I did, my darlin'."

"You have a lot more faith in your compass than I do."

"But you do have faith in me, right?"

"Oh sure, Jonny! Why don't you ask at the next cabin we see? We may be in Africa!"

"We's no's be in Africa, Sissy," said Ella.

"I'm just buggering Jonny, Nanty Ella."

"Well, let's keep these four-legged buggers moving."

"There is another cabin, Jonny."

"We're getting close to something, my love. You see, we are on a road that must lead to a town."

"Are you going to stop and ask?"

"No, keep moving, my pretty plum."

"You are the most stubborn, blunderheaded . . ."

"Be calm, darlin'. I know right where we are."

"Oh, you do? How much further to Nashville?"

"A little over a day, and the river is just ahead."

"That's another bet you're going to lose, you big lummox."

It was starting to get dark as the road led to the river, then turned south along the bank of the Cumberland River.

"See, my pretty plum? Behold, the Cumberland River."

"How do you know it's the Cumberland, Jonny? It's a lot bigger than the river we left in Kentucky."

"Naturally! It's traveled many more miles than we have, my love, and a lot of other rivers have added to it. That's another bet you lose. Let's keep going."

"No, it's not! You said the river was just ahead several miles ago. That's another bet you lost!"

"I knew you would try to wiggle out of the bet. Keep moving, darlin'. The Nashville Road should be just ahead."

Another mile, and the group came upon the remains of an old fort. A cabin was next to it, and a man was outside.

"Hello, mister!" shouted Maggie. "Can you tell us where we are, and how far to Nashville?"

"Hello to you, ma'am. You are at old Fort Blount, and Nashville is about sixty-five miles from here."

"The Nashville Highway is just ahead, right?" asked Jon.

"Yes, sir, about three miles straight ahead to Carthage."

"Carthage? Is that a town?" asked Maggie.

"Yes, ma'am, on the Nashville Road."

"Thank you. And that is the Cumberland River?"

"Yes, ma'am . . . Say, where are you people from?"

"North Carolina, headed for Nashville. You said it is sixty-five miles? That's more than two days," said Maggie.

"Yes, ma'am. The road's in purty good shape. You oughta make it in a couple days."

"Thank you, mister."

"You're welcome, ma'am, but I don't understand how you got up here from North Carolina."

"Thanks to that man there, we took the wrong way!"

"Ya sure did, ma'am. Well, ya can't get lost now."

"Thank you again, mister." Maggie was smiling at Jon.

"You're welcome, ma'am. Good luck."

Maggie laughed all the way into Carthage, Tennessee.

"You mind sharing what is so funny?"

"You, you big lummox! You took the wrong way."

"That's just one man's opinion. He could be wrong."

"He had the right opinion, Jonny. If we had crossed the Blues to Knoxville, we would be Arkansas old-timers now!"

"That must be Carthage ahead. Let's pitch the tent here, Mose."

"Yassa. It be's too dark ta goes further."

Thursday, December 24

"Another fine breakfast, Ella."

"Thank you, Jonny. We has lotsa foods now."

"Then we can go straight through Carthage and head for Nashville."

Maggie began laughing again, as she had the last evening.

"Now what's funny, my love?"

"I can't tell you, Jonny," said a giggling Maggie.

"You can't say because you have no reason for all that cackling! Get up on that wagon and drive."

"You's tells me, Sissy, why's you's laughs," said Ella.

"It's probably not funny to anyone else, Nanty Ella."

"Least of all, to me!" snapped Jon.

"Is orites, Jonny, Sissy tells us."

"Well," said Maggie, between giggles, "remember yesterday, when I said we could be in Africa?"

"Yes, Sissy, I's remembas."

"That was before you found out I knew where we were."

"Orites, Jonny, lets Sissy tells us, shhh," said Ella.

Maggie was still laughing. "Hee, hee, well, Carthage is in Africa! Haha!" Everyone except chuckling Maggie was quiet, staring at her.

"Don't you get it? Carthage, in North Africa!" There was a pause.

"So what, darlin'? It's in Tennessee too. Now you've had your little joke. Please get up on that wagon."

"See, I told you that you wouldn't think it funny."

"Okay, my pretty plum, it's funny, and ironic. But it's probably not very funny to Mose or Ella."

"Oh, I'm so sorry, Nanty Ella, Nunky Mose."

"Is orites, Sissy. I's don' remembas no Carthage. Does you's, Daddy?"

"No's, Mama, I's don' wans ta remembas."

"You two probably remember a lot of carnage!"

"We goes now, Jon," said Mose.

"I'm sorry, Nunky Mose."

"Is orites, Sissy. We goes now."

Carthage was a busy little town with two saloons, and several places to restock supplies. Jon's group rode right through it and turned west on the Nashville Road. It was hard from freezes, and the wagons made good time. By lunch, Jon figured they had traveled fifteen miles. Time to eat!

"Then we only have fifty miles to go yet today."

"What do you mean, my love?"

"Well, if we've gone fifteen so far today, that leaves only fifty more miles to Nashville for Christmas!"

"Did I say that . . . Ella?"

"Yassa, Jonny, you's sho 'nuff did."

"Well, when is Christmas?"

"Tomorrow, you big lummox!"

"Really? Well, I didn't say we would get there before Christmas. We'll be there tomorrow."

"Don't count on that either!" said Maggie. "Every time you've made a statement like that, you've been wrong."

"Not every time! Anyway, we'll be there tomorrow." There was a pause.

"I wonder where the Chasneys are right now," said Maggie.

"I'll bet they've split with those Schinlands and the ex-slaves by now."

"They were all going to Boonesborough, right?"

"No, my love, the Schinlands and the slaves were going there, but the Chasneys were going to Harrodsburg."

"They were not! They're going to Frankfort!"

"I know, darlin', but the Wilderness Road ends at Harrodsburg, just south of Frankfort."

"Smarty pants! How do you know that?"

"Because Charles said so."

"You sure it was Charles? Or Liz?"

"It was Charles. I remember."

"Well, we better get going if we're going to be in Nashville for Christmas."

"Righto, my pretty plum."

The road hugged the Cumberland River for several miles, then the river again disappeared. Jon had to assure Maggie that they would see the river again before Nashville. The gang started to see more traffic on the Nashville Road, so Jon stayed close to them. They met up with a group headed east, in the opposite direction. They stopped to chat.

"Howdy! Where's you folks be from?"

"North Carolina, Salem area," answered Jon. "How about you?"

"We're from Clarksville, on our ways ta Baltimore."

"Wow! That's a long way ta travel in midwinter!"

"Yeah, we knows, but we got aplenty a-time. We figgers ta get there in about a month."

"A month! That's a long way to make in a month. Shoulda started in July!"

"Yeah, we knows. 'Bouts five or six hundred miles, but if'in we makes twenty miles a day, we figgers ta make it."

"We've been two months to here from Salem."

"What's da matter? Dat big horse lame?"

"No, sir, we just went the long way."

"The wrong way, he means," interrupted Maggie.

"I'd say so. Where ya headed?"

"To Arkansas, getting some free bottomland to farm."

"Ma friend, there ain't no such thing as free land, an' I cain't believe yur a-gonna git any bottomland at all."

"Why is that?" asked Jon.

"'Cause there's been lots an' lots a settlers a-comin through here the last couple a years, headin' west."

"Well, I sure hope I find some."

"Where is Clarksville, sir?" asked Maggie.

"On dis river, 'bouts fifty mile above Nashville. Part of what's called Cumberland Settlement."

"How far is Nashville from here?

"Oh, 'bouts forty mile, I rekon, misses."

"Nat very many people going east these days, is there?" asked Jon.

"Naw, we heads ta Baltimore evera winta to sell pelts."

"Wow! Three wagons of pelts?"

"Yup! Hunt an' trap all summas, an' sells it all Winta."

"Well, I have to make Nashville by tomorrow, so I'll say goodbye and good luck to you all," said Jon.

"Thank yee, and good luck ta ya-all. Don't be a gettin' stopped by them waymen."

"Merry Christmas to you," shouted Maggie.

"Thank yee! I don't knows whens that's be, but thank yee."

The three heavy wagons rolled east, past Jon's group.

"Jonny, what are pelts?"

"Fur and skin of wild animals, my love."

"Oh . . . like Nunky Mose did to that panther?"

"Yes, that's right. Let's get on our way, gang."

"Those were big donkeys that were pulling those wagons."

"They were mules, darlin'. They're a cross between a donkey and a horse."

"Firs' I's seen dems, Jon," said Mose.

"They say they can pull like a team of horses, but don't eat as much. Ya hear what I said to them?"

"No. What, Jonny?"

"You should have started in July!"

"Hee, hee! That's funny, Jonny!"

"We's gets crackin' nows, Jon," said Mose.

Diary of Margaret Hamilton

Thursday, December 24, 1835

. . . Here we are, Christmas Eve, and about thirty miles east of Nashville. The road and the climate here have been good, so we should make it there late tomorrow, as Jonny predicted . . . We saw three wagons heading toward Baltimore, full of "pelts" and pulled by mules. I have never seen mules before. They look like overgrown donkeys. The owner said that a lot of people had already moved to Arkansas, and there may be no more bottomland left for us. I know how disappointed Jonny would be, so I hope that's not true. As darkness came, we were close behind another wagon going west. Jonny says we will meet and pass them tomorrow . . . This is my very first Christmas away from the family I love . . . I'm sad!

Merry Christmas and love,
Margaret Rose

Friday, December 25

"Merry Christmas there. Is everything well with you people?"

"Yep, thank ye. Where are you's folks from?" asked the man driving, through a corncob pipe.

"We're from the Salem area, headed for Arkansas."

"Well, I'll be! We're from Salisbury, and we're headin' for Arkansas too! D'ya hear that, Ma? They're a-goin' to Arkansas!"

"I heard, Pa. Maybe we'll be neighbors."

"That's a long way to be travelin' in the winter," said Jon. "You should have started in July!" Jon and Maggie were both smirking, and Maggie covered her face to keep from laughing.

"You did it again, Jonny," she said.

"Couldn't leave afore the crops were in an' shipped out."

"That's our story too. My name's Jonathan Hamilton, and this is my wife, Mag . . . Margaret, and my partners Mose and Ella, and their son Chipper."

"Glad ta knows ya. I'm Henry Hawthorne, and this here's my wife Ann. We'd worked on a plantation in Salisbury, saved our moneys, an' hope ta get land in Arkansas," Henry said, cob pipe dancing.

"What plantation did you work on?" asked Maggie.

"Johnstone Plantation," said Ann Hawthorne. "Have ya heard of it?"

"Have I! They are close friends of my family!"

"Oh, really? What family is that?"

"The McAllisters," said Maggie.

"Samuel McAllister? Bethania?" asked Ann.

"Yes, that's right! He's my father!"

"Oh . . . how interesting! Small world!"

"I lost one of my gang of bounders during a storm at the Johnstone Plantation," said Jon.

"Really? I remember that. I brung some food an' blankets to your . . . what did ya call 'em?"

"Bounders. They got sick from that food you served!"

"I beg your pardon!" said Ann. "I . . . that is, my slaves cooked that food 'specially for you and your bounders."

"I lost two of my gang on that trip, and your boss never made up for their loss."

"I'm afraid y'alls goin' ta hafta take that up wit them Johnstones. Annie an' me quit when we sees the ad in the paper 'bout Arkansas," said Henry.

"Must be the same ad I saw in the Salem paper."

"Sho 'nuff! What part of the country ya plan on movin' to? Maybe we be neighbors there too."

"We're not sure. We would like to get some land on the Arkansas or White rivers, but the people going east we saw yesterday said it may all be taken already."

"Yeah, I sure hated ta get started so late. We were again ta Little Rock, an' then south to the Ouachita River."

"Ouachita? I never heard of it. Have you, darlin'?"

"No, must be close to Texas."

"Well, it runs into Louisiana, then the Mississippi."

"That sounds like a good spot to farm."

"Yup. I has friends there, an' they gets real good money for their crops in New Orleans." The corn cob pipe stuck to Henry's lips.

"New Orleans! That sounds great!"

"Yup. They say England an' France pays good fer our crops theys can't grows there."

"Maybe you wanna join up with us so we can be neighbors," said Ann.

"Well, at least as far as Little Rock, ma'am," said Jon.

"We're in a hurry to get to Nashville yet today, so Jonny can buy me a Christmas present," said Maggie.

"Wha . . . oh yeah. Can your team keep up with us to Nashville, Mister Hawthorne?"

"Just calls me Henry, Jon. They sure can. We will race ye ta Nashville. Ya a-comin', Ma? So long, Jon an' Margaret!" The Hawthornes took off down the road at a gallop.

"Well, what are you waiting for, you big lummox? You said we were going to pass them. Let's get moving!" said Maggie.

"We'll pass them up ahead. Ready, Ella?"

"I's be ready, Jonny."

"Okay, we go at our regular speed. Those horses of theirs will break down soon, and we'll pass them then." As Jon's group struck a fast pace, they saw the Hawthornes far ahead, and increasing their lead. Jon's team continued at their normal speed. It only took a mile or two.

"That's them way ahead, Jonny."

"You bet it is, my pretty plum. I told you so."

"Well, aren't you the smarty pants, Jonny?"

"Dey's be stopped, Jon," said Mose.

"Yeah, and they're going to hold us up."

"Maybe we should blow right past them," said Maggie.

"That wouldn't be neighborly," Jon said, mocking Henry's accent.

"Haha, that's good, Jonny. You sound just like him," Maggie said, laughing.

"We had better stop, gang. Besides, that land he's talking about really sounds good."

"Does that mean they will be traveling with us?"

"I reckon so, my pretty plum."

"Trouble, huh?" asked Jon, who knew the answer.

"Yup, my starboard lead done give out," said Henry.

"Mose, will you take a look at their lead? He's down."

"Yassa, I's do, Jon."

"Should we make dinner, Jonny?"

"No, darlin', it's too early yet."

"I should ne'er raced ye," said Henry.

"Righto! Too late now. That wheel dray don't look good either."

"What are we ta do?" asked Ann.

"Horse don' makes it, Jon."

"Yes, I know. Look at that wheel horse too, Mose."

"He be makes it, Jon. Needs res'."

"There be grass over there," said Henry. "Boy! Unhitch horses an' take over theres!"

Jon was shocked when a teenaged black boy and girl jumped out of the Hawthorne wagon to do as Henry directed.

"We need to water their horses too . . . and ours."

"I's do, Massa Jon," said Chipper, climbing down from Abby.

"Okay, Chip. That's your job. Can they make it to Nashville, Mose? It's a shame to lose that horse."

"Yassa. We's shoots dem horse, rest pulls slow."

"I don't think that wheel dray can pull anything."

"You's rights, Jon. Maybe's we use Conqueror."

"That still leaves only three, when we tie the beat one behind their wagon."

"Yassa. We's ties dem bounty huntas horses."

"And make a team out of them?"

"Yassa, Jon. To Nashville."

"Righto, Mose, let's try it. We'll need to match one of Mister Hawthorne's lead and wheel horses together and have them in the lead, with our two on the wheel. I'll shoot this one."

"Yassa, I's do, Jon. Chips, you's ride wit Mama."

"Abbys can do's pulls wagons, Papa?" asked Chipper.

'Yessum, Chips, bu' we's pulls dem ta Nashville."

"We may as well take the hind quarters and maybe the heart and liver with us, Mose." *BAM!* Jon shot the dray.

"Yassa, Jon, I's do. Soon's I get's horses hitched."

"You are going to eat that horse?" asked Ann.

"Certainly! It's a little tough, but good meat."

"Well, I won't eat any!"

"That's fine, Missus Hawthorne. We'll eat it. Is there room in the trailer, Mose?"

"For somes, Jon."

"Good, put the rest in the carryall. It won't bother Maggie."

"Orites, Jon, I's do."

"Thanks, Mose. Let's get crackin'."

With the spent wheel horse tied behind the Hawthorne wagon, and the two saddle horses helping pull that wagon, the extended group of three wagons and a trailer limped onward to the west. The saddle horses acted up a little, but soon had their pulling job figured out, and pulled what they could. Henry Hawthorne had his "boy" and "girl" running alongside the wagon.

"They are really slowing us, Mose."

"Yassa. Maybe's we's put Conqueror in front."

"And have Corker pull the carryall by himself?"

"Yassa. Corka pulls orites by hisself."

"Okay, Mose. We'll try that after lunch."

Mose found a grassy spot along the Nashville Road, and made a fire for the lunch break. The "boy" and "girl" were very tired.

"Girl! Get a-helpin' that old woman cook!" Without a peep, the girl jumped to help Ella.

"Dis girl be's tired from runnin's," said Ella.

"Ella is used to cooking alone, Mister Hawthorne."

"I don't be a-carin' a damnation how tired she is. When I's says jump, she jump!"

"Or what, Mister Hawthorne?"

"Or I's makes her wish she'd a-listened."

"Not while I'm around, you won't!" There was a pause amidst stares.

"My husban' was only tryin' to control his slave. He didn't mean to upset anyone. We're sorry, Mister Hamilton," said Ann.

"Then let that girl rest while Ella cooks lunch."

"These are very tasty corn dodgers, ah, Ella," said Ann Hawthorne. "You still have corn?"

"We picked up some corn mash a few days ago."

"Oh. Whereabouts, Mister Hamilton? We didn't see any place to purchase food from Knoxville to Carthage."

"We took some from a dead squatter," said Maggie.

"How interesting. Did you see them squatters comin' from Knoxville, Pa?"

"Not by a durnsite, Ma."

"We came another way to Carthage. Through Cumberland Gap."

"Oh, how interesting, Missus Hamilton. Didya hear that, Pa?"

"I heard, Ma. Musta come afrom that Wildness Road in Virginia, huh?"

"Yup! We were in Virginny," said Jon, as Maggie chuckled.

"How long did it take that a-ways?"

"'Bouts two month."

"Two month! Good geeses!"

"We made lotsa stops," said Jon, still imitating Henry's accent.

"It wassa shirt cut!" said Maggie, straight-faced.

"I's get dem Conqueror tied frons a dat wagons, Jon."

"Good, Mose. Let's get on the road to Nashville."

"How far have we come so far this Christmas Day?"

"I'd guess five or six miles, my love. Everybody ready?"

Drivers of all three wagons answered yes, and Maggie led out. Jon rode Prancer forward, then back, checking all the wagons and horses. The Hawthorne wagon was now keeping up and doing well, with the strange assortment of horses pulling it. Jon dropped back to check on the worn-out Hawthorne horse.

"Your wheel horse is doing fine!" he shouted. "You'll need to buy one new horse in Nashville."

"I thank ye fer the helpin' hand," answered Henry.

"You're welcome. I'm going to put your two slaves back in your wagon to rest. These horses can handle it."

"Thank thee," said Henry, as "boy" and "girl" jumped in.

"We surely thank ye fer all yer help, Mister Hamilton!" shouted Ann. "I surely hope you all will decide to travel with us ta the Ouachita River."

"Well, thank you, ma'am. I'll have to see what my gang thinks about that. They may not want to."

"Why would that be, Mister Hamilton?"

"They don't like havin' slaves!"

"Well, ya's got three, ain't ya?" asked Henry.

"No, sir. I have three free partners."

"Free? I didn't a-knowd that!"

After a pause, Ann said, "Well, thank you a lots anyhow, and tell that darkee woman, uh, Ella? Tell her thanks fer the dodgers."

"Ya sa! That sure was good, tasty meats. What kinda mats were it?" shouted Henry.

"Horse!" Jon shouted back, as he rode ahead. "Rotting horse meat from the same dead squatter!" Jon heard an *Eeek!*

The group made good time, but as darkness fell, they were still miles from Nashville. They were now seeing farms and homes, so they had to be close. Finally, Mose found a campsite.

"Chipper, can you stake the horses in the grass by the river, while Mose and I start a fire and pitch the tent?"

"Yassa, Massa Jon."

"Boy! Gatha wood fo' fire! Girl! Help put up the tent!"

"We can all squeeze into our tent if you like," said Jon.

"Thank ye, Mister Hamilton, but we'd prefer to use our own."

"Right, there's a good spot over there, so we can box in our horses."

"That we will. Put that tent a-right there, girl."

"And join us for supner."

"Thank ya," said Ann. "What will ya be servin'?"

"That's up to Ella and Maggie."

"We'll have our girl bring some food too. Hurry up with that tent, girl! Then you can help me cook!"

"I'll see you all in half an hour," said Jon, leaving them.

The Hawthornes had a small tent that attached to their wagon. With it on one side, the Cumberland River on another, and Jon's two wagons and trailer, the horses were corralled to an extent. Ella and Maggie made a stew, and they waited for the Hawthornes.

"When we get to Arkansas, they're headed south, and we are going north, maybe along the White River."

"That's if we can still get land on a river. That river they are going to may be all that's left, Jonny."

"I don't like them very much, especially the way they treat their bounders."

"I don't either, but that's not our business, Jonny. I don't think they will harm them after you warned them."

"But that's only until tomorrow, darlin'. I plan on leaving them in our dust after we leave Nashville. You should have heard her squeal when I told her our lunch was horse meat."

"Really? Well, Nanty Ella's stew is the last of the squatter's horse meat, with some venison. Maybe she won't know the difference."

"We're about to find out. Here they come."

The "girl" was carrying a small pot, and the "boy" had a cloth wrapped around something to eat.

"What did you bring, Missus Hawthorne?" asked Maggie.

"Some beans, and Indian pudding," answered Ann.

"Sounds delightful, and we have some stew."

"Oh, what all did you put in the stew?"

"We had some potatoes and turnips. We will restock our vegetables tomorrow in Nashville."

"What kind of meat . . . is in there?"

"Mostly white tail," lied Maggie.

"How can ya tell the difference?"

"By the taste. The deer has a wild taste."

"Well, let's cut the tongue-wagging and eat, gang."

Jon and Maggie watched, as Ann dipped out only the turnips and potatoes from the stew pot. They looked at each other with wrinkled faces when they tasted Ann's Indian pudding.

"What do you put in your pudding, Missus Hawthorne?"

"Well, I ran outta milk an' corn meal, so I used some rice with spiced water."

"Do you like the stew, Missus Hawthorne?" quizzed Jon.

"Oh, yes, Mister Hamilton. Very special flavor."

"The white tail gives it that. There is plenty for your slaves to eat too, Henry."

"Well, I were just a-gonna give 'em the rest . . ."

"Give them each a bowl of your stew, Ella."

"Orites, Jonny. I's do already," answered Ella.

"And give them seconds when they're ready."

"I's do, Jonny."

"Well! I'm tired and need some sleep. Comin', Pa?"

"In a few minutes, Ma. I'll wait fer our girl to finish."

"No need of that, Mister Hawthorne. Jonny and I will watch them and make sure they get to your tent," assured Maggie.

"Well, in that case, we'll be a-headin' fer bed. See ye all in the mornin'. You's hurries back, understan', girl?"

The girl and boy nodded their heads yes. Jon thought he noticed tears in the girl's eyes.

"Are you happy to be leaving North Carolina?" Jon asked.

The boy and girl didn't answer. They just continued eating.

"Perhaps you wanted to stay at the Johnstones?" Maggie asked. Still no answer.

After a pause, Jon asked, "Would you like to be free, and go with us?"

Both slaves' eyes widened, and Jon detected smiles.

"Jonny! We can't just steal their slaves."

"Maybe, maybe not. I feel like I was robbed of a bounder when I was at their plantation. This would be payback."

"If you've finished, you better return to your masters."

The boy and girl nodded, bowed, and left. Jon was sure he saw tears welling in the girl's eyes.

"Time for all of us to turn in too," said Jon.

"Did you finish your diary, love?"

"Yes, I can't sleep. I've been thinking about what you said to that boy and girl."

"Did you see the tears in the girl's eyes when you told them to return to their master?"

"No, I didn't. I hope that doesn't mean what I think, Jonny."

"Like your father?"

"Yes. I wish you hadn't reminded me."

"Sorry, darlin'. Merry Christmas. Sorry I didn't make it to Nashville today. We'll be there early tomorrow."

"That's alright, Jonny. I love you."

"I love you too, my pretty plum. I'll get someth—"

Suddenly, there was a loud commotion outside, and Jon heard a sound he knew too well, and a scream.

"That was a black snake, darlin'. He's cobbing that girl!" Jon was up and dressed in a flash, and out of the tent. Mose was right behind him.

"I'll be a-teachin' ye not ta disobey me! Now getcha black butt onta that blanket an' spread them legs!" Jon heard Henry's words clearly.

"Please, Massa Henry . . . No . . . Please!" There were loud cries.

"Holt 'er still, boy . . . that be's better," Jon heard Henry say, followed by a scream.

Jon yanked on the tent, and it broke loose from the wagon. "What in damnation is going on . . ." Jon was shocked at the sight of an orgy. Missus Hawthorne was standing with a small blanket. Mister Hawthorne was on the ground with his derriere in the air, and cockelling the girl under him. The boy was holding the girl down. All were naked, except for a silver necklace Henry was wearing, swinging about with his action. "In this tent?" There was a pause.

"How dare you enterin' my tent!" shouted Ann, using the blanket to cover her body.

"Please help me, Massa Ham . . .," said the tearful girl.

"Shut up, bitch! Hold 'er still, boy," said Henry. "Get the hell outta my tent!" he yelled, as he slapped the girl.

Jon grabbed and pulled the aroused boy off the girl.

"What the blazes do ya think yer a-doin'? Go away, an' be a-lettin us be!"

"What in blazes do you think you're doing?"

"I'm a-screwin' my slave!" shouted Henry. "A-gettin' a start on my stock a slaves! Mind yer own business! Henry continued to pump into the girl. Jon stared in amazement, as Mose reached between Henry and the sobbing girl with one arm, and lifted Henry into the air and dropped him to the side. Jon pulled the girl to her feet and hugged her.

"Are you alright?" The girl nodded and reached for her dress.

"A-course, she's alright! This girl will be the head mistress o' my stock!"

"I saw you hit her! Do it again, and I'll hit you!"

"I don' usually hit her. She jest disobeyed me."

"What we do with our slaves is none o' yer business," interjected Ann.

"While you ride with me, I'm making it my business."

"Alrights then, I'll be a-holdin' back on the hittin' fer now."

"You should hold back all the time! Now get some sleep. I'll get you to Nashville tomorrow, but from then on, you're on your own."

Saturday, December 26

The Hawthorne group did not come out of their tent the next morning. Mose and Ella, with Chipper's help, stoked up the fire, had breakfast, and hitched the two wagons.

"You better come on out, Mister Hawthorne, and get a bite to eat so we can be moving on." Jon repeated this call.

"We'll sen' the boy out," came the reply, finally.

The boy came out with two plates, and Ella fed him first, then used wooden plates for the girl and the Hawthornes.

"Thank you. We wan's ta be's wit you's," said the boy.

Jon paused. "Okay," he whispered. "When we leave the town . . . got that? When we leave the town, watch for my signal. Got it?"

The boy smiled, nodded, and walked back to their tent.

"Hurry with that breakfast. We want to get started!" Jon yelled to the Hawthornes, through their tent.

"Yeah," came the reply. "We'll be a-right out."

"Good, we'll hitch the horses up to your wagon. Your wheel hose looks good enough to pull now."

"Then we only need one o' yer horses fer now."

"Yes. We're putting your two-wheel horses back together, and matching our lead with yours to Nashville."

"I'll be a-thankin' ye."

"That's Okay, but you'll need to buy one in Nashville."

"Gotcha! We'll be a-both a-headin' for Memphis, might as well be a-goin' together," said Henry.

"Nah, ah . . . well, maybe. We'll see in Nashville."

"Yeah, be a-right out."

Conqueror was hitched to the lead on the Hawthorne wagon, leaving Corker to pull the carryall, which he did well. It was still before noon when they reached Nashville, one of the original Cumberland settlements. Maggie thought it was the biggest town they had seen on this trip, big enough to buy any and all the supplies they needed.

"Where are you folks headed?" asked a general store owner.

"We're hoping to find some good land in Arkansas."

"Good luck with that. I think you're a little late for that, the way they's been comin' through here."

"So we heard. I guess we should have started in July!"

"That ya should have, sir. What can I get ya?"

"Here, my partner Ella would know best what we need."

"Ella? Your partner?" asked the astonished man.

"Yes, she was my bound . . . my slave, but I freed her."

"Well ya better not let that be known in Arkansas."

"Really? Why is that?"

"They have let it be known that they're a slave state."

"Well, thank you, sir. We'll be mindful of that."

"Yeah, when they ask, tell them she's a slave, Okay? Now, uh, miss, what do ya need?"

"We's needs lots dem foods, Jonny," said Ella. "Flawa, teas, shuggas, coffee, bacon, beans, corn meals, an' vegetables."

"Did you get all that, mister?"

"Yes, sir. Was that sugar? And flour?"

"Yes, and bacon. Maybe some eggs too."

"Yes, sir. We have lots of bacon, and meat of all kinds"

"What do you think, darlin'?"

"Let's get some pork . . . and beef. I'm getting tired of venison and horse all the time."

"Me too. We'd like some pork and beef too, mister."

"Coming right up, sir. Oh, and I have a great price on oatmeal today. It makes a good hot breakfast."

"That's what the bacon is for . . . and eggs."

"But it would be nice to have some oatmeal too, Jonny."

"Then we would need milk, my love."

"Oh, that's right. Too bad we still don't have Abby."

"Yeah, it would be nice to have milk."

"We have everything here you need, sir, including a cow."

"Thanks, but we can't afford a cow right now," said Jon.

"Do you have anything to trade, sir?"

"Hmm . . . how about a horse?"

"I'd say that's a fair trade, sir."

"Let's do it, Jonny. Chipper would love another cow."

"Alright. You have a deal, mister, as long as we can trade the saddle for some of these supplies."

"You're a good trader, sir. Do you have anything else to trade?"

"Well, we have several guns."

"Wonderful. We can always use flints. How many do you have?"

"How many do you need to trade for all this raggery?"

"Hmm . . . I presume the saddle and rifles are in good condition?"

"Yes, sir, they are."

"Well, then, I'll trade you all those supplies . . ."

"And the cow too," said Jon.

"And the cow . . . for the horse, saddle, and five guns."

"You've got a deal, mister."

"I's go's an' tells my son, Jonny," said Ella.

"I have a field in back to put the horse," said the owner.

"And the cow?" asked Maggie.

"My boy, er, helper will bring her around as soon as he helps you load up all this merchandise."

"What kind of cow is it?" asked Maggie.

"A good producer. I think it's a Jersey. I got it in a trade."

"Thanks, mister. I'll get your five rifles."

"Do you have enough powder, sir?"

"I think we do, now that we have five less rifles."

"Just in case, I'll throw in regular and fine powder."

"Thank you, sir. We surely came to the right store."

"And I appreciate that, sir. It's been a pleasure. Is there anything else I can do for you?"

"Yes, now that I think of it. The cow will slow us down, and we are in a hurry. Any suggestions?"

"You have two wagons and one trailer, right? Well, I have an animal transport you can tie to a wagon."

"Animal transport? What is that?"

"It's a long, narrow trailer, wide enough for one horse, and it has sideboards and a feed trough."

"How much for that?" asked Jon.

"Well, if you have another spare rifle . . ."

"Sold! Oh, and there is another family who have been tagging along," added Jon. "Do you have any ideas on how to get rid of them before they eat all our food?"

"Hmm . . . well, a little over two miles west of here, on the main road to Memphis, is a road that goes southwest to the little town of Franklin. From there you can take a road west, a good hundred miles, to Jackson, back on the main road."

"How far south to Franklin?"

"Oh, 'bout thirty five miles. It's 'bout the same distance."

"Really? I suppose the road from Franklin to Jackson . . . Jackson! Does that have anything to do with President Jackson?"

"Yes, sir, that's his home town, named after him. And the road between Franklin and Jackson is Good. In fact, it's the best way! It still has lots of grass for the animals. Grass has been all eaten on the main road. And you can avoid the waymen."

"What are waymen?" asked Maggie.

"Bandits! They steal and then kill sometimes on the main road."

"And not on the back roads?"

"Nobody takes the back roads."

"That settles it, Jonny. We take the back road."

"Okay, darlin'. I'll get the horse and six guns."

"Good. We'll bring the cow and horse transport around front, and throw in some oatmeal. Anything else, sir?"

"Well . . . yes, there is. Do you by chance know an old squatter-corn whiskey maker named Isaak . . . uh, Dre-something field?"

"What field?"

"First three letters are D-R-E, then something field."

"I think it's Drewfield," said Maggie.

"No, sir, I've never heard of him. Why?"

"We found him dead in his shack, couple days east of Carthage. We got his gun and watch."

"The watch was purchased here," added Maggie.

"Well, sir, I'll ask around. If I find somebody that knew him, I'll tell them. Might as well keep the watch."

Out on the street, Mose had hitched the horses up correctly and had the extra horse ready to trade. Chipper was very excited. The Hawthorne slave boy was there as well. Jon figured he must have brought Conqueror back. He heard Henry Hawthorne before he saw him.

"Boy! Hurry up!" Henry yelled from up the street. He had his newly purchased horse hitched, and ready to head west.

"Look for me about two miles out of town. When I signal, jump out of that wagon and come running. Understand?"

The boy nodded yes, smiled, and ran back to his master.

"We have to hurry, Mose. We can't let them get too far ahead. We still have a small trailer coming for the cow."

"Orites, Jon. I's gets rope ta ties un trailer."

"Good. Looks like our supplies are loaded, our wagons are heavy again, and we'll have to run the horses to catch back up."

"Horses ready, Jon, an' five guns."

"Make that six, Mose, one for the cow trailer."

"Yassa. I makes un six," said Mose.

"Chipper, you now have a horse, dog, and a cow! Happy?"

"Yassa, Massa Jon! I's be's happies!"

"Good. Here comes the cow and trailer. Rope it to the carryall."

"I's do, Jon, an' we's gets crackin'!" said Mose.

"Maggie, we look for a road going south to Franklin, about two or more miles west, and take it."

"That would be to the left, right?"

"Right. It would be to the left. Ready, Ella?"

"I's be ready, Jonny. We's runs horses."

"Cow's be tied, an' trailer be's tied too, Jon."

"Great. Get them going, darlin'. Let's catch the Hawthornes, Mose."

"Righto! We catches dem Hawthornes."

Jon and Mose led the race through and out of Nashville. The store owner was correct. The sides of the road were barren, stripped of grass and foliage. The horses kept at a fast gallop, with Corker leading the way. A fast mile passed. A good mile and a half, and still no Hawthorne wagon in sight. Finally, as two miles approached, Jon had Maggie and Ella slow their horses to a trot, and he went ahead with Mose. The road bent left and right, bordering the river. As Jon rounded a turn in the road, he saw the Hawthorne boy and girl running toward him, a couple hundred yards ahead. No sign of the Hawthorne wagon.

"You grab the girl, Mose, and I'll get the boy."

"Yassa. Gets up, Freez."

Freez? Jon wondered, as he saw the road to the left. The sign read "South, Franklin," as Jon rode past it. He got to the boy, grabbed his arm, and pulled. The boy jumped and swung up onto Prancer behind Jon. Mose reached and lifted the girl up behind him, and they headed back to the road to Franklin. No sign of the Hawthornes, as the wagons driven by Maggie and Ella turned left to Franklin.

"Keep going. I'll catch up!" Jon shouted to Maggie. He broke off a branch from a shrub by the road, and began to brush the road clean of wagon wheel tracks. The boy did the same.

"Still no sign of your masters."

"Dem's be's massa no mo'," said the boy.

"Right. Let's catch up to our wagons."

"Chipper, climb up on the wagon with Maggie. I need your Abby for a while."

"Yassa, Massa Jon." The boy climbed onto Chipper's vacated horse.

"I see the girl is with Ella. That's good."

"Anything else, boss?" asked Maggie.

"Just keep rolling. We'll break for lunch in a while."

Break they did in a pleasant, grassy area in the early afternoon. They were about ten miles down the Franklin Road.

"We have plenty to eat, Ella. Come join us."

"I's do un minute, Jonny."

"Are you getting enough to eat?" Jon asked the girl, who smiled and nodded her head yes.

"What is your name?" Maggie asked, but the girl just lowered her head and didn't answer.

"Massa Hawthorne calls dem bitch," said the boy.

"What did he call you?" asked Jon.

"Massa calls me 'Hey' . . . an' 'Boy'."

"Do you have names you would like to be called?" asked Maggie.

"No, ma'am, dem friends calls Snake and Creeps."

"Is it alright if we give you new names?"

"Yassa, Massa . . ." The girl said nothing.

"Don't call me master. I'm not your master. You are now part of our family, Okay?" The boy nodded his head.

"Nanty Ella, do you want to name one?"

"No, Sissy. I's be names 'nuff babies."

"Nunky Mose?"

"No, Sissy. You's names dem goo' names."

"Jonny? Which one would you like to name?"

Jon paused. "Why don't you name them, my love?"

"Well, I've always liked my brother's name, Allston."

"But you call him Ally, don't you?"

"Yes, but it's a nickname, Jonny."

"Is the name Allston, or Ally, for short, Okay with you?"

The boy shrugged his shoulders, then nodded his head yes.

"Then Ally it is."

"Then Allston it is. Should I name the girl?"

"Go right ahead, my pretty plum."

"It's not fair to use both of my family's names, but I have always liked the name Susan for a girl."

"It's a great name. Do you like Sue or Suzy?" When the girl didn't answer, Jon said, "It's going to be a long, boring life if you don't ever talk to us, Susan."

The girl finally looked up and smiled for Jon. "I be's Susan."

"Great! Suzy and Ally, welcome to our family." Everyone applauded.

"I'm surprised the Hawthornes haven't come after them."

"You're right, my love. They are a handsome addition. Now do I get to give them middle names?"

"Jonny! Like you did our first cow, Abby?"

"Like your father did to his bounders."

"Then no! I'd rather they had no middle names."

"Well, we still have one more name to take care of."

"What name is that?"

"Mose's horse, that's what."

"That should be up to Mose, Jonny."

"Righto! It should be a name of strength, to be able to carry Mose all day. Got a name for your horse, Mose?"

"Nosa, but him my frien'."

"Then how about Friend?"

"Orites, Jon, he be names Frien'."

"Well, that takes care of that," said Maggie.

"We haven't named the cow yet."

"Oh, the cow . . . Abby is taken. What do you think, Chipper?"

"How about Crabby, Chip? Or Gabby?"

"I's calls 'er Milky," said Chipper.

"Milky? Is that the name you want for her?"

"Yassa, missy. She be's Milky."

"Good. Let's get all these names on the road."

Diary of Margaret Hamilton

Saturday, December 26

. . . And they were having an orgy in their little tent. Jonny and Nunky Mose broke it up, and we decided we would part with them when we reached Nashville this morning. Jonny said both the boy (Ally) and the girl (Susan) had welts on their backs from cobbing . . . And Nashville is about half the size of Salem. Anyway, we loaded up with supplies, and it didn't cost us one cent! We traded for our spare horse, saddle, and guns. We even got a cow to boot! Chipper named her Milky, because he had already named his horse Abby . . . Anyway, we caught up to them and stole the boy and girl slaves. They are now with us for keeps, and we are taking a different route to Jackson, Tennessee, to avoid the Hawthornes. We named the boy after Ally, and the girl after you, mother. Don't you feel honored? Jonny says we made about twenty-five miles today, and are close to the town of Franklin. Then it's a long stretch to Jackson . . . I know you will be unhappy about our stealing Ally and Susan, but Jonny and I couldn't stand to leave them to the treatment they have suffered. With love to all, and a happy Christmas season. May we soon be together again on holidays.

Margaret Hamilton

Sunday, December 27, 1835

. . . And we made well over thirty miles today, through the town of Franklin, and west toward Jackson, Tennessee. The road is barely manageable, and it looks like we will dodge stumps all the way to Jackson, about one hundred miles west. We are camped at a river we must cross in the morning. We don't know its name. Jonny says it's much too soon to be the Tennessee River, but it runs north, like the Tennessee . . . And not one sign of the

Hawthornes . . . Today was the coldest day we have had in many days. It feels like freezing right now, so I will close and snuggle up to Jonny. Love to all, and to all a good night!

Margaret Rose

Monday, December 28

"Boy, it's cold this morning," said Jon. "Boy, it's sho 'nuff cold! It doesn't look too deep, Mose. Should we swim the horses?"

"Yassa, bu' I's makes raf' for Milky cow an' trailer."

"And float it behind the carryall?"

"Yassa. An' we's ropes tree an' wagons an' trailer wheels."

"Good. It looks like some of Ella's kitchen will get wet."

"Mama put dem bottom shelves in wagon, Jon."

"Good, let's get a move-on. The boy, Ally, can help."

Ally did help prepare the wagons and build a raft for Milky and Milky's trailer, and he volunteered to ride that raft.

"I's takes Corka cross an' ropes line."

"Okay, Mose. Can you take the saddle horses too?"

"Yassa, an' stakes to trees on other side."

"Good. Mose, we'll use this pine to anchor this side."

"Orites. I's goes now, an' brings back Corka."

Mose pulled the line and the three saddle horses across, while on Corker. There was one spot of fifty feet or less that the horses had to swim, touch ground, and emerge on the opposite bank.

"Good job, Mose. It hardly seems necessary to strap on those logs. Only one fairly deep spot."

"Yassa," answered Mose. "Bu' dem one spots spoils food."

"We must wade to the tops of our limbs before the wagons will float, then pull the logs right back off in keister-high water."

"Yassa . . . let's get crackin'!"

Maggie drove the carryall, and the raft carried the cow, the trailer, and Ally. The river covered the hubs of the carryall. Jon and Ally roped the logs to the wheels on one side, and Mose roped the other.

"Are you going to be alright driving them in the deep water?"

"Yes, I'm fine, Jonny. I just hope Conqueror will stay in line."

"Ally! Will you ride the lead . . . oh my god, you have only Conqueror pulling! Damn! Mose!" shouted Jon. "Will you and Corker pull the carryall over the deep spot?"

"Sho 'nuff, Jon. Comes, Corka, we pulls carryall."

The carryall and raft made it across easily, and Mose was able to salvage a couple of the logs from the carryall.

"It's the covered wagon's turn. Bring them in, Ella!"

The same process was used with the covered wagon and trailer. Mose untied the guide line and raced Corker ahead into the deep water to keep Jake, Red, Sloggy, and Smutty in line. Wet derrieres were the only damage, and the group continued west.

"I'd sure like to know the name of that river!" shouted Jon.

"Well, Jonny, you say it's not the Tennessee, so that's still ahead and it will be bigger."

"Yeah. I wish this road was better, and we didn't have to go left and right to avoid stumps and brush."

"How far do you think it is to Jackson, Jonny?"

"It was a little over one hundred miles from Franklin, so we have around eighty more to go."

"Who told you that?"

"That store owner. Didn't you hear him, my love? Traveling like a snake, it's still over a hundred miles."

"Maybe Nunky Mose will pull these stumps out for us."

"Sometimes I think he's strong enough to do just that!" After a pause, Jon continued, "Looks like we're going more westerly now."

"Isn't that the way you want to go?"

"Yes, darlin', but we went south to Franklin, then southwest to that river we crossed, and now we're finally heading west."

"Well, this trail takes us west, so stop complaining!"

"Okay! I will, my pretty plum." There was a long pause.

"Jonny! I'm getting hungry again."

"It's not noon yet, my love."

"So? Your son needs feeding."

"How are you going to do that? He ain't been born yet."

"Well, he's kicking! My food feeds him."

"Alright, my love, we'll find some grass and stop."

The grassy area came with a little creek. Ally jumped off Abby and helped build a fire and water the horses. Susan helped Ella.

"I think we did well, picking up those two."

"So do I, Jonny, even if we had to steal them."

"Gang, we have been making pretty good time lately."

"Except for the squatter, the bounty hunters, the snow storm, and what else? The Hawthornes!" said Maggie.

"Well, at least the last few days!"

"Except for this poor, winding road holding us up."

"As I was saying, we've done a poor job lately, but I'm very satisfied with our progress. I think we'll be in Arkansas early next year, the Lord willing, and the creek don't rise!"

"So's we's get crackin' Jon?" asked Mose.'

"So we get crackin', lots of daylight yet."

The gang kept up their swaying action all day. Eventually, the thick forest of trees thinned, to clusters of mainly pine, much like northeast Tennessee. This meant less stumps for the drays to have to pull around and through, and more progress west. By nightfall, the group had a very large grassy area to camp.

"What a wonderful supner, ladies."

"Wit Sissy an' Susan an' me, dat cain't help ta be's good," said Ella.

"Are those horses staked good, Mose? There's a lot of room for them to roam out here."

"Yassa. Dey be stakes fines, Jon. Ally helps."

"Good. We'll cross the Tennessee River tomorrow."

"How far did we travel today, Jonny?"

"A good twenty-five miles, my love."

"That's terrific, when you consider the conditions we traveled in. I'll get that in my diary."

"Have you been writing down everything that's been happening this whole trip?"

"Yes, I have. It will be a reminder to us and our children, of what we endured these last two months," answered Maggie.

"I hope you left out a few things."

"No . . . your goose is cooked for the rest of your life, Jonny!"

"Who all's going to be reading it?"

"My family, your family, all our friends past and future, and, let me think . . . enemies, strangers, business . . ."

"Okay, that's enough, Maggie."

"In fact, I'm going to turn in now, so I can get my diary all caught up to date. Good night, everyone!"

"Drat!"

Tuesday, December 29

"Good mornin', Mose, Ella. Sure is cold!"

"Yassa. Dems clouden up, Jon. Maybe's snows again," said Mose.

"Good Lord! I hope not. Good mornin', Susan, Allston."

"Goo' mornin's, Massa," said Ally.

"It's not master, Allston and Susan. It's Jon,"

Ally and Susan both nodded their heads yes.

"We are one big, happy family. Now when any stranger asks, then you pretend you're my slaves. Understand?" Again, Ally and Susan responded by nodding yes.

"How longs dat be's fo', Jon?" asked Mose.

"I'm not sure, at least until we get settled on our new land."

"Orites, Jon. You's bes' massa Mose eva hads."

"And you're the best slave! Let's have some breakfast. MAGGIE!"

"I'll be out in a minute, Jonny."

"I'm timin' ya, my pretty plum. Breakfast is getting cold."

"Is it cold out?" asked Maggie, from the tent.

"The breakfast, or the weather? YES!"

"Very funny. You're just a barrel of laughs, Jonny."

"Well, it won't be funny if you get left behind. Better hurry!"

"I told you I'll be out in a minute."

"Which minute is that, my love? A minute before noon?"

"Okay, I'm out," said Maggie. "Burr, it's cold!"

"I hate to see you eat and run, darlin', but we're ready to roll."

"You have to take down the tent first. I'll be ready."

"Good, Gang. let's make tracks."

The gang worked well, and moved at a good pace. That is, until midmorning. Jon noticed the clouds thicken, and soon snowflakes began falling. Within an hour, they were raindrops.

"Mose is getting a tarp to cover the carryall. We don't want to spoil all that meat."

"What about me, Jonny? Will it cover me too?"

"You're already spoiled, my love. Yes, it will cover you too."

"When are we stopping for dinner?"

"About five or six this evening."

"Jonny! Don't be cute. You know what I mean."

"Yes, darlin', I know. If you can hold on, I want to go on a while longer. When we stop, we'll have to hang a tarp."

"I can hold on, but I am getting hungry."

"Okay, hon, you're doing great. Keep them moving."

In the early afternoon, the group came upon the Tennessee River. "Here's where we take lunch. Mose, if you hang the tarp, I'll get wood for a fire."

"Orites, Jon. Ally an' I's do."

"Did you and Sue get wet, Ella?"

"Yassa, Suzie an' I's gets wet, but we's orites."

"Good. We'll all get wet crossing this river."

"Yassa. Riva's pretty bigs," said Ella.

"Can you drive the team from behind the bench? That way, you can stay out of the rain."

"Yassa. After we's lunches, I's do."

"After lunch comes the river. It's going to be a hard cross."

"Yassa. We's makes on full stomachs, Jonny."

"That's the spirit, Ella. I'll get us a fire."

There were trees along the river bank, and Mose picked a group of pine to hang the tarp. Starting a fire was easy, but keeping it burning in the rain wasn't as easy. Corn dodgers warmed the gang up, but the rain dampened spirits.

"Allys, you's helps wit blankets on horses."

"Can we get them further in those trees, Mose?"

"Yassa, we's do, Jon."

By the time the men returned to the tarp, they were soaked.

"I guess we wait out the squall, gang."

"Get by the fire before you all catch your death," said Maggie.

"But the fire is out in the rain, my pretty plum, and if we get any wetter, we will catch our death."

Poor Jonny, thought Maggie. It looked like there was no hope for him either way. But the rest of them would carry on Jon's work!

The rain finally slowed down in midafternoon.

"We have work to do. Getting across this river is going to take all our efforts. Any ideas, Mose?"

"No, Jon. We's do's sames as yesterdays."

"There's probably a ferry across this river on the main road."

"I'm sure there is, darlin', but that won't help us now. Alright, we take this river the same way we took the last."

"Comes, Ally, we's cuts trees."

"Chipper, will you help get the blankets off the horses and get them hitched back up?"

"Yassa, Massa Jon, we's get's horses ready."

Logs were cut, and a raft to carry Milky and her cow trailer was again constructed. Soon Mose was ready to cross the Tennessee with the guide rope. This time, he only pulled his horse, Friend, along with him. The water was immediately chest high on

Corker, who started swimming. Halfway across, Corker started struggling with Mose's weight, so Mose got off and swam beside Corker. Thankfully, a break in the rain for a spell had the current running slower, and the two giants made it across a few yards downstream from their start. Mose quickly lashed the guide rope to a tree after Corker pulled it taut.

"Mose is coming back across. Are you ready, darlin'?"

"You are going to hitch Corker back up with Conqueror, right?"

"Yes, dear. Are you ready to ride that raft with the cow, Ally?"

"Yassa. Jon, I's be's ready," said Allston.

"Good job, Mose," said Jon, as Mose and Corker returned. "Now, if we can get Corker hitched up beside Conqueror . . ."

"I's do, Jon. I's swims wit Corka again, an' we's rest."

"Okay, Mose. You get across again. You deserve a rest."

With Corker hooked back up to the carryall, Mose led the team into the water. It was about chest high to Mose, as he strapped the logs to the sides of the carryall.

"I's rides Abby's 'cross," said Chipper.

"No, you's doun's, son. Daddy!" shouted Ella. "Where's Chips rides? Hims wan ta rides Abbys."

"Son, you's gets in wagons wit Sissy."

"Yassa, Papa, I's do."

Mose swung up on Corker, and quickly headed back down into the water and waded back to the bank.

"What is it, Mose?"

"I's gets four pieces rope, an' ties ta guides rope."

While Jon watched quizzically, Mose made four lengths of rope, made a loop at one end of each length around the guide rope, and tied the other ends to Conqueror, the front of the carryall, the back end of the carryall, and the back of the raft. Then Mose waded back to ride Corker, and started across the river. The lengths of rope, with the loops around the guide rope, slid easily along the guide rope, keeping the horses, carryall, and raft in line.

"I'll be damned!" said Jon, watching the procession glide across the Tennessee River. About midway, Mose again slipped off Corker and swam the rest of the way across. Corker and Conqueror swam and pulled the carryall across easily.

"Now I've got to get this wagon and trailer across myself."

"I's helps, Jonny," said Ella. "I's cuts ropes."

"Thank you, Ella. I'll get the wagon out into the water, and start roping the logs. It's too deep for the horses by the time the wagon and trailer are both in the water."

"Maybe's you's puts traila slants ta side," said Ella.

"You mean have the trailer just in the water at a forty-five-degree angle?"

"I's don' knows, Jonny. Jus' slants traila ta sides an' hooks up in wata."

"Gotcha, Ella, but I can't hook up the trailer to the guide rope. Maybe the front corner."

"Suz an' I's rides traila, an' holds on ta ropes, Jonny."

"Okay, Ella. You're as smart as Mose! Let's see if I can angle the wagon just right."

Jon drove the teams up river before entering the water parallel to the bank. He then drove teams five and fifteen downstream to the guide rope, and turned them sharply into the deep so that the horses and wagon were now facing midstream, but the trailer was still parallel to the bank. Ally then got the lengths of rope, and looped one end around the guide rope, tied one to Jake at the lead, to Smutty at the wheel, and the other two lengths to the front and back of the covered wagon. They looped a longer length around the guide rope, then waded back up to tie Prancer to the back of the trailer. They then proceeded to lash the logs on to the sides of the wagon and trailer, setting them afloat. Jon then helped Susan onto the trailer to grab the guide rope.

"Poor Smutty is in the water up to her neck! But the girl is still holding back from swimming. Good girl, Smutty! I think we're finally ready, Ella."

"I's swims ta cova'd wagons," said Ella.

"No, you won't. I'll carry you to the wagon so you don't get wet, then I'll drive the teams across. Ready?"

Jon carried Ella to the back of the covered wagon. Then he waded to the front of the wagon.

"Ready, Ella?" asked Jon, scrambling onto the wagon's bench with Ally.

"Yes, I's be's ready. I's sees Papa worries 'cross riva."

"Alright, let's get over to him, Ella."

Jon grabbed the rope and attached it to the guide lines on the wagon, and urged teams five and fifteen to swim. The trailer slowly straightened itself behind the wagon, saddle horse last.

"Whoee! It's working, Ella!" Jon shouted. Ella didn't hear. "I hope Maggie puts this in her book, how we conquered the Tennessee River! Whoopee!"

Mose came out on Corker to help Ella finish the crossing.

"Congratulations, Mose. We made it in good shape!"

"Yassa, Jon, we's sho 'nuff did!"

"Let's have a drink of good old corn whiskey."

"Orites, we's drinks, an' we's gets crackin'!"

"What about that guide rope, Mose?"

"I's don' wans ta goes back an' gets ropes."

"Neither do I. The thunder with it! Let's have that drink."

"I don't hear anyone offering us women a drink. Nanty Ella would like a drink."

"Drinking this stuff makes women very horny, and I wouldn't want to take advantage of my wife! Would you, Mose?"

"Nosa! I's sho 'nuff wouldn't wan' that."

"I hear that food does the same thing to men, Nanty Ella."

"Tee hee, why it's surely do, Sissy!"

"Ah, how about a drink, Ella?"

Back on the road, the group was seeing more open country. This would normally mean easier travel, except for a steady rain, which was causing misery. Nature started calling, and Jon motioned to Maggie to keep going, and he looked for a place to relieve himself. *Must be that corn juice whiskey*, he thought.

Just then, Jon saw two men following his wagons. He hid in a cluster of trees and watched, as the two men rode by, pulling a pack horse. He followed them. When they stopped to check their flintlocks to make sure the powder wasn't damp, Jon knew they were about to attack the wagons. He stepped down from Prancer and crept up to a tree close behind. They were about to separate and hit the wagons from two sides. Jon had his Hawken ready, and let out a loud whistle. The two men turned, startled, and not seeing Jon in the rain, started their horses toward him. Jon stood and fired. *BAM!* He hit where he aimed, knocking one off his horse. The other hesitated long enough for Jon to race to another tree, ten or twelve yards away. The second man charged the area on his horse where he thought the shot came from. Jon was hurriedly reloading when he was spotted by the second man. *BAM!* His shot splattered the back of the pine tree that Jon was behind, and chunks of bark hit Jon's body and face, causing him to lose his balance, and he went down on his knees. Seeing this, the second horseman charged with a sword. Jon had the powder down the barrel of his Hawken now, and sprang around the tree to avoid the swing of the sword. He raced back to his original tree in time to avoid another blow of the sword. Jon's hand found a cap in his coat pocket, and he tore the wrapping off with his teeth, still stumbling around the tree trunk, avoiding yet another blow of the sword. Jon fumbled, getting the cap over the nipple, when the next blow hit the barrel of his gun, and it slipped from Jon's hands. The second horseman now raised the sword for a final blow. *BAM!* The bullet sent the man flying off his horse. Jon now had the Hawken capped.

"Get over, on the road, you bastard!"

"Can't . . . I'm hit bad."

"Not bad enough. You're alive!"

Mose rode up and leapt off Friend, rifle in hand. "You's orites, Jon?"

"Yep. Watch him, Mose. I'll check on the other one."

"Help me . . . I . . . I . . . I's dyin'."

"I's helps ya . . . I's shoots ya!" answered Mose.

"Where are you, Nanny boy?"

"Right here!" said the man, rising up from the brush, rifle pointed at Jon.

BAM! Jon's Hawken fired, even though a ball hadn't been tamped down the barrel. The hot powder sprayed the sitting man from head to waist, and he dropped back down, on his side.

"I can't see! I'm blinded! Help."

"You were already blind, or stupid, to attack our wagons."

"We were only going ta pass yer wagons."

"Sure, with guns firing and swords swinging!"

"Honest, we was just a-goin' home!"

"Where is your home?" asked Jon.

"Uh, Jackson. We both lives there."

"Mose!" Jon yelled. "Find out where that man lives."

"Where's you's lives?" Jon heard Mose ask the man. "He be dyin', Jon. He say Franklin."

"Franklin?"

"Yassa, Franklin," answered Mose.

"Looks like you were headed the wrong way, Nanny boy!"

"Uh, he be wrong. We's from Jackson . . . honest!"

"Your partner is dying. I believe him."

"What happened, Jonny?" asked Maggie, as she approached.

"These two were about to ambush our wagons."

"No, no, we was jest a-goin' ta Jackson on business, ma'am."

"What kind of business?" asked Maggie.

"Uh . . . uh . . . Trade! We were a-goin' ta trade goods, honest."

"What are you trading, boy?" asked Jon.

"Uh, house goods, clothes, an' food an' such."

"Where did you get the clothes and food?"

"Uh . . . from Nashville. Honest."

"Wayman, you're a liar!"

"No . . . no. Just ask my partner."

"He be dead, Jon," shouted Mose, by rider number two's body.

"He can't confirm your lies now, boy."

"Honest, we're traders."

"Let's see what you're trading," said Jon.

Jon pulled the large bags off the pack horse and froze.

"Recognize this horse, my love?"

"Hmm . . . no, should I, Jonny?"

"You sure should. It's the horse the Hawthornes bought in Nashville. Mose, come check out this horse."

"Orites, Jon," said Mose, walking over to the pack horse. "Dat horse look likes . . . Hawthorne horse."

"Right, Mose. Let's look in these bags." There were some women's clothes, which Jon thought looked familiar, a corn cob pipe, and a silver necklace.

"What did you do with them?"

"With whose? Whatcha mean, sir?"

"I said, what did you do to the owners of these items?" asked Jon, holding the pipe and necklace.

"Ah!" gasped Maggie. "That pipe! It was his . . ."

"Sure was, darlin', and so was this necklace."

"I . . . I . . . I . . . don' rememba where I got . . ."

"Liar! What did you do with them?" yelled Jon.

"I . . . don' know what you's talkin' 'bout."

"What are you going to do with him, Jonny?"

"I am going to kill him and leave both these bastards here for the wolves."

"Jonny, you can't do that!"

"Watch me!" Jon started loading his Hawken.

"Please, sir . . . don' shoot me again. Help! I'm blind!"

"What did you do to the Hawthornes? Tell me, or I promise I'll fill you with lead balls!"

"I . . . he killed 'em . . . an' threw their bodies in the brush."

"Oh my god," said Maggie.

"What about the other horses?"

"We traded 'em fer money."

"To who?"

"To some older folks . . . passin' by."

"What are you waiting for, Jonny? Shoot him!"

"No, please, sir, I's already shot. D-dat man shot those folks."

"What was his name?"

"I . . . I don' know, we's jest rides home together, honest."

"First, you were going home to Jackson, your partner says Franklin, then you tell us you two were going to trade goods in Jackson. Now you are going home again, and you don't even know him."

"He's a killer and a poor liar, Jonny. Shoot him!" said Maggie.

"What do you say, Mose?"

"Sissy wrong, Jon. We's should don' kill human being."

"If we don't treat him, he'll die anyway," said Jon.

"I am shot, and blind. I'm needin' help. Please!"

"We's takes 'im ta Jackson, Jon."

"Okay, Mose. Will you be responsible for him?"

"Yassa. I's be responsible, Jon."

"Then let's get him back to the wagons and treat his wounds. Looks like we own three more horses and guns."

"Yassa, an' swords, Jon. I's takes care o' him," said Mose.

Mose carried the man to the wagons, where Ella treated a right chest wound from Jon, and treated his eyes by getting the powder out, so he had partial vision. The boy, Ally, helped bury the dead man. Jon found out the man's name was William McCabe, the dead man was his cousin David, and they did indeed live in the Franklin area.

The horse trailer used by the cow, Milky, had sideboards, so while Ella treated Bill McCabe, Mose cleverly built a roof over it so he could put bedding in the trailer and tie McCabe down on top, covered by a tarp. This made eleven horses again, and Jon dug out the eight horse blankets they had and covered the six draft horses and two of the new ones.

"We should tell the McCabe family about these two men, Jonny," said Maggie.

"That means going all the way back to Franklin, my love, and I don't want to do that. There may be more killers there."

"We's tells sheriff in Jackson, Sissy," said Mose.

"Too bad about the Hawthornes being killed."

"Yes, darlin'. We may not have liked them very much, but they didn't deserve to die. Let's get moving."

Diary of Margaret Hamilton

Tuesday, December 29, 1835

. . . And it rained all day. Everyone was soaked by the time we reached the Tennessee River. After dinner, we had to cross that big river. My men are experts at crossing rivers by now, and we managed it in a couple hours with no losses . . . And I heard a shot, then another. Mose raced off on his horse Friend, and I heard a third shot. I was so worried! Jonny had discovered two men who were going to attack our wagons, but Jonny attacked them first. He and Nunky Mose killed one, and wounded the second, who we are now taking to the sheriff in Jackson. Here is the sad part . . . These two men had killed the Hawthornes up on the main road. They both deserved to die! . . . And it's still raining this evening. Hope it lets up soon . . . And Jonny thinks that we traveled only a little over twenty miles today, with the two new family members, three more horses (making twelve total), one criminal in tow, and our starting five. We all send you love.

Maggie Hamilton

Wednesday, December 30, 1835

. . . In just one more day, we will be in a new year. We didn't make it to Jackson today as Jonny wished, but we are close, according to him. I hope so. We are all depressed with this constant rain, and need a change in scenery. Jonny thinks we traveled about thirty miles today . . . And I am anxious to see the president's home, even if Jonny doesn't like him . . . And after Jackson, it is about seventy-five miles to the Mississippi River and Arkansas. I will write you all a long letter then, when we are in our new home.

Love you all,
Maggie H.

Thursday, December 31

"Good morning, gang. Has everyone had breakfast already?"

"Alls bu' you's an' Sissy, Jonny," answered Ella.

"Well, sorry we're holding things up. Maggie! We're late for breakfast! Get a wiggle on!"

"Be right there, Jonny, in a minute."

"Yeah, yeah. Make it a real short minute, my love."

"I will. I'm anxious to see Jackson," said Maggie.

"I'm anxious to pass Jackson, so hurry. Breakfast is cold."

"Cold? Well, heat it up. I'll be right out."

"Well, at least it stopped raining."

"Yassa, stops un night, Jon," said Mose.

"Well, I'm not waiting for Maggie. I'm hungry."

"Here you's is, Jonny, beans an' bacons," said Ella.

"Thank you. I'll probably be saying 'thank you' all day!"

"Ha! Dat not says 'than-que,' Jon, dat says 'go 'way!'" said Mose.

"Yes, Nunky Mose, we're going away as soon as I eat," said Maggie.

"Hee, hee . . . Sissy miss dem joke," said Ella, laughing.

"What joke, Nanty Ella?"

"Dem joke 'bouts beans, Sissy."

"Beans, huh? Must be one of Jonny's jokes!"

"Sure was. Eat them, and let's break ground," said Jon.

"Has our prisoner been fed?" asked Maggie.

"Yassum, missy, we's all ready fo' you's," answered Mose.

"Alright then. Get the tent packed, and I'll be ready."

They were closer than Jon thought to Jackson. Almost instantly, they saw people and houses, then main street of this small town.

"Anything we need in Jackson?" asked Jon.

"Yes, I need to see President Jackson's home, called 'Hermitage.'"

"Why, my love? It's got a roof, doors, windows, and . . ."

"Never mind. I just want to go by it, Jonny."

"So we go by it! No, we don't. We can't afford it!"

The big mansion came into view, huge and beautiful.

"I think it's even bigger than Bethania. Can I drive around?"

"Go ahead, darlin'. Let's unload our prisoner, Mose."

"Orites, Jon, we's do's. We's puts on horse."

"Right! Ally, you're in charge until we return."

"Me? I's be in charge?" asked Ally.

"Yes, can you handle it?"

"Yassa, Mas . . . Yassa, I's un charge."

"Ready, Mose? Let's find the sheriff."

"Ahhh . . . that hurts! Let's shoot the sheriff!" said McCabe.

"You won't be making jokes soon, McCabe."

McCabe laughed. "Yep, I will. Der's no sheriff in Jackson!"

"Good. Then I can just take you out of town and shoot you!"

"That wouldn't be civilized."

"It would be godsend to families of those you killed!"

"I's didn't kill no one . . . honest."

"They just looked at that ugly face and died! Ready, Mose?"

Mose picked up McCabe at his waist and set him on his horse. "Yassa, I's be ready now, Jon."

"Yer mistreatin' yer prisoner!"

"I mistreated you when I let you live!"

"Dem sheriff takes in, Jon, un kills 'im," said Mose.

"When he sees the evidence, he'll hang you, McCabe."

"Told ya, der's no sheriff in Jackson."

"We'll find someone to kill you then, maybe me!"

"Excuse me, ma'am, sir, so you have a sheriff in this town?"

"No, we have a few law enforcers. What did he do?"

"He killed a couple of people west of Nashville."

"You should've took him ta Nashville."

"Where is your law enforcer, sir?"

"Ya'al will find 'em in town hall, mister, block and a half on down this here street."

"Thanks. Come on, McCabe, time to turn in."

"I's be out in no time, uh, Jon, an' I'll be a-lookin' fer ya!"

"You'll find us down in Mississippi. I'll be waitin'."

"Ha, I heard ya talkin' 'bout Arkansas."

"That was where the Hawthornes were headed when you killed them, you bastard!." After a moment, Jon said, "That looks like town hall."

"Yassa. Gets down, bassard," said Mose.

"Cain't . . . I's hurtin' too much," answered McCabe.

"I's puts you's down!" said Mose, grabbing McCabe.

"No, please. Ahh, yer a-hurtin' me!"

"That's nothing, compared to a hangin' rope!" said Jon.

"Said I'd be a-seein' ya shortly, Jon," quipped McCabe.

"Not if I see you first. Let's go in."

"Hello there. Whatcha got?"

"Are you the law enforcer in town?"

"Yes, sir. What kin I do fer y'all?"

"This man killed a couple people this side of Nashville."

"Can y'all prove that?"

"Yes, sir, I can. He tried to kill me and my party, and I have a necklace and pipe here that he had, and that belonged to the people he killed. He admitted it to us."

"I did no such thing! My pardner kilt 'em!"

"And where be yer partner?" asked the lawman.

"They kilt him, an' 'bout kilt me!" said McCabe. "He were my cousin too they kilt."

"What was his name? An' yers?"

"McCabe, William McCabe, an' they kilt cousin Dave."

"Hmmm . . . McCabe, huh? Name's familiar. Let me see . . ." The lawman checked some papers. "Well, what do ya know . . . William an' David McCabe . . . Waymen!"

"Waymen?" asked Jon. "They were waymen?"

"Dis here notes say so. You, McCabe, did theys take anything from ya?"

"Ah . . . yes, they's takes my gun an' my horse."

"Anything else?" asked the lawman.

"Dey kilt me cousin!" answered William.

"What else, Mister McCabe?"

"Ah . . . uh . . . my sword. Dey takes my sword."

"And what did they take from yer cousin?"

"Dave . . . dey takes his gun, sword an' horse . . . an' kills 'im."

'Okay, yer under arrest! You's is wayman."

"No . . . honest . . . I ain't no killa. Please! Dese boot lickers shoots me . . . honest!"

"Dey shoulda killed ya! Waymen . . . how many you's kilt McCabe? Huh? How many?"

"Nobody, sir . . . honest!"

"Yer under arrest, McCabe . . . fer many murders! I'll takes 'im now, mista . . . uh . . ."

"Hamilton. Jonathan, and this is my partner, Mose.

"Howdy! I thinks they be's a reward fer them."

"How much reward, sir?"

"Don' know, hasta contact Nashville. Where I send it?"

"Hmm . . . is your address just town hall?"

"Yes, sir, that will get me alright," said the lawman.

"When we get to Ark . . . our land, I will send you a letter telling you my address."

"Okay. I'll collect an' wait fer yer letter, name's Clem Casey."

"Thank you. So long, Nanny boy!"

Jon and Mose walked out of the town hall, climbed up on their horses, and rode quickly away to find Jon's gang.

"Come on, Maggie, Ella! Get aboard and head out."

"What's the hurry, Jonny?"

"Don't ask questions. Get crackin'."

The women and young ones jumped aboard, and all seven people, with eleven horses and rigs, hurried out of Jackson, and back on the main route to Memphis.

"Don't stop until we make lunch, darlin'."

"What did you do? Get us in trouble?"

"No . . . we may even get a reward!"

"Then what's the big rush?"

"I'll tell you later, my love. Keep them moving!"

"Alright, Jonny. We're at lunch. Now, what was the hurry?"

"We got away with all the stolen goods—the guns, horses, and swords of the McCabes—before the lawman realized it."

"Maybe that lawman didn't want them."

"They were evidence, my love."

"Then he may need that evidence to hang that McCabe."

"Nah, he had all the evidence he needed, darlin'."

"Good. Then stop worrying, Jonny."

The rest of the day was uneventful as the group headed for Memphis.

"Thank you, ladies. That was a great supner."

"You's welcomes, Jonny," said Ella.

There was a long pause.

"I'm sure glad we're out of that Cumberland country."

"So am I, my pretty plum."

CHAPTER VII

—⚬—

Home Sweet Home

Friday, January 1, 1836

"Happy New Year, my darlin'."

"Thank you, Jonny. Happy New Year to you."

"We didn't quite get to Arkansas before the new year, but we came close."

"How close, Jonny?"

"I'd say about sixty miles."

"What do you suppose Arkansas looks like?"

"Hmm, probably a lot like Tennessee, or Carolina."

"Jonny, Tennessee doesn't look like North Carolina."

"Oh? They both have mountains and rivers."

"I didn't see any rolling land like the Piedmont, or any ocean like the Atlantic, or . . ."

"Okay, got it, my love, and they won't see a river like the one we're about to see."

"Yes, my darling husband, I'm anxious to see the mighty Mississippi River," said Maggie.

"Ustanali called it the Great River of the West."

"Usta who?"

"Don't you remember Chief Ustanali Nation? He and his warriors saved you women when you were captured."

"Oh yes, I remember alright. How many wives did he have?"

"Three wives and a slave woman."

After a moment, Maggie asked, "And he had seen the Mississippi?"

"Yes, he had, my pretty plum."

"Well, I want to see it too! Get up, lazy bones!"

"Good morning, gang. Happy New Year, eighteen thirty-six"

"Happy New Year, Nanty Ella and Nunky Mose."

"G'mawnin', Sissy. Breakfass be ready."

"Thank you, Nanty Ella. Good morning, Ally, Susan, and Chipper."

"Let's have breakfast. Maggie and I are anxious to see the Great River of the West."

"We be's ready ta goes, Jon," said Mose.

"Good. Maybe tomorrow we'll see that river."

"How far is it from here, Jonny?"

"Someone said it was about seventy-five miles from Jackson, so I guess sixty miles to go. I told you that."

"Dat be's two days, rights Jon?"

"If we can get crackin', Mose."

"Orites, we's gets crackin'."

Get crackin' they did. The road was in good shape, despite the rains of the last couple of days. The group made good time.

"Shall we stop for lunch, Mose?"

"Der be's no grass an' water, Jon."

"I know. This main route has been stripped of all grass and water."

"I's grains dem, Jon."

"Good, and we have lots of water." To Maggie, Jon added, "Pull up here, darlin'."

"Is this the best you can do? I see no grass or water," said Maggie.

"The best! We're carrying all we need for Memphis."

"Alright. Do we need a fire, Jonny? Let's eat and run."

"Do we need a fire, Ella?"

"Nossa, we's has cold dodgas. Beef be's orites?"

"Sounds wonderful, Nanty Ella. I haven't had beef in ten weeks."

"You had beef at our wedding, darlin'."

"Yes, and that's been ten weeks, you big lummox!"

"Hmm, that's over two months . . ."

"Two and a half months, Jonny."

Jonny paused. "Just think, my love, another two and a half months, and we'll be planting crops on our new land."

"We'll? Who is we, Jonny? I'll be in labor with this child."

The afternoon was just as uneventful as the morning. In midafternoon, the rains came again, but the group was able to continue at a good pace. They were traveling in a southwest direction, so Jon felt this was the last "leg" to the river.

"Those clouds sure look angry, Jonny."

"Yes they do, my love. It's getting late. I'll look for a good place to camp."

"They're coming this way, Jonny."

"I see that, darlin'. Tennessee isn't through with us yet. Pick up the pace, and I'll scout ahead for a camp spot."

"You better hurry, Jonny. It's getting close."

Jon raced ahead and found a clear spot along the road. He hurried back to the wagons. "There's a good spot just around that bend. Run the horses into the trees just past the clearing, to the right."

"Alright, love. It's already raining harder. Get up, Corker!"

"Come on, Ella. There's a spot just around that bend."

"Orites, Jonny, dem bigs storm comes."

"Yeah, there are some trees for the horses. Hurry!"

It was raining hard, as the group raced to get a tarp spread so all could assemble, shivering.

"I's gets fire starts, Jon."

"It's raining too hard to start one, Mose."

"I's builds fire here."

"Under the tarp? You will burn it down!"

"Nossa, Jon. I's builds here, an' raise tarp. Bu' firs', I's gets blankets on dem horses."

"Do we have that many horse blankets?"

"Nossa. We's uses ours an horses."

"Okay, we need our animals. Maggie, can you and Ella grab those blankets out of the big wagon?"

"I's do's, Jonny," said Ella. "We's no wans Sissy ta gets sick an' wets wit' child in dem belly. Suzy, comes. We's get blankets."

"You can get them, Jonny, so Nanty Ella don't catch her death."

"I'll get them, Ella. Stay here, out of the rain." Jon ran to the covered wagon and grabbed a stack of blankets. He gave half of them to Mose, and ran the rest to the tent.

"We need seven, Jonny," said Maggie.

"We's has mo' in carryall. I's gets."

"No, Ella, I'll get them. I'm already soaked."

The men raced around getting blankets, wood for a fire, and putting tarps over the carryall and trailer. They got their coats, and finally wrapped themselves under the tarp.

"Is the cow, Milky, alright, Jonny?"

"Yes. She has food and water, and a tarp over her."

"Good. Then it's time for all of you to get out of those wet clothes, so we can dry them by the fire," said Maggie.

"We don't have any dry clothes to change into, my love."

"You have coats and a blanket to wrap around you, until those get dry. Now get them off before you all take sick!"

"I's gets ropes ta raise tarp an' clothes line firs'," said Mose.

"I, I'm alright, darlin'."

"Jonny, you're not bashful, are you? Ha! You're the one who preached to me about one happy family!" Maggie was laughing.

"I'm alright I said, Maggie. I'm drying out already."

"No, you're not, Jonny. Now hurry up. Off with them!"

"Oh, alright."

Suddenly, the rain slowed to a sprinkle and nearly stopped. It became very quiet for only a couple minutes. Then came a plop, and another plop. The pounding increased, and the ground turned white with an intense downpour of hail. The men heard the horses squealing, and Mose and Ally ran again to the carryall, grabbed the last big tarp, and held it over most of the horses and themselves. Jon was caught with his pants down! He quickly pulled them back up, and ran out in his socks and unmentionables to help. He grabbed the reins of four horses still exposed to the elements, and pulled them under the coverage of the group of pines. The hail turned back to rain, and the white ground disappeared again, but Jon was caught again under the pines. When the rain slowed back down, Jon helped Mose and Ally stretch the tarp out, and rope it to trees for some protection for the horses. He then raced back.

"Are you alright, Jonny? And Nunky Mose and Ally?"

"We's no mo' wets dem we's were, Sissy," said Mose.

"Well, get them off," Maggie ordered, "and get to the fire."

"No sense going any further today, Mose."

"Nossa, it be's too close ta dark."

"Are your feet any better, Jonny?"

"They still feel frozen, my love, but a lot of the redness is gone. Looks like your patient will live!"

"You had me worried for a while. I thought I was going to have to raise your son alone."

"What? After I worked so hard all my life, scrimped and saved all my life, fought the enemy all my life, to father my boy. Did you think I was going to lay down and die?"

"Poor baby! All that working, saving, and fighting, for a boy who may not even be yours! What a waste . . ."

"What? What did you say?"

Maggie laughed. "Gotcha, Jonny! Hee, hee, just kidding, darling. The baby is yours." Maggie was still laughing. "That got your attention!"

"Sure did! Please don't scare me like that, my pretty plum."

"Your son is a strange kicker, that's for certain."

"Hey, boy! How dare you kick your mother like that!"

"I don't think he can hear you, Jonny."

"Well, he will. I'll teach him some manners one day."

After a pause, Maggie asked, "How far do you think we traveled today, Jonny?"

"Well, we made great time this morning and for a good half of the afternoon, so we probably made over twenty miles."

"That leaves forty to go. We won't get to Memphis tomorrow."

"Probably not, my love, but the day after . . ."

"That means Sunday, at the earliest."

"I'm afraid so. Not much we can do about that."

After a few moments, Mose asked, "We's eats now, Jon? Boys be's hungra."

"Good idea, Mose. I'm hungry too."

"I's gets mo' wood fo' dem fire."

"Better put your jeans back on first!"

"Ha, that's a good idea, Nunky Mose. They're dry enough now."

"Thank you's, Sissy. I's puts jeans on firs', an' shoes."

"Good. What do you need from the wagon, Nanty Ella?"

"We's goes see, Sissy. I's makes warm supper tonights."

"Guess I'll put my kentucks back on and help," said Jon.

It was still early, but dark. Ella made a big stew and enough corn dodgers for several days. Susan and Maggie helped. The males then pitched tent, and readied the animals for the night.

"That was the best stew I've ever had, ladies."

"Thank you's, Jonny. We's has lots dem meats," said Ella.

"Yep, and vegetables too. Looks like the rain is stopping. Our stock is fed, and we are alive this New Year's Day."

"Happy New Year, Jonny, and everyone," said Maggie.

"Do I get a New Year's kiss, my pretty plum?"

"You had more than your share this morning."

"Are you rationing kisses now too?"

"I'm not sure what you mean by 'too'!"

"I'll show you tonight in bed, my darling."

"I'll be asleep by then. In fact, I think I'll turn in."

"Why so early, my love?"

"I want to get caught up with my diary, and your baby daughter and I need some rest. Good night, everyone."

"Nites, Sissy. Happy New Years."

"Happy New Year to you all too," Maggie said, as she left.

"I'll see you in a bit, my pretty plum." To Mose, Jon added, "Do you have your harmonica, Mose?" Then it hit Jon. "Daughter?"

"Yassa, I plays a New Year song."

"Good. I need a good song to sleep on."

Mose played several songs before the rest all turned in.

Diary of Margaret Hamilton

Friday, January 1, 1836

. . . And a Happy New Year to all my family. We still have a couple days to Arkansas . . . We had made good time until a terrible storm hit us. We had a heavy hail storm, and buckets of rain. By the time it slowed, it was too late to continue. The three men were soaked, so I made them take of their nether garments to dry over the fire. Ha! Can you believe it? Jonny was bashful! We made twenty miles today, leaving forty more to Arkansas.

Love to all,
Margaret H.

Saturday, January 2

"Good morning, you all. Have you all had breakfast?"

"Yassa, we have, Jon. We's ready ta see Memphis."

"Do you ever get any sleep, Mose? You and Ella?"

"Yes, Jonny, we's do gets 'nuff sleep," answered Ella.

"Mag and me, we're just slow pokes, I guess."

"It's Margaret and I, Jonny," said Maggie, as she also exited the tent. "What's for breakfast, Nanty Ella?"

"It's 'what do we have for breakfast, Nanty Ella'," said Jon.

"Susan make breakfass. She makes oatsmeal an' dodgas," said Ella.

"Great! Isn't it wonderful to have a cow again?"

"It's wonderful to have two . . . three good cooks!"

"I'm not a very good cook, Jonny, compared to Nanty Ella."

"I think you would do in a pinch, my love. At least it's not raining this morning. Might be a good day."

"It be rainin' all nites, Jon."

"You would know that, Mose. You and Ella never sleep."

"We's be fines, Jonny. We's be rested," said Ella.

"The road looks pretty good, after all that water."

"She be's mighty soft groun', Jon."

"Well, I'll grab a bite to eat, and we'll soon find out."

The road proved to be loose, soft, and muddy. There were lots of puddles, and even places where the road was missing.

"Careful, darling, wheel to the right so we don't lose a wheel here. I hope this road isn't this bad the rest of the way."

"I do too, Jonny. Are you sure we can get by that gap?"

"Go real slow, Maggie . . . more to the right."

"I'm scared, Jonny. I can't get by that spot."

"Okay, darlin', scoot over. I'll drive it."

Jon climbed onto the bench and eased Corker and Conqueror forward. The wheels on the left of the carryall, both dipped into the edge of the washed out hold, but Jon snapped the reins over Corker's back and the dray pulled the wagon up over the crevice.

"Mose! Let's tie Corker to the front of that wagon, so he can help pull it past this hole."

"Orites, Jon, we's do."

Roped in front of Jake and Red, Corker pulled the heavy covered wagon with trailer over the crevice at a quick pace. The left wheels of both vessels dipped in and out, causing Ella to bounce off her bench, but she expertly held on.

"Wow, dat be close calls, Jonny!" yelled Ella.

"You did well, Ella. Looks like the cow and horses are Okay."

"Dey be fines, Jon."

"Thanks, Mose. Let's carry on."

This was the continued condition of the road for miles. As the wagons sloshed through the mud, and even some debris, at a much slower pace than normal, they came upon a spot too washed out to get the wagons over.

"What do we do now, Mose?"

"Not worry, Jon. Rememba un Blues Ridge, un we's builds bridge ta cross?"

"Oh yeah! Going up the side of that ridge, near the top."

"Rights. We's do same here, Jon."

"Good idea, Mose, let's get to it."

"Yassa, we's gets crackin'!" said Mose.

Mose cut down two pines, and the bridge was built. Rough planks lay over the log, bridging the gap. Jon and Ally shoveled dirt and mud over the poles.

"Good job, gang." When all were across, Jon said, "It's time for lunch. I'll find a spot up ahead."

"That was a very hard drive, Jonny. Not very many miles covered, did we?" asked Maggie, as the group ate dodgers.

"I would guess about seven or eight, my love."

"Maybe we'll do better this afternoon," Maggie said, as the group continued to eat corn dodgers.

"We have to do better if we want to get to Memphis."

"We'll get there tomorrow, Jonny. I'm sure of it."

"I'm glad to hear that, my pretty plum. I'll be happy to put Tennessee behind us."

The road remained difficult for many miles, but in the late afternoon, as if driving through an invisible curtain, the road was good again. The land opened to swampy areas.

"I wonder if the rain caused those bogs, Jonny."

"I doubt it. Probably made them deeper."

"We finally have good road. Maybe they won't slow us down."

"Those bogs won't bog us down!"

"Cute! But not very funny, Jonny."

Suddenly, the group heard loud, screeching sounds ahead.

"What in the world is that, Jonny?"

"I don't know, darlin'. I'll ride ahead and see. Go, Prancer!" The screeching got even louder, as Jon rode near some swamp trees. Then the screeches stopped and a rushing, flapping sound was heard. Jon then saw a large flock of birds flying.

"Wow! Those are pretty birds. Wonder what kind they are. They are circling around the swamp. I hope Maggie sees them. They sure are noisy, aren't they, Prancer?" Prancer's ears were perked.

"Did you see those parrots, Jonny?" Maggie asked, as she pulled the carryall up to where Jon had stopped.

"Parrots? Are you sure they were parrots?"

"Yes, honey. I think they are Carolina parrots."

"Carolina! You're pulling my leg."

"No, I'm not, Jonny. They were Carolina parrots."

"I've lived in Carolina all my life, and I've never seen any birds as pretty and noisy as those."

"They like warm, swampy areas, close to water."

"I suppose you learned that in college?"

"Yes, I did. I learned all about the birds and the bees."

"Good for you, darlin'. I hope you'll teach me."

"You already know, you big lummox!"

"Parrots, huh? I thought they were all in South America."

"Not all. We may see a lot of strange animals in Arkansas. It has lots of swamps. I've read about them."

As the day darkened, cabins began to appear in spots.

"Does that mean we're getting closer to Memphis?"

"I wish it did, my pretty plum, but we still have a ways to go. We'll be there tomorrow for sure."

"How far have we traveled today, Jonny?"

"Well, not quite twenty, I'm afraid."

"Don't be afraid, Jonny. That's a good day's journey when you consider the road condition this morning. Cheer up!"

"Okay, darlin' . . . there's a good spot to stop."

"We're right behind you, Jonny. Aren't we, Corker?"

Jon could have sworn he heard Corker answer with a snort!

"Another delicious supner, Ella. I think I'll hire you."

"You's gives me steady job, huh, Jonny?" Ella laughed.

After a pause, Maggie said, "I wonder what those people in that cabin are doing."

"Want to sneak over and find out, my love?"

"No, Jonny! That would be a terrible thing to do!"

"Then stop wondering, darlin'. I know what they're doing."

"What, you smarty pants?"

"The same thing we did in barn five."

"What? In barn number fi . . . Jonny! You scalawag!"

"It be's time fo' beds, Chips," said Ella.

"Yassum, Mama. I's takes Isaak ta beds."

"Yes, son, you's take Isaak ta beds. Say nites now."

"Nites, ya all. Comes, Isaak," said Chipper.

"That boy sure loves that dog. They even sleep together."

"Yes, and he takes good care of him. Isaak is really filling back out and looking a lot better," said Maggie.

"Chipper is doing really well. A horse, a cow, and now a dog. He might end up making us rich!"

"Will we ever be rich, Jonny?"

"That's why we're making this trip, my love."

"Oh? We're going to be rich farmers!" Maggie laughed.

"You just wait, darling. We'll make it happen."

"Well, I'll put that promise in my diary. Good night, all."

Sunday, January 3

Jon's gang were all early risers, and were ready to travel as the bright, warm sun made its full appearance. Everyone was anxious to see the river, or Arkansas, or both.

"This is our last day in Tennessee, gang. A whole new life awaits us across the river."

"How do you know that, Jonny?"

"Know what, my pretty plum?"

"That our lives will be any different in Arkansas than they are here? And that we'll be across the river today?"

"I just feel it in my bones."

"If we don't get across the river today, I'll ask Nunky Mose to crack those bones!"

"Well, we don't want that, so let's rumble."

"It be's good days ta rumbles, Jon," said Mose.

With the warm sun at their backs, Jon's team raced southwesterly toward Memphis. The scattered cabins and swamps gradually became farms, and the Nashville-Memphis road became busier, causing excitement for Jon. Up ahead, Jon saw a wagon at the side of the road, possibly in trouble.

"Don't stop, Maggie darlin'. Go by them."

"We can't do that, Jonny. They may need our help."

"Remember what happened last time? The Hawthornes?"

"Yes, Jonny, but stopping was the right thing to do. Look what it got us, Susan and Ally."

"Ah, you're right. We better stop."

"Hello there. Are you in trouble?"

"Naw, just a lame horse is all. I got a man a-gettin' one from one-a these farms," said a white-haired man.

The open wagon had three benches across the bed, and there were five men standing around it with their rifles.

"Are ya migratin', mister?" asked their speaker.

"Yes. We're from North Carolina, and we're hoping to find some good bottomland in Arkansas to farm."

"Well, good luck wit that. We're a-headed fer Texas. We're a-gonna fight wit Huston."

"What's that all about?"

"Ain't ya heard? Texas got a war on 'gainst Mexico, an' they're a-fightin' fer independence."

"Yeah," said another, "we're gonna fight alongside Crockett."

"Ya-all heard o' Davy Crockett, ain'tcha?" said a third man.

"Yes . . . oh yes, I heard of him," said Jon.

"Man . . . look at that big nigger," said a tall, thin man.

"Yep, but ya look at that big horse. How much ya take fer that white horse?" asked White Hair.

"Sorry, he's my breeding stock. Not for sale."

"You jest name yer poison, an' we'll pay it."

"Hey!" said the tall man, "Dat nigga's got a gun."

"Well, good luck wit dat too. Ya sure got a lot o' nice horses there. Would ya like ta sell one?" asked Whitey.

"I have a couple saddle horses I'll sell you."

"Hmm," said Whitey, "I wonder if'n they'd could pull a wagon."

"Sure they can. My par . . . slave can harness them up so they can pull together like a seasoned team."

"Ya let yer niggas carry guns?" asked the tall man.

"Sure do," answered Jon. "An' I got a couple more in dat covered wagon wit guns, an' they be's good shots."

Jon figured these men might try to rob and shoot his gang. "Are ya there, Ally an' Ella?"

"I be's here, Massa Jon," said Ella, poking the barrel of a rifle out the front of the covered wagon.

"I's here too, Massa Jon," said Ally, riding Abby around from behind the covered wagon, rifle in hand.

"We ain't aimin' ta do ya harm," said the white-haired man. "We jest need a horse."

"That's good, and like I say, I got two ta sell ya."

"Will ya trade one for my Guss?"

"Now, what would I do wit a lame horse?" asked Jon.

"Well, he just needs a rest."

"So do I, but I'm a-pushin' on ta Arkansas."

"Aright, what's yer price fer two horses?" asked Whitey.

"Well, I'll sell them fer thirty dollars apiece, two fer twenty-five dollars each."

"Hmm, how much money ya got, Red?"

"Ten bucks, Sol," said the third man, who had dark hair.

"Hokay, un y'all, Arney? How much you got?" asked Whitey.

"I gots two double Eagles, but I's needs 'em, Sol."

"Well, give me one, an' keep the other. That make thirty. I got the rest. Here ya go, sir."

"Mose! Take the saddles off of them two extra horses, and rope 'em to the front of that wagon."

"Yassa, Massa Jon, I's do."

"Good boy! Ally, you's put the saddles in dat there covered wagon."

"Yassa, Massa Jon."

Ally quickly threw the saddles into the wagon, then climbed back on Abby and resumed his guard. Mose expertly combined the single harness into a double, and hitched up the new team of horses to the odd men's buckboard.

"Where'd ya get all them horses?" asked White Hair.

"From dead men who tried to give us jesse!" answered Jon.

"Oh, well, good luck wit the farmin'."

"Thanks. Good luck with the fighting Mexicans, Sol. Move 'em out, girls!" yelled Jon to Maggie and Ella.

"That was a great job, Jonny. I was scared."

"So was I, my pretty plum. Mose, Ally, and Ella sure did a great job, pretending to be my bounders."

"Yes, well, they've had a lot of practice."

"I think I overdid the accent."

"They believed your line, Jonny. Is it time for lunch?"

"Not yet, my love. I'll let you know."

"Another wonderful lunch, ladies."

"Thank you's, Jonny. We trys hard ta please," said Ella.

"How many more miles to Memphis, Jonny?"

"I think it's about ten miles or less, my love."

The group heard the screeching again. They spotted another group of Carolina parrots in some willow trees by a swamp.

"I think they're following us, Jonny."

"Ever heard of parrot stew?"

"My husband, the bird killer!"

"Maybe they'll follow us to our new land."

"Yassa, den we's has parrots stew," said Mose.

"I hope they don't follow. I couldn't take all that screeching."

"Let's go, Jonny. Maybe it will still be light when we get up to the river."

"Okay, gang. Memphis, here we come!"

"It will never be the same, our lives," muttered Maggie.

About midafternoon, the farms became small plots with cabins more frequent. One had a dog that ran out barking and chasing the wagons. Isaak went after it and chased it back.

"Better call your dog back, Chipper."

"Here, Isaak! Here, boy!" yelled the boy, and the dog came running back.

"You got him trained pretty good, Chip."

"I think we're very close now, Jonny."

"What makes you think that, darlin'?"

"Look how close together the cabins are. Look, Jon! There's the Mississippi! Look!"

Jon climbed into the carryall, and there it was. "That's it, my love! Hooray! See those banks way over on the other side? Arkansas! Hooray!"

"I never thought we would make it this far, Jonny."

"Wow! That's one mighty river!"

"How are we going to cross it, Jonny?"

"Look, honey. There are boats out there! See them? That's how we get across."

"Well, get up, Corker! We're going on a boat ride!"

The town of Memphis was smaller than Jon had expected. The main part sat on a bluff overlooking the river, with a road and tow-drag line down to the ferry dock and a few buildings on the river. After an hour wait, it was Jon's turn. The drag gently lowered the wagons and trailers down to the dock with horses still harnessed, and the men walked the others down. There were several wagons parked in a field with horses. Jon figured they were waiting to cross.

A man in breeches approached Jon. "What can I do for you, young man?"

"How soon can you take my group across?"

"I would say tomorra morning," answered the man in breeches.

"No chance yet this evening?"

"Ya see all them wagons there? They's ahead a ya."

"Right, thank you, sir."

"They's all paid ahead. How 'bout ya all?"

"How much is it, sir?"

"Two dolla a wagon or trailer, a dolla per animal or anything that walks."

"Wow, with all my gang, that's a lot of dibbs."

"Ya kin always go north an' cross the Ohio!"

"I see what you mean."

"Or, ya kin go south ta New Orleans."

"Okay, let's see. I have two wagons . . ."

"An' two trailers, that be eight dollas."

"And I have six people, and a boy."

"An' seven makes . . . fifteen . . ."

"And nine horses. How much is . . ."

"An' a cow, an' a dog."

"I even have to pay for the dog?"

"He walks, don' he?"

"But I can carry him, so he takes no space."

"Well, I'll give ya all a break on the dog."

"Thank goodness for small favors!"

"Half dolla fer the dog. Now let me see, two plus two, minus half, plus twelve, times five plus sev—"

"Times five! What times five?"

"Hee, hee, jest a-foolin' ya, mister. It be twenty-six an' a half dollas, sir. Hee, hee."

"Well, you got a high-paying business here. I have twenty-five dollars here, and I'll pay the rest in the morning."

"Then I can't be a-givin' ya no discount."

"What discount am I getting now?" demanded Jon.

"Half dolla. Take it er leave it."

"I'll take it!" Jon still had money. "And two dollars."

"Thank ye. I'll be a-seein' ya."

"Hold it! I got a half dollar and a receipt coming."

"Ain't ya a tipper, young man?"

"Not at your rates, I'm not."

"Oritey, I'll be a-gettin' yer pass ticket an' change, an' I'll try ta get ya all on tomorra."

"Keep the change! Just give me the pass ticket!"

"Rite ya are, young man, tomorra," said breeches, walking away.

"Ya shouldn't fun me like that, mister, I have a brain illness, want to kill when I get nervous!"

"Follow me over to that field."

"We can't go across tonight, Jonny?"

"I don't want to talk about it! Follow me."

"Didn't you pay him enough?"

"I had to pay him too damn much!"

"Don't swear at me, Jonny!"

"I'm sorry, darlin'. Please just follow, and say nothing."

"I didn't want to cross in the dark anyway."

"Another wonderful supper, Nanty Ella."

"Thank you's, Sissy, fo' dem las' day un Tenansee."

"Didn't you like it, Jonny?"

"Huh? Oh yes, darlin'."

"Stop fretting, Jonny. We'll be there tomorrow."

"If we're lucky! All these other wagons are ahead of us!"

"Jonny! Settle down. It's alright."

"We's makes it orites, Jonny," said Ella.

"We's here, Jon. We's makes it ta Arkensaw," added Mose.

"I'm sorry, gang. Sure, we make to Arkansas tomorrow."

"Alright! Let's celebrate leaving Tennessee. Nunky Mose, will you play a few tunes on your harmonica?"

"Orites, Sissy, I's do."

Mose started playing, and Jon cheered up. Soon others from other wagons were coming by and joining in.

"That's what we need, some music to cheer us up," said a lady with a fur scarf around her neck. "May we join you?"

"Sure, come join us. You folks too. Here, by the fire." Soon there was a crowd, clapping and swaying to Mose's music. One man had a stringed instrument, and a duet was born.

"Your slave can really play that harmonica," said the husband of the lady with the fur scarf.

"He's so big. It looks like he swallows that thing," said the fur lady.

"Yes, that buck can do anything," answered Jon. "Ya ought to see him pick people up with one hand."

"Really!" exclaimed fur lady. "How interesting!"

"Our name is Turner, Matt, and Heddy. We're from Crosscreek, North Carolina. Ever hear of it?"

"No, sir," answered Jon. "We're from the Salem area."

"Well, we're practically neighbors! Tryin' to get some free land, huh?"

"Yes, sir, but I hear that most of the good land is taken."

"That's why we're a-goin' south, close to Louisiana. Lots of free, open land down there."

"There ain't no free land nowhere!" said another man.

"I hope you're wrong, sir," said Matt. "I'd hate ta think we came all this ways fer nothin'. Where'd you hail from?"

"I'm from Virginia. Petersburg. We were s'posed ta get free land there, but I got kicked off my land!"

"Kicked off? Fer what?"

"Fer not payin' fer it. They's said it weren't mine!"

Mose and his friend continued to play through the chatter.

"I'm Matt, an' this here's my wife, Heddy."

"Howdy," said another man, shaking Matt's hand. "I'm Jonis Balldin. I'm gonna find some lands in Injun country."

"Ya mean clear past Arkansas?"

"Ya bet yer buns!"

Maggie was visiting with another lady, and Jon caught only an occasional few words.

"For two and a half months! I feel like I fell into a water closet. Promised I would come," he heard Maggie say.

"Poor dear . . . has a job waiting . . . Little Rock."

"Where is your husband?" asked Maggie.

"Asleep in our wagon . . . very tired from . . ."

"Nanty Ella . . . tireless . . . second mother . . ."

"What? Second mother? I never heard . . . Leaving!"

"Goodbye, Missus . . . luck," said Maggie.

It seemed to Jon that he wasn't needed, and he was tired. "If you gentlemen will excuse me, I'm very tired. Mose, see to it all the chores are done before you turn in."

"Yassa, Massa Jon. Nites, Massa Jon."

"Finally got rid of them, darlin'?"

"Finally! I'm too tired to work on my diary tonight."

"Good. Come join me, my love."

"I'll try to get it caught up tomorrow."

"And squeeze like crazy . . . Hmm . . ."

"There should be plenty of time, waiting for our turn."

"You feel so soft and warm, and . . ."

"Go back to sleep. Good night, Jonny."

"Drat!"

Monday, January 4

"Morning! What a beautiful day to leave Tennessee!"

"We's has las' breakfas' ready, Jon."

"Thank you, Mose. Just remember, if anyone asks, it's Master Jon."

"Yassa, I's rememba, Jon."

"What's for breakfast, Ella?"

"Drys beef un' bean, Jonny, an' dey be cold."

"Cold? Why cold?"

"We's don' has fires in parkin' space, Jonny."

"None dem wagons has fires, Jon," added Mose.

"Okay, cold beef and beans it is. I'll go see how long the wait will be as soon as I eat."

"Good morning, sir. How are things going this morning?"

"Jest fine. Are ya plannin' ta cross today?" The man had switched from breeches to pantaloons.

"Yes. Don't you remember? I'm the one with the two wagons, extra horses . . ."

"And a cow and dog! Yeah, I remember," said pantaloons.

"I'm sorry I yelled at you last evening."

"No harm. I think I kin gitcha 'cross today."

"Today? How about this morning?"

The man ignored Jon. The ferry was about four hundred yards out on the river, and was getting closer. "Pantaloons" and two helpers with pulling horses were out on the L-shaped dock, waiting for the ferry. What a ship! Jon had never seen such a beautiful thing. It was big, with big water wheels on each side, but they had paddles on the wheels instead of the buckets that Jon had seen before at a grist mill. The ferry had a flat top that was mostly empty, but in the middle was a cabin with a big round chimney, and it was smoking! There was a loud toot of a horn, and those big wheels stopped and suddenly started again, turning in the opposite direction. This slowed the vessel to a crawl as it banged softly into the dock. A man on board threw ropes from the front, and then from the back of the ship, to the two men with the horses on the long leg of the L-shaped dock. The horses pulled the ferry sideways against that dock, and then the men secured the ropes to posts. A wooden ramp was then lowered from the ferry to the main part of the dock, and the ship was ready to unload and load wagons and people waiting to cross the Mississippi. There were only two wagons to unload, and Jon noticed that "pantaloons" had walked aboard the ferry and seemed to be collecting money from the owners of the wagons, before they started down the ramp.

"That cussed old imp is charging those people twice!"

"No, he's not," said a man who was suddenly standing next to Jon. "The fee is only collected on this side."

"Oh. How much did this cost you, sir?"

"Nine dollars so far, for my wife and I, one wagon, four horses, and a servant."

"What do you mean, 'so far'?"

"Well, I'm going to give him another ten dollars so I can get across today."

"Ten dollars?" asked an astonished former overseer.

"Yes, and I'll be damned glad to pay, so I can get to Arkansas today. I've been waiting for two days now!"

"Why that cheap bastard! I have a notion to . . ."

"Then you may never get across, my friend."

"Yeah, I see what you mean. Thanks, my name is Jon Hamilton. I guess I'd better be damned glad too."

"Glad to know you, Jon. I'm Fred Wilson. My wife, Janet, and I are hoping to find some good bottomland on the Arkansas or White River."

"So was I, but I think we're too late."

"I've heard that too, but I'm not turning back now."

"Well, I've got a wife and two . . . I mean four part . . . slaves, and a boy along with me. Oh, and about ten horses, a cow, and a dog! Plus, two wagons and two trailers!"

"Wow! You're going to need lots of land! You wouldn't care to have three more tag along, would you?"

"Not a bit, Fred. Welcome aboard!"

"Thanks, Jon. I'm in the . . . one, two, three, fourth wagon to the right. Where are your wagons?"

"The last two on the left."

"Oh, didn't you have a party last night?"

"Yeah, that was us. We were celebrating leaving Tennessee."

"Don't blame you, but you haven't left it yet, Jon. I'm going to tell Jan that we have some traveling partners."

"Okay. See you later, Fred."

The wagons and people were now boarding the ferry. Jon noticed that each person, driving or walking aboard, were handing "pantaloons" another tip before climbing the ramp. Jon saw Fred hand "pantaloons" the ten dollars and shake hands.

"I guess I'd better give that bastard an Eagle too."

"Here's something to get us across today."

"Thank ye, sir. I'll be a-gettin' ya on the next ferry."

"How long will that be?"

"'Round noonish. You's in the back row?"

"Yeah, the last two wagons on the left."

"Dat's dandy! I'll be comin' ta get ya when it's time."

"Thanks. We'll be traveling with the Wilsons."

"Which one is that?"

"The fourth wagon on the right. He just gave you ten dollars."

"Oh yeah! I'll be a-gettin' ya both."

Jon headed back to the wagon rows. He noticed that his two wagons were the only two left in that row, and Fred's wagon along with three others were all that was left of his row. Jon looked back. There was still a line of wagons, but the ship was about three-quarters full, and steaming.

"Fantastic!" Jon said to himself. He was thinking that he would introduce Maggie to the Wilsons. "Maggie, darlin', come with me. I want you to meet the Wilsons. They want to travel with us."

"Jonny, we're almost there now!"

"I know, honey, but they . . . er, he . . . seems real nice, and they are looking for the same thing as us."

"Alright, Jonny. We'll be right back, Nanty Ella!"

"And we leave around noon, Mose."

"Orites, Jon. We's be ready."

"Noon, huh? How did you manage that?" asked Maggie.

"I had to give that bastard more money."

"Don't swear, Jonny. Did the Wilsons pay more too?"

"Yes. They've been sitting here for two days."

"So at least we did better than they did."

"Don't know about that, my love. So far this has cost us thirty-six dollars, and there's still a boarding fee!"

"How much is that, Jonny?"

"I'm not sure, but I saw everyone paying as they boarded."

Toot, toot! The ferry's whistle was blowing. Jon and Maggie hurried past the Wilson wagon to watch. There were still two wagons in line that wouldn't make this trip. The flat top of the ferry was full of wagons and horses. The ramp was pulled back onto the ship along with the ropes. The two men had a pole with a flat attachment at one end, reminding Jon of the water poles to drain rain puddles. There was a type of harness on the other end, used by the horses, to push the ship away from the dock. The wheels began turning, as a black cloud escaped from the chimney of the ferry. It then began its journey west, wheels churning and people waving.

"Wow, what a sight, Jonny."

"Yes, my pretty plum. Be sure to put this sight down in your diary. Let's visit the Wilsons."

"Hello there, Mister and Missus Wilson. I want you to meet my wife, Magg . . . ah, Margaret."

"Happy to meet you, Margaret. I'm Fred Wilson, and this is my wife, Janet. This is our servant, Josh."

"Margaret, please come in. It's been so long since I've had the chance to visit," said Jan Wilson.

"Looks like we're next, Fred."

"Danged well better be! I've waited long enough!"

"Where are you from, Fred?"

"Virginia, just southeast of Charlottesville."

"Is that part of the Great Valley?" asked Jon.

"Southern part. It was just getting too crowded for me, and the soil was being overused. So, we headed west."

"Down the Great Valley road, right?"

"Uh-huh! We were close to the road, just had to navigate Rockfish Gap, about five hundred miles from here."

"How long have you been traveling?"

"Less than two months, I think. We left the second week of November. Late start, hey?"

"Yeah. You should have left in July! Ever hear that before?"

"No, but I probably should have," said Fred.

"We've been ten and a half weeks from North Carolina. My wife never ceases to remind me of that."

"Had trouble on the way, huh?"

"Lots of trouble! I'm happy to be leaving Tennessee."

"We got robbed by Waymen, about sixty miles this side of Knoxville. Lucky there were other wagons close, or they would have killed us for sure," said Fred.

After a pause, Jon said, "I can't even see the ferry now. That's a long way to the other side. I could see Arkansas from up that hill."

"Yeah, I guess I should get my wagon hitched up."

"My servants are doing that for me," said Jon.

"Yes, Josh here is a good helper for me too."

"Maggie! Let's head back to our wagons."

"Just a minute, Jonny."

"That's her standard answer," Jon said to Fred. To Maggie, he said, "We've got to get ready for the ferry, darlin'."

"I want to write a short letter home. One can be mailed from here, Okay?"

"Sure, honey, but make it a short one."

"I'm glad you invited them to ride with us, Jonny. I really like Jan."

"Good. I don't know where we'll end up, but neither do they! Maybe we'll all be close."

"That would be nice. I'm hungry, Jonny, maybe Nanty Ella will have something to eat."

"Yes," answered Jon, searching the sky. "It must be eleven o'clock by now. Let's get lunch over with."

"Let's have an early lunch, Nanty Ella, so we won't have to worry about that for a few hours."

"Sho 'nuff, Sissy. Mo' cold dodgers," said Ella.

The parking lot was filling again. More suckers, thought Jon, relaxing with his group. He hoped that bunco artist would come to get them ahead of all those new wagons.

"Stop worrying, Jonny. We'll hear the ferry whistle."

"I hope so. That robber said he would come to get us, but I don't believe him. He's busy down there when the ship docks."

"I'll bet the people we met last night are already on their way to Little Rock. Ha, Mister and Missus . . . what was their last name?"

"Turner, Matt, and Heddy," Jon laughed.

"What's so funny, Jonny?"

"Sounds like Nat Turner!" said Jon. "Remember him?"

"Yes. He killed over fifty people."

"He and his other slaves did." Jon paused. "And Heddy was no head turner," he added, laughing.

"She thought she was. Where were they headed, Jonny?"

"Close to Looosianny! More power to them."

Maggie started laughing. "Ha, that was funny, Jonny! Head turner!" she said, still giggling.

"Did you get that letter written, darlin'?"

"Yes."

Toot, toot! The blast came from the ferry. Jon sprang to his feet. So did several other people waiting by their wagons.

"Come on, ladies. Let's get in line."

"Alright, Jonny. Ready, Nanty Ella?"

"I's be ready, Sissy. Get up, Reds an' Jake! Get up, Slogs an' Smuts!"

The two wagons moved forward, and were quickly behind some late wagons anxious to be near the front.

"Bring them around, darlin'," yelled Jon. Maggie urged Corker and Conqueror around some wagons.

"Hey, woman! Wha' the hell ya think yer doin'?"

"We're going to the head of the line! We were here first."

"Like hell ye are!" the man returned, as he grabbed a whip.

"I wouldn't do that, mister," said Jon, holding a bead with his Hawken on the man. "We've been here since yesterday, and by damn we're taking the lead!"

"I-i-if it means that much ta ya, go right ahead."

"Thanks. We'll do just that," said Jon.

Down the little incline to the dock, Jon, Ally, and Mose kept their rifles ready as they passed the others. Jon waved his arm to Fred and Janet Wilson to follow his wagons, and then stopped beside the two wagons left behind the last trip.

"Hello there. You in a hurry?" said the man driving the first wagon.

"You're darn right I am! We're behind you two," said Jon.

"Alright, mister, thanks. We got here yesterday."

"So did we. Late yesterday."

"Well, it looks like we'll finally get crossed."

"I hope so! Arkansas, here we come!"

There was only one wagon and a couple walkers unloading. "Pantaloons" saw Jon and came over. "I were jest about ta come get ya, mister. I'm a-gonna put ya on, the very first," he lied.

"Good. Here's a little token of appreciation." Jon flipped another Eagle at him. "That's for three wagons and all."

"I be thankin' ye, sir. Go aboard!"

"Will you mail this letter for us, sir?"

"Ya betcha, I will."

"Whoopee! Let's go to Arkansas, gang!" exclaimed Jon.

Jon jumped on the carryall to help Maggie get up the ramp. "Get, Corker. Pull her, boy."

"Looks deep, Jonny."

"I imagine it is, my love. Looks like we're going upriver."

"I hope we don't sink."

"Sink? What made you think of that?"

"It has happened, Jonny. Giant earthquakes hit Arkansas and Missouri, and a lot of boats sank."

"Bet that shook 'em up! When was that?"

"Clear back in eighteen-eleven and eighteen-twelve. I read about it."

"That was before we were born! No wonder I don't remember! And people drowned?"

"Yes. Some said this river ran backward."

"I don't believe that."

"It's true, Jonny. This river made a giant whirlpool, boats sank, and people drowned."

"Ya, but this river couldn't have run backward."

"You big lummox! In a whirlpool, half the river is running backward." This was met with a pause.

"Look, darlin', we're in Arkansas!"

"Jonny! We're still crossing the Mississippi."

"But look. We're over halfway. Those big bluffs, see them? We're almost there! I think I see the dock."

"Don't exaggerate, Jonny. Be patient."

"I *can* see the dock," said Fred, close by, with Janet.

"When we get back on the road, let's stop for a few minutes and celebrate. Okay, Fred? Janet?"

"Sounds good, Jon. We'll follow you."

The bluffs and dock were approaching fast, and it looked like the ferry might crash into it. Jon could now see the men and horses waiting on the dock. *Slam! Screech!* The giant wheels had stopped and reversed, and the force nearly sent Jon and Maggie falling forward.

"Let's get crackin', we're first off the ship."

"We're ready, Jon," was the general response as the gang climbed on wagons and horses. There was another jolt forward, as the ferry bumped into the dock.

The ramp came down, and Jon was just above the dock.

"Jonny, will you drive? I'm scared."

"Sure, darlin', scoot over." Jon jumped aboard his wagon. "Get, Corker!"

After the big dray had eased the carryall down the ramp, Corker and Conqueror, the lead team, surged off the dock and straight up the hill to the level ground on top.

Jon jumped down and watched, as Ella and the covered wagon slowly climbed the hill, the Wilsons following. Mose was helping the horses pull, still up on Friend, his horse. The ferry below was about half empty, as a steady stream of wagons eased up the hill. Ella and Mose were now on top, stopped next to Maggie, and then Fred and Janet pulled their wagon over the top. Suddenly, Jon saw a wagon in line, about a quarter of the way up, in trouble.

"Mose! Unhitch Corker and bring him and rope."

"Yassa, Massa Jon."

Jon raced down the hill, as Chipper, Ally, and dog Isaak reached the wagons. Others were trying to hold the wagon from rolling back down into the other teams.

"I have help coming!" yelled Jon, pushing the wagon from the rear. He saw Mose, on Corker, scooting down to them. "Hold on, men. Help is here."

Mose leaped down with the rope, and harnessed Corker to the lead, in front of the stricken horses. "Gets, Corkas. Go's, big boy," said Mose. Corker, straining at the start, dug in and pulled that wagon over the top, four horses and all!

"I can't thank ye enough!" said the owner.

Jon then saw that it was the same man who was about to use the whip on Maggie. Mose unhitched Corker.

"You better tame your temper, mister."

"Yessir, I'm sorry 'bout me temper, sir."

"I hope so. Now get moving! I don't want to see you again."

"Yessir! Good luck finding land," he said, as he drove off.

Jon dug out a bottle of Isaak's corn whiskey, as Ella found mugs for everyone, including Ally. The women even wanted a drink.

"Here's to a new beginning and a great future."

"Here, here," said Fred, and mugs were emptied.

"Which way do you want to go, Jonny?"

"Well, the only road goes west, toward Little Rock. I guess we'll take it for a ways, like everyone else."

One more look at the mighty Mississippi, and Jon's group fell into the line of wagons headed west.

"Not very pretty, Jonny."

"No, darlin', let's hope the land we get looks better than this."

"Are we looking for land in east Arkansas? West? South?"

"I just don't know yet, my love."

"Are we ever prepared!"

"My first goal is river bottomland."

"But we think that is already taken. So what is your second goal, Jonny?"

"Well, I want to get some wet, marshy land."

"Are you barmy? What would we do with that?"

"Rice, my love, rice."

"Rice? I thought rice needed wet, humid weather, and hot."

"It does, my love. I want to try it here, if I can find the right soil. I don't think cotton would do well, but tobacco, corn, and wheat should do well."

"Then most of the middle part of the state is taken. The west, as well, and you don't seem to want to go south . . ."

"Maybe we should go south, darlin'."

"And the north is mostly mountains, right Jonny?"

"Yeah. That leaves the south. The south, right where the Turners were headed."

"It's a big state, Jonny. Chances are we wouldn't even be within a hundred miles of the Turners."

"With our luck? We'll probably end up buying land from them."

"Well, if we're going to try the south, where do we turn, Jonny?"

"Not yet, my love. Let's wait a day or two."

"Why, Jonny?"

"Well, we may have to go to Little Rock to get assigned our land anyway, and the Turners probably turned south right away. We'll be sure to miss them, going south from there."

"Alright, honey, but I don't want to backtrack."

"I know, darlin'. Let's try passing a couple of these slowpokes ahead of us. I'll go tell the others."

"Alright, Jonny, if you think we can," said Maggie, as Jon let her pass by him.

"Ella! I'm going to try passing a couple wagons. Can you handle that?"

"Sho 'nuff, Jonny. I's be redy."

"Good. I'll tell the Wilsons." Jon moved off in that direction. "Fred! We're going to pass a couple slow wagons."

"Go right ahead, Jon. We can keep up."

"Alright!" Jon raced forward, told Mose, and then went ahead a ways to check the road. He passed by three wagons.

"Hey, mister," said the driver of the slow wagon in front. "Where are you goin' in such a hurry?"

"I'm looking for a spot to pass."

"Am I a-holdin' up the parade?"

"You're doing fine, sir. We're in a hurry, is all."

"Looks like ta me, we're all a-headed toward Lil Rock."

"Yep!" yelled Jon. "But then which way?"

"North, or further west, I reckon."

"Well, that's not for me. I hear all that land is taken. I think we're going south from Little Rock."

"In that case, I'll pull ova as far as I can, so's you can gets by. An' I may be a followin' ye south."

"Thanks, sir, and good luck to you," said Jon.

Jon saw a long, open space ahead, and raced Prancer back to his wagons to get them ready.

"Hey you! Hey!" yelled the driver just ahead of Maggie.

"Yes, sir!" shouted Jon. "What can I do for you?"

"What's goin' on?"

"Nothing much, sir. If you will try to keep to the right as much as you can, my wagons will try to pass."

"Not by a damn site! Who da hell ya think ya are, tryin' to beat us ta the better land?"

"I'm not trying to beat you out. Which way are you headed after Little Rock?"

"North, up the White River. Why ya askin'?"

"Because I'm taking my three wagons south."

"Oh, alright, I'll get over."

"Thanks, mister, and good luck."

"Okay, darlin'. See that wide spot? Pull out there, and pass three wagons before pulling back in."

"But. Jonny, I'm scared!" Maggie shouted.

"Well, scoot over. I'm coming aboard. Ally! Get my horse."

"Yassa, Massa Jon."

Jon grabbed the wagon and jumped up on it, while horses were still on the move. Just as Jon pulled Corker and Conqueror out to pass, the wagon in front did the same, almost causing a collision between Conqueror and that wagon.

"Hey! You ignorant bastard!" yelled Jon.

"Jonny! Stop swearing, or I'm getting off."

"I'm sorry, darlin', but that's what he is!"

Jon hurried his team past the other two wagons, right behind the first wagon that had cut him off. He guided the carryall back in line, and handed the reins back to Maggie. Ella made the pass next, and pulled her wagon and trailer back in line. The wide area was closing fast, and the Wilsons' wagon was running out of room. Mose to the rescue! He rode up to the slow wagon and grabbed the bridle of that wagon's lead, and slowed the lead wagon so that the Wilsons could get past them and back in the line.

"Let go my horse, ya black-ass buck!"

"I's sorry, sir. I's helps Massa's wagon," answered Mose.

"Well, ya got yer wagons by. Now get away."

"Yassa," said Mose, who rode Friend ahead, back to his group, grinning.

Now the three wagons and horses were clear of the slower wagons, and they made good time, until darkness caught them.

Diary of Margaret Hamilton

Monday, January 4, 1836

. . . And the dock worker took the letter to mail to you. I hope you receive it. Jonny was furious over the charges and tips he had to pay to get on board the ferry, about fifty dollars,

he said . . . Such a majestic river, ships, and boats all around. It took close to an hour to cross it, ta the "soils of Arkansas." Had to go upstream on the lovely ferry, so the strong current wouldn't sweep us further downriver . . . And the Wilsons are now traveling with us. They are such a lovely couple, I hope they will settle close to us. They're from the Shenandoah Valley . . . Thinks the best area to look is in the southern part of the territory, close to Louisiana . . . a lot of people settling here. The ferry was full, and the road to Little Rock is full. We are camping close to two wagons right now . . . Just about lost the Wilsons, trying to pass some wagons. They wouldn't have made it if Nunky Mose hadn't stopped the wagon the Wilsons were trying to pass, . . . about nine or ten miles today . . . Love and hugs . . . Hope to see you soon.

Margaret Rose

Tuesday, January 5

"Jon? Jon!" called Mose.

"Huh? What is it, Mose?"

"Dem wagons go by un dark."

"What wagons?"

"Dem wagons we's pass."

"Looks like we'll have to pass them again, Jonny," said Maggie.

"We'll be right out, Mose."

The Hamilton couple dressed quickly and were warming up at the fire, when another wagon came passing by.

"Hey, ya black-ass buck," said the passing driver. "Ya better get yer black ass a-movin' if'in ya wants ta beat us ta Lil Rock!" The wagon went on ahead.

"That was the wagon you held back so we could pass," said Fred Wilson, having some coffee by the fire.

"It's alright, Mose," said Jon, when Mose seemed to want to climb aboard Friend and go after that wagon. "We'll catch back up to them before we reach Little Rock."

"I don' wants un hurts 'em, Jon . . . Massa Jon, bu' I's wans un scares 'em," said Mose.

"You'll get that chance. Morning, everyone."

"Hey, Jan, have you had breakfast yet?" asked Maggie.

"Not yet. We were waiting for you," answered Janet Wilson. "It sure smells good, though. We wasn't going to wait long."

"Good. Let's eat!"

"Sure nice of you folks to allow us to travel with you and share your food," said Fred.

"Our pleasure. Where's your servant?"

"Josh? He's getting the horses fed and watered."

"I'll bet Mose has already done that," said Jon. He turned toward Mose. "Mose, did you feed the Wilsons' horses too, this morning?"

"Yassa, Massa Jon. We's do."

"Then they're being fed twice. Josh! Stop feeding!"

"Tell him to come have breakfast, Fred."

"We were wondering if it would be alright," said Janet. "I see you feed your servants the same time you eat."

Jon and Maggie looked at each other and smiled.

"You might as well know, honey," said Maggie. "These are our friends and partners, no longer boun . . . slaves."

"Josh!" Fred yelled. "Come have breakfast with us!"

"Until we get settled, they are pretending to be our slaves, but to Maggie and me, they are free blacks," said Jon.

"We should do that too, Fred," said Janet, after a pause.

"Maybe, hon, but let's wait until we get settled."

Josh sheepishly appeared by the fire, and Ella filled a plate of oatmeal for him.

"This is Josh, everybody," said Fred.

"And just so you know, this is my partner Mose, his wife Ella, her son Chipper, and Allston, or Ally for short, and Susan."

"I's glad to's meets you's," said Mose.

After a short pause, Jon said, "Okay, gang, let's finish up here and get on the road."

"Everyone voted Jonny as the leader or captain," said Maggie.

"That's alright with us, honey," said Janet.

"Good, maybe we can catch up to those wagons that passed by earlier, so Mose can throw a scare into them."

"He scares me, even when he sleeps," said Fred.

"I've got some news for you. He never sleeps!"

The road to Little Rock was fairly new, so it was in fair shape and Jon's group made good time. Soon they were in swampy areas and crossed several little streams.

"Is this the kind of land you want, Jonny?"

"Yes, something like it, but not on a main road, and we would want some good farmland with it."

"We would need trees too, Jonny, so we could build a home on stilts!"

"Yeah, well, it's about time for lunch. I'll find a spot."

"That Ella is a good cook, Jon. You're lucky," said Fred.

"She sure is, but so are Suzy and my wife."

"Well, your luck runs in threes. I'm glad we met."

"What are you trying to say, Fred?" asked Janet. "That I can't cook?" Janet and Maggie had been gabbing.

"No, honey, you've done well," answered Fred.

"Well, we now have four cooks! Let's see how well they travel."

"How many miles this morning, Jonny?" asked Maggie, on the road.

"A good ten, my love."

An hour into the afternoon run, they spotted wagons ahead.

"There they are, Mose, must be a couple miles ahead."

"Yassa. We's catches dem todays."

"Maybe, Mose. But I don't want to race the horses."

"I know's, Jon. Don' race dem horses."

Late afternoon, and the terrain was covered with a type of pine. The group was now close behind the mouthy driver's wagon.

"Okay, Mose, you want to give him a scare?"

Jon followed behind Mose, as he rode up beside the wagon and driver. Mose then grabbed the halter of the lead horse again, and guided that team to the side of the road.

"You again!" Jon heard the driver say. "I'll fix your black ass!" The man reached for a whip.

"I wouldn't do that!" yelled Jon, now beside the wagon, riding Prancer. "You make him mad, and he'll tear you and your wagon apart." The man saw Jon's Hawken and put down the whip.

"Whatcha want wit me?" The man asked, his wagon stopped.

"I think my man wants to talk to you," answered Jon.

"Takes down yer jeans."

"Is dat boy gone nuts?" the man asked Jon.

"Nope. He means business," answered Jon. "You better do it."

Jon's wagons started by, and Jon waved them on. The man was dropping his jeans, as Maggie drove past, and Jon heard her laughing. He had them dropped when Ella stopped her wagon.

"What you's do, Daddy?"

"Keep going, Ella. We'll catch up." Ella drove her teams forward, and the Wilsons went by, cheering.

"Drops dem unner pans," ordered Mose.

"Ain't ya got no control ova yer buck?" asked the man.

"See how big he is?" asked Jon. "I've got no control over him."

The man dropped his nether garments. He now had no togs on.

"Hans up, un turns . . . rights now."

The man turned away, arms in the air. Mose climbed into the wagon and grabbed a handful of gun powder from his pouch and rubbed it on the man's bare butt, then jumped down.

"Now you's has black ass toos!" said Mose.

Jon was laughing. "Haha, that was good, Mose!" he said as they rode west.

"Maybe's I's use flints an' sets dem ass a-fire."

"Ya did fine, Mose," Jon said between guffaws. "We won't see him again."

"Wha you's do an dem man, Daddy?" asked Ella of Mose, as Jon rode past the covered wagon to the carryall.

"What happened, Jonny?"

"Mose rubbed gun powder on his kazoo, and gave that lummox a black ass! Haha!" Jon was laughing again.

"That's funny! Nunky Mose should have lit it. Ha!"

It was getting dusk when the group noticed a few cabins along the road.

"I think we're about to find a town, Jonny."

"I don't know, darlin'. Let's go a little further."

"Look, Jonny, it is a town."

"Righto! And a good-sized river with a bridge over it!"

"I've never drove a wagon over a bridge, Jonny."

"I'll go ahead and check it out, my love." Jon rode Prancer over the bridge and back. "It looks sturdy, darlin'. Bring them across."

It was a small town, with a few log homes and businesses.

"Do we need any supplies, my love?"

"Ask Nanty Ella. Looks like they're closed anyway."

"That place isn't closed," said Jon, pointing at a store with a loaded wagon outside.

"That looks like one of the wagons on our ship, Jonny."

"Well, pull up, and we'll check it out."

A sign on the door read *Land Office.* Jon went in. The owner of the wagon was just finishing, and about to leave.

"Just follow the river, then southwest about sixty miles," the manager said, "and they will find you a good parcel. It's probably a hundred or so miles to the post. Look for the land office."

"Thank you much. Be a-seein' ya," said the wagon owner, as he left. Jon didn't recognize him.

"What kin I do fer ya all?" asked the manager.

"I guess I'm after the same thing as a lot of others."

"Yeah, rich bottomland, on a river, with three or four months of steamy, hot weather, right?"

"That pretty much describes it," said Jon.

"You all kin find that by catching a boat ta Florida!"

"What do you have in Arkansas?"

"Hills or swamps is about all that are left."

"Got any mixes of swamp and farmland?"

"Hmm . . . how much do ya need?"

"As much as I can get!"

"How many white adults ya got?"

"Four white adults and four free blacks."

"Free blacks? They still don't count. And I would keep that a secret, if' in I were you all."

"Thanks. We are. What's the name of this town, and river?"

"When we become a state, we hope to be the first new town. The talk is Madison fer a name, afta the president. And this here river is the St. Francis. Goes up into Missouri, so some want to call it Saint Francisville."

"Does it run into the Mississippi?" asked Jon.

"Sure does. Say, there's some farmland and swamps on this here river, past the markin' tree."

"What's marking tree?" asked Jon.

"Well, it's a where the river bends, an' where the steamboats cain't go no farther, 'bout thirty or more miles upriver."

"And there's free land past this marking tree?"

"There's land, not exactly free. It's about thirty-two dolla fer hundred sixty acres, hundred twenty-eight a section."

"Where abouts is the free land?"

"There ain't no free land, but ya better buy now, 'cause when we comes-a state, it'll be a dolla an acre."

"No free land?" asked Jon. "I came all the way from North Carolina, because I saw an advertisement saying free land."

"I think I know what ad yer talkin' 'bout, an' it don't say free, mister."

"I have it here with me. Here, take a look," said Jon.

"I seen this here ad a dozen times, mister, an' it don't say free nowheres."

Jon studied the ad from the Salem paper for the first time, and the land office man was right. It didn't say *free*. It used words like *for the taking* and *open to white men or women*, but it didn't say *free*. Jon immediately got mad. He could feel his face become hot, and he was shaking.

"I'm sorry ya misread that ad, sir, but bein's yer here now, might as well get ya some land."

"Give me a few minutes, while I talk to my gang. I'll be right back."

"Sure, mister. Don't take too long, or I'll be a-seein' ya tomorra mornin'."

Jon stormed out of the office and up to the carryall.

"Jonny, what is it?" asked Maggie. Jon was quiet. "Tell me, Jonny, what happened?"

"Must be something bad happened," said Fred.

"I'm sorry, darlin'. I made a big mistake."

"What mistake? What's wrong?" asked Fred.

"There never was any free land." There was a pause.

"I never thought there was," said Fred.

After a moment, Maggie added, "Jonny, it's alright. I suspected it by what other people have said when you mentioned it. We'll be alright, Jonny."

"But I won't be able to buy the land I want."

"Jonny, it's alright! We have money."

"Where? How much?"

"I've got that porcelain Pasha horse, full of double Eagles. And remember, I told you Daddy gave me money? And you still have some money, and that big gold piece."

"An' I's has gold piece," added Mose.

"And Jan and I have money, if you're kind enough to allow us to be neighbors and partners," said Fred.

"Really? You want to be partners with us?"

"Yes, we do," answered Janet. "You are our best friends."

"Okay, thanks. Let's count our pile together, partners!"

"There are over two dozen double Eagles in my Pasha, and Daddy gave me over one hundred dollars," said Maggie.

"Don' forgot un gold rock, Jon," said Mose.

"I have no idea how much gold is worth."

"It's worth a lot, Jon," said Fred.

"Well, I've got a big stone of gold, and I still have thirty-seven dollars of overseer money."

"And Jan and I have a hundred and fifty-two dollars to add to the collection pot," said Fred.

"Wow! Let's see. What's twenty times twenty . . . four, darlin'?"

"That's four hundred eighty, Jonny, and there is more than twenty-four in my Pasha."

"What's a Pasha, honey?" asked Janet.

"It's a porcelain horse. It's just like the real Pasha I had. He died on the trail."

"Oh, I'm sorry, honey," said Janet Wilson.

"Okay, that's five hundred, plus the hundred your daddy gave you, plus thirty-seven is . . ."

"Six hundred thirty-seven dollars, Jonny."

"Yeah, and gold, and a hundred fifty-two is . . ."

"Seven hundred eighty-nine, so we have about eight hundred . . . and we don't need all those horses, do we, Jonny?"

"We'll need them to get to our promised land, my love."

"An' we's has gold toos, Jon," said Mose.

"Righto! Let's go back inside."

"How much did you say land costs, sir?"

"Thirty-two dolla fer hundred sixty acres."

"That's about one dollar for five acres," said Maggie.

"That's fer the betta land. The swamps would be cheapa."

"Swamps? Are you buying some swamps, Jon?" asked Fred.

"Yes. For rice crops, Fred."

"Rice? Hmm . . . that's interesting."

"You will keep quiet about that, right?"

"Nary a peep outta me," said the land office man.

"Good, then, sir, we want to buy about six sections!"

"Not from me. I'm a-here ta direct ya where ta go."

"Well, most of the newcomers are going west, right?"

"The west is mostly taken, sir. I'm a-sendin' 'em south."

"And you have land to the north?"

"Yep, but there are lotsa swamp land, mostly from the big quakes of 'leven and twelve. There's still some land along the Cache River, but it's a bad, muddy river. And the Black River land is bad, so yer best bet be the St. Francis."

"Okay, who do we pay?"

"Ya hafta go ta Batesville on the White River, 'bout seventy-five miles nor'west a-here."

"Haveta?"

"Yep, either south ta the post, west ta Lil Rock, or north ta Batesville ta pays yer money, an' assigns yer land."

"Damn! Well, how do we get there?"

"Ya head straight nor'west, ova swampland an' swampy rivas, till ya hit the White. Then ya follow up the White till ya see the Black Riva empty inta it, then it's 'bout twenty more mile."

"Up the White River?"

"Yep, and you'll pass ova the Cache, so's ya can see it too."

"Thanks, sir. We'll be seeing you."

"Yep! Good luck! Ha, six sections . . . nice! Ha! Swamp! Ha! He'll be a-findin' lots a that."

"That looks like the wagon at the land office," said Jon.

"Yes, it is. It's pretty dark, Jonny. Maybe we can camp by him."

"Hello, sir, mind if we camp next to you?" Jonny asked the older man.

"Nary a bit. Park yer rigs an' join me," said the man.

The three wagons parked, and the colored men went to work unhitching the horses and getting them fed and watered, and raising tents.

"Welcome," said the wise-looking man. "My name is Faulkner, Colonel Faulkner."

"Glad to meet you, Mister Faulkner. I'm Jon Hamilton, and this is my wife, Margaret, and this is Fred and Janet Wilson."

"Well, where ya all from, and where ya headed?"

"We're from Virginia and North Carolina, and we're going north to Batesville to purchase land."

"Not very good land up thata way. I'm goin' south, ta look over some land below the post."

"Post?" asked Fred.

"Arkansas Post, on the Arkansas. That and Fort Smith, by the Indian Territory, were the only towns in this territory when I first come here."

"No Little Rock?" asked Janet.

"Naw, Little Rock is a new town. I don't know why they're gonna make it the capitol, instead of the post."

"Sounds like you know this country well," said Maggie.

"Yep, I'm known as the Arkansas traveler."

"Well, if we don't find anything up north, we may see you again down south, Colonel."

Ella and Susan showed up with food to be cooked on the colonel's campfire.

"This is Ella and Suzy, two of my partners."

"Partners? And you're from Virginia?"

"And Carolina. Yes, they are talented. You'll see."

"I think I see already. That food looks good."

"It is good, and her husband, Mose, is a genius."

"So you made them partners. I would keep that quiet."

"Thanks. We are. Let's eat!"

"Your ah, partner, Ella? Is a genius! This is the best meal I've had since I left New Orleans."

"Thank you's, sir. Have some mo'," said Ella.

The colonel paused. "How many partners ya got?" he asked Jon.

"Ah, the six of us, and three others . . . coming," said Jon. "That is Mose and Chipper, the boy. And Ally."

"All ex-slaves? Hmm . . . There's a settlement of free blacks on the White River, about fifty miles south of Batesville, and one on this river, near the border, I hear tell. They're slaves."

"On this river, huh?"

"Yep, a little settlement called Lou's Landing."

"What do they do up there?"

"Farm, I hear. Say, there may be some good land there."

"That sounds good. Thanks, Colonel."

"You bet. Good luck searchin'. If ya don't find anything up there, come on down near the Louisiana border. Lots of land down there. I'll help ya find some."

"Thanks, Colonel. We may do just that."

"And it would be close to the big market, New Orleans."

"Thanks again. Guess we'll turn in. We leave early."

"Maybe we'll meet again. Good luck."

"Maybe we'll see you in the morning," said Fred.

"I don't think so. I'm long gone by first light."

"Well, Mose and Ella will see you. They never sleep."

"Good night." The rest of the group said their good nights as well.

Wednesday, January 6

"With a breakfast like that, what could be bothering you?"

"Nothing much, darlin'. I was just thinking, what if we don't buy land up this river, or what if the good land is already sold, like most of all the other good land?"

"Then we've wasted a trip, like we've done before!"

"Right, my love. So why don't we go straight up the river first and see the land, then if we like it, go buy it in Batesville?"

"That's a grand idea, Jon," said Fred. "Then if we don't like the property, we don't need to go to Batesville."

"An' I's doun buy's land, rights, Jon?" asked Mose.

"Right, Mose. Wish you could."

"So's we's stays on dem land, an' you's goes to Batesville, Jon."

"Nunky Mose has a good idea, Jonny. Then maybe nobody else will want it while we are buying it," said Maggie.

"That's supposin' we end up wanting it."

"It is that, Jon," answered Fred, "but we must remember we're short of options. Good land is hard to find."

"Okay, gang, we head upriver. Let's get crackin'."

"We's gets crackin'," said Mose.

The three wagons headed north along the St. Francis River, and soon were in pretty good-looking land, large portions, taken by settlers. Some had cabins; others had lean-tos and dugouts on their west side, the river on the right. They saw few trees, mostly open land, with a few swamps. This seemed to be what Jon was after.

"This looks a lot like Bethania land, Jonny."

"It doesn't have the rolling hills, my love."

"True. Are these the kind of swamps you want, Jonny?"

"Yes, but a lot bigger so I can make bogs like your brother has at Chic Wood."

"What makes you think you can grow rice in this climate?"

"It's warm in the summer, and has some rainfall. Perfect!"

"It doesn't need the hot, dry climate?"

"No, darlin'. It grows best in flooded swamps."

"How do you know that, Jonny?"

"Your brother Allston gave me instructions."

"You have met my brother?"

"Yes, my pretty plum. I took my gang down to Chic Wood when a storm knocked out his crops."

"I remember that. And you went to South Carolina?"

"I sure did. Lost two of my gang on that trip, and was fired by your father when I got back!"

"Fired? You bunco bunny! You were there all year."

"He realized he couldn't make it without me."

Maggie laughed. "Bull pile! You're full of it, Jonny!"

"Who's swearing now? If you don't believe me, when you write another letter, ask your father."

"Alright, I will . . . Is it time for supper, Jonny?"

"Not yet, darlin'. Can you go a few miles more? I want to continue on for a ways. No tellin' what's up ahead."

They continued due north, and were soon following a small stream that emptied into the St. Francis. At last, they stopped for lunch.

"This looks like a good spot for lunch, gang."

"It's about time! Your son and I are hungry!"

"We are getting further away from the river. Maybe we should cross this stream and find the St. Francis again."

"That's up to you, Jon. We'd be cutting across people's property if we did," said Fred.

"Yeah, I noticed settlers on both sides of the creek."

"We's maybes an people's lan' now, Jon," said Mose.

"Yes, we may be, Mose, but it's a road of sorts."

"Let's stay on it a ways longer, Jon, and see where it takes us."

"Okay. I hope the good land doesn't end before we reach our goal. What was it? Lou's Landing?"

"That was it," said Fred. "It's full of slaves."

"How are you going to handle that, Jonny?"

"Don't know, my love. Maybe Lou's Landing won't be to my liking."

"I don't think it will be. You don't like having slaves."

"Maybe you don't want us. We have a slave," said Janet.

"We want you, Jan. Jonny and I like you both," said Maggie.

"Thanks, honey. We like you too."

"Maybe we'll talk you into freeing Josh one day," said Jon.

"Maybe. But right now, we travel or we nap."

"We travel, Fred. Everybody ready to go?"

After everyone was ready, Maggie asked, "How many miles did we make this morning, Jonny?"

"I'd say over fifteen, my pretty plum."

As the group raced north, the good flat land became more swampy and thicker with forest. Signs of life became less frequent. Late in the afternoon, they came upon a rough road running northeast, and a high ridge line on their left, running north. Jon wasn't sure which way to go.

"Let's make camp here, and decide which way to go tomorrow."

"Good idea, Jon. This looks like a road going east toward the river. We need to make a choice," said Fred.

"We can decide that over a full stomach," said Maggie.

"Well, gang, this creek continues north, along that ridge. It looks like this new road goes northeast, and another road east to the river. Which one should we take?"

"We's don' takes dem stream, Jon."

"All agree with Mose? Good! We stop following the stream. That leaves either east or northeast."

"You know what, Jonny?" said Maggie. "I'll bet the road there going northeast is the old Military Road."

"Military? What military, darlin'?"

"I think I read it was an Indian trail, made into a road. Runs from St. Louis to Texas."

"Along the St. Francis River?"

"I don't remember, but it must at least meet the river."

"And this one probably goes straight to the river."

"Right," said Fred, "that military must have been swamp critters! We don't know where it meets the St. Francis. I suggest we head straight to the river."

"I don't know," said Jon. "We may get stuck at the river if we take the east road. We know the military will meet the river at some point . . ."

"Do we, Jonny? Maybe it goes straight north."

"Then it would have a side road to Lou's Landing. What do you think, Mose?"

"Hmmm . . . Maybe you's scouts dem riva, while we's goes on dem military roads."

"Good idea, Mose. Wonderful idea." Jon turned to Fred. "See, Fred, I told you he is a genius," said Jon. "I'll leave in the morning and catch up with you along the Military Road."

"Alright, see you in the morning."

Diary of Margaret Hamilton

Wednesday, January 6

. . . Jonny suggested we follow the river north. His suggestions are like orders, and everyone goes along with them. We followed a stream north, until we came upon the old Military Road I had read about in college. Jonny is going to find the St. Francis River again in the morning, while the rest of us take the Military Road. I hope he gets back before we find this "Lou's Landing" tomorrow. Did well today . . .

Love, Maggie

Thursday, January 7

Jon was away at first light. His wife had told him not to get lost. He smiled at that, as Prancer set a gait down the east road. The swamps and pine forests didn't appear very deep, but plentiful. Suddenly, Jon heard that familiar screeching. It was those Carolina parrots again. "I think those damn birds are following me," he muttered with a smile. "Wonder what they taste like." It wasn't long before he came upon a few scrawny cabins, then the river. Across sat a small cluster of buildings, so Jon decided to take a swim on Prancer in water five feet deep.

"What is the name of this place, sir?"

"It's called Marked Tree . . . who're you?"

"I'm just scouting the river, looking for a spot to settle."

"Well, all the good lands are taken. You'd best go south."

"Thanks, mister. No roads north?"

"Ain't none, 'ceptin the Military Road 'bout ten mile west. Ain't no need fer any. They ain't not'in but swamps."

"Thanks again, sir. Guess I'll find that Military Road. Got nothin' much else to do."

"Why don't ya stay, an' get a job! We're lookin' fer good men to build our town up."

"No thanks. I don't like towns. I keep headin' west to get away from them. Be seein' ya," said Jon.

"Not if'in I see ya firs', ya won't."

Jon crossed the river again, and headed north along the bank. It was swampy at first with small cabins, and looked like a constant flood area for the river. There was lots of shrubbery and foliage in the river. Jon then struck out to the northwest to find his group.

"There you are, JH! It's about time. We've already had dinner. Are you hungry?" asked Maggie.

"Nah, I can wait. I don't want to stop the train."

"What did you find out, JH?"

"What's wrong with Jonny?"

"Nothing. I just thought I would call you something else."

"Call me anything but JH, my love."

"Alright, honey, now what did you see?"

"The river, swamps, and no roads. And Carolina parrots."

"Better tell the others . . . honey!"

As the wagons rolled, Jon told each what he had learned. About two hours later, they spotted another road going east.

"I'll bet it's the road to Lou's Landing."

"Let's take it, Jon."

"Yes, honey, let's go see our new home."

As the wagons rolled through some pine trees, the land opened up to nice level ground. Jon stopped and jumped down. He kicked the ground. Nice loam soil appeared. They could now see the river, as it made an S turn on its way south. North of it was beautiful, cultivated land, and to the south and east of the river was a small town, Lou's Landing.

"I like what I see, Jonny."

"So do I, except for no swamps, my love."

"It shouldn't be hard to find swamps in this country."

"This looks like good land," said Fred, "if it's not taken. What do you think, Jon?"

"I like it, but I'd hoped to find some large swamps."

"Well, we've gone through a lot of swamps. There must be some around here too."

"I hope so. That looks like some sort of bridge over the water, north of town."

"Yes, it's a . . . foot bridge, from that barn to town."

The road stopped at the river across from the settlement, where the river finished the S turn, and again flowed south. To their right, they had passed an abandoned farm, which lay west of the river. All along the north was cultivated land, with the big barn across from the town connected by the foot bridge. Jon could see a park, a church, and several other buildings in Lou's Landing.

"What do we do now?" asked Jon.

"We pitch our tents right here, and swim our horses across to town."

"I don't know, Jonny. That river looks awfully swift."

"I don't want to take a chance," said Jan. "I'll wait here."

"I's gets tent built, an' fire fo' suppas, Jon," said Mose.

"Do you like this area, Mose and Ella?"

"Yassa, we's do."

"Okay. Let's you and I go across and check out the town, Fred."

"Alright, but I'm going to take that bridge across."

"Good idea. We'll be back shortly, gang."

"We's has suppas ready fo' you's, Jonny," said Ella.

Fred took the horse, abby, Ally had been riding. Jon rode Prancer around to the bridge, along the middle section of the S in the river, and walked across the bridge into Lou's Landing. The dirt main street first had the park on the right, which took the brunt of the S turn of the river. It was a pretty park with willow trees, and the church sat at the park's end toward the town square. On the left of main street was an unkempt lot with one boarded-up cabin. The one large intersection had an island in the center, a perfect four-way intersection! Straight ahead, to the south, was a very nice home, about three hundred yards away. To the right, about one hundred yards away, was the river, with a dock and a warehouse, or mill. To the left (east), the road had open field to a large house maybe two hundred yards away. About two dozen shacks sat southwest of the intersection, to the river and the mansion, and the southeast corner of the intersection had a small general store.

"It's too late for the store to be open, but there are lights in that big house at the end of the street."

"That seems to be the only light in town," said Jon.

Jon spotted a black slave standing outside his shack. "Hey, boy! Come here a minute." The "boy" ran back into the shack. "I guess we try the house," Jon said.

Jon and Fred walked up to the mansion and knocked at the door.

"Yes?" said an elderly man with white hair and beard.

"Is this Lou's Landing?" asked Fred.

"Sí, who wants to know?" Whitey had a foreign accent.

"We're looking for land to settle on, sir," said Jon.

"There is plenty here. I will sell some to you."

"Is any of it swamp land?"

"Sí, there is plenty swamps to the east. I have three sections. One is swamps, one is field, an' one is town, in the middle. I will sell some."

"Does that include the town?" asked Fred.

"No, no, I keep the town, and the homes. They are in the middle of sections."

"How much do you want for the three sections, sir?"

"Please come inside, and we'll talk."

"Nice home you have," commented Fred.

"I build it from the wood that came from the mill."

"You have a saw mill?"

"Sí, we make furniture and planks. All these houses we build, an' we sell furniture."

"To who?" asked Jon.

"We sell in Sain' Louees."

"Will you sell your shop to us, along with land?" asked Jon.

"Sí. I sell all these, but no the town."

"How much?" asked Fred.

"Hmmm, see . . . three sections, and shop . . . it all for . . . six hundred dollars. That is a real bargain."

"It sounds high to me," said Fred. "We'll pay five hundred."

"Nooo, that is too little. Five seventy-five."

"Hmm . . . we will pay you five fifty, no more."

"Is too little . . . five seventy," said the little old white-haired man, "an' I toss in barn an' machines."

"And animals too?" asked Fred.

"Sí, everything but town."

Jon and Fred looked at each other and nodded.

"Sold! You have a bargain, sir."

"I will want to see all the land before we pay," said Jon.

"Sí, I will show it to you in the morning. You will take dinner with me an' my family now?"

"We have our families across the river, sir."

"Then please bring them to dinner."

"Thank you, sir, but we have black people with us," said Jon.

"Well, we will have food to take to them. We have thirty-seven blacks we feed each day."

"What will you do with all those people when you sell?"

"I shall have to sell them. You will need them. I will sell them to you. No? . . . Yes?"

"We will see tomorrow, Mister . . ."

"I am Don Louie DeValurie, at your service. My wife and daughter live with me."

"Happy to meet you," said Jon. "This is Fred Wilson, who has a wife Janet, and I am Jonathan Hamilton, and my wife's name is Margaret."

"You will bring them to supper, yes?"

"I'm sure you have already taken your dinner?"

"Well, yes, but we have plenty food."

"Thank you, sir," said Jon, "maybe tomorrow, if you please."

"Tomorrow it is, sir. I will see you tomorrow, right here?"

"Yes, sir. And thank you again. Good night."

"We did it, Jan. Look around you at our land!"

"All this, Freddy?" asked Janet.

"Three sections. You're sitting on it. Whoopee!"

"We bought three sections, Jonny?" asked Maggie.

"Depending on seeing the swamps, yes, we did, darlin'."

"How much for three sections?"

"Five hundred and seventy dollars, my love."

"That's about . . . a hundred ninety dollars for a section. Sounds good, Jonny."

"You can thank Fred. He did the gumming. And on top of that, we got the mill, the barn, and the animals."

"Good job, honey," said Jan.

"He has invited us to dinner tomorrow, after he shows us the land. He has a nice, big home."

"Does that include Nanty Ella and Nunky Mose?"

"No, my darlin'. I'm sure it doesn't. He has three dozen slaves of his own. They have shacks on the main street."

"Then I won't go, Jonny."

"We almost have to go, darlin', or we may lose the sale."

"I don't care, Jonny. My Nanty and Nunky are more important."

"Is orites, Sissy," said Mose. "You's goes. Mama cooks for res' o' us."

"I's has food an' fires, Jonny. You's all eats," said Ella.

"Thank you, Ella," said Fred. "One swamp looks like any other, Jon, and we've just bought a section of swamp, right?"

"Yes, but I still want to see it first, alright?"

"Alright. I think we should have a drink on it, though."

"A toast it is. Will you get a bottle please, Mose?"

"Yassa, I's do."

Diary of Margaret Hamilton

Thursday, January 7, 1836

Home, sweet home! We found some very nice land on the Saint Francis River in northeast Arkansas. We are purchasing three sections of land with some swamps, so Jonny can grow rice! It has a darling little town called Lou's Landing. It has the river as big as the Yadkin, a big barn, and a mill, all for five hundred seventy dollars! Jonny wants to look at the swamps before we buy. I don't know why, a swamp is a swamp! Tomorrow we look over all three sections . . . Jonny will have to go to Batesville anyway to record the sale. He is very excited and happy, and that makes me happy . . .

Love to all,
Margaret H.

Friday, January 8

"Good morning, everyone. I hope you all slept better than I did last night."

"You's be snorin', Jonny," said Ella.

"Who, me? I tossed and turned all night! Ask Maggie."

"You's worries 'bouts lan', Jonny."

"I guess so, Ella. Well, today's the day. Let's eat breakfast, so we can see our land."

"We've eaten already, Jon. Where's Margaret?" asked Fred.

"She's getting dressed, I think. I told her if she isn't ready, we would go without her."

"I'll go hurry her up," said Janet.'

"I'm coming. Just a minute!" shouted Maggie.

"Get used to that," said Jon. "Her minutes are very long!"

"I's works on dem house todays, Jon."

"Right, Mose, might as well. I wonder how he gets boards or furniture across the river."

"He has a dock. He must float them across," said Maggie.

"I would like to see some of his furniture," said Janet.

"Well, climb on," said Jon. He turned to Maggie. "You know, my love, we never named this horse." Jon looked back at Janet. "Got a name for him, uh, her, Janet?"

"Good, a mare," said Jan. "How about Lucy? Lucy of Lou's Landing."

"Lucy it is. Here, step up on Miss Lucy of Lou's Landing."

"I'll ride Chippers horse, Ally," said Maggie.

"No, you won't," said Jon. "You're too close to delivering our son. Please wait here."

"Nonsense. I will walk," said Maggie.

"Okay, my pretty plum, you win. I'll will walk with you."

"That's a good idea. Let's all walk," said Janet.

"Let's go. Let's get crackin' across the bridge," said Jon.

"You's takes my gold stone, Jon?"

"We don't need it yet, Mose. We'll use it later."

"Orites. We's be workin', Jon."

At the bridge, Jon and Fred inspected the barn. It was very clean, and it had a large bin of grain for two large, matched work horses that were in stalls. There were many closed doors on opposite walls. Jon thought it was for drying tobacco. There were two cotton gins, and what looked like a kind of baler, plows, and round sharp metal discs fashioned in rows, to be pulled by a team of horses in order to break up the soil. There were other pieces of machinery Jon didn't recognize, and even a pit for blacksmithing and two wagons.

"This is some place."

"It sure is, Fred. I've never seen so much equipment."

"Me either. Looks like he can grow anything."

"Yeah, well, let's get across the bridge. Don Louie is probably waiting for us."

The bridge swayed as the group walked gingerly across. They were struck by the beauty of the park that was on their right.

"We will own this pretty little town with its Valurie Boulevard, and that lovely park."

"Uh, no, my love, the owner keeps the town."

"All of it, Jonny?"

"All but the mill, and I guess the dock."

"We'll need to buy the slaves to run the mill, won't we?" asked Janet.

"Yes, we will, honey," answered Fred, "and to eliminate future problems, we should see if we can buy their homes too."

"Those shacks? Our bounders had better places than these."

"Bounders? What are bounders, honey?"

"Our slaves. My granddaddy thought that was a better name than slave. Nunky Mose and Nanty Ella were our personal house bounders. Jonny gave them their freedom."

"How nice," said Jan. She added, "Look at that lovely church."

"The sign on it says *Mourners Church*," observed Fred. "I wonder what that means."

"Maybe they only use it when someone dies," guessed Maggie.

"And what a lovely intersection and house at the end of the street."

"That's Baron Don Louie DeValurie's mansion, Janet."

"And it is very plush inside, honey," added Fred.

"And that's the mill that is included in the price," said Jon.

"Let's go look at it," said Janet.

"I don't know, honey. Mister Valurie is probably waiting," said Fred.

"He can wait for our money. I want to see the mill."

"Go ahead," said Jon. "I'll go tell him where you all are, and meet you at the mill."

"Alright, Jon. I can handle these two wild women."

"Ha!" laughed Jan. "You can't handle Jack!"

Jon wondered who Jack was as he separated from the other three and walked to the mansion.

"There you here! Where are the others?" Don Louie asked, in his foreign accent.

"They are looking at the mill. We can meet them there."

"Sí. There are three others?"

"Yes, our two wives, sir."

"Excellent!" Don Louie snapped his fingers. "Bring my carriage to the front!" A servant bowed, and left. "We will meet in front of the home, yes?"

"Thank you, sir."

"You have had a morning meal?"

"Yes, sir, we ate an early breakfast."

"Then we shall leave?"

"Yes, sir, we shall," said Jon.

Waiting in front of the home was a beautiful pair of white horses, hitched to a large, open carriage with gold motifs, and a fancy-dressed driver. Jon thought a baron should own this house and carriage.

"Take us to the mill," said Don Louie to the driver. "I think you will want to buy the servants?"

"Well, yes, and their shanties, if we can afford them."

"Yes, I will see to it. I will no longer need them, with theses territories trying to become a state."

"Does that make a difference, sir?"

"I believe it will. They will tax the slave owners and take the slaves of those who will not pay. We will be imprisoned."

"I have been told that they don't like free blacks."

"Sí. They will tax them higher, so they can get them out of the state of Arkansas."

"I see. But we still will need them."

"Sí! I will sell them all."

"And the shacks . . ."

"And the dwellings. Thirty-seven, for . . . three hundred dollars."

"Three hundred . . . I don't know if we have that much money left."

"That is alright. We will make it two-fifty, with fifty dollars payment and twenty-five a year."

"Hmm, that sounds fair. I'll speak to the others."

"Sí. It is very fair, Mister Hamilton."

The luxurious carriage pulled up to the mill. The visitors were waiting.

"We must buy some of this furniture, Freddy," said Janet.

"We'll probably own it anyway," answered Fred.

"We were just going to look at the slave shacks, Jonny."

"Okay, darlin', I'll check out the mill."

"We're going to need the slaves, Jon."

"I know, if we buy the land, Fred."

"What's stopping us? The swamp?"

"I guess. I want to be sure we have some."

"You will see, sir," said Don Louie. "You will see the swamps such as you never see before."

"Mister DeValurie, would you sell the slaves and their houses to us?" asked Fred.

"Sí. I have already told . . ."

"We will not pay over three hundred for them. You will not need them anymore."

"Sí. I have already made a bargain with Mister Hamilton for two hundred fifty dollar, sir."

"Two hundred fifty? Does that include the houses and land?"

"Sí, Mister Wilson, it includes everything."

"That would include more than a block on Mill Street," said Maggie, "and two blocks on the Valurie Boulevard."

"Sí, señora. You are Missus . . ."

"Hamilton, and this is Missus Wilson . . . Janet."

"You have met Mister Cartier?"

"Cartier? I am Jon Hamilton, and these are . . ."

"I have met the others! Are you selling my mill, Mister DeValurie?"

"Sí. I sell my mill, but I am certain these people will need you to manage."

"I have worked very hard . . ."

"He whips the bounders," whispered Maggie to Jon.

"Thinking I would get this mill."

"I have never promised you the mill."

"No, sir, we won't be needing Mister Cartier," said Jon.

"Who will run it, Jon?" asked Fred.

"One of us will do it so we won't need to pay wages."

"Please look through the mill, Mister Hamilton."

"I am Jon, sir, and this is my wife Margaret."

"Two lovely ladies, Margaret and Janet. I will be waiting for you to see the land."

Jon entered the mill, followed by Jacob Cartier. The mill was powered by a large water wheel in the St. Francis River.

"Does this mill operate all year?"

"No. Some in the summer, an' most a-the winter."

"Where do you ship the furniture and lumber?"

"Military Road goes clear to Saint Louis."

"Okay, that's good. Then the barge is used just to get it across the river."

"That's right. I sell lotsa boards to New Madrid. That's where them earthquakes hit," said Jacob.

"That was before I was born."

"Me too, but it made the swamps east o' my place."

"Swamps? Where do you live?"

"Right up ta the end o' this street."

"How big is your home, and how much do you want for it?"

"Old man DeValurie owns it, and the rest a town!"

"And you thought you were going to get it?"

"Yeah . . . when he kicked the pail."

"What about his daughter?"

"If I had ta, I'da married the bitch!"

"Well, you don't have to worry about that anymore."

"I figger ya need me ta handle the niggers."

"I see the way you handle them. That's why I am letting you go," said Jon.

"Oh, a nigger lover, huh? Well, you're not firing me, 'cause I quit!" Jacob Cartier stomped off.

Jon wondered what he should do now. I had to keep these men working. "Say, you, come here please." He looked like the man who ducked into his shack yesterday.

"Yassa!"

"Who is the best, or oldest worker here?"

"I is dem bes'. Jess be dem oldes'."

"Which one knows best how to make furniture?"

"Jess be dem bes'."

"Thank you for being honest. You are now the manager of the sawmill, and Jess will manage the furniture making."

"Does you's own dem mill?"

"After today, yes, and you are . . . manager . . ."

"I's be Murphy, boss," he answered. "Jess! Comes here!"

"Wha' you's wan's, Murf?"

"This be new boss, Jess. He make you's an' me bosses."

"You's an' me bosses?"

"Yas. He owns dem mill."

"No mo' Massa Jacob?"

"No mo Jacob, Jess. You's has furniture, an' I has dem mill. New boss say so."

"Can I count on you two to handle your new jobs until I see you tomorrow?"

"Yassa, boss," said Jess.

"Good, you show me the furniture shop, Jess."

"Yassa, boss-man, dis way."

Jess led Jon to the rear of the warehouse, where he saw some very nice, clean hand-made items.

"Very nice, Jess. You pick a couple skilled workers."

"Murph be bes', bu' I's gets Abe, Curry, an' Goose?"

"That makes four of you. What kind of trees do you use for furniture?"

"Uses pine an' oaks some, cypress, an' pines mostly."

"Right, you will manage and work with the other three, and make the furniture that sells best. Okay?"

"Yassa, boss-man."

"My name is Jon. You and Murph will have a boss tomorrow."

"Dat no be's you, Jon?"

"No, I'll be the owner, the head boss."

"Yassa, head boss . . . Jon."

As Jon walked out the door, he saw the carriage driver on the ground, and Jacob Cartier on top of Don Louie DeValurie, hitting the old man about the face. Jon ran up into the carriage, and pulled Jacob off the "baron" and onto the ground.

"You want to fight someone? Fight me."

"You will be out of my house and town today!" yelled Don Louie to Jacob.

"I will be out when I'm damn ready DeValurie!"

"Your boss said today. That means today!"

"I have no way to get my furniture across the river."

"You have no furniture, Mister Cartier. The house and all the furniture belong to me."

"We'll be a-seein' about that!" hollered Jacob, as he stormed up Mill Street, through the intersection, and beyond.

"You will be out today!" shouted DeValurie. "We must hurry, Mister Hamilton. He will be back."

"I'm going back over the bridge to get my Hawken."

"Sí. Good idea. Driver, take me home."

DeValurie's carriage went one way, and Jon ran the other, past the Mourners Church, the park, and over the bridge. He found Prancer eating grass by the barn, and grabbed his Hawken and pouches from the saddle, and ran back over the bridge. He saw the carriage turn at the intersection, toward the mill. Then he saw Jacob walking down Mill Street with a rifle.

"Jacob!" yelled Jon, trying to catch up to them. As he reached the intersection, he heard the loud *BAM* of the firing rifle. *Oh god, he's shot the Baron*, thought Jon.

As Jon turned the corner, he saw Jacob's back and smoking rifle. The driver was on the ground, and Maggie, Fred, and Janet were about to step onto the street. Jacob pulled a pistol.

"I'm going to kill you, DeValurie! You sold my mill!"

"I wouldn't do that, Cartier. I'll put a ball through you."

"Jake! Jake, don't do it!" yelled a woman, running down the street after Jacob. Jon wondered. *His wife?* As Jon looked back at Jacob, the pistol was now pointed at him!

"Stay out of this," ordered Jacob, "or you die first."

Jon realized he hadn't capped the Hawken, but aimed it anyway. "At this distance, your ball may not even hit me. It damn sure wouldn't kill me. On the other hand, the ball from this Hawken will tear you in half!"

"He's right!" yelled Fred. "There will be pieces of you splattered all over the street."

"Please, Jacob! Put the gun down!" pleaded his wife.

Jacob paused for a long minute, then dropped the pistol.

"Thank God," said the wife, running to Jacob. "Come on, let's go get packed. We'll start all over."

"Wow! That was close," said Fred. "You were steady as a rock, Jon. Would you have shot him?"

"No. I didn't have a cap on the nipple, so I couldn't shoot."

"Wow, that did take some steady nerve."

"I feel sorry for the wife, Jonny."

"So do I, my love. She has to put up with that no good. He shot . . . the driver!"

DeValurie was kneeling beside the driver, who was badly bleeding. Jon thought he saw tears in the baron's eyes.

"He took the ball which was meant for me."

"Where are you hit, driver?" asked Jon.

"I's sh-shots un dem ba-back, sir."

"We've got to stop the bleeding."

"I wonder if Nunky Mose can hear us across the river."

"Try yelling to him, darlin'. Janet, I need . . ."

Janet had already lifted her dress and had torn a large piece of white undergarment out, and handed it to Jon.

"Good girl, thanks. I wish Ella and Mose . . ."

At that moment, things happened. Two women came running from the intersection. Mose was right behind them. Maggie was screaming to Ella, across the river.

"Thank God! Mose, this man is shot bad."

"I's looks, Jon. He be bleedin' bad."

"How did you know we needed you?" asked Fred.

"I's hear gunshot, comes right fast."

"Did you bring liniment, by any chance?" asked Jon.

"No, sir, Massa Jon," said Mose.

"It's alright, Mose. You can talk straight now."

"I's better goes gets horse liniment."

"No need. I just got Nanty Ella. She will bring enough medicine to treat an army."

"You use horse liniment on wounds?" asked Janet.

"Sure do. Heals faster than anything else, honey," answered Maggie.

"Come to think of it, it works great on my horses. Why wouldn't it work on humans?" asked Fred.

"He be bleedin' mo'. Need mo' rags," said Mose.

"Maggie, what are you wearing under those pants?"

"Jonny! I can't talk about that in public!"

"This brave man is dying, my love." There was a pause, while everyone stared at Maggie.

"Oh, alright. Turn your heads, please."

Maggie climbed into the carriage and took off her riding pants and nether garments. She threw the nether garments at Jon.

"Here, you big lummox, take them and be damned!"

"Thank you, my pretty plum. Mose, use this to block the bleeding."

"You would do this for my servant, señora?" asked Don Louie.

"She would indeed, sir. My wife is a caring person."

"Margaret the Magnificent. You have my gratitude," said Don Louie.

Mose saw Ella first, and rushed to meet her close to the intersection. He took her medicine bag from her and carried it.

"I'm sure glad to see you, Ella. See what you can do for him."

"Yassa, Massa Jon."

"How did it happen, Don Louie?" asked his wife.

"He was shot protecting me, Connee. Shot by Jacob."

"By Jacob? Why?"

"Because I sold the mill. He thought it would be his."

"I's has dem bandage, Massa Jon. We's needs gets ta bed, an' gets lead out," said Ella.

"Thanks, Ella. Do you have a place for him, Mister DeValurie?"

"Sí, in the house. Put him in the carriage."

"He will get blood on your seats. Mose, can you . . ."

Mose had picked up the wounded servant and was carrying him toward the intersection, then right, toward the mansion.

"You put horse liniment on his wound?" asked Janet, as the group started walking behind Mose.

"Yassum, I's sho 'nuff do," answered Ella. "Bu' he's needs gets lead ball outs."

"Let's take the carriage back to the mansion."

"Good idea, Freddy. Who's going to drive?"

"I'll do it," said Fred. "Get in so we can catch up. Be careful of that fancy old pistol there. It might go off."

"Whoee," said Ella. "It sho 'nuff be's a fancy gun!"

By the time Fred had the carriage turned around and back to the intersection, Jon, Don Louie, and Mose, carrying the driver, had reached the grounds of the DeValurie mansion. Two more servants came out to help.

"Put him in the guest room," ordered DeValurie. "Will you all take dinner with me, please? Yes? No?"

"Yes, thank you so much, sir," answered Maggie.

"I didn't realize that it was time for lunch."

"Mister DeValurie said dinner, honey."

"I heard what he said, my love. Barons can be wrong."

"He's probably a count, Jonny. With a lovely home."

Mose and Ella took the wounded driver into a back room, joined by Maggie, Jan and a house servant. Soon another servant announced dinner was ready in the dining room.

"The ladies will eat too, no?"

"My wife wants our two dark partners to eat with us."

"Sí, señor, I will allow et. Please bring in the guests. All of them." The servant bowed, and left.

"Nunky Mose and Nanty Ella are operating on the driver, getting the ball out," said Maggie.

"That must be painful," remarked Fred.

"I will see to it they are fed."

"Thank you, sir," said Jon.

"Please be seated." The Hamiltons and Wilsons took seats across from each other, and Don Louie sat at the end. They were soon joined by two lovely ladies, the older one in beautiful Spanish togs, and the other in riding pants and a blouse.

"This is my wife, Señora Constance DeValurie, and my daughter, Señorita Lolita. Please meet our guests, Mister and Missus Hamilton, and Mister and Missus Wilson."

Everyone said hello and shook hands. The ladies took seats across from each other.

"You have a lovely home, Missus DeValurie," said Janet.

"I will show it to you after we eat," answered Constance, smiling.

A wonderful meal was served to the four land speculators.

"This is the most elegant dinner I have had in months," Maggie remarked.

"Thank you, señora. I am happy you like it."

"We are ready to purchase your three sections, sir," said Fred.

"Mister Hamilton will look at the property first."

"Thank you, sir. That shouldn't take long."

"It depends how much you want to see. The swamp is over one hundred sections, of which I own but one quarter of one section, and one-half of another."

"Over a hundred sections?" asked Fred.

"Sí, señor. It was made by the shaking."

"My father means the big earthquake, sir," clarified Lolita.

"That was before our time," said Fred.

"I was but a child," said Lolita, "but I remember them well. I was frightened for ages."

"The earthquakes made the hundred-section swamp?"

"Sí, señor," answered Don Louie, "it also made tall hills."

"There were many swamps, but the earthquake sunk the ground into lakes and streams. Did you come here from Batesville, señor?" asked Lolita.

"No, we came up the St. Francis," answered Jon.

"Well, about twenty miles west of here is Crowley's Ridge, much of it raised by quakes."

"You will cross it when you go to Batesville," said Don Louie.

"Okay, you want five hundred twenty dollars for the slaves, their homes, the mill, and three sections?" asked Jon.

"Sí, señor, except the town."

"Will you sell the town, sir?" asked Fred.

"No, sir! I must keep my dwellings, land, and store."

"What about the rest of the town?"

"You mean you want the church and the park? And my little house?"

"Yes," answered Fred. "If you'll sell them to us."

"Is that your wish, Mister Hamilton?"

"If my partner wants the town, then so do I."

"I see. Hmm . . . We will look at the property and talk about town after, yes?"

"I should stay here and help Nunky Mose and Nanty Ella with the driver."

"No need, Señora Hamilton. My servant is very good doctor."

They all thanked Señora and Señorita DeValurie for the wonderful dinner.

"I wonder if Mose will want to come along."

"I'll go check, Jonny."

"Let us be off now. There is much to see."

A new driver was waiting at the carriage for the five passengers

"I will sit in front with the ladies, so the gentlemen will see better."

"You left this pistol on the seat, sir," said Janet.

"Oh, sí, madam. Protection from Mister Cartier."

"It sure is fancy, sir," said Jon. "What make is it?"

"It is Ripoll Belt pistol. It is from Spain."

"Nunky Mose is operating on the driver. He and Nanty Ella are staying," said Maggie, running out of the mansion.

"Then we will go. Driver, we see the swamps."

The carriage rolled down the boulevard to the river, and turned right. The eastward direction soon ran out of road and turned into a path.

"I hope Mister Cartier has disappeared before we return. He is an angry man."

"Nunky Mose seemed sure the driver will die," Maggie said.

"Then he should be tried for murder."

"We have no courts here, Mister Hamilton. We must perform under our own laws."

"We will have a court," said Jon, "and Mister Cartier will be the first on trial."

"Will you be the judge and jury, Jonny?"

"No. Mose would make a good judge."

"You'll need Nunky Mose for a sheriff . . . and guard, with no jail."

It was just short distance when the swamps came into view.

"There it is, Mister Hamilton, the great swamps."

"Wow, looks big."

"It is, sir. It runs over eleven sections east, and over ten sections south. There are many sections with parcels of good land, like my land."

"Is it ten sections square?"

"No, señor. Think of it as a pie, or a wheel, which you have cut out a quarter. It is square east and south, and a rounded loop. Is one hundred four sections."

"And is it full of water all the time?"

"No, sir. It drains in the summer, but a lake and streams have water all year."

"Wonderful. It even has streams?"

"Sí, señor. The Little River is ten miles to the east, and it flows through the swamps."

"Wonderful. Is it full of cypress trees?"

"Sí, señor. There is some pine and some hard woods, but mostly cypress."

"You have cut some of the trees here already."

"Sí. You see the furniture and mill? This is where we get the lumber."

The carriage drove on along the north line of the swamp.

"This is the end of my section seventeen, seniors."

"I like what I see. Is it like this all hundred and four sections?"

"Yes, sir, señor. The Little River is still nine miles east."

"Do you know how deep the lake is?"

"In the winter, five or six feet, and is nearly gone in summer."

"Is this what you really want, Jon?" asked Fred.

"Yes, I can picture it as rice paddies."

"Wow, you're looking at a lot of years ahead."

"I know," answered Jon. "Can we drive along the west line of the swamps?"

"Sí. Driver, we go back to start of the swamps, and we see the other side."

The driver nodded, turned the carriage around, and rode back to the starting point, then south along the swamp.

"The town is over to the right."

"And this is part of the three sections?" asked Janet.

"Sí, señora, for half mile."

"Is that smoke I see over there, Jonny?"

"It sure looks like smoke, darlin'."

"It is coming from the town. May we go see?"

"Yes, Mister DeValurie. It's your carriage."

"Driver! Turn to the town. Hurry!"

The driver raced west, across the open field toward town.

"It's a house afire!" yelled Fred.

"It is my house. I knew Mister Cartier would do something like this!"

"There's nothing we can do now. The house is gone."

"I hope he is still inside."

"There is Nunky Mose, Jonny. He must have finished the operation."

"Yes, my love, Mose wouldn't leave the driver unless he had finished the operation."

"Or unless the driver was dead," said Maggie.

"Where are the Cartiers, Mose?" Jon asked as the carriage stopped.

"They's nowheres 'round here, Jon."

"I hope that woman isn't inside, Jonny."

"So do I, my love. Have you checked around for them, Mose?" asked Jon.

"Nosa. I's jest gots here, Jon."

"Okay, let's look around. I'll go this way."

"I would hope they ran down Mill Street," said Maggie.

Mose spotted tracks in the soft ground. They were headed at an angle toward the park . . . the bridge.

"I'll get my Hawken." Jon ran back to the carriage. Mose ran toward the park, well ahead of Jon.

"See him, Mose?" Jon asked, after he caught up with Mose crossing the bridge.

"Nosa, Jon. He cross riva here."

"He probably took our horses. Let's see . . . there's Prancer and Ally, and Lucy and Smutty! Did you ride him?"

"Yassa, I's did. They's all here, Jon."

"What did Ella ride?"

"I's don' know, Jon. She be behin' me."

"It was the carryall! See those tracks?"

"We's catches dem, Jon."

Mose climbed aboard Friend, and Jon jumped on Prancer. In short order, they reached the camp.

"Did anyone go by here?" Jon asked.

"Yassa, dey's do," answered Susan."

"Dems horses, you's wagon, Massa Jon," aid Josh.

"Dey goes data way, Massa Jon," added Ally.

Mose and Jon headed west, toward Military Road. It only took a mile or so before they spotted the carryall. *BAM!* A shot from Jacob Cartier whizzed by them. They were right behind the carryall when Cartier showed his face and rifle again. Jon turned Prancer back behind the carryall. *BAM!* Another bullet went by. Now Jon ran Prancer up to Jacob Cartier's side. Mose had already jumped up onto the carryall's bench from the other side. He reached past the wife and grabbed Jacob by the neck. Jacob tried to hit Mose with his rifle. Mose jerked the gun out of the man's hand and lifted him up by the neck.

"Whoa, Corka. Whoa, big boy." The horse recognized Mose's voice and slowed to a stop.

"Let go a-me, nigger! I done nothin' to ya!"

"You's stole my horses an' wagon."

"Let go! You're choking me!" Mose had Jacob in the air with one arm. Jacob grabbed for the knife he kept in his belt.

"Look out, Mose! He's got a knife!" yelled Jon.

Jacob slashed his knife across Mose's arm. Jon saw the blood squirt out. It didn't seem to bother Mose. He raised Jacob over his head with both hands, and threw him into a swampy area beside the road.

The wife screamed and jumped down.

"Are you alright, Jacob?" she asked.

"That big nig . . . a-choked me. I cain't breathe!"

"You're alright! Mose should have killed you and save us the trouble of hanging you!" yelled Jon.

"For what?"

"For burning that house, stealing my horses and wagon, and killing that carriage driver!"

"That nigger were alive when I left 'im!"

"He be dead now," said Mose, confirming the death.

"Well, ya cain't hang me fer killin' no nigger. I should get a medal."

"Let's see if we can make him a metal noose, Mose."

"Please don't kill him, sir," pleaded the wife. "He's all I got."

"Come up outta that swamp! Mose, there must be some rope in the carryall. Let's get them back to camp."

Mose was wrapping his arm with cloth. He grabbed a rope from the carryall, bound Jacob's hands and legs, and put him in the wagon. The trip back to camp was uneventful, and Jon now had a dilemma: what to do with Jacob Cartier and his wife. The rest of group was there.

"What do you suggest we do with them?"

"We should try him for murder, Jonny," said Maggie.

"We's has one room finish, Jon."

"Good, Mose, but let's put the prisoner in the food cellar for tonight. We'll keep Missus Cartier with us."

"What is your name, honey?" asked Janet.

"Dessy . . . Modessa Cartier."

"You can stay in the tent with us, Dessy," said Maggie.

"It's going to be a full tent," chirped Fred. "Maybe some of us can sleep in the house."

"With no heat or cover?" asked Janet.

"We's sleeps un house," said Ally.

"You're the fearless leader, Jonny. You tell us where."

"Okay, my pretty plum. All the women get the tent. That's five, and Chipper makes six."

"And you're not sleeping with me?" asked Maggie.

"Maybe not tonight, darlin'. We'll switch tomorrow night."

"Mama an' I's sleeps in house, Jon."

"Are you sure, Mose?"

"Yassa," answered Ella, now finished treating her husband's arm wound.

"Good. Then Mose, Ella, Josh, and Ally will sleep in the house tonight, and the rest in the tent."

"Too bad, you big lummox. You have to sleep with me."

"We has food here. You's ready ta eats?" asked Ella.

"Thank you, Ella," said Fred. "I'm starved."

"Dig in, everyone. It's late, but it's great," said Maggie.

"What's on the menu for tomorrow?" asked Fred.

"Well, first we pay off Mister DeValurie and try to buy the rest of the town . . ."

"I's wans ta use dem gold rock to buy, Jon."

"That may be a good idea, Jonny. It frees up a lot of the eight hundred we have for other things."

"Alright. We'll see what all your gold will buy, Mose."

"What else must get done tomorrow?" asked Fred.

"We need to work on the house here, and get the lumber and furniture business going at full speed."

"How do we do that, Jonny?" asked Janet.

"Well, I have two of the servants in charge at the mill. One is in charge of furniture making . . . uh, Jess is his name, and Murphy has the mill operation."

"Then what else is needed?" asked Maggie.

"One of us to oversee the operations."

"Nunky Mose would be perfect, Jonny."

"Yes, but we'll need his skills everywhere, darlin'."

"How about my wife?" asked Fred. "She has a lot of skills, and has a great eye for fine furniture."

"Will you do it, Janet?"

"These slaves, Murphy and . . . Jess? Are they skilled?"

"They sure are. I would ask that you handle the operations and the needs of the workers."

"Alright," said Jan. "I'll do it."

"Dat mean we's needs wood, Jon."

"Yes, it does, Mose. I would like you to take charge of the swamp clearing after we return from Batesville."

"When will that be?" asked Fred.

"I hope we can prepare for the trip tomorrow evening, and leave the first thing the day after."

"That would be Sunday, Jonny."

"Tomorrow is Saturday already?"

"Yes, and I want to check out the church," said Maggie.

"Well, I'm ready to turn in. Big day tomorrow."

"Good. I can catch back up on my diary."

"In the morning after breakfast, Mose, Fred, and I will purchase the land. Jan will take over the mill, right?"

"And I want to go along with you, Jonny."

"Okay, my love. Good night, everyone."

"I guess I will check out the Mourners Church alone."

Saturday, January 9

"Good morning, you all. I can smell breakfast from my bed!"

"You cannot! Quit lying, Jonny."

"He's not lying, Maggie. I can smell it too," said Janet.

"Thank you, señora. Let's get eatin' it."

"We can't get dressed with you men standing around."

"Why not, my pretty plum? It's one for all, and all for one."

"Well, all of me is for one to see!"

"Okay, my darlin', Fred and I will leave."

"But you ladies best be ready to go to town when we are."

"You can leave too, Freddy," said Jan.

"Morning, gang. I could smell breakfast from bed."

"Well, you's jest digs right in, Jonny," said Ella.

"I has horses an' carryall ready, Jon."

"Good, Mose. The ladies will be right out, so we can get started. Josh, you and Ally work on the house, and we'll join you as soon as we get back."

"Orites, Massa Jon."

"It's just Jon, Josh."

"How many horses are we taking to Batesville?" asked Fred.

"Good question. We don't need all we have, and we should be able to sell them all in Batesville."

"We's needs three teams, Jon," said Mose.

"Which three, Mose? How well do your horses pull, Fred?"

"I don't know. We bought them just to pull our wagon."

"We's keeps Corkas an' Conquers, Jon."

"Yes, and I have a soft spot for Sloggy and Smutty."

"Maybe's we's keeps two an' Fred's horses, Jon."

"And remember, we have two more in that barn," said Fred.

"That's right! Are you sure we only need three sets, Mose?"

"We should have two teams, at least, for harvest and pulling logs out of the swamp," said Fred.

"An' works an dem mill," added Mose.

"The two we're buying from DeValurie are probably used to that. So we have Slog, Smut, Corker, and Conqueror, and we should keep the two from DeValurie."

"What about the saddle horses? Do we need all of them?" asked Fred.

"Yes, I think so, Fred. I know that Jake and Red are both good pullers."

"So we keep them, and two from my wagon?" asked Fred.

"That sounds like ten to me."

"An me toos, Jon," said Mose. "We's don' needs ten."

"Ha! That means we only sell my horses," observed Fred.

"Looks that way, as long as we can feed that many."

"We's sells Slogs an' Smuts, or Jake an' Reds, Jon."

"Maybe, Mose. I hate to, but we don't need that many horses."

"We'll have to use one field for growing grain."

"Righto, Fred, but if we get those swamps, there are lots of part sections to grow grains and corn, and so on."

"You's wheel horses looks strong, Fred," said Mose.

"Yes, they were stronger than the other two."

"Okay, we'll keep them and sell your two lead horses, Fred. That makes four sets. What are the names of your wheel horses?"

"Cobbler and Flip."

Jon laughed. "Reminds me of Apple and Jack! Remember them, Mose?"

"Sho 'nuff do, Jon. Dem's names a drinks?"

"Yup, Cobbler and Flips are drinks!" Jon was still laughing.

"What's so funny, Jonny?" asked Maggie, exiting the tent.

"We're keeping Cobbler and Flip from Fred's teams, darlin'."

"So? We're keeping Corker from my team! Haha!"

"They are names of drinks, darlin'. Just like Apple and Jack."

"Oh, that's right. Leave it to you two to recognize that!"

"Yeah, well, have some breakfast, ladies, so we can get started before the rain comes."

"Those clouds do look angry," said Janet.

"We're overdue for rain, Jonny. We've had some really good weather lately, for January."

"That's true, my love. How's our prisoner, Ella?"

"I's feeds 'im dis mornin', Jonny."

"May I go see my husband?" asked Modessa Cartier.

"If you promise not to free him."

"I promise."

"Good. Go ahead and spend some time with him."

"Thank you." Dessy left.

"Keep this rifle loaded and ready, Josh. Susan, Ally, you two keep a watch, and yell to Josh if he tries to escape."

"Yessa, Massa . . . er, Jonny."

"Are we ready to purchase a town?"

The answer was a resounding yes, as five people boarded the carryall.

"Good morning, Mister DeValurie. We're here to purchase land and a town from you."

"Greetings, señors and señoras. Please come in to my parlor. You have breakfast? Yes? No?"

"Yes, we have, sir," answered Fred.

"Excellent. You have brought three lovely ladies."

"Yes, sir. They will be part owners."

"I see. Uncommon, but pleasing."

"Now, then," said Fred, "you will sell the rest of the town?"

"Sí, señors, but I must sell for less now. The house, she be destroyed by Mister Cartier."

"By the way, sir, we have him prisoner."

"Excellent! But we have no court or sheriff."

"We will take him to Batesville tomorrow. Alright, sir?"

"Sí, señor, if that is your wishes."

"It is, sir. Now, Mister DeValurie, do you wish to be paid in money or gold?"

"Gold? You have gold?"

"Yes, sir, we do, but we don't know what the value is."

"Trust me, señor, it is worth much, over one hundred dollars for one ounce."

"My partner Mose wants to pay you with gold. He has a stone of nearly pure gold. Show him, Mose."

Mose showed the stone, and Don Louie's eyes were popping.

"For that I would sell everything and be your servant."

"There must be at least five ounces of gold there."

"Sí, maybe six or seven ounces, señor."

"Then you will sell everything to us except your home and acreage behind it?"

"Sí, for that beautiful gold piece."

"Do you agree, gang . . . Mose?"

All agreed to the sale.

"Then we have a deal, sir. Thank you."

"Thank you, señors. I will write a sales slip and place my stamp on it."

"Will the stamp be proof enough of the sale?"

"Sí, señor. I will list everything. Please be seated." Don Louie turned to a servant. "Please bring a parchment and pen." The servant bowed, and soon returned with fancy paper.

"Perhaps one of you will write the agreement," Don Louie said.

"My wife is a very good writer, Mister DeValurie," said Fred.

"And so is my wife, sir," added Jon.

"Excellent! Then each will make a copy."

January 9, 1836

For the sum of one large gold stone, I, Don Louie de Valurie, do sell to Mister Jonathan Henry Hamilton and wife Margaret Rose Hamilton; Frederick Allen Wilson and wife Janet Louise Wilson; Mose Dasilvalentis Hamilton and wife Ella Ellavated Hamilton, all purchasers, the following parcels of land and improvements:

To wit: sections 17 and 18, township 74, range 82 west, and section 13, township 74, range 83 west, with the following exclusion:

To wit: the east one-half of the southwest quarter and the west one-half of the southeast quarter, of the southwest quarter of section 13, township 74, range 83 west, a parcel of forty acres. This sale also includes the remaining town of Lou's landing and all of the town's improvements, such as lumber mill, furniture factory, general store, parks, church, thirty servants (slaves), their homes and property, and all other animals, machinery, and improvements.

Signed this ninth day of January, 1836:

Don Louie DeValurie, SELLER   *Jonathan H. Hamilton, BUYER*
Constance DeValurie, SELLER   *Margaret R. Hamilton, BUYER*

Frederick A. Wilson, BUYER   *Mose D. (Hamilton), BUYER*
Janet L. Wilson, BUYER   *Ella E. (Hamilton), BUYER*

The sales document was signed by all, and stamped with Don Louie DeValurie's seal.

"Thank you for using the name *Hamilton*, Mose and Ella."

"We's be Hamiltons now, Jon."

"Thank you, Mister DeValurie. We will be great neighbors."

"Sí, señors. How much of the swamps will you want to purchase?"

"There are one hundred and four sections?"

"Sí, but many, maybe fourteen or fifteen, have good rich land as well as swamp, señor."

"Then I should try to buy the whole swamp."

"Ah, sí, but they will want more for the good land."

"How much more?"

"They will gladly give away all the swamp, but will charge you for the rest. Maybe you make one offer."

"What do you suggest, Mister DeValurie?"

"Come into my study. I have the map."

"See all these sections that have swamp, but also good soil? You also need these lands along the St. Francis River."

"Yes. How accurate is this map, sir?"

"Very accurate, señor. You can trust it."

"Good. Then I would want to buy a small piece of these sections, where the swamp catches the northwest corners."

"No need, señor. There is a road along the swamp that follows the Little River north, and then along the swamp."

"I see. Great! Where does it go?"

"It starts in Marked Tree, and ends close to the Mississippi and Missouri border."

"Good, then how much should we offer for all the sections?"

"Maybe you start with six hundred, señors."

"Alright, sir, that will be our offer. Thank you."

"My pleasure. Now you will eat and drink with me?"

"Sounds wonderful. What's for lunch?" asked Fred.

"Tortillas and Spanish beans. You like? Yes? No?"

"We have never tried them before," said Maggie.

"What are they?" asked Janet.

"Ha! You are in for a treat, señoras," Don Louie chuckled.

A wonderful lunch followed. Everyone enjoyed it.

"Thank you so much for this tasty lunch," said Maggie.

"You are more than welcome Missus Hamilton," said Constance. "You will need much food to last you and the slaves through the winter."

"Yes. We will have to buy food in Batesville, Jonny."

"Righto, my love. We'll take the trailer and fill it."

"I hope we have enough money after we buy the swamps," said Janet.

"We have a barn full of corn, señors and señoras. You can use all that you need," said Don Louie DeValurie.

"Thank you for your kindness, Mister and Missus DeValurie."

"You are welcome, Señora Hamilton. We will need each other. I will soon leave for Saint Louis, and I will need to use the freight wagon you now own that is in the barn."

"I saw that," said Fred. "What do you use it for?"

"It carries many bushels of wheat and corn."

"You may use it anytime you like, sir."

"Thank you, señor. We will be good neighbors."

"Papa, you have no need of the freight wagon now," said Lolita. "You have sold the land and slaves."

"But I would get supplies for the new owners, for our family, and for the store, Lolita."

"We will pay you for them when you return, sir," said Jon.

"We will see, señor. This stone may cover all."

"I will no longer be proprietor of the store," said Lolita.

"Señorita, will you continue to run the store until we get back from Batesville and decide who will take over?"

"I will be happy to do so, señor."

"Thank you. We haven't looked at it yet."

"Who do you sell to, in the store?" asked Fred.

"There are people who live north and south along the St. Francis River, and along the Military Road."

"I hope they live on the west side of the river," said Jon.

"Sí, they do, and over a mile away from the town."

"Good, because we would like to buy the section just to the south of this one."

"That would be section 24, señor. It is available, as are the part sections on the east side of the river."

"And the swamp is ten sections long to the south?"

"Sí, señor, some sections have but a small amount of land by the river. Others have about one-half of a section."

"Then we will want to buy all those part sections east of the river."

"Sí, señor, that is why I say to offer six hundred for all the sections with swamp and all the ten part sections east of the river. You will need to bargain."

"Then we should start at four or five hundred," said Fred.

"Sí, and be very firm, señors."

Just then, a servant ran into the dining room. "Señor, sir, a shot be heard cross da riva!"

"Uh-oh! That would be Josh. Something has gone wrong."

"Let's get over there, Jonny."

"Righto. Please excuse us, sir. We must hurry."

"Sí, I will see you when you return from Batesville."

"And you return from Saint Louis," said Janet.

"Goodbye, sweet ladies. Please come again," said Connie.

"Bye, and thank you," said Maggie, hurrying out.

Mose and Jon were at the head of the pack, crossing the bridge. Mose kept on running, and Jon waited for the rest.

"Get aboard, quick, before Mose beats us."

Jon raced the carryall around the river bend, and saw that Mose was nearly to the camp. They all arrived together.

"What happened, Josh?"

"Dat bad man, he escapes un dem woods."

"He be's on foot?" asked Mose, breathing fast.

"Yassa, he be's."

"I'll get Prancer. He must not have gone too far."

"I's gets Friend," said Mose.

The two men jumped on their unsaddled horses, and rode into the woods west of the house, making a circle.

"Did you see anything, Mose?" Jon asked, at the circle's head.

"Nosa, bu' he couldn'a gone no further dan dis."

"Are you all loaded?"

"I's loaded, Jon. Is you?"

"Yeah, but we don't want to kill him unless we have to."

"Right you's be, Jon."

"Good, stay in sight. We'll cut through the middle."

The men started forward, in sight of each other, slowly checking the brush and behind trees. Suddenly, Jon was hit on the arm and knocked off Prancer. It was Jacob Cartier, jumping from a tree. Jacob had a wooden club, and as they wrestled, Jacob hit Jon two or three times and then sprang for Jon's horse. *BAM!* Mose's shot grazed Jacob's shoulder, sending him sprawling.

"This one's for your heart, Mister Cartier. Lie still."

From a long distance, they heard Dessy screaming.

"Your wife thinks we killed you. Maybe we should."

"Why should ya? I ain't done nothin' ta ya."

"You stole my horse and wagon, and killed a man."

"A nigger ain't a man."

"You want to tell that to Mose?"

"Keep him away from me. He's mean."

"You better thank the Lord that Mose is gentle and kind."

"Ha! He weren't very kind when he threw me in a swamp!"

"He might have choked you to death. How did you escape from the root cellar?"

"I prayed!"

"Well, you better pray you're still alive when we get you to Batesville."

"Why am I goin' there?"

"They're good at hanging people!" Jon turned to Mose. "Let's head back, Mose."

"Yassa, Jon. Gets up, man."

The afternoon skies had cleared, but the temperature was cool. Jon judged it to be in the forties, as the group huddled around the campfire resting and drinking coffee.

"Are you alright, Dessy?" asked Janet.

"Yes, but . . ."

"But what, honey?"

"He was going to leave me." There was a long pause.

"Maybe not," said Jon. "He was hiding in a tree not very far away. Maybe he planned on sneaking back for you."

"They won't hang him, will they?"

"We don't know. Maybe they will just put him in prison."

"Yeah, this is a slave state," added Fred.

"What will I do if they do hang him?"

"Don't you worry, honey. We'll take care of you," said Maggie.

"You know, I never did see that church or the mill I'm supposed to be in charge of," declared Janet.

"Or the store," added Maggie. "Maybe we should fix up that little abandoned house on the main street for Jan and Fred."

"Would you like that, Jan?" asked Fred.

"We can take a look at it too."

"Let's go back and look while we still have light," said Maggie.

"Okay, darlin'."

"Mama an' I's stays an' watch dat Jacob an' gets carryall ready for trailer," said Mose.

"An' I's cooks suppa," added Ella.

"Sounds good, we have four saddle horses. Let's get them saddled."

"Pretty shaggy-looking place, isn't it, Jonny?"

"Yes, it is, my love, but it could be made livable. I was going to give you the Cartier house."

"That would have been much better, honey," said Janet.

"Maybe in time we can rebuild it," said Maggie.

"Good idea, darlin', but we already have a million or so projects this spring."

"Like what, Jonny?"

"Are you joking? There's the fields to be plowed and readied for planting, the first area of the swamp to be cleared for a rice paddy, the fixing up of two houses, and caring for the needs of thirty bounders, and so on and so on."

"And preparing for the birth of our first child."

"That's right, my pretty plum."

"This place would be close to my work anyway," said Janet.

"Let's take a look inside, Jon," said Fred.

"Yes, and we need to see the rest of the town before it gets too dark, honey."

The group toured the little house and decided it was fixable, then they were off to the Mourners Church across Valurie Boulevard.

"What a pretty little church. It must be used each week, and not just for funerals," stated Janet.

"Too bad we won't be here tomorrow to find out," said Fred.

"Do we have to leave tomorrow, on a Sunday?"

"Yes, my love, so we can tie down all the land and get started with our projects."

"Well, we're coming here the following Sunday."

Next, they looked at the small general store, on the corner of Valurie Boulevard and Mill Street. It was low on supplies, but in good shape. Then it was on to the mill.

"Jesse, Murphy, this is Janet Wilson. She will be the head boss, sometimes with her husband, Fred Wilson."

"A girl boss?" asked Jesse.

"We's seen 'er yesterdays, Jess," said Murphy.

"That's right, Murphy, but you will still be in charge for another week while we're gone."

"You's be's gone a week?"

"Yes, Jesse," said Janet, "and I want to see a lot done when I return. Hear?"

"Yassum," was the answer in unison, "Boss Miss."

"What time do you start and finish work?" asked Fred.

"We's starts un daylights, an' ends un dark," said Jesse.

"Bu' we's be off till Mondays," added Murphy.

"That's fine with me," said Jan. "You're almost finished for the week. Until Monday, then."

"Yassum, Boss Miss," said both Murphy and Jesse.

"I expect to see a lot done by the time I get back."

"Yassum, Boss Miss."

"Do you go to the church on Sundays?" asked Maggie.

"Yassum, Missy."

"Do white people go there too?" asked Fred.

"Yassa, un' after we's un eats."

"The bounders in the morning, and the rest in the afternoons?" asked Maggie.

"Yassum. We's has preach-man here an' mill," said Jesse.

"You's wans un meets preach-man, Boss Miss?" asked Murphy.

"When I return in a week."

"Why is it called Mourner's Church?" asked Maggie.

"We's all mourns an' sings ta preach-man."

"It's getting dark, gang. We better get back to camp."

"Yeah, and some of that great cooking of Ella's," said Fred.

Diary of Margaret Hamilton

Saturday, January 9, 1836

. . . Turned out to be a cold day, but still no rain. It was a big day for us, though. We purchased the three sections, the entire town, except Mister DeValurie's forty acres, and the bounders, businesses and all, and would you believe it? We got it all for Nunky Mose's gold nugget! So we still have our money to spend on supplies and all the swamp Jonny

wants! The prisoner, Mister Cartier, escaped while we were buying the land. Nunky Mose and my Jonny found him and recaptured him. We will take him with us to Batesville tomorrow. Perhaps you will see our town one day.

With love and kisses,
Margaret H.

Sunday, January 10

The rain came very early Sunday morning. Mose had pitched a tarp by the fire so Ella wouldn't drown making breakfast. The downpour delayed any early start.

"We will have the tarps for the carryall and trailer, don't we, Mose?"

"We's do, Jon. I has dem ready."

"Okay, as soon as this rain lets up, we'll put Jacob in the bed of the carryall. I see you have Corker and Conqueror hitched to the lead, with Red and Jake."

"Yassa, an' we's brings Slogs an' Smuts, an' two horses of Fred's."

"That would be my leads, March and April."

"Shouldn't we keep one of the mares, Jonny?"

"We probably should, my love. We'll see how the selling goes in Batesville."

"One dem horses in barn be mares, Jon."

"Oh, great! Then we will have at least one mare. Too bad we can't get another Conestoga."

"Yes, I wonder if that mare of . . . what was his name? Conestoga Joe? . . . got pregnant by Corker?" asked Maggie.

"I's bets she did, Sissy," said Ella.

"We'll probably never know."

"Don't be too sure, my love. Maybe someday we'll go back there to Martins Station and breed both Corker and Conqueror."

"Ha! That will be the day!"

"It will at that, my pretty plum. Get the tarps ready, Mose. The rain is letting up some. When we leave, would you put Cobbler and Flip in the barn?"

"I's sho 'nuff will, Jon."

"If we're keeping Corker and Conqueror, why don't we put them in the barn as well and hitch up one of these teams?" asked Maggie.

"You know, darlin', that's not a bad idea."

"I'm not stupid, Jonny!"

"No, darlin', you're not stupid. Will you change the lead, Mose, and put Corker and Conqueror in the barn too?"

"Yassa. Firs' I's helps loads Jacob."

Mose quickly changed leads on the carryall and put Sloggy and Smutty on lead.

"Thank you, Mose. I wish you and Ella were eligible to get land so you could go with us."

"I's works an' gets house finished, Jon."

"Okay. I guess we're ready to brave the rain. You have rain togs, Fred. Why don't we ride March and April?"

"Good idea," answered Fred. "That way, we won't need to take any more horses. The ladies can handle the wagon."

"We need to tie Jacob up good while he's in the bed of the carryall."

"I's helps do dat, Jon," said Mose.

"Then we're ready. Climb aboard, ladies. You too, Modessa."

In a steady drizzle, Mose rode Corker to the root cellar and grabbed Jacob. Mose put Jacob in the carryall and tied him down.

"You're tying that too tight. Hurts me arms."

"Keep quiet, or I'll hurt your head," answered Fred.

"I ain't done nothin' to ya."

"You burned what was going to be my home."

"That were my home!"

"It were DeValurie's home, now my land." Fred turned to Modessa. "You can ride on the bench, or in the bed with your husband."

"Thank you, sir," said Dessy. "I'll start on the bench."

"I wans ya here wit me!"

"Sorry, Jacob. You were going ta leave me."

"I'da come back, honest, Dess."

"Oh, Okay, stretch that tarp so they're all covered," said Fred.

It was midmorning when the carryall pulled onto the road leading west to the Military Road. Sloggy, Smutty, Jake, and Red were in harness, pulling the wagon and trailer, with drays March and April being ridden by Fred and Jon. They quickly reached the Military Road.

"That looks like a good place to cross, a trail west."

"It's a good thing we have a trail to follow, Jonny."

"Sure is, darlin'. Looks like we got the only good land around. This is all swamps."

Just after noon by Jon's calculations, the gang stopped for lunch. Ella had prepared dodgers to last several days.

"How are you ladies doing?"

"We're pretty wet, but that tarp really helped," said Janet.

"Good. Let's hang the tarp from the carryall to that tree."

"Why do that, Jonny? The seats will get wet."

"I don't think we can all squeeze into the bed of the wagon, my love. Grab a blanket and come down."

"Hey, I'm a-gettin' wet, ya buggers!" yelled Jacob.

"Good," answered Fred. "If you drown, they won't have to hang you."

"Dey ain't a-gonna hang me fer killin' no nigger!"

"If they don't, we will," said Jon. "Now I'm going to untie your legs so you can walk under the tarp."

"How 'bout untie my hands too? They's hurts."

"Then you may try to escape," answered Fred. "Then we'd have to shoot you."

"I ain't a-gonna escape in this here rain."

"We know you ain't. You wouldn't get far before you died!"

Modessa fed Jacob and herself, while everyone huddled under their blankets from the rain and cold.

"Are we about ready to move on?"

"Sure are, Jonny. The tarp isn't keeping out the rain at all. It works better on the wagon," answered Maggie.

"Okay, then. Get back on the wagon so we can stretch the tarp over it again. That means you too, Jacob."

"Too bad we don't have Nunky Mose along."

"Right, darlin'. He could fix the tarp so nobody gets wet."

Thank goodness they had a trail to follow. By midafternoon, the rains slowed, and a mountain came into view ahead.

"Are we going to have to cross that, Jonny?"

"I'm afraid so, my love. Mister DeValurie mentioned it. What did he call it? Crawley Ridge?"

"It's Crowley's Ridge, you big lummox, and it was Lolita who told us."

"Yes, my pretty plum, but we'll worry about crossing it in the morning."

"Good. We can get a big campfire going and get dried off."

"Righto, Jan, this is about twenty miles, all we have made today in this rain. Hope we do better tomorrow."

At the base of the ridge, the group found a small river and trees from which to hang the tarp. Jon started gathering sticks and limbs for a fire, while Fred took care of the horses.

"Look, the skies are clearing, Jonny."

"Yep. It may get cold tonight, but we should still sleep under the tarp or in the carryall."

"Just what are our sleeping arrangements, Jon?" asked Janet.

"Yes. The ground is wet, Jonny. Just where do we sleep?"

"Look in the trailer, Fred. Maybe Mose left something to help keep us dry."

"He did! He put a lot of blankets in the wagon, and our small tent!"

"Thank goodness for Mose. I wish he was here."

"Yes, and Nanty Ella too. You'll be lucky to get a dinner!"

"Looks like Modessa is doing alright."

"Mose sent some smaller tarps to put on the ground, Jon."

"Wonderful! That Mose is amazing! Do you want to sleep with your husband, Modessa?"

"I guess so, Mister Hamilton."

"Good. You must promise not to try to free him, and my name is Jon."

"I promise."

"I don' make no such promises!" shouted Jacob.

"I'm going to make you a promise if you don't shut up!" yelled Fred.

"Okay. We'll put you two back in the carryall. There's room for a couple under the wagon. We can't all sleep in this tent."

"Let's eat before we worry about sleep," said Fred.

"I wonder what the name of this little river is?"

"It's probably the same one we followed coming from Madison, when we strayed from the Saint Francis, Jonny."

"That's a pretty good guess, my love. Maybe it's the west branch of the Saint Francis."

"All my guesses are good, Jonny, and I guess it will take three days each way before we're home again."

"You're probably right, darlin'." Jon looked at Fred. "Let's get Jacob roped back up in the carryall, Fred. I'm pretty tired."

"Alright, Jon. I'll take the first watch and wake you when I get tired."

"I didn't think of that, but it's a good idea."

"Let's sleep here, Jonny, by the fire."

"Okay, my love. Good night, all. Be sure to wake me, Fred."

"I will. Good night. You sleep under the tarp too, Jan, so I can keep close watch on you."

"Alright," said Jan. "But don't wake me when you come to bed."

"You two have been married longer than us!" said Jon.

"Wake up, Jon. I need to be spelled. Can't stay awake."

"Okay, Fred, I'm awake. How's our prisoner doing?"

"He's been snoring all night."

"Good. Hope you can sleep. I'd like to get an early start."

"Are we really going to turn him in?"

"I don't know, Fred. We've got a couple days to think on it."

"Oooh, I thought I asked you not to wake me," said Janet.

"I'm sorry, darling. Scoot over. Here I come," answered Fred.

"Good night. I'll wake you early."

"Hey, you lazy gummers, get your keisters out of bed!"

"Ooh, already?" asked Fred.

"Mmm . . . I smell coffee. Can I have some, Jonny?"

"When you're up! Dessy made coffee, and is cooking now."

"Alright," said Janet. "Let's keep her! You awake, Fred?"

"I am now. Stop bumping me, please."

"Well, get up then, honey. Breakfast is ready."

"Uh-huh, I slept good. All three hours!"

"That's all you need, Freddy boy. Hand me my nethers."

"What? Did you take your clothes off?"

Janet started laughing. "Haha! That woke you up!"

"Keep Fred occupied while I get dressed, Jon," said Maggie.

"How far did you undress, my love?"

"Only the outer layer, Jonny."

"Then don't worry about anyone seeing you, darlin'. We're . . ."

"I know, we're one happy family. With no secrets."

"By George, I think you're getting it, my pretty plum."

"Our first job today is getting over this ridge."

"The trail goes north, Jonny. Maybe it crosses the ridge."

"That's probably our best bet, to stay on the trail," said Fred.

"Okay, I've got everything ready. Let's get the fire out and be on our way."

The group followed the little river at the base of Crowley's Ridge north, until it turned west again. They crossed the stream, and ascended the ridge about ten miles from their camp.

"Now is when we need Corker."

"And Nunky Mose," added Maggie.

"Well, if we need to, we can also hook up March and April."

"And make Jacob walk for a while."

"Right, my love. It isn't too steep yet."

About halfway up the side of the ridge, the trail suddenly leveled, and they found themselves sinking in a white sand. The horses were struggling, trying to pull the wagon and trailer through it. Jon called a halt.

"We're all going to walk until we get through this desert."

"That means you too, Cartier," said Fred.

"I hope I've watched Mose enough, so I can rope March and April ahead of Sloggy and Smut."

"This sure is pretty white sand, Jonny. I wonder how it got up here . . . I'll bet the earthquake did it."

"I don't know, darlin', but it's a pain in the kazoo!"

With six horses pulling and all people walking except Maggie, the wagon made it across the sand trap and found the trail again, heading up.

"This looks steep, Jon."

"It sure does, Fred. We better keep walking."

Jon estimated it to be a 25 to 30 percent grade they were climbing, for over a mile, before the trail leveled to a twelve to fifteen percent grade.

"Can we stop and rest, Jonny? I can't go any further."

"Oh yes, my love. I'm sorry I made you travel this far."

"That's too much for a pregnant woman," said Janet.

"Yes, I'm so sorry, honey. I wasn't thinking."

"I'm Alright, Jonny," Maggie reassured him, "I just need to rest."

"Good, darlin'. Let's rest here. I'll check the horses."

"And I'll fish out a corn dodger for each of us," said Janet.

With rest and a bite to eat, the group was again ready.

"I want you to climb up and drive, darlin'."

"I'm fine now, Jonny. I can walk."

"Don't argue with your husband, honey. Get up there!" ordered Jan.

"Alright. How much further, Jonny?"

"We're not far from the top, my love. Let's move."

Up they went, and soon reached the top. Strangely, the top was swampy, just like the terrain below. The trail ran west for over five miles across the top of the ridge, then started down again.

"Wow! It's just as difficult going down as climbing up!"

"I'm scared, Jonny. Will you drive?"

"The trailer doesn't want to follow the wagon straight," observed Fred.

"Okay. Stop the wagon, sweetheart. Good. Hold the horses right there." Jon turned his attention to Fred. "Fred, let's straighten the trailer."

With the trailer straight behind the carryall, Jon tied ropes from the trailer hitch to each corner of the wagon to prevent the trailer from straying. He then climbed aboard to drive. Jon managed to ease the wagon down the hill by laying on the brake and pulling on the reins of the horses.

"Look, Jonny, there are a few houses at the bottom."

"I see. Doesn't look like a town, though."

"When we get to that house, stop and we'll ask, Jonny."

"Ask what? We're not lost, darlin'."

"How far to Batesville, and how they make a living."

"Okay, we'll ask." They approached the first house. "Whoa, March. Whoa, Sloggy."

"Hello there. Is this a town, sir?"

"One day it will be, I hope. My name's Jones, Julian Jones."

"How far is it to Batesville, Mister Jones?" asked Maggie.

"Oh, about fifty miles, I guess. Where you folks from?"

"Have you heard of Lou's Landing?"

"Over on the Francis. Yep, I've heard of it."

"Well, we bought it, all three sections," said Jon.

"Ya come over Crowley?"

"Yes. Pretty tough goin', but we made it alright."

"Good for you! The big quakes made the ridge."

"We wondered about that," said Maggie.

"Did ya see that sand basin? That were a swamp bottom afor the quakes just lifted in the air!"

"Interesting. You folks farm this land?"

"Yep. We scratch out a livin', growin' corn and squash. Now an' then we grow a razorback.

"What's a razorback, sir?" asked Fred.

"Ha! Ya ain't ne'er heard of a razorback? Ha! Them's mean ole pigs gone wild."

"Mean, huh?"

"As mean as I ever did see mean! Them tusks will kill ya. They kilt me uncle. Sometimes even a ball won't stop 'em from a-chargin' atcha."

"We'll be on the lookout for them," said Jon.

"Ya do that! Be a-seein' ya on your way back."

"Is there any other way around this ridge?"

"Yep, you can go twenty mile north, er south forty mile, an' go round it."

"I guess we'll go back over it here," said Fred.

"How's the travel between here and Batesville, Mister Jones?"

Well, if'n ya go straight west, you'll run into the Black River an' a cliff that's a lot bigger than this here one."

"So we should go south?"

"Just foller this trail, an' take the left fork, 'bout twenty-mile jaunt from here."

"That will take us to the White River?"

"Yes, sir. Y'all knows yer way perty good. Whats ya got that man all hog-tied fer?"

"He killed a man and stole this wagon. We're taking him to court in Batesville."

"I only kilt a nigger!" yelled Jacob.

"That true? They won't do nuthin' ta him."

"Then I guess he's just dead weight," remarked Fred. "I guess we should just kill him now."

"Why don't ya leave 'im here? I'll work 'im ta death," said Mister Jones.

"No, we'll turn him in, like we promised Mister DeValurie."

"Ole Count Lou's still there, huh?" asked Julian Jones.

"Yes. We bought his land and most of the town."

"Do sweet Lolita still live there?"

"Yes, she does. She runs the little store."

"I gotta go see her one o' these days. I'm still sweet on her, an' I thinks she was sweet on me once."

"What happened?" asked Maggie.

"Ole lousy Lou stopped dat."

"Well, we're on our way. Thanks, Mister Jones."

"Ya bet! Don't let them Injuns get ya."

"Indians?" asked Fred. "They mean too?"

"Nah, they's just tryin' ta live, like the rest of us."

"Thanks again. Let's roll, gang. We still have a few hours of daylight."

"Goodbye, Mister Jones. See you on our way back!" yelled Janet.

The group headed west on the trail, over familiar swamp land.

Diary of Margaret Hamilton

January 11, 1836

. . . When suddenly the trail leveled, and we found ourselves hub-deep in beautiful white sand. A "Mister Jones" said that it had been swampy lowland before the big earthquakes, and had "risen up." We met this Mister Jones when we reached the bottom again on the other side. He said the court in Batesville will do nothing to Mister Cartier, but Jonny still wants to turn him in . . . We plan on selling two pair of the three we have. I hope we keep Sloggy and Smutty so we have a couple of mares to breed. Oh, it just occurred to me, I must tell Jonny in the morning. If we sell two sets of horses, that will leave only one pair to pull the wagon and trailer back to Lou's Landing! Uh-oh, let's see him get out of that mess! We are still about thirty miles from the White River, and Batesville.

Love to all my kin,
Margaret Hamilton

Tuesday, January 12

"Good morning, gang. Today we will reach the White River. I think it will be tomorrow before we hit Batesville."

"I have a question, Jonny."

"What is it, my pretty plum?"

"You plan to sell some guns and two sets of horses?"

"That's right, my love."

'Well, how do you plan to get back with only one set of horses, you big lummox?"

"Uh-oh," said Janet, "she's right."

"I hate it when women are so smart," quipped Fred.

"Oh boy, we should have brought Corker and Conqueror."

"Kind of late for should-haves now, Jonny."

"Right. I'll think of something. Let's eat breakfast."

Modessa turned out to be a good cook, and a hearty meal was consumed by all. Then it was back on the trail.

"We've got a nice day to travel, Jon."

"Sure do, Fred. Maybe we'll get lucky for a change."

"Yeah, if we don't run into a razorback . . . or Indian."

"I wonder what tribes of Indians live here."

"Cherokees, I'll bet," said Maggie, from the wagon.

"I don't think so, my love. The Cherokee who left Georgia would be south of here, around Little Rock."

"I would bet you, Jonny, but you never pay up."

"My bets are gentleman's bets. No money involved."

"Well, I am no gentleman, in case you hadn't noticed."

"I sure have noticed, my pretty plum, but I don't think we'll see Cherokee this far north."

"I'll bet you . . . a new bed, with a carved wood headpiece, that we'll see Cherokee Indians."

"Okay, darlin', you have a deal."

Around midday, Jon found a muddy brackish river, and the group stopped for rest and a lunch of cold dodgers. They heard the familiar screech of the Carolina parrot.

"I think they're following us," said Jon.

"They're a pretty little bird," said Janet.

"Yes," answered Maggie. "But awful noisy."

"I wonder how they would taste cooked over a fire," said Fred.

Screeching loudly, the Carolina parrots suddenly flew away.

"Look, darlin', that big bird just scared them away."

"Isn't that a beautiful bird, honey?" asked Janet.

"It's some kind of predator, the way it chased after those parrots," observed Fred.

"Look at that big patch of red on its neck! But I don't see a beak. Do you?"

"Yes, I see it, Jonny. I know what it is."

"How do you know, darlin'?"

"Because I remember seeing a picture of one in school."

"Well, what is it honey?" asked Janet.

"I think it's a woodpecker. Yes, the bill is ivory colored. It's an ivory-billed woodpecker."

"I don't see it pecking a tree," said Fred.

"You will," answered Maggie.

Sure enough, it landed on a pine tree branch and soon began pecking a rhythm on the trunk.

"See, I told you skeptics!"

"Okay, my pretty plum, I believe you. Are we ready to cross this river?"

"Let's hope it's not any deeper than it looks."

"If it is, our prisoner will get his keister wet! Ha!" laughed Fred.

The River Cache was easily crossed, and soon the group reached the fork in the trail that Mister Jones had mentioned.

"The trail heads south along this stream."

"Good thing Mister Jones told us which way to go, Jonny."

"Yes, or I'd have gone straight to the Black River."

The trail went south for a couple of miles, then crossed the creek to a group of well-kept houses. Indians!

"Concede, Jonny?"

"Hello, what tribe are you?"

"Hello. We are Cherokee. I am Oostanaula."

"Are you from Georgia?"

"Yes, many moons ago. Forced to sell, come here. Now Cherokee lose land, no pay, I hear."

"That is right. Do you know Chief Ustanali Nation?"

"I know John Nation. Ustanali his father. He chief?"

"Yes, chief of Smoky Mountain Cherokee."

"Cherokee live in mountains that smoke? Then they lose homes in Georgia. Too bad. Oostanaula sad."

"The chief does well. He has three wives and many followers."

"But he has no money, no land."

"He has gold," said Maggie. She saw the anger grow in Jon's face, and was sorry she had revealed that secret.

"Gold? Where he find gold?" asked Oostanaula.

"On Georgia land," answered Jon. "They took some before they were forced off their lands."

"Now Oostanaula very sad. Maybe gold on land I sell."

"Maybe. Chief Ustanali is my friend. Maybe someday he will come live with me."

"That bad! He maybe try to kill me."

"Why would he want to kill you?" asked Maggie.

"You hear of Blood Law?"

"Yes, I have heard of it," said Jon. "But soon no Cherokee will have land in Georgia, so Blood Law will not matter."

"Oostanaula hope you are right. Where you go now?"

"To Batesville to buy more land," answered Fred.

"Good. You need farmers. Cherokee good farmers."

"Do you own this land?" asked Maggie.

"No own. Cherokee and black no own Arkansas land, just try to live on land."

"President Jackson wants to give all tribes land in the Indian territory west of here," said Jon.

"Cherokee no trust traitor Jackson. He force Chickasaw and Choctaw to Indian territory, now force Cherokee."

"Well, maybe someday you will own land in Arkansas. Maybe we will talk more about land when we return."

"That good, if Cherokee still here," said Oostanaula.

"Are you leaving?" asked Maggie.

"Cherokee no hunt well with old gun and bow. Hungry winter."

Jon and Maggie looked at each other and shook their heads.

"We have a couple rifles, and some powder and balls that you can have. We have three, one for you, and the other two for your best hunters."

"Oostanaula cannot pay for them, cannot accept."

"Maybe you can help us, to pay for the rifles," said Maggie.

"How we help?"

"You have work horses?"

"Yes, but you have horses now."

"Yes," answered Maggie, "but we want to sell four horses in Batesville, and we would only have two left to return."

"Then Oostanaula can help. We will bring four horses to White River and pull you back to your home."

"Wonderful!" exclaimed Jon.

"Oostanaula will bring horses to where Black River meets White River. Leave early two sun-ups from now."

"For this, we will owe you more than three rifles."

"Three rifles means more to Oostanaula than you know."

"Thank you, Mister Oostanaula," said Maggie.

"Oostanaula thank you for rifles. Now we hunt for food."

"Good luck. We will see you when we return."

"You will see Oostanaula at White River."

"Yes, thank you. Goodbye for now."

The trail now continued in a southeasterly direction. Good trail, level land, and fair weather made for fast travel.

"That was brilliant, to get them to help pull us back."

"You mean I'm not a dummy after all, Jonny?"

"I've never said that, or even thought it, my love."

"That new bed is sure going to feel good."

"What bed, darlin'?"

"Don't try to be clever, you big lummox. You lost the bet!"

"Oh, the bet! What was the bet?"

"Jonny! You lost the bet. We met Cherokees."

"Oh yeah. Guess I did lose that bet."

"You bet your derriere you lost."

"I didn't bet . . . my derriere!"

"But you bet a new bed we're buying in Batesville."

"Why Batesville, my pretty plum?"

"Yeah, why Batesville, honey?" asked Janet.

"Because Jonny lost the bet, and he forgets quickly."

"I won't let him forget, honey. I'll be sure to make you one in our new furniture store."

"Oh, Good. That will surprise him, Jan."

"Yeah. Just pretend you forgot the bet. We'll fix your husband, honey."

"Good. It's getting late. I hope he stops soon."

The group found the Black River late, but Jon wanted to press on south to the junction of the White River.

"This is the place, gang. We camp here, where Oostanaula will meet us in a couple days."

"It's so dark. How do you know this is the spot?" asked Janet.

"Jonny thinks he has women's intuition, Jan," said Maggie.

"Well, I hope he's right. This is as far as I go tonight."

"Haven't you already noticed, Janet? I'm always right."

"Hmmm, I noticed alright," answered Janet, smiling at Maggie.

"I'll have to write that in my diary."

"After we eat, honey. I'm starved," said Janet.

Wednesday, January 13

"Good morning, everyone. We'll finally see Batesville today and start our empire."

"Just like that, one easy step!"

"No, I never said it's going to be easy, but it's a start."

"To start with, are we even in the right place?" asked Janet.

"This is where we will meet Oostanaula in a couple days."

"A beautiful spot, but where do the rivers meet?"

"About a hundred yards ahead, just down there."

"How do you know that, Jonny?"

"Just listen, my love. Put your ear to the ground, and you can hear the rivers meet and change direction."

"Oh, ho-ho, I married Daniel Boone!"

"It's Davey Crockett, honey," said Janet. "He's the one who can grin a bear to death, and change a river's course with one slap of his hand."

"I guess you're right, Jan. He's trying to feed us a crocket of bull dripping right now!"

"When you two skeptics finish breakfast, I'll show you the White River, but this is where we cross the Black."

"Where do we cross the White?" asked Fred.'

"See where the trail crosses here? Maybe we won't have to cross the White River."

"Well, let's eat and get to findin' out. The sooner we get to Batesville, the sooner we get rid of Cartier."

"That's right!" yelled Jacob. "The sooner I'll be free!"

"Oh, we're not gonna let you off scott-free," said Fred.

"No, but the court will!" yelled Jacob.

"Then I'll kill you myself."

"I ain't done ya no harm. Let me go."

"You burned down what would have been my home."

"And you stole this wagon and horses," said Janet.

"And you killed an innocent man," added Maggie.

"Please let us go, Mister Hamilton. We will never be a bother to anyone again," pleaded Modessa.

"I'll think on it, Dessy. Let's get crackin', gang."

Crossing the Black River wasn't easy. There was one spot of only a few yards, where the horses had to swim and the wagon and trailer floated a little. Only one got wet.

"Help! You bastards are a-drownin' me!" yelled Jacob.

"Good!" answered Fred. "One less problem for us!"

"Look how the land has changed, Jonny."

"Yes. Did you ladies see where the Black River became the White?"

"We sure did," said Janet. "The color even changed. Look how clear the water is."

"Swift and big too," answered Maggie. "For once you were right, Sir Hamilton."

"Feels good. Yes, the land is that good rich bottomland I heard so much about."

"And we heard it was all taken. This land must belong to that farm house."

"Yes, it does, my love, and there's another farm over there."

"And one across the river," added Fred.

"Well, at least we're on a good road, Jonny."

"We sure are, darlin'. Let's make tracks."

The river country was laced with farms and rich soil. Jon found a nice grassy area along the river for lunch.

"How much further to town, Jonny?"

"I'm not sure, my love. If we see a farmer, we'll ask."

"That's not like you, Jonny. Are you feeling alright?"

"Never felt better, my pretty plum."

"You feel the same to me," said Maggie, pawing him.

"You're just not feeling in the right places."

"Jonny! I'm not Liz, you know."

"No . . . ah . . . thank goodness for that."

"You talked your way out of that, Jonny. Thank goodness."

"While we're in Batesville, why don't you write to them, darlin', and both of our folks as well?"

"I will. They must have mail service here."

"I'm sure they do. Let's get to finding out."

"Hello, sir! Can you tell us how much longer it is to Batesville?"

"Surely can. It 'pends on how fast them horses are."

"Deez horses are fast as wind, plowboy," answered Fred.

"I kin use a couple a dem plow horses, friend."

"Well, now, just maybe we'll be a-sellin' a couple a them on our way back. Now, just how far is it?" mocked Fred.

"'Round ten miles er so."

"Thank ye. We'll be a-seein' ya in a couple a days."

"I'm a-willin' ta give ya tin dollas a piece fer 'em."

"We'll be a-membering that offer. So long, plowboy."

"Take good care a my plow horses, fellas!" shouted the farmer.

"You were funny, honey," said Janet.

"You sure cut him down, Fred," added Maggie.

"Well, he was trying to act smart."

"He's smarting now! Good job, honey."

"If we can't sell these horses in town, looks like we can sell a couple here," said Maggie.

"Yes, but I just think they're worth more than ten dollars."

"So do I, Jon. That's almost giving them away," said Fred.

"Just remember how much it costs to feed them all winter," said Maggie. "We have to sell four of them."

Late afternoon found Jon's group at the outskirts of Batesville, a good-sized boomtown. Nice-looking farms hugged both sides of the White River, which also split the town. Just by first impression, Jon liked Batesville.

"Looks like most stores are closed already, Jon," said Fred.

"Yes, so let's go on in and sleep in a hotel tonight."

"What about me?" cried Jacob. "You're not turnin' me in, 'cause they'd just let me go! Why don't y'all do the same?"

"I got an idea, Jon," said Fred. "Besides burning half the town of Lou's Landing, let's claim he also killed a white man!"

"It will be four of us against one, or two," added Janet.

"Hey, that's a good idea, Jonny. That way, we know he would die for killing that man." Maggie winked at Jon.

"That's what we'll do. Let's go in and find the sheriff."

"You lyin' bastards just would do that, wouldn't ya?"

"We sure will, Cartier. Start saying your prayers," said Fred.

"Please, Mister Hamilton, please let him go," cried Modessa.

"Shut the hell up, bitch!" shouted Jacob. "It's time I tolt ya, Dess, I was a goin' ta kill ya, an' run off wit Lolita anyways, so this saved me the trouble."

"Oh, Jacob, how could you?" cried Modessa.

"You're one sorry excuse for a man!" shouted Janet.

"Take off his ropes, Fred."

"And let him get away? No, thanks, Jon. I want to see him hang."

"Take off his ropes!"

"Yeah, take off deez ropes, ya bastard!" hollered Jacob.

"Please . . . let him go," cried the weeping Modessa.

"Take them off, Fred."

"Why are you doing this, Jonny?"

"He don't deserve to live, Jonny," added Janet.

"All ya bitches shut up! He knows what he's doin'" said Jacob.

Fred untied Jacob, and he swung at Fred, who received a glancing blow.

WHAM! Jon hit Jacob just below the right ear, and sent him to the ground. He got to his knees, holding his face with his right hand. When Jon grabbed him by his shirt and lifted Jacob back to his feet, he hit him flush on the nose. Jacob hit the ground hard and rolled. Jon kicked him in the ribs. "Get up, you son of a bitch!" Jon yelled. Jacob was now a mess, face full of blood and hugging his ribs.

"Please don' hit me 'gin."

"Get up!"

"Please, Mister Hamilton, don't hit Jacob again. We'll do anything you ask," pleaded Modessa.

"You would beg for that bastard, after what he said?"

"Yes, sir. I'm his wife. He'll do what you want."

"Is that right, Cartier?" asked Fred, softly kicking him. Jacob grimaced and nodded his head *yes*.

"Say it. I want to hear it from you, Cartier!"

"Y-yyes . . . any . . . thing . . . you a-a-ask."

"Stay with him for a minute, Dess. Come here, gang." Jon led his group out of earshot from Modessa and Jacob.

"What is it, Jonny?" Maggie asked, now that they were away from the Cartiers.

"Suppose we use them to get an additional three-twenty?"

"You mean extra land?" asked Fred.

"Yes, at the low rate for newcomers."

"And then let them go?" asked Janet.

"How would we do that, Jonny?"

"We offer them freedom if they pretend to be Mose and Ella long enough to add to our holdings."

"That's cheating, Jonny. But Nunky Mose and Nanty Ella deserve to own a part of our land."

"Then would you let that bastard go?"

"Yes, Fred. We couldn't prove he killed a white man anyway."

"But we should ask Dessy to stay with us," said Maggie.

"She is such a sweet lady. I'm for it," said Janet.

"I hate to let the bastard go, but count me in," said Fred.

"Okay. We go to the land office in the morning. If he doesn't go along, we claim he murdered a white man, Got it?" Everyone agreed.

"But I still want Dessy to stay with us," said Maggie.

"Let me rough him up a bit more first," said Fred.

"Alright, you scum, I was chosen to cob you to death," said Fred. *Wham!* He kicked Jacob in the back, then in the plexus, when Jacob rolled over. He then squatted and fisted Jacob in the face.

"Please, Mister Wilson, don't hit him no more, *please!*" pleaded Dessy.

"How about it, Cartier? Ready to cooperate?"

Jacob managed to nod his head yes.

"Okay. Can you hear me, Jacob?" asked Jon.

Jacob again nodded his head.

"Then listen up. Remember my two black partners, Mose and Ella?" Another head nod from Jacob. "Well, you are Mose Hamilton, and your wife is Ella Hamilton. Got it?"

"What are you going to do, sir?" asked Modessa.

"You will sign some papers tomorrow, Mose Hamilton and Ella Hamilton. Then I will let him go free."

"But we would like you to live with us, Dessy," said Maggie.

"Thank you, but I made a vow to my husband."

"But, honey," pleaded Janet, "you heard what he said."

"Yes, I heard. But he didn't mean it."

"You know he did, honey. Your crying proved that."

"Well, thank you all again, but I must stay with my man."

"The invitation will be open to you always," said Maggie.

"You understand what you're going to do?" asked Jon.

Both Modessa and Jacob nodded their heads.

"Now, don't let us down!"

"Or you will be a widow woman, Modessa," added Fred.

"We will not let you down, sir, and thank you," said Dessy.

"Okay. Let's find a stable, get some rooms, and eat," said Jon.

"In that order?" asked Maggie.

"Yes, honey, in that order. Don't worry. You won't starve."

"Hope you're right."

Diary of Margaret Hamilton

Wednesday, January 13, 1836

. . . We talked, and we saw many nice farms, pretty country. We were late getting to Batesville, so the land office was closed. This is a pretty town, and very busy. We had a great supper in an eatery! And a room in a hotel! How about that? . . . Talked the prisoner and his wife into signing Nunky Mose's and Nanty Ella's names to some of our land acquisition tomorrow, then Jonny plans to free them. I hope that Modessa will stay with us permanently, as Mister Cartier said he doesn't want her. Tomorrow is a big day, so will close now.

Love to all,
Maggie Rose

Thursday, January 14

"Is everyone ready to become land-poor?"

"Let's go back to that eatery first, Jonny, for breakfast."

"Oh, I almost forgot breakfast, my love."

"I have Cartier with me, Jon. He better not try anything," said Fred.

"How is he going to explain that face?"

"A razorback charged him," answered Fred.

"We won't disappoint you, Mister Hamilton," said Dessy.

"Good. Let's go eat, gang!"

They had a wonderful breakfast, with eggs! Then they started for the land office.

"Here goes, gang. Let's all keep together."

"We all agree that you'll do the talking, Jon," said Maggie.

"Good morning, folks. How can I help you today?"

"We have some big transactions, along the Saint Francis River," said Jon.

"Certainly. My name is Curtis. Harold Curtis, General Land Office manager for the new state of Arkansas."

"It's not a state yet, is it?"

"No, sir, but soon."

"That won't change any land we buy now, will it?"

"No, sir. Please come into my office."

"Do you have a precise map of the St. Francis area?"

"Yes, sir. It was surveyed just last year," said Mister Curtis.

"So this big map is accurate?"

"Yes, sir. Very accurate, sir."

"Where's Lou's Landing?"

"Ah, right here, sir. Right here."

"You call that accurate? The town is right here, in the bend of the river, in the southeast corner of section thirteen."

"Uh, yes, sir. Ah, how do you know that, sir?"

"Because we bought it. And sections seventeen and eighteen."

"You bought some swamp land, sir?"

"Yes, we did. And we want a hell of a lot more."

"Yes, sir. Th-that can be arranged, sir."

"Good. The six of us are eligible to buy one and a half sections of land at your big discount, right?"

"Yes, sir. I suggest we record the land you've already purchased, and get that out of the way first."

"Good idea! We have a sales slip right here, with the stamp of the seller, Mister Don Louie DeValurie."

"Yes, I've heard of him. You have his signature and stamp?"

"And the legal description of the three sections."

"Good. And a permanent address?"

"Permanent address?"

"Yes, sir. Like Mister DeValurie's address, *301 Valurie Boulevard*, North."

"What address do we use, gang?"

"I guess we use the house on this side of the river, Jonny."

"You mean this one, ma'am?"

"Yes, that's it," said Maggie.

"That would be the physical address of *100 Military Road Access number nine.*"

"Good. Now we can get that taken care of."

"Would it be owned by all three families?"

"Yes, it would. We are all partners."

"Wonderful. Missus Stewart, would you please record this?"

"Yes, sir, Mister Curtis. I'll be right back for their signatures."

"I notice that you are not buying one small piece, forty acres, in section thirteen?"

"Yes, that's right. That is Mister DeValurie's home."

"I see. Alright, Missus Stewart, you may proceed."

"Thank you, Mister Curtis. I'll be back."

"Of course, you know there is a recording fee?"

"How much is that?"

"Ten dollars for large sales, five for smaller."

"Fine. Now we want to buy all the big swamp caused by the earthquakes of eighteen-eleven and eighteen-twelve."

"What? You mean all this worthless swamp here?"

"Yes, sir. All that worthless swamp, and the one hundred four sections the swamp covers."

"Wow! What would you possibly want with one hundred four worthless sections?"

"That's really our business, but there are a lot of cypress trees, and other trees, in those swamps."

"I see. You're right, sir. It is none of my business."

"Would a dollar a section be fair to you?"

"Plus a ten-dollar recording fee, sir."

"Oh yes, I almost forgot," said Jon. "That would be one hundred four dollars, plus the ten-dollar recording fee."

"Yes. Missus Stewart, would you bring me a sales form? We have a large sale."

"Yes, sir, Mister Curtis," she answered from the adjoining room.

"You are one of the Hamiltons?"

"Yes. I'm Jonathan. This is my wife, Margaret, and my partners Mister and Missus Wilson, and cousin . . . Moses Hamilton and his wife Ella."

"Happy to meet you, Missus Hamilton, Mister and Missus Wilson, and Mister and Missus Hamil . . . what happened?"

"Ah, Mose shot a razorback, and didn't kill it. It charged him before we could shoot it."

"Wow, you're lucky, Mister Hamilton. They are mean."

"Yeah, we found that out. But we have pork now."

"Tough way to get it. Well anyway, let's get started on a description for those swamps."

"Here is a sales form, Mister Curtis."

"Thanks, hon . . . ah, we are very informal in this office."

"I see. That's good."

"Are they buying all that swamp land, Mister Curtis?"

"Yes. I gave them a great bargain price of one dollar per section, one hundred four sections."

"That is a great price, sir. A lot of those sections have some good land as well as swamp."

Jon could feel his face getting hot. *The bitch*, he thought.

"Oh yes! Thank you, Missus Stewart. I'm sorry, Mister Hamilton. I must charge extra for the good land."

"Hmm. I understand, Mister Curtis. How much?"

"Well, sir, it looks like one, two, three . . . thirty-one, thirty-two, and thirty-three sections have some good land as part of the swamp sale, sir."

"How much?"

"I'll give you a good deal, sir. How about one hundred dollars for each section with extra land?"

"Too much. I don't have that kind of money."

"Maybe fifty dollars a section, sir?"

"You probably wouldn't be able to sell any of those sections with a swamp on them," said Jon.

"Yes, sir. How about forty dollars a section?"

"Only if you throw in those part sections, along the East side of the St. Francis River, that don't have any swamp."

"I don't know, sir . . ."

"I hear they flood every year," lied Jon.

"Oh, well . . . alright, you have a deal, sir. One hundred four dollars for the swamp sections, and let's see . . . one thousand three hundred and twenty dollars for the good part sections, including ten part sections east of the St. Francis River, and the swamps."

"Two of those part swamp and part good land sections you counted, are sections we already own."

"Oh. Sorry, sir. That makes it only . . . twelve hundred forty dollars, plus ten dollars recording."

"Fine. Now the special land sale for the six of us."

"Yes, sir. Looks like you already have the area tied up, sir."

"Well, we're entitled to a section and a half at the special rate, and we definitely want the west part of section twenty-four here. How about the east halves of sections fourteen and twenty-three, west of these sections we own?"

"Okay, sir. They are available at the special price."

"And what is that?" asked Jon.

"Thirty-two dollars for each one-hundred-sixty-acre parcel. That's one hundred twenty-eight per section."

"And we can have those three parcels for . . . what's one hundred twenty-eight plus sixty-four?"

"One hundred ninety-two, Jonny," said Maggie.

"Plus ten dollars for recording," said Harry Curtis.

"That's a total of fourteen sixty-two, Jonny," said Maggie.

"I'll give you thirteen hundred for the entire package," said Jon.

"Ah, I'm afraid I can't do that, sir."

"How about we forget about the whole deal, then?"

"And you will be stuck again with that swamp!" said Fred.

"You won't find a better deal. You'll never sell most . . ."

"Alright! you have a deal, sir. Missus Stewart?"

"Now, where can I go to sell some gold?"

"Gold? You have gold?"

"You didn't think I would carry all that money around in my pocket, did you?"

"Gold! You have gold!'

"You bet I do, and I need to cash in a big gold stone."

"Ah . . . just how big a gold stone?"

"Oh, it must be four or five pounds of pure gold."

"Wow! Can I see it?"

"You sure can. I have it here, in my shoulder pouch."

"I thought that was gun powder for that rifle."

"My Hawken is always loaded already. Here is the gold."

"Wow!"

"You already said that, Mister Curtis."

"You called, Mister Curtis?" asked Missus Stewart.

"Yes, honey . . . oops! I mean, Missus Stewart. We need to record a couple of large purchases."

"Well, I have the first recorded document for these people to sign."

"Good, and while you're at it, bring money. Lots of money, honey."

"How much money, Harry?"

"Open the safe and empty it! Bring it all here."

"Have you gone barmy, Harry?"

"No, honey, look at that!" Jon showed Missus Stewart the gold stone.

"Wow!"

"That's what I said, honey, and Mister Hamilton wants to sell that magnificent stone."

"I don't think we have that much money, Harry."

"Is there someplace in town that can cash it in?"

"We have a bank, Mister Hamilton, but I can cash it."

"Alright, but I'm not sure what it's worth," Jon was lying again.

"Ah, last I checked, gold was about . . . seventy-five dollars an ounce, sir," lied Harry.

"That must have been when King George still ruled!" exclaimed Fred.

"Where did you say the bank was?" asked Jon.

"Wait! That was . . . a long time ago. Sorry, it's probably . . . ninety . . . five an ounce now."

"He's getting closer, Jon. He's before the eighteen-twelve War now," said Fred.

"It's around one hundred fifty dollars per ounce now," said Jon.

"Oh no, sir. Someone said it was one hundred thirty just a couple days ago."

"Okay, we'll settle for that. How much gold is that, darlin'?"

"Ten ounces, Jonny."

"Let's see, that's the east half of sections fourteen and twenty-three, and all the land west of the Saint Francis River in section twenty-four, in township seventy-four, range eighty-three west," said Jon. "All the land east of the Saint Francis River in sections twenty-four, twenty-five, and thirty-six, in township seventy-four, all the lands east of the St. Francis River in sections one, twelve, thirteen, twenty-four, twenty-five, and thirty-six in township seventy-five, and section one of township seventy-six, range eighty-three."

Harry cleared his throat. "That's correct, Mister Hamilton," he said.

"And then all the sections that have swamp, which includes the entire township seventy-five, in range eighty-two, sections thirteen through sixteen, and nineteen through thirty-six, in township seventy-four, range eighty-two, and sections three through six in township seventy-six, range eighty-two."

"Ah, that's correct too, Mister Hamilton."

"Then there's sections thirteen through thirty-six in township seventy-four, *and* sections two through eleven, and sections fifteen through twenty-one, and twenty-nine through thirty-one, in township seventy-five, range eighty-one." Jon paused. "Oh, and I almost forgot sections one through six, in township seventy-six, range eighty-two west, at the very bottom of the swamp. Is that correct, Mister Curtis?"

"That's correct, Mister Hamilton, all for ten ounces of gold."

"Hmm, I'm still going to have most of this stone left."

"Maybe I could sell you some more land, sir."

"Like what, for instance?"

"Well, sir, this land below the swamps and on the north side of the Little River is still open."

"How about these two part sections beside them, east of the Saint Francis?"

"Yes, sir, they're open too."

"Hmm, I don't know about them. How much?"

"Jonny, they're eleven to twelve miles from town," Maggie pointed out.

"Yes, they are a long ways away from Lou's Landing," said Jon.

"But look, sir. That's two full sections, and four part sections east and north of the two rivers."

"It would have to be a good price, Mister Curtis."

"That's about four and three-quarters sections in all."

"How much, Mister Curtis?"

"How about six more ounces of gold? That would make an even pound of gold."

Jon paused to think, and saw Maggie nod her head yes. "Okay, Mister Curtis, that's a deal. Let's see, so that's all the land east of the Saint Francis River, in sections twelve, thirteen, and twenty-four."

"Ah, sir, only the parts of section twenty-four that are north of the Little River and east of the Saint Francis."

"Right, and all the land north of the Little River in sections seven, eight, and nine, and seventeen and eighteen, of township seventy-six and range eighty-two."

"Everything for the sum total of one pound of gold," said Fred.

"You people drive a hard bargain," said Harry Curtis.

"Now I have to get this chunk of gold sold."

"Maybe we can split that stone, Jonny."

"Maybe so, my love. Do you have a blacksmith?"

"Yes, sir, down the street and two blocks on the other side of the bridge is a stable with a blacksmith."

"Fred, you and Mose watch the wagon, and I'll ride March to the stable. Be right back, Mister Curtis."

"That's fine, sir. It will give Missus Stewart time to write up all these contracts."

"Come on, Mose, let's check out the wagon," Fred said to Jacob.

"Here are your copies of records for your purchase of the DeValurie properties, Mister Hamilton," said Missus Stewart.

"Thank you. Let's go, gang."

"I done yer dirty deed. Now turn me loose," said Jacob.

"We're not finished with you yet. You have more papers to sign, Cartier," said Fred.

"Then we'll let you go," added Jon. "You did well. Keep it up, and we may even give Modessa back to you."

"Keep her! She means nothin' ta me!"

Tears began running from Modessa's eyes, and Maggie hugged her.

"He's not worth sticking to, Dessy. Think about staying with us at Lou's Landing."

"I'll be back," said Jon, as he mounted March. He rode through town, over the bridge crossing the White River, and spotted the livery stable exactly where Curtis said it would be.

"What kin I do fer ya?" asked the heavy-set smitty.

"I have a gold stone that I need split."

"Split? Gold? Who are ya funnin'?"

"Nobody. I would like this gold rock split."

"Whoa! I ain't ne'er seen a rock like that afore!"

"Can you split it in about a third?"

"Well, ya dunt wanna melt the critter. Maybe I can split it wit' a chisel." The smitty grabbed a chisel and mallet, and placed the stone on a large cloth. He split the stone with a single blow.

"Great job, sir. How much do I owe you?"

"Nothin'. Weren't no bother."

"Here, take this gold shaving, with my thanks."

"Thank ye! Come 'gain!"

Jon picked up the rest of the pieces, the two gold portions, and rode back across the bridge to his gang. "I got it cut and weighed, gang. This piece is twenty-point-six ounces, and this one is forty-eight-point-one ounces."

"That makes sixty-eight-point-seven ounces total," said Maggie.

"How many pounds, smarty pants?"

"Hmm, just a shade over four and a third pounds."

"Wrong! I have some tiny shavings that broke off when the smitty split the stone. See?"

"Ah-ha! That makes over four and a third pounds, just like I said, you big lummox."

"You can't beat logic like that, Jon," quipped Fred.

"I don't know why I even try!"

"Let's have some coffee before we go back in there," said Janet.

"She probably won't have those papers ready yet, Jonny."

"I think we should get the signing finished first, so we can get rid of this piece of trash," Fred said, as he pointed at Jacob.

"Yeah, let's get all this over with so I can be gone," said Jacob.

"Right, here we go, gang!"

"Back so soon? I don't think Missus Stewart is ready."

"That's alright. We'll wait," said Fred.

"The gold piece for you is bigger than I needed, so I hope you can pay us the difference."

"Oh, sure. I'll weigh it for you."

Jon bumped Maggie, who was about to speak.

"Alright, Mister Curtis, here. This is it."

"That's a nice stone, Mister Hamilton. Looks like it's large enough to pay the bill," Harry chuckled. "Be right back."

"We have lots of time," said Jon.

"It is plenty big, my friends. It weighs eighteen and six-tenths ounces, so you have money coming back."

"There must be something wrong with your scales, Mister Curtis. I have some scales in our wagon. I'll go get . . ."

"Oh no, sir, that won't be necessary. We'll just call it an even twenty ounces."

"That would make six ounces missing. That hardly seems fair. I'll just go get . . ."

"That won't be necessary. I made a mistake . . . it was twenty and three-eighths ounces . . . I'm sorry for . . ."

"Oh, that's alright. Now, it was twenty-point-six ounces, and we owe you sixteen ounces. That means you owe us . . ."

"Five hundred and ninety-eight dollars," said Maggie.

"At one hundred thirty dollars per ounce," added Jon.

"Yes. I'm sure you're right, Missus Hamilton," said Harry Curtis.

'Isn't she a whiz at arithmetic?" asked Jon.

"She sure is. You're very lucky, Mister Hamilton."

"Oh yes. How well I know that."

"Missus Stewart, please give these people five hundred-ninety . . ."

"Eight!" said Maggie.

"Five ninety-eight, please."

"Okay, Harry. I'm about finished with these sales contracts."

"I may not have a job after this," said Harry.

"Why not, Mister Curtis?" asked Janet.

"When the land office manager finds out how cheaply I sold this . . ."

"Don't worry, Mister Curtis," said Maggie. "He'll be happy when he sees that you sold that big swamp."

"I hope you're right, Missus Hamilton."

After a pause, Missus Stewart was back. "Alright, here are your documents, Harry . . . and money."

"Thanks, honey. If all six of you will please sign all three of these contracts, we can record them so you can be on your way."

"There are places for you to sign too, Mister Curtis?" asked Maggie.

"Oh, yes, ma'am, right . . ."

"I don't see a spot for your signature."

"Well, I guess Missus Stewart forgot . . ."

"That's alright," Maggie said. "There's a spot at the bottom."

"And there is room on these two papers as well," added Janet.

"Yes, of course!"

"Yes, and be sure to note your title, as seller."

"Yes, ma'am. As I said, you are lucky, Mister Hamilton."

"Thank you, Mister Curtis. Good luck to you."

"See to it you don't tangle with any more razorbacks."

"I ain't ne'er goin' ta see a razor again!" said Jacob.

"Ha! My cousin is funnin' again."

"Yeah, well good luck cutting all those trees."

"Trees . . . oh, in the swamps! Thank you. Goodbye."

Once outside the office, Fred exclaimed, "Whoopee! We are land barons! We got all these papers to prove it! All signed, sealed, and recorded!"

"Yes, honey, even if most of it is swamp," said Janet.

"Those swamps are going to make us rich, gang."

"I hope you're right, Jonny," said Maggie.

"Should we go celebrate now?" asked Fred.

"I'm leavin'! Turn me loose!" yelled Jacob.

"Are you going with your husband, Dessy?" asked Maggie.

"I am his wife. I must . . ."

"No! Ya ain't a-comin' wit' me! Stay wit' them!"

"But, Jacob, I'm your . . ."

"Quiet, bitch! I'm a-headed fer them hills, an' I don't want ya. I gives ya yer freedom!" hollered Jacob.

"Don't cry, honey," comforted Janet. "You stay with us. You deserve a lot better than him." Maggie and Jon hugged Dessy as Janet comforted her.

"I done what ya asked. Now I'm a-leavin'."

"Okay, Jacob. Take a rifle and be gone," said Jon.

"And good riddance," added Maggie.

Fred threw a rifle from the trailer to Jacob, and Jacob was gone.

"Don't worry, honey. There'll be others better than him," said Janet.

"Well, let's celebrate, everybody! We just killed two birds with one stone."

"What two birds, Fred?"

"We bought a lotta land, and we got ridda Jacob."

"You're right, honey. What do you say, Jonny?"

"Yes, but first let's get all our shopping finished, then go back out of town and party."

"We can't do that, Jonny. We've got rooms in the hotel."

"You're right, my pretty plum. Well, maybe we can celebrate in the hotel."

"Sure we can," said Maggie. "Come on, let's go shopping."

Diary of Margaret Hamilton

Thursday, January 14, 1836

. . . And as near as I can tell, we own one hundred eighteen sections of land. That's bigger than Bethania! I must confess, I'm drunk! I will finish this tomorrow.

Mag

Friday, January 15

"Come on, get up, Fred and Jan!"

"Oooh, what time is it?" asked Janet.

"After nine in the morning," answered Jon. "Maggie and Modessa are getting dressed right now."

"But I just got to sleep, Jon."

"I don't feel sorry for ya, Fred. At least you got some sleep. I didn't get any."

"Why not?" asked Fred.

"I was worried about our carryall and trailer being full of food and goods."

"You paid that man to guard it."

"Yeah, I guess I did, but I'm still worried."

"Have you checked it this morning?"

"Only about seven or eight times since midnight."

"Are we going to eat before we leave, Jonny?"

"Sure. We still have four drays and as many rifles to sell before we leave too."

"Where are you going to do that, honey?"

"I'll try the stable where I go the gold piece split. I also saw a gun shop on the other side of town."

"And there are lots of farms just out of town," added Fred.

"Right. We'll meet you at the eatery for breakfast."

"Ya. We'll be right there. Ouch . . . my head hurts!"

"This place sure has good meals," said Fred.

"What now, Jonny?"

"You women stay with the wagon. Fred and I will try to sell the horses and rifles."

"I'm ready Jon. I can carry the rifles."

"Good, Fred. We'll take the rifles first, then come back and get the horses."

Jon and Fred walked the three-plus blocks over the bridge to the blacksmith shop.

"Hello, you sellin' those flints?"

"We sure are, all four of them."

"We can use them. I'll give you fifty dollars apiece for them."

"I don't know . . ."

"And I'll throw in all the starter powder, powder, and flints you can use. I assume you have other rifles?"

"What about balls and caps?"

"You have a cap gun?"

"Yes, sir. I have a converted Hawken, fifty-caliber."

"Wow, a Hawkin! I just got some caps from Saint Louis. I would like to see one fired, and I'll add the caps and balls."

"You have a deal, sir. We're headed back to the hotel to sell some horses. Come along, and fire my Hawken."

"Thanks. I'll get your money and close shop."

"Wow, what a magnificent rifle! What will you take for it?"

"They're made in Saint Louis. You can get one there."

"Yeah, I know, but I've been so busy."

"Well, this one's not for sale, but you can shoot it."

"Thank you, sir." The man aimed at a tree branch out of town and fired.

"You hit it! Good shot!" exclaimed Fred.

"That must be five or six hundred yards," said Jon.

"That's the nicest shooting gun I've ever fired! Thanks!"

"You're welcome. Will you reload it, darlin'?"

"Sure, Jonny."

"If you'll excuse us, sir, we need to sell some horses."

"Sure thing. Don't sell them horses too cheap. Yu can get a good price for them from Houston."

"From who?" asked Fred.

"Sam Houston, down in Texas. He needs them to pull his heavy artillery around."

"Who is he fighting?"

"Where have you folks been? He's fightin' the Mexicans."

"No, we haven't heard, sir," said Jon.

"Yeah, Davy Crockett is down there with him. They declared independence from Mexico. A lotta Arkansawyers are there."

"Well, thanks again for the powder and supplies."

"You bet. I'll sell those rifles real quick. Good luck."

"Come on, Fred. Let's get these drays down to the stable."

"Pardon me, sir," said the gunsmith. "If ya sell those three pair, what's gonna pull yer wagon?"

"We're only going to sell two pairs," answered Fred.

"And we have more out of town," added Jon.

"Oh, sorry I asked! Good luck."

Jon felt embarrassed walking six big horses down main street.

"Hello. Yer back. More gold ta pound? Or did ya wanna put gold halters on them horses?"

"No, sir. We want to sell four of them. Are you buyin'?"

"Well, I recon I can use a couple of 'em. How much?"

"I'm not sure what they are worth."

"Well, let's take a look-see." The smitty examined each horse from head to hind. "They's all in good shape."

"Good enough for Houston's army, huh?" asked Fred.

"Maybe, frien', but I's buys fer myself. I'll gives ya a hundred fer them two matched pair."

"They are my two best pair of wheel horses, Jake and Red. They're worth more than a hundred each."

"Wheel horses, eh? Can they pull?"

"You bet your balls they can pull! They're good lead horses as well. I'll take one-fifty each for them."

"Hmm . . . one twenty-five?"

"No, sir. I'm thinking one-fifty is too low."

"Oright! I's gives ya one-fifty."

"Good. Now, where can I sell another pair?"

"Well, I knows a farm east-a here what will take 'em."

"We're going east. Where is this farm?" asked Fred.

"'Bout fifteen mile, on this side-a da river. They has a stone house, and their name's Critin, Al Critin."

"About fifteen miles, huh? How far is it to the Black River from here?" asked Fred.

"A smidgen over twenty mile," said the smitty.

"Good. You now own two excellent work horses, and we wish you well. Let's go, Fred."

As the two men with four horses started back, Jake and Red started to whinny and snort. They knew they were being left.

"I think that they know, and miss ya, Jon."

"Yes. I will miss them too. We have been through a lot together on this journey from Carolina."

"Well, we can always go back and trade them for March and April here."

"Nah, we made an agreement. Let's stick to it."

When they got back to the wagon, the women were not in sight.

"Now where do you suppose they went?"

"Hopefully not too far. Let's get these drays hitched up."

"It's about time you men got back," said Janet.

"We've been waiting for you for an hour," said Jon.

"Yeah, we were about to leave you," added Fred.

"Bunco!" said Maggie. "We've only been gone ten minutes."

"Bunco yourself, my love. Where were you?"

"We got a couple things for ourselves," answered Janet.

"And a few things for Dessy, Jonny."

"Good, but what did you use for money?"

"Those gold shavings from your stone," replied Maggie.

"Oh, okay, let's get crackin', gang."

"You only sold two horses, Jonny?"

"Yes, but we can sell two more in fifteen miles, darlin'."

"How much did you sell Jake and Red for?"

"Three hundred, my pretty plum."

"Isn't it amazing? We're going home with more than we came with, or what we started with in Bethania."

"Well, not quite, my pretty plum. How much did we spend for all these supplies?"

"A little under two hundred dollars."

"And how much did we have to start?"

"Jonny, we had a buckboard, a wagon, five horses, and each of us had over a hundred dollars and my Pasha bank."

"That's all? Wow! We keep this up, we'll be millionaires!"

"Oh, and we had my Pasha, and Abby the cow."

"Yeah, and now we have eight work horses and four other horses, a cow, and Chipper's dog Isaak. Wow!"

"And if we sell two more horses, we'll have about a thousand six-hundred dollars, and about one hundred twenty sections of land . . . and a town, Jonny!"

"Wow! How many acres is that, my pretty plum?"

"Hmm, let's see, Jonny . . . that's a little under . . . seventy . . . seven thousand acres!"

"Whoopee!" yelled Fred, as he and Jon rode the backs of wheel horses March and April. "And we have four businesses!"

"Four?" asked Janet. "The mill, furniture shop, and general store. What else?"

"How about the farming, honey?"

"And the rice-growing gang," added Jon. "That's going to be the biggest moneymaker of them all."

"Whoopee! I'd say let's celebrate, but my head still hurts from last night," smiled Fred.

"And we haven't even mentioned our greatest assets yet."

"What's that, Jonny?"

"Mose and Ella!"

They all agreed to that. With all their chatter, Jon noticed then that they had already ridden about five miles from town.

"Let's ride about ten more miles before lunch."

"Is that where the farm is that we're looking for, Jonny?"

"Yes. Look for a stone farmhouse across the river."

"I saw that house when we were coming this way," said Janet.

"What is the name of the people, Jonny?"

"Ah . . . do you remember, Fred?"

"Yeah, it was . . . Critin? Yeah, Critin."

There wasn't much talking after that. Jon noticed how hard the pull was for Sloggy, Smutty, March, and April, and realized that just one team could never pull the carryall and trailer alone.

"There's the stone house, Jonny!"

"Yep! Let's make a camp right here, gang."

"You mean the tent and campfire?" asked Fred.

"Yes. Let's have a hot lunch."

"But, Jonny, those Indians will be waiting for us."

"I hope you're right, my love, but I'm hungry."

"Me too, Jon. I'll gather some firewood."

"Okay, Fred. I'll get those horses staked in that grass."

"Do we have to cross this river here?" asked Jan.

"I'll take Sloggy across, as soon as I eat," answered Jon.

"Would you like pork and cooked beans?" asked Dessy.

"That sounds wonderful, Modessa."

"Hello over there!" came a shout from across the river.

"Hello!" answered Jon. "Are you Mister Critin?"

"Yes, I am. My brother Doug and I own this farm."

"I hear you want to buy a couple horses," shouted Jon.

"Yes. You got some? I'll be right over."

"Good. We have some pork and beans. Come join us."

"I'll get my brother, and be right with you."

Jon's gang didn't see Al and Doug Critin cross the White River, as they had ridden upstream and crossed before riding into camp.

"Howdy. I'm Albert, and this is Doug."

"Welcome. Step down and join us for lunch."

"We had our lunch, but them beans sure smell good!" said Doug.

"Thanks," said Al Critin. "You folks live around here?"

"Over on the Saint Francis. Came to Batesville to record our land we just bought," answered Fred.

"I'm Jon, my wife Maggie, Fred, Janet, and Modessa."

"Your land down by Marking Tree?" asked Al Critin.

"No," answered Maggie. "Have you heard of Lou's Landing?"

"Sure have," said Douglas Critin. "That's all swamp up there, ain't it?"

"Lots of swamp, but some good land too."

"Well, I hope you got a good price fer it."

"We did indeed, sir. How long have you lived here?"

"Came down from Missouri way three years ago," said Al.

"Sure like the looks of that stone house," said Janet.

"Thanks, ma'am. My brother here is a good mason. This land has such good soil, it took time to gather all them stones," said Al.

"What crops do you grow, and where do you sell them?"

"Lots a cotton an' corn, and some tobacco. Sell 'em right in town. They ship 'em right past here ta New Orleans," said Doug.

"Oh! They don't take them to Saint Louis?" asked Jon.

"Nah, it's a long ways down river to New Orleans, but it pays a lot better'n Saint Louses."

"But you'd have to take yer crops to Saint Louis from the Saint Francis," added Al. "'Cause ya can't navigate the river."

"Hey! Maybe we could bring our crops here to Batesville, Jon, and get more money for them than in Saint Louis," said Maggie.

"Good thought, darlin' . . . Or maybe down Military Road to Little Rock . . . and Texas."

"If you're goin' that far, you might as well go ta New Orleans."

"Yes. Well, we have a couple horses to sell."

"Them ones? What'll you use to pull that load ya got if we buy them horses?" asked Doug.

"We have some other horses waiting where the Black River runs into the White."

"Oh," said Al. "We can let ya use these ones ta that far. I reckon' that's only five or six miles."

"Thanks, Mister Critin. We were thinking of selling just two of these horses, and taking two back home."

"Oh, Okay. Whatever tickles yer fancy."

"You sure?" asked Al. "We'll buy however many you want to sell."

"What do you think, gang? We still have three pair of horses back home."

"Doesn't matter to me, Jon," answered Fred.

"With all our land, I think we're going to need more horses," said Janet.

"That's right, and I'd like another mare, Jonny."

"Yes, my love. We'll sell two, and keep two."

"In that case, we'll take the matched pair," said Al.

"Their names are March and April."

"We'll give you . . ." Al looked at his brother Doug, and flashed two fingers. Doug agreed. "Two hundred each, and help pull your train to the Black River."

Jon's group agreed. "That's a bargain, sir. Thanks. Let's get them hooked up, Fred."

"That sure were a good meal, ma'am," said Doug Critin.

"Why thank you," answered Modessa. She was smiling!

It was late afternoon when the group crossed the Black River and found the spot where they had camped before. The Indians they were expecting were not there.

"Where are the horses ya said would be here?" asked Al.

"They'll be here," answered Jon.

"Are you sure this is the right place, Jonny?"

"Yes, I'm sure, my love." Jon turned to Al and Doug. "You don't need to wait."

"I'd hate to leave ya high and dry," said Al.

"It's alright, sir. Our horses will be here anytime now."

"Well then, here's four hundred, an' I'll get our horses."

"I'll help you unhitch, and thanks again."

"We can wait a while longer, if'in ya like," said Doug, watching Modessa closely.

"No, thanks. We'll be fine."

"Alright, let's go, Doug, so we'll be home before dark."

"Yeah, brother. Bye, ma'am . . . bye, all."

"Next time you're through, stop by our house," said Al.

"Yeah, you'll always be welcome," added Doug.

The Critin brothers headed back across the Black River with March and April.

"Nice people, Jon."

"Yeah. Nice money too!"

"What do we do now, Jonny?"

"We wait for Oostanaula and his horses, darlin'."

"I'm glad we kept Sloggy and Smutty."

"I am too, my love. They were my team fifteen, you know."

"Yes, I know. Maybe we should have kept them all, Jonny."

"We would have trouble feeding them."

"That's true now, but someday we'll probably need them all."

"Let's hope so, my pretty plum. Do you know that Jake and Red didn't want to leave me?"

"How do you know that?"

"Because they made a fuss when Fred and I left them."

"Really? They sure were a good team."

"That they were, my love. Let's make camp again."

The two horses were staked, the tent was set up and a fire was set. Modessa got busy again making supner, with Jan and Maggie's help.

"Better make extra, ladies, in case the Cherokee show up tonight."

"They better show up. It's a long walk to Lou's Landing," said Janet.

"They'll be here," said Maggie. "I hear they can smell food miles away."

"You're right, darlin'. I think I hear them coming."

"What's the matter, honey?" Janet asked Modessa.

"They frighten me."

"Don't worry, Dessy," said Jon. "They're more civilized than most of the whites we'll see."

Oostanaula and two others appeared with six horses. None were as big as Sloggy, but they were close to Smutty's size.

"We have food cooked for all of us. Step down."

"Good. Oostanaula hungry."

"We still have two horses we will keep, so we only need four of yours to pull our wagon and trailer."

"This Oostanaula see. One horse for you and one horse for Oostanaula to ride."

"Okay. We will start out in the morning."

Diary of Margaret Hamilton

Friday, January 15, 1836

. . . Everyone has hangovers this morning. But we are wealthy landowners! We will have forty-seven ounces of gold, supplies to last three months, sixteen hundred or more dollars, lots of animals and equipment, the town, about seventy-seven thousand acres, and what Jonny calls our greatest assets—Nunky Mose and Nanty Ella . . . Jonny says we are about forty-five or fifty miles from our home, camped with three Cherokee Indians and their horses. They are going to pull us home along with team fifteen, which we kept. We sold the others, but we still have four pair of work horses to start. Aren't you proud of Jonny and me? I wrote letters to you all, hope you get them soon . . . and I am very happy, expecting to give birth in early April. I will soon have the diary all filled, and will end writing these notes . . .

With all my love, until I see you again . . .
Margaret Rose

Saturday, January 16

"Our Cherokee friends are up early," remarked Fred, "just like Mose and Ella!"

"Yes. Thank goodness Dessy didn't make them wait too long for breakfast."

"They have Sloggy and Smutty all hitched up with four of their horses, Jonny."

"Yes. You three women and Fred, squeeze into the carryall. Oostanaula and I are riding the other two horses."

"Where are those others riding?" asked Modessa.

"They'll be riding their lead horses. Don't worry, Dessy."

The six draft horses worked hard, pulling the loaded carryall and trailer over swamps and creek to the houses of the three Indians, where they rested and lunched. The three Cherokee all had wives, and the gang ate unknown meat.

"Don't ask, darlin'. Just eat and pretend you like it."

"When will we be back home, Jonny?"

"Well, we can't run down these horses, so we'll see Mister Jones again, probably late tomorrow."

"Then we have to cross back over that Crowley Ridge."

"Yes, and that won't be easy, darlin'."

"But if we start now, we will be there much earlier, Jon," said Fred.

"True." He turned to the Cherokee. "We are ready to go now, Oostanaula."

"You no stay here tonight?"

"We would rather go east toward our homes."

"Then we go. Where other white man prisoner you had?"

"He left us in Batesville. We will see him no more," Answered Fred.

"That good! Now you have two wives?"

"No, I can only handle one wife."

"But she have baby soon. You need two wives."

"I will just suffer when my wife has our baby."

"*You* will suffer, Jonny? You think I will have a picnic?"

"No, my pretty plum. I was trying to be funny."

"You are a barrel of laughs, Jonny!"

"Right. Well, let's get crackin', gang."

Crossing the Cache River was more difficult than before due to the extra weight and different horses, but they made it and soon they were in brushy, swampy land. Jon wondered where the trail was that they had taken before.

"Four days ago, when we met Oostanaula, we were on a trail that leads to the big ridge."

"This Oostanaula know. Oostanaula know of good place to cross ridge to the east. You trust."

"But it's easier travel on trail, friend."

"But not easy to cross ridge! You trust."

"Yes, I trust, Oostanaula."

"Good. We make big ridge today at dark."

"Good! I trust Oostanaula more."

The ground soon became level with fewer swamps, and the load seemed to get easier for the horses to pull.

BAM! The shot from Oostanaula started everyone. Jon rode around the wagons to see if the Cherokee was alright.

"Shits, damn, holy blazes!" exclaimed Oostanaula.

"What happened?" asked Jon.

"Oostanaula not used to gun. Miss bird," he said, pointing.

Jon saw the ivory-billed woodpecker in a tree. He hated to do it, but aimed his Hawken at it. *BAM!* It fell.

"You shoot it, Jon Hamilton. Good shot, I get."

"Why did you do that, Jonny?"

"As a favor, my love."

"Favor? It is not a favor to kill such a beautiful bird."

"Too pretty a bird to kill," said Janet.

"Maybe so, but now we'll keep our own heads!" answered Fred.

"You make Oostanaula very happy. Pecking bird very special to West Cherokee. Bring good luck."

"Wheee, eeeee!" said the other two Indians, as they ran over to the dead woodpecker and began plucking its feathers.

"Did you learn about favors in school, pretty plum?"

"No, I didn't, Jonny. That bird must be sacred to them."

"Oostanaula, what do you use those feathers for?"

"We make ceremony head cover from feather of pecking bird. Decorate hair and dress."

"Those black-and-white feathers are lovely, Jonny."

"They sure are, my love. So is the red . . ."

"We make necklace from beak and feet, and we eat . . ."

Suddenly, there was crashing and grunting noises in the brush. One of the women screamed, and the Indians scrambled to the horses. Jon quickly began reloading his gun.

"Load one of those extra rifles, darlin' . . ."

"What is it, Jonny?"

"I don't know. Maybe Boony," Jonny said, as he poured a charge.

"Very funny, Jonny. I should . . ." *Crash!*

A huge animal of some kind knocked over Oostanaula and his horse, and charged back into the brush.

"What in hell was that?" asked Fred.

"An elephant, honey," replied Jon.

"Are you alright, Oostan—" As Jon was capping the nipple, another huge beast appeared, charging the carryall. *BAM!* Down went the beast, falling against the carryall and almost tipping it over, spilling the ladies.

"Maggie, are you Okay?"

"Yes, I think so, Jonny."

"Did you get that rifle loaded?"

"No, I spilled some gunpowder."

"Well, hand it here and reload the Hawken. Hurry."

Oostanaula was on his knees, rifle in hand. His horse was limping. As Jon quickly worked on loading the flintlock, there was another *crash*. The big beast reappeared from the brush he had run into after bowling over Oostanaula's horse. *BAM!* Jon hit it square in the head and knocked it down, but it started to get back up.

"Here, Jonny!" yelled Maggie, tossing the loaded Hawken. Jon instinctively tossed the flintlock to his wife, and found a cap. *BAM!* Jon's second shot silenced the beast.

"Are you alright, Oostanaula?"

"Think so, Jon Hamilton. You save Oostanaula."

"It looks like a big pig, Jonny."

"They are big pig," said Oostanaula, "call razorback."

"Lord God Almighty!" exclaimed Fred. "They are as big as these horses! This one by the wagon is four hundred pounds!"

"This one is even bigger!" yelled Jon. "At least a quarter ton!"

"Oostanaula thank Jon Hamilton for saving life, and for rifles to kill razorback, get food."

"What do we do now, Jonny?" asked Janet.

"We make camp, and cut up some pork for supper."

"Sounds like a good idea, Jon. I'll get wood," said Fred.

"There's some grass over there for the horses."

"Alright, girls," said Janet, "let's get to work."

Sunday, January 17

"I'm all porked out," exclaimed a tired Jon.

"We have all the pork our wagon and trailer can haul, Jonny, and there is still a lot left."

"I know, darlin'." Jon turned to his friend. "Oostanaula, there is so much meat. What shall we do to get it to your homes?"

"We load two horses, and Oostanaula send them back and put rest in tree. Nickawatie bring horses back."

"Where will you ride?" asked Maggie.

"Oostanaula ride on wagon horse too, with Jon Hamilton."

"Is your injured horse alright, Oostanaula?"

"Horse fine after you put liniment on legs."

"Good. You will be Okay, riding on your work horse?"

"Yes, be Okay. Can walk if need to."

The two extra horses were loaded with wild pork, and the Indian Nickawatie walked them east. There was still a lot of meat, which was roped up in a tree, and the tree marked. It was time to go. Jon was on the back of Sloggy, and Oostanaula on Smutty. The other Cherokee rode a lead horse. The pace was slower, and they made about nine miles before lunch.

"We could use another pair of horses, Jon," said Fred.

"Yes. I guess we should have brought Corker."

"Corker? Name of horse? Strange name," said Oostanaula.

"He is a big, powerful horse, Oostanaula."

"Yeah, he can pull that train load by himself," added Fred.

"One horse pull wagons alone? Like to see."

"Maybe you will see someday, Oostanaula."

"We should get him before we cross Crowley's Ridge, Jonny."

"How would we do that, darlin'?"

"Well, we could camp at the ridge, while you take Sloggy and go get him."

"Hey, that's not a bad idea, my pretty plum."

"That would cost us another day," said Fred.

"Yeah. We were going to that Mourners Church today," said Janet.

"At the rate we're going, it might save a day."

"Then I'm for it," said Janet. "I want to get back to the mill as soon as possible."

"Looks like you will see Corker in action, Mister Oostanaula."

"You have one smart wife, Jon Hamilton."

"Yes I do, sir. Let's get started again, gang. Maybe we can reach that ridge before dark."

Several stops had to be made to rest the horses, and it was dark before they reached Crowley's Ridge. They made camp.

"What would you gentlemen like for supper?" asked Dessy.

"Why, pork, of course!" answered Fred.

"And I'll add some beans. Alright?"

"That sounds wonderful, Dessy. I'll help," said Maggie.

"You're not leaving me alone with these savages!" said Janet.

"Good," said Oostanaula. "We make talk. You make food!"

Sometime during the night, Jon woke, hugged and kissed his wife, and left on Sloggy for Lou's Landing.

Monday, January 18

"Jonny? Jonny? Where are you?" asked Maggie, running out of the tent after she woke with no husband.

"He must have left for Lou's Landing," answered Janet.

Everyone was already up, sitting around the fire and eating breakfast.

"Jon Hamilton leave during night. My friend Elias on guard, see Jon Hamilton leave on horse, Sloggy," said Oostanaula.

"Want some breakfast, honey?" asked Janet.

"Which 'honey' are you asking?" asked Fred.

"Oh, yes. I'll finish dressing," answered Maggie.

"No hurry, honey. We're not going anywhere today."

"I'll be out soon and have breakfast, then work on my diary. I wish Jonny would have woke me when he left."

"He probably tried, honey. You were deep in sleep."

"Do any of you have some cloth and sewing gear?" asked Dessy.

"It just so happens we have some in our supplies for the general store. Why?" asked Janet.

"After I finish cleaning up from breakfast, if it's alright, I would like to make something for the baby."

"What a wonderful idea! Maggie would love that. Would you mind if I help?"

"Not at all, Jan. Thank you."

"Alright. Us women have work to do," said Janet. "You men just keep out of our way."

"Oostanaula and Elias make headdress from feathers of pecking bird. Make Nickawatie jealous."

"That leaves me to rest! I could grain the horses and keep the fire going, I guess," said Fred.

Jon and Sloggy made it up Crowley's Ridge in the darkness. Now, as the first rays of light appeared, Jon raced Sloggy across the top and down the other side. *Oostanaula was right*, he thought. This was an easier crossing. He still didn't think the horses would have made it over. Maybe all eight of them could have made it. As the sun got high, Jon ran into the old Military Road. He turned Sloggy north, and soon found the road east, to home.

"Where's Mose?" Jon asked Josh, as he reached his land.

"Be's working un house," said Josh, pointing to the old farmhouse on the west side of the St. Francis River.

Jon made his way over to the farmhouse. "Mose! Are you in there?" The house looked different.

"I's here, Jon. You be's orite?"

"Yes. We need your help! We need Corker to pull us."

"Orites. Where be dem carryall?"

"It's about half a day's ride from here, over a big ridge."

"Orites, Jon. I's has horses ready. How many you's sell?"

"I have only Smutty and Sloggy here, and some Cherokee work horses. They are about worn out."

"Den we's takes Corka an' Conquers, an' Coblers an' Flip."

"That's four, and Smutty is there. That's enough."

"Orites, Jon. We's leaves Slog here. He needs res'."

"You's needs foods, Jonny?" asked Ella, from the house.

"Food? Gosh no. We have stacks of food! Let's go, Mose."

"I's tells mill workas ta work alone!" yelled Ella.

Mose and Jon kept the four drays at a steady pace to Military Road and over Crowley's Ridge. It was past noon, and Jon now thought he should have taken some food from Ella. They made their way down the west side of the ridge, and in less than an hour's gallop, the carryall and camp came into view.

"Here they come!" yelled Fred. "Hello, Jon, Mose. You sure made good time. You brought my horses."

"Yes. We grabbed Corker and Conqueror and your two. We were in a hurry to get back here."

"Hi, Jonny!" Maggie hugged her husband. "I was worried when I woke and you were gone. Why didn't you wake me?"

"I don't think a herd of razorbacks could have woke you!"

"Razorbacks! Hi, Nunky Mose! You should have seen how big and mean they were," said Maggie.

"Yeah, look here Mose, at the size of their heads!" exclaimed Fred. "We think that one weighed six hundred pounds or more."

"Laudy! Dey be's wild pigs? From farms?" asked Mose.

"Grow wild," said Oostanaula, "here forever."

"Oh, Mose, this is Oostanaula and Elias, and this is . . ."

"Nickawatie," said Oostanaula.

"Nickawatie. They are Western Cherokee. They live a few miles west of here. And this is our partner, Mose."

"Razorback pigs have been here for three hundred years. They originally became wild here when some escaped from the Spaniards, Nunky Mose."

"Did you learn that in school too, my love?"

"Yes. They were from a gang of Spanish explorers, looking for gold. Their leader was named DeSoto. He died around here."

"And that was three hundred years ago?"

"Yes, Jonny. Have you eaten?"

"No, and I could eat one of those razorbacks!"

"I'll warm up food for you," said Modessa.

"This the big horse you say, Jon Hamilton. He is giant!"

"And he is powerful," added Fred.

"We shall see. He pull that wagon?"

"Yes. I will show you after Mose and I eat."

"This Oostanaula want see, Jon Hamilton."

And see he did! After eating some pork, Mose and Jon hitched Corker to the carryall, with trailer, both loaded with food and supplies. The giant white horse pulled them, and even after people piled on, Corker still pulled them around the campsite with little trouble.

"Oostanaula never see such power! Would like to own."

"Sorry, Chief, not for sale," said Fred. He turned to Janet. "Just think, honey, we own a part of that horse!"

"Well then, get him hitched to the wagons, and let's go home!"

"Good idea, Jan. We might even get there tonight."

"Not when we have to cross Crowley's Ridge, Jonny."

"This way is easier, just like Oostanaula said."

"Why you name giant horse Corker?"

"We didn't name him, but 'corker' means remarkable and clever."

"You will not need Oostanaula and horses now."

"No we won't, Oostanaula. Thank you very much for your help. We couldn't have made it here without you."

"Thank you for food and rifles, Jon Hamilton."

"Wait . . . Fred, do you know where the gunpowder is?"

"It's on that side of the trailer, Jon."

"Let's give Oostanaula some extra powder and balls."

"Good idea. I'll get some."

"Thanks, Fred." To Oostanaula, Jon said, "Don't forget the tree with the pork in it."

"Oostanaula not forget. And not forget new friends."

"Come and see us anytime. You will be welcome," said Jon.

"Goodbye, friends. Oostanaula see you again soon."

The Cherokee loaded the razorback heads on two of their horses and waved goodbye before heading west.

"You's gives pig heads away, Jon? Dey's makes good food."

"Yes, Mose. They use the head, eyes, and tusks. We have all the pork we need for months!"

"And we're rich, Nunky Mose! We have money, gold, the town, and about seventy thousand acres of land!"

"Whoeee! We's do be rich, Sissy!"

"A lot of the thanks should go to Chief Ustanali for the gold he gave us. Did you write to him, darlin'?"

"No, Jonny. How would we reach him in the Smokies?"

"I don't know, my love. Someday, maybe. Let's move, gang."

Mose hooked up Cobbler and Flip at the wheel, Conqueror and Smutty ahead of them, and Corker in the lead. The wagon and trailer rolled East at a good speed. Jon rode Corker at the front, and Mose and Fred rode the wheel team, Cobbler and Flip. In very little time, they reached the ridge and crossed it easily.

"Too bad we won't see that lovely white sand again," said Janet.

"Or those people . . . the Joneses? Maybe some other time," replied Fred.

"There's the Military Road, gang. It's about eleven or twelve miles to our turnoff. We can make it."

"It's getting pretty dark, Jonny."

"I know, darlin', but once we make the turnoff, we can make the rest in the dark."

"Do you see our road, Jonny?"

"Not yet. We must be close, though."

"It be's just ahead, Jon, 'bout fo' hundred yards."

"How do you know that, Mose?"

"I's knowed dem trees." Mose pointed. "There, Jon, just turns rights."

"There! I see it now." Jon turned Corker right.

"I can't see, Jonny."

"I can now, my love. We're on it. Whoa, Corker."

"Why are we stopping, Jonny?"

"Because Mose and I are walking to guide you." Jon turned to Fred. "Fred, we'll free Corker, and you ride ahead and bring back lanterns."

"Sure, Jon. It will be interesting to ride in the dark."

"Don't worry. Corker knows the way."

"Good, be back soon."

The group "felt" their way down the road. The moon would appear occasionally from behind the clouds, and the gang could see to press forward. At last they heard Fred returning, along with someone else. Mose was able to light the lanterns.

"Who is that with you, Fred?" asked Janet.

"It's Josh, honey. He's on Sloggy. Ella is here too."

"A-ha! Finally, we can see," remarked Maggie. "Get up, Smutty."

After a short ride, Jon announced, "Here we are, gang. Home at last!"

"What are we going to do with all this food, Jonny?"

"Will it be alright overnight, Ella?"

"I's hopes so, Jonny. It be's cold."

"Good. How much salt did we buy, my love?"

"A sack. Why?"

"Okay, early tomorrow morning, we men will dig a food cellar, a big one. You ladies gather all the barrels we have. We are spending the day working to preserve all this food."

"Bu' I's has hot food fo' you's tonights," said Ella.

"Good. We'll feed and stake the horses tonight, and get an early start tomorrow."

"Did you see how much Nunky Mose did while we were gone, Jonny? This old house is finished inside!"

"That's wonderful, my love. Can all of us live inside?"

"There are five separate rooms, two down and three up."

"Good, let's let Mose and Ella decide which room we get."

"I'll sleep in the tent," said Modessa.

"No need, honey," said Janet, "if you don't mind sharing a room for now with Susan."

"I don't mind at all. Does everyone have a room, then?"

"Yassum, dey's do," answered Ella. "Jonny an' Sissy takes one room downstairs, an' Daddy an' I goes up."

"And Nunky Mose dug out the old well, Jonny, so we now have good water."

"Great! Thanks, Mose! Now let's eat," said Jon.

"Should I be at the mill in the morning?" asked Janet.

"I's check un mornin', Jonny. Dem mill do goods," said Ella.

"Help with the barrels of brine first, Jan, then maybe later you can check in at the mill."

"What if we're short of salt, Jonny?"

"Then we will try something else. We may even have to make a run to Marking Tree for more salt."

"In the meantime, let's eat some of Ella's hot food," said Fred.

Diary of Margaret Hamilton

Monday, January 18

. . . And when I awoke, Jonny was gone. He left in the middle of the night to get help, horses, and Nunky Mose . . . lazy day. Janet and Dessy made a pretty set of clothes for

my baby. They are so sweet. . . . The three Cherokee left with the ugly heads of the two razorbacks that Jonny killed, and we headed for home. It was very late, and very dark when we arrived home.

Love to all,
Maggie

Tuesday, January 19

The day of preservation arrived early. Jon was thankful that it was near freezing overnight, and all the meat was fine. Mose and Josh were digging at dawn, and Fred soon joined in. Jon helped the women find and clean six barrels. They filled them with water down at the Saint Francis River, and hauled them in the carryall to the old root cellar, where they poured salt into five of the barrels. That took all of the salt. Ella poured molasses into the barrels to add flavor. The barrels were filled with pork and covered.

"I'll try to find more salt, ladies, but it's time to start cutting meat into strips."

"What should we do with the strips?" asked Janet.

"We'll take lengths of rope, and, Modessa, you unravel them. We'll string lines overhead, and hang the strips to dry."

"Like we did around the covered wagon?"

"Righto, my love. Mose will help string up the lines. I'm going to find more barrels and salt."

Jon saddled Prancer, and rode around the river toward the barn, where he walked over the bridge and into town. Luckily, DeValurie had purchased salt on his last trip to St. Louis, and the store also had used barrels, so that worry was over. Next, Jon headed to the mill.

"You's massa toos?" asked Jesse.

"I am an owner of this mill."

"Un dem alls buckras an' missy's massas toos?"

"That's right, Murphy, but Missus Wilson will be the boss."

"Massas, missys, boss miss, buckras . . . Dem all's boss," said Jesse.

"Yassa," said Murphy, "toos many chiefs."

"Yassa, Murph, an' not 'nuff Injuns," added Jesse.

"Now, I need you to ship more boards and posts across the river today and tomorrow. Understand?"

"Yassa, we's un'stan', Massa. Big, big brudda sens boards 'cross riva tree times," said Murphy, signaling three fingers.

"He be's big black boss orites," added Jesse.

"And send the bag of salt and empty barrels in front of the store across the river too,"

"Yassa. Dems all, Massa?" asked Murphy.

"In your spare time, start building a big, fancy bed."

"Fo' dem house an' puts bed in," added Jess.

"Yes! That too! Maybe later. We need to fix that little house across from the church, but those boards first."

"Yassa, buckra boss!"

By day's end, the gang had finished a large addition to the original food cellar, and had stored most of the food purchased in Batesville. Mose and Ella took a room downstairs, along with Jon and Maggie. Fred and Janet, Josh and Ally, and Modessa and Susan took the three rooms upstairs. Chipper stayed with his mother and father. They all made their beds on the floor with lots of blankets.

"We got a lot done today, my love."

"Yes, isn't Nunky Mose a wizard?"

"He sure is. I think I'll put him and Josh to building a water cooler over at the river tomorrow."

"What is that, Jonny?"

"It is sort of a big box that water flows over and under to keep food very cold. We saw one that old corn whisky farmer had built."

"The one that died and owned the dog. Isaak?"

"Yes, and it worked good."

"But doesn't this river flood a lot, Jonny?"

"Oh yes, that's what I hear. Maybe he can build the cooler where the river won't harm the food."

"Well, if it can be done, Nunky Mose can do it!"

"That's for sure, my pretty plum. Didn't he do a great job on this house?"

"Yes . . . our first home, Jonny."

"There will be more, darlin', bigger and better."

"But I want our first child to be born right here."

Wednesday, January 20

"Good morning, everyone. Did you all sleep well in our new home?" asked Jon. The rest of the group all answered yes.

"What are our plans for today, Jon?" asked Fred.

Jon looked at the women. "Well, I thought you women should go into town, and get the bounders, the servants, all squared away for food and housing. Modessa, you see Lolita about that, and then you can take over the store. Jan will handle the mill, and Maggie will be Lou's Landing's first mayor and get the town running smoothly. Sound Okay?" The women all agreed.

"So what are you men doing?" asked Janet.

"Well, I have a big job for Mose to tackle. Mose, remember the water cooled box that old man with Isaak had?"

"Dem ones in dem stream, Jon?"

"Yes. Can you build one here? Somewhere where it won't do damage when the river floods?"

"I's do, Jon. Bu' we's needs to build banks so's riva don' flood our house."

"That should be our first project, Jon," said Fred.

"Yes, I agree. We'll start on that today right after breakfast, and worry about the water cooler later."

"Let's eat!"

In the big barn, the men found two wagons they could use along with the carryall to haul rocks and dirt. Mose hitched up the new, matched pair of horses to one wagon, Cobbler and Flip to another, and Sloggy and Smutty to the third. This left Corker and Conqueror for Jon to use where needed. Mose hitched Corker to the disc contraption and made a path back and forth along the final bend in the river, and along the west bank, a length of two miles. Jon walked into town and recruited ten servants from Janet's mill crew to help haul rocks. They knew where to find them, up the river a mile north of the barn. Jon and Fred went there, and Fred was put in charge of loading wagons with stones of various sizes. Mose dug a trench and a large hole, and built his water cooler with a waterline from and back to the river, to flow over and under the water cooler box. He then built the five- to six-foot rock wall over it.

The same rock area had banks of clay. Jon, now determined to see this project through, piled clay, then dirt over the wall of rocks, from a point south of his land, north around the river's bend, to a point about two-thirds of a mile north of the barn, all on the west side of the St. Francis River. The project took over three weeks of hard work.

Friday, February 13

"Well, darlin', tomorrow we can start on a new project."

"It will soon be too late to bed the tobacco seeds, Jonny."

"I know. There are beds for seeds just outside the barn."

"Where do we get the seeds, Jonny?"

"I hope Mister DeValurie has some from last year. I've been too busy to check the seeds I brought in the covered wagon."

"You brought some?"

"Sure did, my love, and some cotton and rice seeds."

"So what is your next project?"

"To get the beds ready and bed tobacco and rice seeds."

"Susan and I can do that. Nanty Ella has a full-time job keeping everyone fed, including the bounders."

"Doesn't Susan help her?"

"Yes. I guess I can sow the seeds with Ally, and I think Fred will help."

"Well, I can get the beds ready."

"What will the others be doing?"

"I need Mose to start clearing a paddy or two of swamp."

"I thought he was going to strengthen the bridge."

"I know, and remodel the little house on the boulevard."

"Well, he can't do three things at once, Jonny."

"I'm not too sure about that, darlin'. He's magical!"

"Will you help me bed the seeds we have, Fred?" asked Maggie.

"Never work on Friday the Thirteenth!"

"We have lots of cotton seeds for you, and rice, and tobacco seeds."

"Cotton?" repeated Fred. "In that case, I'll help you tomorrow."

Diary of Margaret Hamilton

Friday, February 13, 1836

. . . And the men finally finished the dike along the river, and some bounders are planting bushes on it to strengthen it. Now Jonny has three more jobs to do! It never ends! And I can feel it kicking. A boy, I am sure.

Love, Maggie

Saturday, February 14

They came just after dawn, down the road leading to the river, and Lou's Landing. Eight men in all, looking mean to Mose. Their hairy faces were illuminated in the early morning light. They stopped their horses when they saw the farmhouse to their right. The men saw six or seven slaves running about doing chores, and decided to disregard them. What they wanted was in town. They rode up to the dike, which protected the farmhouse from the river, and peered across at the town. Again, the men saw several slaves working at a mill along the water. Logs were being pulled out of the water and into the mill by a team of horses.

As the men rode north along the dike and around its bend toward the huge barn and bridge, they didn't notice the "slaves" at the farmhouse scurrying about with rifles. *BAM!* They knew they had made the mistake of not raiding the farmhouse when they heard the shot coming from it. After a pause, three of the men rode back around the bend and raced toward the farmhouse. They saw a huge slave stand and then saw the bolt of fire from his rifle. *BAM!* One of the men departed from his saddle. Another black man and woman then rose and fired from about one hundred yards. *BAM! BAM!* A second man yelled something as he fell from his horse. The third man did a quick U-turn and raced back around the bend and out of sight from the "slaves."

Jon and Maggie were at the DeValurie mansion, checking on cotton and tobacco seeds, when they heard the warning shot from the farmhouse. Always ready, Jon grabbed his Hawken and ran down the boulevard toward the main intersection of town. Over the dike, on the other side of the river, he saw the three men on horseback racing toward the farmhouse. He then saw Mose cut one down, then two more shots, and another fell. He thought those shots probably came from Ella and Josh.

"By damn, that's cutting them down!" Jon yelled. Jon then saw Janet and two others, possibly Jesse and Murphy, as he ran for the bridge just in time to see several other men starting toward him on the bridge.

"Hold it right there," Jon huffed. "Who are you and what do you want?"

The lead man on the bridge raised his rifle to take a shot at where he thought Jon's voice had come. *BAM!* Jon's ball ripped into the lead man's chest, lifting him off his feet and sending him into the river. The others ran for shelter behind the dike, covered by their friends who shot twice, missing Jon completely.

"I said, who are you and what do you want?"

"Ya ain't got no powder in yer gun now," came a voice.

"Well, step on the bridge again, and you'll get the same thing your partner got."

"He must have 'nother gun, Abe," said another voice.

"Do as I says, an' ya won't get hurt," said the one named Abe.

"He ain't got no balls in his gun, Abe. Let's rush 'im."

"Shet up, Hedge. I'll do the talkin'! Hey, y'all, throw yer gun cut, an' y'all live. We won' kill ya."

During this conversation, Janet, Murphy, and Jesse arrived. Jan had an unloaded flintlock with her. The three then began to load both rifles for Jon, using his powder bag.

"What did you say?" Jon yelled.

"I says, toss yer gun out, an' we won' kill ya!"

"Who are you?"

"Ne'er mind who we are. Jest do as I says!"

"Well, what do you want?"

"We want yer golt!"

"Gold? We don't have any gold," Jon answered.

"Quit yer lyin', bub. We're here ta getcha golt!"

"I said we don't have any gold!"

"We're a-gonna kill ya fer lyin'! Ya gotta big ole stone o' solid golt, an' we want it!"

"Where did you hear that?" asked Jon.

"Shet up, an' han' yer gun out, or we're a-comin' at ya!"

Janet handed Jon the loaded flintlock. "Well, you want to die. Come on!"

"Let's go, Abe. He ain't got no loaded gun."

"Ya asked fer it! Here we come!" yelled Abe.

Three men rushed up onto the bridge and faced a rifle. *BAM!* The ball hit the lead man in the midsection, and he fell back against the others. They let him down and continued to come at Jon.

"Now he be's outta balls. Get 'im!" yelled the new lead man, shooting his rifle. His ball sprayed the dirt in front of Jesse.

"Oooeee!" shrieked Jesse. His eyes were as big as saucers.

Jon grabbed his Hawken and dug for a cap. *BAM!* The ball tore through the front man's stomach, and knocked down the man behind him. The last man stumbled back to the dike. *BAM!* A shot came from behind the dike.

"That's Mose!" yelled Jon. "He's got another one of them."

"There can't be many left," said Janet.

Jon heard the sound of the wagon and hoofs. Maggie and Mister DeValurie rode up on two of his horses.

"Are you alright, Jonny?"

"Yes. You're just in time. I think the war's over."

"Who were they, Jonny? What did they want?"

"I don't know who they are, but they wanted our gold."

"Someone in Batesville told them."

"Yeah, guess you're right about that." Jon saw Mose near the farmhouse. "Are you Okay, Mose?"

"Yassa, Jon," came the response. "We's gots two, one hurt bad. Mama goin' get horse lin'ment."

"Right," Jon yelled. "We're coming over."

The man who had been hit with the same ball that killed the man in front of him had crawled back to the dike along with the last man standing. Mose and Fred were guarding them.

"Well, ye men are plenty fierce defenders," said Don Louie DeValurie.

"Yes. Next time, they better send an army," said Jon.

"Let's hope there is no next time, Jonny."

"This man is dead too," said Modessa, who suddenly appeared.

"No need for the liniment now," said Fred.

"That leaves just you, mister. Talk!"

"Ah . . . ah . . . we's heard ya had a big golt piece."

"Who told you?" demanded Maggie.

"I don' know. I's heard it from Abe," he said, pointing to Abe's dead body.

"Why don't I just kill him? I didn't get to kill any," said Fred.

"No! Don' kill me . . . I won' tell nothin'." There was a pause.

"We don't have any more gold! Do you hear?"

"Yes, sir . . . n-n-no golt. I hear!"

"Good. Get on your horse and ride! Don't come back!"

"We should have killed him too, Jon. So we never see more of them again," said Fred, as the last man disappeared.

"I have a feeling we won't see him again," said Janet.

"Well, gang, we've earned a break before we get started on the job again. We'll bury the dead first thing."

"And now we have seven more horses to take care of."

"And seven more rifles, my pretty plum."

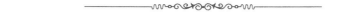

"Well, gang, we've rested enough. We have work to do."

"You name it, Jon. We're ready."

"Okay, Fred. You have experience planting, right?"

"I do. I've planted all my life."

"Right. Your crew is going to be small, I'm afraid, Janet. Fred is going to take ten men and women and plant all the cotton seed we have in the east half of sections fourteen and twenty-three, west of the farmhouse. Okay, Fred?"

"All the land we have, those are the two half sections?"

"That's right. Come right up close to the root cellars. Not counting the road, that will make two miles long of cotton."

"Wow, by over half a mile wide. Do we have that much seed?"

"I hope so. Do as much as you can, Fred."

"Pick your crew, honey, and go to work," said Janet.

"Take your team of Cobbler and Flip, and that disc."

"That should cut the ground up, but what about all those trees?"

"Take an axe, cut them down, and plant around them. Leave room to come in later and pull the stumps out."

"Takes branches off trees. I's comes an' halls trees ta riva fo' mill," said Mose.

"Alright. I'm on my way. This should take several days. I'll plant everything west of the farmhouse. Wish me luck."

"See you tonight, honey," said Janet. "I'll give you four men and six women."

"Here, you's takes plenty foods," said Ella.

Fred hitched Cobbler and Flip to the disc machine and left.

"Who's next, Jonny?"

"Jesse, Murphy, how are you at swimming and walking on logs?"

"We's dem best, buckra boss."

"Who's the best, Jesse?"

"Uh . . . Jimms be bes', an' Murph—"

"Okay, you stay at the mill, Jesse. Murphy and . . . Jims will float all the logs on the river to the mill."

"We's do's, buckra boss," said Murphy.

"That leaves Jesse and the rest of the female bou . . . uh, servants to help you, Jan."

"What about the rest of the men?" asked Janet.

"Most of them will go with Mose to the swamps. I'll need a good carpenter and Josh with me."

"Daddy be's un swamps?" asked Ella.

"Yes. Mose, I would like you to start clearing the closest corner of the swamp. Take Corker and Conqueror and one other team with you, and pull out all the stumps. We need clear dirt paddies for our rice, our future."

"Orites, Jon. I's gets crackin'."

"And pull the logs to the river, to Murphy, Mose."

"That leaves you and me, Jonny, and I guess I'll be bedding tobacco and rice seeds with Ally."

"Righto, my love, and Josh and I will get you started."

"Then what are you doing the rest of the day?"

"Josh and I have a million things to do, my pretty plum. We start by making a chute to get Mose's logs into the river."

"Yes? Then what, Jonny?"

"Well, there will need to be a chute on the other side for Fred's logs, and I want to widen the bridge so we can ride horses and wagons over it."

"That's a lot of work, Jonny. You'll need Nunky Mose."

"If I do need him, I know where to find him, darlin'."

"Where do you plan to plant tobacco, Jonny?"

"I'm not sure, darlin', but I'll get it figured out."

"Why not on all that cultivated land in section thirteen? That's where Mister DeValurie had his tobacco crop."

"Well, I want our animals near the barn, and I'm thinking of planting some wheat in section thirteen."

"Wheat? What do you know about wheat, Jonny?"

"Not much, my love, but it's big up north."

"Then tobacco will go in along the river?"

"I guess, and maybe north of the swamp. Don't worry, my pretty plum. We have a lot of room!"

"Yes, we do. And we'll need to plant a lot of corn."

"You know, darlin', we now have seven more horses. That's enough for each of our group, including you."

"No, Jonny . . . I don't want another horse."

"Why, hon? Just because you lost Pasha?"

"There will never be another Pasha."

"I know that, darlin', but you'll still need one. They're fun to have. Come on, Mag, pick one out."

"I don't . . . well, Okay, Jonny. That one is nice."

"Then it's yours, my pretty plum. We'll surprise the rest of the gang tonight with a horse for each of them."

"You better get to work, Jonny, before we fire you!" Maggie joked.

The remainder of the day went very well. In the northern part of section fourteen, Fred found a heavy forest of pine trees, so he started his clearing and discing about a quarter mile south of the north property line. He finished the day about a quarter way from his starting point to the Military Access Road to his south. Jon figured it would take Fred about eight days to clear and plant all of the cotton. Maggie, Ally, and a female servant finished the beds of tobacco and rice that day. There were a lot of tobacco seeds left, so Jon and Josh had to build two more large beds for Maggie's seeds.

With Sloggy and Smutty, they hauled timber from the mill for a new bridge, and got started digging holes to place the timbers so the new bridge would be "higher over the dike," Jon decided.

Mose had the best day. He and his seven male servants from the mill cleared enough land for a large paddy, pulled cypress logs to the river, and cut out and pulled the stumps from the paddy. They even helped Jon and Josh build a ramp that the horses could pull logs onto before they rolled them into the river, where Murphy was waiting to float the logs to the mill.

"Wow, what a day! I'm bushed."

"As soon as we finish eating, I'll wash you, honey, then we'll hit the hay," said Janet.

"Every one of you did a great job, so I've got a surprise for you all. In the morning, each of you pick a horse of your own."

Diary of Margaret Hamilton

Saturday, February 14, 1836

. . . And I'm just about all out of pages in my diary, so I will try to be brief . . . There were eight of them, come to rob Jonny of his gold nugget, or kill us all. Jonny and Nunky Mose killed six, and Nanty Ella killed one. Only one was left, and Jonny let him go . . . Have seven more rifles, horses, and saddles. So now we all have a horse. I still miss my Pasha, though . . . We got a lot done today. Jonny was happy. My last entry will be after my son is born . . .

With love,
Margaret Hamilton

Chapter VIII
The Empire Cometh

Tuesday, May 25, 1836

"Someone be's comin', Auntie Margaret," said Chipper Cheechako, racing into the farmhouse with Ally.

"How many, Chip?" Maggie was nursing the baby, David.

"Only one, missy."

"Well, ring the bell, Chipper, so the men will come running."

"Orites, I's do." The boys ran back out and rang the bell.

The man on the horse, leading a pack mule, stopped on the road.

Jon and his two helpers were carefully hoeing weeds from around the thick rice plants when they heard the bell ringing.

"Keep working, men. We can finish this today."

"Yassa, buckra boss. Then you's wan' wata back?"

"Right, Dunner. I'll be back to reflood this paddy."

"You's goes ta checks bells, buckra boss?

"Yes. I'll be back as soon as I can."

Jon jumped aboard Prancer and raced into town. He crossed over the new bridge that Mose had just finished, and he rode over the path along the dike. When he rounded the last bend in the river, he spotted a man sitting on his horse next to a pack mule. The man was watching the farmhouse.

Jon was sure glad he had his Hawken. "Hello. What do you want?"

"Don't shoot that thing. I'm peaceful," the man said.

"Good. Welcome to Mose's Landing."

"Mose's Landing? I thought I was at Lou's Landing."

"You are, sir. We just changed the name before Arkansas becomes a state."

"Are y'all a religious colony?"

"No, sir. We named the town after the man who bought it, my partner Mose. What can I do for you?"

"Well, my name is Matt Chandler, and I'm the constable for northeast Arkansas. You had some killings a while back."

"Yes, sir, we did indeed. There were eight men who attacked us one day. They were looking for gold."

"And you killed seven of them?"

"Yes, sir. They're buried in the church grounds."

"And none of y'all got hurt?"

"We were lucky, alright. Their leader was a fella named Abe something," said Jon.

"Abe Jutland was his name. I don't know if I can believe you. Those men were criminals."

"Well, any of my partners will tell you the same."

"I caught the eighth man. They hung him in Batesville a couple weeks ago for murder. He said that your group ambushed them, and he was the only one who got away."

"My partner Mose is coming now. I don't see my other partner yet. He is checking on the cotton bolls for picking."

"Already?" asked Matt. "This must be really good soil. Most crops are just starting to flower."

"I know. We may be able to start a second crop," said Jon.

"Yeah, yer crops all look good."

"Thank you, sir." Jon turned in Mose's direction. "Mose! Come here."

"A big colored man? Your partner? He bought this place? Am I getting conned?"

"No, sir. He earned his money fair and square."

"He must have bought it straight from Don Louie DeValurie, but how on earth did he record it in Arkansas?"

"The land office just approved it, no questions asked."

"Well, I'll be damned."

"Mose, this man is the law around here, and he wants to know what happened to those eight men who came here."

"Deys came to robs us, an' we's kills dem!" explained Mose.

"How do y'all know they were going to rob you of gold?"

"They said so when I asked them what they wanted," answered Jon.

"An' deys come attackin' an' firin'. Dems no friends," added Mose.

"Alright. If I can see their graves, I'll be gone."

"Oh, no sir, Mister Chandler, we would like you to stay a while and rest, and have something to eat."

"That's kind of y'all. Thanks. Tell me, why would they come here looking for gold?"

"I guess because that's how Mose here paid for this land."

"Oh? Then DeValurie would have that gold."

"Why yes, I suppose he does. Let's go into town, and I'll take you to his home, Mister Chandler."

"Fair enough. And I'll look at the graves," said Matt.

The three rode over the new bridge into the town of Mose's Landing. They stopped at the Mourners Church.

"Mourners Church. What kind of religion is that?" asked Matt.

"Just a regular church," answered Jon, "but you oughta hear them mourn. They can wake the dead!"

"Well, it doesn't look like they woke anyone buried here!"

"No, thank goodness for that! We'd hate to have to fight them again. They looked like criminals."

"I could get you their names, but we wouldn't know which name went with which grave."

"Except this one's name is Abe . . . Jutland?"

"That's right. Alright, take me to DeValurie's home."

"It's that one at the end of the boulevard, sir."

"Yep. That's quite a house, leastwise from here."

"It sure is. I'll introduce you to DeValurie."

"Hi, Jonny. Who have you got there?" The question came from Janet, who was outside the mill and walking toward the intersection.

"Hi, Jan. This is Matt Chandler. He's investigating those men who attacked us in February."

"Did you witness what happened, Miss . . . Jan?" asked Matt.

"I sure did, right from that bridge. They'd have killed us all if it hadn't been for Jonny's good shooting."

"Did they say what they were after?"

"Sure did." Jan saw Jon's nod of Okay. "They were after some gold that we no longer had."

"Thank you, Jan. You're a great help."

"You're welcome, honey, anytime. I was just going to have some coffee with Dessy. Care to join us?"

"Well, maybe we'll all have a bite to eat as soon as we get back from DeValurie's house."

"Sounds good. See you later, honey."

"Ah-ha! It's you, Jonny. Please come in. Maybe you like some tea or coffee? Yes? No?"

"Not right now, Don Louie. Thanks. This is Mister Chandler. I told him about the gold piece that we bought this place with."

"Yes. We make excellent deal, sí?"

"May I see the gold piece, Mister DeValurie?" asked Matt.

"Sí," said Don Louie, after getting a nod from Jon. "It is in the safe. I will get it. A moment, please."

"This is quite a place, alright," said Matt, as they waited.

"Here it is, sir, bright and shiny."

"Yes, it is. Thank you, Mister DeValurie."

"You wish to touch? Wish to hold, maybe?"

"No, thanks. I just wanted to see it."

"You are not going to steal it later, I hope?"

"No, sir. This is the last you'll see of me."

"Good. I mean you are welcome to visit again, señor."

"Thank you for your time, sir," said Jon.

"Come see us again, Mister Hamilton. Your crops are looking very well."

"Thank you. They're keeping us very busy."

"Sí, we know. Remember to store the corn here."

"I'll remember, sir. Thank you. Goodbye."

"I seen all I need to," said Matt Chandler.

"Good. Come to our house, Matt, and have a bite to eat."

"Thank you, Mister Hamilton. Then I'll be on my way."

As they rode down Valurie Boulevard, Modessa and Janet met them at the intersection.

"Want some coffee now, gentlemen?"

"We're going to the house, ladies. Come on over and have an early lunch."

"Alright, you asked for it. We'll be right over."

"All of us partners live in this house until we can build separate homes. Come in."

"Thank you. It's a big enough house," said Matt.

"Yes, but that doesn't stop me from getting on everybody's nerves once in a while."

"I do that myself. What's this? Hi, little fella."

"This is my wife, Margaret, and our son, David Alexander."

"Hi, Davey! What a big boy . . . and all that red hair."

"Yes, there is no question who the mother is!" said Jon.

"You're not funny, Jonny. Will you have lunch with us, Mister . . ."

"Chandler, ma'am, Matt. Yes, I will, and thank you."

"Good." Maggie shouted to the other room, "How is lunch coming, Nanty Ella?"

"I's not ready's yet," came the reply. "It be's early yet."

"Well, Looks like they're all coming early."

"Wells, dey's jest has ta wait," said Ella.

Maggie turned back to the men. "Looks like it will be a little while yet, Mister Chandler. Please come in and sit a spell. I'll get you some coffee."

"I'll do it, my love. You have your hands full."

"Thanks. Don't get Nanty Ella too upset."

"How old is your boy, Missus Hamilton?"

"Fifty-one days today. His name is David Alexander, after his grandfather and great-grandfather on his daddy's side."

"This sure is a nice farm, picking cotton already."

"We'll be starting soon. Most of it has a few weeks to mature yet before we pick it. We've also started topping tobacco plants," Maggie replied.

"Tobacco! I didn't see tobacco plants."

"They're just east of here, along the north side of the big swamp. We have three sections of tobacco, more or less."

"Three sections! My Lord, how much land do you have?"

"Over one hundred sections. Most are swamps."

"My oh my, cotton and tobacco. I notice all that cultivated land across the road is bare."

"Yes. Jonny wanted to plant wheat there, but it's too late now."

"I'll get some seed this fall," said Jon, returning from the kitchen, "when I sell our crops in Batesville. Have some coffee."

"Why in Batesville?"

"Well, it was either there or Saint Louis, which pays less."

"They barge it to New Orleans, and we get better returns," added Maggie.

"Why not take it to Memphis?" asked Matt.

"Memphis? Tennessee?"

"Yep. I hear they ship it to New Orleans at no charge."

"Well, thank you, Mister Chandler. That's closest yet."

"You're welcome. The Saint Francis is blocked with brush and stuff from just above Marking Tree to above the Little River, or you could ship it yourself."

"Someday, maybe. We own land along the Little River."

"You do? That must be ten miles from here."

"Orites, lunch be ready. I hurries!" yelled Ella.

"Thanks, Ella. Let's eat, friend. Yes, it's about twelve miles."

"Whatcha gonna do with all that land?" asked Matt.

"Don't know yet. Just hold it for now," answered Jon, as they sat at the table.

"Well, we'll soon be a state. Maybe I'll get some help patrolling all this area," said Matt.

"We haven't heard anything up here," said Maggie. "Could you tell us what is going on around the country?"

"Well, Ambassador Sevier is in Washington, trying to get a bill signed to make Arkansas a state."

"Just think, independent from Missouri," said Jon.

"And Texas is independent! They are now a free country."

"Really? How did that happen?"

"What? Ya ain't heard of the war? The Alamo?"

"Like I said, we just don't get any news around here," said Maggie.

"Well, a couple years ago, a fella named Austin was captured by them Mexicans and held prisoner for over a year. That made them Texans mad. Then last fall, they got mad enough to drive them Mexicans out of Texas, and down past the town of Antonio. This made them Mexicans mad, and they attacked a place in Antonio called the Alamo, and killed all the men defending it. Davy Crockett was there, and got killed as well. That made the Texans real mad, and just last month, Sam Houston's Texas army whipped them Mexicans and took their general Santa Ana prisoner, and declared Texas a free nation. A lot of Arkansawyers fought with Houston."

"Maybe we should have settled in Texas, Jonny."

"We're settled here now, my love, and here to stay."

"I was hoping you would say that, darling. We've already put too much time and work in this place to move."

"Well, I must get on the road," said Matt. "Maybe I'll be stopping back someday, but I'm closing the book on those eight."

"Thank you, sir. Come back again, anytime."

"You're welcome, and thank that colored woman for that great lunch. You're a lucky man, Mister Hamilton."

"And thanks for all the news," added Maggie.

"You're welcome. Don't forget to take your great crops to Memphis. They'll give you a good, fair price."

"Thanks again. Goodbye for now, Mister Chandler."

As Matt Chandler rode away, Jon saw Fred and his crew coming in for lunch.

"Who was that, Jon?"

"A lawman, wanting to know about those eight men."

"Did you tell him I didn't kill any of them?"

"He was happy with our answers. I guess it's time for us to get back to our crops, Mose."

"I'm hungry! We'll get back when we've eaten," said Fred.

"Okay, Fred. See you all later," said Jon.

"Bye, Jonny . . . Say goodbye to Daddy, Davey!"

"Bye, son. Take good care of your mother!"

Old Farmhouse
Sunday Dinner
August 29, 1836

"Come in," said Maggie to the DeValuries. "Dinner is almost ready. I have places for you at the dinner table."

"Thank you," answered Lolita. "This is my friend, Jules, who lives over the Crowley Ridge."

"Oh yes, Mister Jones. Welcome to our home. I saw you come up the road this morning and ring our warning bell."

"Yep. That was what dat bell were fer," said Jules.

"Yes. Do you remember us? We passed through your place in January on our way to Batesville."

"Oh yeah. You's had dem horses ta sell."

"That's right. Come to our table. It's so nice to see you, Missus DeValurie."

"It is so nice of you to invite us," said Constance, her Spanish accent very evident.

"You are welcome anytime. It seems so seldom that we see you. We are so busy."

"We should see each other more often," responded Connie.

"Yes. I was at church earlier today. Perhaps we should meet on a Sunday after church for tea and conversation."

"It would be wonderful. Next Sunday?"

"Yes. Each first Sunday after church, about two thirty?"

"Wonderful, Missus Hamilton, next Sunday. I will be at the church."

"Please join me at the table. Is everyone ready to eat?" Everyone was."

There were eleven people gathered at the long, new table of oak and pine with a middle extension of cypress wood. The extension had shown a crack that presented itself when new, before a heavy plant oil was applied. Mose was seated at the end nearest the kitchen, with an empty chair to his left for Ella, who busied herself in the kitchen. Maggie then Jon took seats next to Ella's chair. Across from them sat Fred, Janet, then Modessa, who sat across from Jon. Lolita and Jules finished Jon's side. There was an empty space across from Lolita, and Constance was seated across from Jules, with Don Louie DeValurie at the end, opposite Mose.

"Let us start with a drink from Mister DeValurie's stock of wine," said Jon, "to celebrate our first crop to market."

"Here, here," said Fred.

"Victory!" added Mister DeValurie.

"Tomorrow, I train to Memphis, and rewards, for hard work." There were shouts of joy.

"You have three wagons loaded, Jonny. Who is driving?"

"Well, good question, my love . . ."

"I thought so too! And, do we have enough horses, since you sold those two teams in Batesville?"

"Yeah. That only leaves four sets for three wagons," added Fred.

"DeValurie will solve the problem," said Don Louie. "You will, of course, use my team of excellent stallions, Madrid and Granada, along with two servants."

"That is asking a lot of you, Mister DeValurie."

"Nonsense! It is my pleasure. Besides, you will need them to handle the very big market wagon you have."

Jon was taken aback upon hearing that word he hadn't heard for so long. Maggie noticed the look on her husband's face.

"Dey has pulled dem big wagons befo', Jon," said Mose. "We's need dem, an' Venus an' Saturn."

"Saturn? Venus? What is . . . Paree an' Calie?"

"We changed their names, Mister DeValurie."

"Yes," said Maggie. "We didn't know their names, so we named them after those planets, big and strong."

"Sí, big and strong. They be also beautiful."

"Yes. I hope they breed," said Maggie.

"If they do, I will get first offspring?"

"Yes, Mister DeValurie, I promised you that," answered Jon.

"They are so pretty. Black and white. Your other two all white stallions are pretty too," observed Maggie.

"Sí! They pull your cotton to market."

"Thank you. Then we're all set. I'll take Josh. Any of your partners want to go?"

"No, thanks," answered Fred. "We have too much work here."

"I's cuts tobacca plants, an' works on little house. An' maybes plows wheat fields," said Mose.

"We can wait a while yet to plant wheat, but we are going to need another barn, just for tobacco."

"Maybe we can get started on that before the little house for Dessy. We need to remodel the ferry system too."

"You's takes train ta market, Jon. We's has plentys un works here, Fred an' I's," said Mose.

"I hope we have some mail at Madison, Jonny."

"That reminds me, my love, I want to see if we can have mail delivered here, to Mose's Landing."

"You have changed the village's name," said Mister DeValurie.

"Yes, sir, in honor of Mose, who bought it."

"We still kept your street names, Mister DeValurie," said Maggie.

"This is good, Señora Hamilton. You have the cotton, tobacco, and food?"

"Yes, we have hulled brown rice and squash."

"The squash be waste of time, but the rice will be very good market. So very new here."

"I hope you are right, Mister DeValurie. I have four sacks of about one hundred pounds each."

"Do not let them buy too low, my friend. They will try."

"I won't, but I need to know what price is fair, sir."

"Last year in Saint Louis, I received ten cents per pound for cotton, and a good price for tobacco is from twenty to twenty-five cents a leaf. You maybe get more in Memphis for cotton."

"I hope so! And I hope we do well with rice."

After a pause, Constance said, "What a wonderful meal, Missus Hamilton. What is the dish we had first?"

"It's called macaroni pie, and mostly flour and butter."

"I thought they were onions," Jules said to Lolita.

"Don't be silly, Jules. You've had onions before, remember?"

"You might have onions and other vegetables that come out of our garden behind the house," said Maggie.

"I's be servin' dem now," said Ella.

"Thank you, Nanty Ella. Anyone else have news?"

"Jackson will no be president for very long," said DeValurie.

"Yeah, but they ain't no difference," said Jules. "Van Buren will be da same."

"He's vice president now, ain't he?" asked Fred.

"Yes," said Maggie. "He'll have to be better than Jackson."

"Well, Jackson signed bill to make Arkansas a state."

"Let's drink to that!" exclaimed Fred.

"Yes, but he's also forcing all the eastern Indians through Arkansas to west of here," added Maggie.

"Jules and I worry that Jackson will cause a depression, and we will not be able to afford to wed," said Lolita.

"Wed? Are you about to wed, honey?" asked Janet.

"Yes, about Thanksgiving. Jules will live here in Lou's . . . Mose's Landing."

"Where, in Mose's Landing?" asked Fred.

"Maybe just on the boulevard, if you will sell a lot," answered Lolita.

"Our town is growing, my pretty plum."

"What about the town you wish to start, Jules?" asked Maggie.

"My brodder Jonus is trying to start one, now that we are a state."

"Do you have a name for it, honey?" asked Janet.

"Well, my brodder Jack say Jonesbora," said Jules.

"How many brothers do you have, Jules?"

"Eight brodders, an' tree sisses, all a-startin' with the letter J."

"My goodness," said Constance, "all of this food is wonderful."

"Thank you. All the vegetables are from our garden."

"There's squash, potatoes with gravy, carrots, turnips, and . . ."

"Corn and cabbage, honey, and turkey and wild hog," finished Janet, when Maggie paused.

"Don' forgets dem desserts," said Ella.

"It is de best meal I ever eat," said Mister DeValurie.

"Susan is serving sweet potato pie, made by Nanty Ella."

"Is good thing we bring carriage. I will sleep," said Don Louis.

"Please have your servants and horses here early, sir," said Jon.

"We will, and good luck, Mister Hamilton."

"Thank you."

Outside Madison, Arkansas
Wednesday, September 1, 1836

"Wake up, darlin'. It's time to roll."

"I'm awake, Jonny. Ooh, this ground is so hard. I didn't sleep at all last night."

"Then what was all that noise you were making?"

"What noise? I wasn't making any noise."

"The ground under this tent was shaking so bad, I thought them earthquakes had come back."

"It was not, you big lummox! Will we make it to the river today, Jonny?"

"The Mississippi? I'm not su—"

"No, the Amazon! I'd like to get back home this month."

"What for, my pretty plum? We'll just have to pick the rest of the tobacco, or the second crop of cotton, or work on . . ."

"Hold it! Let's enjoy this trip for now."

"We really need a bigger barn for tobacco."

"Maybe Jules will help Nunky Mose and Freddy with that. I hope Lolita will be happy."

"She will, my love. Jules is a good man. Besides, she's no spring chicken anymore. She needs to have young'uns now."

"Am I a spring chicken, Jonny?"

"I'd say you are a momma goose!"

"Well, you're a turkey!"

"Come on, darlin'. Josh is ready. I'm stopping in Madison."

"Hello, can I be o' some hel . . . say, don't I knows ya?"

"Yes, sir. Last January, you directed me to some land up this river, and look outside at the results."

"My oh my! Three wagons! Tobaccy, stacks a cotton . . ."

"Yes, and rice and squash. Headed across the river."

"So ya bought land up riva, huh? Swampland?"

"Some. What I wanted. But good, rich soil too."

"How much ya get?" asked the land manager.

"About a hundred thirty or so."

"It must be durned good land to get three big wagons full a crop, in only hundred thirty acres."

"A hundred thirty sections."

"*Sections!* My Lawd! Them all recorded?"

"Yes, sir, and we own the town of Mose's . . . Lou's Landing."

"Well, what kin I do fer you's? Ya ain't a-wantin' mo' land?"

"No, sir, I just want to thank you and see if we can get mail shipped to our town."

"Well, the mail comes here from Lil' Rock, an' goes up dis riva ta Markin' Tree an' Saint Louie on da Military Road."

"Can you get them to stop at Mose's Landing?"

"You'll hafta go next door ta the mercantile. They has the post office. Ya gotta post office?"

"I'll build one, as soon as I get home."

"Well, good luck ta ya. Hope ya get a good price in Memphis."

"I don't know what a good price is."

"Needer do I, but good luck."

"Thank you, sir."

"Are you the postman?"

"Postman, barber, land seller, blacksmith, bartender, preacher man, bear hunter, an' town drunk! What ya need?"

"I live in the town of Mose's Landing, formerly Lou's Landing, up this river."

"Ne'er heard of it! An' we got no mail fer ya."

"Well, sir, I would like a mail stop at my town."

"A mail stop? In Mo's Landin'? Where's it at?"

"About fifty miles north of here, maybe twenty miles below the boot heel of Missouri."

"And it's a town?"

"Yes, sir. A growing town with a mill, furniture store, lots of farmers, and a rice-growing paradise!"

"Hmm, that means swamps."

"Yes, sir, but also good land. Just look outside."

"Wow! You grew all that?"

"That's just my first load. Now, can we have the mail delivered and picked up there?"

"Hmm, you have a post office in this town, uh . . ."

"Mose's Landing, sir, and yes, we have a new post office at the farmhouse by the river. The town is across."

"Okay, ya got it, Mr . . . what's yer name?"

"Hamilton. Jonathan and Margaret."

"Hamilton! One minute, I may have some mail fer ya."

"No one's heard of this town," said Jon. Must be someone else."

"Here they are! I remembered 'cause they was three . . ."

"Three letters? For me? My god . . ."

"Don' swear, Mister Hamilton, or ye won't get dis mail."

"Sorry, sir. Wow, three letters!" Jon checked them. One was for "The Hamiltons," care of Little Rock, one to Lou's Landing, and one to Memphis.

"They all were transferred here," said the postman.

"Thank you very much, sir."

"You's welcome, Hamilton. With mail like that, you need a post office in Mose's Landing. I seen one had Lou's."

"Yes, it's the same place. We changed the name."

"I'll remember. Good luck sellin' that crop."

"Look, darlin', three letters."

"Three? Are you sure they're for us?"

"Yes. We'll read them when we make camp tonight."

"Like hell, Jonny! You drive. I'm reading!"

"Okay . . . Josh, you ride Prancer a while. I'm going to ride this wagon for a while with my wife."

"Yassa. It be's fun ta rides Prancer."

The two servants of DeValurie's were doing well, so Jon climbed aboard Maggie's wagon.

"This first letter is from my mother. She got the letters I sent from Pineville and from home, but not the others I guess."

"That's strange. What does she have to say?"

"Daddy is retiring! He's splitting up Bethania. Sammy is getting the main part, and it sounds like Virgie and Miles are getting large portions of land on either side."

"What about us? You? Don't you get anything?"

"Just a second." Maggie continued reading. "Oh, here. We get the west four and a half miles to the Yadkin River."

"Oh great! We get Hamilton Hill!"

"Yes, Daddy wants to give back that worthless gold mine to you."

"He does, huh? Well, good! Someday we'll just go dig that worthless mine and hit the mother lode."

"Everyone's fine. Someday they may come visit."

"I can hardly wait!"

"Be nice, Jonny. Daddy helped us a lot, you know."

"Yes, you're right, darlin'. What else?"

"That's about it for that letter. Here's one from the Chasneys."

"The Chasneys! Great," said Jon.

"You just want to know about Liz."

"Liz? Liz who, darlin'?"

"Don't try to bamboozle me, you big lummox!"

"Oh, you mean Elizabeth! Yes, I want to know about her, and Chuck and Dave."

"Surrrre . . . well, they both have one hundred sixty acres along the Kentucky River, across from Frankfort . . ."

"Then they made the journey alright," observed Jon.

"Ah-ha! Listen to this! Liz is engaged!"

"To Chuck? Or Davy?"

"She says she just couldn't wait any longer. She wants to have kids. She wants to tell you she's sorry. For what?"

"I'm sure I don't know, my pretty plum."

"I'm sure you do, Jonny. I said, don't bamboozle me!"

"What else do they say, my love?"

"Hmm . . . that's about it. Their address is Route 1, Frankfort, and they say to write soon, and someday we'll meet again."

"Yeah, maybe. I wouldn't count on it, though. Who is the last letter from?"

"This last one's from your folks."

"Wonderful! Read it out loud."

"Hello, how are you? We are fine. Alex has a cold . . ."

"On second thought, just read the good parts out loud."

"Alright. Your brother Drew has taken over the farm, and he acts like he didn't want it."

"That's strange. We used to argue about who is getting it."

"Both Drew and your dad want to come to Arkansas."

"To live? Wouldn't that be great?"

"I don't know, Jonny. We were trying to get away from them."

"Yeah, both our parents," said Jon.

"How about this? Your sister has a baby!"

"A boy or girl?"

"Well, they named it Jonathan Drew."

"I guess it's a boy! They run strong in our family!"

"Where does she live?" asked Maggie.

"In Savannah, Georgia, last I heard. What else?"

"Hmm . . . they're having a nice spring. My goodness, this letter was mailed April first!"

"Express mail, I guess. April Fools!"

"You're the April fool, Jonny . . . and August! Lummox"

"I'm Okay now. It's September."

"Oh, I almost forgot!" exclaimed Maggie.

"Almost? Here, you take the reins, darlin'. I like the looks on these people's faces when they see our full wagons."

"What people?"

"Haven't you noticed? They're still pouring into Arkansas."

"No, I hadn't noticed. You've had me reading, Jonny."

"Well, they have. See, here comes another wagon."

It was three wagons in a row. Jon and Maggie got a kick out of the way people stared with envy at the crops.

"Poor souls," said Maggie, "the lands have been taken already."

"Well, my love, maybe they'll get lucky. We did!"

"Thanks to you, Jonny . . . and Nunky Mose and Nanty Ella."

The Great River
Noon, September 2, 1836

"How much will it cost to get these three wagons across?"

"Lessee, two dolla fer wagons, an' a dolla fer all else."

"Righto. That's six, and . . . fifteen, makes twenty-one. Get out your money, darlin'."

"I gets twenty-two dolla, sir," said the toll collector.

"Twenty-two? The extra is the tip?"

"Nosa, that one wagon is extra big. The tips ain't been a-counted yet."

"The extra dollar *is* the tip, mister!"

"Alright, alright, don' get a-fired up! I'll be a-tryin' ta get ya aboard today yet."

"Damn it! There ain't no one else waiting to go across! You get me on this next ship, hear?" said a heated Jonathan.

"Jonny, don't swear! Here's your money, sir," said Maggie.

"Alright, here's yer ticket."

"There wasn't any toll on this side before, remember? I'll bet ole pantaloons will charge us again on the other side."

"What are you going to do if he does, Mister Hot Head?"

"Where's my Hawken? I'll take twenty dollars out of his kazoo!"

"Jonny! Calm down. We're Tennessee-bound again."

"Yeah, you're full of good news."

"Jonny, will you please settle down?"

"I'll try, my love, but I'm sick of these bunco bastards!"

"Stop it! Let's enjoy this boat ride."

"We better! It costs enough!"

The ferry snuggled up to the dock. It was loaded with people, wagons, and animals, all of which were having trouble getting up the bluff.

"Okay, Josh, you go first. Then the cotton wagon, and Maggie and I will bring up the rear."

"Orites. Here's I go."

Josh's wagon went right up onto the dock. The big market wagon with the heavy cotton was having trouble. Jon quickly hooked Corker in front of the white team of DeValurie's and pulled them right up. Then, back with Conqueror, Corker finished the task.

"Brr . . . it's cold on this river."

"What? It was in the nineties on land. At least it's a little cooler on the water."

"I didn't see any place before to drop off crops over there."

"I didn't either, my love. We'll ask first thing."

The boat ride was very smooth, and soon the ferry was easing up to the Memphis dock. A couple of small jolts and stop, and who should be first on board? Ole Pantaloons! Jon grabbed his Hawken and made sure Pantaloons saw him cap the nipple.

"Wel-welcome to Tennessee. My, what great lookin' crops. Are y'all together?"

"Yes, sir. We have tickets right here."

"Well, goody for ya! There's just a little fee fer usin' the pulley ta gets yer load up into town."

"I knew it," said Jon, who raised his Hawken. "How much?"

Pantaloons eyed the rifle. Maggie saw sweat on his brow. "I gives y'all a special deal. I won' charge nothin' fer the horses an' slaves, but my boss says I gotta charge fer the wagons an' load . . . and stabilizin' the cotton load."

"How much?" Jon was now aiming the Hawken.

"Well, lessee . . . three times two, plus ten, times six, plus five, minus two, times seven . . ."

"What in damnation are you counting?" yelled Jon.

Pantaloons cackled. "Hee, hee, just foolin', just foolin'!"

BAM! Jon fired into the air, frightening everyone. Pantaloons dropped to his knees.

"So was I! This time! I don't take too kindly to foolin'!"

"Yes, sir . . . uh, two dolla each wagon an' load."

"That's twelve dollars, Jonny."

"Thanks, darlin'. Now, where do I sell my crop?"

"Tur-turn right at the top o' the bluff, 'bout two mile south o' here." Pantaloons turned his attention to the dock crew. "Men, get these wagons up the bluff."

"Thanks." Jon flipped an Eagle at Pantaloons.

"Howdy! That is the best-lookin' crop a tobacca I've seen yet. Cotton looks good too."

"I was told I could get a better price here than at either Batesville orSaint Louis."

"That you can, sir, even better'n New Orleans."

"Really? Well, you can see I have lots of cotton and tobacco leaves. I also have some rice and squash."

"Yessir, I'll get my niggers to unload 'em and weigh 'em. Would you like some cold tea or water?"

"Cold tea? That sounds good," said Maggie. "How much would . . ." Maggie saw the look on Jon's face. "How much would it cost to ship this stuff all the way to New Orleans?"

"Oh, it would cost you a pile. But we pay better. Come on in outta the heat. It's gonna take a while to unload."

"Thank you, but I think I will watch the process. I have two grades of tobacco, primed and stemmed."

"Yes, sir. My niggers know the difference. They will sep—"

"Stop calling them niggers!" yelled Maggie.

"Sorry, ma'am, what would ya have me call 'em?"

"How about bounders? Or servants?"

"Bounders? What is that?"

"The name we called our Negroes on the plantation," answered Jon.

"Oh. Bounders. I'll try to remember."

"Do you weigh the tobacco?" asked Jon.

"Yes, sir. We weigh all the different crops, then put them right on the steamboats over there."

"Then it doesn't matter how good or clean the crop is if you weigh and pay them all the same, right?"

"Ah . . . well, we inspect them for quality too."

"I hope so! I have the best quality you'll ever see here."

"Ah, yes, sir. Very good quality, sir."

"That great big scale is for cotton, right?"

"Yes, sir. Some cotton is crated and heavy like yours."

"Mine are clean, too. Very little trash!"

"How do y'all manage that, sir?"

"We handpick the leaves and stems both in the field, and while it's ginned."

"Amazing! Here is your tea, sir."

"Your scales are off, sir. They're not setting on zero."

"Ah . . . yes, sir. That allows for the crating and the trash."

"Over two pounds? My crates weigh less than a pound."

"Y-yes, sir. I'll see to the adjustments."

"Good. Where do you weigh the tobacco and rice?"

"On these scales over here. I see they need adjusting too."

"Yes, they do indeed."

"We don't get rice, so we have no scales for it. This is the first rice I seen," the buyer said.

"Well, those are hundred-pound sacks, and I have four of them, filled to the brim. At least a hundred pounds each."

The servants easily maneuvered the huge cotton wagon under a giant block and tackle, which lifted the crates directly to the scales, then to large keel boats. The block and tackle pulley was on wheels! Jon had never seen that. His crates of cotton were about four by five feet, and the big, heavy wagon held three layers of five crates, fifteen in all.

"He's has five, three, six, five cotton, sir."

"Are you sure o' that, Dance?"

"Yassa, I's be sure."

"Well, that's five thousand three hundred and sixty-five pounds of cotton, minus the crates, sir."

"My crates are not two pounds, sir."

"Alright, let's say a pound and a half . . . times fifteen equals twenty-two and a half pounds of crate, sooo . . . you have fifty-three hundred and fifty-two and a half pounds of cotton.

Jon got a yes shake from Maggie. "Alright. How much per pound do you pay?"

"I pay ten cents a pound for clean cotton."

"Well, you won't find any cleaner."

"That is five hundred thirty-five dollars and twenty-five cents."

"Thank you, my love."

"Wow! That woman is good!"

"Yes, she is. Now for the tobacco. These are the nicest looking leaves I've ever grown."

"Do you have the weights, Dance?"

"Yassa, massa. Twos, trees, seva, five, massa."

"Are you sure?"

"Yassa, I's be sure, massa," answered Dance.

"Two hundred thirty-seven and a half pounds."

"How much?"

"I generally pay twenty cents." There was no reaction from Jon. "But these leaves are so nice, I will pay twenty-five."

"That is your best offer for this beautiful load?"

"Yes, sir. That is my best price ever."

"Fifty-nine thirty-eight, Jonny."

"What about the rest?" asked Jon.

"I pay ten cents," said the buyer.

"Ten cents? That's hardly worth planting it!"

"Oh . . . it is very nice. I pay twelve. Best offer."

"How much is that, darlin'?"

"Uh, fifty-nine dollars," answered Maggie.

"That's almost the same as the prime."

"Yes, but over twice the tobacca, sir."

"Alright. What about the rice?"

"I do not know the price of rice, sir."

"If it is so new, you should get a good return, sir."

"I don' know that sir," said the buyer. "I will give you ten cents. No more. Take it or leave it!"

"I think we should take it back home, darlin'."

"Then we would have to eat it, Jonny."

"Hmm . . . I guess, I'll sell, but I want it weighted."

"Yes, sir. Dance, weigh those big sacks."

"Yassa, massa."

"Would ya like more tea, sir?"

"No, thanks, I'll watch the weigh-in."

The bags weighed a total of four hundred eight pounds.

"Fo', no pound, eight, massa," said Dance.

"That's forty dollars and eighty cents, Jonny."

"Yes," said the buyer, "and the squash, I don' know . . ."

"Weighs . . . five, two, two, massa," said Dance.

"Hmm . . . I give ya five cents a pound."

"Take a look at them, sir. One can feed a family," said Jon.

"Okay, Okay. Six cents, final."

"How much is that, darlin'?"

"Thirty-one dollars and thirty-two cents, Jonny."

"Sold out! It's a pleasure doing business with you, sir," said Jon.

"That makes seven hundred twenty-five dollars and seventy-five cents, Jonny."

"I am sure she is right. I will get the money." The buyer left, and soon returned with the money.

"Thank you. Where is the best place to buy machinery, sir?"

"Farm machinery? Saint Louis, or New Orleans."

"And you are taking my crops to New Orleans soon?"

"As soon as we can get ready," said the buyer.

"Can we go along with you?"

"I don' know, what 'bout yer nig . . . bound . . . servants?"

"If you will let us, I will keep one wagon here, and send the other two home."

"Jonny, we need to get home too. The others are doing our work while we travel at leisure?"

"This is a good chance to buy some needed equipment, darlin', and to see New Orleans."

"Jonny, what would happen if those three escaped with our horses and wagons?" There was a pause.

"Hmm, I guess you're right, my love."

"You know I'm right, Jonny. Some other time."

"Right, my pretty plum."

Farmhouse Dinner Table
Saturday, November 27, 1836

"Well, folks, we haven't been together like this since we celebrated our first crop ready for market."

"Is this a celebration of our second crop?" asked Fred.

"Good question. I guess it's the finish of the first and second!"

"Explain that, Jonny," said Janet. There was a lot of noise coming from the kitchen. Janet looked toward the kitchen. "Ally, Chipper, Susan! Quiet down in there!" She turned back to Jon, who continued his explanation.

"Well, we finally finished our first crop of tobacco, corn, and rice . . ."

"An' dem crops in dem garden out back," said Ella.

"And we finished the second crop of cotton," said Jon.

"Thank the good Lord for that," added Fred.

"And we finished planting a hundred sixty acres of winter wheat."

"An' some un dem rice be secon' plants, Jon," said Mose.

"That's right, and on top of all that, we have a new bridge to town and a good ferry system across the river."

"How about the new extension on the barn?" asked Maggie.

"And the work done on my little house," added Modessa.

"All thanks to Mose," said Janet.

"All of us helped when we could," said Fred.

After a pause, Jon said, "Anyway . . . a toast to a super first year."

"What about all the things Jan had made in the furniture store," said Dessy, "like those pieces in my house?"

"An' dis tables," added Ella.

"And my bed," Maggie continued.

Everyone was cheering and sipping wine with each item said.

"Tomorrow we take our second train to Batesville!" This was met with more cheers all around. "But today we also celebrate the marriage of Lolita and Jules. We will start their new home next year. Everyone cheered even more.

"That was such a lovely wedding," said Modessa.

"And the DeValuries are such wonderful hosts," added Maggie.

"My wife has a very important announcement," said Jon.

"Today we received our first letter in our new post office!"

"We were saving it for this occasion," said Jon.

"Read it, read it, read it!" was said in unison and excitement. Margaret started reading the letter from Little Rock:

November 9, 1836

My Fellow Arkansawyers:

Congratulations on becoming a part of the newest state of these United States. This was a long, persistent struggle, as we were labeled a slave state.

Arkansas is not a slave state! We are a free, independent state who wishes to govern ourselves, and who is tolerant of the institution of slavery, and will not condone interference.

In line with this policy, we must conduct our first public census, and your assistance is needed. We would like as near an accurate count of men, women, and children under the age of sixteen in your area, including Negro, Indian, nonwhite, and Caucasian, as you can provide.

Also, if you wish the corporation of your town of Lou's Landing, please submit a separate accounting of its population, and the individual numbers of the races listed above.

Once again, fellow Arkansawyers, welcome to the latest and twenty-fifth state in the country. Our new capitol building has been started, and soon will be ready for your visit.

Yours Truly,
James Sevier Conway, Governor
State of Arkansas

Please remit responses to:
The Governor, State of Arkansas
Little Rock, Arkansas

As this letter was read, all eyes were on Mose and Ella.

"Notice that they didn't ask if the Negroes were slaves or free, like Nunky Mose and Nanty Ella," said Maggie.

"Nor their names," added Jon, "so Mose, Ella, are you alright with being on such a list?"

"Yes, we's orites, Jon. This be's no difference from Nort Car'lina, an' we's pretends ta be's slaves here."

"Only when strangers are present, Mose. Sorry, but to us you two will always be equal partners."

"A toast to our partners, Mose and Ella," said Fred.

"Thank you's, all. You's goo' partnas."

"Which raises the question, partners. Do we, or when do we, free all the servants?" There was a pause.

"Can we afford to free them?" asked Janet.

"You all know how well we did in September," said Maggie.

"Yes, and we're about to deliver a second big crop," added Jon.

"So, we can afford it. I guess I have no objections," said Fred.

"What do you think, Modessa?"

"I'm not a partner, Jonny," Dessy answered.

"I make a motion that we make Modessa a full partner."

"For once I agree, Jonny," said Maggie. "I second."

"Thank you, but I'm happy here. I don't need to be . . ."

"Quiet, honey, you have no vote. Let's vote," said Janet.

"Okay, all those in favor, raise your . . ." All hands were already up. "New partner, what do you think?"

"Well, as long as we have good crops like this year . . . but what if we have some bad years?"

"She's right," said Maggie. "What if we pay them with, say, three or four shares of our profits?"

"That's a good idea, honey. Then they prosper when we do."

"And we still give them their houses and food?" asked Fred.

"Yes. That way they can prosper. Now, while we are all gathered here, how do we figure the shares?"

"Sissy be's goo' wit figures, Jonny. Sissy pays moneys, an' we's all prospas," said Ella.

"Do we all agree with Ella, let Mag handle the finances?" Everyone immediately agreed.

"I'll make this motion," said Fred, "that Maggie . . . I mean, Margaret, be our treasurer."

"I'll need a second, before we vote."

"I'll second, honey," Janet said to Jon.

"Okay. All in favor?" All hands went up. "All agree."

"Alright, I accept. Now, who all gets full shares? And I think we should also have half shares," said Maggie.

"Then I should get half a share," said Modessa.

"Bunk! We voted you a full partner," answered Jon.

"Right, honey. You deserve a full share, same as the rest of us," said Janet.

"I's thinks Jon shoul' get two shares," said Mose.

"Me's too, Daddy. He's frees us, an' takes us ta Arkansas."

"Thank you, Ella, but I think if any should get two shares, it should be Mose."

"Nosa, Jon, jus' you! I makes motion."

"And I, Fred Wilson, second that motion. He brought Jan and I into this partnership. Let's vote!

The vote was unanimous. Jon abstained.

"Alright. Two shares for Maggie and I, and . . ."

"No, honey, three shares for Maggie and you, and one each for Freddy, Mose, Ella, Dessy, and I," said Janet.

"What about Josh, folks? And Ally?"

"An' Suzy toos," added Ella.

After a pause, Fred said, "I think we should give them half shares for now, until they're adults."

"And Jules has been helping a lot," added Modessa.

"Right. For now, we give Jules, Josh, Susan, Ally, and Chipper half shares. Okay, gang?" Everyone agreed.

"Can we end up with an odd amount of shares?" asked Janet.

"I think we can, Janet, but let's keep it even. I'll take one and a half shares. That's more fair," said Jon.

"Now, that makes seven and a half full shares, and four and a half part shares. That's ten and a half, and we give all the free servants three shares, and spend three shares on equipment?"

"How much would the servants get then, my love?"

"Well, if we do as well this second load, with thirty free servants, they would get . . . hmm . . . over three dollars and change."

"For a full year, Maggie?" asked Fred.

"I think so, Fred. We'll be dividing sixteen shares."

"That doesn't give them much, my love."

"Bu' it be's betta den nuttin'," said Mose.

"Well, if I take only one share and we give the servants four, and our equipment is paid before we divide up . . ."

"Jonny, we will have nothing to buy that equipment with," said Maggie.

"Either that, or no money left for shares," added Modessa.

"And we voted two shares for you, Jon," added Fred.

"Well, is there anything wrong with me giving a part of my share?"

"Jon, three dollas be goo' pays when you's has none," said Mose.

"Okay, Mose. Everyone agree on sixteen shares?" All were in favor with no motion being made.

"We haven't heard from our guests, the DeValuries," said Janet.

"Here's to our special guests, the DeValuries," toasted Fred.

"Welcome to our shareholders meeting," added Maggie.

"Thank you. We're enjoying this wonderful meal," said Constance.

"And the meeting. We never pay servants. What will become of them with money?" added Don Louie DeValurie.

"Maybe they will work even harder," answered Fred.

"Jonny would set everyone free," said Maggie.

"That is good. Everyone should be free," added Lolita.

"Even my servants?" asked Don Louie. "How would we pay?"

"Just the way these people do, Father."

"We no longer have land, Lolita," said Constance.

"Then what need have we of six servants, Mother?" asked Lolita.

"They are our friends, daughter," said Don Louis.

"Then consider freeing them, Father."

"We will need more workers, Mister DeValurie."

"We will talk more of this, Mister Hamilton."

"But now, let us enjoy this wonderful food," said Constance.

"I have one thing more, while we eat dessert," said Maggie.

"What do you have, my pretty plum?"

"Well, we are celebrating Jules and Lolita's wedding, and a couple days ago it was Thanksgiving. My family celebrates it."

"I'll drink to that," said Fred.

"Let's all celebrate our good fortune, Lolita and Julian's wedding, and Thanksgiving."

"I'll drink to that too."

"I think you're doing too much toasting, honey," said Janet.

"And I had a birthday a few months ago. I'm now twenty-one years old," added Jon.

"An' free, an' whites," said Mose.

"And you forgot my birthday, Jonny."

"When were your birthdays, honey?" asked Janet.

"Jonny's was July eighteenth, mine was April twenty-first, just seventeen days after our son was born."

"Hey, we have you surrounded, honey," said Janet.

"I'm sorry, darlin'. Guess I was just too excited about little Davey being born." Jon turned to Janet. "When are your birthdays?"

"Our birthdays are just two days apart," said Fred.

"Yes, plus seven years, honey!" added Janet. "You were born in seventeen-ninety-four, and I in eighteen-oh-one?."

"Any children?" asked Maggie.

"Yes, two, honey. They are both married and in Virginia."

"You must be older than you look," said Maggie.

"Thanks, honey. I'm thirty-five, and he's forty-two."

"Our birthdays are in July, the seventeenth and nineteenth," said Fred.

"How about you, Mose? And Ella?"

After a pause, Mose said, "We's don' knows when we's has birddays."

"Do you know what years?" asked Fred.

"Nosa. In's Africa," answered Ella.

"What days would you like best for birthdays?"

Mose paused as he considered the question. "Dem day we's left Bethania, Jon," he answered.

"What day was that, my love?"

"October twenty-fourth, Jonny."

"Alright. From now on, your birthdays are October twenty-fourth."

"Thank you's, Jon an' Sissy."

"Let's drink to everyone's birthdays, all in the past!" suggested Fred.

"How many are leaving with you tomorrow?" asked Janet.

"Jules and I will visit his family," said Lolita.

"Good. They need to know about your wedding. I want to take Modessa along so she can get her divorce."

"Why don't we all go, Jonny?"

"We will handle your business when you leave," said Don Louie.

"Mama an' I's stay, Jon."

"No, Daddy," said Ella, "you's goes an' has fun. I's has plenty work fo' Suzy, Ally, an' Josh."

"We do have a little time to relax," said Jon.

"We women can do a little shopping in Batesville," said Janet.

"You girls deserve some fun," observed Fred.

"What about freeing the bounders?" asked Jon.

"We'll do that in their church tomorrow morning, Jonny."

"Hmm . . . and you don't want to go, Ella?"

"Nosa, bu' takes Daddy."

"Okay, we'll do it, or have fun trying!"

Sunday, November 28

The moaning stopped cold, and over three dozen sets of eyes turned and watched the procession enter and walk up to the altar and face the crowd. Jon spoke.

"My friends, all except Mister DeValurie's servants, we are here to tell you some good news. Mose and Ella here are former slaves like you, but Mose and Ella are now free blacks. Because we are in a state where free black people are not welcome, they *pretend* to still be slaves when strangers are around. How would you like to be free, except when strangers are around?"

There was a very long silence, then whispers, then talk. One stood.

"How's we knows we's be free?"

"Good question. Today we take three wagons to market, and the money we get for the crops you helped raise will be split many ways. Some of it will go to each of you."

"How's much we's all gets?"

"It won't be much, but it will be yours to keep. You will own your house, and still get your food and clothes."

"We's owns house toos? An' whats we's do's fo' moneys?"

"The same things you do now, nothing different." This statement was met with a lot of chatter.

"We's do! We's be free men!" was exclaimed amidst cheering and dancing.

"We will be gone for two weeks. Jess and Murph are in charge."

Batesville, Arkansas
Monday, December 6, 1836

"Three wagons, huh? That's a lot of crops. Ye musta owns lotsa land."

"Yes, we do, sir. This is our second load just like this."

"Oh, no wunda you's so lately. I don' remembas any other loads like this'n," said the buyer.

"We took the other one to Memphis."

"Memphis? Dey's don' gives ya no bargains."

"We'll see about that," said Fred. "They gave us good fare."

"Orite, what's day gives ya fo' cotton?"

"No," said Fred, "what do *you give* for cotton?"

"Anywheres from eight ta ten cents."

"Memphis gave us 'leven and a half," Fred lied. "This here cotton is all hand-cleaned."

"Hmm . . . It do look clean. Eleven an' a half, huh?"

"That's right, and we figure it's worth more. That's why we're here." Jon watched in amusement as Fred spoke.

"Hmm . . . alright, I gives ya twelve cents a pound."

"What do you have to weigh with? We think we have over four hundred pounds a crate."

"Fo' hundred? No ways!"

"Just try liftin' one."

"Fo' hundred! Why half dems woods crates!"

"The wood's about a pound," lied Fred.

"No ways . . . two poun's, fella."

"No way, fella! We split the difference."

"Hmm . . . Orite. Dat's three ninety-five poun's each."

"No way! Them crates weigh over four hundred each."

"Orite, we's calls it fo' hundred. How many crates?"

"Twelve crates of clean cotton."

"Sold," said the buyer. "What's next?"

"Just the finest tobacco you will ever see, all cured by air and hand-picked," said Fred.

"A lot of primed leaves are smoke and air-aged for a couple months," said Jon.

"That's five hundred seventy-six dollars for cotton, Jonny," said Maggie.

"I'm glad you're along, darlin'."

"I gives ya twenty cents fer tobacca, that's it."

"No way, fella. They gave us a lot more in Memphis," said Fred.

"Twenty cents, takes er leaves," said the buyer.

"Why, that's robbery! I ought to . . ."

"Hold it, Fred! I'll take over. You cool off," said Jon. Jon turned to the buyer. "He's right, sir. They paid us twenty-five cents."

"Hmm . . . twenty-five, huh? I'll pay twenty-two."

"Well, sir, this is the best tobacco you can get. They should pay plenty for it in New Orleans."

"Twenty-two, that's it," said the buyer.

After pausing, Jon said, "For all the tobacco I have?"

"That's right, fella, fer alls you has."

"Okay, you can weigh it. We did," said Jon.

"Hows much ya got, fella?"

"Seven hundred and ten pounds total weight."

"Orite, I takes yer word fer it."

"That's one hundred fifty-six dollars and twenty cents."

"Thank you, my love. Let's get it unloaded."

The tobacco was half unloaded when the buyer saw his mistake. "Hold it! This here ain't all prime tobacco!"

"Are you sayin' we lied?" asked Fred.

"Nosa, I jest thought it were all prime. I has ta pays less fer them stem-cured leafs."

"How much less?" asked Jon. "You gave your word that you would pay twenty-two cents a pound."

"I's knows that, fella, bu' I cain't go flat broke!"

"How much?"

"Ten cents."

"Ten cents?! Get my Hawken, I'll gut him out!"

"Gut? Orite, fifteen cents. I cain't go no higher."

"Alright, you liar, I'll take it."

"How much do we have, Jonny?"

"We have a hundred sixty-eight pounds of prime and five hundred forty-two pounds of stem-cut."

"Hmmm, that's . . . thirty-three dollars and sixty cents for the prime, and . . . eighty-one dollars and thirty cents for the stem, Jonny."

"Thanks, darlin', how much total?"

"One hundred fourteen dollars and ninety cents."

"Right, and I'd better get an honest price for rice."

"Rice? Ya gots rice? Ya grows it here?"

"That's right. Hundred pound sacks of clean, hulled rice. Three full ones, and a half-full sack," said Jon.

"I ain't sure they even takes rice," said the buyer.

"They will. They said so in Memphis."

"Oh, they's did, huh? How much they pay ya?"

"Too much! Fifteen cents," lied Jon.

"Too much?" The buyer's face lit up. "I'll gladly give you twelve a pound."

"Hmm . . . twelve fifty."

"Orite. Twelve fifty, sold, but only da full sacks."

"Why not the half sack?"

"Cain't sell part sacks. Takes dem three sacks."

Jon and Fred huddled out of hearing range.

"We can feed it to the servants to give them a change from corn," said Fred.

"Right, and we'll try the store in town," said Jon. Jon and Fred reapproached the buyer. "Okay, I'll sell just the three full sacks."

"Orite, a hundred pounds each, ya says?"

"They were about a hundred two pounds each in Memphis."

"Hmm . . . that be orite, I guess."

"That's thirty-eight dollars and twenty-five cents, said Maggie.

"Thanks, darlin'. What's the grand total?" Jon paused as Maggie did the addition.

"Seven hundred twenty-nine dollars and fifteen cents."

"Hmm, about the same as Memphis."

"Same? I's pays better'n Memphis," said the buyer.

"We're happy. Let's go to town."

"What 'bouts wheat, Jon? Wat dem pays un wheat?"

"Oh, thanks, Mose." Jon turned back to the buyer. "What do you pay for wheat?"

"Hmm. Don't gets wheat neither. 'Bout ten cents."

"Okay," Jon said. "We'll have some next time. So long."

"So long, fellas."

"Hello, ladies. What have you there?"

"Christmas presents," answered Janet. "I'm glad you're back with the wagons. These packages are getting heavy."

"Where did you get the money, honey?" asked Fred.

"I lent them each ten dollars from the shares they have coming, Freddy," answered Maggie.

"I's wans ta gets presen' fo' Mama," said Mose.

"And don't forget Chipper, Nunky Mose! Let's you and I go shopping for Nanty Ella."

"Orites, Sissy, we's do."

"I'm hungry. Let's all eat lunch, then shop. That selling crops is hard work," said Fred.

"It's not quite noon, gang. While you're shopping with Mose, Fred and I will put the horses and wagons in the stables, and we can get Modessa's divorce taken care of."

"Alright, Jonny, but I would like to be there for Dessy."

"Thank you, but we can do it, Margaret," said Modessa.

"Alright, then we'll all have lunch together at the eatery in say, an hour and a half, Jonny?"

"Okay, my love. Put your packages in this wagon."

"See you later, honey," said Janet.

"Lessee, three wagons an' horses . . . 'bout three dollars for boarding for a couple days," said the man running the stable.

"Okay, here you are. Where can we find a judge?"

"Gettin' married, huh?" The man chuckled. "Good luck. You'll find a judge back across the riva an' right two blocks."

"Thank you, sir. Take good care of my horses."

"And wagons, and presents," added Fred.

"Don' worry. They's all safe here."

Once the wagons and horses were stabled, it was time to get Modessa divorced.

"Let's start walking, gang."

Jon, Fred, Janet, and Modessa headed over the bridge into the center of town and turned right. The courthouse sat along the White River. It was just a tired-looking, wood-framed building. They entered and approached the clerk.

"We would like to see the judge, please."

"He is busy this morning. What's it about?" asked the clerk.

"This lady wants a divorce."

"From one of you two?"

"No, ma'am, from her husband who abandoned her."

"Hmm, how long ago?"

"In January," answered Modessa, "right here in Batesville."

"Oh? What was his name?" asked the clerk.

"Jacob Cartier. I am Modessa Cartier."

"Cartier . . . Cartier . . . I've heard that name."

"He probably robbed your bank!" quipped Fred.

"I'll think of it. I'll go see if I can work you in. Who are the rest of you?"

"They are support for me," answered Modessa.

"And we all witnessed his treatment of Modessa, honey," added Janet.

"Take a seat. I'll be right back," said the clerk.

"Thank you."

"The judge has an opening. Come this way, please." The clerk led them all into the courtroom.

"Your Honor, this is Modessa Cartier, who wishes to divorce her husband, Jacob Cartier, for desertion."

"Are one of you men the husband?" asked the judge.

"No, sir . . . Your Honor," answered Jon.

"Then what the Sam Hill you doin' here?"

"We are witnesses, Your Honor."

"Witnesses? He must be a terrible bastard, this . . . Jacob Car-Cartier . . . I know that name! *Lucy!*"

"I'm looking, Your Honor." Lucy poked her head in the door.

"That woman is always two steps ahead of me. Well, it says here he deserted you in January. That's eleven months! Did he beat ya?"

"Well, he's hit me several times," answered Modessa.

"Did any of y'all see him beat her?"

"Hitting her is beating her, honey," said Janet.

"Thank you, Counsel. What's yer name?"

"Janet Wilson, hon . . . Your Honor, and this is my husband of twenty years, Freddy Wilson."

"Happy ta meet ya . . . honey! What about you?"

"I'm Jonathan Hamilton, Your Honor, and I heard Jacob say he didn't want to be married to Modessa anymore."

"He did, huh?"

"We heard that too, Your Honor."

"You're Wilson? And you heard it too, huh?"

Just then, Lucy poked her head in the door again. "Your Honor? Jacob Cartier is wanted for murder. You issued a warrant on October tenth."

"Thank you, Lucinda. Do you know where we might find him, Missus Cartier?"

"No, Your Honor. He said he was going up into the hills."

"Alright. Your divorce is granted. The clerk isn't here today, so just sign this, with witness, at my secretary Lucy's desk, with a ten-dollar fee."

"Thank you, sir," said Modessa.

"Yer welcome . . . honey!"

"Now do we eat?" asked Fred.

"Yes. That eatery is on the main street. Maggie and Mose are probably there already."

The eatery had a big sign that read *Van Buren Elected*.

"I wonder what will happen now with a new president."

"Not much, honey. Jackson handpicked him," said Janet.

"Jules don't think much of him, but I'm glad to see Jackson finally go," said Jon.

After a pause, Dessy asked, "This is where we meet Maggie, isn't it?"

"She likes to shop, honey," said Janet.

"Well, while we wait, let's toast the new single lady."

"Good idea, Jon. I'll drink to that!" exclaimed Fred.

Fred had a buzz by the time Maggie and Mose appeared. "'Bout time you's showed up! I'm hungry!"

"You're loaded, honey. Why waste it with food?" asked Janet.

"How did the shopping go, my love?"

"Wonderful, Jonny. Mose has all his shopping done, and I got some things for us."

"Let's see them, honey."

"They're in the wagon, Jan, but I'm not through."

"How much money do you have, darlin'?"

"I brought plenty, Jonny. I knew this would be our only chance to shop before Christmas."

"Okay, but what about some machinery and things we need for the farm?"

"Well, I brought two hundred . . ."

"Shouldn't those things be paid for from our shared money from the crops?" asked Modessa.

"They sure should," answered Fred. "We have three shares going to expenses, and we need more equipment."

"What if it costs more than those shares are worth?"

"Then each of our shares will be less, Jon," answered Fred.

"How did you do today, honey?" asked Janet.

Maggie answered, since she had kept track of the money. "A little better than Memphis, so our total from crops came to fourteen hundred fifty-four dollars and change."

"Hallelujah! I'll drink to that!" exclaimed Fred.

"I've changed my mind, honey. You need some food!" said Janet.

"An' remembas, we's still has wheat in dem fields, an' tobacca in dem barns, an' seeds fo' springs," said Mose.

"And any money from the store and mill. Should that money go to our shares?" asked Modessa.

"Yes," said Jon.

"You bet, honey," added Janet.

"Wow," said Fred, "this is more money than what we paid for the land."

"Well, not quite," said Maggie. "We paid over two thousand dollars, all in gold. Remember?"

"Yeah, we remember, honey, and we owe it all to you two and Mose."

"Anyway, we have had a great year. Doesn't matter how much the stuff costs. We need it. Let's eat!" said Fred.

"What would ya li . . . sorry, we don't serve people of that race in here," said the waitress.

"He's our partner!" yelled Fred. "And he is just as good as any man in this town!"

"Sorry, sir. I just work here."

"Orites," said Mose. "I's goes out un . . ."

"No, you don't, Mose. Where do people of that race eat? Is there another eatery in town?" asked Jon.

"We have a room in back for him to eat."

"How about another eatery?" asked Maggie.

"There is one by the courthouse, but he wouldn't get ta eat there either."

"I's eats in back rooms, Jon," said Mose.

"Then let's all of us eat in the back room," said Fred.

"Sorry, sir, it's a tiny room just for black people." There was a pause.

"I know. Let's go back to the stables and cook some of our own food, like we did on the trail," said Maggie.

"Good idea. The hell with this place, and this town!" said Fred.

"Sorry, I wish I could help ya," said the waitress.

"That was the best lunch I have ever had!" said Fred.

"It did have a special flavor, Dessy," added Maggie. "Did you like it, Nunky Mose?"

"I's sho 'nuff did, Sissy," chuckled Mose.

"Yeah, eating with all these cows added extra aroma."

"I would like to buy a couple of those cows."

"What for, Jonny? We have Milky."

"I know, darlin', but if we had a bull and another cow, we could have some manure for the crops."

"An' milks an' cow meats fo' everyones," added Mose.

"I suppose that means chickens and pigs too," said Maggie.

"Why not? They all poop, honey," said Janet.

"And maybe some goats or sheep," said Fred.

"Oh sure! Then we wouldn't need to buy any dresses!" quipped Jan.

"Nothing like being completely self-sufficient," said Maggie.

"How about it, gang? Do we buy some farm animals?" asked Jon. He received unanimous positive answers from the group.

"An' don' fo'gets dem plows, Jon."

"I won't, Mose. Let's do that now, while the ladies go finish their shopping," said Jon.

"We haven't got rooms at the hotel yet," said Maggie.

"Get them too, my pretty plum. I need some money."

"What if they don't let Mose have a room, honey?"

"Hmm . . . Get the rooms, and we'll sneak Mose in."

"Alright, Jonny. Have fun!"

"Yeah, have fun, honeys. We will!"

"Dat machine shop is right behin' me, 'long wit the feed store an' animal buy-n-sell," said the smitty.

"Thanks. I see you have some extra wheels."

"I do. Lotsa wheels an' no wagons, ha!"

"I'll give you a dollar each."

"Whatcha do with 'em? Ya got wheels!"

"Yes, but we can use some extra. One dollar each?"

"Sold. They's three sets, so I throws in the extra."

"Good. Just throw them in the wagon. How about bellows for our pit, sir?"

"I have dis one, feet pumper, an' tools."

"I'll take them too. Here's a couple more dollars."

"I trades all these fer da rice in yer wagon," said the smitty.

"Righto, that's a deal. The machine shop is next, men."

"Hello. How are you gentlemen?"

"Fine. We're looking to buy some machinery."

"Well, we have the best. What do you need?"

"Well, a couple plows, a gin, and a spreader."

"Spreader? What is that?" asked the salesman.

"It sows the seeds, and spreads seeds and manure."

"Never heard of it, but we got plows an' the latest gin."

"How much?"

"Ah, well, sir, the plows are ten dollas each, an' the gin . . . a hundred dollas."

"What? I can buy two gins in Carolina for a hundred."

"That's a long way ta pull one here. Look, it separates the seeds real clean and blows trash away."

"I'll give you seventy-five for it."

"Make it eighty, an' it be yers."

"Okay. What is this?"

"Called a reaper, the latest. It cuts wheat at the groun', an' brings it out here ta be bundled."

"Think it will work on rice?" asked Jon.

"Rice? We ain't got rice here."

"I grew rice this year, sir."

"Yeah? How did it do?"

"Pretty good. I think a reaper might work for rice. What do you think, Mose?"

"We's plants rows an' makes wheels bigga, Jon."

"How much?"

"Hundred twenty dollas."

"Make that one hundred, and it's sold."

"It says McCormick. Didn't he invent the gin?" Fred asked the smitty.

"That was his father, I think. Yours at hundred dollas."

"Okay, put sold signs on them, and I'll pay you tomorrow."

"That's two hundred total, an' thank you."

"Do you have fence wire?"

"Wire? No, sir. We use wood rails an' rope."

"Which one do we use to hold cattle, Mose?"

"Dem woods rails, Jon."

"Good, I think that's all for now, sir."

"Thank you again. These machines will be waiting."

"Sounds like Count Louie," smiled Fred, once they were outside.

"Yes. Now we buy some animals."

"Welcome, we buy, sell, or trade."

"We sure don't have nothin' to sell or trade," quipped Fred.

"Alright. Horses, cows, pigs, sheep, chickens?"

"Maybe some of all of the above."

"Do we need more horses, Jon?" asked Fred.

"We's needs othas mo'," said Mose.

"Alright. Bulls or cows?"

"Maybe one of each, cattle, pigs, and sheep?"

"Our two bulls are fifty dollars each. The cows are thirty, the pigs are twenty, sheep ten, and chickens a dollar."

"How about we get a discount if we buy some of each?" asked Fred.

"Sure thing. What ya need?"

"A bull and a cow. Pigs and sheep, Mose?"

"We's shoots big pigs, razaback, Jon, an' takes lots dem sheep ta make clothes for alls," said Mose.

"Probably cheaper to buy cloth, Jon," advised Fred.

"Hmm . . . Okay, a bull, a cow, and ten chickens."

"A rooster too, sir?"

"Yes, a couple roosters. We'll give you eighty dollars for the lot, sir."

"Eighty? Alright, eighty it is. Thank you. Here's some feed. Come again."

"Will you make a cage to hold a dozen chickens?"

"Sure will. Chickens, huh?" asked the smitty.

"Yes, and a bull and cow. We can pull them."

"Very slow! I's makes ya side rails too."

"Thank you, sir. We'll be needing them tomorrow."

"Good. I keeps thinkin' I's knows ya."

"You do. In January, you split a chunk of gold for me."

"Oh yeah! An' a bought a pair o' horses from ya."

"That's right. I sure miss those two drays."

"Well, ya oughta go gets 'em! Their owner ain't carin' for 'em. Not feedin' 'em!"

"Where are they, sir?"

"On a farm up-riva, 'bouts mile an' half."

"Mose! Grab Corker and Conqueror, and our guns."

"Yassa, Massa Jon."

"Ya gots 'em trained purty good. Name's Hollsworth, get dem work horses," said the smitty.

"I'm going too, Jon. I'll ride Sloggy."

"Sure, Fred. Who's going to tell the women?"

"If'n they's shows, I'll be a tellin' 'em," said the smitty.

"Right! Let's get crackin' to see Hollsworth."

The men knew they had the right place when they saw Jake in the pasture. The horse was limping, favoring his left front leg. They stopped, and Mose stepped over the fence.

"Comes, Jake. Here, boy. Comes, boy."

Jake recognized Mose's voice and whinnied. He hobbled over to Mose, who checked his leg and body.

"His ribs are showing, Mose."

"Dis worse, Jon. Ankle's cut. He be's cobbed, toos."

"Why that dirty bastard! Find Red, Mose."

"Where are you going, Jon?" asked Fred.

"To get my horses back, and to kill a farmer!"

"I'm right behind you."

Jon and Fred heard Mose calling Red as they galloped the hundred yards further to the log farmhouse.

"Got your flintlock, Fred?"

"Sure do. Why?"

"Get ready to use it. I'm gonna knock on his door."

Fred hid behind a tree as Jon approached the house. Suddenly, the door sprang open, and Hollsworth appeared.

"That's far 'nuff, stranger! Who are ya? Whatcha want?" asked the farmer, pointing a muzzle at Jon.

"Is your name Hollsworth?"

"That it be. What's yers?"

"Hamilton. I owned two horses that the smitty sold to you. He said I might buy them back."

"Ya might. One ain't no good ta me. Turns up lame."

Jon was having trouble holding his temper, even with a flintlock pointed at him. He was thinking he should have his Hawken with him. "I saw one. Where is the other?" Jon asked.

"Be a runnin' out there in that pas . . . Hey, what's dat big nigga doin' wit my horses? I fixes him good!" The farmer brought his rifle to his shoulder.

"I wouldn't do that, mister!" shouted Fred, aiming at a startled Hollsworth. He hesitated just long enough for Jon to spring at him, body-slamming him against the log wall of the house. Hollsworth dropped his rifle, and Jon hit him as hard as he could on the right ear and ducked as the farmer tried to swing back. As he stooped, Jon grabbed the rifle by the barrel and swung it at Hollsworth, hitting him in the groin area. As Hollsworth bent down in pain, Jon again swung the rifle, the butt striking the farmer flush in the face, sending him to his knees with blood gushing.

"Had enough, you bastard?"

"What did I do ta you?" muttered the bloody farmer.

"You starved and beat my horses."

"Them's my horses."

"Not anymore. I'm taking them back."

"I don't wanna sell," said the bloody Hollsworth.

"No, you just want to kill them," said Fred.

"You don't have a say, Hollsworth. I'm taking them back."

"Jon," said Mose, now approaching with Jake and Red, "dem Reds in bad shape toos."

"Can they make it back to town, Mose?"

"Reds can. Jakes maybes can."

"Listen to me good, Hollsworth. I'll leave some money with the blacksmith for what these horses are worth now. Don't you come in for a couple of days, or this will be a picnic compared to what you'll get if you come in sooner. Got it?"

"Yer a-stealin' my horses."

"You don't deserve to have horses!" yelled Fred.

"Just remember, don't come to town for a couple more days."

"Get off my property!"

"We're leaving. We'll drop your rifle off at the next farm. Mose, you have yourself a couple horses to mend."

"We's fixes dem ups, Jon."

"Look, honey, they have Jake and Red," said Janet.

"They have! Jake is limping. I wonder what's happened to him. Hey, Jonny, where have you been?"

"We got back Jake and Red, and we bought a lot of things for the farm. Need some money, darlin'."

"How much do you need?" asked Maggie.

"Around four hundred, my love."

"Jonny, I only have about one hundred left."

"It comes from the shares of our year's work," said Fred.

"Okay, Fred, we'll take about three hundred from crop money."

"That will be a lot more than three shares worth, Jonny."

"Dat be's orites, Sissy. We's needs 'em," said Mose.

"And that helps make more money next year," added Fred, as they walked back to the blacksmith.

Mose applied liniment to Jake's leg and fed and grained all the horses at the blacksmith's shop.

"Here is money for the boarding of our wagons and horses, and for the remodeling of that one."

"Nope, it a-covers all with that sack a rice, good grain," said the smitty.

"Thank you. When Mister Hollsworth comes in a couple days, will you pay him this fifty dollars? Twenty is for Jake, thirty for Red."

"Yes, sir. If'n ya need liniment, the animal store has it."

"Thanks, Smitty. I'll go look tomorrow."

"Let's have our late supper. I'm starving, Jon."

"Freddy, honey," said Janet, "I'm surprised you stay slim."

"I work it off, my pet. It's hard work stealing back our horses!"

"Steal? Jonny?"

"We didn't steal them, my love. I gave money to the smitty to cover what they are worth now, after they were beaten and starved."

"That's what happened to Jake?"

"Yes. He hobbled Jake's leg until it cut through the skin."

"Are we going to eat?" asked Fred.

"Right now! We'll eat at the wagon, just like lunch."

"I's eats in back room, Jon."

"That's alright, Mose. Dessy is a good cook."

"Let's try the other eatery, Jonny. Maybe they are more friendly about Negroes."

"Good idea, it's back over the bridge, across from the courthouse."

"I'm sorry, folks, but you all can eat together in the colored people's room. It's empty," said the maître d'hôtel.

"That's where we will eat supner!"

"Good meal! I'm stuffed!"

"But you'll be hungry again before long, Freddy," said Janet.

"Now we have a real job!"

"What job, Jonny?"

"Yeah, what job is that, honey?" asked Janet.

"Getting Mose up into a room."

"Why don't we just get our rifles and march in?" asked Fred.

"I's sleep in dem wagon, Jon," said Mose.

"You deserve a nice soft bed, Nunky Mose."

"You leave this job to me," said Janet. "Get ready to walk Mose in. Us girls will distract the clerk."

"Hi there, honey. Got a room for three horny girls?"

"Y-yes, we do. It's the best room in . . ."

As the clerk was speaking to the women, the men snuck up the stairs. Once they were safely out of sight, they heard Janet say, "Forget it, honey!"

Between Batesville and Mose's Landing
Thursday, December 9, 1836

"It's time to switch animals again, Jonny."

"Right, darlin', let's see. It's the bull's turn to walk, and Jake goes back up in the wagon with the cow."

"That's right, honey. How's Jake's leg?"

"It's better, Jan. Mose greased it again during the last stop."

"Look, honey, Mose and Freddy have made the change already, and Mose is feeding the animals," said Janet.

"That means we can get down and stretch our bones," said Maggie.

"Someone's coming! I'll go see who it is," said Jon.

"We's has dem rifles ready, Jon."

Jon, with his loaded Hawken, rode ahead to see what turned out to be the noisiest clamoring wagon in Arkansas! A single old nag was laboring to pull the wagon, while an old scrubber was walking beside it.

"Howdy, I'm yer travelin' salesman. I got anything ya need fer sale, anything at all," said the peddler.

"Howdy yourself! You're going to need another horse soon."

"Ahh, ole Boss has been a-pullin' this wagon fer years. Always looks like he's on his las' leg."

"Well, what do you have of interest to me?" asked Jon.

"Nails, screws, hinges, ropes, gunpowder, hats . . ."

"Mose! Come look at this stuff!" yelled Jon.

"I sees womens. I get Boss closer."

"No need. They're coming on the run. Check out this stuff, Mose. Maybe there is something we need."

"Howdy, ladies. I have cloth, bonnets, blankets . . ."

"Dem horses need grains," said Mose, "an' we's has grains."

"Nah, see dat? Dat's oats, an ova there's ryes."

"That's oats? And rye over there?" asked Jon.

"Ya betcha! Deys' wild in Arkansas, good grain."

"I didn't know that! It's all over!"

"I's lets dem animals feed, Jon," said Mose.

"That's why them razorbacks get so big, Jon," said Fred.

"Hold it! I thought I just heard one now," said Jon.

"Yes, I heard something too," said Modessa.

"Got your flintlocks, Mose and Fred?"

"No, we left them at the wagons," answered Fred.

"I's go gets 'em, Jon."

"Too late, Mose. It's right behind that bush." Jon took aim with his Hawken, while everyone else was quiet. Suddenly, something furry streaked across the clearing close to the group, and ran up a tree in a flash.

"Why didn't you shoot, Jonny?"

"He was too fast, my love. It was small. Let's take a closer look." The three men slowly circled the tree.

"Well, I'll be," said Fred. "It looks like a fox."

"It be's grays, Jon. Sho 'nuff, it be's a fox," said Mose.

"I never heard of a tree-climbing fox."

"Shoot it, Jon," said Fred, as Mose went after his flintlock.

"No, Fred. It's so small and harmless. Let it go."

"Alright, Jon. I wonder what startled that fox like that?"

"Hmm . . . You're right, Fred. If it was us, why did he jump out toward us?"

"There must be something else in those bushes. Mose! Will you bring my rifle too?" yelled Fred.

The women suddenly screamed and ran around the back side of the trader's wagon. The old horse, Boss, never flinched.

"What is it, my love?"

"It's ah . . . Jonny, look!" Maggie was pointing.

Jon ran to the women and heard the low growl.

"It's a panther, Jonny," said Modessa.

"Eeek! Help! Jonny!"

BAM! The ball from Jon's Hawken tore into the chest of the big cat at the shoulder. It turned two or three times in a circle and charged at Jon, leaping and knocking down the group leader. Jon tried to grab his knife from his belt, as the cat tore at his shirt and back. Jon saw Mose running toward him.

BAM! BAM!

The panther dropped on top of Jon with a final growl.

"Is you's hurts, Jon?" yelled the approaching Mose.

"Oh . . . Jonny! Are you alright?" Maggie was weeping.

"I think so. My back feels hot. Where did those shots come from?"

"They came from Oostanaula and Nickawatie." The three Cherokee emerged from the brush.

Mose grabbed his knife and started to cut.

"Hold! Nickawatie and Elias cut big cat. We shoot."

"I'm glad you did, Oostanaula. You saved my skin."

"Jonny, it made some deep lines in your back."

"I's gets dem liniment," said Mose.

"Here, let me clean the wounds first," said Modessa.

"I's has just the thing to heal them cuts," said the peddler.

"No, thanks. We have liniment," said Jon.

"You came at the right time. Thank you," said Maggie.

"Oostanaula trail cat, hear banging in wagon."

"My noises scared away animals," said the peddler.

"Let's put our pots and pans together then, ladies," said Fred.

"If'n ya don't have no pots an' pans, I has them here."

"Did you ladies find anything you need from him?" asked Jon.

"Lots of things, honey. Perfume and a bonnet," answered Jan.

"Do you need money?" Jon asked, as Mose applied liniment.

"No, thanks, honey. We still have some left over."

"How about stuff for the farm, Mose?"

"I's looks, soon's I be finished here, Jon."

"I'll take a look too," said Fred. "I saw some metal things and some wire, and . . ."

"Wire? We can use some wire. We may need to spend a little more of that money, my pretty plum."

"Alright, Jonny. Get what we need."

"How about you, Oostanaula? Need anything?"

"Need blankets. Get cold now."

"I has four blankets left. A dolla each," said the peddler.

"Maggie, will you please buy those last four blankets for Oostanaula?"

"Alright, Jonny. That puts us out of business for a while."

"Oostanaula has gift for you, Jon Hamilton."

"Thank you, friend. What is it?"

The chief snapped his fingers, and Elias brought the horses up. "Oostanaula has bird for each friend."

Draped over the horses' necks were several turkeys. He gave one to each of Jon's group, minus a few feathers.

"Thank you, friend. You wish to travel with us?"

"No. We must hunt for winter, Jon Hamilton."

"Then you will need these wild turkeys."

"No. Wild bird easy to find here. You take home."

"Thank you, Chief," Jon said, as the Cherokee disappeared.

"We has wire an' box o' metals, Jon," said Mose.

"They total ten dollars, Jon," added Fred.

"Okay, take ten more dollars from our shares money, darlin'."

"I be thankin' ye all. Have a safe trip home," said the peddler.

"That was a big panther, Jonny. I was so scared."

"Scared? He came after me, not you, my love."

"And I suppose you didn't get scared?"

"I didn't have time to get scared, my love."

Maggie paused. "He sure was a pretty color, wasn't he, Jonny?"

"Yes, and a big cat. Lucky Oostanaula came along."

"He'll probably make a coat out of that skin."

"Yeah. Winter is on its way. I can feel it, darlin'."

"He sure had a pretty color to him."

"You said that already, my pretty plum."

"Did I? Guess that means I would like to have a panther skin like that."

"Yeah. Someday I would like to hunt in those mountains north of Batesville. Someday, when, *if*, we ever get caught up with all the work!" Jon chuckled. "Let's go home."

DeValurie Dinner Table
Saturday, December 25, 1836

"Merry Christmas, e'eryone," said Don Louie.

"Merry Christmas!" Everyone answered in unison.

"Ahh . . . That is very good wine, Mister DeValurie. What is it made from and where did you get it?" asked Fred.

"It is from the grapes in my garden," he answered, his Spanish accent still very evident.

"Papa makes very good wine," said Lolita.

"I will toast my grandbabe!"

"Grandbaby?" asked Janet, glancing at Lolita.

"Sí, my Lolita is with babe."

"Already? That Jules is a fast worker," quipped Fred.

"So were you. Remember, Freddy, honey?" asked Janet.

"We tried very hard. I am getting old for children," said Lolita.

"You still look young and pretty, Lolita," said Modessa.

"Anyway, here's to the new addition to the Jones family," toasted Jon.

"I'll drink to that! Where's the bottle?" asked Fred.

They all toasted Jules, Lolita, and Christmas.

"Chipper is anxious to open his presents," said Maggie.

"Dey kin waits till afta we's eats," said Ella.

"I have never seen a decorated tree before. Have you, honey?"

"We had them all the time at Bethania, Jan. I guess it was a German tradition. Right, Jonny?"

"Yes, my love, and there are lots of Germans around Salem."

"It sure is lovely, Missus DeValurie," said Modessa.

"Thank you, Dessy. It's pretty with the presents all around it," answered Constance DeValurie.

There was a pause while everyone admired the tree and presents.

"You serve such an elegant meal, Missus DeValurie," Dessy said.

"Yes, you sure do, honey. Your china is lovely," said Janet.

"Thank you, ladies. It was all my mother's."

"I's has somethin' ta ask you's all," said Josh.

"What is it, honey?"

"Uh . . . I's wans ta marries Suzy."

"What?" cried Fred. "You *what*, Josh?"

"I's wans ta marries Suz—"

"You're too young! I forbid it!"

"Now, Freddy, just relax," said Janet. "How old are you, honey? And Susan?"

"I's be ninetee', I thinks. Don' knows 'bouts, Suz."

"That's much too young. I forbid it."

"Hold it, honey. Remember how old we were?" asked Janet.

"I was . . . twenty-five," answered Fred.

"You lie, honey. I was sixteen and you was twenty-two."

"See? I was an adult!"

"But I wasn't. Susan! Come out here."

"Y-y-yessum, Missus Wilson?"

"How old are you, honey?"

"I's not sure, ma'am . . . maybe's three fives."

"See honey? She's as old as I was . . . and Josh is almost as old as you were."

"I still forbid it. Where would they live?"

"I think we should divide some of the town into lots."

"Good idea, my love. We're going to have to divide them anyway, if we plan to give the servants their homes."

"Those shacks are laid out in a pattern, so it would be easy to make them into lots," said Fred. "Yeah, let's do it."

"The two blocks between the intersection and Mister DeValurie's forty acres are long enough for probably twelve lots," said Maggie.

"And four deep, to the park and path along the river. That make forty-eight lots, more than we'll ever need," said Jon.

"I's starts work in dem lots tomorra, Jon."

"Okay, Mose. While we're at it, we might as well lay out some sites on the east side of the boulevard."

"Including one for Jules and Lolita, honey," added Janet.

"You are making verra big town in Lou's Landing," said Don Louie.

"Yes! It is now Mose's Landing. But let's call the two blocks of servants' lots *Lou's First Addition*."

"Great idea. That will make everyone happy," said Fred.

"Excuse, please, bu' Suz an' me's wans ta marries," said Josh.

"I'll drink ta that!" slurred Fred.

"Then we's can marries?"

"Yes, you can, honey. Freddy just gave permission."

"Suzy! We's can marries!" Josh rushed into the kitchen and hugged Susan.

"What? I didn't say that . . ."

"You just toasted their wedding, honey," said Janet.

"Did I? Oh well." There was a pause.

"Before the dessert, let's get to the main business at hand. The share money." Everyone cheered and clapped their hands.

"Mag . . . er, Margaret has the figures for the crops."

"Alright, partners. The total take from the trips to Memphis and Batesville was fourteen hundred fifty-four dollars and ninety cents." This was met with more cheers from the group.

"Modessa, do you have the general store sales?"

"Yes, I do. After costs, we cleared four hundred seventy-nine dollars." There was more celebrating by the group.

"How about the mill, Jan?"

"We sold about one hundred twenty dollars in lumber, and two hundred five dollars of furniture." Everyone was excited about all the good news they were receiving, and continued to clap and cheer.

"Okay, that totals one hundred forty-one dollars and eighteen cents per share," said Maggie. The group cheered again.

"How much was the total take, honey?" asked Janet.

"Twenty-two hundred fifty-eight dollars and ninety cents."

"Wow! That's two hundred and eighty dollars for us," exclaimed Fred.

"More like two hundred eighty-two and change, honey."

"The thirty servants each get fourteen dollars and eleven cents."

"And a certificate of freedom, and ownership of their homes," added Jon.

There was a standing applause after Jon's statement.

"If my figures are right, after the three hundred ten dollars we spent on machinery, the balance left over in the three shares for expenses is one hundred thirteen dollars plus," said Maggie.

"What should we do with that money, gang?"

"I's thinks you's shoul' has it, Jon," said Mose. "You's spen's mo' than alls res o' us." Everyone was in agreement with Mose's statement.

"Hold it! I would rather see it dispersed among you all or the servants than given to me . . . please."

"That would be a problem. Let's leave it in the expense account for next year," said Fred. The group agreed with Fred's suggestion.

"Now, I'll pass these certificates around to free the servants *except* when other people are around, while Maggie pays you all your money. And thanks! A job well done!"

The signatures and payoffs took some time before the dessert.

"We would like to offer our happy pleasure on your good prosperity," said Don Louie DeValurie.

"Thank you, sir. And thank you for selling your land to us," said Fred.

"This is the ten dollars I owe you, Maggie," said Modessa.

"Oh, that's right! Here, honey. I'm glad Dessy thought of it," added Jan.

"An' I's owes Sissy toos, Mama. Mo' than ten dollas," said Mose.

"Orites, Daddy. I's gives back . . . how much, Sissy?"

"Nothing, Nanty Ella. You made this dress for me."

"Dat be's par' o' work shares, Sissy. Take dem ten dollas."

"No, Nanty Ella. I'll pay the servants at church tomorrow."

"Connie and me will be freeing two, maybe three of our servants. Maybe they will work here for you," said Don Louie.

"We will hire them if they wish to stay. Thanks."

"May we still use your horses Grenada and Madrid?" asked Fred.

"Oh, sí, señor, anytime you need them."

"Thank you, Mister DeValurie. We may not need them now. Our Jake and Red are getting well again. But we will pay your freed servants in shares and give them a house, like the others."

"I will tell them. We will miss them."

"Okay, gang, let's all gather at the tree for Christmas presents."

Everyone got something, and Maggie had even remembered to get a gift for all the DeValuries. Jon was shocked when he opened his.

"A pistol! Look, the chamber revolves! How much did . . ."

"Never mind how much, Jonny. It's a new Colt revolver."

Black River
January 20, 1839

"Damnation, that fire feels good!" exclaimed Fred.

"Shore does," said Julian Jones, "but I reckon' it'll get colder."

"You see that ridge we have to cross tomorrow?" asked Jon.

"We's gots ta climbs dat?" asked Josh.

"Shore do, if'n we want ta hunt them Ozarks," said Julian.

"Yeah, that was a great idea, this hunting trip, Jon," said Fred.

"Might as well do it now. Maybe we can shake the blues."

"It orites, Jon. We's do's orites," said Mose.

"We can thank Andrew Jackson fo' not getting any money fo' dem crops," said Jules Jones. "Rememba when Lolita an' I predicted that Jackson was goin' ta hurt us?"

"How'd he hurt us, Jules?" asked Fred.

"Don't ya rememba a coupla years ago, when he fought again' Congress, an' broke the big bank? Ah, the Specie Act were the name he used. Them banks goin' broke is what caused all the hardship everybody is facin'."

"All I know is that nobody has any money. It almost didn't pay to put seeds in the ground," said Jon.

"What were the prices we got, Jon?"

"We got only nine cents for the primer tobacco, and six cents for wheat and cotton. Rice was only five cents."

"All dem tobacca down da drain," said Mose.

"Yep! Over nine hundred pounds of fine tobacco, and eleven hundred pounds of cotton and rice. Hardly anything."

"Well, the store did alright. People gotta eat," said Fred.

"Maggie and I got ninety-three dollars, but those poor workers of ours got only a little over a dollar for a whole year!"

"Dat be's a dolla mo' den dey had, Jon," said Mose.

"And they got their food an' clothin' an' a place ta stay," said Jules.

"We's comes here ta forgets dem moneys, Jon."

"That's right. So what's our plan for tomorrow, Jon?" asked Fred.

"Well, we cross the Black River here, climb that cliff, and we'll be in the Strawberry River country."

"How far is that from Batesville?" asked Jules.

"I'd say about thirty miles north of Batesville."

"Dem Strawberrys Riva be's froze," said Mose.

"Yeah. The bears are probably in their winter sleep," added Fred.

"We's jus' wakes dem," said Josh.

"Ha! That be right, Josh, we just wake 'em up! Ha, ha!" laughed Jules.

"Well, whatever we get doesn't matter. It's just getting away from the hard routine and money panic."

"And thanks to you, Jon, we already have our bellies full of turkey and venison," said Fred.

"Yeah, Jon, give us a chance ta shoot tomorra," added Jules.

"I's gets sleep now, big days tomorra," said Mose.

"Let's build that fire back up first. It's going to be cold," said Jon.

January 21, 1839

"Get up, Fred! You're going to miss breakfast!"

"It's too cold to leave these blankets."

"You shoulda brought Janet along ta keep ya warm," said Jules.

"I'll bet that Lolita keeps *you* warm."

"Yes! She can do that fandango layin' down!" joked Jules.

"Ha, ha!" roared Fred. "I asked Jan one time if she remembered the names of the minuet!" Fred was laughing hard.

"What did she say to that?"

"Nothing, but she knows how to kick the can-can! How's that redhead, Jon?"

"She needs me. She says it takes two ta tango!"

"You's men's talks cheap, bu' alls I's needs ta do's is snaps dem fingas, an' Mama comes a-waltzin'," said Mose.

The men were all laughing. "That leaves you, Josh. What kind of dancin' do you and Susan do?" asked Fred.

"We's toos young. Cain't dance, so's we's plays leap frogs."

"Jus' don' croaks, boy," laughed Mose. They all had a good laugh over their jokes.

"Well, saddle up, men. We've got this murky river and that big cliff to climb before we can get some good hunting."

"Can't saddle up. We left our horses with the chief," said Fred.

"I mean, load up! Oostanaula's not going to bring horses."

Mose swam the murky Black River with a rope tied at his waist, and everyone got good and wet using the stretched rope to guide them across. Another fire had to be built to dry the hunters out. It was well past noon when the group at last reached the top of the cliff, and the landscape opened up to a beautiful pine-forested plateau with very little brush. After a short hike up the Strawberry River, the group spotted five or six whitetail deer scampering away from them.

"You have to be quick to shoot a buck here, Jules."

"Yeah, too many trees ta hide behin'."

BAM! "I's tinks I's got a deer!" exclaimed Josh.

Mose was in the trees in a flash after the deer. *BAM!*

"Get him, Mose?" yelled Fred.

"I's gots 'em!" answered Mose. "Josh gots 'em!"

Josh's ball had cracked ribs, and Mose finished the buck.

"Well, now we have food again," said Fred.

"Yeah, but we wan's big game. Bear, pantha," said Jules.

"Meantime, let's eat some venison,?" said Fred.

"You better get a fire going then, Freddy."

"That hit the spot, Mose," said Fred.

"Sho 'nuff did. We's goes up riva, Jon?"

"Why not? Let's see where it takes us."

The traveling was fairly easy, and many loud noises were heard. Heard, not seen, because there was too much forest. Five weary hunters made camp, ate venison, and told jokes that evening.

"It's your turn, Fred. Know any good jokes?" asked Jules.

"Well, there's one I heard in Virginni. This farmer was tending his cows when a stranger walks up. 'That's some nice cows ya got there. Is it true that cows can predict the weather?' 'Why yes,' said the farmer. 'If'n the cows are standing, it's not gonna rain for twenty-four hours. But if'n they lay down, you'd better find some shelter.' 'Bull,' said the stranger. 'Look there, half of yer cows are laying down, and half are a-standing. What's that mean?' 'Well,' said the farmer, 'that means half the cows are liars!'"

Everyone except Mose was laughing hard at Fred's joke.

"I's thinks we's needs some shelta. Looks at dem clouds."

"You're right, Mose. Let's get back under those trees."

The men hurriedly made their new camp under a thick growth of fir trees, just in time. Heavy rain hit the Strawberry.

"That was close," said Jules.

"Yes, I hope it lets up before morning. If it keeps up this hard, it will ruin our hunting trip. Nothing will come out, and I'll have to shoot all the cows I see standing!"

"Well, let's not let it spoil our evening," said Fred. "Let's worry about hunting tomorrow! Who's got another joke?"

"I will tell you one, but don' tell Lolita I said it."

"Okay, Jules, let's hear it."

"Two Spanish hunters in the woods came upon a naked lady sitting on a stump. The first hunter asks, 'Are you game?' The lady answers yes, and the second hunter shoots her!" The men all laughed.

"Come on, Jon. Don't you have a joke?" asked Fred.

"Well, my brother told me one that I thought was dumb."

"Let's hear it, Jonny."

"Well. Uh . . . A man stopped to eat at an eatery, and a dog inside kept growling and barking at him. The man finally asked the waitress why the dog don't like him. 'Oh, it's not you, sir, that's upsetting the dog.' 'Well, what is it, then?' 'You're eating out of his dish!'"

"I gots a slave joke," said Mose.

"Great, let's hear it!"

"Dem ovaseer had a new slave, suppose ta be's fast an' good worker, so's dem ovaseer say, 'Where dat bucket be's, you's carries dem rocks an' fills all dem holes in dem field, an' I's gives you's one hour ta finish.' So dem black boy runs an' works fast, an' first half hours he done fill twelve holes, an' dem ovaseer be very happy. Den in next ten minutes, he do only three holes, an' den next ten minutes he only do two's, an' den next ten minutes he do only one. Dem ovaseer say, 'What dem problem?' An' dem boy say, 'Dem bucket too fa' away!'"

"Ha, ha, that was a good one, Mose."

"It be's good, Jon, 'cause you's be ovaseer," Mose laughed.

"I just thought of an old hunting joke. Want to hear it?

"Yeah, Fred, let's hear it," answered Jules.

"Well, if I can remember it . . . There was a Norwegian and a Swede out hunting without any luck, and the Swede said, 'Shut up, Eric. I hear somethin' in them trees.' Eric looked and said, 'There ain't nuthin' behind them trees, Henrich.' A little while later, Henrich said, 'Shut up, Eric. I hear somethin' behind them rocks.' So Eric looked and said, 'There ain't nuthin' behind them rocks.' A little later, Henrich said, 'Shut up, Eric. There is somethin' in them brushes.' Eric started to look when somethin' jumped up, and Henrich shot and wounded it. Eric was on it immediately with his knife. 'What is it, Eric?' called Henrich. 'I be . . . uh oh! It's a man!' said Eric. Henrich was scared as he ran to the brush. 'I got some cloth to stop the bleedin'.' 'It's too late, Henrich,' said Eric. 'He's dead.' Henrich looked at the body and said, 'You dummy, he'd a-lived if'n ya hadn't gutted him!'"

As the rain and laughter slackened, Jon saw a set of eyes glowing in the dark. He reached for his Hawken. *BAM!*

"What was that, Jon?"

"I don't know. I hope it wasn't a man! Light a stick, Mose."

After a search, they found a big panther, shot between the eyes.

"Wow, that's a big one, Jon. It must be eight feet, nose to tail!"

"It probably smelled our venison. Will you skin him, Mose?"

"I's do, Jon. Den we's hide dem cat from wolves."

"Let's build up the fire. They're all around us, and it's cold!" said Fred.

A sleepless night was spent watching for wolves.

January 22, 1839

"Y'all awake, Josh?" asked Jules.

"How's can you's sleeps? All dem howls an' tawks."

"Brrr, you're right, Fred. It is cold. If'n we had our horses, I think I'd ride outta here right now," said Jules.

"Yeah. Hunting sure is fun!" said Fred.

"My brave partners, hunting *is* fun!"

"We's goes on up riva, Jon?"

"Why not, Mose? Let's give it another day, and if we don't get a bear, then we can change routes and maybe head southwest toward that mountain and the White River."

"What mountain? I didn't see no mountain," said Fred.

"We're in the Ozarks, Fred. There are mountains all around, but there is one fairly close that I got glimpses of."

"I's saws it toos Jon."

"We should be decidin' before long," said Jules. "This riva is getting' real small, an' we're a-gonna run out soon."

"Okay, so we eat venison breakfast, and follow Strawberry Creek for half a day,"

"Sure, Jon, don't get all worked up about it. Let's have breakfast."

"Sorry, Fred. I guess this rain is upsetting me."

"Dem rains not hard, Jon. We's hunts orites."

"And today, we has good luck. I feels it in my bones."

"I hope you're right, Jules, but how would we get our game out and back to the Black River?"

"Let's get the game first. Next time we'll bring the horses," said Fred.

"The traveling was easy through stands of pine, fir, and several other species of trees, some Jon had not seen before. About midmorning, the group came to a grass and brush clearing.

"Hold it! What kind of animal is that?" asked Fred.

"I'm not sure. They almost look like cattle," said Jon.

"Out here, Jon? Dems no farms here," said Mose.

"They be wood buffalos," said Jules.

"Wood buffalo? They don't have a thick heavy coat."

"It gets worn off in all these brush an' vines."

"Who wants to shoot one first?"

"I will," answered Fred. "See that big one over there?" *BAM!*

"You got him, but you didn't kill him, Fred."

"Just give him a minute. He'll die as soon as I reload."

"I's shoots it, Jon? Please? I shoots it?" asked Josh.

"That Okay with you, Fred? It's your call."

"Go ahead, Josh. Get closer, and get a head shot," advised Fred.

Josh walked up close, aimed, and fired. The bull kicked and rolled, until Fred had reloaded and finished him.

"I'll be durned. The rest didn't run away!"

"I will kill the one ova by da big tree," said Jules.

Jules's shot got a large cow. She kicked, screamed, and died.

"There's one for you, Mose, over there."

"No, Jon. Maybe's them can carry dem shot meats."

"Really? Think we can tame them enough?"

"We's tries, Jon. We's ropes dem to's trees later."

"Right, let's try it, Mose."

"We's waits, Jon. Too early. We's come back."

"Right, Mose. Let's skin the two we got. I'll bet they're good eatin' too."

As they were skinning, there was a shot in the distance.

"Must be another hunter close by," observed Fred.

"I'll go see, while you all are cutting and skinning." Jon walked north over a mile when he spotted smoke and then a clearing, and a big log cabin with a man standing in the doorway.

"Hello! I heard your shot," said Jon.

"Yeah, your shots sounded like a war. Come on in, stranga."

"We killed two wood buffalo. My men are cutting meat."

"Those are my buffalos! I plans ta domesticate 'em."

"Oh, I'm sorry, sir. We thought they were game."

"Game hell! Yer a-killin' my cattle!"

"Sorry, sir. There were a couple others. We thought maybe we could tame them enough to carry our pile."

"What? Ya ain't got no horses?"

"No, sir. We left them at the Black River."

"Then ya were gonna jus' leave 'em fer the wolves."

"We hoped to tame a wood buffalo enough to carry them."

"Tell ya what. Ye catch an' tie 'em ta a tree, an' I'll let ya use one o' me pack horses."

"That would be wonderful! But how would we get the horse back to you?"

"They knows these woods like the back a me hand. Jus' let 'em go, an' they's come trottin' home!"

"Good! Thank you for the offer. I'd better get back."

"Hold on now. I's get my horses, an' we goes back together."

Jon fired his Hawken just before entering camp. "Men, this man lives just over a mile from here."

"Welcome, mister. We got lots of meat you can have," said Fred.

"Dem's me buffaloes ya kilt."

"Oh, and you live here, in these mountains?" asked Fred.

"I do! I hope ta start a herd wit dem buffs."

"He will lend us this horse if we catch those other beasts."

"Really? Well, let's get crackin'."

"Dem's Jon's words, Fred," said Mose.

"Mose, you come with me. That big bull can't be far, and one is in those trees. The third is . . ."

"Ova der, Jon. I saw 'em a little while ago," said Jules.

"Good, we'll, try to herd them to this clearing. Ready, Mose?"

Jon rode into the brush and trees, and found the big wood buffalo grazing. Jon chased after him and ran right past Mose. The creature jumped when he saw the black giant.

"Get that rope around his neck or horns, Mose."

"Orites, Jon. I's gets 'em."

"Good job, Mose. I can pull him to the clearing." A screaming, lunging animal was tied to a tree by his horns.

"Now the one in those trees!"

The search was on. It took a while to find the cow.

"There it is, over there. I'll circle around."

The two horsemen soon had the beast running to Mose.

"That makes two, and you saw the other, Jules?"

"Yeah, in those bushes, Jon."

The smaller animal was easy to corral. Josh got water from Strawberry Creek, and the creatures calmed down some. One by one, they herded the stubborn animals to the mountain man's cabin, where there was a field with a small corral.

"I shore do thank ye all. Would ye come ta stay the night here in me cabin?"

"No, thanks, sir. We're just sorry we killed them two," said Fred.

"We still have some light. We're hoping to get a bear."

"Well, ye goes north 'bout ten mile ta Spring River, then some east, an' ye'll see some rock caves. Bears there."

"Thank you, sir. We head north, gang."

"Pay no mention! Good luck. Stop by 'gain."

"Must be lonely, living alone like this," remarked Fred.

"Naw, I'm a-courtin' a widow woman a few miles south a here."

"What would a widow be doing in these mountains?" asked Fred.

"These Ozarks be full o' widows an' children."

"Too bad we's all has wives," said Jules.

"Well, good luck to you with your widow, sir."

"This must be Spring River," said Jon.

"Looks jus' like Strawberry Creek," observed Fred.

"It run dem same ways in Strawberry," added Mose.

"Let's go east, like the man said."

Along the little creek, Mose suddenly stopped the group.

"Wow, what is that?" asked Fred.

"I don't know. I've never seen such a beautiful animal."

"It be lookin' un big deers," said Josh.

"Very big! Look at that big body. Must be a male."

"Should we shoot it?" asked Jules.

"We's oready has big load un meats," answered Mose.

"Let them go, gang. We're after bear."

"Yeah, I'm hungry. Let's eat here," said Fred.

The men were enjoying their break, when suddenly a muzzle shot rang out from close range.

"Dat be's close!" said Josh.

"I'm going to check it out. I'll be back soon,"

"I'm coming too, Jon," said Fred.

"I's be comin' toos, Jon," added Mose.

The three men moved quietly through the trees. Soon they spotted a man with a face full of hair, cleaning the big deerlike animal they had so recently seen.

"Hello! You with the kill, we're coming out."

"Just a damn minute! What does ya want?"

"Just to say hello and congratulations for shooting that big deer."

"This ain't no deer! It be's an elk," said the hairy man.

"Elk! I've never seen one of them," shouted Jon.

"Well, ya can come take a look if'n ya like."

As the three men walked out into the open, the hairy man jumped up and aimed his rifle at them.

"Hold it," said Jon. "We have three rifles on you to your one, which I'm betting is unloaded."

Click. The man lowered his empty musket and stared. "Hello, Jon . . . M-Mose, ya founded me."

"Found? How do you know our names, mister?"

"Don't y'all know me? I'm Jacob Cartier."

"Cartier! You're Jacob?" asked Fred.

"Yep. Ya turnin' me in? Uh . . . keep him away from . . . please," Jacob said, as he pointed to Mose.

"Small world, isn't it?" asked Jon. "We're here on a bear hunt. Never thought I'd ever see you again."

"I lives here. Yer not gonna turn me in?'

"No. We won't even tell Modessa we saw you."

"H-how is she doin'?"

"She's fine. Doing well," answered Fred. "We'd hate to give her a setback by telling her we saw you!"

"Do you live around here?" asked Jon.

"Yep. 'Bout ten mile west a here. Got meself a home an' a widder woman."

"Let's be's goin', Jon. I's be getting' sick," said Mose.

"Right, Mose. I can't say I've enjoyed this meeting."

"Ye kin take some meat if'n . . ."

"We'd starve before we'd take your meat," said Fred.

"All the more fer me! Don' get lost!" Jacob said, as the men left.

"If that don't cap the climax! Meeting him here!"

"Who was he?" asked Jules. They were now back at Spring Creek.

"He was Modessa's mean husband."

"Yeah. He murdered one of your father-in-law's servants and would have killed DeValurie if Mose and Jon weren't there."

"I's didn't reco'nize him wit all dem hair," said Mose.

"And he burned down the house that Janet and I were going to move into," added Fred.

"Well, you have a better one now, Fred."

"Sure do, thanks to you two."

"We's go gets bear now, un still light," said Mose.

After traveling only a couple miles, the men found a tall bank of big rocks. They could see entrances to two caves.

"It be's awful quiet," said Josh.

"They be's sleepin', Josh, bu' dey's be der," said Mose.

"See all those footprints, Josh? And look, there are some hairs of his coat from when he rubbed against those rocks," said Jon.

"It be's a he-bear?"

"We're going to find out, Josh. Let's make some torches. It may be really dark in there."

"Who's going in first?" asked a shaky Fred.

"You are, Fred. Alone!" Jon winked at Mose.

"Naw, not me. Alone? I can't see in the dark."

"How about you, Jules? Want to go first?"

"I don' think so, Jon. I follow you with torches an' extra gun, Okay?"

"Well then, I guess Josh will have to go it alone."

"Me? Oh . . . Orites. I's goes shoots bear," said Josh.

"Ha, ha! You're a good sport, Josh. I'll go in first."

"An' I's goes wit you's, Jon," said Mose.

Both Jon and Mose carried a torch in their left hand and a rifle in the right. This worked well for a ways, where they could walk bent at the waist. But soon they were on their hands and knees as the cave became even smaller. From time to time, they would stop and listen for any noises, but heard none. At about one hundred yards in, they were on their bellies crawling, propelling forward, inch by inch, and still no noise but their own breathing.

"How's can dem bear gets through dis little holes, Jon?"

"I don't know, Mose," replied Jon, at the lead and trying to whisper past his left shoe, "but they do."

At last, Jon saw what looked like a room ahead. "Get ready," he whispered. "We're coming to an opening."

"I's be ready, Jon. What's I do?"

"I'm going to crawl into the room. You come up here to the entrance, ready to shoot. Okay?"

"Orites, Jon. I's be ready. Bu' no bears here, Jon."

"How do you know that, Mose?"

"I's hear dem bear makes noise un der sleeps."

"Well, I've never heard them sleep, so be ready."

"I's ready, Jon."

Jon inched forward. When his head and arms were clear in the room, his arm circled the room with his torch. "I don't see anything, Mose," he said, as he crawled in.

"Dem room be's empty, Jon." Mose also scanned the room.

"Look at the ground. They've been here."

"Ova der, Jon. Dems be bones."

"Oh my god. Some of them are human."

"Dey be's bear an' human, Jon. Dey's fights ta death."

"Here's the man's knife, rusty and all old blood. I wonder how long ago this happened."

"Twos, maybe's tree years."

"Should we take the bones out and bury them?"

"No, Jon. Man's spirit un bones stays here. Bad lucks ta moves 'em."

"Okay, Mose. Let's get out of here."

Darkness had long since come when Jon and Mose finally made it out of the cave. The fresh, cold air felt good.

"What did you find in there?" asked Fred.

"Dead bodies."

"Dead bear bodies? No live ones?" asked Jules.

"Dead bear an' dead man," answered Mose.

"You's jus' tries ta scare us," said Josh. "I's skeered!"

"Should we bring them out?"

"No, Fred. We'll just leave things as they are and try the other cave tomorrow morning."

"Sounds good. I think our campfire should be in front of that cave, so nothing can get out."

"Go ahead, Fred. Then y'all can crawl ova them hot ashes in the mornin!" quipped Jules. They all laughed.

"Is there anything better than a meal of venison, turkey, wood buffalo, coffee, and corn bread? This is living!"

"Yeah, where's the dessert?" asked Fred.

"Did yer mother have any children that lived?" asked Jules. They all laughed.

After the laughter died down, Mose said, "Dis be's long day. I's gets dem sleeps."

"Me too, Mose. I'm really beat."

"See you all in the mornin'. You no sleeps, Fred?"

"Uh, no, Jules. I'm staying awake to watch that cave."

January 23, 1839

Morning found the fire still burning high, and Fred propped against a rock, rifle in hand, and sound asleep.

"Poor man was worried a bear might come out at night."

"A lot a good he'd do, bein' sound asleep," said Jules.

"Fred! Get up and have some breakfast."

"We's gots coffees, Fred. Dat wakes you's up," added Mose.

"Maybe Fred had the right idea. These marks by this cave are really fresh."

"Hear that, Fred? We needs ya ta guard us today," said Jules.

The men finally woke Fred enough to take hot coffee and eat breakfast. All was now ready for the second cave.

"Are you sure ya want ta go in there?" asked Fred.

"Isn't this what we made this trip for?"

"Ya, it is, Jon, but it be very dangerous," said Jules.

"We need some torch sticks, Mose."

"I's got em, Jon. We's ready. I's goes firs' todays."

"Are you sure, Mose?"

"I's be sure, Jon. Let's gets crackin'."

Into the cave they went, torches burning, rifles at the ready. There were fresh bear signs all around, and they walked bent-down and very cautiously for a long spell. Then the cave made a slight turn to the right and shrunk to crawling room only. In time, the two men were facing a split. One path continued straight, and another path veered to the left. This brought the trek to a temporary halt.

"Dey's fresh signs both ways, Jon," whispered Mose.

"Yes. It's hard to tell which is fresher."

"I's thinks we's splits, Jon."

"No, Mose. We need each other. Let's both take one path and see where it goes. If we hear nothing, we'll crawl back here and try the other direction. You choose which way."

"Orites. We's goes left."

"Right! Let's light a torch and leave it here."

Mose led the crawl again, which soon made a turn to the left. Jon figured that they had already crawled much deeper into this cave than the one yesterday evening. Now, with the left turn, he figured they must be coming in behind the other cave. They listened, but heard nothing. The crawlspace seemed to be getting even smaller, and the men found themselves again flat on their stomachs, inching forward with their elbows and toes.

"We's be crawlin' jus' like yestadays, Jon."

"Yes," whispered Jon, "and with the same results."

"We's keeps crawlin', canno' turns 'round."

The inching was hard, smelly work, and very slow moving.

"I's sees sometin', Jon."

"What is it, Mose?"

Mose didn't answer immediately. He just crawled faster, pulling away. After a moment, he said, "It be's a big room, Jon."

"Got your flintlock ready?"

"Sho 'nuff do," Mose said, as he poked his head and torch into the room. He stood behind some large stones and peeked around as Jon came out behind him.

The men circled the pitch-black room with their torches.

"Der be no bears in here, Jon."

"This looks a lot like the back room in the other cave."

"We's knows hows ta find out." Mose circled the room.

"Good thing you have that torch, Mose. I can't see you."

"Ova heres, Jon. Looks wha' I's finds."

There, in a corner, were the bones of the man and bear, right where Mose and Jon had left them the previous evening.

"Well, I'll be cobbed! The other path we took yesterday must be over this way."

"Yassa, it be's. We's leave, Jon. Be's bad lucks ta be here."

"Okay. I think the first cave is the easiest way back."

"Sho 'nuff be. I's goes firs'."

"We'll scare the hell out of them coming out of cave one!"

As Mose peeked his head out of the first cave, he saw Fred, Jules, and Josh sitting around the campfire facing the second cave. Jon and Mose snuck up close, growled, and roared.

"Holy heaven!" shouted Fred.

"Ahhh!" yelled Jules. "I think I wet my bloomers!"

Click. Josh was the only one to grab a rifle.

"Don't shoot, Josh. We're peaceful."

"What the . . . how'd you get out there?" asked Fred.

"You's be's sleeps when we's come out dem cave," said Mose.

"No, sir, I didna sleep! Josh didna sleep!" said Jules.

"No, Josh was awake. He's the only one who grabbed a gun."

"Where you's comes from?" asked Josh.

"From that cave over there, like magic."

"Then the two caves connect . . . like magic!" said Fred.

"Dat cave dun splits, an' we's took dem wrong ways," said Mose.

"Are you going back again?" asked Fred.

"Yes, but we need to change. Look at our togs."

"Ya must be hungry. We has coffee and meat," said Jules.

"Sounds good. Josh, will you wash these shirts down at the creek and hang them here to dry?"

"Sho 'nuff, Jon. You's eats an' I's wash."

"Tell us about the cave. Find anything this time?" asked Fred.

"A lot of very fresh signs."

"I's knows dem bear be's in dem cave," said Mose.

"It's gettin' late. Maybe you go in 'gain tomorra?"

"No, Jules, you can't tell night from day in there, so I want to go back now and get the filth over with."

"Alright. Have something to eat first," said Fred.

"I've got another shirt, but what about Mose?" asked Jon.

"I's wears same, Jon. It be's wet, bu' clean," said Mose.

Guns and torches clean and ready, Jon took the lead back. They soon made their way to the split and found the torch they had left burning, but was now out. Mose and Jon relit the torch.

"Mose, This time, we get us a bear."

"Dis time, we's do, Jon."

Jon squeezed into the hole and started crawling forward, with Mose close behind. The smell almost gagged Jon, but he pressed forward on elbows and knees. The light from his torch showed fresh bear signs all around. They were now deeper into this cave than the other cave, or the other branch of this cave, when Jon suddenly stopped.

"Listen, Mose. Do you hear that?"

"Do's I hears wha . . . yassa, I's hears."

The men heard a distant whining sound ahead.

"Do bears make that sound?" whispered Jon.

"I's don' knows, Jon. Maybe's female has babies."

"Maybe. But if it is a sow with cubs, do we shoot her?"

"I's don' knows. If you's shoots, I's shoots."

"Okay. Just don't shoot me. Are you ready?"

"I's be readys, Jon. Gets crackin'!"

As Jon and Mose inched forward, the whines grew louder. Finally, Jon saw the opening ahead. He cocked and capped his Hawken. The click of their hammers must have startled the beast, as it stopped whining and made some teeth-gnashing sounds. It roared when it saw the light of the torch.

"We've been spotted, Mose."

"Yassa. Stays low, Jon, so's I's shoots ova you's."

Jon flashed the light all around and saw nothing. Sweat was rolling down his face. Suddenly, the bear roared again. It was right above Jon at the entrance to the room! Jon looked up and saw teeth snapping. He tried to bring his Hawken forward, but was cramped. He saw the giant raise his arm to swing.

"Back, Mose! Back!"

The blow caught Jon's shoulder and ripped his shirt off him. It was in shreds. Jon dropped his torch and Hawken at the room's entrance as he sprang backward against Mose. The enraged bear was roaring so close that the fire of the torch went out from the beast's slobber. Mose leaned forward over Jon and fired point blank. *BAM!*

Sparks, unused gunpowder, and hot smoke fell on Jon; and he screamed. The room ahead was filled with thick black smoke. Mose picked up his torch and tried to spot the smoke and sparks on Jon's shirt and rub them out. The tunnel was now filling with smoke, and both Mose and Jon slapped at it with their hats. Jon was now feeling the pain in his shoulder and upper arm.

"Is you's orites, Jon?"

"Take a look at my shoulder and arm, Mose."

"Oh, he dun gotcha, Jon. You's shoulder an' arm be bleedin'. I's try ta wraps wit shirt."

"It's Okay, Mose. I think it was a glancing blow. No bones are broken. Do you think you killed him?"

"I's sees dem face an' shoots. He don's be in front dem hole, Jon."

"Yeah. So we probably just wounded him. I wonder if I can reach my Hawken and the torch."

"Jus' dem minute, Jon. I's reloads. Orites, I's redy."

Jon crept forward the few feet to the entrance and felt around the ground. His fingers felt the torch stick, and he drew back his hand and tried to rub his shirt. "Ugh," he whispered, "it's full of slime!"

"Dat be's orites, Jon. I's has mo' sticks."

Jon felt around again and found his Hawken. He pulled it to him and could tell that it was slimy as well. Mose reached past Jon with a stick and lit the new torch almost in Jon's face. It stung for a minute, and somewhere in the dark the bear roared again and bared his teeth. Jon could now see gobs of the bear's blood on the ground.

"You wounded him, Mose."

"An' dat makes him mo' mean!"

Jon circled the room with torchlight, but saw nothing. He heard the loud click and chomping of teeth. He heard the clicking again. Jon concentrated the light straight ahead and saw a tiny movement. As his eyes became a little more accustomed to the dark and the gun smoke lifted a little, Jon saw the glowing eyes, then the head, against the far wall, between thirty and forty feet away. The side of his face was bloody, and his head was swinging from side to side. Suddenly, the bear sprung up with a roar and charged. Jon dropped the torch and tried to position his Hawken to his bleeding shoulder as he again sprang back against Mose, who did not fire this time. The bear stopped and jumped back a little, not wanting to touch the burning torch on the ground. He roared at it and finally slapped it out of the way.

"Do's I shoots, Jon?"

"Just hold it a minute, Mose. He can't quite reach us, unless he comes into the cave, and the smoke from our shots may choke him or us to death!"

The growls and roars told Jon that the bear was right at the entrance, although he couldn't see it. The tunnel finally grew quiet again, and the men were able to catch their breath. Several long minutes passed before they once again heard the clicks from a short distance away. Once again, Jon braved the painful heat as they lit another torch. The bear made a halfhearted roar as he bared his teeth. Jon again inched forward, until his torch was in the room. The bear was on his haunches against the opposite wall, growling and clicking, tossing his head from side to side.

Jon slowly brought his Hawken to his burning shoulder and took careful aim. Mose was almost on top of him, and was breathing fast and loud. Jon then realized how hard *he* was breathing, and how hard his heart was pounding. He swallowed hard and tried to relax. The bear's head was thrashing from side to side, and Jon just knew he would only get one shot. He wondered if he should try for the heart, but decided against it, as it would ruin the fur coat. "Hold still, buster!" he whispered.

"You's gots un now, Jon," whispered Mose.

"He won't hold still, Mose."

"Maybe's you's shoots dem bear ins chest."

After a moment, the answer suddenly came to Jon. He puckered his lips and gave a deafening whistle, which echoed loudly. The bear stopped tossing for a brief moment and growled. *BAM!* The room again filled with smoke. Jon grabbed the torch and again pushed back against Mose.

"You's gots 'em, Jon!"

"I'm not sure, Mose. Keep watch, while I reload."

"Orites, Jon, bu' you's gets 'em! You's good shots, bu' we's puts fire in fronts, Jon, bear don' likes."

It took several minutes for the smoke in the room to lift.

"I don't hear anything, Mose. Do you?"

"Nosa. I's knows you's gots 'em, Jon."

"Look, Mose," said Jon, holding out the torch. "There he is."

"Yassa. He be's dead, Jon. Let's crawls in dem room."

"Be careful, Mose. He may not be finished."

"Orites, Jon. Comes. I's cuts dem neck."

"Okay. I got a bead on him. Do it quick."

The bear was curled in a huge ball, so Mose couldn't cut its throat. Mose buried his knife in the back of the neck. "He be's dead, Jon." Mose rolled the big beast over, and was then able to open the bear's throat, then its belly.

"How do we get him out of the cave, Mose?"

"Hmm . . . We's needs ropes, Jon." Mose then grabbed the bear's arms and pulled it to the tunnel entrance.

"You're right. We need rope. We'll have to leave it until morning, then all of us will pull it out."

"Yassa. We's leaves 'im here, Jon."

"Where's the bear?" asked Fred, as the hunters appeared.

"Yes, we hears the shots," added Jules.

"We were shooting at bats."

"Bats? You are batty, Jon," said Fred. Jon laughed.

"Did the bats rip your shirt, Jon?" asked Jules.

"Jon gots big bears, almos' gets Jon! I's gets liniment."

"Wow, he did put some creases in you, Jon!" exclaimed Fred.

"Bu' Jons put dem holes in dem bears!" said Josh.

"Mose damaged him, and I finished him off . . . Ooh, that liniment smarts!"

"So tomorrow you bring him out?" asked Fred.

"No, tomorrow you bring him out. Mose and I rest."

"We will tries," said Jules. "How far in is the bear?"

"Oh, about a mile."

"Mile? I say we leave him!" exclaimed Fred.

Jon was laughing. "We were just funnin' you."

"Yes, it be's less 'an hundred yaads," said Mose.

"Well, there's food to heat, and a place to sleep," said Fred.

"Thanks, Fred. Stoke up that fire. I'm going down to the creek to jump in! I've got slime and blood all over me."

"Me toos. Den we's eats an' sleeps."

January 24, 1839

"Another fine breakfast, but I would like some bacon," said Fred.

"Why? So you can pork out?"

"Let's eat some bear bacon, señors," said Jules.

One at a time, Jules, Jon, Fred, and then Mose entered the cave with torches and rope. Jon had his Hawken just in case.

"The split should be just ahead, Jules."

"I think I see it, Jon. Two tunnels."

"Yes, we'll all gather there and take the rope the rest of the way to the room where our prize is."

Mose took the rope, crawled through the tunnel, and bound the bear. He then scooted back, and all four men pulled the bear through. The four men then crawled outside and tied the end of the rope to the pack horse, and pulled the bear out.

"I's skin dem bear an' cuts dem meat," said Mose.

"Good. Then we rest today and find the Strawberry River tomorrow."

Spring River
January 25, 1839

"This is a nice clear little river, isn't it?" asked Fred.

"It gets bigger as we follow it," said Julian.

"It starts in Missouri. That's not very far north."

"It be's come from Missouri. It has quicksan' an dem bottom," said Mose.

On this cold damp day, wild turkey and whitetail deer were seen all over, but the pack horse and backpacks of the men were full. The men suddenly came upon dozens of mounds on the ground.

"I wonder what they are?" asked Fred.

"They look like burial mounds, but they're long."

"If we had shovel, we will find out," said Jules.

"If we had a shovel, who would carry it?" asked Fred.

Presently, they came upon a log cabin with smoke coming out of the chimney. A grubby man came out to greet them.

"Howdy! Looks like ye been a-huntin'."

"Yes, sir, and it took four days to get our bear."

"What ya been doin'? Sleepin'? I sees bear ever day!"

"Yeah, well, we're headed for the Black River."

"Is 'bout forty miles down riva, but I'd a-go the last ten miles southeast. Easier ta get ta the Black."

"Why is longer easier?" asked Fred.

"'Cause ye don' hafta climb down the cliff."

"Oh, we thank you much, mister . . ."

"Ye welcome. Ye boys take care them bear don' getcha!"

"Say, what are all those mounds we passed?"

"Ye ain't ne'er heard a them mammoths?"

"No we ain't heard," said Jules. "Tell us 'bout it."

"Well, thousan's years ago, giants lives here, even bigger than that nigger. Those peoples was nine an ten feet talls. Dey be buried in them mounds."

"He's connin' us, Jon," Fred quietly said.

"Ya don' believe me, huh? Come, take a look, I shows ye."

The man disappeared into his cabin and came right back out with a long bone. "Dis here be's a leg bone."

"Wow, that bone would go a foot above my knee!" exclaimed Fred.

"Where did you find that bone?" asked Jon.

"I digs up one-a them mounds."

"Then you must have a lot more bones."

"Yep! I's found lotsa things in a mound."

"But you won't show them to us?" asked Fred.

"Nope! But ya goes north 'bout fiftheen mile, an' ya can see lotsa bones."

"Is that in Missouri?" asked Julian.

"Jus' about."

"We believe you, sir. Good luck to you."

"Well, good luck ta ye too."

The men rode in a southeast direction along the Spring River.

"Should we go north an' get some bones, Jon?" asked Jules.

"They'd be great keepsakes, Jon," added Fred.

"Okay. We have time. Let's do it," said Jon.

North the group traveled. About midday they came across very large bones scattered here and there on the ground, but which finger and which toe belonged to which body?

"Nothing is all together, Jon."

"It looks that way, Fred, so take a few and let's go."

After lunch, the men started east. Ten miles later, they came upon a small stream flowing due south. They had just followed it a short distance when they spotted many tents and roughly built tee-pees. The Indians were ragged and downtrodden. They waved as Jon's group approached.

"Are you Cherokee?" asked Jon.

"Yes, we are Cherokee on way to new territory."

"Why are you camped in the middle of the day?" asked Fred.

"We travel many hundred mile, very tired and sick."

"Many hundred . . . where did you start your journey?"

"New Echota, forced to move west over Great River."

"This be more of Jackson's doings," said Jules.

"Yes, Jackson enemy of all the five great nations."

"Nations . . . Do you know Ustanali Nation?"

"Ustanali . . . I have heard of John Nation."

"John Nation is dead. His father is Chief Ustanali."

"John Nation dead! I have not seen John Nation for many winters."

"Ustanali and many others escaped from Georgia and live in the Smoky Mountains."

"I have heard of Cherokee in mountains that smoke."

"I have seen them, and we are friends. Do you know Oostanaula?"

"Yes, I know Oostanaula. You know him too?"

"Yes. He lives close to the Cache River, about forty miles east of Batesville."

"Bateville town? I have heard of it. How I see Oostanaula?"

"Hmm . . . you go back, cross Black River, then go south about thirty miles. You will be following the Cache River."

"He's going to bring our horses to us, Jon," said Fred.

"Oh, that's right! We will meet Oostanaula on the Black River in about three days," said Jon.

"Keostanto wishes to greet Oostanaula, but must wait until sickness leaves us."

"You are Keostanto. I am Jon Hamilton. I will tell Oostanaula that you are here."

"What is your sickness?" asked Fred.

"It is from long trail. We call trail where they cried. Many Cherokee women and children die on trail from cold, hunger."

"We will share some meat with you."

"We have seen many deer on the Spring River," said Fred.

"Yes, but soldiers take our guns, leave Cherokee to starve."

"I's gives 'em my gun, Jon," said Josh.

"We have more rifles at home. I'll give them mine too."

"Okay, Fred, but we should keep a couple."

"I will give them dis rifle. That make three," said Jules.

"Good, and we have enough powder and balls."

"You would do this for Cherokee?" asked Keostanto.

"Yes, and we will share our meat."

"Just enough to feed children, Jon Hamilton. We will shoot guns at deer."

The pack horse seemed extra happy to be relieved of some of his load. The men then prepared to leave.

"Do not forget to tell Oostanaula we are here, and wish to talk and smoke."

"I will tell him, Keostanto. Good luck to you all."

"Cherokee thank you, Keostanto thank you."

"Men, we can make the Strawberry River before dark."

The stream the men were following flowed due south, so Jon thought it would connect with the Strawberry River. Soon daylight began to wane, but the men pressed forward.

"I would like to make camp on the Strawberry River."

"How much farther is that, do you suppose?" asked Fred.

"We should be very close."

The last rays of light reflected on the rushing water of the Strawberry River. The men immediately spotted two whitetails grazing at the river's edge. Mose and Jon stole closer, rifles ready.

"We don' needs mo' foods, Jon."

"Let's get them for those Cherokee."

"Orites, I's takes dem deer on dem right."

"Okay, Mose, but we must shoot at the same time or we'll just scare one away. I'll count to three, and on three, shoot!"

"Orites, Jon, I's be's ready."

"One, two . . . three." *BA-BAM!* Because Jon knew his compression cap fired faster than Mose's flintlock, he had hesitated a half second before firing.

"We's got's 'em, Jon! I's cleans dem out," said Mose.

"Good. We'll make camp right there by the river."

The Cherokee were happy and thankful for the venison. Two days later, the men were camped at the meeting place. They turned the pack horse loose at the mouth of the Strawberry River and got their horses from Oostanaula, who continued north to meet Keostanto. Three more days found the men home, welcomed by hugs and kisses.

"Guess what?" said Maggie. "I fell off the porch roof again!"

Mose's Landing
Old Farmhouse
May 30, 1846

"How's our patient, Ella?"

"Sissy be's betta den yestadays, Jonny."

"What about the little girl?"

"I's don' knows, Jonny. She be's verra sick," said Ella.

"I guess she was born early. She has no hair!"

"Yassa. Lil' missy tiny. I's feeds her goats milk."

"Is Maggie feeding little Mary at all?"

"Nosa, Jonny. Sissy too weak, got no milk. We's wans Sissy ta lives, Jonny. No mo' childs."

"Well, we have four boys and little Mary makes two girls. I guess that's enough."

"Bes' be, Jonny. Sissy be thirty-two now, an' weak."

"I see what you mean, Ella. That's six leg biters in ten years. Wow, what a woman I have!"

"Yassa, bu' no mo', Jonny. Sissy verra sick."

"Can I go in and see her?"

"Yassa. Doun talks too long."

"Hello, my pretty plum. How are you feeling?"

"Not pretty, Jonny," said Maggie, in a very weak voice. "But sour like a plum, I suppose."

"I love the taste of plums! And I love you."

"That's the first time you've said that this year, Jonny."

"Is it? That's about . . . eighty, hundred."

"A hundred fifty days, Jonny!" Maggie said with a weak voice, but a big smile.

"I'm sorry, darlin'. I thought about it every day."

"Sure . . . ugly, fat old dame! You're probably getting tired of seeing me pregnant and ugly."

"The most beautiful woman in Arkansas is the mother of my six children."

"Seven, Jonny. S-seven."

"Well, Okay, my love, seven with Jonny."

"He lived six days, Jonny. He was alive in me!"

"I'm sorry I put you through all that pain and stress."

"I'm not, Jonny. We have six beautiful children, but I'm afraid about having more."

"We've had plenty, darlin', and you're right. They are beautiful, even the newest little lady, Mary Margaret."

"Born on May twenty-fifth, eighteen-fourty-six! Tomorrow she'll be as old as . . . Jonny was."

"Don't think about that, my love. Think about our lives and happy children. There's Davey, and . . ."

"Born April fourth, eighteen-thirty-six. He's ten years old now," said Maggie.

"Yes. Then it was Sammy. Samuel Fredrick, born July tenth, eighteen-thirty-nine. Then there's pretty little Suzy . . ."

"Susan Martha, Jonny, after our mothers."

"Yes. She was born on the fifth . . . or sixth?"

"June sixth, eighteen-forty. She'll be six in a week. Then there was Jonny . . ."

"I know, darlin'. But you bounced right back, and had Andrew Mose. My brother is proud of that."

"So is Nunky Mose. He's already spoiling Andrew."

"Born October sixth, eighteen-forty-three. Then our baby boy, Miles Allen, born July eighteenth last year, on my birthday."

"Just eleven months and about twelve days ago, Jonny. That's too soon. I need to gain back my strength."

"We'll make little Mary our last, my love, as your birthday present."

"If she lives! I think she is two months early, maybe more."

"Yes, she is so tiny and looks funny with no hair. Do you know where Ella puts her? In the side oven, to keep her warm!"

Maggie laughed. "Oh, that's funny. Nanty Ella knows what to do."

"She's feeding little Mary goat's milk. I don't like it."

"I know. Nanty Ella says that will make her strong."

"Then how would you like some goat's milk, darlin'?"

"Shh. I tasted it when I was feeding Mary," said Maggie.

"I won't tell Ella if you don't. Are you taking food away from our little angel?"

"Nanty Ella feeds her plenty."

All the members of the "family" now started showing up for dinner, and all checked on Maggie before sitting down at the long dining table. Jon sat at one end, the head of the table.

"I've called you all together to bring up a couple of matters needing attention. First, as you have heard, our country is now at war with Mexico. It shouldn't take long to win, since Zach Taylor has already whipped them in Texas. Jules here is thinking of joining the army and fighting."

"He better not. I am Spanish," teased Lolita.

"If you join up, Jules, you'll have a bigger war at home."

"I see that, Fred," said Jules. "Maybe is better I remain home."

"So, I guess my question is unimportant now," said Jon.

"What was the question?" asked Fred.

"If Jules joins the army, does he keep his share?"

"I's say yes, Jon. Jules work hard plantin' crop," said Mose.

"Yeah. Someday all young gummers may have to go to war! Jules, Josh, Davey, Sammy. We should pay them if we can."

"But what if they just move away, honey?" asked Janet.

"How about . . . If they work part of the crops, they get their shares, even if it's just the planting or harvest?"

"That sounds fair to me, Jon," said Fred.

"Is anyone opposed to that?" There was no answer.

"Okay. That's how it will be, so long as we can afford it."

"What else, honey?" asked Janet.

"Well, Mose's Landing now has over one hundred people, with a couple dozen leg biters. Isn't it time for a school?"

"Fo' all dem childrens?" asked Ella.

"For all the children, Ella, including Josh's, and someday Chipper's, and the servants' children."

"We would have to pay a teacher," said Janet.

"We do, Jon. Modessa would be a perfect teacher."

"Hey, yes!"

"Modessa would be perfect!"

"Sounds great!"

"Would you be willing, Dessy?" asked Janet, once the table quieted down.

"If that's what everyone wishes."

"Who would build it, and with what money?" asked Fred.

"The same way we built your house, Fred, and Jules and Lolita's house, and this house."

"An' Dessy already get share fro' dem crops," Ella pointed out.

"Maybe's takes two years ta built, Jon," said Mose.

"Well, the sooner we start, the sooner we finish!"

"Where do we put it?" asked Fred.

"Well, there's room by the Mourner's Church. Or how about the property between the river and DeValurie's forty acres?"

"I thought you were saving that for businesses," said Janet.

"Yes, along the river front, but there's plenty of room behind."

"What about the addition of servants' homes?" asked Modessa.

"There is still room for a big block of servants' homes *and* school grounds, bordering the section line and DeValurie."

"Yassa, dat be's big property, room fo' all," said Mose.

"That would be better than by the church," said Janet. "By the cemetery and all that mourning!"

"Okay, all in favor of a school bordering the DeValurie property and section line, say aye." Everyone agreed.

"You could all be teachers," said Modessa. "You plan and execute by majority vote and share the rewards."

"Speaking of shares," said Janet, "I would like to see the original six get a raise in shares."

"Yeah," agreed Fred, "and we should add a few names to the shareholders, like Lolita and Chip."

"All agreed?" asked Jon. Once again, all were in agreement.

"Right, as soon as Maggie gets to feeling better, she will make the changes, including a little more for expenses and servants."

"Can we eat now?" asked Fred.

"You have been eating, honey. Your plate is empty!" said Janet.

"Oh . . . I've got some more items to bring . . ."

"You said a couple, Jon."

"I know, Fred, but I just thought of more."

"Alright, honey, let's hear them. Eat, Freddy."

"Well, the prices for our crops are finally going back up to where they were before the panic, so it's time to take our crops down to New Orleans and get the best price."

"That's a long ways to haul wagons," said Fred.

"We don't! I propose we buy a couple of river boats and ship our cotton, tobacco, and vegetables by boat."

"River boats?"

"Boats?"

"Our own boats?"

"We's cain't goes down dem riva, Jonny," said Ella.

"There's an area about four or five miles long that is clogged by shrubs and bushes down by the Little River. We clean that out, and it's clear sailing all the way to New Orleans."

"We just decided to build a school next," said Modessa.

"Dessy, every year, between planting and harvesting, we have worked on several projects at the same time."

"We's cleans riva in summas, Jon. Water low," said Mose.

"I'm sure we'd get a better price in New Orleans for rice than we get anywhere else," said Fred. "We always have a lot of rice left over."

"Not for long, Fred. It's our crop of the future."

"Yes, Jon, but even with sales going up, we still had rice left over."

"What's you's knows an' we don', Jon?" asked Mose.

"Well, in our two years of selling little bags of *Aunty Ella's Golden Rice*, sales have climbed. Now there is a new machine that removes the layer of brown and leaves a white rice. We can name it . . . how about *Uncle Mose's White Rice?*"

"Wow! That sounds great!" exclaimed Fred.

"And we expand our sales. I think our women can go to Nashville, Cincinnati, Louisville, Natchez, New Orleans, and St. Louis, and open new markets."

"How much does this machine cost?" asked Janet.

"I'm not sure. Whatever the cost, we need it. We are way ahead of the other farmers in the west. Let's stay ahead!"

"We's starts by clearin' dem Francis Riva," said Mose.

"I guess now the question is, will we have enough rice?"

"Have you checked lately, Fred? Mose's crew has about five sections of swamp cleared, and a hundred or so paddies ready for planting."

"Wow! What do we do with the other hundred sections of swamp?" asked Fred.

"Someday we may need it. By the way, we are getting a lot of farm animals. Why don't we use the big pastures north of the barn for another barn and seeding beds?"

"Where would we put all those farm animals, honey?" asked Janet.

"Well, we have lots of land south of here, along the banks of the river. Or, remember we purchased half of sections fourteen and twenty-three, west of here? We can buy the other half of those sections."

"And we own a lot of land on the Little River, right?" asked Janet.

"Yes, dear, but that's a long ways to tend cattle," answered Fred.

"Why don't we run the cattle down along the river for now, and think about those other two half sections in a few years?" asked Janet.

"Then the price would be too high, honey," answered Fred.

"How much is it now?"

"I checked the last time we were in Batesville, and it was two dollars an acre now," answered Jon.

"Wow, it's gone sky-high! How much is that per acre?"

"He just said two dollars an acre, dummy!" Janet said to Fred.

"Well, it would be a section total. That's six hundred and forty acres, times two dollars is . . ."

"Twelve hundred and eighty dollars," said Modessa.

"See? We need Dessy as our school marm!" said Fred.

"Okay, do we purchase one or two river boats?" Everyone agreed to purchase two.

"We maybe can pay them over a couple years," said Fred.

"They build them in Saint Louis and New Orleans."

"We's checks dem prices when we's finish clearin' riva," said Mose.

"We're finished with the planting for now, so we can start on the river. Right, Mose?" Mose nodded. "By the way, you all know why Susan is not here. I propose a toast to Josh and Susan's second child."

"Here, here!"

Old Farmhouse
Mose's Landing
December 5, 1856

"We could have had this dinner at my place," said Janet.

"We had our Thanksgiving there, Janet," said Don Louie DeValurie, in his Spanish accent.

"We could have had it anywhere, but we had some special reasons for asking you all here," said Jon.

"We know the reason. It is for Lolita and yours truly's new baby, Rosita," said Julian.

'That's part of it, Jules. Congratulations! That make five?"

"When are you going to stop? Keep it up, and you and the Hamiltons will fill the school!" said Modessa.

"Dessy, you're not a good one to talk," answered Maggie. "I know your little secret. It's another reason for this party."

"Well, what is it, Dessy? Come out with it!" urged Fred.

"I . . . I . . . I think I'm . . . pregnant."

"What?"

"No, that can't be!"

"Well, I declare!"

As the responses and excitement quieted down, Modessa continued, "And I'm scared."

"Of what, honey?" asked Janet. "Martin is a good man."

"Yes. We are getting married before Christmas," said Dessy.

"You'll be having it just before school next year," said Maggie.

"If I can keep it alive that long."

"Oh, is that what you're worried about?" asked Janet. "We don't care about the other problem, honey. We love you!"

"How old are you, sweetie?" asked Fred.

"I'm . . . I'm forty-five years old!" sobbed Dessy.

"Well, don't worry, Dessy. You're very healthy and young for your age. Would you like us to find another teacher?" asked Maggie.

"No, not this year. I only have about three more months of school."

"Yeah," agreed Fred. "Then it's back to planting."

"I's sends Susan ta checks on Dessy e'ery day," said Ella.

"I think Dessy deserves her full shares continued," added Jon.

"Naturally, you big lummox, we got our shares every time you knocked me up!" said a sarcastic Maggie.

"You're going to have a healthy baby, honey. Congratulations."

"And anything you need, *anything*, just holler," added Maggie.

"Thank you, Jon and Maggie. Thank you all. I love you."

"We love you too, honey," said Janet.

"Now, are you going to need a bigger house?" asked Jon.

"No, Jon, we like our little house," answered Modessa.

"We'll add a room next year, Jon," said Fred.

"Good idea. We need to get Mose well now."

"Yeah, I hear he darn near drowned in that swamp when he passed out. Took all his helpers to carry him out," said Fred.

"He gets betta now, jus' need rest," said Ella.

"That ague is no easy thing to cure. He may have some bad spells the rest of his life."

"Yeah, and it snaps the strength right out of a man. How he avoided it all them years in the swamps amazes me," said Fred.

"Mose with lil strength is like all the ress of us with plenty strength!" said Julian.

"I know you're taking good care of him, Ella."

"Yassa, Jonny. I's gives Daddy castor oil an' coffee, den colomel in dem coffee. He's don' knows which be worse!"

"I was sure that white man sitting in Mose's chair wasn't Mose!" quipped Fred. "That the next surprise?" he asked.

"The biggest surprise was little Jonny," quipped Janet. "I remember you both saying after Mary was born that she was the last, no more leg biters!"

"That's what happens when you make up," said Maggie. "If you ever get in a fight with your man, girls, don't make up!"

"Ah, but I'm proud of my little namesake, he's a good boy. But you almost guessed our next surprise. Tell them, darlin'."

"Today is Jonathan Ashley's sixth birthday, and I assure you that he was the last!"

"We didn't bring anything for him. We are sorry," said Lolita.

"He already has his best present of all, his grandfather!"

"Everyone, this is Jonny's father, Alex Hamilton," said Maggie.

"And little Jonny's grandfather, from Salem."

"Just in time to be too late for harvest!" joked Fred.

"This is the first time any of my brood has seen their grandfather," said Maggie, "either of them."

"Very happy to meet you, Mister Hamilton," said Modessa. The welcome was echoed by everyone else. "Glad you're here," "Wonderful to see you," and "Welcome" were all heard around the table.

"And we have one more surprise. Mom?"

Out of the kitchen came a white-haired, smiling woman.

"And this is my mother, Martha Mary. My father and mother have retired, and are going to live with Maggie and me."

"The empty seat there must be for you. Welcome," said Fred.

"Thank you," said Martha. "Thank you all."

"My son has told us of his wonderful partners," said Alex.

"He was connin' you," smiled Fred.

"Missus Martha be's goo' cook," said Ella.

"We didn't have any Ellas around. Mom had to do all the cooking for our family."

"He thinks I can't cook! Maybe someday I'll poison him," quipped Maggie.

"Sissy cook goods too. We's cooks togetha," said Ella.

"Thank you, Nanty Ella. Somebody likes me!" said Maggie.

"I like you, my pretty plum."

"And I like you, Mother," said young David A. Hamilton.

"That makes me feel better. My children like me," said Maggie.

"All of us love you, honey," said Janet.

"How did you come out, Mister Hamilton?" asked Fred.

"By train! There's a spur that goes from Salem to Abingdon in Virginny that ties to the Chattanooga line, and continues all the way to Memphis. Then we took a ferry across the big river and caught a ride with the postman to here."

"Wow, how long did that take?"

"Hmm . . . Two weeks, Martha?"

"Sixteen days, Father," answered Martha.

"Jonny! Remember your promise when we married?"

"Promise? I've kept all my promises."

"All but one, lover. You promised I could go home to visit when traveling got better."

"Oops! I did! I'll send you in the spring."

"Spring?" asked Fred. "We need all hands in the spring."

"I make a motion we send her now," said Janet.

"I seconds!" shouted Ella. There was a pause.

"Well, come on, honey, call for the vote!" said Janet.

"He won't do that. He knows what the vote will be!" said Maggie.

"Oh . . . All in favor, raise your left hand!"

Jon said those last words very fast, and all raised their right hands. Again very fast, he said, "Opposed, right hand! Motion defeated!" Jon was laughing.

"Thank you, partners, I'll leave as soon as Nunky Mose . . ."

"You better leave now, honey, so you'll be home for Christmas and New Year's."

"She is home, Janet. This is her home."

"Yes, Jonny, but you promised I could visit Bethania."

"You's has our permission, Sissy," said Ella.

"Thank you, Nanty Ella. Maybe I'll take little Jonny along, so my parents can meet one of their grandchildren."

"Alright, my love. Let's bring him in . . . Jonny!"

"What?" answered the six-year-old boy from the kids' room.

"Come in and have your birthday dessert, darling," said Maggie.

Everyone enjoyed pandowdy, and little Jonny got some candy.

"I'll check out our property on the Yadkin River, Jonny."

"What property is that, my darling?" asked Alexander.

"Daddy split up Bethania, and gave us, I think, either four or five sections by the Yadkin River."

"Remember it, Dad? We have your old mine."

"By God! I've always regretted selling it," Alex said.

"Why, Alex? It bought the farm!" said Martha.

"I'd like to try digging it again."

"You're too old, Alex. You'd kill yourself!"

"Maybe someday we will, Dad."

"Better hurry. I'm seventy-one years old."

"Wow," said Fred, "no wonder you retired."

"You'll like our little town, Daddy," said Maggie to Alex.

"We would like to see it tomorrow, Margaret," said Martha.

"We all call each other by our first names, Mom."

"Margaret *is* her first name, honey!" said Janet.

"I mean, everybody calls her Maggie," said Jon.

"It's alright. Mom, call me whatever you like," said Maggie.

"Maggie and I will take you all around tomorrow, Mom and Dad."

"Our town has over two hundred people now. It grows almost every week," said Janet.

"Yeah, we got a new church, a doctor, an apothecary, a post office, a big merc . . . general store, a school, a wagon maker, hardware store, a pub, a barber, a blacksmith, and a stable with an animal doctor," said Fred.

"You know what you forgot, honey?" asked Janet.

"No, what, honey?"

"You forgot the mill and furniture store, where I work!"

"We need a circuit court. We're growing so fast," said Jon.

"How much land do you own here, son?"

"Probably a hundred thousand acres, but about seventy thousand is swamp . . . our rice fields!" answered Jon.

"We just bought two more half sections on our west border so we can run cattle on them," said Fred.

"And your crops are able to support you?" asked Alex.

"Righto, Dad. We have several crops, so if one goes sour, we have others to fall back on."

"What kinds of prices do you get, say, for cotton?"

"We ship our crops from here to New Orleans now. We bundle cotton in five-hundred-pound bales and ship them. We got sixty-seven fifty a bale this year, and it's going up again next year. We sold twenty bales."

"You have your own boats, son?"

"Right, Dad. I'll take you for a ride on one, if you'd like."

"Thanks, Jon. Martha and I would like that."

"Do we have more to get settled?" asked Fred.

"Daddy say we's need 'nutha reapa, Jonny," said Ella.

"Yeah, they have a more modern McCormick now," said Fred. "It won a gold medal at the world fair in New York."

"And I would like a new sewing machine, Jonny," said Maggie.

"I just bought you one, my love."

"Ten years ago! They have a modern Singer now too," said Maggie. "It's called the shuttle machine. Nanty Ella and I are not able to keep up, with the old Singer, and do all the sewing, cooking, and watching children."

"Okay, my pretty plum. A reaper and a sewing machine."

"Whad else we talk about? These discussions are verra stimulatin'," said Julian Jones.

"I hear Buchanan won the president's race," said Fred. "What's that gonna do for the economy?"

"I hear he's a bachelor," said Janet.

"He has no new policy on slavery. That will keep us on the same path to war," said Lolita.

"Better than Freemont! His policy to stop slavery would surely mean war," answered Maggie.

"There already is war up in Kansas and Missouri," said Jon.

"Did you hear about the attack on the town of Lawrence and the return massacre of homesteaders?" asked Jules.

"It's really getting nasty up there," said Jon.

"Yeah, and Sammy wants to go fight for the slavers," said Davy.

"He what? Samuel Frederick Hamilton, come here!"

"What is it, Dad?" Sammy came into the dining room.

"What's this I hear about our wanting to fight in Kansas?"

Sammy glared at Davy. "I was just joking with Dave."

"You'd better be! We're staying neutral."

"If you say so, Father, but we won't be neutral very long," said Sammy.

"Sammy thinks there's going to be a war, Dad," said Davy.

"I think so too. It is coming. You will see," said Lolita.

"The Compromise of eighteen-fifty was supposed to settle the issue of slavery, I thought," said Fred.

"It do nothing, Fred. It make it worse!" said Jules.

"The border fights are the result of the Kansas-Nebraska Act, letting each state vote on slavery," said Lolita.

"Maybe the Union will put a stop to all the killing up in Kansas. I hear troops are coming to Saint Louis and New Madrid," said Jon.

"New Madrid? That's where the great earthquakes hit," said Maggie.

"I guess we should have elected that know-nothing candidate for president, Fillmore," said Fred.

"Boy the Supreme Court are a bunch of know-nothings. They ruled that slave Dred Scott couldn't stay free, even though he had escaped slavery," said David Alexander.

"Yes, and they ruled that the government could not stop slavery. Even the new states! It is a mess," said Lolita.

"I tell you, we are facing trouble," added Jules.

"Well, maybe Buchanan can do something to cool both sides."

"I hope you and Mom like it here, Dad," said Jon.

"We can see there is plenty to do. I think Martha and I will fit in fine here," answered Alex.

"I've never had a sewing machine, but I'm good at repairing and cleaning clothes. Had to be with Jonny and Drew," said Martha.

"Hey, I've got an idea for another business! How about we start a combination laundry, clothing repair, and nursery?"

"Who would run it? Maggie?" asked Fred.

"How about Mother Martha, my daughter Susan, and maybe one or two servant girls?" asked Maggie.

"Looks like another building project. Where do you want it?"

"There's a spot close to Dessy, across from the new church. Better yet, down with the new businesses by the river, on Valurie Boulevard extension."

"And you do shareholders' clothes and babysitting free?"

"Yes, and still make money from all the new families here."

"Okay, my pretty plum. We'll try to have it ready when you return from Bethania."

DeValurie Mansion
Mose's Landing
November 25, 1860

"Welcome! Happy Thanksgiving, everyone!" greeted Mister DeValurie, his Spanish accent still evident after so many years.

"Happy Thanksgiving!" most everyone said in response.

"What be happy 'bout it? We'll soon be at war!" said Jules.

"Lincoln is president. We will secede," added Lolita.

"He won't be president until next March," said Fred.

"And a lot of good people in Washington are trying to find a way to avoid war," added Jon.

"You will see when President Lincoln is installed, we will see war! South Carolina will be first to secede," said Jules.

"And our son, Louces, will have to go," added Lolita.

"Yes, and Jonny and I will lose Davy and Sammy right away."

"Mom, I want to go now," said Sammy Hamilton. "Those damn Yanks have just invaded our state, and are in Little Rock."

"How do you know that, Sammy? And don't swear!"

"I saw it on the new bulletin board at the square," answered Sammy.

"Suzie said that Jim put it up the day before yesterday, so we can keep up with all the happenings," said David Hamilton.

"But how did Jimmy know?" asked Maggie.

"Jim's dad got his new telegraph machine hooked up," said Dave.

"Well, Samuel, you can't go to Little Rock. We need you here to finish the harvest," said Jon.

"Dad, I'm twenty-one years old!"

"I know, son. You and David are adults and will have to make a choice soon, but I'm still hoping war can be avoided."

"You're dreamin', Dad," said Sammy.

"Maybe a war would pass us by," said Janet.

"Not likely, honey," Fred responded. "They know we're here."

"Yes, we's s'posed ta be gone a'ready," said Mose.

"We's s'posed ta be gone firs' un year," added Ella.

"We already fixed that, Nunky Mose. All our workers, Josh, Chipper, Ally, Susan, Nunky Mose, and Nanty Ella, are all our slaves when anyone asks!"

"All our workers better know that too, darlin'."

After a pause, Maggie said, "Jim will have to go in too, if we go to war."

"Maybe even his dad," added Fred.

"We don't have enough Negroes to exempt everyone! Let's see, I guess it will take twenty or more, and we have over a hundred."

"We have one hundred thirteen, not counting children."

"Wow!" said Fred. "We started with thirty, remember?"

"Yes, but that would only cover five or six of us," said Jon.

"Well look, Jonny, there's you, Fred, Julian, David, Sammy, Martin and maybe even Andrew . . ."

"That makes seven, my love."

"And we have about enough workers to exempt six, Jonny."

"I don't want to be exempt!" said Sammy.

"I hope they don't recruit women," quipped Janet.

"Please don't say that, Sammy," pleaded Maggie.

"Mom, war is coming, and we've got to save the South."

"Maybe the South needs to be taught a lesson," said David.

"Who's gonna teach 'em? Those blue bellies?"

"Those blue bellies have more people, troops, guns . . . you name it, they got it," said David.

"Yeah, but their way of life isn't threatened! We have the crops that England wants, and they will get us the guns and help we need."

"You're nuts, Sammy. If England comes into our war, France will join the north . . . and Germany!"

"There are a lot of Germans around here," said Fred.

"Let 'em come! We whooped 'em in the war for liberty, and we can whoop 'em again!" exclaimed Samuel.

"Can we talk about something else? This is our Thanksgiving!"

"Yes. Are we shipping our crops to New Orleans?" asked Fred.

"Certainly," answered Jon. "Why not?"

"There's already a lot of big guns all up and down the river."

"Yes, honey, but no war yet."

"You didn't want to talk about war, Jan!" laughed Maggie.

"Oops, I'm sorry," said Janet.

"That's the only thing there is to talk about," said Sammy.

"Let's talk about our crops," said Fred.

"Okay, Fred, why don't you start with cotton?"

"Yeah, well, we have already had our first pickin', and we got eighteen crates of good, clean cotton."

"That's wonderful, Fred. We may have to buy another boat just to ship cotton."

"Lolita's helping us make clothes to sell at the mercantile store with a lot of that cotton," said Martha Hamilton. "She's a good seamstress."

"How will we sell our cotton if the north blocks the Mississippi?" asked Janet. "Or our furniture?"

"We may have to buy more wagons and horses, and haul everything to Saint Louis," said Jon.

"What about Memphis or Batesville?" asked Fred.

"They would be blocked too, if we were."

"Dat be right, Jon. Dey sends crops ta New Orleans," said Mose.

"Nobody should shoot at us. There's no war yet," said Jon.

"We're not talking about war, Dad," said Sammy.

"Okay. What about tobacco, Mose?"

"Dem's be all picked, an' hangs in dem barns."

"Then what are you doing now, Mose?" asked Fred.

"Workas works on Jon's house."

"Yes. They've got the basement and foundation done," said Jon.

"It will be a big house," said Jules.

"Has to be, with all us Hamiltons," said David.

"Will it be bigger than mine?" asked Don Louie DeValurie.

"Yes, Papa," said Lolita. "It will be a mansion."

"We want you to live there too, Nunky Mose and Nanty Ella. It is for all the Hamiltons," said Maggie.

"Thank you's, Sissy, bu' we's likes our home here," said Ella.

"We wrote to Sammy McAllister, Ella, and asked for your Danny and maybe a couple others."

"You did? Oh, bless you's, Jonny an' Sissy!"

"Danny be comin', Jon?" asked Mose.

"I don't know yet. We haven't got an answer."

"We asked my Sammy, my brother Sammy, to catch us up on all your children, Nanty Ella."

"Thank you's, Sissy," Ella said with tears filling her eyes. "Thank you's."

"How would you get them out here, Dad?" asked Davy.

"Hmm, I guess we would send Maggie again, and have them pretend to be her slaves."

"Again? It's been four years, Jonny!"

"Better send Mom quick, before the war starts!" said Sammy.

"Sammy, we's don' talks 'bouts war," said Ella.

"And we have bales of wheat, bags of beans and rice, corn, flax, and . . . you name it, to sell."

"Enough to feed an army," quipped Fred.

"We're not talking army or war, honey," said Janet.

"We's need mo' horses, Jon, jus' in case," said Mose.

"Yes, and we need to go to Martins Station . . . Cumberland Gap, and find Conestoga Joe. Remember him? He has a horse of ours, sired by Corker."

"Dem horse be's twenny-five years olt and gone, Jon."

"I know, Mose, but they probably have had foals that would be ours."

"Corka sho 'nuff sired good offsprin'," said Mose.

"Were you out to section fourteen to see them, Dad?"

"Yes, you're getting a pile of animals out there."

"Good. As long as we have plenty to feed them."

"Dey's sho 'nuff makes plenty crops grows," said Mose.

"Why aren't your Susan and Jimmy here, Maggie?" asked Dessy.

"Her baby Jimmy was fussing. They may be over later."

"Congratulations, Grandma and Grandpa Hamilton, and the baby's great-grandparents are here too," said Fred.

"Daddy un me, we's great granparents toos," said Ella.

"What is the baby's last name, Maggie?" asked Janet.

"James Virgil Rosewell, the Third."

"Rosewell, that's right. They're putting out a newspaper, aren't they?"

"That's right, Jan," answered Maggie. "I hear they are calling it the *Mose's Landing Liberator*."

"*Liberator*? That's a strange name," said Fred.

"Not so strange, Fred," said Modessa McConnell. "The original Moses liberated the Jewish people from bondage in Egypt."

"Suzie said she suggested *Mose's Landing Commandment*."

"That would be an even stranger name for a newspaper!" said Fred.

"If it doesn't say newspaper, it's strange to you, honey," said Janet.

"What else do we talk about?" asked Jon.

"The big fire at Fort Smith," suggested Don Louis.

"That was only two months ago," added Lolita.

"Mister Rosewell said it was started by escaping slaves," said Sammy.

"It was only one of a lot of fires in northern Texas and Arkansas," said David. "They think it's abolitionists and freed slaves doin' it."

"Not freed slaves, Davy. Escaped slaves starting an insurrection. The free slaves are all gone from Arkansas," corrected Sammy.

"All but a hundred and thirty of them here," quipped Fred.

"But nobody but us knows that, honey."

"Dat be why Conway ordas alls us free niggas out!" said Josh.

"Sho 'nuff glad he be gone," said Mose. "Dem new Gov'nor Rector too busy ta chase afta us free Negroes."

"It would have been a lot better if Bell and Everett would have been elected U.S. president instead of Lincoln," said Jon.

"Or Douglas," added Fred. "Even Breckenridge may have been able to void a war."

"They're both Democrats, honey. One of them should have stepped down so they wouldn't split that party," said Janet.

"Would be no difference. We still be at war," said Jules.

"We're not talking about war, remember?" said David.

"Funny, Lincoln got no votes at all in Arkansas, but he was still elected president."

"That means we leave the Union, Dad, and I'm ready!" said Sammy.

"I guess I'd better start getting ready too," said David.

"No need, boys. We have enough workers to cover you."

"Good thing we got our crops to New Orleans when we did," remarked Jon.

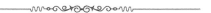

The Old Farmhouse
Mose's Landing, Arkansas
September 17, 1861

"Don't cry, darlin'. She lived a long life."

"I . . . I . . . c-can't help it, Jonny," Maggie sighed in between sobs. "She was like a second m-mother to me."

"Me too, my love. On second thought, go ahead and cry all you want. Can I get you anything?"

"No . . . maybe another hanky."

Jon left the bedroom of Mose and Ella. Mose was sitting just outside the bedroom door with his head in his hands.

"Sorry, Mose." Jon hugged the giant man. "Is there something I can do for you?"

"No . . . thank you's, Jon. I's sits here an' thinks."

"I'll be back in a minute, Mose. Maybe we can talk."

"Orites, Jon. Thank you's."

Thanks to Mose, the farmhouse had some warm water from the kitchen stove. Jon dampened a cloth and found a handkerchief for Maggie, then came back out to Mose.

"Ella was a fine woman, a great woman! She did a lot of work to make this place a success." Mose didn't comment. "She sure could cook. Sure glad Maggie went back to Bethania and brought Danny out. Where is Danny?"

"He be upstair in blue room," replied Mose, his head still in his hands.

"He's sure been a great help since he came out here. Ella was happy to see him." Mose again did not comment. "She was happy to hear about her family, even though she didn't get to see them again, except Danny. At least she didn't have to suffer long. I wonder how old she really was." Jon was still doing all the talking. "Do you want Ella buried in the graveyard behind the Mourner Church, Mose?"

Still no answer, but Mose nodded his head yes.

"Alright. I'll see to it, and I'll be sure a letter is sent to Bethania to let everyone know."

Fred, Janet, and Modessa came into the house to offer their condolences, and crowded into Mose's bedroom. After a few minutes, Fred came back out.

"Sure am sorry, Mose. Boy, she was the head cook, ran the house, worked in the laundry and rice plant, did a lot of the sewing, and ran the vegetable garden. How do we replace her?"

"We don't, Fred. Guess we'll put Susan in charge, and get her more help."

"Your Susan, or Josh's Susan?"

"Josh's Susan. My Susan is caring for little Jimmy, and is worried about big Jim. There's been no word from him since his company took Fort Smith. He probably fought in Oak Hill, too, like Dave and Sam did."

"You haven't heard from them either, have you, Jon?"

"No, I haven't. I hope the board is accurate down at the square. It didn't list any of our boys dead."

"Damn the war," said Fred. "You got Davy fighting for the north and Sammy fighting for the South!"

"Yes, and I haven't heard from either one, but I know they fought against each other at Oak Hill."

"Don't feel bad. I've got two offspring and Lord knows how many grandkids and maybe even some great-grandkids, and I ain't heard a word from any of them in twenty-five years!"

"That makes you how old, Fred?"

"I'm sixty-seven now, and Jan's sixty."

"Well, you won't have to worry about being called up."

"Hope not. Our state has contributed enough! The state says Arkansas has fifty-eight thousand troops," said Fred.

"Yes, and six thousand Union soldiers. Davy is one." Jon turned to Mose. "You doing alright, Mose?"

"I's orites, Jon. I's be glad I gots no children."

Susan Wilson, Josh's wife, came in and announced that dinner was ready.

"Come on, Mose. Food will do you some good."

"You's goes ahead, Jon. I's be wit you's in minute."

Gathered at the table were Fred, Janet, Jon, Josh, Susan, Modessa, and Chipper, who was now thirty-six years old. Also at the table were Alex, Martha, and Ally.

"I would like to propose a toast to Ella," said Fred. "To Ella, may she rest in peace."

"Here, here," everyone toasted.

"Aunty Ella's rice has been such a good seller these last few years, and now the namesake is gone," said Janet.

"But the name don't need to go," said Fred.

"I think this year the white rice will outsell the brown."

"Thank goodness we still have that namesake . . . Mose," said Dessy.

"All our crops are doing well again. It will be something, getting them down to New Orleans in a couple of months."

"Worse than last year, Jon?" asked Alex.

"Yes. Last year wasn't too bad. We were stopped and boarded by a Confederate gun ship, and another time passing Vicksburg. I thought I was being shot at."

"What happened?" asked Fred.

"They were just testing their new batteries."

"But you made it alright to New Orleans," said Alex.

"That I did, Dad, but this year may be different."

"It would be a shame to lose the beautiful crops you have here, just because of a Civil War you didn't start, son"

"We may not have started it, Dad, but we're in it all the way with Dave, Sammy, and Jim all fighting against each other."

"Do you have any idea where they're at, Jon?" asked Fred.

"Well, Dave was with Lyon's Union forces at Oak Hill. They were beaten and retreated to Springfield. Sammy was part of McCulloch's forces, still in Missouri after winning at Oak Hill, as are Sterling Price's forces, somewhere in Missouri with Jim."

"There are a bunch of fights in Missouri right now," said Fred.

"That's a barmy state," said Alex. "First that Union man Freemont declared all Negroes Emancipated, gets fired, then the Confederates declare Missouri a Southern state, but they don't secede like Arkansas did. Now both sides claim it!"

"They sho 'nuff ain't like us here," agreed Fred. "When Arkansas decided to leave the Union, it was a sixty-nine to one vote."

"Yes, Governor Rector told President Lincoln that his call for federal troops from Arkansas was an insult," added Jon.

"I wonder where our boys will be fighting next?" wondered Alex.

Maggie entered the dining room and sat next to Jon. Her eyes were red from crying.

"Are you alright, my love?"

"Yes. Nunky Mose is with her now."

"Mose wants her buried in the graveyard by the Mourner Church. I'll prepare a spot tomorrow."

"Maybe close to the river, Jonny. What should we put on the headstone? We don't know her age or where she was born."

"Your father gave her the name Ellavated. We know one important date to her, October twenty-fourth."

"We could say Mother of thirteen children, and Nanty to one. Born in Africa, freed October twenty-fourth, and died on September seventeenth, eighteen-sixty-one."

"Sounds good, honey," said Janet. "What difference does it make how old she was?"

"Age makes a difference sometimes, honey," said Fred. "If we weren't such old fogies, we might be fighting in this war!"

"True. Maybe we are all safe. You're sixty-seven, Dad is seventy-six, and I'm forty-six. There's our exemptions!"

"You must put the famous Aunt Ella's Rice on the stone," said Dessy.

"That stone's going to be pretty large, ladies," said Jon.

"Jonny, I was going to mention we received two letters yesterday."

"And you're just telling me now? What were they?"

"Well, Mama thinks my bothers are all exempt from the war due to their ages, as well as all of the bounders. The other letter was from the Chasneys. Charles and Dave have joined the Southern Militia of Kentucky. They're pretty old, aren't they, Jonny?"

"Yes, as old as I am, I guess. Did Liz get married?"

"She didn't say. Only that she is alone. No! She can't come here!"

Mose came in during this discussion and took a seat at the table.

"Are you alright, Mose?"

"Yes, Jon. I's goes back, work on mansion tomorra."

"Take a few days off, until after the funeral, Mose. The house can wait. You've got it just about all framed already. It's looking good!"

Mississippi River
Aboard M. L. Transport #1
November 29, 1861

"How do you like this, being on the river, Mose?"

"I's likes, Jon. Jus' gots ta rememba, I's yer slave."

"Yes. I hope Danny remembers too, on that other boat."

"Dis be's big loads, Jon."

"Right, Mose. We have two more to go. We'll be at Vicksburg pretty soon. Then you'll see strong defenses."

"Dey be attack, Jon?"

"If they ever are attacked, they think they can withstand it."

"Massa Jon, what be's withstan' means"

"That was good, Mose. You really sounded like my slave. Call the other boat over so we can remind them."

"Yassa, Massa Jon." Mose blew a horn and *M. L. Transport #2* steered close beside.

"Hi, Marty!" Jon yelled into the horn, "Remind Danny that from now on, he's your slave."

"Okay, Jon," responded Martin McConnell. "For the entire trip, right?"

"Righto! We're coming up on Vicksburg, Mississippi. They are making a fortress, in case the feds attack them."

"Gottcha, Jon. I'll be right behind you!" yelled Martin.

As the Mose's Landing transports, loaded high with crops, came into view of the Vicksburg compound, Jon and Mose stood in awe over the forts and batteries designed to get an enemy ship in a deadly trap.

"When I wave, pour on the steam!" yelled Jon.

'Right, Jon, I'm ready. Let's go," answered Martin.

Jon's lead vessel eased down the river, past the first fort and the battery on the opposite shore in Louisiana. Two-thirds of the way past the town entrenchments, Jon observed big guns being positioned to shell him, and a uniformed man yelling from the ramparts. Jon waved frantically at Martin and yelled, "Go!"

Mose poured on the pressure and stoked the fire. Black smoke billowed from his chimneys, as the transport picked up speed.

Boom! Bzzz! The big ball whizzed over the bow of *M. L. Transport #1.* Jon turned the wheel to port. *Boom! . . . BAM!* Two more heavy shots splashed into the river behind and to his port side. Jon swung the wheel back to starboard. He looked back at his other boat. It was following Jon's lead. Three shots were all that the rebs fired at him. Jon let out his breath.

"Wow, that was scary!" yelled Martin, as his transport number two eased up alongside Jon.

"Too close for comfort," answered Jon, through his horn.

"Why are they shooting at us?"

"I'm not sure, Martin, but I'll bet we find out when we come back upriver."

"Okay, I'll follow again. I've got to check my unmentionables!"

Jon laughed. "Our next obstacle is Fort Hudson, just a short way downstream."

As Jon rounded another bend, there sat two Confederate gunboats. The captain was waving at Jon to stop, so Jon stopped.

"Are these all your crops?"

"Not all. About half, headed for New Orleans. Why would those bird brains shoot at us?"

"They want to stock up to the hilt with food and other supplies in case they get surrounded."

"And they'd *kill* for it?"

"They'll pay dearly for it. Our job is to see to it that they don't get surrounded."

"They pay even more than New Orleans?"

"I think they will, if you're good at connin' 'em!"

"Well, thank you, sir, I'll remember that."

"There's a good bank to pull up to for the night just ahead. I'd advise you to use it. It's barmy on the river at night."

"Okay, sir. Thank you very much," said Jon, as they left.

"Hi, I'm Steve, and this here is Ben. We'll gettcha unloaded, an' atta heer, as quik as we can. Them damn Yanks have been a-shellin' us fer two monts."

"Thanks, Steve. I'm hopin' to get by Fort Hudson and Vicksburg alive," said Jon.

"We'll put a couple a Reb flags on yer boats. That'll help," shouted Steve.

"Great, thanks. We'll be gettin' to hell outta here, soon as you get us unloaded."

"Not sure if weel be a-seein' ya next year, so good luck to ya!"

Eighteen sixty-two was another bumper crop at Mose's Landing. Jon was worried about selling his crop in New Orleans, but he planned to try, as Vicksburg was still in the hands of the Confederacy. On his way down to Mississippi, Jon counted thirty-eight Confederate gunships. The Confederates were happy to see supplies headed for New Orleans to counter the Union's blockades. Jon's flotilla made it close to New Orleans, with their cargo intact, but were quickly unloaded in a little community called Kenner.

The morning of November thirteenth was warm and dry, but the water made it seem cool to Jon. It reminded Jon of last year's trip to New Orleans. Very little power was needed to steer the heavily laden boats down the big river once they navigated the bend at Port Hudson, Louisiana.

"I don't see how the Union can ever take Mississippi from Vicksburg to Baton Rouge with all these guns aimed at them, unless they starve these people."

"Tha's why dey wan's our foods, Jon," said Mose.

"I guess so, but they can't eat cotton and tobacco."

"Dey's really wan's our next boats o' veggies."

"Yeah. We may have to give them up next trip."

"Wha's place dat be, Jon?"

"That's Kenner. Doesn't look like there's very many guns there! I guess they figure the feds will never get past New Orleans from the Gulf, or to Baton Rouge from the South, Vicksburg from the north.

"Maybe's starvin' dem only way, Jon," said Mose.

Kenner was bustling. Jon and Martin had trouble winding their way through all the boats on the river. As they passed, the people on the boats and town-dwellers cheered.

"Why dey cheer, Jon?" asked Mose.

"They're happy to see our load of cotton and tobacco, Mose."

"Dey see's dem befo'!"

"I guess they need the money our crops could bring, if they make it out."

"Hello, Mister Hamilton. We've been waiting fer y'all."

"Hello, Steve, Ben," answered Jon from his boat. "Are you ready to unload us? We'd like to head back tomorrow."

"We're ready, orite. See dat big gun-ship a-sittin' there? It's a-gonna take on yer crops the now, an' be a-gettin' fer England."

"Good. Well, anchor us down, and she's all yours," said Jon.

"Have any trouble on yer way ta here?"

"They shot at us at Vicksburg, and a couple gunboats stopped us and asked a few questions. I thought it was last year all over again. I see they've taken New Orleans."

"Well, we're a-glad ya made it here," said Steve.

"Where's your farm machinery store?" asked Jon.

"Head out Canal Street right ova der, just outta Na Orlans an dem Blue-Belleys."

"What ye be a-needin' there, Mister Hamilton?" asked Ben.

"Ya, It purty close to thum basards," added Steve

"Wagon an horses, we may not make it down the river next year, so we'll have to haul it over land to Memphis or St. Louis."

"Gads, I hope not," said Steve, shaking hands with Jon. "We be a-needin' all the cotton an' tobacco ye can bring."

"Well, as soon as we get back home and can finish harvest, we'll have at least one more boatload for you," said Jon. "By the way, this is Martin McConnell, my boat number two skipper."

"Glad ta knows ye," said Steve. "Welcome ta N'Olans."

"Thank ya, sir. I ain't never been here before," said Martin.

"Do you have some horses we can use, Steve?" asked Jon.

"Ya betcha," said Steve. He turned toward a young kid. "Boy! Bring a couple of buggies fo' Mister Hamilton an' his men . . . all hitched!"

"Yassa, Massa Steve!" The slave boy ran off.

"Ya men mus' be hungry! Foller me, Thurs a good eatin' hole down da wharf. My workers will feed yer niggas, even that big'un there. He mus' eat a ton!"

"Are you hungry, Mose?" Jon asked with a smile.

"Yassa, Massa Jon. I's be's soo hungra, I's can eats three dockmans!"

Jon laughed. "Well, don't eat them, Mose. They have to unload our boat so we can get back home."

"Yassa, Massa Jon. Maybe's jus' one?"

"I want to take both my slaves along to buy a wagon, Steve. They're both experts on wagons and horses."

"That'll be fine. Massa Jon!" Steve was laughing.

After a plateful of seafood, Jon, Mose, Danny, and Martin rode onto Canal Street with its beautiful big mansions.

"Look at that place, Mose. It's something like our house will look like soon."

"Yassa, we's gettin' close, Jon. It be's finish soon."

"That's fine, Mose. You'll have a corner all your own."

"Hello, welcome ta our *Plantation Pieces*. Whatcha need?"

"A big, sturdy wagon to haul crops, and maybe a couple horses to pull it."

"Yessa, we're a-sellin' some good 'uns. Lookee here, this 'uns da latest Studebaker."

"Studebaker, huh? They good ones?"

"Da bes', stranger. All da corners has metal enforcements, an' dems is heavy wheels."

"How much?"

"Wellsa, 'bouts hundred fifty dollas."

"Hmm . . . hundred fifty."

"Worth lots mo' den dat! I kin get two hundred . . ."

"Then what's it doin' sittin' here?" asked Martin.

"Ah, lookee here, has new-fangled metal axel."

Jon looked over at Mose, who nodded his head yes.

"Make it a hundred twenty-five, and it's sold."

"Ah . . . that be cash, sir?" At Jon's yes nod, he said, "Sold!"

"What have you got for drays to pull it?"

"Come out a-here, I'll show ya. Take yer peek."

"You don't have much here. I want some good work horses."

"Don't have much? Dem damm yanks take my horses! Maybe y'all gives me yer address, an' I'll find ya some."

"Don't have time, mister. I leave tomorrow for Arkansas."

"Well . . . no, I . . . well, orite. I'll show ye somethin' y'all will love. Come wit me." They entered a hidden side barn. "This here is da bes' y'all will e'er get."

"Beautiful . . . what are they?" asked Jon.

"Y'all likes dem? They's a-gonna cost ya lots."

"Yes, I like them. How much?"

"Dey's come from Scotlan'. Dey called Clydesdales."

"They sure are pretty. Well matched," said Martin.

"Take a good look at them, Mose. You too, Danny."

"Dey's bred by a Duke-a-Hamilton."

"By who?"

"By Duke-a-Hamilton, in Scotlan'."

"Are you conning me?" asked Jon.

"Nosa, I swear! Had 'em snuck in."

"How much?" Jon asked, when Mose and Danny both signaled yes.

"Five hundred apiece."

"Five hundred?"

"Yassa. Dat's what dey's cost me."

"I think he's lying, Jon," said Martin.

"So do I. They didn't cost you more than two hundred!"

"Oh, yassa, dey's cost me lots! Fo' hundred each?"

"Hmm . . . Okay, but if I find out you cheated me . . . see this big man? I'll have him tear you limb from limb!"

"Th-thank ye, sir. Dey's be da bes'!"

"They better be able to pull this Studebaker full!"

"Tha's nine hundred twenty-five dolla, sir."

"I'll pay you when I get back to the docks."

"But . . . how's I knows?"

"You don't trust me? Come with me back to town."

"Yassa, I do dat. I will close up shop."

"You and Dan want to drive them back to the boat, Mose?"

"Yassa, Massa Jon. Wit pleasure, Jo . . . Massa Jon.!"

"Well, do it fast, and quiet, before we're spotted"

"There y'all are, Jon," said Steve. "We done loaded yer crops on dat gun ship, an' got yer money . . ."

"Thanks. How did it break down?"

"Hundred sixty-five a bale fer cotton. Dat's forty one twenty-five fer twenty-five bales. Thirty-four seventy-one an' ninety cents fer tobaccy. Dat makes seventy-five ninety-six an' ninety cents total."

"Okay, thanks, Steve. I owe you about nine hundred twenty-five dollars."

"Yowee! I's reckon' yer a millionaire, sir!"

"Naw, this money is shared with a lot of people," said Jon.

"Ya paid that much fer these horses an' wagon?"

"Yes. You know my name, Steve?"

"It be's Hamilton, ain't it?"

"Yes. And these horses came from the Duke of Hamilton in Scotland."

"They's shore is beauties. One male and one female."

"That give ya any ideas?" asked Martin.

"No . . . yeah! Better get a couple stalls made on Jon's boat."

"Thanks, Steve. It won't be much trouble getting them up this river, but the Saint Francis can be a little rough this time of year."

"How long do ya reckon it'll take fer ya ta get back down here with yer next load?"

"Probably a good week, providing we don't take a few shells from Vickburg or Port Hudson."

"I'll try ta sen' word ta let ya through," said Steve.

"Can I take one of your servants with me? I'll pay you for the few days I have him."

"What ya want one fer, Jon?"

"To help with the wood fuel, and to watch my horses."

"Yassir. How's 'bout a dolla a day?"

"That's fair, Steve. Thanks. Are we about ready?"

"Ya outta stay the night, Jon. Dem riva's a bugga at night!"

"Well, thanks, but the sooner we start, the sooner we get back down here. How are we fixed for wood?"

"I gotcha loaded wit wood ta start, Jon," said Ben.

"Okay, thanks. What's the servant's name?"

"Jus' call 'im Jazzy, Jon. Bring 'im back," said Steve.

"Right. Are you ready, Marty, Mose, and Danny?"

"I'm waitin' on you, Jon" said Martin from boat two.

"We's ready, Massa Jon," said Mose.

"Ready, Massa Jon," said Danny.

Jon let his boat drift a little, then put her in half power to pick his way upstream.

"Jazzy, I want you to tend the fire. Keep steam up, Okay?"

"Yassa, I's do," said Jazzy, heading below deck.

"They make a great addition, don't they, Mose?"

"Dey sho 'nuff do, Massa Jon."

"I's sees ya pass Baton Rouge, Jon. You's tries fo' Port Hudson ta's dock?"

"Yes. We'll probably have to dock at Port Hudson. I'd like to make Natchez tonight."

"Dat be's awful dark, Jon."

"Yeah. You're right, Mose. Natchez is such a beautiful little town. I wish you could see it."

"Maybe some days, Jon. We's stops un Port Hudson."

"Hello down there. Wanna come up into the fort?"

"Hello . . . no thanks. We'll sleep on our boat."

"Where ya headed?"

"Arkansas, our home."

"Well, we seen ya a-comin', so's we didn't fire. But good luck gettin' past Vicksburg."

"Thanks, we'll need it. Good night," said Jon.

"G'night. Hope y'all get back home."

December 1

Early the next morning, December first, the *M. L. Transports* one and two were churning the river waters upriver. Soon Vicksburg came into sight, as did gunboats coming toward Jon.

"Pull yer boats ova ta the dock, and no tricks!"

"Tricks? We wouldn't think of pulling any tricks."

"Jus' get them ova there,' said the officer in the gunboat.

The boats all docked, and Jon found his crew covered by several rebs with rifles pointed at them.

"We are not criminals!" shouted Jon. "Or feds!"

"You acted like criminals a couple days ago, when ya ran by here with both boats loaded," said an officer, a captain.

"We were afraid you would sink us."

"We coulda sunk ya easy, but dat woulda spoiled the food ya had aboard."

"We had tobacco and cotton."

"Nothin' else? No food?"

"Just cotton and tobacco this trip," said Martin.

"What about otha trips?"

"We'll have more cotton and tobacco next trip too," said Jon.

"What else?" asked the captain, sternly. Nobody answered.

"Lieutenant Anderson, line these swamp jocks up against that wall and shoot 'em!"

"Yes, sir, Captain! Ya heard 'im, line 'em up!"

Jon and his crew were pushed and herded against the wall.

"Is this what we get for working so hard to support you?"

"Ya didn't stop with yer cargo when we told ya to. That's not no support!" shouted the captain.

"Yes, but the crops go to money for the Confederacy."

"Money in yer pocket! Shoot 'em, Lieutenant!"

"Yes, sir! First company to the line! Drum roll!" Reb riflemen quickly lined up, facing Jon's crew.

"Ready on the left . . . ready on the right . . . aim!"

"Wait! Hold it! What do you want from us?"

"We want food! A boat load we can store."

"Okay, but you can't use cotton or tobacco. I'll get food."

"That's better! Put your men at ease, Lieutenant."

"Yes, sir! Squadron at ease."

"I'm coming back with another load. I'll try to get a load of wheat, rice, and anything else I can gather."

"Now yer talkin'. Where's this food a-comin' from?"

"Arkansas, up the Saint Francis River."

"So ya should be back this a-way in 'bout a week."

"My crews are harvesting it now. It will take a few days to get it all loaded onto these boats."

"I'll give ya till the tenth, an' don't try ta run the gauntlet. We'll shoot ya down an' sink ya!"

"Captain, sir?"

"Yes, what is it, Lieutenant?"

"If'n we lets 'em go, how's can we be sure they'd return?"

"Good question, Lieutenant, very good question. It all will go good on your record. We hold one of them, ya stupid numbhead!"

"You have my word, Captain. I'll be back," said Jon.

"Hmm, which one we keep . . ."

"I's stay, sir," said Mose.

"Naw, yer too big. It'd take half my command ta guard ya, an you'd eat up half our store! Naw, maybe I'll hold the white man with ya."

"He's the only one that can operate my boat, Captain," said Jon.

"Alright, I'm a-takin' this one here." The captain pointed to Jazzy.

"Me's? I's be dock worker in N'Orleans," said Jazzy.

"Don't worry, Jazz. We'll be back to get you," said Jon.

"I's comes back too, Jazzy," said Mose.

"Quiet, ya big nigga, or we shoot ya!"

"Oh, yassa, missa osifer, I's sorry, sa," mocked Mose.

"Ya has ten days ta come back an' exchange food fer nigga!"

"Alright, Captain. I'll be back with food."

"I's thoughts we's was dead, Jon," said Mose.

"It was close, alright. Now we have until the tenth to get back."

"Dis be's firs' a Decemba, Jon?"

"Yes. That means we will only have about five days to load the boats for our return trip."

"Fives, Jon? I's swear da captain say ten."

"He did, Mose, but we still are a couple days back to Mose's Landing, and about three days back to Vicksburg."

"I's hopes dem boys gets dem crops picked."

"So do I, Mose. How's Marty doing?"

"Marty an' Danny do's good, Jon. Dey's right behin'."

The boats pulled up to the dock at Mose's Landing on December third.

"Welcome home, honey," said Janet. She was standing with Modessa at the dock. "Well, look at those beautiful horses!"

"Hi, darling!" yelled Modessa to her husband. "Any trouble?"

"Lots of it, honey. Are we ready to reload?" asked Martin.

"Why the hurry, honey? You've earned a rest."

"No rest for the wicked, Janet. We need to get loaded," said Jon.

"What? Alright, honey. I'll get the loading crew together."

"Thanks, Jan. You get to name our new team."

"They are lovely! And a new wagon . . . are the old ones in bad shape?"

"We will have to have Mose check them out, but we can use this Studebaker. We're not going down river next year!

"That bad, huh?" asked Janet, as more people, including Maggie, started showing up to greet the boatmen.

"Hello, my pretty plum. Here's your money, minus nine hundred twenty-five dollars for the horses and wagon."

"A thousand dollars? Do they have gold teeth?"

"No, but they're the start of our new breed from Scotland."

"Scotland! Are we getting too good for American horses?"

"I'll tell you all about it tonight, my love, but now I need to get these boats reloaded in a hurry."

"They're holdin' our slave hostage in Vicksburg, and we gotta get a load of food to them, or they will kill the slave," said Martin.

"Slave? Hostage? What the hell's going on, Jonny?"

"You left with four, and the same four are back," said Janet.

"I'll explain it tonight! Now get our loading crew, dammit!"

'I'll get the supper started, Jan, while you start loading."

"Alright, honey. Your husband is a grouch!"

"I know, Jan. I'll get the story from him later," said Maggie.

"We'll put the rest of the cotton and tobacco all in boat number one, and the wheat, beans, corn, and rice in boat two."

"Orite, Jon. I's checks on dem tobacca," said Mose.

"And I'll get the cotton rollin', Jon," said Martin.

"Good. I'll get Josh and Susan to help get the vegetables here to the dock, and let's get Jules on the wheat."

"I guess Jon is right, honey, no rest for the wicked!" said Jan.

"We hold off everything else, and get the boats loaded," said Jon.

Everyone present got busy. Maggie, Janet, and Modessa just shrugged shoulders and got busy too. Jon rode the new Studebaker and team to find Jules, then Josh and Susan.

Martin rode with Jon across the river to the barns, and got a team of his own. He headed for the cotton fields, while Mose did the same, but he headed for the tobacco fields. By the end of the day, crops were piling up at the Mill dock. In the evening, the table at the old farmhouse was packed.

"First of all," said Jon, "our first run on New Orleans made seventy-five hundred, ninety-six dollars and ninety cents. They are clamoring for supplies to feed and clothe the Confederacy. I spent nine hundred and twenty-five dollars on the wagon and the team of Clydesdale horses."

"They are so beautiful, but why so much, Jonny?" asked Dessy.

"We are getting into the start of a new breed of work horses, and I'm hoping we can develop them. They are bred and shipped here by the Duke of Hamilton in Scotland. We are among the first to own them here in the states. If our company don't want them, I'll pay for them myself."

"I make a motion we pay for them from our shares," said Fred.

"An' I's seconds," added Mose.

"All in favor?" Everyone raised their hands. "Good. The wagon is also a new, improved breed called the Studebaker."

"It is really a sound, strong wagon," said Alex Hamilton.

"I move we purchase it on shares," said Modessa.

"I'll second. We need another good wagon," said Fred.

"All in favor of buying the wag . . ." All hands were raised before Jon finished his sentence.

"Okay. Before I tell you about this trip, and I know how anxious you all are to hear about it, is there any other business?"

"By the way, New Orleans was taken by the Yankees. We unloaded in a town called Kenner," said Martin.

"Have you seen your new home, Jon?" asked Alex.

"Just from the river."

"It is looking beautiful, Jonny," said Martha.

"It's probably better'n the Duke's castle!" said Alex.

"Yeah, well, we can't worry about that now. Anything else?"

"Don't' you want to know about the boys, Jonny?"

"Oh, yes, darlin'. What news is there?"

"Nothing on the toll board in the square!"

"Maggie! Why scare me like that, darlin'?"

"I'm sorry, Jonny, but I thought you'd want to know. Sterling Price is still in Missouri, and we think Jimmy is still with him. General McCulloch and Sammy are back in Arkansas, maybe Little Rock. I don't know where Davy is."

"Thank you, my love. I'm sorry I got upset."

"Now tell us about your adventure down the Mississippi," said Fred.

"Okay, well, every place on the river is real busy, trying to prepare for a possible invasion from the North. On the way to New Oleans . . ."

"That's *Orleans*, Jonny, with an *R*. New Orleans."

"Thanks, dalin'. Anyway, We were fired at when we passed Vicksburg. Luckily, they missed, but they were close. Then we were stopped by Confederate gunboats, asked questions, then let go. Finally made it to this side of New Orleans. Man, what a busy place that is! We bought the Clydesdales and the Studebaker wagon there, and they leased us a dock worker to help us get back home. On the way back, we saw the biggest and strongest lines of guns all along the river that you can hardly imagine! Right, Mose and Martin?"

"That's true, Jon. They were all over," answered Martin.

"I's don' knows how dem Yankee boats can runs on down dem riva," added Mose.

"Get back to the story, honey," said Janet.

"Alright. We spent the first night coming back to Port Hudson, in Louisiana, and it's a stronghold at a bend in the river. The next day, we came to Vicksburg again, and they were waiting for us. They took us prisoners and lined us up against a wall and almost shot us dead!"

There was a very long pause.

"That's not funny, Jonny! Quit lying, you big lummox!"

"They probably serenaded them all day," said Fred.

"No, they lined us up and threatened to shoot us if we didn't supply them with food. They took the slave boy hostage, and will kill him if we don't return in ten days."

"How much of that is the truth, Jonny?" asked Maggie.

"All of it," said Martin. "They were gonna keep me hostage until Jon told them I was running a boat."

"So now you're gonna cow down to them and bring them back our food, honey?"

"And we lose all that money?" asked Fred.

"We never asked them about money," said Martin. "They were about to shoot us if we didn't agree to bring food."

"All for a . . . a man we don't know, who ain't even one of our men?" asked Fred.

"It's the honorable thing to do," said Alex.

"That's right, Fred, and we've only got a few days to get back to Vicksburg with a full boat load."

"I move we get the boats loaded and sacrifice a load of food to exchange for the slave man," said Modessa.

"Second," said Martin. "All in favor?"

Everyone raised their hands, though some were slower than others.

"Okay. We already have all the rice bagged and boxed. We need someone to get it down to the dock."

"Get me a wagon team and some helpers, and I'll get rice to the dock," said Alex. "The processed rice too, Jon?"

"Yes. We'll try to sneak some rice to Kenner."

"I will get the wheat from the barn," said Jules.

"Good. And Josh and Susan are boxing the vegetables."

"Some a dem, Jon. We's sacks dem beans an' squashes," said Josh.

"Alright! Mose is handling the tobacco, and Martin the cotton, and I'll run around and help wherever needed. Do you have enough help with the loading, Janet?"

"Sure do, honey. Don't worry about my crew."

"Good. Get the cotton and tobacco all in boat number one, and try to hide boxed rice below deck, Jan."

"You have Martin workin' cotton. Where do you want me?" asked Fred.

"Hmm . . . start on the dock with Janet, Fred. I'll let you know if I need you elsewhere. Okay, gang, we've got our work cut out for us, and we'll do it!"

"I'll drink to that!" said Fred.

Near the mouth of the St. Francis River
December 7, 1862

"We're going to make it in plenty of time, Mose."

"Yassa, we will, sho 'nuff, Jon."

"We got all of the wheat, beans, squash, a lot of the rice, and a couple bales of cotton on Marty's boat."

"An' loads a corn, Jon. We's be's short fo' winta."

"Well, DeValurie may have extra corn for the animals."

"An' we's has tobacca an' cotton in dis boat."

"Along with a lot of boxed *Uncle Mose's* rice, well hidden."

"We's be ready, Jon. Marty's be right behin'."

"Right. Mississippi River, straight ahead!"

"Yassa, Massa Jon!"

The transports eased into the darker channel of the Mississippi, crossed over to the calm Tennessee side, and skimmed the river at a quick pace. As darkness approached, Jon searched the now Mississippi bank for a place to stop.

"There's a little town. We'll dock there."

"Hello. What is the name of your town?"

"Greenville, Mississippi," was the response.

"Is it alright if we dock here for the night?"

"Y'all can. I was jus' a-gonna help get ya wood."

"Well, thank you. That's mighty kind of you."

The young man gathered an armload of wood and took it aboard Martin's boat.

Martin suddenly yelled, "Come back here, ya damned thief! Come back, or I'll shoot!"

"What did he take, Marty?"

"An armful of corn."

"Let him go, Marty. His family is probably starving."

"Right, but I'll be more watchful from now on."

The next morning found the two transports whizzing down the river toward Vicksburg and the exchange for Jazzy. Jon called Martin forward and spoke on his horn.

"When we see Vicksburg, you go in front of me and dock first."

"Alright, Jon. I'll get shot at first!"

"Ya did come back! That slave mus' mean more ta you than I figured," said the captain.

"And he's not even mine! He's a loaner," said Jon.

"You got men to unload your goods, Captain?" asked Martin.

"Sure do. Both of 'em! Sergeant . . . a detail ta unload these boats."

"Yes, sir! Corporal, a detail to unload those boats!"

"Yes, sir! Private Anderson, a detail . . ."

"Hold it just a minute, Captain. Our agreement was one full boat load of food in trade for that slave."

"Things change in this here army, Skipper."

"But, Captain, a load of tobacco and cotton would only take up valuable space. You can't eat it!"

"But I maybe could sell it."

"To who? I loaded two bales of cotton with your food, just in case you could use it. That's a thousand pounds."

"I like that, skipper, thanks. I'll tell you what . . . We have a general here. I'll ask him if we keep both boats."

"I'd like to speak to him too," said Jon.

"Come with me, skipper," said the captain.

"Sir, I have the skipper of the two supply boats."

"Thank you, Captain. What is your name?"

"Jonathan Hamilton. I have a farm up the Saint Francis River in Arkansas."

"And all them bales of cotton and tobacco are yours?"

"Yes, sir. I made a deal with your captain, and he is turning tail on his bargain!"

"Oh? What was the bargain, Mister Hamilton?"

"Your captain held one of my men captive until I returned with one boat load of food for your men. I kept my end of the deal, sir. It took all of my food for the winter to fill the boat, and now your captain is taking away my means to make a living, my boat full of tobacco and cotton."

"In other words, my captain is not honoring his part of the bargain. Well, Captain, what do you say for yourself?"

"Sir, we can use the tobacco and cotton to sell."

"Hmm . . . we would have to ship it to Baton Rouge to sell, and they are Confederate military, just like us. The money would go to our common cause, meaning we get nothing!"

"May I add to that, General?" asked Jon. "The dock workers, including the Negro you held captive, all know my boats and would refuse to buy from your men."

"Well," said the general. "we don't have the time or the extra men to waste shipping the load to Baton Rouge, so we have to depend on you, Mister Hamilton. You do understand the importance of this post, and the urgency to finish its defenses?"

"I do, sir," said Jon. "And I feel I have been more than helpful to you by bringing you a boat load of food."

"Alright. You're free to go, Mister Hamilton. Take your slaves and your cotton and tobacco, and go in peace."

"Thank you, sir! And good luck to you and yours," said Jon.

"You's a good talka, Jon, ta gets us outta der," said Mose.

"Thank you, Mose. I thought we might lose this load of tobacco and cotton . . . and rice, to them."

"Hello, Jon!" yelled Martin. His empty boat had pulled up beside Jon's. "Congratulations on getting us out of there in one piece."

"Thanks. There's a Port called Grand Gulf a short ways ahead. Let's leave your boat there and just take this one to Kenner."

"Right, Skipper, will do."

"Hello, Jon!" yelled Steve. "Glad ta sees ya made it past Vicksburg alright. How'd my man do?"

"He did great! Jazzy is worth a boat load to me!"

"We held up that ship for England, jus' fer you," said Ben.

"Well, let's not make him wait any longer. I'm anxious to get back home. I have three of my family at war."

"Yep, this jus' may be the last time I sees ya fer a spell."

Home of Fred and Janet Wilson
Mose's Landing, Arkansas
June 23, 1863

"Welcome to my humble little home," said Fred.

"Humble? Little?" commented Martin. "If you want to see a humble little home, come and see Dessy and me!"

"We were comparing this house to Maggie's mansion, honey."

"Jan's right. The White House is even humble, compared to Jon and Maggie's place," remarked Fred.

"When will we see it, Margaret?" asked Lolita.

"We'll have a picnic there for Independence Day," answered Maggie.

"Mmm, we love picnics, Maggie," said Jules.

"Well, folks, we're not here for any picnic," said Martin.

"It be's serious matta, right, Jon?"

"That's right, Mose. We just saw the board at the square. Memphis fell to the feds on the sixth, and now the gunboats have captured Helena and are on our river."

"Helena? What happened to the new army that General Hindman built with the conscription?"

"I guess they headed west to Little Rock. They may try to take back the Elkhorn Tavern at Pea Ridge," said Maggie.

"And maybe head back up into Missouri to help Price," said Jon.

"That's where Jimmy is, right?" asked Fred.

"We think so, Fred, but we don't know for certain," said Maggie. "And now Andy wants to enlist."

"How old is Andrew now, honey?" asked Janet.

"He's almost twenty, and Miles will be eighteen next month," answered Maggie.

"We's almos' lost Jules an' Marty when dem soldiers come here an' dem conscriptions," said Mose.

"What did ya say ta gets away fro' dem soldiers, Marty?" asked Josh.

"I lied and told them I was fifty-five, and had twenty-five slaves, same as Jules."

"I think he do not believe me," said Julian. "He say he be back ta prove I be lying."

"Well, you both should be alright," said Janet. "The conscription ages were from eighteen to thirty-five."

"Yes, but they can expand that age limit anytime," said Modessa.

"Were any of your boys at Shiloh, Jon?" asked Fred.

"We don't know, Fred. After McCulloch lost at the Elkhorn Tavern and got killed, we think Sammy went under the command of Van Dorn, and he was sent to Shiloh."

"What a bloody mess that was!" added Fred. "They say both sides had over seventeen thousand men killed, and at least eight thousand wounded."

"That's not a battle. It's a massacre, honey," said Janet.

"Dear God, I hope none of our boys were there," said Maggie.

"That's what hurts," said Jon. "We don't know where any of them are. We think David is with General Grant, and he's at Shiloh, and we think Jim is still in Missouri with Price."

"We're not going back to New Orleans with our crops anytime soon. That's all Yankee territory now," said Martin.

"Yes, Vicksburg is all that's left on the Mississippi."

"So where do we take this year's crops, Jon?" asked Alex Hamilton.

"To Saint Louis, I guess."

"That's Yankee territory too," said Martin.

"Yeah. They may take some prisoners too, like the rebs did to us in Vicksburg," added Fred.

"Where do you suppose we can get ahold of a cannon?"

"A cannon? Have you gone barmy, Jonny?"

"No, my love, the feds are on the White River, and worse yet, they are on our river up to Marking Tree."

"Dey comes closa, an' we's don' have ta worry 'bout Saint Louis."

"That's right, Mose. We need to figure a defense here."

"We's block dem riva, Jon," said Danny Doubleclutch.

"That's a good start, Danny, but we surely need a cannon."

"But we have no slaves, Jonny. Why would they harm us?" asked Maggie.

"As far as anyone is concerned, we have slaves, darlin'. Besides, they know we trade commerce with the South."

"This be's bad year for Mose's Landing. You will see," said Lolita.

"Please don't say things like that, Lolita. I am praying that my boys will be safe and can come home soon," said Maggie.

"After all these setbacks, the South cannot last much longer, Margaret," said Modessa. "Maybe they will come home soon."

Mose's Landing, Arkansas
The shareholder's cornfield
July 10, 1863

"How's the battle going, Fred?"

"The battle is about won. It's the biggest crop of corn we have ever had."

"Wonderful," said Jon. "We have really been hurting for corn, after we had to give most of it away last year."

"Yeah. I'll bet whoever controls Vicksburg still has our corn."

"Wheat too, but we have lots of wheat now."

"It's funny how we can survive when we have ta."

"You mean the wild oats, Fred?"

"Yeah, Jon. I think we cut and hauled every doggoned wild oat and rye plant in the state of Arkansas this summer!"

"Well, the animals can eat good now!"

"You been out to the west section lately, Jon?" asked Fred.

"Not lately, why?"

"All our old horses are gone now. Sloggy, Smutty, Flip, Venus, Saturn, Red, Cobbler, and Jake, all dead, as well as Conqueror and Corker. Those two were the best horses we ever had!"

"You talk about battles . . . Corker was in some good ones with Mose and me when we were coming out here."

"Yup, that's all water under the bridge, Jon. The good ole days! Things have changed for the better now."

"Well, I hope they're better. Not sure, though, with the war going on and no word from our boys."

"Jon, have you heard about Gettysburg? The telegraph says it's the biggest battle yet fought. Bigger than Shiloh, or Vicksburg."

"I wish the damn war was over," said Jon.

"Say, who's dat ridin' out here so fast?"

"It looks like . . . Jim Rosewell."

"He's your son-in-law's dad, ain't he?" asked Fred.

"Yes, he is. Must be important, he's coming fast."

"Jon! There you are," said Jim Rosewell.

"Hello, Jim. What can I do for you?"

"Just came in. Lincoln has emancipated the blacks, and Union gunboats are headin' up the river from Marking Tree!"

Jon told Fred to get his crew together and into the Mourner's Church. He told Rosewell to get any women in town into the new church. Jon raced his horse to the farmhouse and got everyone there inside, and then rang the warning bell. He then galloped into town, where he instructed Josh to get all the guns and ammo from his mansion, and to get Maggie and twelve-year-old Jonny Junior and Jon's parents into the basement of the mansion. Jon saw Janet, and asked her to get all the workers to their homes or the Mourner's Church. He found Julian, and instructed him to get his family into the DeValurie mansion and to bring all the rifles. Then Jon and Martin headed for the dock and fired up *M. L. Transports one* and two, took them downriver past his mansion, lined them up, sunk the transports, and stretched a heavy chain across the river from tree to tree.

"You two are soaked! Come here, Martin, and change clothes," said Modessa.

"I don't have time, honey. You get to the house."

"Let's see . . . we have Jules, Fred, Mister Rosewell, Mister Thompson, Ethan and Emil Grady, Ned Baxter, Josh, Ally, Chip, and Danny. I told them they didn't have to fight, but they wouldn't listen. We also have you and I, Marty. That makes a total of thirteen to battle the Union navy. We're ready!

"They don't know that we have no slaves, right?" asked Martin.

"That's right. As far as I know."

"Let's hope they recognize a white flag when they see one."

"We have a white flag and a blocked channel. That should confuse them a bit," said Jon.

"Maybe they'll get so confused, they'll turn tail and run!"

"Somehow, I rather doubt that."

"So do I! What now? Just wait?" asked Martin.

"Yep. Let's get our baker's dozen spread out."

Everyone seemed ready, and settled in for the big show.

It was a hot July day. Jon marveled at the sight of thirteen outwardly brave men with their crazy, wide assortment of weapons, from flintlocks to percussions. Jon had chosen his double barrel muzzleloader, and loaded it with bird shot. He knew he couldn't kill a bundle of blue bellies, but he sure could strike misery on a few.

They all heard them coming before they saw them. Three ironclad gunboats appeared in a line, striking fear into thirteen hearts. The chains didn't even slow them down, pulling the anchor trees over and into the water. *Crunch!* The lead gunboat crushed the deck of Jon's sunken transport. *BOOM!* The shot destroyed the back end of the new church in the park. As the lead gunboat ran up onto the bank just a few yards in front of Jon, the second gunboat fired. *BOOM! Sssszzz!* The shot hit Hamilton Street behind Valurie Boulevard and sent a blast of fire into the air, destroying homes and, Lord knows, killing people. The second warship slid up the bank behind the first, and a troop carrier followed behind. Out jumped Union soldiers.

"Don't shoot, men! Don't shoot!" yelled Jon, but the blue-bellies fired. Jon saw Ned Baxter and one of the Grady brothers die in splashes of blood. He then saw a federal soldier fall, from whose shot, Jon wasn't sure. Jon frantically waved his white flag.

"Kill dem rebel bastards!" yelled someone from the gunboats, and more shots rang out.

Jon saw Josh fall, wounded. He screamed, "Stop! Stop!"

"Don't shoot the Negroes!" yelled someone.

"Why the hell not? They're shootin' us," said a soldier.

Jon saw a group of three or four Union troops coming toward him. One shot, and a mini ball struck Jon in that same side where he had been hit before. He threw down the white flag, grabbed the double-barreled rifle, and fired both barrels at the group. They fell in a pile, screaming bloody murder, tossing in agony on the ground. There was no chance to reload, so he grabbed his Colt pistol from his belt, and fired two or three more times, hitting one soldier as he was about to shoot Danny. Another shot from somewhere hit Jon's pistol and hand, sending the Colt flying. Jon raised his hands into the air in surrender, and luckily was noticed by some troops and by his own people. Martin raised his arms and came out of hiding, and one by one, so did the others.

"Hold your fire, men! They surrender!"

"We surrendered before you started firing at us!" shouted Jon.

"How was we supposed to know that, Jonny reb?"

"Don't you blue-bellies know what a white flag is for?" asked Fred.

"I don't see no white flag, ya rebel scum."

"I was waving it all the time!" yelled Jon.

"Why are yer niggers shootin' at us? We came ta free ya."

"We's already free," said Chipper.

"Come on out, all you Negroes," yelled a soldier. "You're free."

"This one says they are already free."

"Tha's right. We's all free," said Mose, just showing up.

"There you are, Mose. I . . . I was wonderin' where . . . you were."

"You's been hit, Jon. How bad is ya hurt?" asked Mose.

"I'll be alright, Mose. Can someone check out those hou-houses on Hamilton Street?"

"I's do it, Jon," said Danny.

"I's check dem church," said Ally.

"Corporal . . . casualty report," said a lieutenant.

"Three dead, six wounded, sir."

"What about your losses, reb?"

"We aren't rebs. And we aren't feds. We are neutral."

"It's been reported that you supply the Confederates with food and crops. That makes you a sympathizer."

"We sell our crops to anyone willing to pay our price."

"An' that means Batesville, Saint Louis, anyone!" said Martin.

"And all these Negroes are free? I don't believe it."

"We's all has papers ta proves it," said Mose.

"Bring out your freedom papers!" yelled Jon to the workers.

Several disappeared to their homes to get their papers. By this time, all the townspeople were gathered.

"Jon . . . Josh has been hurt," said Modessa.

"How bad is it, Dessy?"

"Pretty bad. He has a chest wound."

"Jon be's hurt toos. I's gets dem liniment," said Mose.

"How bad you hit, honey?" asked Janet.

"I'll be alright. Is Danny back?" asked Jon.

"Yes, he's here," said Fred.

"There be's two dead, Jon, an' one wounds," said Danny."

"No one in dem church," said Ally.

"That makes four of my people dead, Lieutenant, and two, uh, three wounded, and it was all unnecessary," said Jon.

"Here be's free papas, buckra boss."

"Show them to the lieutenant, Murphy."

"Orites, buckra boss. Look, sa, I's be free," said Murphy.

"We's all be free," said Jesse.

"Well, I'll be. But didn't Arkansas expel all you free Negroes?"

"Yes, but they have never come to enforce that law."

"Lincoln has emancipated all black people anyhow," said Fred.

"That took effect January the first," said the lieutenant.

"They's still sellin' ta the South, sir."

"Yes, I know, Corporal, that ends now! Corporal, four parties of three. Destroy the crops in the field."

"Yes, sir! Four parties of three, front and center!"

"No, please, ya cain't do this ta us," cried Jules.

"This crop was going to the Union at Saint Louis," said Fred.

"You's puts all un Negroes outta work," said Danny.

BOOM! BOOM! The big cannon from the second gunboat startled everyone, even the lieutenant. Jon looked with horror, as the blasts hit his mansion and exploded. Parts of the house collapsed, and fiery chunks flew into the air. Instantly, the house was aflame.

"MAGGIE! Oh, God, no!" Jon pushed his way through the crowd, tears coming from his eyes. He spotted a horse and ran to it, knocking someone down. Somehow, he was now aboard the horse, racing toward his mansion.

"Maggie . . . Jonny . . . Please, God . . . Don't . . ."

Jon could see soldiers walking on the grass, rifles drawn, headed for the mansion. He dug his heels into the horse's sides. "Got to beat 'em there," he said. "Please . . . please, let them be alive!" He saw his father emerge from the burning home, leading his mother. Alexander Hamilton was carrying a gun. *BAM! BAM!* "Oh no, Dad! Mom!" Tears continued to flow from Jon's eyes and run down his cheeks. He couldn't see, but he slammed his heels into the horse's side again. His eyes finally cleared enough to see that his father lay still on the grass by the porch stairs, and his mother kneeling over him.

"Dear God, help me!" He was now on the lawn, one hundred fifty, then one hundred yards away. Then he saw red hair. Maggie! She and little Jonathan were on the porch. Maggie had a gun. "NO! Nooo!" he yelled, as more shots rang out. Both his wife and son fell. "Noooooo!" Jon ran the horse straight at the officer.

"He's coming right at us! Corporal! Men! Shoot that reb bastard, now!"

"Yes, sir. Fire at will, men!"

"You dirty son-of-a-bi . . ." *BAM! BA-BA-BAM!* Lights out . . . falling . . . "Where . . . am . . . Mag . . . can't see . . . Black . . . am I . . . h-h-he . . . Dead?" . . . Bright . . . tunnel . . . lights . . . fading.

END

Edwards Brothers Malloy
Oxnard, CA USA
December 18, 2015